The Chalk Giants

After the apocalypse the hazardous evolution of mankind continues. And in primeval response to the disaster, humanity's solutions to catastrophe carve the harsh new world in violent patterns of magic and myth, rite and religion. Brave images scar the ancient hills, the clash of swords and the ageless power of sexuality signpost another, bloodsoaked path to civilisation.

Kiteworld

The Realm of Kiteworld has survived nuclear catastrophe and is governed by a feudal and militant religious oligarchy – the Church Variant.

In the outer Badlands, real or imagined demons are kept at bay by flying defensive structures of giant interlocking Cody kites piloted by an elite and brave Corps of Observers.

Through a series of Kite stories we are drawn compellingly into a strange but recognizable world where loyalty to the Corps is everything and non-conformity is a sin. Keith Roberts depicts the fortunes, passions and failings of his characters against this background of a fragile and superstitious society. As the fanatical Ultras embark on a religious campaign of destruction, the Realm starts to disintegrate fast.

The Grain Kings

'We reap and we thresh; grain for half the world. We are the Grain Kings raised of old.'

They call them the Grain Kings. Gigantic mechanical monarchs of the wheat-bearing plains that were once the frozen Alaskan wastes. Whole eco-systems in themselves, they can supply the food so desperately needed by the teeming millions of our overpopulated planet. But even now, as the whole world waits in hungry suspense, the great powers battle for control of the prairies and two competing combine harvesters find they are heading on a course of collision. A collision with catastrophic consequences – not only for the hundreds of crewmen aboard each massive machine but for the future survival of all mankind.

Also by Keith Roberts

Novels

The Furies (1966)
Pavane (1968)
Anita (1970)
The Inner Wheel (1970)
The Chalk Giants (1974)
Molly Zero (1980)
Kiteworld (1985)
Kaeti & Company (1986)
Gráinne (1987)
Kaeti On Tour (1992)

Collections

Machines and Men (1973)
The Grain Kings (1976)
Ladies from Hell (1979)
The Lordly Ones (1986)
Winterwood and Other Hauntings (1989)

Keith Roberts

SF GATEWAY OMNIBUS

THE CHALK GIANTS
KITEWORLD
THE GRAIN KINGS

GOLLANCZ
LONDON

First published in Great Britain in 2013 by
Gollancz
An imprint of the Orion Publishing Group
Orion House, 5 Upper St Martin's Lane,
London WC2H 9EA

An Hachette UK Company

A CIP catalogue record for this book
is available from the British Library

ISBN 978 0 575 10522 5

1 3 5 7 9 10 8 6 4 2

Typeset by Input Data Services Ltd,
Bridgwater, Somerset

Printed and bound by CPI Group (UK) Ltd, Croydon, CR0 4YY

The Orion Publishing Group's policy is to use papers that are natural, renewable and recyclable products and made from wood grown in sustainable forests. The logging and manufacturing processes are expected to conform to the environmental regulations of the country of origin.

www.orionbooks.co.uk
www.gollancz.co.uk

CONTENTS

Introduction from The Encyclopedia of Science Fiction ix

The Chalk Giants 1

Kiteworld 207

The Grain Kings 439

ENTER THE SF GATEWAY . . .

Towards the end of 2011, in conjunction with the celebration of fifty years of coherent, continuous science fiction and fantasy publishing, Gollancz launched the SF Gateway.

Over a decade after launching the landmark SF Masterworks series, we realised that the realities of commercial publishing are such that even the Masterworks could only ever scratch the surface of an author's career. Vast troves of classic SF & Fantasy were almost certainly destined never again to see print. Until very recently, this meant that anyone interested in reading any of those books would have been confined to scouring second-hand bookshops. The advent of digital publishing changed that paradigm for ever.

Embracing the future even as we honour the past, Gollancz launched the SF Gateway with a view to utilising the technology that now exists to make available, for the first time, the entire backlists of an incredibly wide range of classic and modern SF and fantasy authors. Our plan, at its simplest, was – and still is! – to use this technology to build on the success of the SF and Fantasy Masterworks series and to go even further.

The SF Gateway was designed to be the new home of classic Science Fiction & Fantasy – the most comprehensive electronic library of classic SFF titles ever assembled. The programme has been extremely well received and we've been very happy with the results. So happy, in fact, that we've decided to complete the circle and return a selection of our titles to print, in these omnibus editions.

We hope you enjoy this selection. And we hope that you'll want to explore more of the classic SF and fantasy we have available. These are wonderful books you're holding in your hand, but you'll find much, much more … through the SF Gateway.

www.sfgateway.com

INTRODUCTION

from The Encyclopedia of Science Fiction

Keith Roberts (1935–2000) was a UK author and illustrator long resident in the south of England, where most of his best fiction was set. After working as an illustrator and cartoon animator, he began publishing sf with 'Anita' and 'Escapism' in the same issue of *Science Fantasy*. He served as associate editor of *Science Fantasy* 1965–1966 and edited its successor *SF Impulse* for the whole of its run (March 1966–February 1967). His first novel, *The Furies* (**1966**), is the most orthodoxly structured and told of all his work, sf or otherwise, most of his later novels being fixups, recrafted assemblies of earlier work told from a brooding, slantwise, intensely visual point of view. *The Furies*, on the other hand, is a traditional tale in the mode of the UK disaster, in which a nuclear test goes awry, inspiring an onslaught of space-spawned giant wasps which ravage England and come close to eliminating mankind. Beyond a certain sultriness of tone, it could have been written by any author familiar with the UK Cosy Catastrophe mode.

With his second book, however, Roberts came fully into his own as a writer. *Pavane* (**1968**) superbly depicts an Alternate History in which – Elizabeth I having been assassinated, the Spanish Armada victorious and no Protestant rise of capitalism in the offing – a technologically backward England survives under the sway of the Catholic Church Militant. The individual stories here assembled are moody, eloquent, elegiac and thoroughly convincing. *The Inner Wheel* (**1970**) deals with the kind of gestalt Superman-cum-Telepathy theme made familiar by Theodore Sturgeon's *More Than Human* (**1953**) and is similarly powerful, though tending to a rather uneasy sentimentality, perhaps endemic to tales of such relationships but also typical of Roberts's handling of children and women. *Anita* (**1970**) is fantasy; the stories it contains had appeared much earlier in *Science Fantasy*. *The Boat of Fate* (**1971**), an historical novel with a Roman setting, shares a painterly concern for primitive landscapes with the far more ambitious *The Chalk Giants* (**1974**) (see below).

Roberts's early short stories were assembled in *Machines and Men: Science Fiction Stories* (**1973**) and *The Grain Kings* (**1976**) (see below). Later work was assembled in *Ladies from Hell* (**1979**), *The Lordly Ones* (**1986**) and *Winterwood and Other Hauntings* (**1989**). As in his later novels, these stories increasingly display an entangled – though sometimes searching – unease with human nature and sexuality, an unease he associates with the moral condition and fate of the UK.

Roberts's first novel after a gap of some years was *Molly Zero* (**1980**), a tale in which the classic sf tale of the growth of an adolescent is – typically for Roberts – subverted by a sense that the Dystopian world into which the young female protagonist enters – an oppressive class-ridden demoralized Little England whose inhabitants are barred from the sea by metal fences – is dismayingly corrosive. It is a sense that variously though unspecifically serves as background for the shadowy escapades of the eponymous heroine in the **Kaeti** sequence comprising *Kaeti & Company* (**1986**), *Kaeti's Apocalypse* (**1986**) and *Kaeti on Tour* (**1992**); and the life of the haunting *femme fatale* depicted in *Gráinne* (**1987**). In the sullen quietism that underlies the tales told, these books have little of the feel of sf. Much more sf-like is the **Kiteworld** sequence comprising *Kiteworld* (**1985**) (see below) and the relatively minor 'Drek Yarman', which invokes the atmosphere of earlier work in its depiction of an ominously transformed homeland.

As an illustrator, Roberts did much to change the appearance of UK sf magazines, notably *Science Fantasy*, for which he designed all but seven of the covers from January 1965 until its demise (as *SF Impulse)* in February 1967, and also *New Worlds* for a period in 1966. His boldly Expressionist, line-oriented covers paralleled the shift in content of these magazines away from Genre SF and Fantasy towards a more free-form, speculative kind of fiction. He later did covers and interior illustrations for the book editions of *New Worlds Quarterly* edited by Michael Moorcock, for some of whose novels he designed covers. He also illustrated several of his own 1980s titles, and published three works of nonfiction: *The Natural History of the P.H.* (**1988**), the initials referring to the 'Primitive Heroine' who appears throughout Roberts's work, a figure men may treat as a *lamia* but who is in truth a figure of charismatic, self-reliant integrity; *Irish Encounters: A Short Travel* (dated 1988 but **1989** chap); and *Lemady: Episodes of a Writer's Life* (**1997**), an uneasy memoir. In the unease of that memoir, and the associated note of regret for a sterner past that marks so much of his fiction, Roberts presents himself and his work as emblematic of the state of his native land: deeply emotional under a stiff facade (that often fractures); patriotic about the soil and selfhood of his country during the years of its retreat from an unsustainable imperial era; smiling through unshed tears.

The Chalk Giants, the first title presented here, almost certainly encapsulates more thoroughly and deeply than any other work Roberts's complex relationship to his selfhood and his native land. The separate tales here presented elegantly embody a cyclical vision of the island of Britain, from the future back to the explanatory past. The Near Future protagonist of the framing narrative (who appears only in this UK edition) drives to the south coast to escape an indistinct disaster, goes into hiding, and (depending on one's reading) either cycles the rest of the book through his head or can be seen as himself emblematic of the movement the tales portend, from Post-Holocaust chaos through God-ridden Ruined Earth savagery back to a state premonitory of his own wounded condition. The whole of *The Chalk Giants* is greater than its considerable parts.

In *Kiteworld,* the second title here reprinted, Britain is dominated by religious fanatics; the greatest pleasure of the tale must lies in its elated Steampunk rendering of the life of the crews who man the Kiteships, which are the size of Airships, whose task it is to guard the frontiers against 'demons', as the ballistic or cruise missiles of a former technological era are now called. It is a kind of parody of the Pax Aeronautica theme, in which those who command the airwaves command the country, and keep it at peace. Underneath, however, lies the portrait of a land, in the grips of a religious elite, at odds with itself.

The title story of *The Grain Kings,* the collection of independent tales that is the third title presented here, fascinatingly describes life on giant hotel-like grain harvesters in a world of vast farms. In the same volume, 'Weihnachtsabend', perhaps Roberts's most radical single story, hallucinatedly depicts an Alternate History, a Hitler Wins world where the Nazis have triumphed, and explores the cheap ersatz decadent paganism of the victors; the tale climaxes in a corrupt Wild Hunt whose prey is a woman. This is the most savagely dark of all Roberts's tales. Elsewhere, the dark is softened in visions of the author's much-loved England, of places to live in peace, and stories that dream of peace.

For a more detailed version of the above, see Keith Roberts's author entry in *The Encyclopedia of Science Fiction:* http://sf-encyclopedia.com/entry/roberts_keith

Some terms above are capitalised when they would not normally be so rendered; this indicates that the terms represent discrete entries in *The Encyclopedia of Science Fiction.*

THE CHALK GIANTS

Foweles in the frith,
the fishes in the flod—
And I mon wax wod.
Much sorw I walke with
for best of bon and blod.

Anon.,
thirteenth century

The patrol car is moving again, edging up past the stalled south-bound traffic. Its loudhailer is working; the words come crackling and flat, distorted by the heat of Salisbury Plain in August.

Stan Potts watches the blue flasher revolve, and sweats and rubs himself and swears. He wants to pee, and has wanted to pee for an hour or more, and dull pain has grown to sharper pain, then to all-consuming need. He slicks the gearstick forward and back and stares through the Champ's blotched windscreen and tries to think of nothing, nothing at all.

The observer has left the Wolseley, is working his way from vehicle to vehicle along the jam. Uproar breaks out somewhere in the distance, car horns and shouting. The loudhailer is saying, 'You will not be admitted to restricted areas. If your journey is not essential, return to your home. You will not be admitted to restricted areas.' *Stan wipes his face with the back of his hand and gropes behind him. Somewhere, clanking about, is an old bait tin. He finds it, works it down behind his heels.*

The observer leans on the window-sill. His arms are covered with short golden hairs. He says, 'Where to, sir?'

Stan says, 'Wareham.'

The policeman shakes his head. He looks very young. He says, 'It's restricted, they won't let you in. Better turn round.'

Stan Potts's voice says, 'I have to try. My father's very old.' They are just words, and not important.

But the patrolman has gone on anyway. He isn't really interested.

The Wolseley draws level and stops. The driver is talking on the r/t. He says, 'Four miles north of Amesbury. Yes, O.K.' The car moves forward, radio whistling. Stan grips the can between his knees, pulls at his flies. The relief makes his head spin a little.

The man at the window says, 'I've got to get petrol.'

Stan jerks, trying to cover himself. He says, 'Nobody's got any.' He lies back, in pain.

'Ninety miles I've come,' says the man. 'I've got to get petrol. What's in those?'

'Water,' says Stan. 'They're water.'

'You dirty bastard,' says the man. 'You were pissing in that can.'

The Escort ahead has moved up twenty yards. Stan twists the starter. The engine fires. It sounds ragged. He says, 'I'm sorry. I haven't any petrol.'

'You dirty bastard,' says the man. 'I've got my wife and family back there.'

The Ford moves again. The traffic behind the Champ is hooting, trying to force its way. The man grabs for the door-catch. He says, 'Get out. Get on your feet.'

Stan lets the clutch in. Something thumps against the Champ's side. He looks back. The man who needed petrol is wrestling with the two shirt-sleeved policemen. A uniform cap bounces in the road. The figures sprawl across the boot of the patrol car. Beyond, a convertible is trying to butt its way through. The driver is slapping at the door-panel with his open hand, and shouting. One wheel rises and falls over an obstruction. Somebody screams. Stan drives fifty yards, brakes. It seems the fight continues, but its details are obscured by overtaking traffic. The can tips, spillings its contents darkly. He reaches for it again, and groans.

ONE

The Sun Over a Low Hill

1

Always on a long trip it was like this. First he'd worry for a while and listen for big-end knock and differential whine and noise from the dynamo bearings, then boredom would set in and he'd start working out times and mileages in his head; and finally driving would become automatic and then it was like getting tunes in his brain only the tunes were sights and scenes sometimes from years back, things he didn't want to remember but had never managed to forget. No rhyme or reason to them; like the faces you're supposed to see in a glowing fire. Only he'd never managed to see the faces, not even when he was small.

The Champ rumbled steadily, clocking twenty, twenty-five. He was south of Salisbury now, clear of its bottleneck of old streets, the hooting and fumes and din. The city had been bad; there were broken windows, in one place he'd seen riot troops with guns and shields. Somewhere a building was burning; the smoke cloud rolled down thick and black and evil-smelling, obscuring the cathedral spire and the lines of hooting, panicking cars. It was car horns and shouting, and forcing your way yard after yard. A Vauxhall rammed him, on the new roundabout on the outskirts; the big towing hook on the Champ smashed through the stoneguard, left the car sputtering, wheezing water and steam. There had been armed troops; but he had still been lucky to get clear.

He gripped the wheel, trying not to think any more. Ahead, a bare five miles away, was the coast road that skirted Bournemouth. In old times he would have been at his destination inside the hour, but the traffic was slowing again to a halt. To either side stretched the glades of the New Forest. He swallowed. He'd caught himself wondering if the ponies would survive.

He told himself for the dozenth time how if he had a dash compass he would risk driving cross-country. He'd tried to get hold of one, a week before; but he'd been too late. Maybe they'd been banned. He stared round and licked his mouth. He had the vehicle for it, he had his maps; but he wasn't going to make it, even now. He didn't have the guts.

The fear was welling again, jamming his throat. He made himself be calm. He found a handkerchief, wiped his forehead, then the wheel rim. He sat listening to the throb of the Champ's big engine. After a time he switched off again, to conserve fuel.

How and when the idea had come he couldn't say. At first, like all such things, he had thrust it away; but it returned insidiously, time after time. It got into his brain at work, again like a tune that wouldn't be dismissed, came between him and sleep as he lay night after night, hearing the clock tick and his mother's restless coughing from across the landing. He told himself it was useless, useless, till he was sick of the sound and very taste of the word; but it didn't help.

His first buying had been tentative, tins and packets picked up here and there, smuggled back to be transferred later to the garage where he kept the Champ. He spread them on the floor, working by the light of the one dim lamp, saying to himself, 'You're never going to do it. You haven't the guts; and if you tried, you'd fail.' Finally he sat himself in the cab with a pencil and scratch-pad. Some overall system was needed; that much at least was obvious.

He realized nearly at once how random and senseless his purchasing had been. Most of the foodstuffs, bought in a species of hysteria, were too bulky for his purpose, too liable to spoiling. He set himself mentally to explore the shelves of his local supermarket, ticking off unit after unit. He'd read somewhere rice kept more people alive than any other staple; so far it hadn't figured in his lists at all. Flour was another obvious basic; to transport and store it he would need damp-proof containers, either of plastic or metal. Butter he supposed was a necessity; it could double as cooking oil. That at least was readily available in tins. Salt would be vital; it too would need an air-tight container. Most canned meats were unsuitable; too little bulk, too much slosh. Corned beef, though, was ideal; greatly daring, he risked buying in bulk. Soups tempted him; he settled finally for the dehydrated variety that comes in foil-lined packets. Later he added baked beans to his list of possibles, and remembered the peculiar merits of dehydrated potato. He never stopped asking himself, 'What are you doing it for? What do you think you're going to do?' But the back of the Champ began to fill.

He packed each box and carton with consummate care, grudging every inch of unused space. He added his fishing rod with two spare top joints, a box of hooks and heavy lines. Camp accessories followed: a two-ring burner, plastic cups and plates, forks and kitchen knives, a hand lantern, containers of gas. The bottles were bulky, he had to cut back on the space allocated for bedrolls and blankets. He told himself, 'You're never going to turn the starter. You're never going to drive down there and you're never going to do what you think you'll do because it's mad.' And still he didn't stop.

A trip to a second-hand dealer yielded a dozen five-gallon fuel cans; they accounted almost wholly for the remainder of the space. Then he remembered he'd made no provision for the most vital necessity of all, a supply of drinking water. He had to start again, nearly from the beginning, revising his priorities, discarding this, cutting down on that. With the Champ empty he drove her down to the workshop, oiled and greased and checked her over. The sealed power unit he didn't touch, but it was good for a hundred thousand miles. He made up an emergency kit: fuses, lamps and bulbs, rotor arm and distributor cap, spare coil and condensers, plugs, fanbelt, hoses, jubilee clips. An iron frame, spot-welded hastily under the chassis, received a second battery sealed in polythene; lastly he took the locked case from his bedroom drawer, slid it behind the driving seat. Topcoat, boots, toolkit and second spare wheel would have to travel with him in the front. He stowed them experimentally, walked round the big motor. There was room for nothing else; the Champ was full.

The traffic was moving again. Ahead on the main road were blue and amber flashers; somewhere an ambulance was yelling its strident double note. A saloon car lay on its side, there was a jack-knifed artic. Beyond, the road was a hooting jam of vehicles.

He'd discounted for the moment any means of heating. In emergency the burners would have to serve. He hadn't smoked a cigarette in years; he'd packed five hundred, all the same, in sealed tins of fifty. Another fifty lay in the dash cubby for immediate use. He prized the lid off, lit up. The first drag made him cough; he inhaled again carefully, lay back in the seat. He couldn't stop the shaking in his hands.

The pictures had started, as they always did. He rubbed his face, tiredly; but Form 3Q was still laughing, and Sledger Bates standing with the register under his arm, eyes bright blue beneath tufted ginger brows. 'What for?' he said. 'What for? When I give lines, you don't ask what for. For what you were doing before I came in …'

The seat edge hit the backs of his knees. He was holding the desk-top, stammering, vision swimming. 'Sir, I …'

'Another fifty, Potts!'

'I … I …'

'A hundred and fifty, Potts! Going up!'

'Sir, I …'

'And another fifty. Got the score, Chapman?'

'Yessir!'

'*Sit down!*' The voice was thundering, defeating him.

'Sir …'

'*Potts! Sit down!*'

His legs gave way, traitorously. He held his head down, all of him shaking, the exercise book sparking and spangling six inches from his eyes.

'Two hundred and fifty,' said the Sledge. 'Fifty for luck, the rest for cheek.

Don't rub that out.' The chalk scraped the corner of the board; the register slammed on the desk. 'You must be mad, Potts,' said the Sledge. 'You must be mad. Turn to a hundred and twenty-three.'

His hands were aching where they held the wheelrim. He flexed his fingers. The light was fading now, the tail-lamps of the stalled vehicles ahead winking like jewels. He closed his eyes and tried to work out how long he'd been in the car. Horns set up bedlam behind him. He jerked awake. The line had moved; he shoved the Champ into gear, drove forward. The hooting stopped.

He lit another cigarette. The taste was coming back. He remembered how when you drove past the castle and up out of the valley you drove back into sunlight. You got it on the last bend, full in the eyes; then the road snaked away between dry-stone walls and there was the pub and the yellow and red caravan outside and the hanging sign rich-lit against the deepening sky. Sometimes too the May mist lay across the curve of hills, long angled stripes of it moving fast down toward the village. Driving through it was like driving through clouds, and the sun on top made it look like fairyland.

The Champ barked, breasting the slope in second; he swung into the pub yard with a clash and jingle and sat and listened to the engine tick as it cooled. And the paddock was there and the grazing donkeys, nothing changed; the great dimming sweep of hills and the castle brooding miles off in the dusk and house lights and headlights showing in sparks and twinklings and Poole on the horizon and the air moving huge and clean and old. He listened to the silence, then his own feet on the gravel as he walked toward the door; and Ray was inside and the rest, John with his clipped posh voice and the artist with the beard who drank from a pewter pot with a lid to it, and the frightening fierce-eyed girl who played the guitar and sang the song about working, all the bloody work and no pay, he wouldn't have minded her. And the fossil fish in its glass case on the wall, the pots hanging over the bar and the yard-glass in its chain slings and the lit signs for Devenish draught and keg and the cigars and cigarettes and the placards advertising English Country Wines.

Something in his chest gave a hot jump, for she was there too. She wore a shirt checked in amber and sage green and a short canvas-coloured skirt and sandals that left her feet bare, just a sexy little strap between the toes. Her hair and eyes were dark, her skin brown-gold in the lamplight and her hands like butterflies, as deft and slight. She was perfect, head to feet. He wondered sometimes how anything could be that perfect, somehow it seemed nearly wrong. He swallowed and wondered what to say, but there was no need because Ray called from the bar as he always did, 'Same place,' and grinned and jerked his head at the ceiling. So he hefted his stuff upstairs and unpacked, he knew the furniture in the room now and the bed with its immaculate, tight-stretched sheets. The window stood ajar on its big old-fashioned stay and beyond was the castle, the great shell of ruin blue in the dusk. He would unpack quickly and put the camera and light-meter in the one drawer that locked and go and eat his meal because afterwards he could sit in the bar. And once she talked to him a whole ten minutes, asked what he did for a living and whether he'd had a good trip and how long it had taken getting down. After that he had a good time, although she didn't speak to him again; instead he heard how John's boss planted the wrong strain of wheat and the wind had flattened it, and how the caravan had taken first prize in a carnival and how the coastguards log a boat all round the shores of Britain. Driving back, it seemed the hours flew; it was as if she was with him, he'd brought her back like a wonderful catch from a wonderful shifting sea. He smiled, in the dark; and the Champ took a roundabout gently so as not to wake Martine, asleep a hundred miles away.

He got the Champ from Chalky for a straight ton, God knew where he had picked it up; but when he got tired of her and said she was using too much bloody juice and went for an old Magnette Stan took her over and cleaned her up and had new side-screens made and a hood at Trade and got himself a garage again. After that she was good for him because he could sit inside her and dream, though when he got her down to Purbeck the first time Ray Seddon took the pleasure out, right out, saying he thought the bloody coal had come.

They all laughed, the people he knew, and he had to laugh with them, but afterwards it wasn't too bad because she came out to see. She was wearing a white shirt and the canvassy skirt and her hair had been cut, though he preferred it that shade longer. The Champ was standing on the skyline, angled on the rough car park behind the pub; the sun was glinting on her dark green paint, she looked big and tough and smart. Martine had her arms folded and a cardigan over her shoulders. She said in her brittle little voice, 'What are all those knobs?' and he said, 'Four-wheel drive,' and then his voice stuck in his throat because the chance was there, anybody else in the world would have said, 'Nip in, I'll give you a run,' but he couldn't speak. So time stopped for a bit; then she was walking back saying, 'I have to get on now,' so he went round to the back of the car and fiddled with the jerrican lock as if it didn't matter, and the afternoon was still and warm and he felt like death. After which Northerton was hard to take; his mother's house and the doctor coming and the workshop and the fish-and-chip place on the corner and the birds on the telly and in the Sunday papers, all reminding him of her. Winter was coming on; and Chalky was hard to take, the Sunday walks down past the garden fields and the new Grammar School to Drawback where they ran the dogs. The grey sky and the rough brown fields, the silence and leafless trees, all were hard to take, though what he had inside him locked away he couldn't speak of, least of all to Chalky. Though he owed the castle to him and the valley and Martine; to a week's holiday, years back now, Chalky between women, with time on his hands for once. What had haunted Stan had left him unimpressed. The beer was good, he had pronounced; the castle all right, if you liked that sort of thing; and Martine all right, though she didn't look like a very good fuck. Stan pondered, frowning; while Chalky swore and cursed and the greyhound put up hares it never caught, and cut itself on hedgerow wire. And sometimes it was good to get back in the Champ and drive down past the gasworks to his place and shut the curtains and put the Box on and get his mother's tea.

The traffic was halted again; and lights were flashing, amber and blue. There were cars drawn up and lorries; it looked like a road-block and he couldn't think any more what he meant to do.

All the tech lights were on, so the side of the building looked like a shining yellow cliff. The canteen was cold and nearly empty, stinking of lunchtime's bacon rolls. They'd pulled two tables together, though the fat woman had yelled through the serving hatch not to, and Tasker was there from the Boot and Shoe, the only leather bloke they got on with, and Quatermain and Briant and Tony Sidgwick and half a dozen more. Mist was closing in and the odd bangs were starting already and they were all making a row, and it was Guy Fawkes Night.

He sat with the rest, feeling a hot breeze blow on the back of his neck from the table at the far end where the art school girls were sitting. The tall blonde was there, Annette Clitheroe, thirty-five, twenty-three, thirty-six, and the little Irish one they reckoned did turns with the Pakis, and the other one, Helena, the one they nearly had the jumper off in the corridor that night and she didn't have a stitch on underneath. Tony Sidgwick kept cheeking them, saying to come down on the tech table and they'd show them how, then he started on Annette Clitheroe, her people had this big furnishing shop in town centre. She was wearing her hair up round one of those felt former things and Tony kept shouting what was it on her head; and she said finally, 'That's my business,' and Sidgwick said, 'That's a bloody funny place to put it,' and they all started shrieking, Stan included, because he couldn't help himself. Then Sidgwick lit a jumping jack under the table, they didn't see him do it till it was fizzing and went off; and Stan Potts's brain worked with lightning speed so that he grabbed it and threw it over his head and ducked. The fat woman was yelling over the counter about the Principal, and Sidgwick was choking himself he was laughing that much.

Her heels on the concrete floor were very distinct and sharp. She walked the length of the canteen, carrying the plate, and set it down in front of him. He had to look up, though he couldn't stop the laughing; and her eyes were snapping and glinting behind her glasses, there were red spots of anger on her cheeks. In the centre of the spoiled cakes, embedded in a meringue, were the remains of the cracker; and there were little white splashes of cream on her sweater, and one on her jaw.

She said, 'My cousin lost his eye through one of these, you big fat bloody thug. *You must be mad* ...'

He'd passed the road-block but he'd had to lie, he'd said he was going to Dorchester. The traffic was lighter now, the cars spaced out and moving at forty, sometimes forty-five. But nearly nothing was coming up from the west.

His mind was empty; so to fill it, and keep away the things he didn't want to see, he set himself to remember the road ahead. Wimborne, and the left turn by the Dorset Farmers, the little bridge, the long straight in the trees with the notice saying Welcome to Poole although you never really touched it; and the new roundabout at the bottom with the filling station, he could remember it being built. Then there was the other roundabout by the Bakers' Arms and the research place, Admiralty they said it was, with the miles of high steel fence. Then the turn into Wareham, the siding where the oil tankers stood; and beyond, over the bridge ... but his heart was thumping again, hammering, it seemed, painfully against his ribs, and he checked the thought half-formed.

After that first chance trip he went back to Purbeck time and again; though the journey from the Midlands was a long one, five hours and more on a bad day. It left little from a weekend; just one night, and the following morning. The nights he spent in the bar; he would rise early on the Sunday, drive down to the castle or out on to the heath. The castle drew him, the vast shell of ruin topping its hill, the village straggling and crouching at the foot of the mound. Foursquare it stood in a great pass, flanked to either side by bulging heights of chalk. Once he climbed the nearer of the hills, sat an hour or more staring down at the ruined walls and baileys, the gatehouse with its leaning towers of stone. A chalk stream ran beside the mound. Tall trees arched over it, bushes clothed its banks; and here in autumn the glow-worms came, like cold green stars in the grass. He longed to take them back to her, jewel her fingers with them and her dark, rich hair.

Other times he drove across the hills themselves, over the range road that was so often closed. There were hidden bays there, and empty, forgotten villages; and once he saw a horseman ride the forbidden cliffs, a mile or more distant, outlined against the pearly haze of sea. He discovered Kimmeridge with its blackened beach, the great house that overlooked the bay; Worth, its gnomish cottages hidden in sea mist, and Dancing Ledge with its lovely rock-carved pool. He was learning, too, the people who used the pub;

John, as much a mystery to his friends, who knew, it seemed, every country you cared to mention and yet drove a tractor for a living; Martin Jones the hippie, with his floral shirts and wispy shoulder-length hair; Maggie who played guitar for the tourists sometimes in the Barn Bar, who lived in a white bungalow down the road with a birdbath on the lawn and a stone rabbit with broken-off ears, and Richard Joyce who painted for a living and who must have Private Means. He knew them, though he couldn't talk to them; and for their part it seemed they looked askance at the fat man in the corner, with his pained half-smile and always-furtive eyes.

These folk formed, as it were, an inner circle of acquaintanceship. But there were many others; Andy who worked with John, Andy with his tanned good-looking farmer's face who went with Penny who helped out sometimes in the bar; Ted and Arthur and the locals and Vicky who was tall and blonde and wore an Army uniform, they said she was a nurse; she knew Richard, he'd seen her with him a couple of times. And the tourists, the leggy warm brown summer girls who sat in the hayloft in the Barn with their men and laughed and drank cider and lager and sometimes wine. He liked the Barn Bar best, with its high cool walls hung with implements and harness and the thatched roof over the counter and the door standing open to the dusk and the moths circling in the pools of yellow light. He saw the place in dreams; and always Martine was there, Martine with her great dark eyes. Sometimes too he saw her in the hills, in the hidden villages and by the great rock pool. Then he would wake and realize that once more he was home, that he had been alone, that he would always be alone; he would stare into the mirror, at the balding head, the faded, heavy-lidded eyes, and know he would never go to that golden place again, that Northerton was where he belonged and where he must stay. But the simplest truths are the hardest to accept; so he would pack his things, just one more time, and hear his mother's complaints, and the images would swirl hour on hour till he saw the hills again, the sea-mist striping their flanks. He would drive into the remembered yard; and always he would know as he pushed through the hotel door that this time she was gone, gone for ever. Yet always she was there.

In the intervals between his trips he studied. He read the geology of the region; and its history, prehistory and architecture. Every fact that touched upon the place touched, it seemed, on her, made him feel fractionally less alone. So, increasingly, she towered in his consciousness; her face glowed above the hills, her slender hands cupped bays and sea. He discovered the Hardy novels, and in time the painter Nash; the hills and trees and standing stones, flowers that broke from their moorings to sail the sky, fossils that reared in ghostly anger from the rocks. Suns rolled their millstones of golden grain; and it seemed he heard, far off and far too late, the shock of distant armies. He became at times transfigured; then he would remember, and Northerton would claim him and the garage, the oil changes and grease-ups and job cards and MOTs; Chalky and the dogs, the telly and the dreary Sunday nights. His mind, circling, would balk once more at the inevitable yet wholly unacceptable fact: that he was fat, and bald, and forty, and that life was ended.

This inner pain was such that greater issues tended to pass him by; so that it was with some surprise that he entered the Barn Bar one summer night to find the place unusually quiet, a handful of regulars and visitors clustered round a tranny that stood on the counter-top. The words he heard seemed no less and no more than the many uttered before; but the silence that followed them was intense.

Martin Jones broke it. He sat hugging his knees, head back against the wall of the place, fair hair brushing the stone. 'Well,' he said in his quiet, carefully modulated voice, 'it's all happening. This is what we've been waiting for.'

Ray stood frowning behind the bar, one hand laid, it seemed protectively, on the shoulder of Martine. 'Charming,' he said. 'Come on, Martin, we've heard it all before.'

The hippie shook his head. He said, 'Not quite like this.' He glanced round lazily. He said, 'I'm looking forward to it. So's Vicky. It's what she joined up for.'

The blonde woman turned to stare at Joyce, but did not speak.

Jones always seemed exceptionally well informed. 'This will be a primary retaliation zone,' he said. 'They'll want to be sure of Winfrith. I expect we'll be shipped out before too long. They've cleared one of the caravan parks at Sandbanks as an embarkation area. They're keeping quiet about it, of course. That won't be a sight of good, unfortunately. Far too flat.'

Somebody said, 'Tell us where would be any good.'

'Quite a lot of places,' said Martin. 'One thing's certain; I shan't be waiting it out in Poole.' He yawned. 'I'd tend to look for somewhere between the hills and the sea,' he said. 'You'd get good blast protection from the Purbecks; and I can't see anybody lobbing anything into the Channel. They're much too accurate these days.'

Maggie said, 'There'd still be fall-out.'

Martin said, 'I shouldn't think there'd be much to worry about there. You only get fall-out with ground detonations. If we get anything it will be air blasts; they're far more destructive anyway.'

Maggie said bitterly, 'Maybe they'll want some good dirty blasts while they're at it.'

'It's possible,' said Jones politely, 'but I think strategically unlikely.' He brushed the light hair back from his eyes. 'After all, they – and don't forget "they" could be the Americans – will want to occupy the territory afterwards. Otherwise the whole thing's pointless.'

Richard said, 'It's nice to know there's some point in air blasts. It makes it all seem more worth while.'

He turned. As if in emphasis, a rumbling had sounded from outside. The noise intensified; then past the open door ground yellow headlights, dark green armour. The vanguard, it seemed, of a considerable column, moving up towards Worth and the sea. They watched the first vehicles pass; then Ray shrugged. He said, 'That's it then.' He picked a cloth up expressionlessly, hung it over the pumps. A shocked pause; and somebody laughed. They said, 'It's not Time yet.'

'No,' said Martin. 'Not yet. But soon …'

Stan Potts had not spoken. His mind was working furiously; for he knew just such a spot as the other had described. He remembered the lane that wound down from the range road, the lane they only opened once a year, in summer when the Gunnery School closed down. The dead village behind its ten-strand fence, ruined, bullet-pocked gables of barns; and the great shuttered farmhouse by the sea, close under the brooding cliffs. The hippie had spoken, as usual, with calm conviction; and the unthinkable had come to seem, for a space at least, a practical reality. He glanced at Ray, under his lids; at Joyce the painter, and at Martin Jones. Lastly, he saw Martine; and something caught his breath, made his heart begin to pound. Though the notion that later came was not yet fully formed.

The tail-lights ahead brightened. He braked automatically, stared round. For a moment he was disorientated. He brought his mind back from distance, saw with something like a shock the railway siding to his left, the bulky line of tankers. Ahead was the bend that took the road into Wareham; and on the bend they had set up their block. The Army this time; he saw the lorries drawn up, figures moving purposefully behind the red-and-white striped pole. Handlamps bobbed, he caught the gleam of a steel helmet. A car was turned back peremptorily, another waved to one side. So he wasn't going to make it, after all; but he had known that from the start.

Where he sat at the tail of the queue he was a quarter-mile or more from the checkpoint. The vehicles in front of him moved forward, stopped again. He saw a car directed into the side road that runs inland, across the heath to Wool. Another followed it; and something seemed to snap inside his head. He thought, 'This is an army vehicle.'

It seemed his hands and feet had acquired a purpose of their own. He swung out, horn blaring, drove fast down the outside of the queue. He saw a man turn, surprised; another unslinging a Stirling from his shoulder. He braked with a squeal, shoved his driving licence from the window. He said,

'Territorials.' The man stepped back; and he sounded the horn again.

A lamp flashed into his eyes. Somebody said, 'Get out of that thing. Keep your hands in sight.'

He was lined up for the barricade. He let the clutch go, clamped his foot on the floor. The Champ bellowed, took the pole across the bonnet. A cracking; the wheels hit the level-crossing tracks, slewed. He saw a man running, waving his arms. Then the street was full of din. He glimpsed lorries drawn up, civilians being herded aboard a coach; and the noise came again, a metallic hammering from behind. His vision starred; he swerved, held the car. White walls showed the house-fronts stained with neon; and the bridge was ahead. Beyond, a lane forked right. He stamped the brake, clawing at the wheel. His mirrors blazed; he accelerated, swung on to the rough. The suspension bottomed, sickeningly. Bushes showed ahead; he clawed at the dash, and he was driving blind. The wheels sucked, spun, gripped again. The lights jazzed on the skyline; then he was swaying and racketing down a long slope, and behind him was darkness.

Ten minutes later he braked to a halt. He killed the engine, opened the cab door. His ears were singing; water was trickling, somewhere close, but there were no other sounds.

The shaking started then. He sat and hung his head and wanted to be sick. In time the fit passed. He raised his face, stared round. Beside him the Champ loomed against the night, parked at the crest of a little rise. To the east an orange haze reflected the lights of Poole; and ahead, dimly visible, were the hills. The night air moved cool against his skin.

The trickling was not water; he could smell, now, the raw, rich stink of petrol. He unstrapped the nearside screen, groped inside, found a torch. He lifted the jerrycan down, poured what remained into the tank and slung the thing into the bushes. Then he walked round to the Champ. Cracks had radiated across the windshield; in the corner was a neat round hole. He touched it, shakily. He said, 'Oh my Christ.'

His head still felt swimmy, and his throat and mouth were dry. He climbed back into the driving seat, twisted the starter, heard the engine catch and bark. The main road ran somewhere to his left; but he dared not risk it again. He drove forward slowly, eyes more accustomed to the gloom. Near at hand the heath stretched broken and undulating, mist clinging to the hollows of the ground like thick white smoke. The hills grew higher, outlining themselves against the night; and in time he heard gravel crunch under his wheels. He had found a lane, or quarry track. He lit a cigarette, closing his eyes against the flare of the match, and set himself to climb. The fear had gone; in its place was a curious sensation, almost like elation. For he had achieved the impossible; crossed a crowded, panicking country to reach her. Now he was almost there; and now he knew how long she had been with him. He'd seen her in cafés and restaurants and supermarkets and pubs, on beaches and hills and in the street; she'd laughed at him from hoardings, kicked her legs on the Box, shown him her belly in the Sunday rags. While he worked his allotment, and walked with Chalky and the dogs, and drank his halves on Saturday nights. Now life was altering, the world breaking up, Sledger and Annette Clitheroe and school and tech blowing away to dark. He was going to her in a stone-built pub where the bar lights burned amber and a fossil fish hung on the wall; and if she wouldn't come he would beat her, because he'd waited long enough and he was tired. And if she struggled he would tie her, and if he had to tie her he'd brought the rope, and maybe that way it would be better yet.

The moon rose, flooding the horizon with dull golden light. The mist banks gleamed; through and between them the Champ picked its way, a big, cautious shadow in the night.

2

To see the scene that follows through the eyes of Stanley Potts you must imagine extraordinary things; colours that throb and spark, hills that roll and tilt, haloed with light beneath a sky of smoky milk. You must hear the calling of night birds across that haunted space, the crash of the sea like blood pounding in the ears; you must hear too the singing of all the choirs of heaven. And can you not see the Champ as she breasts each slope, floats from cloud to cloud of glowing mist?

Now she halts, at the steep mouth of a little lane; and Stan Potts waves from the window to the car that follows. The station waggon backs up, driven by Richard Joyce; and the Champ charges the fragile gate that blocks the way, the splinters fly in graceful moonshot arcs. And there is the track beyond, winding between fences of bright wire; the field where army hunters used to graze, the empty village with its empty barns, church tower lost in trees, the thistled Great House with its empty windows, washed in brown moonlight. He points wordless; and she nods and smiles, her face with its great eyes underlit by the dash. He is remembering the parties at the tech, each the same; and how one never saw it happen but suddenly everybody would be paired off, he never knew how it happened but it was every time the same; and he would sit and sip his beer, alone in the centre of the room, and try not to hear the giggles from the shadows and the whispering, and try not to care that he was Potts the Pot and nobody wanted him. He is remembering too that it cannot happen any more, that they are four now, in an empty land. He is remembering that she is with him, and that Richard Joyce is following and Maggie who played guitar, once in a lifetime long gone by.

He has made no error in his route. There ahead is the bay with its amphitheatre of cliffs, pale and vast in the sinking light. Below the cliffs a great half-moon of turf, stretching to further rockfalls and the sea. And at the sea's edge, foursquare against its shimmering plain, the farmhouse with its lines of dark windows, its chimney stacks of burly stone. The joy that fills him makes him want to shout aloud; but he says, 'We're nearly there,' and she laughs and says, 'It's beautiful.' She moves, rustling; and he smells her scent. How ashamed he is, now, of the thoughts that filled him; when she came so sweetly, and made no demur. They all but burn his mind!

He coasts the Champ to a halt, by the boarded-up door of the place. His senses, it seems, are unnaturally acute. The Cambridge pulls in beside him; he hears the crunch of tyres on shingle, the squeak and whimper of the fanbelt as the engine dies. His own boots rasp on rock; he hurries to the passenger door; and Martin Jones says, 'Good evening!'

Have you imagined his mood? Have you heard the angels sing, felt the tremulousness that filled him like bubbling wine, till it seemed he was floating on air? Now you must imagine a further change; a reversal of his fortunes, no less!

How the sea spins, inside his Potty old head; how the sky whirls, and the cliffs! He sees her run to him; he sees the arm that curls about her; he hears her say, 'I didn't know how to get here. But he brought me.' Now they are five, and the world is comprehensible again; the smile has already fixed itself protectively about his lips. He feels he should sing light tunes, *Dah-dah dee-dee-dee dah-di-dah*, as he unpacks the Champ, as he carries in the sleeping bags and the stove and the food and the tins and cases and boxes and cans. Jones has brought what he has not, blanketed the windows of the long-disused rooms, set out chairs and a folding table. A fire of driftwood crackles in a hearth; Tilly lamps hang green and hissing, even the floors have been swept. It's a real little Home from Home! He sees how carefully it has all been planned; he sees how she clings to him as he goes from room to room, rubbing him with her little brown hands. He's glad he's had so much practice at keeping the half-smile clamped to his mouth, at lidding his eyes and at staring at the ground; for nobody has guessed his secret. It was all his fault, right from the start. He has been silly; men with fat bottoms should never fall in love!

There is even a tablecloth, gay-checked in white and blue. They make a meal, using his stove; there's no question but that they're going to let him stay. He blushes, smiling at the cloth, as they thank him, thank him for what he has done; and the party is quite gay. Afterwards the cars are hidden, driven from sight in a ruined outhouse, and bracken and brushwood heaped round their fenders to make them invisible from the air. Stan fetches his handlamp because there are only two Tillys, and naturally they will be needing three rooms. But there is a spare room, at the end of a cold, cluttered corridor;

Martin leads the way to it, Tilly lamp held high, the light glancing from his soft blond hair. He calls the place the Bachelor's Suite, and they all laugh, and Stan joins in. There is no water, explains his host; but he has found a jug and basin, and set up an old packing crate as a wash-hand stand. He was expecting more visitors, he tells him, more than in fact arrived. He hopes he will be comfortable, and leaves him.

There is an awkward moment then because she stands in the doorway and smiles as if she means it and says, 'Thank you,' again and for a moment it's almost as if she's going to peck his cheek. But Martin calls from the corridor, and adds something Stan doesn't catch, though he hears the artist laugh. So she turns away, and he pushes the door to and hangs the lamp from a hook in one of the ceiling beams. Then he spreads his bag out and turns the liner back, and Gets Undone.

He doesn't feel he can really bother to shave.

He lay for a while unsleeping, though now that he and the Champ had both done their bit he supposed they had earned a rest. The sea lapped and whispered outside the place, the still, damp air of the room stung his cheeks. For a time the traffic noise dinned in his ears; the shouting and hooting, revving of engines, bawling of the many loudhailers. Then he wished that he could become angry, but his inhibition was too great. Men with large bottoms look funny when they are annoyed. From this his thoughts drifted to other things, none creative, some positively counter-productive. He remembered how one day in Biology Chapman discovered his resemblance to the duck-billed platypus, and passed a note to Smythe about it, so from Potty Potts he became Potts the Platypus, which he did not like. Though the name didn't take too well till the Sledge found a drawing on the board one day, and realized the direction of the sniggerings, and said, 'How rare is the platypus, Potts?' and there was this great roar of laughing. So he had to stand up, 'on his back legs', as Sledger put it, and stammer out all he knew about the creature, and after that the nickname was assured. Then the R stream got hold of it, the yobboes, so each break time and each afternoon it was *Platypus, platypus*, in chanted rhythm while he was jostled and shoved and had his balls grabbed from behind, at the centre of a ring of races, unable to get away, waiting for the prefect's bell to end the torture. He thought perhaps he could beat one of them up till he saw Tompkins, who was the worst, fight in the boxing tournament and realized what would happen to him if he tried. And so the half-smile was born. It had stayed on his face for twenty-five years.

Platypus, platypus. Potty-the-rarimus-plat ...

The moon sank, beyond the ridge of cliff. With its setting, clouds drew across the sky; and for a time the summer night was at its darkest. In the darkness came wisps and tendrils of mist. They thickened steadily, coiling up from the water in half-seen skeins. The amphitheatre, the level space between cliffs and sea, began to fill. Then the mist rose higher, lapping the tall rock, spilling across the undulating ground above. With the dawn a watery light-burst showed for a time, low down. Shadows were visible, for seconds together; but the fog was not dispelled. Nor did it clear on the following day, or the day after that.

The colony, if such it had become, worked steadily. Latrine pits were dug, in the dry scree below the cliffs, the house rendered more habitable. Joyce, the artist, rigged movable screens for the windows, replacing the blankets that had hung there; the women cooked and rearranged the stores while Martin Jones made an expedition along the foreshore, God knew to where, returned rowing a boat. They heard his hail out in the mist, rushed down to admire the prize. He seemed well versed in nautical matters, running her up on to the beach and securing her with a rope fixed to a spike driven into a crack in the rock. Stan took his rod to a little spit of land, well out in the mist, where he could be away from the others; Maggie with her brilliant dark-fringed eyes, and Martine, trim in a chunky sweater and neat, tight-fitting jeans. He was unused to sea-angling, but at his second attempt he landed four fine silver fish. Jones pronounced them grayling, and showed how they could be scaled by rubbing a knife-blade from tail to nose. They ate them that night, grilled and fresh, and listened to a tranny blurt out its endlessly worsening news.

Increasingly it seemed Jones had taken over the leadership of the group. He it was certainly who ordered their days, organizing rota systems for such chores as chopping wood. What little lay about the farmhouse and the barns was rapidly consumed; so he produced from somewhere a creaking handcart, with which he would set off for the headland that closed the bay to the west, return with load after load of bleached, brittle planks. Also he located a spring of fresh water, some half-mile from the farmhouse. It came welling and bubbling out of the cliffs, cold and crystal-clear; and it became Stan's job to trudge forward and back each morning till the containers were refilled.

A part of his mind was nearly happy with the turn events had taken. The other thing had, after all, bristled with difficulties. He had no practical experience of lovemaking, but doubted as an engineer whether two bodies would fit together as neatly and automatically as in the paperbacks he had read. Also, what did you say? What *could* you say to them? To lay one's hands on the body of another seemed suddenly a monstrous thing; so he was glad in a way the problem was not his, he performed his duties with no complaint and spoke little to the rest. Martine in particular he avoided, lowering his eyes when she came near so as to give no cause for offence. He was realizing how narrow his escape had been. He remembered the rope, and what he had thought he might do, and blushed in the dark for shame.

But the even pattern into which his days had fallen was not destined to last. It was Martin Jones who brought matters to a head, one pearly, still-grey afternoon. They had taken the boat out, into the drifting mist, to fish the deeper water a little offshore; now sky and land alike were hidden, the vessel slapped and drifted in the void while Stan sat patiently, head down over the butt of the rod, aware of the other's stare. Jones lolled in the bows, in reefer jacket and an ancient, battered cap; he watched for a time, eyes narrowed, before flicking a cigarette butt overboard. 'You know, Potts,' he said pleasantly, 'I've been thinking. The food's getting a bit down; and there are loads of other places round about. I think it's time one of us moved out.'

For an instant a thought, as wild as it was absurd, flickered in Stan's mind. He said, 'What do you mean?'

'Well, look at it my way,' said Jones. 'You've got the vehicle for it, we'll stake you to a couple of days' grub. Should be good pickings up by Kimmeridge. They had a general shop.'

Stan said dully, 'Maybe I could go and see what I could find.'

Jones shook his head. 'No,' he said, 'that's not what I mean.' He leaned forward. 'Fuck off, Potts,' he said. 'Nobody wants you here.'

Stan smiled, and kept his eyes down. He said, 'I'll think about it.'

Jones lit another cigarette. His woman's face was thoughtful. 'I expect you will,' he said. 'But you won't go.' He paused. 'You're a funny sod, Potts,' he said. 'Why did you come down here in the first place? What was it you wanted?'

The flush was starting at the roots of Stan's hair. He kept his eyes on the sea with desperate casualness, and hoped the other would stop.

Martin blew smoke. 'I don't think you're a ginger,' he said, 'so it wasn't Richard. And it certainly wasn't me. You don't like me much, do you?'

Stan said, 'I wouldn't say that.'

'Well,' said Jones, 'I don't like you.' He blew smoke. 'I wonder if we've got what you wanted,' he said. 'I hope it wasn't Maggie. She wouldn't be any good to you. Shall I tell you why?'

Stan didn't answer; and the other began to laugh. 'No,' he said. 'I don't believe it. But it's true, isn't it? I know who it is. You never take your eyes off her.'

Stan said, 'Oh, shut up …' He could have bitten his tongue instantly; but it was too late, the childish remark was out.

Jones went into fresh peals. 'Potts,' he said, 'you will be the death of me …' Then he became serious. 'Stanislaus,' he said, 'have you ever had a woman?'

No answer.

'You haven't, have you?' said Martin. 'And I'll tell you something. I don't think you ever will.' He shook his head. 'Poor old Potts,' he said. 'It's going to take more than the end of the world to change your luck. *You must be mad ...*'

He heard his mother's voice on the stairs, and the door slam as he stood crimson and shaking with shame.

His life had not been easy. He remembered how years back, before he left school, it had been the same. His father used to take him to the Variety sometimes, his father had been an expert on Variety; he said he liked the cleverness of the turns, though if there were nudes he always leaned forward a little in his seat. And Stan would sit and pretend to tuck into his ice cream and watch up under his lids at the girls who ran about in their little pants and bras and showed their belly buttons, sometimes he couldn't forget for days. He used to think if only he could have one of those girls, just one, only once to know what it was like, it wouldn't be too bad. Afterwards, when he knew that wasn't going to happen, the Variety was finished; and you didn't have to open the Sunday papers and see it there, or watch it all on the Box. Only as he got older, it got worse again because it started happening everywhere, on the streets; some of them were only kids but you could see their nipples and the whole lot if you looked. It made him more furtive, more secret; it brought the smile back nearly all the time. And the office girls at work, when they came up through the Stores you could see the lot, you sometimes couldn't help it. Then they'd glare as if it was your fault, something you'd done. So the need came back, stronger than before, till he must assuage himself, though he groaned and cursed. Then he met Martine, and for a time held her image pure. But the dreams would come; till one day, only to stop them, he thought how wonderful it would be if he *was* her, to live inside her body and have it for his own, to walk with his head up and have the world at his feet. He knew it was wrong, but once started the thoughts wouldn't stop. Any more than the other thing had. Then one morning he found – what he found, slung over the front garden wall.

It seemed his heart stopped. Just stopped. He didn't want to see; he tried not to see, but it was there, *they* were there. He couldn't leave them; he had to snatch, and scrunch the lacy ball in his palm, drive his hand deep into his donkey jacket out of sight. He was terrified then that somebody had seen; but it still wanted twenty to eight and the street was empty, blue in the half-light. He hurried off, shoulders hunched, face burning, heels banging the paths. He wrapped the shame in a handkerchief; and it was as if he held her, her herself, tight in his fist. It was a Mystery, the first he had encountered. His heart hammered, through the day, when he thought what he had done, what he owned. He hid the terrible discovery in his wardrobe, pushed right at the back of the topmost shelf. He tried not to think of it, of what lay there, but it was no use. The thing had to be done, the experiment performed.

They were smaller even than he'd imagined. He drew them up, over his white thighs; then his face flamed; then it was done, the transformation complete. And he was panting, he could hardly breathe, he was angling the mirror to see. He had become the enemy, the thing he feared; and fear was banished.

Then of course the door swung open; and he was covering himself, his belly, the scrap of see-through lace about his loins. A cry was echoing, which was his own cry of fear and shame; and his mother backing away, and her voice sounding on the landing.

'*You must be mad . . .*'

A pale chink to one side of the shutter told him dawn was in the sky. He moved his eyes round the little room. He had been dreaming; he was almost sure he had been talking to Chalky then, and Chalky had given him some excellent advice, though he couldn't quite remember what it was. Also it had seemed he had been back at school. He remembered the form room vividly; afternoon light lying across the walls and beyond the tall windows the cattle market with its empty pens, the pines in the cemetery, the buses grinding up to London Road. He had been standing, and the Sledge had been shouting questions and he had been shouting back the answers, confident and assured; and the face of Sledger Bates was altering, with amazement and delight, while Chapman and all the rest sat stunned and quiet. He sighed, because such things could never be. Then he frowned. The frown was the outer sign of the great leaping jolt that had struck his chest; it was as if he had slept to dream of the thing he most desired, and woken to find that thing clutched in his hand.

He rose, and dressed himself. He eased the door open, peered out. The corridor lay quiet and grey, nobody stirring. He guessed it wasn't more than six a.m. He tiptoed past Martine's room, listened again.

He was used to the place now. His hand found the door-catch in the half-light, twisted. He crossed the yard to the barn, still stepping carefully. He opened the driving door of the Champ, groped behind the seat. For a moment he was afraid the thing would be gone; but it was still there. He lifted the case, went back the way he had come.

He sat in the meagre light, resting his hands on the lid, smelling the faint antiseptic tang of oil; and it all came back, the little range beside the Masonic Hall, the firing-point with its pinned-up targets, the massive cupboards where the rifles were stored. Though he and the other pistol men pretended to look down on the rifle section. This lying on the floor and strapping yourself rigid, that wasn't shooting. Besides, there was something about the feel of a pistol, the balance and the way the grip snugs into your hand. And the target wavering and dim, pinned by the clumsy foresight; the good feeling when you know you're shooting well and the spotter is calling them out beside you and the eights and nines start coming in. He had been a steady member, improved a lot over the years; till he gave up using the old club clunker and went a bit mad and got himself a ten-shot Browning. He developed a new feeling for weaponry; and by and by another gun came to haunt him, he was never quite sure why. Certainly it looked like no other ever made; he came to know its lines by heart, the deep-cusped trigger, steeply sloping stock with the lovely curve that takes the base of the thumb, the knuckle bar with its knurled grips like the eyes of a crocodile, or fossil. He made himself an expert; he learned every model from '08 to '43, when the Reich was feeling the pinch and the new gun came in, the sheet-metal gun, the PPK. Only once again it seemed fate had dealt him a blow; because he couldn't hold the pistol on his ticket, you needed access to an outdoor range and for that he had neither the inclination nor the means. So he was reduced to talking about the toy to Chalky, who'd used one in the Mob in Germany; till one night Chalky came in more mysterious than usual – Christ, the people he knew – and asked him if he'd like to see a certain thing, and Stan of course said no he didn't dare. Though later when he held the gun he knew he wasn't going to be able to let it go. So he bought it, for thirty-five, off the Yank who'd brought it in, and a box of Swedish Parabellum thrown in as well. And after that he sold the Browning and gave up the club, because he daren't belong any more. He stood, for the first time in his life, outside the law; a new experience, and one not wholly pleasing.

He'd fired the thing just once, on a Bonfire Night. Later he was disgusted with himself; he'd never handled a heavy pistol before, nervousness made him take a bad grip. The Luger spat a leaf of dark orange flame; and a flying house-brick caught his palm and he stood appalled, ears ringing, hearing the cartridge case go clipping up through the branches of a tree.

He unlocked the lid and opened it, sat staring down. Then as ever he hefted the pistol, feeling its weight, seeing the slate blue of the barrel, the *Erfurt* stamp with its crown, the wooden handgrips each held by a screw, the only screws in the action. He divined then a part at least of the Mystery; that this was a gun a group of men had built, when they wanted to fight the world. He frowned, remembering what he had read of the smashing power of a heavy bullet; then the room seemed to spin a little. He had remembered how once at the Club they put a cake of soap up for a laugh, and the Browning drilled a cone out of it two inches across.

The fit passed; and he marvelled at his steadiness. He opened the box of rounds, fed the fat cartridges into the magazine, clicked it into the butt. He pressed back on the muzzle to check the recoil spring and cocked the gun, saw the shiny bullet driven home. He checked the *Geladen* telltale, and pushed the safety on. Then he put the thing aside, and waited.

He was shivering by the time the others rose; but his brain felt clear. They were sullen, unspeaking; he wondered if the prospect of his leaving had been discussed. He brewed himself coffee, heating a saucepan on the camping stove. He saw they were down to the last gas bottle. He drank, holding his hands round the cup for warmth, and heard the squeaking as the wood-truck passed the door. He waited a moment longer, and walked into the yard.

The fog was thick as ever, and the light strange; yellowish, and dull. A path wound up across the grass, rising to the cliffs that fringed the bay. He followed it, keeping well back, guided by the sound of creaking.

The ascent was less steep than he had expected. The path led through a gully in the rock, dank stone close to either side. At the crest, the light was brighter; and he glimpsed in the mist the moving shadow that was Jones.

His heart was thudding faster; but the calm remained. He took the gun from his pocket, seated the grip into his palm, clicked off the safety and laid his forefinger alongside the trigger guard. The path swung left, dipping again toward the sea. He hurried the last few yards, and saw the other had turned. Behind him stretched a ragged crest of ground; the light, breaking through the mist, showed the pale gleam of his hair. He was cocking his head, staring back the way he had come. He called, uncertainly; then as Stan closed with him he relaxed. 'It's Potty Potts,' he said. 'What are you doing, Potty Potts?' Then his face altered.

His stance was good; and the action of a Luger is precise. He took up first pressure, squeezed. This time he was holding well; the weight of gun and clip absorbed the recoil. The muzzle rose, dropped back to the mark. Echoes ran, barking; but the second round missed. For Jones was no longer there.

He walked forward slowly, and stopped. The paradox was explained; the crest of ground, dim in the mist, was the edge of a seaward-facing cliff. He peered into the void at his feet and heard, mixed with the seething in his ears, the distant roar of the tide. A sea bird wheeled, complaining; there were no other sounds.

He sat on the grass, seeing the rag-doll figure flung out into space as if punched by a massive fist. Then he looked down at the gun. Strange how at the end it had been so easy. No range at all.

He pressed the magazine release, ejected the chambered round. Then he stood up, walked to the truck. A heave, and it too vanished. The faint noise of its falling reached back to him.

It took an hour to find a path to the beach. He moved slowly, climbing between piles of shattered rock. As he climbed, he sang. The tune he chose was his favourite: 'O God our Help in Ages Past'. Light moved round him, wheeling; and the angels joined in with the descant.

He found the truck lying smashed beside a great flat-topped rock. Near it a spur of stone showed a smear of sticky red, but there was no sign of the body. The sea sucked and lisped, surging round the outcrop; the narrow beach of dark fawn sand was empty and smooth.

He sat a while, letting his eyes drift closed. He felt very tired. He heard the sea roar, and the mewing of the gulls. Then the mewing stopped.

He opened his eyes. As he did so the mist above him glowed. Then the water. The brightness grew, till the sea was a mirror of silver, reflecting a hidden sun. Afterwards, the sound began; a sighing at first and rumbling, like the passage of great wheels across the sky. The rumbling deepened to a growl. The cliff vibrated; boulders and stone rained down, from somewhere came the boom of a heavier fall. He ran out into the sea, saw the mist fly ragged, as if driven by the passage of great masses of air. Distant headlands gleamed, alien in bright sunlight; then the noise died away. In its wake came another; but fainter and far-off, like an echo. When that was gone too he turned eastward, began to pick his way once more below the cliffs. An hour, and the bay opened out ahead; he saw the grey bulk of the farmhouse, the barn where the cars were parked.

He had been gripping the butt of the gun in his pocket. He made himself relax, climbed to the sloping turf. The place was silent; and at the door sat Richard Joyce.

He went past him into the building, knowing already what he would find. The rooms deserted, beds and sleeping bags sprawled anyhow. He walked back to the other. He said, 'Where are they?'

The artist looked at him tiredly, resting his head against the stone. There were dark rings under his eyes. He said, 'They've gone.'

'What do you mean?' said Stan. 'Where?'

'Gone,' said Joyce. 'Just gone.' He heaved himself to his feet and walked away.

The sounds came again, in the night. After which he dozed. Toward dawn he was visited by a dream. First it was as if she called to him, her voice mixed with a soughing wind. Then it seemed he stood on some eminence, placed high above a rolling plain. He saw the heath and hills, then all the country; the blue-grey sea, fossil-haunted cliffs. He saw the castle and the village, small as children's toys; and other villages and towns, and others and still more. Then white flame leaped, devouring; and when he could see again they were blotted out. Wiped clean, every one. And the sea creamed against empty beaches, the wind hissed through the grass. Her voice came again, high and mournful as a sea bird. The sound rushed out to lose itself in the vastness of the west; and the sun rose, over a low hill, bringing an empty dawn.

TWO

Fragments

Maggie

Somebody wrote to me to say I'd killed my parents. If that's true I suppose I did them a favour. It got them out of this.

Did I kill them?

In fact, no. You don't die of grief. You don't die of anything except stoppage of the heart. But that's the trouble with emotions. People don't understand them. They miss what they can do, and make a lot of noise about what they can't.

Certainly nobody understood me. After what I'd done I was supposed to be – oh Christ, distraught or something. That's what they could never understand. I wasn't distraught. I wasn't anything. Not even sorry. Given the same chance I'd have done the same again.

I suppose I got off lightly. Never teach again of course, but who the hell wants to? If you'd seen that school …

Imagine a great, echoing, glass-and-concrete box. Or a stack of rabbit hutches, fifty or sixty feet high. And all round, reaching into distance, the roofs of the New Model Estate. Grass showing here and there, the grass they hadn't destroyed. And little tamed trees. I felt I was suffocating. Like a goldfish in a bowl.

I can still hear the kids if I want to. All the hundreds of kids, footsteps and chattering filling the place like splashing water. I can see the Links, long glass corridors stifling-hot in summer, the geometric troughs of peonies and geraniums. It was a Model School. Model School and Model Estate. That was what was wrong with it.

They said I had no feeling for the children. That was the biggest laugh. I was the most popular staff member there, it used to get up the others' noses. Then they said I had no morals. That stung. The only thing that did. Morals are of the mind, not the body. But that's two thousand years of Christian ethos for you.

I wonder what's happened to that school. Flattened, I should think. Those noises …

What did I actually do to that girl?

At least that's one thing I can still be precise about. The Estate was going to take her, like it took all the rest. She was going to marry, like all the rest. And beget children; decently, with the lights out, like all the rest. And shorten her husband's life for a bigger fridge or a bigger car or new lounge curtains or a trailer cabin cruiser or a colour TV. Instead I opened her eyes, for a little while. I taught her, before the little houses took her, to swim in the wine-dark sea. She sat at the feet of Sappho; she heard the thunder from Olympus, knew Pan and all the fauns.

Only that, of course, isn't what they called it.

I think there's a time for everybody when feeling runs out, the tears just dry up. It's another theory I had, something else that sent me wild; that emotion isn't a bottomless well, that we're all of us born with a measured amount and when we've run through that there's no more to come. So if we squander it on unworthy things we're squandering the only part of ourselves that has a meaning, that sets us apart from trees and the brute beasts. Holmes used to say the brain was like an attic, it could only hold so much lumber. So he never bothered to remember whether the earth went round the sun, or the sun went round the earth. Because it didn't matter to him. I believe the same of the heart.

So when I came back down here I wouldn't let myself be moved. To anger, or to joy. They said I was cold, what I'd done showed I had no feelings. But it wasn't like that. It was nothing like that at all.

At least my mother gave me a roof. I suppose I should be grateful. I suppose I was. She let me sit about, and stopped talking to the neighbours, and the whispering died away in its own good time.

I suppose that's why I closed myself up. The things that hurt most people passed me by; and the things that wounded me, they couldn't understand. Nobody will, in this epoch. Not any more. Maybe when people start again, in a thousand years when the ash has blown away, there'll be a new society; one that will care. And maybe in those times there'll be no wars, or need of them. Sappho will come again.

Long thoughts for a scandal in a Comprehensive! I suppose if I told them to anybody they'd think how hard I was working to justify myself. One thing's certain. They wouldn't listen.

I think Richard understood. But men are odd. Most of them can't stand their own sort of homosexuality but ours turns them on. I talked about it to him once. He reckoned the aesthetic counted for a lot, that it was male practice that offended him, not the morals. But I don't know. I think there's more to it than that.

He was good for me. He'd been through the mill himself, he didn't expect … oh, standards, anything. There were some afternoons I just couldn't cope. I'd lie on the bed with the blinds pulled, see the sunburst on the linen, shadows moving on the floor, hear the summer noises of the Island …

He never tried for me. I think he understood. Sometimes he'd paint, or just potter. Sit and read, make tea. And knowing if I called him he was there …

They wouldn't have understood a relationship like that either. Just presumed I'd turned Normal.

The pub saved me too. I often wondered whether Ray knew. If he did he never showed it. He didn't pay me, for the singing. Not that I wanted him to. But I could always eat there. It all helped out.

I suppose I wasn't badly off. I'd got Richard when I needed him, and enough money to scrape by on. Even managed to keep the Cambridge going. I think I was settling down to an uneventful spinsterhood. Sounds queer. It's all a state of mind. Like the other. I've known spinsters who'd been married for years. Raised families.

Only one thing scared me. Right deep down. I was afraid my feelings were dead, despite the penny-pinching I'd still got through the stack. It was enough for me just having a living. And going to the Barn, watching the people come and go. I wondered sometimes if I should have killed myself, a long while back when it all blew up. Talked about that to Richard too. He said no, he reckoned nobody sane ever really wants to die. He said there'd been a time when he didn't care about living, but that was a different thing.

Pity about Vicky coming down. Don't know how he felt about that. He went into his shell a bit. Pity it had to happen. Nearly makes you believe in personalized Fate.

I told him I thought I might be dead emotionally. That was queer too. Like tempting providence. I don't know what I feel now. What I want. Maybe the bombs shook me more than I realized.

I knew what I wanted then. When Marty came. But I wouldn't admit it. Not at the start. That was silly. When you stop being frank with yourself that's when you really do start getting old.

Never known about her folk. She's got an auntie in Bournemouth somewhere but she hardly ever sees her. She's more withdrawn than most girls of her age. Twenty-three now, coming twenty-four. She was nineteen when I met her.

I wonder if she knew? From the start? So much rubbish talked about female intuition. Excuses for empty heads. Some have it, though. The pretty ones. Or maybe they've all got it. I never tried to find out about the others.

She was fond of me, I know that. I've got a certain quality, I can project. And age has made it easier. That's why I would have made a good teacher.

That's why I *did* make a good teacher …

I used to sit up with her some nights. In her room. Drink coffee. Slept there once. That was a strain. She surely knew then …

She's lovely. I used to think she had Spanish blood, but I changed my mind. Now I think she's pure long-headed Celt. She fits here. Belongs. A Goddess, in a mini and an amber shirt.

Something moving in the notion. But this is a moving country. The past isn't dead. Least, not till today. Till today, they remembered the Bloody Assize. Now, we've all been tried.

Trying to find a place for sorrow. But it's all too much to take in. Maybe I'm still in shock.

Wonder if that bloody fog's still there? I'd give a lot to see the sun. The wind's been rising anyway. That should clear it.

Wonder if he was right, about the fall-out. Trying not to think …

He was the worst thing that could have happened. From my point of view at least. Heard he'd got a wife in Poole anyway. Teacher. I kept my mouth shut. It would have looked like preaching morals. And I'm hardly the one to start that. Too many cheap answers available.

Wouldn't have liked him anyway. Walking, talking Image, new-style bourgeois. All the fine emotions of a rattlesnake. But that's done with now. That and a lot more things.

Wonder if the pub's still there …

Silly thought. Of course it's there. It's all there, in the mist. Those … epicentres were miles away. Up in the Midlands maybe.

Wonder if it's all over …

I remember those trips down to the beach. The Ledges. Thought they were a mistake, at the time. Silly, but I just didn't think she'd show so much. Must be getting old-fashioned. This is – this was – the seventies.

I oiled her once. She was brown. Never saw a girl get so brown. Then when she stripped for the shower, the little white band across her behind …

I thought it was over for me. Dead. I wasn't to know.

The afternoons were always the worst. When Richard had gone into Bournemouth. Or when he was down on the beach. Those beach scenes of his were starting to be something else …

He went up to London once. To set the big exhibition up. I could have gone with him. But I couldn't leave, I couldn't stand being that far from her. It had hit me, by then. Nothing like I'd ever known before.

There's a spinney down the road. Half a mile on from the pub. I used to walk to it sometimes, sit where I could see the roofs over a swell of land and the tall chimneys, the stone slates orange-patched with lichen. I'd wonder what she was doing; if she was lying down, or changing, or stocking the bars maybe for the evening. Or if she wasn't there at all, she'd gone into the village or across to Poole. It seemed I should be able to tell. I used to try to see through slates and walls, into her room; or send my thought out, over the grass in the sunlight. Sometimes I'd get drowsy. Then the guns would start, behind the hills, I'd wake and hear the insect noise, hum of cars maybe a long way off; and the big iron doors slamming in the sky. It was a total experience, something Nash might have understood. I think Richard was brought up on his painting …

Odd thing happened once. The Stan Potts man turned up, came and parked that great lorry of his just off the road, sat and looked back as well. He was there an hour or more; but he didn't see me.

Wonder if he had a thing about her too? I wouldn't be surprised. Queer man. Comes from the Midlands somewhere, I think. Never talked to him. Didn't really feel much inclination. I don't think I'd have got through. One thing I'm sure of, though. If ever there was an unhappy soul, it's he …

I used to get dreams about her. Always the same sort of thing. I found her in a brook once. Just lying there, among the golden reeds. A bit like Ophelia. Her dress was open; her skin was still brown, her bra looked very white by contrast. Salt-white. No mark on her; and her eyes were closed, as if she was asleep. But I knew she was dead.

Another time it was worse. Much worse. She was lying in the road. Not much of her left; but you could see she'd been wearing that lovely checky shirt. A tuft of her hair was moving in the breeze; the rest of her was … flattened, as if car after car had gone over her, like they go over cats. As if there'd been some terrible panic, and nobody had tried to stop.

Dreams? They're like prevision now …

That broke me up. I hadn't been going to the pub that night. But I had to. To see that … I know it was silly. She was there of course, talking to Arthur and Teddy King. I sat a bit; then something she said, I don't know what it was, but she was laughing, holding a glass. I wanted to tell her … what was coming, what was somehow going to happen if we didn't all take special care. I couldn't of course. Couldn't speak. I went out to the loo instead, sat and bawled for about half an hour. I don't think I'd ever felt so bad. Of course Martin Knowsit Jones had moved in by then, I was just cat-jealous …

She was worried, afterwards. Wanted to know what was wrong. I said it was nothing, I'd got an upset stomach. Which I suppose was true …

Started fantasizing, after that. Couldn't help it. I pretended sometimes she was living with me at the bungalow. Others, we'd got ourselves a boat; narrow-boat it was once, I remember. I'd dress her, and undress her, any way I fancied; and we were together, always together, I had her for my own.

It wasn't easy waking up to what would happen. In a way, she'd helped me through my thirties; but any day now she was going to be away and gone like all the rest, measuring curtains and having babies, and the old man down at the boozer; or sitting watching telly with her every night, the good and dutiful husband, that would have been worse. I thought it would almost have been better if – well, she could die like that, in the stream, like Ophelia. That's what comes, when you love somebody that much.

I've heard it said we can't love. Creatures like us. The people who say that are wrong.

I'd sit sometimes and read Shakespeare; or Homer, John Donne, anybody with a soul. Then I'd think, 'They're talking to me, down all the centuries.' And I'd start to cry. Sometimes I'd go on all night. Hardly a fit occupation for a grown mother of none.

Strange how Potts turned up. The more I think about it … but it doesn't matter. I think I'd have tried to do the same sort of thing anyway. Better than being shipped out to Poole. Easy too, when it came to it. All the confusion …

Somehow, it's absurd but I feel sorriest for Ray. And the pub.

I wonder if … but we shan't ever know. Those shots … They were shots, living down here you hear enough small-arms fire. And they were both of them out there, in the fog.

Queer, how she reacted. As if she knew.

At least I knew what she was going to do. That's prevision, if you like. I don't think she'd have taken anything with her. Not even a coat …

Strange, too, how we didn't talk. Just walked like that, side by side in the fog.

Feeling bad now about Richard. Maybe … what I thought happened, didn't. But it did, I don't know why I'm so sure but I am. Martin Jones isn't coming back. So Richard's alone there, with that creepy man. But she didn't know what she was doing. She was … strange, I had to go with her. He'll understand …

It wasn't really all that far. She started crying once, after the flashes. Thank God we'd left the cliffs. I held her, till the noise stopped. I'd never held her before.

If I'd let her go, on her own. She might have gone mad …

At least you couldn't miss this place. That black, littered beach; and the cliffs, bulging, lines of stone set in them like lines of teeth … I thought there might be people at the house. I thought we could get a night's rest, something to eat.

It took us an hour to get in. Inside, it was strange; the mist pressing against the panes, and the odd light, and the furniture still and stark, reflecting in all the polished floors. If you called there were echoes, you heard them run through room after room; but nobody was there to answer.

We went up the big staircase, through the bedrooms. Then the attics. It's weird, the great white house in the mist, all the things inside it and nobody to come, perhaps nobody to come, perhaps nobody will ever come again. So different from last time …

On a normal day, you could see across the bay. There's a wood, on the high ground to the west; in one place somebody had felled the trees, made a sort of notch. You could see the sea through it, like a pale blue eye. They told me they used to put a lamp in the window, for the smugglers. But there'll be no lamp tonight …

There's food in the larder, tins and tins of it. And we found a woodpile in one of the outhouses, and some coal. There was a gun rack too, it took me another hour to find the cartridges. Maybe they weren't supposed to keep them here.

Whatever happens, we're all right. For a day or two at least. I still can't get round to feeling afraid …

I'm beginning to see now, she ran away from him. I don't know why. Not yet.

I laid a fire in one of the bedrooms. Hung sheets round it to air. We'd found candles, I lit some for her. Then I got her to bed. She looked beat. I told her I'd stay down here for the night, in the kitchen. I'd got one of the shotguns, and a pocketful of cartridges. Felt very tough.

Well, wasn't it the best thing to do? There could have been prowlers, anything, somebody had to watch. And I didn't want to be close to her, I couldn't afford to be close. I was trying to do the best I could.

I don't know when the noise came. I was dozing. Don't know what it was either. Something caused by … this afternoon.

I sat up. The fire was low. Pink light reflecting from the walls, and the big grey squares of the windows. I listened, and it came again. Soft and booming. Almost summery. Like those strange sounds you used to hear far off, on a warm, still day. Then there was another, closer; and another, they seemed in line. And then … I don't know what it was like. A monstrous horse galloping, straight for the house. The windows shook, the doors swung and rattled; then it was past, fading over the sea. When it had gone I heard her scream.

I'd never heard anybody scream like that. For a moment I thought … you know, there was something. Something really there. I'd found a torch, I took the stairs three at a time. She ran into me on the landing.

She was … well, in a state. She wouldn't go back to the bedroom, not at first. I got her back eventually, I told her it was nothing, it couldn't hurt her, it was gone. She'd had a dream I think. He was coming for her, out of the sea. So she knows he's dead too. The candles had burned down; I lit some more, and built the fire. But she wouldn't let me leave her again. I held her till she was quiet; and maybe it's true that fear is communicable, for that was the first time I was really afraid. I'd shot the bolts on the door, I sat there staring with the gun across my lap. Don't know what I was waiting for, what

I expected to see; the handle turn, jump, something like that. Nothing happened of course; I broke the gun finally, set it to one side. I said – this is the silliest thing – 'If he's been killed once, he can be killed again.'

Then I looked round at her. She was watching me, in the flamelight; and I think quite suddenly we both of us knew.

Martine

I don't know why I went with him in the first place. Well, I suppose I do; but you don't like admitting that sort of thing, even to yourself.

In a way I wish he'd never come. But then I wish so many things, I wish life could have gone on just like it was. I loved the pub, the hours were a bit long but there was always a laugh, always something going on. And Ray was good to us, good to all of us. I wonder where he is, I hope he didn't …

Mustn't think like that, mustn't get scared again. I'm warm and safe, I'm all right, nothing's going to happen tonight. Not now. The noise has gone, it was only a noise …

Keep wondering where they all are. Can't help it. Don't know what happened …

Remembering the good times. Crabbing at Chapman's with old Teddy, used to have to get up about five. And the carnival, everybody did their own costumes, some of them were terrific … And when they got the cricket team going, Ray knocked the ball right through Mrs. Dangerfield's greenhouse roof …

Always liked Maggie. Don't know what it was about her. Everybody liked her, Ray liked her a lot and he'd known her for years. Lot longer than me. And Richard, he was round her place nearly all the time. They weren't lovers, she told me once. I remember I felt embarrassed somehow. Her just coming out with it like that.

Richard used to stay on sometimes, when we hadn't been all that busy. I think he was a really good painter. Ray had bought one of his of the castle. We were going to have it in the Barn …

Something funny about him and Vicky. Never found out. I think they used to know each other before …

Don't know how old Maggie is. In her thirties somewhere. I think she's older than she looks, but she's got a terrific figure. And she was sort of … alive. Can't explain it. I used to love to hear her play. Used to try and get Ray to put me in the back, he was always having me on about it. But the front bar got so crowded anyway, you never stopped running …

She'd got this sort of husky singing voice. And she was a terrific guitarist. She used to say though, listen to Segovia. She didn't like what she played for the tourists all that much, it was only because it was good for trade.

She said once she used to try and remember not to wash her feet.

Perhaps it's over now. The ... bombs. Please God make it be over. Perhaps we'll all go back, they'll just let us go back. I don't care if the country gets ... taken over, or whatever. I never did ...

I suppose it was really my fault. What happened. Well, part of it ...

I always knew she liked me. Don't know how I could tell. I used to know whether she was in the pub, I could always tell if she was there. Sometimes you could feel it more than others, a ... breeze, or a prickling. Used to wonder sometimes, if it was something she did herself. Like switching something on. Used to think perhaps I'd got a crush on her. That was silly though. I mean you don't just go round getting crushes. Not after school anyway.

That day after the beach was worst. That was the day I wore the new bikini. Martin said the first Bikini started all the rest. I don't know what he meant, something about a bomb ...

I wanted to get a new swimsuit anyway. And it was in this lovely sort of off-brown. What there was of it. The girl said it was all right, they were all like that that year. I said well, if it was the only one in that colour ...

Don't want to lie. Not any more. I wanted her to see me, I wanted to ... show off, I suppose. It was like ... well, being admired.

Afterwards, when she came up, I wasn't dressed. She was helping with the bar that night, Ray was in Bournemouth at the cricket and Penny wasn't coming in till seven. I said to come in. I mean, it didn't matter. Not with another woman. And I'd got this mother thing about her anyway, at the time.

I felt ... well, funny round the knees. She didn't *do* anything, she was just sitting talking, smoking a cigarette. Then in the bar, she had to stoop past me to get a bottle, she put her hand on my hip. Just lightly, to steady herself. I thought I was going to pass out, I don't know what was the matter with me. I wanted to ... I don't know, do a striptease, something crazy, just have her look at me again.

She went off when Ray came in, she said she'd got somebody to see. I was miserable, afterwards. I wanted ... something, but there was nothing you could do. Just nothing. I thought, I don't know, if she'd been a man ... But that was wrong too. I didn't want her to be like anything else. Just what she was ...

I never liked Martin all that much. He was too ... well he was a right smoothie, to start with. That accent; and he'd never been near a public school, he told me himself. I never knew where he got his money, he never used to do a stroke. But he used to reckon if you once started working that was the end, you'd work the rest of your life. He used to spend a lot of time in Bournemouth, he said if you hung round money long enough some of it would rub off. He'd been ... oh, a steward on a liner, thousands of things. I never could decide how much of it was true.

He used to say he knew women. I expect he did. He certainly got what he wanted out of me. But talk about fast, that first time we hadn't been in the car five minutes ...

He made me really mad once. Asked me if I'd got any ... things with me. Straight out, just like that. He said that was the only way it was worth doing. I said what did he think I was, I mean you don't just carry things like that about in your handbag, it's like walking about with a loaded gun. I said it might be all right for Americans, but it wasn't all right for me. Anyway after that he'd always got them with him. Don't know where he got them from. Can't see him walking into a chemist's for them. I suppose he did.

I only went with him because – well, I suppose I wanted to prove I was ... normal and all that, I wasn't what she thought. But afterwards, her face that night. I didn't think she'd take it like that. She said she'd got a bug but it wasn't that, she'd been crying. I didn't want to hurt her, not like that, I ... well, I suppose I loved her. In a way. But I'd got myself in so deep ...

I wouldn't have gone down there. To that place. And with *him*, of all people. But Maggie wanted to, and she was coming anyway. She said ... oh, thousands of things. It all made sense at the time. Or seemed to. I didn't know what I wanted to do, I was so scared, I'd been scared for days. I thought I'd be safe with her.

And then Martin being there, I never thought ... I didn't think I'd ever see him again, I didn't want to see him again. I couldn't think. And the very first night, he said something ... well, foul about her. I was that mad, I kept trying to get up but he was holding me, the madder I got the more he laughed. He thought it was all funny, the war, me, everything. Then those shots, I know they were shots. They were sort of loud and yet distant, you heard them echo round all the cliffs. I thought he was going to come staggering back all pouring with blood or something, I couldn't stand it, I couldn't stand any of it any more. I just ... well, started walking. I didn't know where I was going, I couldn't think. Then she came after me and made me wait, she said at least I had to have a coat. She said she'd come with me, if I'd ... trust her. I started getting uptight again, I thought she hated me somehow because of Martin. But I ... wanted to be with her, I wanted her to come, I didn't feel scared any more. Not till the bombs ...

I couldn't stop shaking, afterwards. But she was terrific. She told me ... where she thought we ought to go, and that we'd be all right. Then she took my hand. It seemed ... well, quite all right, I just felt about six. I kept thinking about the bombs, and how the sea all lit up. It sounded as if the country was breaking in halves.

She said there'd be ... people at the house. But there weren't. We walked all round it, in the fog. It was huge, great round white towers at either end and all the lines of windows ... Then she said we'd have to get in because I was cold, she was going to get me warm. She'd found this big iron bar, she started in on a set of shutters over a window, when she got them open we had to break the glass. I got scared again. I mean, you can't just go round doing things like that. I kept thinking somebody would come, we'd both get put in jail. She said there was nobody there, at least we'd have heard a dog. But it all stayed quiet.

She got the window up finally and got inside and pulled me up after her. Then … it's ridiculous, but we both started laughing. Because you see we were standing in this huge lavatory. I mean a huge lavatory, it was a great high room about forty feet long with a huge wooden door and this one little pedestal set in the middle of the wall. The pipe went up about a mile, all covered with felt and lagging; then she said something about cavaliers sitting there practising their target shooting and I started falling about, I didn't think I was ever going to stop. Then suddenly it wasn't funny any more because we were standing in this great empty house and you could hear the silence, sort of pressing down. Anyway she took my hand again and opened the door and we started exploring, through all the rooms. She was terrific. She must have been scared as well, but she didn't show it. She'd got the iron bar, she kept saying, 'It's all right, there's nobody here. You can see there's nobody here.' It was a lovely house too, all the rooms high and white and full of marvellous furniture.

There was one thing I didn't like. In one of the big round rooms, the tower rooms, there was a case of dolls. Wax dolls, I'd never seen any before. Not close up anyway. Most of them were children but there was one of an old woman dressed in black. Least I think it was an old woman, it was very old, the face was all yellow and cracked. It was holding its arms out to the windows and the silvery fog, all you could see was the fog and just the grass for a yard or two round the house. I know I started shivering again, Maggie took me back through to a big kitchen. There was a larder there with shelves of stuff and a gas stove, when she turned the taps the rings lit. It only meant there was gas left in the pipes or they hadn't turned the supply off yet but somehow it cheered me up. Then she turned the water on, that worked as well though there wasn't any electricity. She said they must have forgotten about the gas but it didn't matter anyway, there was an Aga in the corner, she'd get it going later on. We got a fire lit then she found a big box of candles, she said it was lucky there'd been so many strikes.

I felt better when I got warm. She made some soup, I didn't think I'd want to eat because I'd been sick once on the way but when it was warming it smelled so good. Then we went upstairs again, she said she was going to fix a bedroom for me. I wanted to stop down in the kitchen but she said there was no reason I couldn't sleep in a proper bed.

She chose a room at the end of a long corridor. It was on the other side of the house; but most of the bedrooms were stripped, this one had curtains you could draw. She lit another fire, it was so cold for August, and set the candles round. She even aired some sheets. She said I could have a bath in the morning, there'd be hot water when she'd fixed the Aga.

It was dark by the time we'd finished, I hadn't realized it had got so late. I said wasn't she going to stop but she said no, she'd go downstairs and watch. She'd found a shotgun, she said it was the best thing we could have, better than a rifle, nobody would face a shotgun. She said the doors were all locked anyway, nothing could get in. She said I was a ... big girl, and the bombs were finished, there wouldn't be any more. She waited till I was in bed, then kissed me and said to get a good night's rest. Then she went downstairs.

So much had happened, I was really tired. I lay and watched the candles for a time. It was all so cosy and snug, it was wonderful to be lying there, I thought we'd all be dead or something. I thought of her downstairs and wondered what she was doing, whether she was asleep or not. Then the wind started, you could hear it gusting round the house, I wondered if it would clear off all the fog. You could hear the sea too. The candle flames were moving, very slightly, in a draught.

She'd seen the house before, they used to open it sometimes. That was how she knew about the gap in the trees, and the smugglers. I was sorry she'd told me about that though I know she didn't mean any harm, because the sea was the last thing I thought about before I slept.

I had this dream. I don't know where I was standing but I could see the notch in the trees and the sea beyond. The sea was vivid blue, I'd never seen such an intense blue. You could see some of the trees, the branches and trunks, it seemed it lit them up. As if it was luminous.

I stood there for a time just watching. Then I realized – I don't know how I knew but I did – that there was a path up from the water, up the other side of the hill, and somebody was climbing it. I got frightened. I don't know why but I knew I didn't want to see him, I *mustn't* see him. I started trying to run but I couldn't move fast enough, my legs wouldn't work. I was looking back, I saw him come scrambling through the gap. Then he was close. His face was all eaten away, eaten flat, you could see all the holes in it, the tubes and veins, some were opening and closing as he breathed. I knew it was me he wanted, he was angry with me because I'd got him killed. I sat up in bed, I was screaming. Then there was this terrible knocking and banging, it sounded at the door. I knew he was in the house. Then I heard Maggie calling, I had to get to her and warn her, tell her he was here. I was wrenching at the door but it was locked somehow or jammed, it wouldn't open. Then I didn't know where I was, I thought he was in the room with me after all, I couldn't get away.

I don't know what happened, after that. I think she slapped me, I can't remember. She made me come back in, she'd got the gun, she went all round the room but there was nothing there. She opened the curtains, the fog was still thick outside. She said the other thing was nothing, she'd heard it before though never close like that. She said it was to do with the bombs, that it was a meteorological thing, like thunder, something called Barrisal Guns. I don't know why but that frightened me again. I knew by then I'd had a dream, but I wouldn't let her go. She said it was all right, she wouldn't leave me any more. She closed the bolts on the door and sat a long time, on the bed. She was still holding the gun.

Warm, and safe …

It was as if there was a part of my mind that just stopped working. A part was saying 'right', and 'wrong', but I couldn't understand any more. I couldn't understand what it was saying, what the words meant. Then it was as if Martin was loving me, and I was loving him back; but better than it had been, better than it had ever been before. Then it seemed – she'd changed, or I'd changed, I could kiss her on the mouth, all the dreams were happening. Then things started spinning, inside my head; Dancing Ledge and the pool, the bungalow, boats on the sea, the pub, the hot white rocks in the sun. Then it was as if I was at the cricket match again and something terrific had happened and Ray was laughing and all the people I knew; Penny and John and Andrew and Richard and old Ted. And I was pushing close, I couldn't get close enough, I wanted to do everything with her, climb the castle and walk, and run and swim and drive; everything, all at once. And never be frightened again.

I thought the morning after was going to be terrible. It wasn't though. She was downstairs, doing breakfast. She'd found a tin of sausages and there were hens out in the yard, she'd been out and found some eggs. I just walked up to her and kissed her. It didn't feel strange at all.

She went over to the sink and started scraping some plates. When she turned back, she'd been crying. But she didn't talk about it. Neither of us talked about it, not for the rest of the day.

The mist didn't go. I thought it would be here for ever.

When the wood ran short we gathered driftwood again from the bay. There was enough of it. I didn't think about Martin. Not any more. Later on we walked up the hill to the village. There was a post office, it had been a general shop as well. I think we'd got quite used to breaking in.

We brought so much back it took us all our time to carry it. Getting back to the house was nearly like coming home.

I should have loved to live in a place like that. I don't know how old it was. Eighteenth century, I suppose. I could see Maggie as an eighteenth century lady. You know, making up and putting those sexy patches on they used to wear. Another time I thought we should have been fishergirls. All poor and ragged. I think between us we lived through all the ages.

There were cows in one of the fields behind the house. One morning they were all bellowing, I thought they were ill but she said they wanted milking. I don't know whether she'd done it before but she was very good. She said it must be rotten for them. Like wanting to spend about six pennies at once.

We had so much milk we didn't know what to do with it. We boiled it all at first because of TB. Later we just stopped bothering.

Then she showed me how to use the guns. They're easy, you just open the little latch and put the shells in and they're ready. And you've always got another shot if the first one misses. She made me promise never to carry one closed. She showed me what might happen if I did. There was a dead hare in the field, she fired at it and it was horrible. There was nothing left …

There's a little concrete pillbox in the bay, I think it was left over from the war. We made love inside it once. Nearby there was a stack of lobster pots, we found a boat pulled up and got it down to the sea and sank them out in the bay. We didn't catch anything for a week but she said to keep on trying, we just hadn't found the proper place.

I remember the first one we caught. He was huge; and they're so dark here, because of the black-coloured rocks. I didn't want to kill him, I don't think she did either. But she said it was him or us, and anyway it was no different from eating meat.

He was so beautiful, when he was cooked. I couldn't believe it. And there were lettuces in the kitchen garden, enough for a salad. She made a wonderful sauce, out of ketchup and thick cream, and fed me the claw meat, put it in my mouth. I think that was the sexiest meal I ever had.

Only one bad thing happened. I saw that Stan Potts man again, one day.

I couldn't believe it. I was going down to the beach, I wasn't taking much care. And there he stood, in the mist, in this horrible old macintosh. He was staring up, toward the house, I thought he'd seen me or heard the noise I made. But I don't think he had.

I sort of skulked back, behind a rock. I closed the gun, as quietly as I could. I thought, 'If he starts to climb. If he starts to come up …' I knew what would happen if I fired it but I think I'd still have shot him. I think I'd turned into a sort of little animal. What we had was so good, nobody was going to take it away.

Anyway he didn't come up. Just stood there looking miserable, as if he'd lost something, he was looking for it. Finally he walked away.

I followed him for a bit. In the mist. He kept going, round the bay. I left off when he got near the western cliff. I suppose he was going back to the farmhouse. I hadn't thought, about him still being there.

I didn't tell Maggie. Perhaps I should have, but I didn't. It was just that … I didn't want anything to spoil it. Not even a little thing.

Another night there was some gunfire. It sounded close. We sat up all night listening, but nobody came near.

She said I always had to take a gun with me. Everywhere I went, even if it was only a step.

I should have done. I should have listened. But nobody ever came. Apart from just that once. It was as if people didn't exist any more, we'd have the place to ourselves for ever.

I'd come down to the shore, to go out to the pots. She was still asleep, I didn't want to wake her. I forgot, I honestly did. I remembered when I was going across the yard. But I was only going to be gone a little while, it only took a few minutes to row out. It wasn't worth going back.

The mist was bad. I don't think it will ever clear. I'd pushed the boat off, I was getting in. Then I heard this pebble scrape.

I looked up. I could just see him. I thought for a minute it was Stan Potts again. But he was too tall.

I suppose I panicked. If I'd just got into the boat, he'd never have followed me. I could have landed anywhere, run back to the house …

I backed away instead. Up the beach. I didn't say anything. All I could think of was, I hadn't got a gun.

He said, 'It's all right. Don't run away …' But I ran anyway. I heard him following.

He was between me and the house. I couldn't get past him. Then I caught my foot, landed in some bushes. I thought he'd get me; but I got away just in time.

He was still following. I couldn't scream, it wouldn't be any good. She wouldn't have heard me, she was too far away.

I didn't know what he wanted. He kept on calling but I wouldn't answer. I was climbing as quietly as I could. But he still knew where I was.

There's another path up by the pillbox. It crosses a stream, goes up where the cliffs are lower. Like big steps, all grass and clay. I think he'd lost me; but I slipped and he heard me again. I thought perhaps the bombs had sent him mad. I was sure he was mad, I don't know why. I kept thinking how upset she was going to be. I was crying, I hated to think of her that upset. It was all my fault because I hadn't taken the gun.

He shouted up to me. 'I own this place. Who are you?' But I didn't believe him.

There was a place where the path went up between two mounds of rock. I'd climbed one before I thought, I lay there panting. There was a big piece of stone, I picked it up. I knew he wouldn't see me, against the rock.

The light was brighter. Almost as if the sun was bursting through. I waited. When he came, I was going to hit him with the rock. Then I heard his feet below me on the path. He was closer than I'd thought.

Richard

Remembering afternoons at bungalow. Lawn bald under cypress tree, stretching to rockery. Purple and yellow bedding plants, sunken lane beyond. Birdbath, stone rabbit patched with lichen. Shadow of pedestal stretches across grass. In my painting I would solve such an equation.

Remember doing series that was nothing but the lichen. Orange scumble over olive green, old faces from hills peering through.

Castle visible from lounge windows. Stone shell set above valley, open to air and light. Wild sun's nest. View framed by white glazing bars. White house, smelling of nineteen-thirty-five. Made me feel nearer to him. Middle phase before Junkers, rolling suns.

Pity about Maggie. She didn't live there. Don't know if she ever lived anywhere. Talked a lot about the school. Angry image, wasp-hive. Gone now. One-second slum clearance plan.

Glad castle still there. Wonder how long it will last. Can't imagine dissolution. But can't imagine dissolution of anything. Playing music the last day. Reger, Buxtehude. Read spec, on record sleeve. Tierce and blockflute, quintflute. *Rohr Gedacht*. Take a book to describe death of one church organ.

Remembering rest of room. Fleecy half-moon rug in front of grate, slip mats on wood-block floor, leather-covered Spanish chest in corner. Silver on sideboard, white china swan. Framed pastel, head of saluki. Whisky in side cupboard, as aid to concentration. Carved Swiss hat-rack outside door, family of climbing bears.

Remember her lying on bed. Afternoon sun on blinds. Drenching light, green-gold. Remember tumbled blankets, lovely planes of body. Thrust of hip, knotted sheet pulled between thighs. Lorelei, or Jennifer. Should have painted her. But am not Picasso. Can't paint tears.

Could have had her. But take her once and spatial relationships destroyed. Vital to preserve image of castle, china swan. Sooner flog bishop.

Remembering flat in Cheltenham. Tried to work there but was stifled. Relationship between creativity and fucking. Vicky understood latter but couldn't follow former any farther than the rest. Perhaps procreation a major art form. In which case all painting frustrated sex.

Definition of philosophy. Pastime unfitted for grown men.

Remember rage at refusal to seek divorce. Think she used to go up to Town to meet hubby. Handsome allowance; her reluctance understandable. Her coming down here bad luck on both of us. But also understandable. Was bound to be Army or Church. For aye to be in shady cloister mew'd.

Tried to develop philosophy of shallowness. Greed, indifference, etc., wholly admirable, integrity the only crime. But new order would develop own integrity, therefore fail. Could never understand partial involvements. As Vicky. Emotion in cast iron frame. Passion can be trained like fruit tree.

Potts a great creative artist. Firing of gun a major Surreal act. Quieter and cheaper to have simply pushed him off cliff.

Have seen gun. Luger. Keeps it in sleeping bag. Spends hours cleaning, etc. Distinctive smell of miscible oil. Wonder what Leader said to make poor bastard flip. Can't get up much feeling for Jones. One shitbag so much like the next.

Can't get up much feeling for anything. Remember discussion with Maggie. Overstocked attics, etc. Maybe right.

Maggie an interesting woman. Life failed socially, had to fall back on intelligence. Liked her ideas on moral sense. Unfortunately only applicable at low culture levels. Table of Affinities end result of need to regulate birthrate, Holy Matrimony handy for generating virgins. Will maybe have her chance in next hundred years.

No primary objection to lesbianism. Act only disgusting when participants ugly or fat. Coition between consenting beauty queens. Hold similar views on pederasty but don't think I was believed. Hope she made Martine. Would like to have been fly on ceiling, shouting yippee.

Martine a very moreish girl. Wouldn't have minded conventional rummage myself. But didn't try for her. From him that hath not, shall be taken away.

Must be something in sea air. Remember identifying castle as lingam-yoni motif. Male pillar upholding sun-drenched cup. Had been reading programme notes on *Parsifal.* Tried a painting but didn't think it worked out. Gave to Maggie for lounge. She liked it.

Am no Symbolist. Also, Miró and Munch an infertile cross.

Missing those afternoons. Would welcome views on current relationship with Vicky. Three times round a bit of a bloody joke.

Quiet week, after bombs. Fished, brought up wood from beach. Pity he had to ditch the truck as well. Heard plane once, above mist. Droned round half the day. Wondered what reconnaissance was for. Found out later.

Woke to noise of engines, grinding of tracks. Whole place shaking, wondered what in hell was going on.

Debarking took three hours. Fog dense, could barely see lights of landing craft. Heavy tanks, one-twenty-millimetre turrets. Markings were a surprise. Each made thunderous turn on beach below farmhouse, shouldered off up into mist. Strange primal movement of tracked vehicles. Must have seen house; but fortunately has preserved deserted appearance.

Seemed to have no infantry support. Lucky for us, unlucky for them.

Firing started just before dawn. Cannonade sporadic at first then continuous, thundering through mist. Cliffs of amphitheatre ringing in dark. Last weird battle in the west.

Don't know where Potts took off to. Think he went to earth. Walked to where I could see small-arms flashes, orange points sparkling in fog. Our people deployed before high ground, where lane joins old range road. One tank burning. Remember foundry chimney seen at dusk. Open hatch looked like it.

Four tanks in paddock below lane, presenting low profile. Others moving through spinney to left, trying to outflank. Watched for a bit. Stink of cordite, shaking of ground to noise of cannon. Then rounds started slapping into grass beside me, with a zip and whick. Got down, and stayed that way. Got out as soon as I could, went back to house.

Voices on beach during day. But nobody came near. Been cursing fog. Blessed it. After midday no more firing from hill. Heard guns farther west. Sounded to be down on heath.

Walked up again in evening. One tank slewed through wire in front of old manor house. Track poking up like looper caterpillar, something on turret side looking like dark red rag. Didn't examine too closely. Others still in field. Iron exo-skeletons, like old shelled beasts. But silent now. All dead. Look'd up for heaven, and only saw the mist.

Would like to have been War Artist. But little point this time. No sale for results.

Poetic for there to be survivor. Just one. But not Medraut.

Great patch of blood across her shoulder and sleeve. Not hers. Face gaunt, walk listless. Didn't seem to care where she was going. She said, 'There was nothing we could do.' Can't remember any surprise at seeing her.

Stink from burned-out tanks making me puke. Got her away, down track to house. Said Birmingham and Glasgow had gone.

Made her strip off uniform jacket. Her shirt soaked as well. Looked at blood incuriously. As though noticing it for first time.

Queer about blood. Could never stand it. Or earthworms, giant trees. If haemoglobin had been green, wouldn't have cared. Should have seen shrink while I had the chance.

She was starting to shake. Gave her whisky and hot water. Used to give her whisky at the flat. On bad days. Thank God we brought crates down from pub. Kept me going.

She took toddy when I made it. Sat and held cup. I latched shutters across window, made up fire. She didn't want to eat. Said to her once, 'What are you going to do?' But no answer. Always used to say, was bad at making decisions.

Had kept her hair at old length. Said once she'd never cut it again.

Helped her let it down. Was as I remembered it: strands vari-coloured, gold, brown, red, white. Made her another drink. Said then she wanted to go outside. Didn't think she'd come back. But she did.

Potts had come in. Didn't say much. Just looked at her with queer, ashamed little grin. Wondered what he was thinking. If anything. Doesn't talk a lot. Not any more.

Laid out sleeping bag for her. She sat and looked at it a bit. Wondered if she was thinking about Maggie. But she didn't ask.

Got in with her, to get her warm. Put my arms round her. Queer to feel her again. But my hands didn't need her breasts. We'd gone through all that once.

Remembered, used to ache when kept apart. She said it was the same for her. Used to make me promise to sleep on left side. She'd sleep on right and pretend I was there, used to call it Lefts and Rights.

Maybe that was what was wrong. Coming back like that, getting in way of memory.

Used to put one arm under pillow, so I could cradle her and not muss her hair. Did same again. Habit dies hard.

Woke later. She was warm. Slid into her, slowly. She started moving hips. Nearly like good old times.

Asked me in the morning if I'd been painting any more. That was like old times too. Said I'd been getting by. Knew she wouldn't want details. Always liked my paintings fine, stuck on a wall. It was the rest she wasn't keen on. But had never had an artist before of course. Was all going to be Parturition without Pain.

Still plenty of fish. We ate them. Nothing else to do. Imagined sometimes running Geiger over them, hearing roar of clicking. Dreamed about it.

Had a lot of dreams. Saw her once combing hair. Was all coming out as she tugged, in chunks and swatches. Yelled at her to stop, but she wouldn't. Kept saying it would be better when it was gone. Mad with her when I woke up. Somehow seemed the sort of thing she would do.

Like the blood. Didn't seem to care whether she was soaked in it or not. So she hadn't changed.

Never knew woman with such an affinity. Remember day in Cheltenham when she dropped Pyrex dish. She's still got white line across wrist. Standing there when I went through letting blood spurt through open window. Didn't want to get it on the floor. Said, 'I shouldn't have tried to save it. I shall let the next one go.' Put dressing on when she'd streamed enough. I took her up for stitching. Probationer's face in Casualty. But seemed to think the whole thing was a laugh.

Wondered if she still had the other haemorrhages. Maybe Army medical not as fundamental as I thought. She used to say it was cancer. Those were the bad days. Doesn't matter what I thought. Not any more.

Think I'd seen enough of her when I left Cheltenham. She was Goddess of course, we all find one of our own. Even Potts, poor bugger. But mine bled from the backside.

Think it was the inactivity that caused first rows. Sitting day after day in fog, waiting for what was coming next.

Couldn't get off beach. She said they'd set up a cordon, on the rising ground. Couldn't cover all the coastline, but anything moving up from sea would be shot. No way of knowing if troops still in position. Didn't feel like finding out the hard way. Went across to Kimmeridge instead, to little village. Not much good. Only one shop, which had been cleaned out. Proved there were still people about somewhere. But they never came near us.

Nearly sure sometimes there was nothing up there. Dead tanks, dead houses, dead hills. Other times wondered if had been killed myself, the day they took Birmingham out and lit the Channel. And traffic had been heavy so filing clerks were slow, getting me up for Judgment.

Wondered where Potts took himself off to. Used to wander out into mist, in dirty old belted mac. Sometimes be gone all day. Never took gun, not any more. Had feeling one time he wasn't coming back.

She used to say she thought a lot of him. But that was old stuff too. Like tramps. Could never resist tramp, filthier the better. Used to feed them, try and get them to come up to the flat. Swore it was result of hospital training. But never did a good work that was private. They used to call them Penances with Hooks.

She never understood about my painting. And I was closer to her than any other woman I ever met. Not many disappointments like that in one lifetime.

Said once she was sorry for me, because men could never have babies. Maybe she was just as disappointed in me.

Subject of Potts really caused final row. Said she was sorry for him, way he looked at her she could tell he was lonely, never had anybody to love. Love the greatest experience, etc. Said I'd always had enough to do feeling sorry for myself. Anyway, had seen her sympathy once or twice. Another trained fruit tree. One thing led to another, Christ knows why. Probably both dog-tired. Said in the end I didn't want her, never had. Said she'd sleep with him instead, at least he'd show some gratitude. Said O.K. fine, to carry on, then had to hold her back when she started getting up. Was always her trouble. No sense of the grotesque.

Looked rough in the morning, said she didn't feel too good. Said to take it easy for the day but that wasn't right either. Said it didn't matter how she felt, had always had to work. Got fed up with the whole bloody thing, went down to boat. As I pushed off heard her walk across yard, slam of big house door. Started to work off temper chopping wood.

Stayed out most of day. Took half a dozen grayling, more than we'd need. Didn't fancy going back so rowed on west, thought I'd see if I could find some decent wood. Made fire in cranny in rocks, cooked own lunch for once. Didn't enjoy it. Went through all the moods I used to go through before, whenever I walked out on her. Used to be mad to start with, tell myself I was being ruined anyway, we were better off apart. Also other insidious thing, that I was handy as lover but no good for a spouse. Used to remember her face then, calm, frozen look she always used when she was hurt. Would want to run back like bloody fool, or find phone. Then would get mad again because I knew that look as well, it was standard part of armoury. Then I'd remember things we'd done together. Like first week's camp on Purbeck, cracking up crab with tentpeg mallet, drinking white wine by moonlight. And it would all start again.

Tide was setting, when I started back. Made it a hard row. Getting dark when I beached boat. Walked up to farmhouse with conviction something was wrong.

Lamp was lit and she'd prepared decent meal, out of scraps we had left. She was sitting in corner, by fire. Blanket round her, thought how white she looked. Said she was O.K., just fine. Tang in air, like hospital. Even then it didn't click.

Took dish across to the sink we'd rigged. Nearly threw up. Bottom of sink one big puddle of blood.

Ran back to her, grabbed her hand. Had been keeping it out of sight. Dressing she'd put on was sopping but could see how short it was.

Don't think I've ever been so mad. Was scared of course, when I realized what she'd done. That now I had a Goddess with a finger missing. She'd got a meal ready then. Done it specially well, I expect while she was pouring blood.

Wasn't angry with her, was angry *for* her. Asked like a fool was it still bleeding, was there anything I could do. She started pulling at dressing on stump, said there wasn't but she expected I'd like to see. Hit her then, hard across face.

She steadied up. Stood and looked at me. White marks on cheek. Then said if there was nothing else, was going to bed. Asked if I was sure I didn't mind.

Covered her with the blankets. She didn't argue, just lay clutching poor reddened hand. Made fire up, asked if she wanted whisky. Didn't answer. Cleaned sink, couldn't leave it like that. Got spare lamp, went into Martine's room. Sleeping bag still there, her bits scattered about. Air felt like a tomb but once in bag it wasn't too bad. Took a long time to sleep. Stomach felt queer, and had got the shakes.

She'd gone in the morning. Didn't seem possible at first but suppose I should have expected it. Run through each other a long time back, each taken what the other had to give. Thought when I killed it first time nothing could ever be as bad again. But was wrong. When ghost is killed too, nothing left at all.

Didn't try looking for her. Instead started on whisky. Don't know what I was celebrating. Perhaps that Death is King.

Don't know what happened to me after that. Had run through feelings, no emotion left. So don't know why I was on hands and knees in front of door, why tears pouring down face. Searched shingle, inch by inch. Then realized I was looking in wrong place. Think whisky had got to me.

Went to barn. Blood on floor, and on wheel of Maggie's car. But still couldn't see what I was looking for.

Couldn't believe it when I found it. Don't think I believed till then any of it was real. Wrapped it in handkerchief. Then couldn't see straight. Realized had taken all she had to give, then asked more. So started giving pieces of her body. Nothing else left.

Potts back midmorning. Shuffled about, poked head round door of barn. Asked what was the matter then said, 'I'm sorry.' Bloody fool sounded as if he meant it. Started laughing then, couldn't stop. Shoved out past him, ran into mist. Made for lane. Knew she'd have gone that way. Seeing her face now as it used to be, forehead and firm cat-muzzle, big calm dark blue eyes. Had to find her and explain. Knew if I could find her it would be all right. Never know loneliness and pain again.

Reached dead village before I realized. Tank still there, heeled over in ditch. Beyond it could see trunks of trees lining main road.

Couldn't believe it. Realized mist thinning, light brightening round me. Ran again, up to road. Sky pale blue; sunlight, golden rust on wrecks, hill ahead with golden grass. Air cool; and down below, mist stretching out like sea.

Curious conviction of total emptiness of land. But started in again, running toward hill.

Dusk has fallen, the long, blue dusk of summer; and Potts is alone. It does seem a shame …

He lies in his room at the end of the ruined corridor. He's wearing his old mack; his back is against the chill stone of the wall, his head sunk forward on his chest. He feels empty inside somehow, as empty as the farmhouse. He's been trying to get cynical about it all. But he's just too tired.

There's a noise somewhere, a creak or a scuff. Like the scuff of a foot. He tries to imagine what it would be like if the door opened slowly and she was standing there, she'd come back. Just her, on her own. But the picture won't form. It won't form because he knows that's not the way things happen. People never come back.

The noise wasn't anything of course. He imagined it. Or maybe it was a rat.

It seems impossible somehow that life could be so empty; that the farmhouse should be empty, and the cliffs. Not just wrong, impossible. He reaches out to where he laid the gun. He wants to put the barrel in his mouth and pull the trigger, stop all the emptiness once and for all. But he daren't. In spite of everything, he's still too scared. That's nearly the worst of all.

The light has almost gone now; and surely that was her, she turned her foot on a pebble just outside, he heard the scrape. He calls out, as loud as he can; but nothing answers. He lies back; and this time his eyes stay closed.

He frowns. There are the sounds at last, the sounds he's been waiting for; a clopping and pattering of footsteps, and something else. A high-pitched squeaking; erratic, like … it must be, the wheel of a truck!

He's certain he isn't dreaming; he sits up, and at once a curious equipage jerks itself into sight. For a moment, he's disappointed. He'd almost thought … but it doesn't matter what he thought. Something odd is happening, something very odd indeed. He watches, intently. Quite what his altered viewpoint is, he's not sure; but it doesn't matter. At best, viewpoints are subjective things …

THREE

Monkey and Pru and Sal

To Monkey, the movement of the sun across the sky always seemed essentially a sideways matter. It was this innate feeling – a thing of the blood rather than the intellect – that helped him in his first uncertain attempts at map reading. For years, the maps he owned had been meaningless to him. He would draw them from the wooden pocket in which they were kept, steadying himself against the lurching movements of Truck, and fold and unfold them, admiring the rich light blue of their edges, the patches of green and brown overlaid with delicate networks of marks and lines. And he would blink and frown, grappling with something more nebulous than memory.

The sea gave him his first real clue; the great blue presence of it, looming and dazzling between the shoulders of watching hills. How Truck, in its erratic career, came to be in sight of the water will never be known; but Monkey crowed with delight, extending blackish, sticky fingers to the brightness. Then he fell wholly quiet.

He remained quiet for a day, a night and part of another day. All that time, Truck veered and rattled along within sight of the vastness. Then a dead tree, sprawling grotesquely across the road, caused Pru and Sal to swerve aside. They fled, backs humped, from the clutching, bleached branches; and Monkey lay frowning, thoughtfully oblivious, sucking at his fingers. In time, he began to doze. He dreamed of formless shapes that hovered aggravatingly just beyond reach. When he opened his eyes again, Truck was passing along a narrow sunken lane. Walls of reddish-brown rock jerked past on either side, hung here and there with the translucent green leaves of ferns. Above, the foliage of over-arching trees shone golden in sunlight.

Monkey, still bemused, lay seeing the green and brown and blue; and suddenly it was as if a great idea, already formed somewhere in his brain, pushed itself forward into consciousness. He stopped his thumb-sucking, drew out once more the precious, grubby sheets; and the truth burst on him. He bawled his loudest, bringing Truck to a precipitate halt; sat up crowing and dribbling, a map clutched destructively in one great fist. He waved his arms, startling Pru and Sal from their immemorial indifference; and Truck turned, jerkily obedient, under control at last.

Monkey, his mind buzzing with new ideas, stopped Truck when the blueness was once more in sight. He sat a long time frowning, screwing his eyes against the miles-long dazzle; then finally, unsurely, he waved to the right. Though 'right' at that time was a concept beyond his grasp; rather, he turned his destiny five-fingerward. To his left, or three-fingerward, lay the water; in his hand, still tightly and juicily gripped, was the map. His intention was as irrevocable as it was strange. He would follow, or cause Truck to follow, the edge of the sea.

Through the day, and on into the night, Pru and Sal kept up a steady pace. For a time, Monkey lay restless; finally their steady pounding soothed him to sleep. Dawn light roused him, streaming over the high canvas flap of Truck. He sat up, mind instantly full of his great design. The spyholes of Truck, ahead and to either side, afforded too narrow a field of view. He stood precariously to his full height, hands gripping the edge of Truck's bleached hood; and crowed once more, with wonder and delight, at what he saw.

He was parked on the crest of a great sweep of downland. Ahead the road stretched away, its surface cracked and broken, bristling with weeds. Across it lay the angular shadow of Truck, topped by the small protuberance that was Monkey's head. Beyond, and far into the distance, the land seemed to swell, ridge after ridge pausing and gathering itself to swoop saw-edged to the vagueness of the sea. Below him, a great distance away, Monkey saw the curving line of an immense offshore beach. Waves creamed and rushed against it; above it were hovering scraps of birds, each as white as the foam. The noise of the water came to him dimly, like the breathing of a giant.

He collapsed abruptly, huddled back to the darkness and protective warmth of Truck. Later, gaining courage, he traced with one finger the little green line that was an image of the mightiness. He sat proudly then, chin on fist, the master of all he surveyed.

At midday the great beach still stretched ahead. Behind the long ridge of pebbles, lagoons lay ruffled and as blue as the sky, dotted with the bobbing pinpoints of birds. The lagoons too Monkey traced on the map, and hugged himself with an un-communicable excitement.

His good mood was tempered in the days that followed. Always, relentlessly, he urged Truck on toward the sunset; always, at dawn, he stared anxiously ahead, expecting to see the narrowing of the land, the blue glint of sea five-fingerward. But the land went on endlessly, leaping and rolling; and his faith was sorely tested. To Monkey, the notion of scale was as yet as hard to grasp as the notion of God. He became aware, for the first time, of the frustration of helplessness. His thought, lightning-swift, outran the stolid jogging of Pru and Sal. Sometimes he urged his companions on with high, cracked shouts; but they ignored him, keeping up their one stubborn pace.

It was a dull, drizzling morning when Monkey reached the end of the world. The sea, grey as the sky, was fretted with long white ridges; a droning wind blew from it, driving spray like hail against the impervious hood of Truck. Monkey, woken from a grumbling doze, sat up blearily, crawled to the forward spyhole and yelped with triumph. The land on which Truck stood ran, narrowing at last, into the ocean; the water had swung round five-fingerward, barring further progress. Monkey crowed and howled, bobbing till Truck shook on its tall springs; for after all, the great idea was true. He had understood a Mystery.

North, or headwards, was a concept already relegated to the state of things known. Headwards Truck turned, then five-fingerward toward the sun and three-fingerward again. During his first great journey the notion of contour had also come to Monkey; he studied his maps, fitting each painstakingly to the next, and in the depth of winter was undismayed to see, rising ahead, the outlines of hills greater and more terrible than any he had known. Pru and Sal stopped at the sight, clucking and stamping in alarm; but he made no further move to urge them forward. For a time Truck wandered as it had always wandered, aimlessly; and Monkey was content. Snow came, and the long howling of the wind. In time the snow passed. The sky grew blue again, buds showed green against the stark twigs of trees. Then the maps were once more produced; and once more, Truck went a-voyaging.

In this way Monkey came to understand the land in which he lived. The concept of 'island', though suggested by the maps, was more difficult to grasp. The many sheets, placed edge to edge, alarmed with their suggestion of headward immensity. At first, Monkey's brain tended to spin; with time, he grew more assured. He kept tallies of his journeys now, scratching the days carefully on the greasy wooden sides of Truck. Soon he found his head could tell him, nearly without thought, the time of travel between any two points on his maps. Also the drawings themselves grew other marks, made by Monkey with the yellow drawing-stick that was his greatest treasure. He sketched where wild wheat grew, and where the land was good for hunting; and Pru and Sal, though they betrayed no outward gratitude, became sleek and well-filled. The larder of Truck was stocked to capacity; and Monkey, as is the way with men, looked about him for fresh worlds to conquer.

The adventure on which he decided almost proved his undoing. He turned Truck headwards, or north, resolved to travel as far as possible in this as yet unexplored direction; though he no longer harboured illusions as to the magnitude of the journey. Pru and Sal clopped steadily, day after day, indifferent as ever; and day after day Monkey squatted on his little rubbery heels, staring through the forward spyhole in breathless expectation of wonders. The tally lines grew again, wobbling across the dark wooden sides of Truck; hills appeared obediently to either hand, each in its allotted place. Monkey knew them now at a glance, reading their brown thumbprints on his maps. For a time, all went smoothly enough; then difficulties started to arise.

The first had to do with certain areas on the maps where the roads ran together in ever-thickening jumbles. Monkey steered for one of these, curious to see what such oddness could portend; but a whole day from his destination Pru and Sal stopped abruptly, stamping and shivering, giving vent to little hard anxiety-cries. Monkey, irritated, urged them forward; but his howls and bangings went unheeded. Pru and Sal danced with distress, shaking their heads and snorting; then, abruptly, they bolted. Truck, turned willy-nilly, jolted and crashed while Monkey clung on grimly, rolling from side to side in a confusion of legs and arms and maps. Dusk was falling before the wild flight eased; the tallies were ruined, and Monkey himself was lost.

He lay a day or more in a dull stupor of rage before he again took heart. As ever, the sidewaysness of the sun encouraged him; he spread the maps out once more, while Truck ambled slowly between rolling, gently-wooded hills. In time a higher hill, rearing dark against the sunset, gave him a reference. His good humour returned; for Pru and Sal jogged submissively, and the tallies were not wholly lost. The sideways or three-fingerward projection to which he had been subjected during their flight counted for little; he marked the map, using his drawing-stick, and turned Truck again on to its proper heading.

Twice more, the odd confluences were avoided by Pru and Sal; these times Monkey, prepared for their defection, found it easier to redirect their course. Whatever lay at the mysterious junctures must, it seemed, be avoided; for the present, he bowed to the inevitable.

For five more days the journey proceeded smoothly; then came the greatest shock of all. Far too soon – barely a half of the tally was complete – Monkey found the way impassably barred. Ahead, and to either side, stretched the sea.

The shock to his overstrained nerves was considerable. For a time, stupidly, he urged Truck forward, as if refusing to acknowledge the impossibility; the water was hissing round the axles, and Pru and Sal were keening with dismay, before he came to his senses. He sat a whole half day, glaring and fretting, staring at the map and back to the great blue barrier. Then he turned Truck three-fingerward. Two days passed before the sea once more swung round to bar his path; the proper sea this time, in its designated place. Monkey turned back, every hour adding to his alarm. The green and brown, green and brown of the map went on; yet still the lying, deceitful land shelved to the water, vanished beneath the waves. The tally grew again, senseless now and wild. Monkey howled and sobbed, picking his nose with rage; but the salty goodies brought no comfort. He threshed impotently, till the springs of Truck groaned and creaked and Pru and Sal stooped clucking, voices harsh with concern. But Monkey was unconsolable. His bright new world was shattered.

He felt himself losing control. His hands and limbs, wobbly at the best, refused to obey him. His nights were haunted; he wetted himself uncontrollably, till Truck exuded a rich sharp stink and half a whole map was spoiled. Madness, had it intervened, would have been a merciful release; but he was saved, finally, by a curious sight.

For a day or more the ground had been steadily rising; now, just after dawn, Monkey saw ahead of him the crest of a mighty cliff. The land, no longer gentle, broke away in a great crashing tumble of boulders and clay round which the sea frothed and seethed, flinging streamers of foam high in the air. Monkey huddled back, waving Truck on, anxious to be gone from the place; but at the height of the rise he began to thump and squeal. Pru and Sal stopped indifferently, their hair whipping round their heads, their curved, hard fingers hooked across the handle of Truck. The wind seethed in the grass; clouds sailed the early, intense sky; but Monkey had eyes for nothing but the Road.

It had been a great road, the widest and finest he had seen. It came lancing out of distance, its twin broad ribbons dark blue and cracked and proud. It soared to the edge of the cliff; and at the edge, on the very lip, it stopped.

Monkey raised himself, cautiously; then banged the side of Truck, ordering it forward. Pru and Sal moved slowly, unwilling now, straining back from the lip of the cliff; but Monkey's fear was forgotten. He stared, seeing how the road ended terrifyingly in a sudden, jagged edge. Below, white birds rode the updraught, tiny as scraps of paper. The sea crashed and boiled; and Monkey, screwing his eyes, saw what in his misery had eluded him. Far across the water, dim with distance but unmistakable, the brown and green, brown and green started again, marching out of sight.

He fell back; and relief was like a balm. Once more, he had understood; and the second Mystery was stranger than the first. The land had been changed after the maps were made.

The maps lived to the right of Truck, in their shallow compartment. Each part of Truck, each fragment of the tiny inner space, was apportioned with equal care. To Monkey's left was the area designated, in later times at least, Garage Accessories. The Accessories themselves didn't amount to much. There was a sleekly polished red oil can; beside it, tucked in tightly to prevent unpleasing rattles, the piece of rag with which Monkey furbished the metal, keeping it bright. Next to the oil can lived a tin of thick brown grease, with which Monkey anointed the axles of Truck whenever the elements conspired to draw from them high-pitched, irritating squeaks. Other Accessories were even less prepossessing. There was the galvanized nail with which Monkey prised up the lid of the tin (seconded lately for the important function of journey-marking) a small rusty spanner which fitted nothing about Truck but which Monkey kept anyhow, and an even more curious fetish: a little yellow wheel, made of some substance that flexed slightly in the fingers and was pleasant to hold and suck. Like the spanner, it served no discernible function; but Monkey was equally loth to throw it away. 'You can never tell,' he would bawl sometimes at the unresponding heads of Pru and Sal, 'when it might Come In.'

At Monkey's feet a locker closed by a rusty metal hasp constituted the Larder. Here he kept the flat grey wheatcakes that sustained him, and his bottles and jars of brook water. Other chunks of rag, stuffed carefully into the spaces between the containers, checked the clinking that would otherwise have spoiled his rest. Next to Larder, a corner compartment was crammed with spare rag, blankets and a blackened lace pillowslip. It also housed a broken piece of mirror, carefully wrapped and tucked away. Once, Monkey had gashed himself badly on its edge; now it was never used.

To either side of his head as he lay were the Tool Chest and the Library. The Tool Chest contained an auger, a small pointed saw, three empty cardboard tubes and a drum of stout green twine. The Library was full to overflowing, so full its lid could scarcely be forced down. Sometimes Monkey would take the topmost books out, lie idly turning the pages, marvelling at the endless repetition of delicate black marks. The marks meant nothing to him; but the books had always been there, and so were accepted and respected. Like Truck, they were a part of his life.

Between its several compartments Truck was fretted by a variety of holes, all seemingly inherent to the structure. The spyholes, covered when not in use by sliding flaps of leather, afforded Monkey sideways and frontal vision. Beneath him, concealed by a hinged wooden trap, was the Potty Hole; to either side smaller apertures, or Crumb Holes, enabled him occasionally to clean the littered interior of Truck. He would spend an hour or more carefully scraping together the mess of wheatcake crumbs, twigs and blanket fluff, pushing the fragments one by one through the holes. The activity had enlivened many a grey, otherwise unedifying afternoon; it cheered him, giving him a sense of purpose.

Pru and Sal formed the other major components of Monkey's mobile world. How they had come to him, or he to them, he was unsure. Certainly there had been a time – he remembered it now and then in vague, dreamlike snatches – when there had been no Pru and Sal. And also, he was nearly certain, no Truck. He remembered firelight and warmth, and lying on a bed not enclosed by tall wooden sides. He remembered hands that touched, a voice that crooned and cried. Also he remembered a bleak time of wailing and distress. The figures loomed round him, dim and massive as trees; there were other deeper voices, harder hands. One such pair of hands, surely, had placed him for the first time inside Truck. He remembered words, though they made little sense.

'Lie there, Monkey. You're with me now. Poor bloody little Monkey. You're with me …'

He didn't like the dream to come too often. It woke him alone in Truck, miserable and cold, crying for the hands and voices that had gone.

Maybe Pru and Sal had stolen him, as he lay supine in his bright new Truck. No one else would ever know; and they, perhaps, no longer remembered or cared. They too had become a part of his life. Always, as he lay brooding or contentedly dozing, their shoulders and heads were visible, outlined darkly against the sky. Their brown thin hands were clamped, eternally it seemed, round the wide handle of Truck; their feet thumped and pattered down the years.

In appearance, Pru and Sal were not unalike. Their hair, long, frayed and bleached by the sun, hung stiffly from their small rounded skulls. Their skin, tanned by the outside wind, had assumed the colour of old well-seasoned wood. Their eyes were small, slitlike and blank; their faces, untroubled by thought, ageless and smooth. Their fingers, over the years, had grown curved and stiff; good for killing, useless for the more delicate manipulations at which Monkey excelled. They dressed alike, in thick kilts of an indeterminate hue; and their voices, when they troubled to use them, were also alike, as harsh and croaking as the voices of birds.

For Monkey, secure in his endlessly roving home, the seasons passed pleasantly enough. Pru and Sal, in their motiveless fashion, tended him well. On rainy days, and in the dark cold time of winter, they drew across the open hood of Truck a tall flap of stiff grey canvas. Then Monkey would crawl invisibly in the warm dark, sucking and chuckling, groping among the crumbs of Larder, tinkling his jars of ice-cold chill, while the feet of Pru and Sal thudded out their comfort on paths and roads unseen. These, perhaps, were the best times of all; when snow whirled dark against the leaden strip of sky, and ice beaded the high hood of Truck and wolves called lost and dim.

Sometimes the snowflakes whirled right into Truck, tiny unmelting stars from outer air; and fires would leap, in clearings and unknown caves. In the mornings Pru and Sal must smash and crash at the ice of brooks while the wind whistled thin in thin dead grass.

Though springtimes too were good. The breeze stirred gentle and mild, rich with new scents; the sky brightened, filling with the songs of birds. Pru and Sal, clucking and mumbling, would draw back the canvas cover, allowing the cheesy air to whistle cheerfully from Truck; and Monkey would sit up, chuckling, feeling the new warmth on his great blotched hairless face. Summers he would lie naked, rubbing pleasure from his mounded belly while the warm rain fell, sizzling on his heated flesh. At night the stars hung lustrous and low, and trees were silent mounds of velvet cloth.

But the map reading changed, for all time, Monkey's life. The great adventure ended, it seemed a hollowness formed in his mind. Truly, he was satisfied with his conquered Island; and not unmoved by his discovery of its truncated state. New sights and sounds presented themselves each day; a waterfall, a forest, a bird, a lake. But novelty itself can pall. Monkey, mumbling and frowning, hankering for he knew not what, began, irritably, the formal tidying of Truck. Each object he came to – so known, once loved – seemed now merely to increase his frustration. His wheel, his drawing-stick, his spanner, lay discarded. The axles of Truck set up an intermittent squeal, but Monkey merely sneered. He tidied Larder and Blanket Store, dipped desultorily into Garage Accessories. Nothing pleased him. Finally, he turned to Library.

Almost at once he discovered a curious thing. The locker was deeper than it had always appeared. The blockage was caused by books that had swelled with damp, jamming their covers firmly against the outer wooden skin of Truck. Monkey puffed and heaved, straining unaccustomed muscles. Finally the hindrances came clear. He emptied the compartment to its bottom, sat back surrounded by books he had never seen. He opened one at random and instantly frowned, feeling a flicker of excitement for the first time in weeks.

The book was unlike the others in one major respect. Monkey huddled nearer the light, crowing and drooling, turning the pages with care. Some were glued irretrievably by damp; on others he saw, beside the squiggling marks, certain drawings. They were detailed and complex, many of them in colour; he had no difficulty in recognizing flowers and trees. Monkey, who had invented drawing, felt momentarily abashed; but the rise of a new idea soon drove self-awareness from him. He stared from the drawings to the little marks, and back. He tilted his head, first to one side then to the other. He laid the book down, picked it up, opened it again. Later he sat for an hour or more peering over the side of Truck, seeing the stony ground jog and jerk beneath. In time he made himself quite giddy. He closed his eyes, opened his mouth, laid his gums to the hard wood edge. Small shocks from the wheels and springs were transmitted to his skull.

From all this pondering, one idea emerged. He opened the new book once more, studied the flowers and trees. After a while he spread a second beside it. He discerned, now, certain similarities in the little black marks. Some of them, he saw, rose above their fellows, like tall bushes among lesser. Something in his brains said 'head' to that, or 'north'. It was the first key to a brand new Mystery. Illiterate, Monkey had divined which way up one holds the printed page.

For a season, and another, and part of a third, Truck squeaked and rumbled aimlessly while Monkey lay absorbed. The whole equipage might have become irretrievably lost had not the sinews of Pru and Sal remembered what their scorched brains were unable to retain. They followed, faithfully, their course of previous years. They harvested wheat, pounded and husked the grain, baked the flat hard cakes; they hunted rabbits and deer, ate and drank and slept. They came finally to the New Sea again, and the broken road; and there, triumphantly, Monkey added his own gull-cryings to the wheeling birds. The words floated down, vaunting and clear, to lose themselves in the roar and surge of the water.

'Even so our houses and ourselves and children have lost, or do not learn for want of time, the sciences that should become our country . . .'

How the wonder had come about will never be wholly explained. It was an achievement comparable to the first use of fire, the invention of the wheel; but of this Monkey remained unaware. Certainly, the concept of a map aided his first steps to literacy. That the books in his keeping were maps of a curious sort was never in question; though what such charts expressed he was wholly unable to define. He was conscious of an entity, or body of awareness; something that though vastly significant was yet too shadowy for the mind wholly to grasp. He grappled with it nonetheless while his bones – the bones of genius – divined the inner mysteries of noun, adjective and verb. It was slow work, slow work indeed; 'tree', for instance, was simple enough, but 'oak', 'ash' and 'hawthorn' baffled him for months. 'Green tree' was likewise a concept fraught with difficulty, though he mastered it finally, adding to it the red, blue and violet trees of his mind. The noises he made, first fitting breath to cyphers, were less comprehensible than the utterings of Pru and Sal. It was patience that was needed; patience and dogged, endless work.

Truck rolled on, while Monkey bleated and yelped. Seasons, hours, moods, all now brought forth their observation. To Pru, sucking at a scab on her leg, he confided his opinion that 'lilies that fester smell far worse than weeds'. Sal, seen piddling into a deep green brook, provoked an equally solemn thought. 'In such a time as this,' mused Monkey, 'it is not meet that every nice offence should bear his comment.' Staring into a leafy sunset reminded him of the lowing herd, while a sight of the sea brought forth memories of Coastwise Lights. 'We warn the crawling cargo tanks of Bremen, Leith and Hull,' he expounded gravely. Yet for all his learning he remained centrally baffled; for despite Kipling he saw no ships, despite Shakespeare he met with no great Kings. In the beginning, God might very well have created the heavens and the earth; but God, it seemed, was no longer an active agent. No spirits sat on thistle tops, in flat defiance of Tennyson; and though Keats's nightingales still sang, indubitably Ruth no longer walked.

Monkey found himself sinking once more into despondency. The books he owned he had read, from cover to cover; yet understanding seemed as far away as ever. Pru and Sal jogged as they had always jogged; the sun rose and set, rain came and wind, mists and snow. The sea creamed and boomed; but Monkey's mind was as rock-girt as the coasts. Nowhere, in any book, had he come upon a description remotely resembling Truck, or himself, or Pru and Sal; while all those things on which books most loved to dwell – armies and Legions, painters and poets, Queens and Kings – seemed lost for ever. 'Left not a rack behind,' muttered Monkey balefully. He lay sucking his wheel and brooding. Somewhere, it seemed, some great clue had evaded him. The books showed a world unreachable, but sweetly to be desired. As the maps had showed a world, incomprehensible at first, that now lay all about him.

He frowned, wondering. Then for the first time in many months he pulled the maps from their compartment. He unfolded them, tracing the confluences of roads, the strange knots he had never been permitted to explore. Their meaning was plain enough now. They were of course towns; their very names lay clear to read. He sat puzzling, and was struck by a wholly new thought. What if all the wonderful things of which he had read – the ships and Kings, the castles and palaces and people – still existed? What if, all this time, they had been waiting for him in the never-visited towns? He lay sleepless well into the night, turning over the brilliant, unsettling idea. Everywhere, glowing prospects opened; and when he finally dozed, he was visited by a splendid dream. He seemed to stand outside himself, and outside Truck; and Truck was bowling, unaided, along a great broad highway. To either side, half lost in a golden haze, reared towers and steeples; and everywhere, as Truck moved, there seemed to rise a great and rolling shout. It was as if all the people in the word – the glittering, wondrous people of the books – had come together to greet him; and there were hands and eyes, cheering and laughter, voices and the warmth he had so seldom known.

He sat up, peering from the confines of Truck. Dawn was grey in the sky; overhead, a solitary bird piped. Monkey's whoop of triumph sent it scuttling from its branch. 'Away toward Salisbury!' he cried to the sleeping land. 'While we reason here a Royal battle might be won and lost . . .'

The intention, once formed, was irrevocable; but at first the practical difficulties seemed impossible to overcome. For all their stolid obedience, on one point Pru and Sal stood firm; neither threats nor cajolery would get them near a town. Monkey tried the experiment several times more, always with the same result. As Truck neared each objective they would move slower and slower, keening and wailing in distress; and finally they would balk completely, or bolt like startled deer. Eventually, Monkey was forced to accept the obvious. Whatever was done must be done by his own efforts.

For several days more he lay frowning, puzzling at the problem. Finally a decision was reached, and he started work.

What he contemplated – a modification to the fabric of Truck itself

– seemed at first like sacrilege. Eventually he overcame his qualms. Certain measurements, made for the most part secretly after dark, confirmed the practicability of his scheme. He worked carefully with his drawing-stick, scribing two broad circles on the side of Truck. When the work was marked out, the auger came into play. With it he bored carefully through the planking on the circumference of one of the circles. When half a dozen holes had joined he was able to insert the tip of the little saw. The job was slow and tedious; more difficult, he imagined, than learning to read. His hands, unused to such exercise, grew blisters that cracked and spread; he bore the pain, keeping on stubbornly with his task. Finally he was successful. A circle of wood dropped clear; beyond, an inch or so away, revolved the battered, rusty rim of one of Truck's wheels.

He stared awhile, fascinated by the unusual sight; then set to, puffing, on the other side. The second job was finished quicker than the first; the wood here was partly rotten, aiding the saw. The new holes let in a remarkable amount of draught and dampness; but Monkey was content. It was a small enough price to pay.

The next phase of the plan was more difficult still. Wheedling, coaxing, using all his skill, he persuaded Pru and Sal nearer and nearer to the town of his choice. He had selected it mainly for the flatness of the surrounding ground; that he deemed a vital factor in eventual success. The last stage of the approach was the most delicate of all. Pru and Sal were stamping and trembling; the slightest mismanagement could have sent them wheeling back the way they had come, and all the valuable ground gained would have been lost. When it was obvious they would go no farther Monkey allowed them to camp, in a spinney adjoining the road. He lay quietly but with thudding heart, waiting for night and the start of his greatest adventure.

The vigil seemed endless; but finally the light faded from the sky. Another hour and the moon rose, brightening the land again. Very cautiously, Monkey sat up. The springs and axles of Truck, well greased the day before, betrayed him by no creak. He inched forward, a fraction at a time. His height when fully erect was little more than a yard; but his arms were of unnatural length. Squatting in Truck, well forward of the hood, he could easily reach through the new holes he had made, grip the wheel rims with his great scabbed hands.

He pushed, tentatively. To his delight Truck moved a yard or more. Pru and Sal lay still, mouths stertorously open. Another shove, and Truck had glided the whole distance from the little camp site to the road. Monkey, without a backward glance, set himself to steer his clumsy vehicle toward the distant town.

An hour later he was panting and running with sweat, while every muscle in his body seemed on fire. His hands were raw and bleeding from contact with the rusty rims; he had been obliged to stop, and bind his palms with rag. But progress had been made. Crawling to the spyhole – the rearward spyhole now, for Truck was technically moving in reverse – he saw the copse where Pru and Sal still lay as nothing more than a dim smudge on the horizon. Ahead, close now, lay the focus of his dreams.

By dawn, Truck was bowling merrily if jerkily along a smooth, paved road. To either side, dusty and grey, rose the remnants of buildings, their roofs and wall-tops bitten and nibbled away. Grass sprouted and bushes, here and there stunted, unhealthy-looking trees. The sight both appalled and fascinated Monkey. He thrust at the wheelrims, harder than before, staring round anxiously for signs of life; but a total hush lay over all the acres on acres of ruin. Apart from the trundling of Truck's wheels, there was no sound; even the wind seemed stilled, and no birds sang.

The sunrise proved Monkey's undoing. His eyes, weak at the best of times, were dazzled by the pouring light; he failed to observe and heed the steepening gradient ahead. Truck moved easily, without apparent effort, steadily increasing its pace. By the time understanding came it was too late. Monkey wailed despairingly, clutching at the wheelrims; but the flying iron tore the rags away, ploughed up the skin of his palms in thick white flakes. He shrieked, snatching his hands away; and instantly Truck was out of control. The rumbling of the wheels rose to a roar; Monkey, howling with pain and fright, felt himself banged and slewed before, with a heart-arresting jolt, Truck stopped dead. Monkey was propelled, catapult-fashion, in an arc. The blurred road rose to meet him; there was a crash, and the unexpected return of night.

He woke, blearily, a considerable time later. For a while, understanding was withheld; then realization came, and with it a blind terror. The sun beat down on the hot white road; behind him, seeming a great distance away, Truck was upended in a heap of rubble like a little foundered ship.

The panic got Monkey to his feet. He tottered, wildly, the first three steps of his life, stumbled and fell. He crawled the rest of the way, grazing his knees on the unfriendly surface of the road; but when at last he clutched the tall spokes of a wheel with his lacerated hands, some measure of sanity returned. A wave of giddiness came and passed. Monkey lay panting, staring round him at the awesome desolation.

From his low viewpoint little was visible but the bases of ruined walls. He raised his head, squinting. It seemed taller ruins reared in the distance. He thought he caught the glint of sunlight on high, bleached stone; but his head was spinning again, and with his streaming eyes, he could not be sure. He lay still, gathering strength; then, with a great effort, pulled himself to his feet.

Truck seemed to be undamaged, though the crash had mortally

disarranged the lockers and their contents. Books and blankets sprawled everywhere inside, mixed and confused with the remnants of Larder. Monkey, scrabbling, managed to retrieve a few scraps of rag, and an unbroken bottle of water. He plumped back, gasping, in the shade. Unscrewing the cap of the bottle hurt his hands again; but the liquid, though lukewarm, restored his senses a little. The rag he bound, as tightly as he was able, round his palms. He rested an hour or more; then, painfully but with dogged determination, he drew himself to his hands and knees. He began to crawl slowly away from Truck, into the ruined town.

Some hours later, an observer stationed beside the broken road would have witnessed a curious sight. The night was black as pitch, neither moon nor stars visible; but despite the overcast the road was by no means dark. It was lit, in places quite brightly, by a wavering bluish glow that seemed to proceed from the ruined shells of buildings themselves. By its aid, a small wooden truck was jerking itself slowly along. Its method of propulsion was curious. From a hole at the rear of the vehicle protruded two long, smooth poles. Each in turn, to the accompaniment of grunts and labouring gasps, groped for the cracked surface, found a purchase and heaved. Truck, under the influence of this novel motivation, lurched and veered. Sometimes, as if its occupant were very, very tired, it rested for long periods motionless; but always the upward movement was resumed. In time, the slope eased; and there could have been heard, rising from the ungainly little vehicle, a cracked but triumphant refrain.

> *'Silent the river, flowing for ever,*
> *Sing my brothers, yo heave ho . . .'*

Pru and Sal were waiting beneath the fringe of trees.

For a while, as Truck laboured toward them, they stood poised as if for flight. The hailing of Monkey, and his shouted exhortations, steadied them. His face, blackened and terribly peeling, loomed moon-like above a mound of tattered, browning paper; his arms terminated in dark red balls of rag; but it was Monkey, still indubitably and defiantly Monkey, who greeted them.

They ran to Truck with hard, gabbling cries, seized their long-accustomed handle and fled. Their feet galumphed, up hill and down dale, away from the sinister, shining town; and as they ran Monkey, his brain burning with strangest visions, regaled them with news of the world.

'Subscribers' dialled trunk calls are recorded at the exchange on the same meters used for local calls,' he carolled. 'These meters are extremely reliable, *and are regularly tested.*' He flung down the pamphlet, grabbed another. His eyes swam; fierce shooting pains stabbed suddenly through his head. 'How to take care of Your New House,' he shouted. 'Taps and Ball Valves, Gulleys and Gutters. Paths and Settlement Cracks ...' Pru and Sal shrieked back; but Monkey's voice boomed triumphantly, overriding them. 'What is Shrinkage?' he cried cunningly. 'Is an Imperfection a Defect?'

Truck heeled, struck a stone and righted. Monkey leafed at the jizzing papers. 'These are your Service Authorities,' he intoned. 'Rating Authority, Water Supply Authority, Gas Board, Electricity Board!' He snatched up another paper from his hoard. 'I never wanted to be a Star,' he bellowed. Then, turning two pages at once, 'Separates that Add Up in your Wardrobe ...'

Truck slowed at last, in the sun and shadow of a dappled wood where a grassy road ran between grassy banks.

Monkey wasn't feeling too good any more. He gulped and blinked, fighting the rise of a sudden swelling pain. 'Goodbye,' he said sadly, 'to the Bikini Girl of Nineteen-Seventy-Five. Next year will be Cover Up Year ...' The pain centred itself into an acute epiglottal knot; and Monkey burped. The burp was red and bright, and ran across his chin. He groaned, and brought up his wind again. The second belch was worse than the first. He splashed the wetness with his hands, and started to shriek.

The attention of Pru and Sal was riveted. They stooped, staring and mumbling. Their hands, iron-hard and hooked, scrabbled concernedly; and the cheeks of Monkey fell wholly from his face, lay on the pillows as bright as flower petals!

A mask, whether it be of blood or another substance, is a form that depersonalizes. Now, new triggers operated within the curious brains of Pru and Sal. The red thing that writhed and mewed was no longer Monkey, but a stranger that had taken Monkey's place. They seized it at once, shrieking with rage, and hurled it to the ground. Still it cried and wailed, its fear-smell triggering in turn desire to kill. Pru and Sal stamped and leaped, keening, their unused grass-dry bosoms joggling beneath their shifts. In time the sounds stopped, and what was on the path lay still. They gripped then the handles of the empty Truck and fled, backs humping, knees jerking regular as pistons. When they had gone, the lane was quiet.

The day was warm, and still. Flies buzzed, steady and soothing, through the afternoon. Toward dusk a wild creature found, in the path, something to its liking. For a time it chewed and mumbled warily; then leaf shadows, moved by a rising wind, startled it away. It retired to its hole, under the roots of an elderly, spreading oak; there it cleaned its fur, washed its nose and paws, and died.

Clouds piled in the sky, amber-grey in the fading light. Overhead, the leaves of trees glowed pale against the thunderous masses of vapour. The first rainspots fell, heavy and solitary, banging down through the yielding leaves; and the storm broke, with a crashing peal. In time it passed, grumbling, to the east. It left behind it, in the cleansed lane, a great new smell of earth and wet green leaves.

Stan is deeply troubled. He knows now the land is empty; all the rolling miles of it stretching out beyond the little bay. He's seen for himself; and she has gone for ever.

Somehow it's as if it was all his fault. Maybe if he'd never driven down, never thought … what he thought, none of it would have happened. Not the bombs, not anything. If only he'd known, if only he'd realized in time. He'd have given everything away, the gun and the Champ, the lot; just sat and been glad to be what he was and that she was happy, though not with him. He feels he would like to cry; only his eyes are so gummy, they've nearly glued themselves shut.

He gets them working by rubbing with his fingers. The room is just the same, he sees a packing crate with plastic cups and saucers standing on it and the camping stove and his stuff scattered about. The light is bluish and dull; it's either dusk or dawn. But seeing is really too much effort; after a while his eyes close themselves again.

But listen! Is it possible? In the darkness behind the lids, there are new sounds. Many sounds. The gloom brightens; and he is amazed. In that minute – it couldn't have been more – whole forests have sprung up; and there are men again. Real men, and women too. Villages stand protected by stockades; there are fields of barley and wheat, he sees animals grazing, carts jolting along dusty white tracks. He thinks of all he has missed; he can't afford such inattention, such ingratitude, again. He's sorry now the thought of doing away with himself ever entered his mind.

His viewpoint alters. He sees a hill, one special hill. On it lies the tiny figure of a girl.

It seems he swoops closer. He sees the bushes that clothe the slope, the very blades of grass; then he catches his breath. He can't believe; but neither can he mistake her. It's happened, after a weariness of time; his prayer has been answered. There is a God; and he's wise, and just!

FOUR

The God House

1

If you had lain as Mata lay, stretched out on the wiry grass, and pressed your ear to the ground, you would have heard, a long way off, the measured thud and tramp of many feet. If you had raised your head, as she now raised hers, you would have caught, gusting on the sharp, uncertain breeze of early spring, the heart-pounding thump and roll of drums. Since dawn, the Great Procession had been winding its slow way from the sea; now, it was almost here.

She sat up quickly, pushing the tangled black hair from her eyes; a dark-eyed, brown-skinned girl of maybe thirteen summers. Her one garment, of soft doeskin, left her legs and arms bare; her waist was circled by a leather thong, on which it pleased her to carry a little dagger in a painted wooden sheath. Round her neck she wore an amulet of glinting black and red stones; for Mata was the daughter of a chief.

The valley above which she lay opened its green length to the distant sea. Behind her, crowning the nearer height, was a village of thatched mud huts, surrounded by a palisade of sharply pointed timbers. In front, rearing sharp-etched against the sky, was the Sacred Mound to which the Procession must come. Here the Giants had lived, in times beyond the memory of men; and here they had once reared a mighty Hall. The top of the Mound was circled still by nubs and fingers of stone, half buried by the bushes and rank grasses that had seeded themselves over the years; but now none but the village priests dared venture to the crest. The Giants had been all-powerful; their ghosts too were terrible, and much to be feared. Once, as a tiny child, Mata had ventured to climb the steep side of the Mound toward where Cha'Acta the Chief Priest tethered his fortune in goats; but the seething of the wind in the long yellow grass, the bushes that seemed to catch at her with twiggy fingers, the spikes and masses of high grey stone half-glimpsed beyond the summit, had sent her scuttling in terror. She had kept her own counsel, which was maybe just as well; and since that day had never ventured near the forbidden crest.

The sound of drumming came sudden and loud. The head of the Procession was nearing the great chalk cleft; any moment now it would be in sight. Mata frowned back at the village, pulling her lip with her teeth. The other children, placed under her care, had been left to fend for themselves in the smoke and ashes of the family hut; chief's daughter or not, she would certainly be beaten if she was discovered here.

Nearby a tousled stand of bramble and old gorse offered concealment. She wriggled to it, lay couched in its yielding dampness; felt her eyes drawn back, unwillingly, to the Sacred Mound.

At its highest point, sharp and clear in the noon light, stretched the long hogsback of the God House; reed-thatched, its walls blank and staring white, its one low doorway watching like a distant dark eye. Round it, the fingers of old stone clustered thickly. Above it, set atop the gable ends, reared fantastic shapes of rushwork; the Field Spirits, set to guard the house of the Lord from harm. Mata shivered, half with apprehension, half with some less readily identifiable emotion, and turned her gaze back across the grass.

Her heart leaped painfully, settled to a steady pounding. In that moment of time the Procession had come into sight, debouching from the pass between the hills. She saw the yellow antennae and waving whips of the Corn Ghosts, most feared of all spirits; behind them the bright, rich robes of the exorcizing priests, Cha'Acta among them in his green, fantastic mask. Behind again came Cymbal men and drummers, Hornmen capering in their motley; and after them the great mass of the people, chanting and stamping, looking like a brown-black, many-legged snake. She bestowed on them no more than a passing glance; her whole attention was concentrated on the head of the column.

She wriggled forward once more, forgetful of discovery. She could see Choele distinctly now. How slender she looked, how white her body shone against the grass! How stiffly she walked! Her hair, long and flowing, golden as Mata's was dark, had been wreathed with chaplets of leaves and early flowers; she held her head high, eyes blank and unseeing, lost already in contemplation of the Lord. Her arms were crossed stiffly, in front of her breasts; and from the crown of her head to the soles of her feet she alone was bare. Quite, quite bare.

The whole Procession was closer now. The Corn Ghosts ran, skirmishing to either side, leaping fantastically, lashing with their whips at the bushes and old dead grass; the animal dancers pranced, white antlers gleaming in the sunlight. Mata edged back in sudden panic to the shelter of the bushes, saw between the stems how Choele, deaf and unseeing, still unerringly led the throng. Her figure, strutting and pale, vanished between the bushes and low trees that fringed the base of the Sacred Mound. The people tumbled after, exuberantly; the drums pounded ever more loudly; then suddenly a hush, chilling and complete, fell across the grass. Mata, screwing her eyes, saw the tiny figure of her friend pause on the causeway that led to the Mound. For a moment it seemed Choele turned, looking back and down; then she stepped resolutely on, vanished from sight behind the first of the rearing stones.

Already people were breaking away, streaming back gabbling up the hill. Mata rose unwillingly. Her father would be hungry; like the rest of the village, he had been fasting since dawn. She remembered the neglected bowls of broth, steaming on their trivets over the hut fire, and quickened her pace. At the stockade gates she paused. Below her, folk toiled up the slope; others still stood in a ragged black crescent, staring up at the Mound. The priests in their robes clustered the causeway, tiny and jewel-bright. From this height the God House with its long humped grey-green roof showed clear; Mata, shielding her eyes with her hand, saw a tiny figure pause before the doorway of the shrine. A moment it waited; then slipped inside, silent and quick as a moth, and was lost to sight. A heartbeat later she heard the rolling cry go up from all the people.

Once again, the God Bride had entered the presence of her Lord.

Mata ran for her hut, legs pounding, not feeling the hardness of the packed earth street beneath her feet. The fire was low; she blew and panted, feeding the embers with dried grass and bunches of sticks, and for the moment heat and exertion drove from her the thought of what she had seen.

The drums began again, late in the night. Great fires burned in the square before the Council Lodge; youths and men, fiercely masked and painted, ran, torches in hand, in and out the shadows of the huts; girls swayed in the shuffling, sleep-inducing rhythm of a dance. On the stockade walls and watchtowers more torches burned, their light orange and flickering. Old men and crones hobbled between the huts, fetching and carrying, broaching cask after cask of the dark corn beer. The other children were sleeping already, despite the din; only Mata lay wide-eyed and watchful, staring through the open doorway of the hut, seeing and not seeing the leaping grotesque shadows rise and fall.

Every year, since the hills themselves were young and the Giants walked the land, her folk had celebrated in this fashion the return of spring. They waited, fearfully, for the hooting winter winds to cease to blow, for the snow to melt, for the earth to show in patches and wet brown skeins beneath the withered grass. Little by little, as the year progressed, the sun gained in strength; little by little vigour flooded back into trees and fields, buds split showing tiny, vivid-green mouths. Till finally – and only Cha'Acta and his helpers could say exactly when – the long fight was over, the Corn Lord, greatest of the Gods, reborn in manhood and loveliness. Then the hill folk gave thanks to the Being who was both grain and sunlight, who had come to live among them one more season. A Bride was chosen for him, to live with him in the God House as long as he desired; and the Great Procession formed, milling round the God Tents on the distant shore.

Choele had been a season older than Mata, and her special friend. Her limbs were straight and fine as peeled rods of willow, her hair a light cloud yellow as the sun. To the younger girl she had confided her certainty, over half a year before, that she would be the next spring's chosen Bride.

Mata had shrugged, tossing her own dark mane. It was not good to speak lightly of any God; but especially the great Corn Lord, whose eyes see the movements of beetles and mice, whose ears catch the whisper of every stem of grass. But Choele had persisted. 'See, Mata; come and sit with me in the shade, and I will show you how I know.'

Mata stared away sullenly for a while, setting her mouth and frowning; but finally curiosity overcame her. She wriggled beside the other girl, lay sleepily smelling the sweet smell of long grass in the sun. The goats they had been set to watch browsed steadily, shaking their heads, staring with their yellow eyes, bumping and clonking their clumsy wooden bells.

Mata said, 'It is not wise to say such things, Choele, even to me. Perhaps the God will hear, and punish you.'

Choele laughed. She said, 'He will not punish me.' She had unfastened the thongs that held the top of her dress; she lay smiling secretly, pushing the thin material forward and back. 'See, Mata, how I have grown,' she said. 'Put your fingers here, and feel me. I am nearly a woman.'

Mata said coldly, 'I do not choose to.' She rolled on her back, feeling the sun hot against her closed lids; but Choele persisted till she opened her eyes and saw the nearness of her breasts, how full and round they had become. She stroked the nipples idly, marvelling secretly at their firmness; then Choele showed her another thing, and though she played in the dark till she was wet with sweat she couldn't make her body do it too. So she cried at last, bitterly, because Choele had spoken the truth; soon she would be gone from her, and there was no other she chose to make a friend. For a year, each Bride lived with the God; but none of them had ever spoken of the Mystery, and all afterwards avoided their former friends, walking alone for the most part with their eyes downcast.

But next day Choele was kinder. 'This will not be true of us,' she said. 'For a time I shall live in the God House, certainly; but afterwards we will be friends again, Mata, and I will tell you how it is when you are loved by a God. Now come into the bushes, and let us play; for I am a woman now, and know more ways than before to make you happy.'

The drums were still beating; but the fires, that had flickered so high, were burning low. The Corn Ghosts were dead, driven by Cha'Acta's magic from the fields; their old dry husks, empty as the shells of lobsters, had already been ritually burned. In the winter to come the old women, who had seen many Corn Processions pass, would plait new figures; for next year, too, the God would need a Bride.

Mata gulped, and swallowed back another thought half-formed.

She slipped from the hut, moving quietly so as not to disturb the little ones. From the Council Lodge, set square facing the end of the one street of the village, sounds of revelry still rose; for the moment, she was safe. She shadowed between the huts, heading away from where the fires still pulsed and flickered. By the stockade, the outer air struck chill. She climbed the rough wooden steps to a guard tower. As she had expected, the high platform was deserted. She stood shivering a little, staring down into the night.

The moon was sinking to the rim of hills. Below, far off and tiny at her feet, the Sacred Mound was bathed in a silvery glow. Across its summit, black and hulking, lay the God House. It was still, and seemingly deserted; but Mata knew this was not so.

She tried to force her mind out from her body, send it soaring like the spirit of Cha'Acta. She heard a hunting owl call to its mate; and it seemed she flew with the flying bird, silently, across the moonwashed gulf of space. Then it was as if for an instant her spirit joined with Choele, lying waiting silent on the great brushwood bed. She heard a mouse run and scuttle on the floor, thought it was the scratching of the God; and giddiness came on her so that she staggered, clutching the wood of the watchtower for support. Then, just as swiftly it seemed, she was back in her body; and fear of the God was on her so that she shook more violently than before. She pulled her cloak closer round her throat, staring about her guiltily; but none had seen, for there were none to watch. She huddled a long time, unwilling to leave her vantage point, while the fires in the street burned to embers and the moon sank beneath a waiting hill. Its shadow raced forward, swift and engulfing, half-seen; and the God House was gone, plunged in the blackest dark.

She licked her mouth and turned away, groping with her bare feet for the edges of the wooden steps.

The God, as ever, was pleased with his Bride. Cha'Acta announced it, before all the people; and once more the horns blew, the drums thundered, the vats of corn beer were broached and drained. Every day now the sun gained visibly in strength, the hours of daylight lengthened. A burgeoning tide of green swept across the land, across the forest tops in the valleys, across the little patchwork fields where the corn pushed sappy spears up from the ground. The time of breeding came and passed; the coracles ventured farther from the coasts, bringing back snapping harvests of sea things, lobsters and crabs. The villagers, from headman and priests to the lowest chopper of wood, grew sleek and contented. High summer came, with its long blue days and drowsy heat; and only Mata mourned. Sometimes, as she lay watching her father's goats, she wove chaplets of roses for her hair; sometimes she joined in the children's play and laughter; but always her thoughts slid back to the great house on the hill, to Choele and her Lord.

In the mornings she woke now before it was light, with the first sweet piping of the birds. Always, the Sacred Mound drew her irresistibly. She would sit and brood, in some hollow of the grassy hill, watching down at the long roof of the God House, still in the new, pearly light; or she would run alone and unseen, down to the brook that meandered softly below the Mound. Trees arched over it, cutting back the light, their roots gripping the high banks to either side; between them the water ran clear and bright and cold. Her ankles as she walked stirred greyish silt that drifted with the current like little puffs of smoke. The coldness touched first calves and knees, then thighs; then as she dipped and shuddered, all of her. Sometimes she would look up, unwilling, to the high shoulder of the hill, and see the nubs and spikes of stone watching down, run scurrying to drag her clothes on wet and sticking. Then she would bolt from the secret place to the high yellow slope of hill below the village; only there dare she turn, stare down panting at the Mound and the God House, rendered tiny by distance and safe as children's toys. And once, on the high hill, a whisper of cool wind reached to her, touched her hot forehead and passed on into distance, to far fields and the homes of other men. She sat down then, unsteadily; for it seemed to her the God had indeed passed, laughing and glad, to play like a child among the distant hills. A gladness filled her too so that she rose, stretching out her arms; for the Lord speaks only to his chosen. She turned, excited, for the village, bubbling inside with still-unadmitted thoughts.

Later, she was vouchsafed more convincing proof.

Toward the end of summer she was set to gathering reeds; the village folk used them in great quantities for thatching both their own homes and the God House. The sacred hut, alone of all buildings, was refurbished every year. For its great span, only the finest and longest reeds would serve; so Mata in her searching wandered farther and farther afield, hoping secretly her harvest would adorn the home of the God, and that he would know and be pleased. The afternoon was hot and still; an intense, blue and gold day, smelling of Time and burning leaves. She worked knee-deep for the most part, shut away among the great tall pithy stems, hacking with a keen, sickle-bladed knife, throwing the reeds down in bundles on the bank for the carts to pick them up. In time the endless, luminous-green vistas, the feathery grass-heads arching above her, worked in her a curious mood. She seemed poised on the edge of some critical experience; almost it was as if some Presence, vast yet nearly tangible, pervaded the hot, unaware afternoon. The reed stems rubbed and chafed, sibilantly, water gurgled and splashed where she stepped. She found herself pausing unconsciously, the knife blade poised, waiting for she knew not what. Unconsciously too, later with a strange rapture, she pressed deeper into the marsh. Its water, tart and stinking, cooled her legs; its mud soothed her ankles. The mud itself felt warm and smooth; she drove with her toes, feeling them slide between slimy textures of root, willing herself to sink. Soon she had to tuck her skirt higher round her thighs; finally, impulsively, she drew it to her waist. She fell prey to the oddest, half-pleasurable sensations; and still the magic grass called and whispered, still she seemed drawn forward.

She heard the wind blow, a great rushing rustle all about; but her vision was narrowed to the brown and yellow stems before her eyes. Her free hand now was beneath the water; and it seemed in her delirium a great truth came to her. The grasses, in their green thousands, were the body of the Corn Lord; and his body, mystically, the grasses. She cried out; then her own body seemed to open and she knew the Magic Thing had happened at last. She pressed the reed stems madly, awkward with the knife, sucking with her mouth; and life ended, in a wonderful soaring flight.

The world blinked back. She opened her mouth to gasp, and water rushed in. She threshed and fought, fear of the deep mud blinding reason. Dimly, she felt pain; then she had dropped the knife she carried and the bank was close. She reeled and staggered, clawed to it, rolled over and lay still.

The sun was low before she opened her eyes. She lay a moment unaware; then memory returned. She half sat up, pushing with her elbows against a weight of sickness. Somewhere, there were voices. She saw a waggon moving along the river bank. It came slowly, one man leading the ox, a second stooping to fling reed bundles on to the already towering pile.

Her chest felt sore and sharp. She stared down, frowning. Her dress was stuck to her, glued with dark red; the rest of her was muddy still, and bare.

The waggoners had seen her. It seemed they stood staring a great while; then they stepped forward carefully, placing each foot in line. One of them said in a low voice, 'It's the headman's child. She who was sent to cut the reeds.'

She laughed at them then, or showed her teeth. She said, 'I harvested more than reeds. The God came to me, and was very passionate.' She fell back heavy-eyed, watching them approach. They fiddled awkwardly with her dress, giving her more pain. At last the fabric jerked clear; and the villagers huddled back frowning. Across her chest ran deep, curving gashes; the marks the Corn Lord gave her, with his nails.

The wounds healed quickly; but the dullness of spirit induced by the God's visit took longer to disperse. For many days Mata lay in the family hut, unmoving, drinking and eating very little; while all the village it seemed came to peck and cluck outside, stare curiously round the doorposts into the dark interior. Meanwhile prodigies and wonders were constantly reported. Magan, Mata's father, saw with his own eyes a great cloud form above the God House, a cloud that took the baleful shape of a claw; the marshes glowed at night with curious light, sighings and rushings in the air spoke of the passage of monsters.

Finally, Cha'Acta came. He arrived in considerable state, three of his priests in attendance; he wore his official robes, blazoned with the green spear of the Corn Lord, and Mata as she saw him stoop beneath the lintel huddled to the farthest corner of the bracken bed. Never before had Cha'Acta acknowledged her directly; now he seemed terrible, and very tall.

Lamps were brought, the other children banished; and the High Priest began his examination. The wounds were subjected to the closest scrutiny; then Mata told her tale again and again, eyes huge in the lamplight, voice faltering and lisping. The thin face of Cha'Acta remained impassive; the dark, grave eyes watched down as she talked. But none could say, when he rose to take his leave, what decision he had come to, or what his thoughts had been. Later though he caused gifts to be sent to the hut; fresh milk and eggs and fruit, a tunic to replace the one the God had soiled. All knew, perhaps, what the portent meant; only Mata, it seemed, could not believe. She lay far into the night, eyes staring unseeing in the dark, clutching the soft fabric to her chest; but as yet her mind refused to make the words.

Autumn was past by the time her strength returned; the harvest gathered, the animals driven into their stockades. Round the village the fields and sweeping downs lay brown and dry, swept by a chilling wind. Eyes followed her as she moved through the village street, cloak gripped round her against the cold. She flushed with awareness; but held her head high and proud, looking to neither left nor right. She climbed to the stockade walk, stared down at the God House on the Mound. Cloud scud moved overhead; the pass between the hills lay desolate and bleak, grey with the coming winter.

Usually the God House was empty well before this time, its doors once more agape, its walls ritually breached. But Cha'Acta remained silent, and Choele was not seen. The village muttered curiously; till finally word came that the Corn Lord had once more left his valley home. The men of the village scurried on to the Mound, fearful and slinking, dragging after them the long grey bundles of thatch. Through the shortest days they worked, renewing the great roof and its framing of timber and poles. The walls of the God House were patched and re-whitened, its floors pounded and swept ready for the coming spring. Mata, who now did little of the housework, watched all from the rampart of the little town. She saw the Field Spirits carried down the street, hoisted distantly to their places; two days later, she saw Choele walking alone through the village.

She ran to her gladly; but a dozen paces away she faltered. For her friend's face was white and old, the eyes she raised toward her dark-ringed and dead. And Mata knew with certainty that despite the promise of Choele the

Mystery had come between them, as blank and impenetrable as a wall.

She ran, dismayed, to her father's hut. An hour or more she lay on her pallet, squeezing the hot tears; then she rose, wiped her face and fell to with the household chores. A decision had formed in her, cold and irrevocable; and at last the forbidden thoughts were freely admitted. Next year, Mata herself would be the Corn Queen. Afterwards, when she too knew the Mystery, she would go to Choele; and all between them would be as it had been before.

Mata was often seen about the village in the brightening days that followed. She took to placing herself, consciously or unconsciously, in Cha'Acta's path. Always she moved with becoming modesty; but her downcast eyes missed nothing. Sometimes, wrapped in talk or bent upon his own affairs, the Chief Priest seemed not to notice her; at others he turned, watching her as she moved on her errands, and Mata felt the keen, impenetrable stare burn on her neck and back.

Her father finally sent for her late one night. He sat in some state in the Council Lodge, a pitcher of corn beer at his elbow. Cha'Acta was also present, and the elders and priests. Mata stood head bowed in the smoky light of torches while her father spoke, sadly it seemed, saying the impossible words; and later, when she left, there was no sensation of the earth beneath her feet. Already it seemed she was set apart from normal things, the chosen of the Lord.

She lay sleepless till dawn, watching the embers glowing on their shelf of clay, listening to the breathing of her sisters and her mother's rattling snore. A score of times, when she thought of what would come, her heart leaped and thudded, trying it seemed to break clear of her body. At length the longed-for dawn broke dim and grey; she rose and dressed, went to seek a hut at the far end of the village. In it lived Meril, the old woman who instructed the God Brides and for many years had preserved their Mysteries.

Mata stayed a month with the crone, learning many things that were new and by no means wholly pleasant. Choele, it was true, had often taken her to the hills for purposes not dissimilar. But Choele's fingers were brown, and sweet as honey; Meril's were old and horny, sour-smelling. They left her feeling unclean. Mata shuddered and stiffened, sweating; but she endured, for Choele's sake and the sake of the God.

Cha'Acta she now seldom saw. There was still much to be done; grain to be prepared for sowing, beer to be brewed, pens and stockades repaired, the God Tents and all the paraphernalia of the Great Procession made ready once more. In most, if not in all of these things the Chief Priest took an interest. Meanwhile, the buds swelled perceptibly. Rain fell, waking new grass; and finally came a time of clear, bright sun. The skies dappled over with puffy, fast-moving white clouds; the wind came gusting and warm, lifting trails of dust from hilltops and the sloping fields, and Mata knew her waiting was all but ended.

Then came tragedy, stark and unexpected. Choele was missed from the village. For some days uneasy bands of men desultorily searched the hills and surrounding ground; then one morning an oldster came gabbling and puffing up the hill, shouting his incoherent tidings to the sleepy guards on the gate. In the brook that ran below the Mound, the grey, cold brook where Mata once had bathed, floated a sodden bundle of cloth and hair; all that was left of the Corn Lord's Bride.

The omen threw the village into a ferment. Drums beat before the Council Lodge, where Cha'Acta and his priests prayed and sacrificed to avert the undoubted wrath of the God. Men rose fearfully, watching up at the clear skies; but strangely the weather remained fine, the land continued to smile. So that by the week of the Great Procession the death was all but forgotten; only Mata felt within her a little hollow space, that now would never be filled.

She already knew her duties, and the many ways existing to please a God. What remained after Meril's rough instruction had been imparted by Cha'Acta in his harsh, monotonous voice. For two days before the great event she fasted, drinking nothing but the clearest spring water, purging her body of all dross. On the day before the ceremony she made her formal goodbyes to her family. A waggon was waiting, decked and beribboned, drawn by the white oxen of Cha'Acta; she mounted it, stood stiffly staring ahead while the equipage jolted out through the broad gates of the stockade. The guards raised their spears, clashed a salute; then the village was falling away behind, the wheels jerking and bumping over the rough turf of the hill.

Every year, so ran the litany, the God came from the south, drawn by prayers across the endless blue sea. The little camp the priests had set up by the shore already bustled with activity. Hide tents had been pitched; over the biggest, on a little staff, hung the long green Sign of the God. Here Mata would lie the night. Some distance away the nodding insignia of the Chief Priest marked where Cha'Acta would rest on this most important eve; beside his quarters, waggons unloaded more bundles of hides, the poles and withies on which they would be stretched. Other baggage was stacked or strewn around; Mata saw the motley of the Hornmen, the antlers and hide masks, by them the green lobster-shells that in the morning would become the Corn Ghosts, and shivered with a medley of emotions.

Difficult now to retain even the memory of Choele. Her tent was ready for her, its lamps lit, the grass inside strewn with precious water bought at great expense from the traders who sometimes passed along the coast. She was bathed, and bathed again; then lay an hour, patiently, while the fluffy down her body had begun to grow was scraped from her with sharpened shells. Her breast-buds were stained with bright dye, her hair combed and stroked and combed again; and finally, she was left to sleep.

She slept soundly, curiously enough, tired out by the time of fasting and preparation; it was a shock to feel her shoulder shaken by old Meril. A cloak was held out to her; she crept from the tent, into the first glow of dawn. The sea lay cold and flat; a droning wind blew from it bringing with it the harsh, strange smell of salt.

The God Tents were triangular and black, built not of hides but of thick, impermeable felt. The flap of the nearest was raised for her; she crept inside, shivering, already knowing what she would find.

On the ground inside the little booth had been placed a great copper bowl. In it, charcoal smouldered and the magic seeds of plants. The little space was thick already with an acrid, pungent-smelling smoke; she coughed, catching her breath, leaned her head over the bowl as she had been taught. Instantly she heard the sighing as the bellows, worked from outside by an attendant priest, forced air over the burning mass, bringing it to a glow.

The smoke scorched her lungs; she retched and would have vomited had her stomach not been empty. She inhaled dutifully, closing her streaming eyes; and in time it seemed the fumes grew less sharp. Then strange things began to happen, her body, she was sure, had floated free of contact with the earth; she groped awkwardly, pawing the hard ground for reassurance. Then the bowl and its contents seemed to expand till she felt she was falling headlong and at great speed toward an entire world on fire. The inside of the booth, small enough for her to span, likewise enlarged itself to a soundless black void, infinite as the night sky. In it, sparks and flashes burned; there were stars and moons and suns, comets and golden fruit, God-figures that passed as fleeting as they were vast. She opened her eyes, screwed them closed once more; the forms still swam, in the darkness behind the lids.

Lastly it seemed that Mata herself had grown to immense stature; she felt she might grasp with her arms the headlands that closed the bay, stoop to catch up the running figures of men like ants or grains of sand. She rose slowly, swaying, knowing she was ready.

Outside the tent the light had grown. She felt, dimly, the presence of the people; heard the shout as the cloak, unwanted now, was drawn from her. Muffled fingers touched her, plaiting the green wreaths in her hair; and already she was moving away, angling with difficulty her mile-long legs and arms, stepping up the rocky path from the bay. Behind her the Procession jostled into order; cymbals crashed, horns shouted, the drums took up their insistent thudding. Her ears registered the sounds; but disconnectedly, in flashes and fragments, mixed with a roaring like the voice of the sea.

The wind blew, steady and not-cold, pressing to her tautened body close as a glove; while from her great height she saw, with wonderful acuteness, the tiniest details of the land across which she passed. Pebbles and grass-blades, wet with sea-damp, jerked beneath her bright as jewels. She sensed, in her exalted awareness, the rising of mighty truths lost as soon as formed, truths that her body nonetheless understood so that it laughed as it moved, exulting; while stepping so far above the ground a part of her mind marvelled that she did not fall.

The Corn Ghosts skipped, lashing with their whips, chasing their half-terrified victims from the path. The priests chanted; Cha'Acta, eyes implacable behind his bright green mask, blessed the land, casting spoonfuls of grain to either side. The sun, breaking through the high veils of mist, threw the long shadow of Mata forward across the grass. She glanced down, along the length of her immense body to the far-off, forgotten white tips of her feet. The vision was disturbing; she raised her eyes again, rested them on the distant line of the horizon.

Already – it seemed impossible – she saw before her the high pass in the hills. On the right was the village with its stockade; to her left, close and looming, the Sacred Mound and the waiting house of the God. She could feel now, faintly, the textures of grass and earth beneath her feet; but the intense clarity of sight remained, she saw tiny flowers budding in the grass and insects, sticks and bracken and dead straw. The way steepened, beside the Brook of Choele; she pressed on, hurrying the last few yards. And here was the causeway, built of ancient stone; beyond, the Sacred Mound, empty and desolate and vast.

Never before had she been so high. Subtly she had expected grass and bushes, the very stones, to be changed here somehow, so close to the home of the God; but even to her exalted sense they seemed the same. At the causeway end she remembered to turn, showing herself again to the people. She heard them cry, felt their stares against her like a prickling wind; then she was alone, threading her way between the spires of stone.

She climbed now in earnest, using her hands to steady herself. She rounded a lichened buttress, trudged across an open space where dead grass tangles stroked her thighs; and the God House was ahead, awesome and close. She faltered then, hands to her throat; and memory flooded her dulled brain, she wished herself for one heart-stopping moment back at her father's hearth, smutty and unknown, and all she had done, undone. Then the time was passed; she paused once more to wave, heard the scattered shouts from the hill and stepped inside, to darkness and quiet.

The quietness, at first, oppressed her worst; a singing silence, heightened by the rushing of the blood in her ears. She stood still, clutching her shoulders, trying to draw herself into a tiny compass. The long house was empty, and quite bare. The floor, swept of all but the tiniest grains of dirt, gleamed a dull grey-brown; the walls rose, rough and cobbled, to shoulder height; the long gable stretched away above, thatch-poles showing equidistant and pale. Between them the reeds lay even and close, filling the place with the scent of grass and ponds.

She walked forward, slowly, still with her arms crossed in front of her. As her eyes became used to the gloom she saw that what she had taken to be the end wall was in fact an open wattle screen, pierced by a narrow entrance. She stepped through it. Beyond, an arm's span away, was a second screen, also pierced. The entrances she saw were staggered, blocking from sight the great outer door. Beyond the second screen was a chamber, small, square and dark. She saw a couch of thick-piled bracken; beside it a water jar and dipper, standing on the smooth, beaten floor.

And that was all.

Her legs shook suddenly. She unwound the garlands from her hair, clumsily, tossed them down unnoticed. She knelt by the pitcher, dipped water. It was clear, sweet and very cold. She drank deeply, slaking herself; then rolled on her back on the bracken bed. She was conscious, now, of a rising weariness; she let her limbs subside, luxuriously, her eyes drift closed. In time the singing in her ears faded to quiet.

She woke in darkness. The little chamber itself was pitchy black; she turned her head, slowly, saw the intervals of the wattle screens lit by a silver-grey glow. For a time, she was confused again; then she realized the hours she must have slept. The cold, metallic light was the moon.

The effects of the seed-smoke had wholly left her now. She shivered, wanting a coverlet; but there was nothing in the hut. Then she remembered she was not there to sleep.

She swallowed. Something had roused her, surely. She listened, concentrating her whole awareness. The wind soughed across the Mound, stirring the grass and bushes. A timber creaked, somewhere in the great hut. Her heart leaped, it seemed into her throat; but nothing further came. The God House was as silent as before.

She frowned, brooding. Were all the tales, the stories, false? Her training, thorough as it had been, stopped short of this. What if no God ever really came, to live in the house on the hill? Or what if – terrible thought – the Corn Lord had rejected her? What if he had already come, in the darkness and quiet, found her unpleasing as a Bride and passed on? Then he would leave the valley for ever; and the corn shoots would rot in the ground, the people starve. She would be stoned, disgraced … She clenched her fists, feeling her eyes begin to sting. The disgrace would be the least of her pain.

She made herself be still again. He would come in his own time and fashion; for who, after all, could command a God? Once, already, he had visited her in the reeds; what more did she need, in proof? It had been a mark of favour such as no other, in her memory, had received. He would come; because he always came, and because he had chosen her.

The thought brought fresh fears in its train. What would he be like, when he came? Perhaps he would be burning hot, or terrible to look on. Perhaps his eyes would be like the eyes of a beast … She willed her mind to stop making such thoughts. It was hard, this time of waiting. She wished for the magic smoke again and the strength it gave, the great thoughts that in the morning had seemed so clear. In time she slipped, unwillingly, into a doze.

The moon was higher, when she woke again; and this time, she knew without doubt, she had been roused by something more corporeal than the wind. She lay still, trembling, straining her ears. Almost she cried out; but the thought of her voice echoing through the dimness of the hut choked the sound in her throat. Then she heard them; the stealthy, padding footfalls, coming down the moonshot dark toward her.

She rolled over, scrabbling at the bracken. Her vision swam and sparked. A blur of movement, sensed more than seen; and a figure stepped into the chamber. She stayed crouched and still, glaring up. The moon, touching the wattle screens, gave a dim, diffused light. For her eyes, tuned to blackness, it was enough; she could see, now, every terrible detail.

The creature before her was naked, seeming taller than a man. Round calves and thighs ran delicate, scrolling lineworks of tattoo; above the thighs the manhood swung, a great, thrusting, forward-jutting column. More tattoos marked the breasts; while in one hand the figure gripped a Staff of Power, topped by the Sign of the Corn Lord. Its head alone was invisible, covered by a great fantastic mask; black in this light but green she knew, green as the sprouting grain. She did scream then, high and shrill; and the creature growled impatiently. 'Be quiet, little fool,' it said. 'The God is here.'

The form was Godlike; but the voice, though muffled by the mask, she knew too well. It was the voice of Cha'Acta.

Her limbs, that had been stiff with fear, were loosened. She scuttled for the doorway, ducking, fending off the clutching arms; but the High Priest caught her by the hair, flung her heavily back to the couch. She lay panting, tried to roll aside. He stooped above her; the mask caught her a bruising blow on the cheek. She scrabbled, biting and scratching; and the thing fell clear, showed her Cha'Acta's contorted face. She flung herself at him then, beating and pummelling with her fists; but her wrists were caught, blows rained on her body. She curled whimpering, wrapped round a bright ball of pain; she was lifted, thrown down and lifted again. Lights spun before her eyes, like the magic lights of the seed-smoke. When the beating was over she could no longer see; and her mouth felt loose and stinging. She lay dully, unable to resist, feeling the great weight of Cha'Acta press across her. After that the dream or nightmare was repeated many times, till the middle of her body felt one great burning pain; but toward dawn, the High Priest let her be.

2

She moved slowly, in the cold grey light, hanging her draggled hair. Rolled over, groped with her heels for the hard earth floor. The movement caused giddiness, and a vast sickness; she hung her head again and tried to vomit, but nothing came.

In time the sickness passed a little. She opened her eyes blearily, stared down. Her body, that had been smoothly white, was ugly now with bruises, marked with dried blood. She panted, holding her hands out in front of her face. They were dark-striped too.

She set her teeth, edged to her knees beside the pitcher. The water, splashed over shoulders and head, brought a little more awareness. She worked clumsily, rubbing herself clean. Lastly she drank, swilling the metallic taste from her mouth.

Lying across the bed was a tunic of fine bleached linen, decorated on the breast with the motif of the God. She stared at it for a while then stood, worked it painfully over her head. She peered out between the wattle screens. The dawn light showed her a huddled shape by the outer door. She began to creep toward it, an inch at a time, setting her feet down noiselessly.

Some sixth sense roused Cha'Acta. He sat up, holding out an arm; and the great mask of the God crashed against his skull. He groaned, gripping his hands round the ankles of the Bride. Mata struck again, frenzied, bringing the mask down from a height. The eyes of Cha'Acta rolled upward, disclosing the whites. The High Priest arched his body, breath whistling through his nose; but his fingers still held firm. The third blow opened the skin of his scalp in a white half moon that flooded instantly with red. He fell back, head against the pale rough wall; and Mata ran.

Fear lent her speed. Only at the bottom of the Mound she paused, doubled up, hands gripping beneath her kilt. The spasm ebbed; she stared up fearfully, certain she had been seen. But the village and the high rough slope of grass lay deserted.

She set off again, walking and running by turns, rubbing to ease the stitched cramps in her side. For a time she followed, more or less blindly, the path of the Great Procession. Once out of sight of the pass and the Sacred Mound, instinct made her turn aside. In the low ground between hills and sea, an arm of forest thrust black and ragged in the early light. Here her people never ventured; for the forest was the haunt of wolves and bears, wildcats and savage ghosts, and shunned by all right-minded dwellers on the chalk. By mid-morning she was deep among the trees, safe for the time from observation.

Her fasting, and the terror of the night, were rapidly taking their toll. She fell often, stumbling over creepers and unseen snags. Each time it was longer before she rose. She stopped at last, staring round her fearfully. About her the trees had grown higher; their vast shapes, black and looming, cut back all but a glimmer of light. Between the gnarled trunks the ground was rough and broken, carpeted with old briars; branches and twigs hung motionless, and there were no sounds of birds.

She rubbed a hand across her wet face, staggered on again. Her blindness led her finally to the head of a little bluff. She saw it too late; the rank grass slope, sheen of water and mud ten feet below. She landed heavily, with a thudding splash. The soft ground saved her at least from broken bones; she crawled a yard, then two, lay thinking she would never rise again.

The wind blew then, stirring at last the tops of the trees, whispering in the tangled undergrowth.

She lifted her head, frowning, trying to force her mind to work. The breeze came again; and she seemed to see, with great clearness, the yellow slopes of the hills she had left forever.

She raised herself, moaning. Here, between the trees where nothing came but Devils, no God would ever search to find her bones. Her limbs jerked puppet-fashion, outside her control; tears squeezed from her eyes; but her mouth moved, whispering a prayer. To the Corn Lord, the Green One, the Waker of the Grain.

The way lay across a shallow marsh, its surface streaked with bands of brownish scum. She crossed it, floundering. The sun was higher now; her mind recorded, dully, the impact of heat on back and arms. On the far bank she rested again, thrust half from sight beneath a tangle of lapping briars. Beyond, the ground sloped smoothly upward; and it seemed her Lord called from ahead, ever more strong and clear. She toiled forward, sensing the thinning of the trees. She broke at last from a fringe of bracken, stumbled and dropped dazedly to her knees.

Ahead of her, bright in sunlight, stretched a long, smooth ridge of chalk. Across it, curving close to the forest edge before swinging to climb to the crest, ran a rutted track; and crowning the ridge at its farthest end was a village, fenced about by watchtowers and a stockade. In such a place she had been born, and reared; but this was not her home. She had never seen it before.

She lay a while where she had fallen, face against the soft, short turf. She was roused by a jangling of harness, the trundle of wheels. She sat up, thankfully. Along the track, jogging gravely, moved a bulky two-wheeled cart, loaded high with faggots. Its driver reined at sight of her; and she forced her bruised lips to make words. 'Bring me to your headman,' she said. 'And my God will reward you, granting you great happiness.'

The driver stepped forward cautiously, bent over her. She twisted her face up, trying to smile; and for the first time, saw his eyes.

Gohm, the woodman, had never been too strong in the head; he bit at a broken nail, frowning, puzzling his sluggish wits. 'Who are you?' he said slowly, in his thick voice. 'Some forest spirit, fallen from a tree?' He turned her over, roughly; then snatched at the top of the filthy tunic. The fabric gave; he stared at what he saw, and began to giggle. 'No spirit,' he said. 'Or if you are, you have no power here.' He drove two calloused fingers beneath her kilt; then, because she screamed so, kicked her in the mouth. After this he did several more things before tossing her into the cart, covering her roughly with bundles from the load. 'Now certainly,' he said, 'the Gods have smiled on Gohm.' He shook the reins; the cart lurched, trundling on up the steep rise toward the village.

At the far end of the muddy street the woodman reined. 'Woman,' he bellowed, 'see what the Gods have sent. A slave to scour your pots and blow the fire; and better still for me.'

The woman who peered from the low doorway of the hut was as grey and lined, as thin and lizard-quick as he was bear-like and slow. 'What are you babbling about, you old fool?' she grumbled, scrambling on to the rear step of the cart. She pushed the faggots aside; then stayed stock still, eyes widening, hand pressed across her mouth. Gohm too was arrested, his wandering attention riveted for once; for the bag of bones and blood with which he had cumbered his life still owned two white and blazing eyes, fixed on him now in a stare terrible in its intensity. 'This is your evil day, Gohm Woodchopper,' it whispered. 'Those fingers, first to defile, hew no more sticks; no water will they draw for you, not if you lie dying.'

With that the shape collapsed abruptly, lying still as death; and the woman reached thin fingers to the mud-stained cloth of the tunic, traced there beneath the dirt the Mark of the Lord.

To Mata existence was a dull and speechless void, shot through with flashes that were greater pains. She was lodged in a fresh-swept hut, and women were appointed to wash and heal her body, minister to her needs; but of this she was unaware, and remained unaware for many days to come. Meanwhile the Fate called down on Gohm worked itself out swiftly enough. A bare week later, while cutting wood at the forest edge, he gashed two fingers deeply with his hook. The wounds, instead of closing, widened, yellowed and began to stink; while the pain from them grew so great it drove him wild. One day he took an axe and, going behind the hut, struck the agonized members from him; but the wild surgery did little to improve his condition.

He took to wandering by himself, grey-faced and mumbling, and it was no surprise when his body was brought in from the trees. The corpse was much disfigured, torn as if by bears, and the face quite eaten away. This happened within a month of Mata leaving the wood; and the village that sheltered her grew silent and fearful. Men crept to the hut where she lay, avoiding its shadow, to leave rich gifts; so that when she finally woke it was to considerable estate.

The news at first meant little to her. She lay in the hut, surrounded by her women, eating little, watching the sailing clouds in the sky, the rich waving green of trees. Summer had come once more; the Corn Lord, though thwarted of his Bride, had yet fulfilled his promise. She frowned at the thought, revolving many things; then rose and sought an audience with the headman.

He received her in the Council Hut; very similar it was to the Lodge in which her father had once sat. Beside him stood his Chief Priest; and at him Mata stared comfortlessly a great while. Finally she turned, tossing her head. 'Chief,' she said, 'what do you wish of me?'

The headman spread his hands, looking alarmed. The tale of Gohm had not been lost on him; this pale-faced, brilliant-eyed child made him uneasy in his chair of office. 'Our wish,' he said humbly enough, 'the wish of all my people, is that you stay here with us and let us honour you. Also if you will speak well for us to your Lord, our crops will grow straight and tall.'

The Chief Priest had begun to fidget; Mata turned back to him her disquieting stare. 'This is good to hear,' she said carefully, 'and pleasing to the God. But I have heard of other towns where though fine words are spoken they are not supported by deeds.'

The headman burst into voluble protests, and Mata was pleased to see that sweat had formed on his forehead. 'Look, then, that it be so,' she said. 'For my Lord loves me well, and invests much strength in me. My touch brings death and worse; or pleasure, and great joy to men.' She stretched her hand out, and was secretly amused to see the other draw back. 'Now this is the wish of the God,' she said. 'You shall build, on the hill beside the town, a great house. Its length shall be thirty paces, measured by a tall, strong man, its breadth five and a span …' She went on, as well as her memory served, to give a description of the God House of Cha'Acta. 'Here I shall live with my Lord,' she said, 'and such women as I choose to gather and instruct.' She glanced sidelong at the growing darkness of the Chief Priest's face, and spoke again rapidly. 'Here also,' she said, 'your holy Priest shall come, and many good things will happen to him. Also he must bless the work, and oversee each stage of building; for he is loved by the God, and a great man in your land.' She dropped to one knee before the priest, and saw his expression change from hatred to wondering suspicion.

So a new God House was built; and there Mata lived, in some luxury. She took as bedmate a slim brown child, Alissa; her she taught carefully, instructing her in Mysteries and the pleasuring of Gods and others. There also, when the mood was on her, she summoned Cha'Ilgo, the Chief Priest; and made herself, with time, most pleasing to him.

They were good days, in the Long House on the crest of the hill; but all summers reach their end. The leaves of the forest were changing to red and gold when Mata once more called the priest and the headman to her. 'Now I must leave you,' she said without preamble. 'For last night my God came to me in the dark, while all the village slept. His hair was yellow as the sun, brushing the rafters where he stood beside my bed; his flesh was green as rushes or the sprouting corn, his member greater than a bull's and wonderful to see. He told me many Mysteries, not least this: that out of love for you I must leave Alissa, who is dear to me as life, to be your new Corn Queen. In this way you will be happy, when I am gone; the barley will spring and you will have your fill of beer, cheese and all good things.'

They heard her words with mixed emotions. Cha'Ilgo at least had come to regard her presence highly; yet it was not without relief he saw her litter pass, for the last time, the armed gates of the town. She had come friendless and alone; she left in mighty state, Hornmen and fluters before her and a company of spears. Her kilt was white as snow; necklaces of pebbles and amber adorned her throat, round her slim ankles were rings of bright black stone. Behind her swayed other litters with her treasures and going-gifts; seed grain and weapons, jars of honey and beer, money-sticks of fine grey iron. Behind again came trudging sheep and oxen, and a great concourse of villagers.

Cha'Acta was warned of her approach by the horns and thudding drums. He came to the village gates to see for himself, while Mata's folk lined the stockade walls with their spears, biting their beards uncertainly. It was Magan the headman who first recognized his daughter; he rushed to greet her rejoicing, amazed at her return from the dead. The gates were swung wide, the company tramped through; and there was a time of great rejoicing. For the Corn Bride was reborn; the Gods could smile again on the village in the steep chalk pass.

For a time Cha'Acta and his priests held aloof, huddling in the Council Lodge talking and conspiring; till black looks from the villagers, and a plainer hint from Magan, forced the issue. The High Priest entered the hut where Mata was lodged suspiciously enough, leaving a handful of armed followers at the door; but she ran to him with cries of joy. She brought him beer, serving him with her own hands; afterwards she knelt before him, begging his forgiveness and calling him her Lord. 'My eyes were blinded, till I could not see the truth,' she said. 'I saw Cha'Acta, but could not see the

God; though he blazed from him most splendidly.' She poured more beer, and more, till his eyes became less narrow, and he unbent toward her fractionally. Across his brow ran a deep diagonal scar, the mark she had given him with the mask; she touched it, tenderly, and smiled. For this I was punished, and justly so,' she said. She showed him the white half-moon on her chin, where Gohm's boot had torn the lip away, the crossing weals on legs and thighs from her wild flight through the wood. 'Also,' she said, lifting her kilt still further, 'see how I have grown, Cha'Acta my priest. Now the God has ordered that I return, to love you better than before.' Then despite himself the manhood in Cha'Acta rose, so that he took her several times that very night, finding her sweet beyond all normal experience. 'The God first entered me when I worked at cutting his reeds,' she said later. 'Now he comes to me again, in you. Let it be so forever, Lord.'

The trees blazed, slowly shed their leaves. For a time the air remained warm; but when the first frosts lay on the ground, whitening the long slopes of the fields, news came that disturbed the new-found tranquillity of the tribe. Strangers appeared in the valley, refugees from the unknown lands that stretched beyond the Great Heath. They brought with them wild tales of a new people, a race of warriors who lived not by the peaceful tilling of the soil but by plunder, by fire and the sword. Some said they came from the Middle Sea, some from Hell itself, braving the roughest seas in their fast, long ships. Each warrior, it seemed, was a King in his own right, claiming kinship with certain Gods; wild Gods, rough and bloody and dark, whose very names sent thrills of fear through the storytellers as they uttered them. There were tales of whole villages destroyed, populations wiped out; for the invaders preyed on the land like an insect swarm, leaving it bare and ruined behind them. The elders shook their heads over the stories. Nothing like them had ever come their way; but there seemed little to be done, and with the first real snow the trickle of refugees stopped. For a time, nothing more was heard.

Mata paid little attention to the tales. Her power with the people had increased; for her wanderings had taught her very well how to win respect. Always now she was at Cha'Acta's side; and always behind her stood the great Corn Lord, warming her with his presence. Children and babes in arms were brought to her; for it was believed magic dwelt in her touch, the young ones she blessed would grow up healthy and strong. Yet always she was careful to defer to Cha'Acta, so the Chief Priest had little cause for complaint. Each night he came to her in the God House; for the child who had once proved such an able pupil was now a willing mistress. So much was she to his liking that when the seed time was nearly due again and the ploughs went out to scratch the thin-soiled fields, the question of a new Bride for the God had not been raised.

It was Cha'Acta who broached the matter, late one night. The sea mist lay cold and clammy on the hill, eclipsing the torches on the village watch-towers, swirling round the fire that burned in the great hut. Mata heard him for a while; then rose impatiently, flicking a heavy shawl across her shoulders, and walked to the hut door. She stood staring into the void, feeling the cold move on stomach and thighs. After a while she spoke.

'Where will the God find a Bride to equal what he loses?' she asked amusedly. 'Can another do the Magic Thing, that pleases Cha'Acta so much? Will another be loving, and as warm? Will the barley spring better for her than me?'

The High Priest waited, brooding; for he knew her power. Also, he was loth to lose her. He made no answer; and she turned back, walked swaying toward him, her eyes dark and huge. 'Also,' she said, 'what would become of me? Would I be found too one day face down in a pool, with the brook fish nibbling me?'

He stirred impatiently. 'Let us have no more of this,' he said. 'For all your beauty you are still a child, Mata. You do not understand all Mysteries.'

She felt the God inside her, giving her strength. She kicked the fire barefooted, sending up a shower of sparks. 'This I understand,' she said. 'That there are Mysteries best not told, Cha'Acta priest; or spears would be raised, and sacred blood would surely make them unclean.'

Cha'Acta rose, eyes smouldering with rage. He moved toward her, lifting his hands; but she stood her ground, flung the shawl back and laughed. 'Look, Cha'Acta,' she said. 'Look before you strike, and see the Magic Thing.'

He stared for a time wild-eyed. So easy now to strangle her and cut, show what was left for the work of some wild beast . . . Sweat stood on his forehead; then he fell back, rocking and groaning. 'Do not taunt me, Mata,' he said hoarsely. 'I mean no harm to you.'

His chance was gone; and they both knew it. She stood a moment longer, smiling down; then dropped to her knees beside him. He gripped her, gasping; and she was very loving to him. They lay all night, in the close light of the fire, and Mata gave him no rest; till toward dawn he slept like one of the dead. She roused him in due course, feeding him broth and beer; afterwards she dressed, came and sat obediently at his feet. 'My Lord,' she said, 'tell me now of these thoughts that I am to go, and another take my place.'

He shook his head, eyes hooded. 'No one will take your place, Mata,' he said. 'You know that well enough.'

She pursued him, gently. 'But, Lord, the people will wish it.'

He said, 'The people can be swayed.'

'I would not bring grief to my Lord Cha'Acta.'

He said hopelessly, 'You can persuade them, Mata. If no other.'

She stared up under her brows, eyes luminous. 'Then do you give me leave?'

He banged his fists on his knees, pressed them to his forehead. 'Do what you will,' he said. 'Take what you wish, speak as the Lord moves you; but for my sake, stay his Bride.'

She sat back, clapping her hands delightedly. 'Then let Cha'Acta too swear his constancy,' she said. 'By the great God, who stands at his shoulder as he stands at mine. For I have seen him many times, my Lord; his prick is long as a rush bundle, and as hard and green.'

He groaned again at that; for she had a way of rousing him with words even when her body was quiet. 'I swear,' he said finally. 'In the God's own house, where he must surely hear.'

So a pact was made between them; and Cha'Acta found he could not break the invisible bonds with which she had tied him.

By early summer, the people had begun to murmur openly; for the planted corn was springing and still no Procession had been called, no new Bride chosen for the God. Mata herself stilled them, speaking from the step of the Council Lodge; an unheard-of thing for a girl or woman to do. 'Now I tell you,' she said, 'the Procession will take place, as always before. Also the God, speaking through Cha'Acta, has let his choice be known. It is this; that I, and no other, will lead his priests, his Bride of a second summer.'

There were shocked mutterings at that, and some fists were shaken. She quelled the disturbance, instantly. 'Listen to me again,' she said. She raised her voice above the rest. 'In another place, a man once lifted his hand to me; the flesh dropped very quickly from his bones. My Lord, who is swift to bless, is swifter yet to punish; for his voice is the rolling thunder of heaven, his anger the lightning that splits the stoutest trees.'

The villagers still growled uncertainly. Men stared at each other, gripping the handles of their daggers and pulling at their beards.

'Now hear another thing,' said Mata. She spoke more quietly; by degrees, the crowd stilled again. 'Your grain will sprout higher and stronger than before,' she said. 'Your animals will thrive, and you will prosper. No evil shall come in all the season, while I rule the God's House. And if I lie, I tell you this; you may fling me from the Mound and break my bones.' She said no more but turned away, pushing impatiently through the crowd. It parted for her, wonderingly; and no man raised his voice when she had gone.

Her words had been bold; but when Cha'Acta taxed her with them she merely smiled. 'The God spoke truth to me,' she said serenely. 'As you will see.'

The summer was such as the valley had never known. The grain stood taller than the oldest villager could remember, waving and golden and rich.

No wind or rain came to spoil the harvest, so that the storage pits were filled to their brims and more had to be dug, lined with wickerwork and clay. The cattle and sheep grew fat on the valley pastures, the harvest celebrations were the finest ever known; and after that all made way for Mata as she walked, stepping respectfully clear of her shadow.

To Cha'Acta also it seemed she was possessed. She had taken to sniffing the magic seeds again; she used them constantly, claiming they gave her clearer sight. Often, now, she had visions of the God. Also he came to her more frequently; and once took her in full sight of all the people, so that she lay arching her back and crying out, and spittle bearded her chin. At that even the Chief Priest fled from her, in more than religious awe.

Then more signs of the raiders began to appear.

Once again, bands of wanderers started filtering through the valley. All were ragged; many bore gaping wounds. The villagers fed them from their own supplies, turning troubled eyes toward the north. Some nights now the horizon glowed an angry red, as if whole towns were burning far across the Plain. Once a party under Magan ventured in that direction, several days' journey; they came back telling of scorched fields, blackened ruins where once had stood peaceful huts. At this Cha'Acta sat in council with the priests and elders of the tribe; a long and solemn council that went on a whole day and night. Mata attended for a time; but the smoke that filled the big Lodge annoyed her, stinging her eyes, while the babble of so many voices confused her brain. She ran away to her own great house on the Mound, lay all night dreaming and watching up at the stars. At dawn she sniffed the Magic Smoke again; and a vision came to her so splendid she ran crying to the village while the sun still stood red on the hills, throwing her long flapping shadow across the grass. The news she told sent men scurrying, uncertainly at first and then more eagerly, toward the Sacred Mound. Today, she proclaimed, the God held open house; and the people trooped after her, not without superstitious shudderings. Cha'Acta, emerging with his followers, found the watchtowers empty, the street deserted save for the witless and the very old; while the crest of the Sacred Mound was black with folk. There was nothing left him but to follow, raging.

The people had gathered in a great half-moon on that side of the Mound that faced the village; the space before the God House was filled by them. Mata herself stood facing them, outlined sharply against the brilliant sky. Beneath her heels, a sheer stone face plunged to the yellow cliff of grass; beyond, tiny and far-off, rose the russet heads of the trees that lined the brook.

Cha'Acta, panting up the last incline at the head of his troupe, was in time to catch her final words.

'And so by this means we shall be saved; for none will dare raise a hand against us, while the God himself watches from the hill and his limbs are scoured and bright. It will be a work like no other in the world. By its aid, and my Lord's protection, you will become famous, and wealthier than before; for men of other tribes will surely journey many days to see.'

Cha'Acta had heard more than enough. He marched to the centre of the circle below the wall, holding up his arms for quiet. In his robes of office, blazoned with the Mark of the God, he made an impressive figure. The hubbub that had risen was stilled; Mata alone remained smiling, hands on her hips. She watched indifferently from her wall, the black, long hair flicking across her face.

'Come down from there,' said the Chief Priest sharply. 'And hear me, all you people. This is an evil thing that you have done.'

The villagers buzzed angrily; and he turned, pointing, the sleeve of his robe flapping in the wind. 'This is no time for toys,' he said. 'To the north, not five days' journey away, are many warriors; more warriors than you or I, any of us, have ever seen. Where they come from, no man can tell; but they bring with them death and fire, and that you know full well, as well as I. Now for a night and a day we have sat in the Council Lodge, debating many things, always with the safety of the people in our hearts. For a time, we were unsure; then there came among us a certain God, who was green and tall . . .'

'That is surely strange,' piped up an old, grizzled-bearded man. 'For the God was with his Bride, with Mata here. From her own lips we heard it.'

Cha'Acta had never in his life been contradicted by a commoner; his brow flushed with rage, for a moment he considered striking the other to the ground. He swallowed, and forced himself to remain calm. 'I am the High Priest of the God,' he said coldly. 'You forget your station; thank the God that in his mercy he lets you keep your tongue.' He raised his arms again. 'I am your Priest,' he said. 'Have I not counselled you wisely, and brought you to prosperity? Is this not true?'

A roar cut him short. Voices shouted, above the din.

'Mata . . . Mata led us . . .'

Cha'Acta felt sweat running beneath his robes. The mob surged forward; he checked it, imperiously. 'Hear me,' he said. 'Hear me, for your lives. The people from the north have told us, and some of you have seen, that a stockade is no defence against these warriors. For they press so thick against it, cutting and stabbing with their swords, that the stoutest fence is finally thrown down. Now what we must do is this. We must ring the village, on its weakest side, with a great bank and ditch. The chalk we shall pile high, so it is steep and slippery to climb; and in the ditch, planted close together, we shall set forests of pointed stakes. The stockade we shall line with our best slingers and archers, and hold the enemy away until he tires. This the God revealed to me; and this we must do at once.'

'And this the God revealed to me,' shouted Mata. She stooped and snatched up something that lay at her feet, held it out for all to see; a goat hide, cured to suppleness, bearing in great black charcoal strokes the figure of a man. The club he carried he brandished fiercely over his head; his eyes glared; his great member rose proudly, thrusting up before his chest. "See the God's own shape,' said Mata. 'For so he appeared to me not two hours since, as I sat here on the grass. While you and your greybeards, Cha'Acta, wagged your silly heads in the Council Lodge and talked long, stupid words.'

At that the blood seemed to flow from Cha'Acta's face and arms, leaving him icy cold. 'Mata Godbride,' he said, 'you lie ...'

Mata's eyes were sparkling at last, brilliant with hate. 'And you lie, holy priest,' she shouted. 'Before the people, and in sight of the God.' She danced on the wall, wrenching at the neck of her tunic. 'In the reedbed, before he took me to wife, the Corn Lord put his Mark on me,' she said. 'This is a great Mystery; greater than Cha'Acta's ...'

The crowd bellowed; and the Chief Priest, face blazing white to the lips, called hoarsely. 'Mata, as you love me ...'

'As I love you?' she squalled. 'For this I have waited, Cha'Acta, many moons, and suffered your weight on me ...' She flung out an accusing arm. 'Cha'Acta Priest,' she shouted, 'took me against my will, forcing me in the Sacred House there when I was promised to the God. And Cha'Acta took the Bride Choele, killing her afterwards to seal her tongue—'

Cha'Acta waited for no more. He ran with surprising speed across the grass, up the swell of ground to the wall. In his hand gleamed a short, curved knife. Mata didn't move; she stood contemptuously, feet spread on the wall, hair flogging her bare white shoulders. Ten paces he was from her, five, three; and something flickered in the high, warm light. Few saw the flight of the spear; but all heard the thud as it struck home, full between the High Priest's shoulder-blades.

Cha'Acta had gained the base of the wall. He stood quite still for a moment, eyes wide, ashen face turned toward the girl. One hand was to his chest; across the fingers, where the iron tip of the weapon pierced the flesh, ran a thin, bright trickle of blood. He raised the knife, uncertainly; then his legs lost their strength. His body toppled, crashing through the bushes below the wall; then it was bounding, faster and faster, down the sheer slope of grass. The onlookers, rushing forward, saw it strike the base of the Mound, fly loose-limbed into the air. A stout tree shook to its top, a splash arose; then he was gone, and the stream was rolling him away.

For a moment longer the crowd stared, pale-faced and shocked, edging back from where Magan stood wide-eyed, glaring at the fingers that had made the cast. Then Mata raised her arms.

'Build the God ...!'

The shout spread, on the instant; she was seized and swung from hand to hand, carried by the surging, rejoicing mob down the long slope of the Mound.

Through the rest of the day the villagers scurried across the face of the great hill, roping out a grid pattern two hundred paces deep, nearly a hundred and fifty broad. At nightfall, fires sprang up at a score of points around it. The work went on far into the hours of darkness; women and children toiled forward and back across the slope, bringing fuel for the beacons. At first light Mata, who had not slept, began her part. Men followed her, wonderingly. She carried the tiny drawing of the thing to be; over it, they saw, she had inscribed a network of the same fine crossing lines. She worked methodically, with many pauses and checks, pressing lines of white pegs into the ground; by midday nearly half the Giant was visible, and work had started on the cutting of the head. Men tore at the turf with hatchets and antler picks; others shuffled forward and back up the hill, doubled over by the weight of baskets of chalk rubble that were tipped out of sight among the bushes of the Mound. In the village hearths burned low, babies cried unfed; while lines of women both old and young, scurried across the hill, wearing a maze of new tracks in the grass, bringing platters of fish and meat to the workers, and jugs of milk and beer. At nightfall Mata left her marking-out to supervise the digging at the shoulders. The trenches, she proclaimed, were everywhere too narrow; she ordered them widened to the span of a tall man's arm, and deepened by a foot or more. Fresh shifts of workers scurried to the task; and by the second dawn the head and shoulders were complete.

With the dawn came a little group of strangers. They stood far off below the Sacred Mound, well out of the longest bowshot, and stared up at the hill. Magan marked them worriedly, shading his eyes with his hand. They were too distant for details to be clear; but their clothes seemed not to be the clothes of chalk dwellers, and on their heads he caught the gleam of iron. Also he saw that each had come on horseback, a nearly unheard-of thing; he could make out the animals grazing, farther down the slope. A party was detached to investigate; but long before; they came within hail the strangers wheeled their mounts and trotted away.

Mata, dark lines of tiredness under her eyes, still scurried from point to point, directing every detail of the work; and slowly, sparkling-white, the Giant grew. The arms developed hands, the hands burst into fingers; then the great club came into being, vaunting across the grass. But by midday the valley floor was once more a-straggle with refugees. They shuffled past in groups, staring in wonderment at the toiling villagers; and one of them called up. 'What are you doing, fools who live on the chalk?' he said. 'Do you think the Horse Warriors will be frightened of your little picture? Will they run with hands above their heads, crying "Oh"?'

Magan, poised on a slight eminence with the spears of his bodyguard clustered round him, answered loftily enough. 'Get to the sea, old man, and do not trouble us with chatter. This is God's work, and a magic thing.' But even as he spoke the headman lifted his eyes worriedly, scanning the vacant outlines of the hills.

By the third evening, the trickle of refugees had once more thinned; but fires burned close, reflecting angrily from the clouds. Also, carried on the wind, came the dull throb of drums; and for the first time folk paused uneasily in their work, stared questioningly at each other. Then it was that Magan sought out his daughter; but she brushed him away. 'Be silent, Father,' she said. 'You have already killed a Chief Priest; hold your peace, or perhaps the God will kill you too.'

By the fourth dawn the Giant's great prick lay proud and gleaming across the hill, and the diggers were working on his feet and calves. The drums had beat throughout the night; now they fell ominously quiet. One scout, posted by Magan a mile or more out on the heath, returned swearing he had seen the glint of armoured marching men; the others never came back at all.

Then Magan frowned, seeing where faith had led them; but there was no time left for further reflection. From over the skyline beyond the Sacred Mound galloped a column of riders. They came with terrifying speed, fanning out across the turf, banners and standards fluttering; from them as they swept closer rose a harsh, many-throated roar.

Magan, shouting despairingly for his spears, ran down the hillside, whirling his own sword above his head. Everywhere men flung down their mattocks, grabbed for weapons. A line formed, packed and jostling. It checked the charge; though the weight and pace of the riders tore great gaps in the villagers' ranks. The warriors, fighting well, re-formed; and a desperate retreat began, up across the sloping grass to the stockade gates. Behind the fight women and old folk scurried across the hill, flinging their baskets of rubble aside as they ran. Mata, hacking wildly at the turf, glared up to find herself nearly alone. The Giant was all but complete, part of one foot only remaining to be worked; but her voice, shrill as a bird, went for the moment unheeded.

Magan, fighting his hardest, heard behind him a fresh sound of disaster. He glanced back, appalled; and a groan burst from him. Over the stockade black smoke climbed into the sky, fringed at its base with leaping tongues of flame; on the ramparts tiny figures swayed, locked in deadly combat. The attack had been two-pronged after all; the second column of raiders, approaching unseen, had already taken the all-but-deserted village, and fired the huts.

Hope had gone; now only one thing remained. The headman raised his voice in a great shout.

'The Giant … Fight to the Giant, and stand …'

The lines reeled, locked and breathless; a battling half-moon formed, withdrawing step by step across the grass. Against it the raiders charged again and again, with reckless skill. Everywhere men had fallen, lay tumbled in ungainly heaps, half-seen through the drifting smoke. Magan opened his mouth to shout again; and a lance, wickedly barbed, took him in the throat, stood out crimsoned a foot beyond his head.

Behind the fighting men, almost between the legs of the horses, a frenzied little group still hacked at the turf. Sweat ran, blinding, into Mata's eyes; her hair hung across her face; and arbitrarily it seemed, two trenches met. The God was finished.

She turned, yelling defiance, sent the mattock spinning at the face of a mounted man. She ran upward, diagonally across the hill. Her hair flew round her; her breasts, uncovered, swung and jolted from her dress. The grass, close before her eyes, raced and jerked; but the frenzy in her brain blinded her to all else. Level with the Giant's head she turned, squalling with triumph, staring down at the great thing Cha'Acta hadn't lived to see; and the line below her broke, the last men of the village went over in a writhing heap.

Something hummed past her, and again. She ran once more, doubling like a hare; for only her own folk used the sling. Beside her a woman staggered in mid-stride, twisting to show her shattered forehead. Mata glared up, at the stockade and watchtower; and there was the dark blur of a descending missile. For a moment, while sense remained, she wondered how the sky could have made a fist, hit her so terribly in the mouth; then her legs buckled, she rolled back with the slope. She fetched up, finally, in the Giant's heel; behind her on the grass stretched wavering spots of red.

He came floating at last from agony and dark, brighter and more lovely than she had seen him before. He stooped above her, frowning, his great gold eyes compassionate. Shudders shook her, racking her ruined body. It seemed she raised her arms; and his entering was first the greatest pain she had known, and afterwards the greatest peace. She sighed, yielding; and the Corn Lord took her up, flew with her to a far place of delight.

The invaders were well pleased. The storage pits of the village, undamaged by the flames, had yielded grain for an entire season; the valley was sheltered, opening to the south; and in all the land there were no enemies left. Their chieftains strutted, jangling the trinkets they had stolen from the dead; while those who took other pleasures from the wreckage on the hill found many of the bodies still warm.

Potts has had a most unpleasant dream. In it – could it have been a picture he saw once – there was this wheel. A great golden wheel rolling across the hills, shooting out rays like sunbeams or spurts of yellow grain. He thought how fine it looked rushing along there against the bright blue sky, and the grass and bushes swaying to the wind it made. Then all at once it turned and was roaring at him, all the weight and vastness; and when the golden flame had passed she lay there broken and bloody like a doll, he couldn't believe it when he saw her.

He has woken to darkness. In the darkness is the sound of the sea. Also it seems a bird is wailing somewhere. But that's not possible; so the noise must be in his head.

He wants to move, but he can't. His arms feel heavy, like lead; and there's this tight pain across his chest, it makes breathing difficult. When he coughs there are sparks of colour behind his lids, and the pain is worse. So things are going wrong again.

He thinks if he could only get himself more upright his breathing might be easier. He tries pushing with his heels, and his palms against the floor. It's difficult; but it will be worth it. Anything would be worth it to stop the pain.

There, he's managed it. And his breathing is better, much better; it was smart of him to think of doing that. Though the wall is uncomfortable against his shoulders and the back of his head. What would be good would be to have a pillow behind him. One of the blankets would do, rolled up; but not for a minute. He'll get his breath back properly first.

He's feeling guilty now; the pain made him forget the Wheel, and what happened to her. He feels bad about the whole thing, naturally; but he's also baffled. He's certain this time it wasn't his fault. It was nothing to do with him; it just happened, out of the blue. Nothing anybody could have done.

He'll get the pillow in a minute. Right now he's in a sweat. Funny, he was shivering when he woke. He opens his mouth, drawing in deep breaths; but the air itself feels hot. And there's this roaring in his ears. Like thunder.

FIVE

The Beautiful One

For weeks now the heat had not abated. Day after day the hard sky pressed on the rounded chalk hills; the leaves of trees hung listless and dry, the growing grain yellowed, rivers and ruins shimmered with mirage. The nights were scarcely cooler. Men tossed and grumbled in the stockaded towns, dogs ran snapping and foam-flecked. At such times tempers are short; and the temper of the Horse Warriors was at its best an unsure thing.

Toward the end of one such baking day a column of waggons and riders rumbled steadily between hills of smooth brown grass. At the head of the cavalcade rode a troop of Warriors, their skins tawny, their beards and flowing hair dark. They carried bows and spears; and each man wore a skullcap of burnished steel. Behind them jolted an ornate siege engine, the tip of its throwing arm carved in the likeness of a great horse's head. More Warriors brought up the rear, driving a little rabble of wailing women. Clouds had thickened steadily through the day, trapping the heat even closer to the earth. Thunder boomed and grumbled overhead; from time to time men glanced up uneasily, or back to the skyline where showed the palisade and ruined watchtowers of a village. Flames licked them, bright in the gloom; a cloud of velvet smoke hung and stooped, drifting slowly to the south.

Behind the tailboard of the last waggon staggered half a dozen men. They were naked, or nearly so, and streaked with dust and blood. Their wrists were bound; ropes of plaited hide passed round their necks, tethering them to the vehicle. Two more wretches had given up the unequal struggle; the bodies towed limply, jolting over the ridges and boulders of the track.

Shouts from ahead brought the column to a halt. The pale dust swirled, settling on men and horses; the prisoners dropped to their knees, groaning and fumbling at the nooses. A group of men cantered down the line of waggons, reined. They were richly dressed in trews and tunics of figured silk; and each wore a mask of woven grass, fringed with heads of green barley. Their leader carried a gilded Staff of Power; on his chest, proudly blazoned, was the great spear of the Corn Lord.

He nodded now gravely to the Horseman at his side. 'You have done well,' he said. 'The spoil of the first waggon, the grain and unbleached cloth, is forfeit to my God. Also one in ten of the draught animals, and what sheep and goats you drive in from the hills.' He held his palms up, fingers spread.

'The rest the God returns to you, to do with as you choose. This the Reborn ordered me to say; will it be pleasing to you?'

The other showed his teeth. 'Cha'Ensil,' he said, 'it will be as your Mistress desires. The Horse Warriors too know how to be generous.'

But the other had stiffened, eyes glittering through the mask. He said, 'What have we here?'

The Horseman shrugged. 'Prisoners, for the sacrifice,' he said. He glanced at the lowering sky. 'Our God becomes impatient when the nights are sultry,' he said. 'Have you not heard his hooves among the clouds?'

'I heard the Corn Lord chuckle in his sleep,' said the priest crushingly. He pointed with the Staff. 'Show this one to me,' he said. 'Lift his face.'

The Warrior grunted, waving an arm. A man dismounted, walked to the prisoner. He twined his fingers in the matted hair, yanked. The priest drew his breath; then reached slowly to unlatch the mask. 'Closer,' he said. 'Bring him here.'

The victim was dragged forward. Cha'Ensil stared; then leaned to place strong fingers beneath the other's jaw. The cheekbones were high and delicately shaped, the nose tip-tilted and short. The green-grey eyes, glazed now with pain, were fringed with black. Blood had dried on muzzle and throat; the parted lips showed even white teeth.

A wait, while the oxen belched and grumbled, the horses jangled their bits. Then the priest turned. 'He is little more than a child,' he said. 'He will not be pleasing to your God.' He reached again to jerk at the leather noose. 'The Corn Lord claims him,' he said. 'Put him in the wagon.'

The Horseman glared, hand on his sword hilt, face flushed with anger; and Cha'Ensil raised the glittering staff level with his eyes. 'This is the God's will,' he said. 'A little price to pay, for many blessings.'

Another wait, while the other pulled at his beard. The priest he would have defied readily enough; but behind him stood One whose displeasure was not lightly to be incurred. The thunder grumbled again; and he shrugged and turned his horse. 'Take him,' he said sardonically, 'since your God gains such pleasure from striplings. The rest will serve our needs.'

The priest stared after him, with no friendly expression; then turned, gesturing once more with the Staff. A knife flashed, severing the noose. Released, the prisoner stood swaying; he was bundled forward with scant ceremony, slung into the leading cart. The tail-gate was latched shut; and Cha'Ensil rose in his stirrups, with a long yell. Whips cracked; the waggon turned jerkily from the line of march, lumbering to the south.

In the last of the light the vehicle and its escort reached a pass set between high chalk hills. The cloud-wrack, trailing skirts of mist, alternately hid and revealed the bulging slopes, crossed with sheep tracks, set with clumps of darker scrub. On the nearer crest, smears and nubbles of black showed the remnants of a village. On the flanks below sprawled a great chalk figure, while foursquare in the pass rose a steep and grassy mound. Across its summit, revealed by flickerings from above, curved a long ridge of roof; round it, among spikes and nodules of stone, straggled a mass of secondary building, pale plastered walls, gables of green-grey thatch. There was a stockade, topped with disembowelling spikes; and a gateway fronted by a deep ditch and flanked by vast drums of stone, themselves leaning till the arrow slits that once had faced the valley stared sightless at the green jungle below. Between them the party cantered, with a final jangle and clash. Torches were called for and a litter, the gates re-manned; and Cha'Ensil moved upward across the sloping lower ward. The rising wind fluttered at his cloak, whipping the pine-knots into screaming beards of flame.

The little chamber was windowless and hot, hazed with a blue smoke heavy with the scent of poppies. Torchlight gleamed on white walls and close grey thatch, flickered on the Chief Priest's face as he stood expressionlessly, staring down. Finally he nodded. 'This is well,' he said. 'Prepare him. Clean the dirt away.'

A rustling of skirts, whisper of feet on the bare earth floor; clink of a costly copper bowl. The limbs of the sleeping boy were sponged, his chest and belly washed with scented water. Lastly the stained cloth-scrap was cut away.

The priest drew breath between his teeth. 'His hands and feet,' he said. 'Neglect no skill.'

The nails of the sleeper were cleaned with pointed sticks, the hair scraped from beneath his arms. His head was raised, his hair rinsed, combed with bone combs and rinsed again. Thunder grumbled close above the roof; and Cha'Ensil whitened his knuckles on his Staff. 'Prepare his face,' he said. 'Use all your art.'

Stoppers were withdrawn from jars of faceted crystal; the women, working delicately, heightened the eyelids with a ghosting of dark green, shaped the full brows to a gentler curve. The lashes, already lustrous, were blackened with a tiny brush. The sleeper sighed, and smiled.

'Now,' said Cha'Ensil. 'Those parts that make him like a God.'

The nipples of the boy were stained with a bright dye; and the priest himself laid fingers to the groin, pressing and kneading till the member rose and firmed. Belly and thighs were brushed with a fine red powder; and Cha'Ensil stepped back. 'Put the big necklet on him,' he said. 'And circlets for his arms.'

The dreamer was set upright, a cloak of fine wool hung from his shoulders. The women waited, expectantly; and Cha'Ensil once more gripped the boy's chin, turned the face till the brilliant drugged eyes stared into his own. 'You were dead,' he muttered, 'and you were raised. Blood ran from you; it was staunched. Mud dirtied you; it was washed away. Now you go as a God. Go by the Staff and Spear; and the God's strength be with you.' He turned away, abruptly. 'Take him to the Long House,' he said. 'Leave him in the place appointed, and return to me. We must pray.'

The rumbling intensified, till it seemed boulders and great stones were rolled crashing through the sky. Lightning, flickering from cloud to cloud, showed the heads of grasses in restless motion, discovered hills and trees in washes of broad grey light. The light blazed far across the sea, flecking the restless plain of water; then the night was split.

With the breaking of the storm came rain. It fell not as rain customarily falls, but in sheets and solid bars; so that men in far-off villages, woken by the roaring on their roofs, saw what seemed silver spears driven into the earth. The parched dust leaped and quivered. Rivulets foamed on the eroded flanks of hills; twigs and green leaves were beaten from the taller trees. In the chalk pass, the brook that circled the base of the Mound raced in its deep bed; but toward dawn the violence died away. A morning wind moved across the hills, searching and cold as a knife; it brought with it a great sweet smell of leaves and fresh-soaked earth.

At first light two figures picked their way across the Mound, moving between the fingers and bosses of stone. Both were cloaked, both masked. Once they turned, staring it seemed at the flanking slope, the ruins and the chalk colossus that glimmered in the grass; and the taller inclined his head. 'My Lady,' he said in a strong, musical voice, 'when have I injured you, or played you false? When have my words to you not become true?'

The woman's voice when she answered was sharper-edged. 'Cha'Ensil,' she said, 'we are both grown folk; grown older than our years perhaps in service of the God. So keep your tales for the little new priestesses; their lips are sweeter when they are afraid. Or tell them to the Horsemen, who are little children too. Perhaps there was a Great One in the land, long ago; but he left us, in a time best forgotten, and will scarcely return now. It isn't good to joke about such things; least of all to me.'

They had reached the portal of the great hut crowning the Mound. Above, green rush demons glared eyeless at the distant heath. To either side stood bundles of bound reeds, each taller than a man; the Signs of the God. The priest laid his hand to the nearer, smiling gravely. 'Lady,' he said, 'wise you are most certainly, and wiser in many things than any man. Yet I say this. The God has many forms, and lives to some extent in each of us. In most men he is hidden; but I have seen him shine most gloriously. Now I tell you I found him, lashed to a Horseman's waggon. I knew him by the blood he shed, before I saw his face; for all Gods bleed, as penance for their people. I raised him with these hands, and placed him where he waits. As you will see.'

She stared up at him. 'Once,' she said coldly, 'a child came here, hungering for just such a God. Now I tell you this, Cha'Ensil; I raised you, and what is raised can be thrown down again. If you jest with me, you have jested once too often.'

He spread his arms. 'Lady,' he said humbly, 'my hands are at your service, and my heart. If I must give my head, then give it I shall; and that right willingly.' He stooped, preceding her into the darkness of the hut.

She paused, as always, at sight of the remembered place. She saw the floor of swept and beaten earth, the gleam of roofpoles in the half dark; she smelled the great pond-smell of the thatch. At the wattle screens that closed off the end of the long chamber she stopped again, uncertain; and his hand touched her arm. 'Behold,' he said softly. 'See the God . . .'

The boy lay quiet on the bracken bed within, his breathing even and deep. A woollen shawl partly covered him; the priest lifted it aside, and heard her catch her breath. 'If I mistook,' he said, 'then blame the weakness of my eyes on gathering age.'

She took his wrist, not looking at him. 'Priest,' she said huskily, 'there is wisdom in you. Wisdom and great love, that chides me what I spoke.' She unfastened her cloak, laid it aside. 'I will wait with him,' she said, 'and be here when he wakes. Let no one else approach.' She sat quietly on the edge of the bed, her hands in her lap; and Cha'Ensil bowed, slipping silently from the chamber.

Beyond the fringe of trees the hillside sloped broad and brilliant in sunlight. Above the boy as he lay the grass heads arched and whispered, each freighted with its load of golden specks. Between the stems he could see the valley and the tree-grown river, the reed beds where dragonflies hawked through the still afternoons. Beyond the river the chalk hills rose again, distant and massive. On the skyline, just visible from where he lay, stood the stockade and watchtower of his village.

His jerkin was unlaced; he wriggled luxuriously, feeling the coolness of the grass stroke belly and chest. He pulled a stem, lay sucking and nibbling at the sweetness. He closed his eyes; the hum of midsummer faded and boomed close, heavy with the throb of distant tides. Below him the sheep grazed the slope like fat woollen maggots; and the ram moved restlessly, bonking his wooden bell, staring with his little yellow eyes.

The boy's own eyes jerked open, narrowed.

She climbed slowly, crossing the hillside below him, gripping tussocks of grass to steady herself on the steepening slope. Once she straightened, seeming to stare directly toward where he lay; and he frowned and glanced behind him, as if considering further retreat. She stood hands on hips, searching the face of the hill; then turned away, continuing the long climb to the crest. On the skyline she once more turned; a tall, brown-skinned girl, dark hair blowing across face and throat. Then she moved forward, and clumps of bushes hid her from his sight.

He groaned, as he had groaned before; a strange, husky noise, half between moan and whimper. His teeth pulled at his lip, distractedly; but already the blood was pounding in his ears. He glared, guilty, at the indifferently cropping sheep, back to the skyline; then rose abruptly, hurrying from the shelter of the trees. Below the crest he stooped, dropping to hands and knees. He wriggled the rest of the way, peered down. The grass of the hillside was lush and long, spangled with the brilliant cups of flowers. He glimpsed her briefly, a hundred paces off; ducked, waited, and scuttled in pursuit.

There was a dell to which she came, he knew it well enough; a private place, screened with tangled bushes, shaded by a massive pale-trunked beech. He reached it panting, crawled to where he could once more see.

She lay on her back beneath the tree, hands clasped behind her head, her legs pushed out straight. Her feet were bare, and grimy round the shins; her skirt was drawn up, showing her long brown thighs. He edged forward, parting the grasses, groaning again. A long time she lay, still as a sleeper; then she began. She sat up, passing her hands across her breasts, squeezing them beneath her tunic. Then she pulled at its lacings; then shook her head till the hair cascaded across her face and rolled again and again, showing her belly, the great dark patch that meant now she was a woman.

His whole being seemed concentrated into his eyes; his eyes, and the burning tip of him that pressed the ground. He saw the shrine, unreachable; he saw her fingers go to it, and press; he saw her body arch, the vivid grass. Then sun and leaves rushed inward on him as a centre, the hillside flickered out; and he lay panting, fingers wet, hearing the echo of a cry that seemed as piercing as the long cry of a bird. After which he collected himself, ran with terror as he had run before, jerkin flapping, to the valley and trees and the safe, crunching sheep. Later he sobbed, for the empty nights and days. His neck burned, and his cheeks; he begged her forgiveness, she who could not hear, Dareen whose father was rich, owning fifty goats and twice that number of sheep; Dareen whose eyes he never more could meet, never, in the village street.

The dream disturbed him. He moved uneasily, wanting it to end; and in time it seemed his wish was answered. A fume of acrid smoke seared his lungs; voices babbled; hands were on him, pressing down. It seemed he had descended to one of the Hells, where all is din and lurid light. He fought against the hands, bearing up with all his strength; and a bowl was thrust before his face. In it coals burned; their fiery breath scorched his throat. He writhed again, trying to pull back his head; but his hair was caught. The coals loomed close then seemed to recede, till they looked like a whole town burning far off in the night. After which the hard floor no longer pressed his knees. It seemed he was a bird, flying effortlessly upward into regions of greater and greater light. Then he knew he was no bird, but a God. And Dareen came to him, after all the years; he sank into her, rejoicing at last, and was content.

He was conscious at first of cool air on his skin. He rolled over, mumbling. The dream-time, though splendid, was finished; soon he must rise and dress, start his morning chores. The soup-pots must be skimmed, the fire stoked; billets waited to be split, the two lean cows must be milked. He wondered that he did not hear his father's snores from the corner of the hut. A cock crowed, somewhere close; and he opened his eyes.

At first the dim shapes round him made no sense; then, it seemed on the instant, all memory returned. He leaped, trembling in every limb, to the farthest corner of the bracken bed. The movement woke the woman lying at his side.

Her body was brown; as brown as the remembered body of Dareen, and crusted on arms and legs with bands of gold. Save the rings she wore nothing but a mask of kingfisher-blue, through which her dark eyes glittered with terror in their gaze; but her voice when she spoke was musical and soft. 'Don't be afraid,' she said. 'Don't be afraid, my lord. No one will hurt you here.' She stretched an arm to him; he shrank farther into the angle of the wall, pushing shoulder-blades into the rough wattle at his back. She chuckled at that and said again, 'My Lord . . .' She pulled at the shawl he held gripped. He resisted, knuckles whitening; and it seemed behind the mask she might have smiled. 'Why,' she said, 'you are proud and shy, which is as it should be. But the God has already entered you once, and that most wonderfully.' She fell to stroking his calf and thigh, moving her fingers in cool little sweeps; and after a while the trembling of his body eased. 'Lie down,' she said, 'and let me hold you; for you are very beautiful.'

Truly it seemed the effects of the Magic Smoke had not yet left him; for despite his fear he felt his eyelids droop. She drew his face to her breasts, crooning and rocking; and lying with her was like lying with a great rustling bird.

The sun was high when next he opened his eyes, and the chamber empty. He sat up seeing the light stream through the chinks of the wattle screens. He rose shakily, staring down at the gold that ringed his own body, the great pectoral on his breast. This last on impulse he slipped from his neck, holding the shining metal close up to his eyes. The face of a stranger or a girl watched back. He laid the thing aside, frowning deeply, walked a pace at a time to the hut door. He cringed back then, terror rising afresh; for he knew the manner of place to which he had come. After which he needed to piss;

this he did, trembling, against the wattle wall. An earthenware water jug stood beside the bed; he drank deeply, slaking his thirst. Then he wrapped the shawl round him and sat head in hands on the edge of the bed, and tried to think what he could do.

She came to him at midday, bringing food and drink. She helped him dress, washing him with scented oil, tucking his glory into a cloth of soft white wool. Although he cringed at first her hands were gentle; so that he all but overcame his fear of her. The fruit and bread he ate hungrily enough; the drink he spat out, expecting the taste of beer, and she laughed and told him it was Midsea wine. His head spun again at that for none of the village had ever tasted such a thing, not even T'Sagro who was the father of Dareen and who owned fifty goats. He drank again, and the second sip was better; so that he drained the cup and poured himself more, after which his head spun as it had spun when he sniffed the Magic Smoke. Also the wine made him bolder so that he said, 'Why am I here?' These were the first words he had spoken.

She stared at him before she answered. Then she said, 'Because you are a God.' He frowned at this and asked, 'Why am I a God?' and she told him in terms of forthrightness the like of which he had not heard, least of all from a woman. Also she had a trick of speech that seemed to go into his body, hardening it and creating desire. When she had left him he lay on the bed and thought he would sleep; but her words returned to him till he pulled the cloth aside and stared down at himself wondering if he might be as beautiful as she had said. Then he remembered his father and sister and the manner of their deaths, and wept. Toward nightfall he sat at the hut door and saw far off below the great fall of the hill smoke rise from where perhaps the Horsemen burned another village that had refused its dues, and felt lonelier than ever in his life. Then tiredness came on him strongly so that he lay down once more and slept. She returned by moonlight, flitting like a moth; he woke to the cool length of her pressed at his side, her hands working at his cloth. He did as he had done in the dream, entering her strongly, making her cry out with pleasure; till she had taken his strength, and he slept like one of the dead.

Later, when she brought his food, he said to her, 'What are you called?' and she said in a low voice, 'The Reborn.' The fear returned at that; but night once more brought peace.

The days passed, merging each into the next; and though he dared not wander far from the hut he found himself anticipating her visits more keenly than before. Also no fear is wholly self-sustaining; he slept more soundly, colour returned to his cheeks. She brought him a polished shield, in which to see his reflection; he took to posing secretly before it, admiring the slender strength of his body, the savage painted eyes that stared back into his own. At such times he grew big with thinking of her, and fell to devising new means of pleasuring. Also he wondered greatly at her age; for at some times she seemed old as a hill or the great Gods of the chalk, at others as young and fragile as a child. He thought how easy it would be, one day, to pull the mask away; but always his hand was stayed. He talked now, when she came, with increasing freedom; till one day, greatly daring, he told her his wish that she could always be with him in the hut. She laughed at that, a low, rich sound of joy, and clapped her hands; after which she was constantly at his side, and a green-masked priest would come or a girl to bring their food, scratch the doorpost and wait humbly in the sunlight. She talked at great length, of all manner of things, and he to her; he told her of his life, and how he had herded sheep, and how it was to live in a village and be a peasant's child.

She said, 'I know.' She was sitting in the hut door; it was evening, the grass and tumbled stones of the hill golden in the slanting light. Goats bleated, on the slopes of the great Mound; and the air was very still.

He laid his head in her lap; she stroked him awhile, then pulled back her head. He sat up, meaning finally to speak of the mask; and she rose, stood arms folded staring out across the hill. After a while she spoke, back turned to him. 'Altrin,' she said, 'do you truly love me?'

He nodded, watching up at her and wondering.

'Then,' she said, 'I will tell you a story. Once there was a little girl; younger than your sister, when you loved her and used to stroke her hair. She was in love too, with a certain God. He came to her in the night, promising many things; so that in her foolishness she wanted to be his Bride.'

She half turned; he saw the long muscles of her neck move as she swallowed. 'She came to a certain House,' she said. 'She lay in that House, but there was no God. So she ran away. She became rich, and powerful. When she returned it was with gold and money-sticks, and soldiers of her own. Because of her wealth her people loved her; because of their love, she gave them a Sign.' She nodded at the flanking slope, the sprawling giant with his mighty prick. 'While the Sign lay on the hill, her people would be safe,' she said. 'This the God promised; yet he turned away his face. The Horse Warriors came; the people were killed, the village put to the fire. The servant of the God was killed, there on the hill.'

He stared, swallowing in his turn; and the hut seemed very still.

'I was that child,' she said. 'I am the Reborn.'

She stepped away from him. Her voice sounded distant, and very cold. 'I lay on the hill,' she said. 'The God took me, and was very wonderful. Later, when he grew tired, he returned me to life. It was night, and there were many dead. I was one of them; and yet I crawled away. I crawled for a night and part of a day. I did not know where I was, or what had happened to me.

I could not see, and there were many flies. I lay by a stream, and drank its water. Later I ate berries and leaves. I did not know what had happened to me. One day I decided a thing. I crawled to the stream and looked in, over the bank. The sun was high, so I saw myself clearly.'

She shuddered, and her hand went to the mask. 'I knew then I must die again,' she said. 'I had a little knife; but I lacked the strength to put it into myself. I got into the water, thinking I would drown; but the pain of that was too great also. I lay a day and night trying to starve; then I thought my heart might stop for wishing it. But the God refused my life, holding me strongly to the earth. I ate berries and fruit; and my strength returned.'

The boy frowned, toying with a necklace she had given him; golden bees, joined by little blue beads. He reached forward, trying to trap her ankle; but she moved aside. 'Can you think what it was like?' she said bitterly. 'I had been beautiful; now the Gods had taken my face away.'

He flinched a little; then went back to playing with the necklace, frowning up under his brows.

'I thought then, how I could get revenge on men,' she said. 'For men it was who had brought me to this pass. Then one day the God came to me, stirring me just a little. I had forgotten my body, which was as beautiful as ever. Also I couldn't find it in me to hate Him, who is yet the mightiest of Men. I clapped my hands; and he sent another Sign. A fishing bird flew past, dropping a feather on the water. I took it in my hand, seeing how it shone. I knew I could be beautiful again.'

She twined her fingers, still staring at the great hill figure. 'I made a mask, of grasses the sun had dried,' she said, 'and a crown of flowers for my hair. I bathed myself in the stream, and washed my clothes. I walked to where there had been huts and fields; but they were burned. So I walked to where there were other towns that the Horsemen had not destroyed. Near one of them I saw a girl-child herding geese. "Leave your flock," I said, "and come with me. I am the Reborn, and the God is at my side."

'Truly, he was with me; for she came. We lay together, and she pleasured me. Her fingers were shy, like flowers. In the morning she brought me food. I saw a young man sowing winter wheat. "I am the Reborn," I said. "Come with me, for the God is at my side."

'So we came to where a village had stood, in a chalk pass by the sea. The Horse Warriors burned it; but being simple folk they had not dared my Hall. Nearby they had camped; for as yet they built no towns. I went to them. Thunder followed me, and fire-drakes in the sky. "Put down your weapons," I said. "I am the Reborn, and the God is at my side." The gold they had stolen I took from them, and cloth from the Yellow Lands to dress my priests. So I came home; in a litter, as of old, with Hornmen before me and my own folk round about. Yet there were none to welcome me. Instead were many ghosts;

Cha'Acta, whom I killed, and Magan, whom I killed, and many more. They would not let me be.

'The Horsemen came, asking what tribute the God desired. I made them fetch me skins of fishing birds. The sower of wheat came to me. I asked how he was called. "Ensil," he said, "if it please my Lady." "Then you are Cha'Ensil," I said, "and a mighty priest. Be faithful, and you shall be mightier."

'Yet my Hall was empty; he whom once I knew had fled. The wheat sprang green and tall; naught sprang from me but tears. The Horsemen brought me tribute; yet I grieved. Then one day Cha'Ensil came to me again. He told me how he had found the God. I did not believe. He brought me to his house; and there he lay, young and beautiful, with no cloth to cover him.' She turned suddenly with something like a sob, fell to her knees and pressed her face against his thighs. 'Never leave me,' she said. 'Never go away.'

He stroked her lustrous hair, frowning through the doorway of the hut, his eyes remote.

The long summer was passing; mornings were misty and blue, a cold chill crept into the God House of nights. Faggots were brought and stacked, a great fire lit on the hard earth floor of the hut. Some days now she would barely let him rise from the couch. Many times when he was tired she roused him, showing a Magic Thing her body could do; when all else failed there was the seed-smoke, and the yellow wine. She bathed him, stroking and combing his hair; wild it was and long, brushing his shoulders like silk. Finally these things palled. Winter was on the land; the fields lay sere and brown, cold winds droned through the God House finding every chink in the wattle walls. He brooded, shivering a little beside the fire; and his decision was reached. Custom had taught him her ways; he broached the subject delicately, as befitted his station.

'Sometimes,' he said, 'as you will know better than I, even Gods desire to ride abroad and see something of the country they own. I have such a desire; perhaps the God you say is in me is making his wishes felt.'

She seemed well pleased. 'This is good,' she said. 'When the people see you they will be glad, knowing the God is with them. I will ride with you; we must speak to my priest.'

In the months that had passed he had rarely seen Cha'Ensil; now the priest was summoned in haste. He came in state, resplendent in his robes of patterned silk. With him he brought his women; but at that the Reborn demurred. 'I will prepare the God,' she said. 'I and no other; for his is no common beauty.'

His hands, which had been calloused, had softened from idleness. She pared and polished his nails, tinting his palms and feet with a dark red stain. His hair she bound with delicate silver leaves, and clothes were brought for him; a cloak of dazzling silk, a tunic with the Corn Lord's broidered Sign, boots of soft leather that cased him to the knee. Lastly she gave him a strong white mare, tribute from a chieftain of the Horse People. He sat the creature gingerly enough when the time came, being more used to plough-oxen; but she was docile, and his ineptness went unremarked.

So the party set out; Cha'Ensil with his priests and soldiers, his Horn and Cymbal men; the Beautiful One on his splendid mount; the Reborn and her favoured women in tinkling litters, borne on the backs of sturdy bearers and swaying with the God's gilded plumes. They crossed the Great Heath to the villages of the Plain, curved north and west nearly to the lands of the Marsh Folk, who pay no taxes and do strange things to please their Gods. Everywhere the Horsemen bent the knee, placing hands to their beards in awe; for the Corn Lord was a mighty spirit, his fame reached very far. For Altrin, each day brought further earnest of his strength; and Mata watched with pride to see the young Prince she had made dash happy as a puppy, circling to her call.

Chieftain after chieftain hastened with gifts; and the tribute from the grim towns of the Horsemen was richest of all. The treasure waggons towered toward the end, while behind them trotted a bleating flock of goats. The eyes of the Beautiful One grew narrow at that, his mind busy; till he summoned Cha'Ensil, more curtly perhaps than one should summon a Chief Priest, to demand an accounting of the God's dues.

Cha'Ensil frowned, holding up the notched sticks on which he carved his marks; but the Prince pushed them scornfully aside. 'Everywhere I see villages that are rich,' he said. 'Both our own folk's towns and those of the Horsemen. Yet we are poor, owning barely five hundred goats and scarce that number of sheep. The Corn Lord brings this prosperity; let his tallies be increased.

Cha'Ensil set his lips into a line. 'That is for the Reborn to decide, my Lord,' he said gently. 'For she is your Mistress, as she is mine.'

But Altrin merely laughed, flinging the bone of a game bird into the fire round which they were camped. 'Her will is mine,' he said, 'and so mine is hers. Increase the tallies; I will have a thousand goats by autumn.'

Cha'Ensil's face had paled a little; yet he still spoke mildly. 'Perhaps,' he said, 'even Princes may overreach themselves, my Lord. Also, favours freely given may freely be repented.'

The boy spat contemptuously. 'Priest, I will tell you a riddle,' he said. 'I have a certain thing about me that is long and hard. With it I defend the favours that are mine; and yet I carry no sword. What do you think it could be?'

The other turned away, shuddering and making a very strange mouth; and for the time nothing more was said.

Later, Altrin had a novel idea. First he loved the Reborn with more than usual fervour, making her pant with pleasure; then he lay with his head against her breasts, feeling beneath him the swell of her belly that was so unlike the belly of a girl. 'My Lady,' he said, 'it has come to me that you have been more than generous in your gifts. Yet one thing I lack, and desire it most of all.'

She laughed, playing with his hair. 'The God is greedy,' she said. 'But that is the way with Gods; and I for one am very glad of it. What do you wish?'

He drew his dangling hair across her breasts, and felt her tense. 'Cha'Ensil, who is a priest, has many soldiers,' he said. 'They defend him, running to do his errands, and are at his beck and call. Yet I, in whom the God himself lives, have none. Surely my state should equal his, particularly if I am to ride abroad.'

She was still awhile, and he thought perhaps she was frowning. Finally she shook her head. 'A God needs no soldiers,' she said. 'His strength is his own, none dares to raise a hand. Soldiers are well enough for lesser folk; besides, Cha'Ensil is my oldest servant. I would not see him wronged.'

He sensed that he was on dangerous ground, and let the matter rest; but later he withheld himself, on pain of a certain promise. That she gave him finally, when she was tired and her body could no longer resist. He slept curled in her arms, and well content.

The party returned to the high house on the chalk. Once its walls would have been ritually breached; but that was in the old times, long since gone. In every room of the complex fires roared high, fighting the winter chill. The days closed in, howling and bitter; and the snow came, first a powdering then a steadier fall. Deep drifts gathered on the eaves of the God House, blanketing the demons that clung there. But rugs were hung round the walls of the inner chamber, a second fire lit before the wattle screens; and the Reborn and her Lord dined well enough night after night, on wild pig and wine. Sometimes too the priests of the household, or their women, arranged entertainments; at devising these last the Prince showed himself more than usually adroit, and in his Mistress's heart there stirred perhaps the first faint pang of doubt.

With the spring, Altrin rode out again. He took with him a dozen men of his new bodyguard, later recruiting as many Horsemen into his train. The party rode east, to where fishing villages clustered round a great bight of the sea, and the Black Rock begins which none may cross, Divine or otherwise. Everywhere folk quailed before the young God with his cold, lovely eyes; and what those eyes happened on, he took. Grain he sent back and goats; and once a girl-child for his Mistress, to be trained in the rites of the God. Two weeks passed, three, before he turned back to the west. The Horsemen he dismissed, paying them with grain, hides and gold from his own supply; later that day he strode back into the hut on the Sacred Mound.

She was waiting for him, in a new gauzy dress of white and green. What expression her face held could not be told; but she was pacing forward and back along the beaten earth floor, her arms folded, her chin sunk on her chest. He hurried to her, taking her hands; but she snatched herself away. 'What is this?' he said, half-laughing. 'Are you not pleased to see me?'

She stamped her slim foot. 'Where have you been?' she said. 'What are you thinking of? I cried for you for a week. Then I was angry, then I cried again. Now – I don't care if you've come back or not.'

A bowl and a cup stood on an inlaid table, part of his winter spoil. He poured wine for himself, drank and wiped his mouth. 'I sent you a pretty child to play with,' he said. 'Wasn't that enough?'

'And I sent her back,' she said. 'I didn't want her. What use are girls to me now? It was you I wanted. *Oh* ...'

He flung the wine away, angrily. 'You tell me I am a God,' he said. 'I wear a God's clothes, live in a God's house. Yet I must answer like a ploughboy for everything I do.'

'Not a ploughboy,' she said, 'a sheep herder. A peasant you were, a peasant you remain. *Ohh* ...' He had turned on his heel; and she was clinging to him with desperate strength. 'I wanted you,' she said. 'I wanted you, I was so lonely. I wanted to die again. I didn't mean what I said, please don't go away. Do what you choose; but please don't go away ...'

He stood frowning down, sensing his power. As ever, her nearness roused him; yet obscurely there was the need to hurt. His fingers curled on the edge of the brilliant mask; for an instant it seemed he would tear the thing aside, then he relaxed. 'Go to our chamber,' he said coldly. 'Make yourself ready; perhaps, if my greeting is more fitting, I shall come to you.'

Cha'Ensil, stepping to the doorway of the hut, heard the words and the sobs that answered them. He stood still a moment, face impassive; then turned, walking swiftly back the way he had come.

Some days afterwards the hilltop began to bustle with activity. A new Hall was rising, below the God House and some forty paces distant; for the Reborn had decreed the older structure too chilly to serve another winter. Also extra accommodation was needed for the many hopefuls flocking to join the priesthood. The fame of the God was spreading; all were anxious to share his good fortune. The Prince himself took a keen interest in the newcomers, selecting (or so it seemed) the comeliest virgins and the least prepossessing men; but Cha'Ensil held himself aloof from the entire affair. Later the Beautiful One rode north, and again. An extra granary was built, a new range of stables; and still the tribute waggons trundled down to the great gap in the chalk. The Horsemen bore hard upon the land; and where they rode, there also went the ensigns of the God. Smoke rose from a score of burning villages; and at last it was time, high time, to cry enough.

Cha'Ensil, seeking an audience with the Prince, found him in the New Hall, where he was accustomed to take his ease. He lay on a divan draped with yellow silk, a wine jug at his elbow and a cup. He greeted Cha'Ensil casually enough, waving him to a seat with a hand that flashed with gold. 'Well, priest,' he said, 'say what you have to quickly, and be gone. My Mistress waits; and tonight the strength of the God is more than usually in me. I shall take her several times.'

The priest swallowed but sat as he was bidden, gathering his robes about him. 'My Prince,' he began reasonably enough, 'I, who raised you to your estate, have every right to counsel you. We live, as you know full well, by the good will of the Horsemen. They fear the God; but they are children, and greed may outrun fear. This show of magnificence you seem so set on will end in ruin; for you, and for us all.'

The Prince drained the cup at a gulp, and poured another. 'This show, which is no more than my due, makes you uneasy,' he said. 'You lie jealous in your bed; and for more reasons than the ones you state. Now hear me. My strength may or may not come from the God; personally I think it does, but that is beside the point. Behind me stands One whose will is not lightly crossed; while I satisfy her, and satisfy her I think I do, your power is ended. Now leave me. Whine to your women, if you must; I am easily tired by foolishness.'

Cha'Ensil rose, his face white with rage. 'Shepherd boy,' he said, 'I saved you for my Lady. For her sake have I borne with you; now I tell you this. I will not see her and her House destroyed. Take warning . . .'

He stopped, abruptly; for Altrin had also risen to his feet, swaying a little from the wine. A cloak, richly embroidered, hung from his shoulders; save for a little cloth, he was otherwise naked. 'And I tell you this, sower of winter wheat,' he said. 'That when the strength goes from me I may fall. But that is hardly likely yet.' He squeezed, insultingly, the great thrusting at his groin, then snatched at his hip. 'Priest,' he jeered, 'will you see the power of the God?'

But the other, mouth working, had blundered from the chamber. Behind him as he hurried away rose the mocking laughter of the Beautiful One.

The horse drummed across the Heath, raising behind it a thin plume of whitish dust. Its rider, cloaked and masked, carried a great Staff of Power. He crouched low in the saddle driving his heels at the beast's sides to urge it to even greater speed. While the fury gripped him Cha'Ensil made good time; later he slowed the weary animal to a walk. Midday found him clear of the Great Heath; at dusk he presented himself at the gates of a city of the Horsemen, a square, spike-walled fortress set above rolling woodland on a spur of chalk. There he instituted certain inquiries; while his status, and the gold he bore, secured him lodging for the night together with other services dearer to his heart. For the Chief Priest had by no means wasted his opportunities since taking service with the God of the great chalk pass. The morning brought answers to his questions. More gold changed hands; and Cha'Ensil rode north again, on a mount sounder in wind than the one on which he had arrived. Half-way through the day he bespoke a waggon train; the drivers waved him on, pointing with their whips. At nightfall, out in the vastness of the Great Plain, he reached his destination; the capital of the Horsemen's southern kingdom, a place resplendent with watchtowers and granaries, barracks and royal courts.

Here the power of the Corn Lord was less directly felt. Cha'Ensil fumed at the gates an hour or more before his purse, if not his master, secured admission. He made his way through rutted earth streets to the house of a Midsea merchant, a trader who for his unique services was tolerated even by the Horsemen. Once more, gold secured admission; and a slave with a torch conducted him to the chamber of his choice. A heavy door was unbolted, chains clinked back; and the priest stepped forward, wrinkling his nose at the odour that assailed him. To either side in the gloom stretched filthy straw pallets. All were occupied; some by women, some by young boys. The slave grunted, gesturing with the torch; and the other called, sharply.

Nothing.

Cha'Ensil spoke again; and a voice answered sullenly from the farther shadows. It said, 'What do you want with me?'

He took the torch, stepped forward and stared. Dull eyes, black-shadowed, watched up from a pallid face. The girl's hair sprawled lank on the straw; over her was thrown a ragged blanket. Cha'Ensil raised his brows, speaking gently; for answer she spat, turning her face from the glare.

The priest stooped, mouth puckered with distaste. Beneath the blanket she was naked; he searched her body swiftly for the signs of a certain disease. There were none; and he sat back on his heels with a sigh. 'Rise, and find yourself a cloth,' he said. 'I am your friend, and knew your father well. I have come to take you away from this place, back to your home.'

Cha'Ensil returned to the God House alone some few days later, and hastened to make obeisance to his mistress; but it seemed his absence had not been too much noticed. He served the Reborn well in the weeks that followed, and was unfailing in his courtesy to Altrin when chance placed the Beautiful One in his path; for his heart was more at rest.

Two months passed, and a third; the green of summer was changing to flaunting gold when he once more rode from the Sacred Mound. He headed south, to a village well enough known to him. Here, on a promontory overlooking the sparkling sweep of the sea, stood just such a Hall as the one he had quitted. He presented himself at the stockade, and was courteously received. Later he was conducted by tortuous paths to a tiny bay, closed on either side by headlands of tumbled rock. A dozen children played in the crash and surge of the water, watched over by a priest and a seamed-faced woman who was their instructress in the Mysteries. A purse changed hands; and the woman called, shrilly.

Cha'Ensil peered, shading his eyes. A lithe, brown-skinned girl waded from the water; she stood before him boldly, wearing neither cloth nor band, returning his scrutiny with a slow smile. He spoke, uncertainly; for answer she knelt before him, lowering her head as the ritual dictates.

He nodded, well pleased. 'You have worked excellently, Cha'Ilgo,' he said. 'The God defend and prosper you.' Then to the woman, 'See she is dressed, and readied for a journey. I leave inside the hour.'

That day a new priestess arrived at the Hall of the Reborn; and Cha'Ensil, whose office it was, conducted her to the Presence with pride. Altrin, seated grandly to one side, did not speak; but his eyes followed the girl as she moved through the forms of greeting and Cha'Ensil, watching sidelong, saw his brows furrow into a frown.

The opportunity for which the Chief Priest had waited was not long in coming. He was sent for, brusquely enough; a few minutes later, his face composed, he stooped into the presence of Altrin.

The Beautiful One, it seemed, was more than a little drunk. He eyed Cha'Ensil balefully before he spoke; then he said roughly, 'Who is she, husbandman?'

Cha'Ensil smiled soothingly. 'To whom,' he said, 'does my Lord refer?'

The other swore, reaching for the wine bowl. Its contents spilled; the Chief Priest hastened to assist him. The cup was recharged; Altrin, flushed, sat back and belched. He said again, 'Who is she?'

Cha'Ensil smiled once more. 'Some child of a chalk hill farmer,' he said. 'An apt pupil, as I have been told; she will no doubt prove an asset to the House.'

'*Who is she?*'

'Her name is Dareen,' said the Chief Priest steadily. 'The daughter of T'Sagro. Your father's neighbour, Prince.'

The other stared. He said huskily, 'How can this be?'

'I found her, in a certain place,' said Cha'Ensil. 'I freed her, thinking it would be your will.' He extended his arms. 'The enmity between us is ended,' he said. 'Let her happiness be my peace-gift to you, Lord.'

Altrin rose, his brows contracted to a scowl. He said, 'Bring her to me.'

Cha'Ensil lowered his eyes. 'Sir, it is hardly wise …'

'Bring her …!'

The other bowed. He said, 'It shall be as my Lord desires.'

The night was windy; the growing complex of wooden buildings groaned and shifted, alive with creaks and rustlings. Torches burned in sconces; by their light the pair negotiated a corridor hewn partly from the chalk, tapped at a door. A muffled answer: and the Chief Priest raised the latch, propelling the girl gently forward. He said, 'My Lord, the priestess Dareen.' He closed the door, waited a moment head cocked; then padded softly away.

She faced him across the room. She said in a low voice, 'Why did you send for me?'

He moved forward, seemingly dazed. He said, 'Dareen?' He reached to part the cloak she wore; and she knocked his arm away. She said furiously, '*Don't touch me.*'

He flushed at that, the wine buzzing in his brain. He said thickly, 'I touch whom I please. I command whom I please. I am the God.'

She stared, open-mouthed; then she began to laugh. 'You?' she said. 'You, a God? Who herded sheep on the hillside, and dared not lift eyes to me in the street? Now ... a God ... forgive me, my Lord Sheepdrover. This is too sudden ...'

He glared at her. He said, 'I did not choose to raise my eyes to you. You were a child.'

She snarled at him. '*You did not choose ...*' She swallowed, clenching her fists. 'Day after day I walked to where you lay,' she said. 'And day after day you watched me, like a silly little boy, and played with yourself in the grass because you were afraid. I humbled myself, in sight of you; because I wanted you, I wanted you to come and take me. But you never came. You never came because you dared not. Now leave me in peace. You are no man for me.'

He grabbed the cloak, wrenched. Beneath, she wore the green and gold of a priestess. Her waist was cinched by a glittering belt; her breasts jutted boldly at the thin cloth of her tunic. He gripped her; and she swung her hand flat-palmed. The slap rang in the little chamber; he doubled his fist, eyes swimming, and she staggered. Silence fell; in the quiet she probed at a wobbling tooth, rubbed her lips, stared at the smudge of red on the back of her hand. Then her bruised mouth smiled. 'I see,' she said. 'Now I suppose you will beat me. Perhaps you will kill me. How very brave that would be.' She circled, staring. 'Now you are a God,' she said. 'What happened to me, when you became a God? And Tamlin, and Sirri, and Merri, and all the others? Do you know?' Her eyes blazed at him. 'Tamlin died on a treadmill,' she said. 'Sirri was sold to the King of the Horsemen, who beat her till he broke her back. Merri has the sickness the Midsea people bring. I went to a whorehouse; while a certain God, whose name we will not speak, dressed in silk and called himself a man.' She wiped her mouth again. 'Well, go on,' she said. 'Beat me; or call your priests to do it for you. Then you can lie in peace, with your fat old woman who doesn't have a face ...'

She got no further. His hands went to her throat; she tore an arm free, struck at him again. A wrestling; then her mouth was on his. She was groping for him, pulling and wrenching at his cloth.

Much later, when all was over, he began to cry. She cradled him then in the dark, pressing his mouth to her breast, calling him by a name his mother used when he was a tiny child.

He woke heavy with sleep, and she had rolled from him. He groped for her, needing her warmth after the many years. She nuzzled him, smiling and stroking; and the door of the chamber swung slowly inward.

He sat up, appalled. He saw the mast of glittering blue, the Chief Priest at her side. He sprang forward with a shout; but he was too late. The door banged shut; he wrenched it back, but the corridor beyond was empty. The Reborn and her minister were gone.

The light grew, across the Heath. Above him the high hill and its buildings lay deserted; and a drizzle was falling, drifting from the dull void of the sky.

He moved with a desperate urgency, stooping low, fingers clutched round the wrist of the frightened girl. The stockade was before him, and the high lashed gates. He climbed, scrambling, reached back to her. Her skirt tore; she landed beside him with a thud, glared back and up. He took her wrist again, slithering on the steep grass of the ditch, pushing aside the soaked branches of trees.

From a chamber high on the Mound, the Reborn stared down. No quiver, no movement betrayed her breathing; beside her, Cha'Ensil's face was set like stone. The fugitives vanished, reappeared on the farther slope. The woman stiffened; and the priest turned to her, head bowed. He said, 'My Lady?'

She turned away, hands to the feathered mask. She said, 'He must come back, Cha'Ensil.'

He waited; and her shoulders shook. He said gently, 'And if he will not?'

The muffled words seemed dragged from her. She said, 'Then none will sit beside me. None must know our secrets, priest. Or what power we have, is gone …' She waited then; till the latch clicked, the sound of his footsteps died. She dropped to her knees, crept to the corner of the little room. She pushed the bird-mask from her, and began to sob.

Beside the great mound the brook ran swift and silent between fern-hung banks. A fallen tree spanned it, stark in the early light. He crossed awkwardly, turned back to the girl. Sweat was on his face; he stared up at the Mound, plunged on again. Beyond the brook grew clumps of waist-high grass. He staggered between them, brown bog-water about his calves. There was a swell of rising ground; he fell to his knees, the girl beside him, hung his head and panted.

A voice said quietly, 'Where to now, my Lord?'

He raised his face, slowly. Round him the semicircle of figures stood grey against the sky. A few paces beyond, masked and cloaked, was the priest. The Beautiful One glared, licking his mouth, and raised a shaking finger. 'Eldron, Melgro, Baath,' he said. 'You are my men. Save me from treachery …'

The man called Eldron stepped forward, stood looking down. 'Wake the thunder, Prince,' he muttered. He whirled the heavy club he carried, struck. The Prince collapsed, setting up a hoarse bawling.

Melgro wiped his face. 'Bow the trees down, Lord,' he said, and struck in turn.

Baath, smiling, drew a heavy-bladed knife. 'Rouse the lightning, ploughboy,' he said, 'and I will call you God.' He drove with the blade; and the little group closed in, hacking in silence. Bright drops flew, spattering the rough grass; the bawls changed to a high-pitched keening that was cut off in its turn. The body rolled a little way, back to the water; shook, and was still.

The girl crouched where she had fallen, unmoving. As the priest approached she raised a face that was chalk-white beneath its tan. 'Why, priest?' she said, small voiced. 'Why?'

Cha'Ensil stooped above her, drawing a small dagger from his belt. He said, 'I loved him too.' He pulled her head back quickly, and used the knife.

Potts has been dreaming again. First it seemed he was a child once more, back at home and in bed. He'd probably had asthma, he often used to get asthma. He knew he was a child, certainly, because of the pace at which his mother ran upstairs. She used to run like that to bring his tea, a bowl of tinned fruit salad (both cherries in his portion), buttered bread sliced thin and a half tablet of ephedrine hidden in a spoonful of jam; though over the years her feet had slowed and slowed. Later it seemed he was better because his mother said with all her old rough jocularity, 'Out you go then, there's bugger all up with you,' and he left the house and went to the car – how the years did fly – and the car was the old MG he once owned, not the Champ. His first motor, she had been. Where he drove he wasn't sure; but she ran better than she had ever done, engine note humming through little towns, tacho needle flicking as he climbed hill after sunlit hill and the gear lever clicking smoothly, snicking forward and back.

He's feeling better about the other business too. He might have guessed of course she wasn't dead. Now time, that had borne so heavily on him, has ceased to be a factor. Beyond the worlds he has glimpsed stretch others and still more; in one of them, assuredly, he will see the light shine in her eyes, feel her arms at last. Till then, he is content.

He puts his fingers to his face. If she was to walk in now, he's afraid he'd look a mess. He seems to have developed a rash of little pimples round his mouth; and his breathing sounds queer, bubbling and thick. Also he wetted himself in the night; but he's sure she'd understand. He's got the pillow rigged now behind his back; and the pain doesn't seem half as bad.

He's not going to worry any more; there's far too much to see. Already a new colour has entered his world. He holds the image that has come to him, the image of the ships. Soon, surely, he will see her again; she's skipped down all the ages so far at his side.

SIX

Rand, Rat and the Dancing Man

1

It had rained all night and on into the morning, so that long puddles lay everywhere about the wharves of Crab Gut and the crowd that had assembled to see the greatship leave plashed ankle-deep in oozing yellow mud. Drifts of vapour obscured the sea-filled cleft in which the village stood; above the huts with their roof-combs of painted wood the Tower of the Crab loomed, a gaunt, pale silhouette. More than one of the watchers frowned at the omens, making beneath his cloak the sign that wards off evil luck.

Looker lay ready at her berth, as she had lain all night. Her bow and stern posts, tall and intricately carved, were rigged in their sockets, the great truss that was her strength strained to humming tightness, her yard in place above the tripod of spars that served her as a mast. Trim she was and beautiful, low in the water and broad in the beam, as fine a fighting vessel as any in Sealand; but the shields strapped to her bulwarks were whitened in sign of peace, white cloths covered her sides and fighting top so that she already looked like a ship of the dead. The crowd muttered, shuffling its feet, turning from time to time to stare up at the stockade surrounding the Tower.

It was from the stockade that the expected procession debouched. First came Matt the Navigator, burly and bearded, a bearskin draped across his shoulders, the curved lever of the steering oar carried like a staff of office. Behind him walked Egril Shipmaster, oldest servant of the House of the Crab, and his two tall sons. Then came Ranna the priest; at his elbow walked a boy with caged cockerels for the shipblessing. There followed the forty-odd rowers and crew, muffled and hooded against the downpour. Last of all strode Rand the Solitary, onetime Prince of Crabland, with Elgro the Dancing Man at his side.

Alone of all the company, Rand was bareheaded; also the watchers saw he carried neither axe nor sword. The rain plastered the long fair hair to his skull, gleamed on cheekbones and throat. He held his face high, seeming unaware of the downpour; his eyes looked grey and vague as the sky.

Drums thudded on the wharf. Matt swung to the platform above *Looker*'s stern cabin, shipped his lever, drove home the wedges that secured it to the great shaft of the oar. Clattering rose from amidships as the rowers took their places, eased the blades of the long oars through the ports. *Looker* rolled slowly, shedding water in streams from the awnings rigged above her deck. Men ran forward skidding and slipping; ropes splashed into the sea.

The drums stopped. Ranna, knife in hand, held up a struggling cockerel; and Rand spoke quickly from the greatship's stern. 'No blood,' he said. 'Wine if the Gods must have it, or water; but spill no blood, Ranna. It is not my will.'

In the stillness, the hiss of rain sounded clearly. The great-ship surged and creaked, feeling already the lift of the open sea. A rope groaned, tightening. Egril swore, circling finger and thumb beneath his cloak; Elgro shrugged, and spat. The priest turned his masked face to the ship; and a shout from Matt brought the oars crashing down. The last lines snaked away; the blades rose once in salute, dipped again. *Looker* steadied and began to gather way, trailing a greyish sheen of wake. The last the villagers saw of her was the rhythmic flash of her rowing banks, the last they heard the thudding of her drum. Then she was gone, vanished like a spirit into the shadowy sea.

She pulled hard and steady the rest of the day, following the vague loom of the nearer shore. All day till evening, the rain roared unceasing. The bows fell and rose, slicing the sea; spray flew back in stinging sheets, mingled with the slosh of rainwater on the decks. The drum beat, timing the strokes; the rowers leaned their weight forward and back, monotonously, faces blank. Their passage was unobserved; no fishing boat would put from shore in weather such as this, no warlord in his proper mind leave the shelter of his haven.

Below decks, the little cabin stank of wet leather and cloth. Rand groaned and tossed, the hammock in which he lay swaying to the movements of the ship. The timbers of *Looker* creaked and squeaked and talked; the drumbeats echoed in the tiny space, becoming the ringing of a fearsome gong, the smashing of an iron-clad ram against an oaken door. He muttered, rubbing at his face, fumbling for the amulet round his neck. In time, the fever that had gripped him abated; he fell into a troubled sleep.

A strange thing happened. It seemed the stout sides of *Looker* grew clear as glass, so that through them he could see the waves and restless sky. The waves lapped and hissed, foam gleaming on their crests; through and between them a nightmare swam, trailing its complex body, holding up long skinned arms.

His shout, ringing through the ship, startled the rowers on their benches. He sat up convulsively, crashed his head with bruising force against a deck beam. Hands gripped his upper arms. He threshed, wildly; and intelligence came back to his eyes. He lay panting and sweating; and the Dancing Man smiled. 'The rain has eased, my Lord,' he said. 'We have made a good offing; will it please you to set a course?'

The greatship lay motionless in the water, steadied by her oars. Rand stared round him blinking, feeling the evening air move cool against his skin. Astern, dimly visible in the growing night, were the ragged mountains of Sealand. Ahead the edge of the cloud-pall loomed low across the water, seeming more solid than the land. The sun was setting, in a miles-long tumble of copper light; the sea was calm, and empty.

He climbed to the forward grating, stood clinging to the stempost. He ran a hand across his face, swallowed. 'South,' he said. 'South and west, Elgro. Take me to the Islands of Ghosts.'

Men scurried into *Looker*'s rigging. Her sail, with the great red Mark of the House, fell and bellied; ropes flew and cracked as the canvas was sheeted home. Water bubbled under her stem; and at last the long oars came dripping inboard. The breeze blew steadily; she gathered speed, on course for the Lands of the Dead.

Rand stayed on the lookout platform, feet apart, one hand gripping the stempost, the wind moving his hair. The sun sank crimson and angry, the mountains veiled themselves in dark. The rowers prepared their evening meal, stretched tired limbs, rolled beneath the benches. Once Elgro brought food for his lord, a bowl of rich-smelling soup; but Rand refused it, gently, turned his eyes back to the sea. Elgro, cursing under his breath, padded the way he had come; and overheard the seaman Dendril mutter to his friend Cultrinn Barehead. 'The nights are full of wonders,' he said, 'when the favoured of the Gods turn their hands to wetnursing. Who can tell; when we return to Sealand, perhaps we shall find all the nursemaids have become priests.'

Elgro tripped over the butt of an ill-stowed oar, flinging the contents of the bowl with some accuracy at the speaker's head. Dendril swore, clawing the scalding mess from his face and beard; when he could see again Elgro's vicelike fingers were gripping his shoulder, the pale eyes of the Dancing Man staring into his own.

'I heard you curse the spilled soup, friend, and that is all,' said Elgro softly. 'Which is as well for you ...'

The rigging of *Looker* creaked in the night wind. The rowers snored, wrapped in their sealskin cloaks; and the drum was quiet. For Rand, the great ram had ceased to beat.

Her eyes were blue; light, clear blue like the horizon of the summer sea. Her hair hung to her waist, pale as foam, garlanded with flowers and berries. Her hands were slender, her hips broad. She broke bread for him, laughing, at ease in her husband's Hall, while the kept-men of King Engor snored with the dogs on the rush-piled floor. The firelight flickered, bronzing her skin; her hand brushed his arm, cool and soft as a moth. She raised her cup to drink; his lips shaped her name, Deandi.

He moved in the hammock, muttering.

He had been Prince of the Crab, in that far-off time; a tall, inward, powerful young man, given to strange fits of brooding, to hunting and wandering by himself, to little company. On feast days, when mead and metheglin and beer ran like water, when the great Hall of the Crab shone red and smoky with the glare of torches and big-breasted girls pranced and jiggled on the table-tops, Rand sat apart, listening as like as not to the tales of fishermen. He had never been known to pay attention to any woman, much less seek her bed; so that his father the King put scorn on him, taunting his cowardice, calling him less than a man. He sent him finally to tend the crab pots for a month, saying they seemed to be his greatest love; and folk grinned behind their hands to see the Prince in the trews and apron of a fisherman. Rand performed his duties gravely, neither sad nor gay, rising early on misty mornings, sculling out in a borrowed coracle to haul at the rough black lines, fill his fish tubs with the wriggling catch. The warboats passed him, on their great way to and from Crab Gut. Sometimes their crews hailed him, much amused at his expense; but Rand merely smiled and waved back, balanced in the rocking chip of a boat, showing his even white teeth. He was without doubt a very strange young man, particularly for the son of a King.

Cedda, though powerful, was old, nearing his sixtieth year. His health was not what it had been; so that when he laid siege to the tower of his neighbour Fenrick many shook their heads, declaring it would be the last war he would wage. In that they were correct; for after a month Cedda, cursing feebly, was carried on a great litter from the scene of his endeavours, a marsh fever in his bones. He lived long enough to see the stronghold breached, its defenders sworded and its cattle driven to new fields; then he passed to the Gods, leaving Rand as patrimony a Kingdom and a blood feud, neither of which it seemed the young man much desired. For the halfbrother of Fenrick was Engor the Wolf; and the wife of Engor was Deandi, of the cool white arms.

He called her from the hammock, time and again, beating his fist on the cabin's wooden side.

He opened his eyes. Grey light seeped into the little space; in his mouth was a taste like blood. He swung his legs down, stood gripping a stanchion. *Looker* rolled slowly. The tension of the great truss thrilled in the woodwork; timber creaked and shifted, whispering.

He pulled a cloak round himself, unlatched the cabin door. He stepped into a shadowed world. The water lapped and bubbled; the sky was grey as new iron. The rowers clustered on their benches, still wrapped in their cloaks; the sail slapped idly at the mast. Astern, the land had vanished; *Looker* was a speck, in the great waste of the sea.

He walked forward, stood shivering a little and chafing his hands. A touch at his arm made him turn; he stared into the Dancing Man's long eyes, seeing the strange head with its frizz of hair, half red, half badger-grey. Elgro said, 'Good morning, my Lord.'

He looked back at the water, and smiled. He said, 'It's like the frozen world the priests talk about, where men are as old as mountains.' He leaned his back to the stempost, stared up at the tall mast struts. He let his eyes move down to the truss and the long ash poles that tightened it, the awnings rolled on their spars, the cramped complexity of the deck. He said, 'Elgro, how old is this ship?'

Elgro considered, running blunt fingers through his thatch. 'Your father built her, in his own youth,' he said, 'to fight a war. That was two seasons before the great flood, when the roof blew off the Tower and the sea monster came ashore. And five years before he took the throne himself, and made a war with Dendril and the sons of Erol of the Fen.' He shrugged. 'Many years, my Lord,' he said. 'Too many to count in the head.'

Rand nodded, slowly. His skull felt hollow and empty, as though he had been drinking Midsea wine. He closed his eyes; and the rocking of the vessel seemed intensified. He said, 'It all comes back. I dreamed again last night. Elgro, was it right? For such a little sin?'

The other pursed his lips. He said, 'I danced the ghosts away the night you were born. Don't ask me to answer for Gods.'

Rand frowned, as if at some effort of memory. He said, 'We stand close enough; yet we are so far apart. Sometimes it seems I stand apart from all men; even you, Elgro. As if there's no one in the entire world but me. At others … it's as if we were ghosts ourselves. Wailing and chattering, none able to hear the next.'

Elgro watched stolidly, not answering. A silence; then Rand sighed. He said, 'I remember the first time I sailed with my father. I was five. We went to Seal Hold, where Tenril had his Tower. Do you remember?'

The Dancing Man nodded.

Rand said, 'It was summer, so the sun never set. There was a big tent, on the shore. You could hear the shouting from it, and the dancers' bells. I sat and watched the seals out on the rocks. The light was strange. It was as if it came from inside things. From everything.'

Elgro waited.

Rand said, 'Later, the sea was blue. You could smell the land, miles out across the water. Like hay, and flowers. That was the night she came with me.'

Elgro said, 'My Lord, you must eat now.'

Rand shook his head, eyes vague. He said, 'She wanted to sail north, for ever. To see the Ice Giants, and find the Bear King's Hall.' He turned. He said, 'What do they say of these Ghost Islands? Tell me again.'

Elgro shrugged. 'They say the spirits fly there, after death. And that the cliffs are lined with wailing Gods; and Kings from old time thick as sprouting grass.'

Rand smiled again. 'And you?'

Elgro shook his head. 'I say most lands are much the same, my Lord. The sun sets and rises, the people wake and sleep. Some scratch the ground, some fish. Others make war.'

Rand said, 'And we do none of these.' He leaned his elbows on the greatship's curving side, stared at the sea. He said, 'When she came with me, it was all new again. I thought I could live for ever.'

Astern, the sun was like a blind bright eye. The rowers stretched, scratching themselves. Somebody laughed; a crewman swaggered to the ship's side to piddle in the sea. Rand straightened. He said, 'To have such nights, as make you pray for dawn. Elgro, dance one Ghost for me. I'd give you half the world.'

The wind rose, through the day. *Looker* made good speed, hissing her way south, trailing a wake of brilliant foam. Once mountains showed high and faint to the east; once the lookout called for a strange sail. The greatship stood well clear. By nightfall, the sea was empty again. The wind still blew from the north, strong and cold.

A medley of sounds roused Rand from sleep. Water boomed and seethed, timbers groaned, spray flew rattling across the planking overhead. *Looker* was in wild motion; rising, rolling, sliding headlong into the troughs of waves. He reeled his way on deck, stood clinging to a mast strut. Away to the west stretched a ragged coast. He screwed his eyes, shouted a question; at his side Egril nodded sombrely, the long hair flying round his face. He said, 'The Ghost Islands, my Lord. But we make no landfall here.'

By midday the weather had worsened. Squall after squall swept down; the greatship laboured, rolling lee scuppers under, pitching in a welter of white. Twice Egril ordered the crewmen aloft to take in sail. The wind yelled in the rigging, plucking at their backs as they climbed. *Looker* fled south, under a rag of canvas; and still the wind increased. The yard was braced round, and again; but the tide was setting now toward the coast, sweeping the vessel to leeward. Egril called for the oars to be unshipped; and a weary struggle began. Rand set himself to row with the rest, the Dancing Man at his side.

The drum throbbed, urgently; he flung his weight forward and back, hearing the hammer blows beneath the hull, feeling the planking shake under his feet. Blisters formed and broke on his palms; but the pain and labour were antidotes to memory. For a time, he felt nearly happy.

Through the day, the vessel held her own; but toward nightfall the wind, gusting as violently as ever, veered to the east. Matt and Egril held anxious counsel, clinging to the lee of the wildly tossing poop. To the south, dim in the fading light, stretched a long spit of land. Beyond, if *Looker* could weather the point, lay the deepwater channel separating the north and south Ghost Islands. Once through it a vessel might run for days; to the edge of the world, if need be.

The crewmen scurried again. The sail was furled, the great yard lowered inches at a time to the deck. The feat accomplished, *Looker* lay a little easier. Her truss was tautened; and the rowers bent themselves once more, wearily, to their task.

For an hour or more the issue stood in doubt. Across the sea, above the medley of other sounds, could be heard the boom of surf. The moon, gliding between ragged clouds, gave glimpses of close rock. *Looker* pitched and rolled, falling off into the troughs of waves, rising through a welter of spray. A surge carried away the sternpost, another half the shields of the weather rack; the cloths with which she had been draped had long since flogged themselves to tatters. In time, the roar to leeward seemed to grow less. The rowers stared, unwilling at first to believe their senses; and the land was falling away, ahead showed a waste of sparkling water. The greatship yawed again, swept sideways by the crabbing of an enormous tide.

The respite was brief. The wind blew now from dead astern; and the channel was narrowing. Once a cliff-wall reared to larboard, its top lost in darkness. Waves crashed at its base, seething upward two or three times the height of *Looker*'s mast. The vessel jarred and shook, caught in a yeasty boiling, before the undertow plucked her clear. The channel widened once more, narrowed again. The lookouts clung to prow and mast-head, eyes red-rimmed, glaring into darkness. The greatship rolled, water gurgling and sloshing in her hold. Her crew, bone-weary, lost all track of time; they groaned and muttered, praying for the dawn.

The sky lightened, by imperceptible degrees. The masthead became visible black against scarcely lighter grey, and the battered length of the deck. Men slumped across the oars, gasping with relief. Elgro, his hair caked and spiky, gripped his young master's shoulder and grinned; Egril, relaxing for the first time in many hours, permitted himself the ghost of a smile. The strange tide, still flowing, bore the greatship effortlessly to the west; it was as if the storm, blowing so long and violently, had piled up untold masses of water, which now must find release.

The voice of the masthead lookout was as thin and desperate as the cry of a bird.

Ahead, growing from the dark, stretched a long mounded spit. At its base the sea frothed round jagged teeth of rock; beyond, a beach of smooth grey sand sloped to low cliffs. The current, setting across the channel, drove the vessel down fast as a running horse.

A fresh ship, with a fresh crew, might have weathered the hazard; but the seconds that were lost while the rowers struggled with the oars were irreplaceable. The blades rose and flashed; but the pull was ragged. *Looker* surged sideways, recovered, wallowed again. Then it was too late; she swept forward helplessly, already among the rocks.

A bellow from Egril brought the blades down once more. In every place save one the reef thrust up grey and dripping, pounded by spray. Matt swung his weight at the steering oar; the greatship steadied, rushed for the gap.

For an instant, it seemed the manoeuvre would succeed. Black water slid past, bubbling; then the oars of the larboard rank struck rock. The butts swept forward across the packed thwarts; a concerted shriek, and the benches were empty. *Looker* slewed, struck with a pounding roar.

For Rand, it was as if time was slowed. The impact flung him headlong across the deck; he gripped a tangle of rigging while water surged round his waist. Something struck his thigh; an oar-shaft rose end over end, hung turning. The vessel rolled, pounded again. The truss flexed; and the long levers that tightened it spun from their crotches. He saw a man hurled backward, a bright mash where his face had been; then the bow planking rippled and burst.

The dissolution of the greatship was bizarre in its suddenness. Lacking the tension of the truss, the hull seemed to explode on the instant into its component fragments. The mast-spars, wrenched apart by the springing of the bulwarks, crashed into the sea. Oars, benches, gratings, hatch covers, tossed in confusion. A wave creamed forward, dotted with casks, planks and bobbing human heads. A bird wheeled, its voice lost in the noise of the surf; the wave licked the foot of the cliff, expended itself in a fading fringe of lace.

Water rushed into the lungs of the King. His ears roared; he rose flailing, sank again toward stillness. He was aware, vaguely, that hands gripped his arms; then his knees struck sand. He staggered forward, rolled full length, lay groaning and retching salt. Over him, chest heaving, stood the red and grey, bow-legged man who had snatched him from the Gods.

The survivors huddled moodily on the beach. Of forty men, just twenty-one remained; and of those Cultrinn crouched whimpering, glowing rags clutched to the splinters of an arm. Below the cliff Egril lay grey-faced and coughing. His sons stooped over him; at his side knelt Rand, and the Dancing Man.

Dendril walked slowly to the group. He stood feet spread, hand on the pommel of his sword. 'King of the Crab you are called,' he said, staring down contemptuously. 'But I see no King worthy of the name.' He raised his voice. 'I see a fisherman,' he said. 'Who fished too long and well, robbing among other things his neighbour's pots. Who in his arrogance denied the

Gods their due, and now expects us all to share his punishment. Half of us are gone already; shall those that are left die with him? Rather we will leave him here to mope, and I will lead you. His kept-man will bring him soup.'

Rand turned, shaking his head as if in pain; and Elgro stepped forward smiling. 'Now, Dendril,' he said. 'And all you others sworn to follow the Crab. A new tune has come into my head. I feel my feet begin to itch; will one of you partner me? For ghosts are hovering just above our heads; a sacrifice will soothe them.' He crouched, eyes raw-rimmed with salt, flexing his long arms. A silence; then one of the rowers, a burly blond-bearded man called Egrith, spoke up. 'Well you know I make no cause against you, Elgro,' he said. 'Also what vows I take, I keep. But this much is true. We sailed with neither mark nor sacrifice, which is contrary to any priestly law I ever heard; and see where it has led us.'

'Why, Egrith,' said the Dancing Man, 'I see indeed where it has led you; through a time of mortal peril to a most well-found beach, where we shall shortly dry our clothes and gather some food, and conduct ourselves like Sealanders rather than squabbling children. If you are dissatisfied with that you should perhaps walk back into the sea; or come with me and I will hold your head under water till your honour is appeased.'

Somebody laughed, abruptly; and the tension broke. Dendril, turning to rally the rest, saw his support already melting away. He clenched his fists angrily, and stalked off.

'This is well,' said Elgro after a pause. 'Now, all the rest of you; fetch wood to build a fire. And Egrith, climb the cliff a little way and watch. My spirits tell me there are many tribes in this land, not all of them friendly.'

The party set to work. Timber from the wreck abounded; sparks were coaxed from flint and steel, a blaze kindled in the shelter of the rocks. An iron pot had been salvaged from the water; and Matt, wading out, secured a cask of salt meat and another of Sealand herrings. They lolled on the beach more cheerfully while their sealskin cloaks, propped on sticks round the warmth, steamed and stank. An hour passed; then Galbritt and Ensor called from below the cliff. Rand, hurrying to them, saw the Shipmaster raise himself. Twice he made to speak, extending his arm; then the coughing shook him again. He fell back, eyes fixed and blank. Blood showed between his teeth, and he was dead.

'This too was well,' said Elgro quietly. 'Now, we will make a cairn here for him. He can lie in sight of the sea; and no fox or bird will visit him, annoying his sleep. Also I will dance the strongest dance I know, so his rest will be the sweeter.' He turned, quickly, to the sons. 'Will you be satisfied?'

They stood frowning, pulling at their lips; and Galbritt, the elder, answered. 'He spoke strangely, before he died,' he said. 'We didn't understand him. Something there was of witchcraft, and a Fairy woman who entranced the King; but he called for no blood in vengeance. We shall be satisfied.'

The Sealanders scurried again. A mound of rocks was raised above the Shipmaster, twenty feet or more long and six feet high. At its head they set the great stempost of *Looker*, which the waves had washed up on the beach. Elgro, inspecting the work, pronounced it satisfactory. He danced a wild, stamping song, forward and back across the How; when it was done he walked to Rand, who stood as ever a little apart, his chin sunk on his chest. 'Now, my Lord,' he said softly. 'We are twenty strong, and in better temper than before; though one of us, it is certain, would be best elsewhere.' He jerked his head to where Dendril sat scowling by his injured friend, and whetted a knife significantly on his palm.

Rand stared, and shook his head. 'Elgro,' he said, 'you know the vow I took. I have spilled blood enough; now more lives are on my head. Let it be.' He pulled his cloak round him, looked at the sea. 'We will leave this place,' he said. 'Let the men take what they can carry, from the wreck; it may be some time before we can find shelter.'

The party wound upward slowly, Rand leading with the sons of Egril. Matt followed, taciturn as ever; then came the rowers, well hung about with weapons, some with bulky packs on their backs. In the rear Cultrinn, white-faced and moaning, was half carried, half dragged up the steep cliff path.

The sun was high by the time they reached the crest. Behind them the sea stretched into distance, calm now and mockingly blue; to the south the land ran broken and rolling, hill after hill dotted with bracken and carpeted with heather. No smoke rose, anywhere; there were no sounds, no signs of human habitation.

Rand shaded his eyes, uncertainly. 'Elgro, I lean on your counsel again,' he said. 'You know my need; which way shall I go?'

Elgro scowled. 'I know the ways of ghosts to some extent,' he said. 'I dance for life, and death. But your business is with the Gods. For that you need the priests we left behind.'

Rand glanced at him sharply, and shrugged. 'In that case,' he said, 'one way is as good as the next.' He struck out across the short turf, head bowed, not looking back. The Sealanders followed, in a straggling line.

At midday they rested in a sheltered hollow, eating a little of the food they had brought with them. Rand, now, was impatient to be gone. They rose without undue complaint, and once more shouldered their loads.

The sun dropped toward the west. Their shadows lengthened; and still the empty hills marched to either side. The sky was reddening when they came on a curious sight. At the crest of a sweep of grassland was set a little stone hut, no more than waist high. Round it at a distance of twenty paces or so stood a circle of upright stones. The wind had dropped, through the day; now no leaf stirred. The place was utterly still.

Elgro approached sniffing like a dog, as was his custom when puzzled or suspicious. 'This place stinks of Gods,' he said finally. 'So some sort of folk live in these hills.' He walked forward carefully, setting his feet in line, squatted at the entrance to the shrine. He stared a while; then straightened, with a short laugh. 'A fine spirit,' he said. 'If he is the greatest the land can offer, I think we shall come to no harm.'

Rand, stooping, made out an image in the shadows. Eyes of polished stone winked at him; above were two tall ears. He shook his head, frowning. Wild and ragged though the carving was, the figure was undoubtedly a hare.

'Now,' said Elgro, 'people who worship hares must be very odd folk to meet.'

At Rand's side, Galbritt touched his arm. He drew, with a scrape of steel.

Facing them some twenty paces off, where a moment before had been empty heather, was a little group of men. They were short, barely reaching to the shoulders of the Sealanders, but sturdy and powerfully built. They carried light spears, no thicker at the tips than twigs; and three or four held drawn bows.

The Sealanders bunched, muttering; but Rand raised an arm. He walked forward slowly, palms spread. 'We are sailors, shipwrecked on your coast,' he said. 'We come in peace, desiring only shelter for the night. Also one of us is very sick. If your priests can bring him to health, we will pay with gold.'

The strangers stared, stolidly; then one, who seemed to be their leader, grunted. 'Those are very peaceful swords I see in your folk's hands,' he said. 'And peaceful axes and spears. Also you have defiled a holy place, the punishment for which is death.'

Rand said mildly, 'We meant no harm; we approached not knowing it was the house of a God. Show us how he will best be pleased, and we will make an atonement. Also I will sit at your fire and talk, for I see you are an old folk, and very wise.'

The strangers grunted together; then the leader turned back. 'Sealanders seeking peace are wonderful folk,' he said. 'Yesterday at noon the sun turned cold, hanging the land with icicles. Tonight, undoubtedly, the moon will become green.'

Rand turned. He said, 'Elgro, tell them to put their swords away.'

The weapons were sheathed, unwillingly. The little people jabbered once more among themselves; in time it seemed a decision was reached. The bows were lowered; and a guard formed up, at a circumspect distance from the Sealanders. The party moved on, following a well-trodden track across the shoulder of the hill.

The village they eventually reached was curious in the extreme. There were no fine buildings, no Chief's hut or High Priest's Lodge; in fact from a distance no dwellings were visible at all, so well did the low roofs, overgrown with bracken and turf, blend with the valley floor on which they stood. Smoke rose here and there; at the hut doorways as they passed, women with babies at their hips stood staring sullenly. All were unclothed to the waist, and as dumpy and unlovely as their menfolk.

There was a council hut of sorts; a long, low structure, as overgrown as the rest. Outside it the Sealanders waited suspiciously, it seemed an interminable time. Within, voices could be heard raised in argument. Finally their guide reappeared. 'I, who am called Magro, bid you welcome,' he said importantly. 'Our God, who is very wise, has evidently sent you to be his guests and keep him company. In one week's time, we hold his high festival. Then you will worship him; and your promise will be fulfilled.'

He led the way to a hut taller and longer than the rest, set a little apart on a mound overlooking the shallow stream that supplied the place with water. 'Here you will rest,' he said. 'Food will be brought you, and drink; but we use no skill in healing. I will speak of your friend to the Fleet One; after that, if he dies it is the God's own will.'

Soup of a sort was brought, and jugs of flat, stale-smelling beer. Elgro, sitting moodily at the doorway of the hut, took a mouthful and spat it at the grass. 'Well, my King,' he said, 'I hope your penance has so far brought you joy. It would seem to have cost us a ship and half a company, and very nearly our lives into the bargain; and I think others of us will not see Crab Gut again. For my part, I would trade heartsearching for one mouthful of Sealand mead, drunk at ease in our own Hall, with folk we can trust at our backs and within sound of the sea.'

Rand made no answer; just jabbed at the turf with a pointed stick, and frowned.

Later that night they sought out Magro in his hut. The little chief sat swigging beer in front of a smoky fire, surrounded by his women. He scowled as the Sealanders entered, greeting them with a belch; but Rand squatted beside him in the ashes humbly enough. 'Here is gold,' he said, 'for my people are grateful. Also a great treasure; a magic stone, by which we cross the sea. It points always to our homeland, wishing to fly back across the water.'

The chief took the needle on its slender thread, glanced at it incuriously and tossed it aside. 'The gold we will keep,' he said. 'Magic stones are of no particular use. We are an old people, too wise to trouble with toys. It can hang from the neck of one of our babies, or a woman.'

At Rand's side, Elgro hissed like a snake. The Prince laid a hand on his arm. 'First I will tell you how we were shipwrecked,' he said. 'We sailed from Sealand with peace-cloths on our sides; for I had heard there are many Gods in this country. I am a King in my own land; this is my Dancing Man, a friend of ghosts. We came for counsel.'

'Then you are fools,' said the little man frankly. 'As befits Sealanders, and pirates. There are such Gods, as I know very well; but their land lies to the south, many days' journey away. You will not live to reach it; if you do, it will be the worse for you.' He shouted, harshly; and more beer was brought. 'Drink,' he said. 'We are kindly people, returning good for evil; whatever you may or may not have heard.'

Later he condescended to discuss the subject of Gods.

'Once there were many Gods, and ghosts too,' he said. 'Some lived in rocks, some in trees and streams, some in hollows in the ground. Then we were one people throughout the islands; living in peace, harming no man, remembering the wisdom of the Giants.' He cleared his nose, coarsely. 'Then the Horse Warriors came,' he said. 'From where, nobody can tell. They took the North Land; our cities, which were wonderful, were destroyed. Then they came here. Our cities were destroyed. Some of us fled, to where the pasture is thin and the ground bad for the plough. With us we brought one God, the oldest and strongest of all.' He held up the figurine that hung round his neck, and burst into a singsong chant. 'The Hare fights no man, being fleet and wise,' he said. 'The Hare strikes down his enemies, being cunning in the night. The Hare is Lord of the hills, and the high pastures by the sea.'

He reapplied himself to the beer. 'Now the Sealanders come in their turn,' he said. 'They fight the Horse Warriors on land, and harry their ships. Like them, they burn and kill. You, who are Sealanders, we have no cause to love. Yet we have taken you in, and sheltered you. Here you will remain. In one week, it is the festival of our God. You will worship him.'

Rand frowned, drawing with a finger in the ashes. 'Chief,' he said, 'how will this be?'

But Magro merely belched again, and shrugged. 'In your own way,' he said, 'you will worship him.'

Later Elgro spoke bitterly, in the darkness of the communal hut. 'With regard to wisdom,' he said, 'I should have taken that sawn-off little viper's neck between my fingers, to teach him if nothing else the wisdom of civility.'

Rand lay wide-eyed, staring into the blackness. 'I came for peace, not killing, Elgro,' he said. 'For peace.'

Elgro snorted. 'Your desire for peace, I have no doubt, will be fulfilled,' he said. 'For it will end in the deaths of us all.'

Rand turned, crackling the bracken bed. He lay a long time, hearing the steady breathing of the rowers, the whimpering of the wounded man. Toward dawn, the sounds ceased. In the morning light they saw the Hare had made his answer; Cultrinn was dead.

In the days that followed, they learned the ways of Magro's folk and their God. His shrines abounded, dotted everywhere about the surrounding hills. From hollowed trees, from caves, from the little huts, the tiny mask winked and glinted at the light. He was fleet, and weak, and watchful; and he owned the land.

On the fourth morning people from the surrounding countryside began flocking into the little moss-grown town. There was a great coming and going, a clattering and splashing by the brook. Dogs barked, women chattered, children yelled. Tents sprang up by the score, rough affairs of hides slung over bending willow poles. Stacks of fuel were cut and transported; and a vast fire built, on the outskirts of the village. Elgro viewed the proceedings with growing distrust. 'As to this business of worship,' he said, 'it seems to me we have enough Gods already. Also the way of the thing has not been made clear enough for my taste. Some modes of adoration can be less than comfortable; as you, my Lord, are very well aware.'

But Rand shook his head. 'These are hospitable folk,' he said. 'Their manners are not all that could be desired, but they have offered us no harm. We should be churlish to leave now, or refuse to see their God-rites. Besides,' – he smiled, gently – 'a Dancing Man of Sealand has little to fear, surely, from a Hare.'

Elgro scowled, and shrugged; but for the remainder of the day, and the day that followed, he went conspicuously well armed.

By the fifth morning, the tents sprawled to the valley rim; and by nightfall a strange procession had begun. Everywhere, the hare images were gathered from their niches. More arrived and more, each propped in a litter of cloth and willow poles, in charge of a chanting group of men with torches and flutes. The fire was lit; round it clustered a growing congregation, a sea of alert ears, unblinking yellow eyes. Drums set up a pounding; beer jugs were passed more and more freely, and the dancing began. Priests, naked save for furred headdresses, whirled and shrieked; chanting girls, the hare-symbol swinging between their breasts, wound in and out among the seated people, scattering drops of blood and honey.

The noise redoubled. Heat from the fire beat back; and Rand felt his own head begin to throb. The ram was swinging again; he grabbed for beer, gulping eagerly, anxious for oblivion. Sweat burst out on his body; the dancers swayed, surging forward and back, hair flying, faces orange-lit by the flames. Then it seemed the whole world spun. He rose with a cry; plunged headlong, barely felt the hands that dragged him to the hut. He sprawled across the bed, shaking and groaning, the noise still in his ears like a distant sea. In time the sounds receded. The dance went on all night, till earliest dawn; but he was far away.

They crowned him King, in the great Hall of the Crab, setting him on the painted wooden throne. A day and night he sat, his father's sword across his knees, while round him the drinking and feasting went on. The greatships creaked and tossed, clustering in the harbour and along the wharves of Crab Gut; on the hill the Tower blazed with light, where Rand the Solitary held open house for all the world. To him came messengers from every court of Sealand; from Seal Hold to the Blue Fen, Orm Rock to the scattered Lakes of the Bear. Each swore friendship in the ancient way, with blood and salt; he received them smiling, giving a golden ring to every man. But as the night wore on his eyes turned more and more to the windows set beneath the high roof-eaves. Vat after vat was broached, and jar after jar of Midsea wine; and still the voice he wanted most to hear was silent.

They came with the dawn; a dozen grim-faced men, stamping up from the harbour to pound at the stockade gates. Beer was sent for and meat, the King's advisers summoned or shaken rudely from their snoring. He received the messengers in state, seated with Elgro and Ranna the High Priest. They strode in haughtily enough, armour jangling, glancing to neither left nor right; and the Staff of the Wolf was planted in Cedda's Hall.

For a further day and night the King withdrew himself, ordering the strangers cared for with all courtesy. He sat in his high chamber, watching the sun patterns move on the rug-hung walls, hearing the clank of milkpails from the sheds, the shouts of children at play. At length his decision was reached, and the Council reconvened.

The messengers chose to hear him fully armed, each with a red war-lanyard on his belt. Hubbub rose, in the Hall; the King stilled it, holding up his hands. 'Let us be patient,' he said. 'Wrong has been done; blood will not wash out blood. Now, let our friends approach.'

He stared at each man thoughtfully before he went on. 'Hear me well,' he said, 'and take back careful word to your master. Fenrick put shame on my father, Cedda King, claiming certain grazing lands, and rights of chase in others owned by the Crab. For this we went to war, and Fenrick's Tower was breached. With Engor we made no quarrel; nor do we seek one now. Yet a blood price was incurred, which the Wolf has every right to claim.'

Muttering rose again; once more, he stilled it. 'The Tower of Fenrick we keep, by right of conquest,' he said. 'This by all Sealand laws is just. Also those of his lands adjoining ours, from the Tower to Steffa's Rock. Let a line be drawn between these points, and clearly marked with posts. The lands beyond, to his own borders, we give to our brother Engor. Let his people possess them in peace. The cattle taken I cannot return, for they are spoils of war. But for my part ...'

Uproar, in the hall. He rose; and by degrees it stilled.

'For my own part,' he said, 'I give my father's spoil. The cloth from the Yellow Lands, the Midsea wine; the chest of spices, and eight bars of gold. Also the weapons from the armoury, both axes and swords; and the great-ship *Seasnake*, with her shields and fittings of war. This I will put in writing for your King. The lesser things you may take with you when you go; we will prepare *Seasnake* for her voyage, and provision her for one week at sea. If your master will send a crew to man her, it will be honourably received.' He smiled down at the messengers. He said, 'Will this be pleasing to King Engor?'

They looked at each other in stunned silence, and shrugged.

Later, from the rampart walk, the Dancing Man watched the last of the waggons jolt down toward the harbour. Then he turned, showing his teeth. 'My Lord,' he said, 'remember what I say. This day's work will be paid for many times, in blood.'

Rand shook his head, frowning. 'Elgro,' he said, 'can we not live in peace? The sun is free for all; and the mountains, the green things in the spring, fish in the sea. I have put my hand out, which no King before me did. Let us enjoy these things, while we can. The days are short enough, for all of us; and darken with shadows, whether we will or no.'

Elgro shrugged and turned away, muttering.

For Rand's people, they were troubled times; for word of the giftmaking spread, from the southern marshes to the bleakest northern Tower, where the aurora flickers and the Ice Folk come to trade. Everywhere men shook their heads, and solemnly agreed the King of the Crab was mad. But mad folk who are rich make useful friends; and delegation after delegation presented itself at the Tower, armed with demands for this and that. Sometimes Rand chided them and sent them packing; but usually, he gave. He sent tapestries to the Prince of White Bear Lake, gold to Ulm of the Fishgard, a dancing woman to the Lord of the Nine Isles. Meanwhile, the boundary stakes were planted. Engor occupied the ceded lands, with a conspicuous show of force. Two days later news was brought that the fence was down, the standard of the Wolf advanced to the very edge of Rand's territory. He frowned, but made no move against his neighbour.

Warboats took to sailing Crab Gut in broad daylight, robbing the fishermen of their catch, adding insults to the injury of theft. Rand soothed his people's indignation, from his own pocket. Armed strangers appeared on the pastures of the Crab, frightening the field-thralls from their work, stealing cattle, trampling the standing grain. To their Kings, Rand sent remonstrances couched in the mildest terms; and more gifts, to ensure the peace he craved. In this way the uneasy summer passed. Autumn gales lashed the coasts of Sealand; and for a time, the Kingdoms were quiet.

Spring brought the disaster Elgro had foretold. For days, while the sun grew slowly in strength, news came in of raids and pillagings, the murder of peasants, burning of outlying huts. Engor, parading Rand's boundaries with all his strength, made no secret of a boast that before another winter he himself would sit in the Hall of the Crab. Rand spent a night in noisy council. Ranna spoke bitterly and at length; Elgro chided; Egril stamped the floor of the Hall, swearing before he stomached further insult he would sell his services to a foreign lord. Through it all, Rand remained immoveable. Wolfhold held all he found dear; for Deandi's sake, he would make no war with Engor.

The people muttered, darkly. There was talk of defiance, of rebellion; even, at the end, of the raising of a new King. Then one morning matters came to a head. A band of refugees presented itself at Rand's gate; women and some men, bloodied and in fear of their lives. The tale they told, of torture and killing and rape, sent Rand stumbling grey-faced to his room, calling for Elgro and a scribe. An ultimatum was sent out by the hand of a Midsea trader, a swarthy little man who it seemed valued gold more than he feared for his life. The village by Crab Gut settled uneasily to wait its answer.

It wasn't long in coming; for Engor had camped a bare dozen miles from the fortress of his enemy. A shout was raised that very night; and a grim-faced Elgro summoned the King from his room. Rand rose without a word, and followed; down the winding wooden steps, across the Hall to the stockade.

Round the great gates stood it seemed all the people of the town. The crowd opened silently, for the King to pass. He stood staring, the wind moving his hair and cloak, while his skin turned white as salt-crusted rock.

At the gates stood a cart, drawn by a span of bony oxen. On it had been erected a stout wooden post. The thing bound to it was reddened from head to foot. Its tunic, tied up soddenly above the waist, displayed the ruined groin. The eyes of the messenger glared appalled above a mask of flesh. From the mask the manhood swung, and dripped.

Drums beat, in every village of the Crab. Fires burned, and torches; by their light men polished armour, honed axes and swords. The messages flew, to Orm Rock and White Bear Lake and the satrapies that clustered round Long Fen. Fighting ships rode at Crab Key, patrolled the mouth of the Gut. The land seethed, like a boiling pot. Day and night, the soldiers streamed in; and finally, Rand was ready. He showed himself to his people; and folk marvelled, seeing Cedda come again in youthful glory. Then the gates creaked back, the King and his bodyguard rode through. Behind them, an army streamed north to war.

The din, the shouting and crack of whips, creak and rumble of wheels, faded. His shoulder was shaken, and again. He groaned, rolled over, tried to stand.

Grey light was in the sky. Outside the hut, in silence, stood the Sealanders, drawn swords in their hands. Six of them would not rise again; they lay stark in the dawn, their eyes rolled up beneath the lids. Beside them was the body of a priest. In his hand he still gripped a furry paw, its claws dipped in some brownish substance. Long scratches on the faces of the dead showed where the Hare had taken his revenge.

Round them, the village slept.

'Now,' said Elgro, 'I hope your thirst for wisdom is slaked, my Lord. Before we leave, we will show some skills of our own. I will speak with this little Chief.'

In Rand's brain the drugged fumes of the beer still spun. He stared round him, at the dull eyes and trembling hands, and shook his head. He said bitterly, 'Do that and we are all dead, Elgro. All we can save is our lives.'

The little party straggled grimly, in the growing light. No further words were spoken till the valley was behind them. By midday they were deep among the hills. For an hour or more clouds had been thickening on the higher slopes; now they crept lower, bringing a thin, chilling rain.

The mist saved them. Twice they heard the voices of pursuers below them; twice the shouts, and jangling of weapons and harness, passed them by. That night they sprawled beneath an overhanging rock, too weary to seek proper shelter. At dawn some sixth sense roused the Dancing Man. He rose quietly, narrowing his eyes. One place in the heather was empty; Dendril had gone.

The weather worsened. The rain fell steadily, day after day. Above and to every side sounded the roar of waterfalls, invisible in the driving mist. The Sealanders moved south blindly, living as best they could on stream fish, eggs of wild birds. They would have starved; but on the fourth morning they came on the ruins of a town.

It had been of considerable extent. They wandered uneasily along paved, grass-grown streets, between shells of ragged stone. Watchtowers reared gaunt and desolate, the dim sky showing through their windows; to either side, stretching into the mist, ran a great ditch and mound, once topped by a palisade of sharpened stakes. It was the finest and highest fortification they had seen; but like the city it had been overthrown. More watchtowers had stood at intervals along it; now their stones lay tumbled and fire-blackened on the grass.

On the outskirts of the place Egrith made a discovery; a patch of curious fleshy-stemmed plants, tubers growing thickly round their roots. Raw, the things had a sweetish, earthy taste; cooked, they were better. A fire was coaxed into life in one of the roofless buildings; the Sealanders sat all day boiling pan after pan of the strange earth-fruits, burning fingers and mouths in their haste to gulp the things down. Their hunger appeased, they stoked the fire again, making some shift to dry their clothes. They passed an uneasy night in the ruins, starting at the slightest sounds; the splash and drip of water, calls of night-flying birds. The desolate place seemed thronged with ghosts; even the Dancing Man sat frowning, a drawn sword by his side, a spear laid ready to hand.

Morning brought a cheering gleam of sunlight. They gathered the last of the tubers, cramming what they couldn't eat into their packs. At last it seemed their luck was changing; for they were leaving the hills. Beyond the ruins the land swept down to a great green plain. Along the horizon ran a strange dusky band; beyond, very sharp and clear, peaks jutted into the sky, laced with the rolling blue and silver of clouds. The sight further heartened them; and Elgro smiled, gripping Rand's arm. 'There, my Lord,' he said, pointing, 'is as fine a place as I have seen, to search for Gods.'

They started down, in good spirits; but the promise of the morning was not sustained. Before they had cleared the hills, clouds were once more climbing to obscure the sun. The distant mountains vanished; and rain began to fall, as heavily as before. They plodded on dourly, pausing once to eat. Shortly after Matt, who was leading, stopped and pointed. Rand joined him, and Egrith and the Dancing Man. They stood staring, frowning up at the obstruction that blocked their path.

It looked like nothing so much as the crest of a vast, frozen wave, twenty feet or more in height and as black and shiny as polished jet. It seemed the land sloped up to the lip of the bluff; in places too the rock of which it was composed overhung slightly, heightening the curious impression. Elgro, approaching carefully, struck with his spear-tip; gently at first, then harder. Chips flew; he picked one up, stood turning it in his palm. Its edges were sharp as the blade of a knife.

The party moved to the right, seeking a way round or over the obstacle. A mile or so farther on, the cliff edge was split by a series of deep cracks. They climbed, carefully, one of the little ravines so formed, stood once more staring. In every direction save the one from which they had come the rock lay bare and glittering. No tree grew, no blade of grass; the wind, rushing across the emptiness, made a thin, persistent moan. Stretching into distance were more of the curious wave-like forms, like ripples on a gigantic pond, each crest the height of a man. It was as if the land itself had burned, flowing outward from some focus of unspeakable heat.

Rand pushed the wet hair from his eyes and frowned. He said slowly, 'The Hare King told me, there were once Giants. Elgro, could this be?'

The Dancing Man pulled a face. 'That I do not know,' he said. 'But if this was their work, I shouldn't have cared to meet them.'

The party trudged south, through the grey void of the still-falling rain.

The strange place was vaster in extent than they had realized. Water had collected in every dip and hollow of the rock; they splashed knee-deep through lake after lake, some of them scores of paces wide. Darkness overtook them far from shelter. Lacking fuel, they could build no fire; they ate the remainder of the tubers raw, huddled miserably in the lee of one of the curious ridges. Round them the wind howled and zipped like an entire legion of spirits.

The rain eased toward morning. The sun climbed blind and red, throwing long spiky shadows across the rock. To the south rose the peaks they had struggled to reach. They drank a little water from the pools, squeezed out their cloaks as best they could and staggered on.

The hours that followed were torture of a different kind. The sun, strengthening, brought steam boiling from the rocks; the strange landscape blurred and shook, hazed with vapour. Also the ridges to the south were steeper than any they had seen. The land rose in swell after swell, each terminating in a vicious, jagged little cliff. They detoured and backtracked wearily, stumbling and skidding, gashing hands and knees on the sharp rock. The place, most certainly, was cursed; for strive as they might, the hills drew no closer.

It was past midday before they reached the final crest; and another hour before a safe descent was discovered. They ran and leaped the last few yards, rolled gasping in unbelievable grass. They lay a time seeing the high rock they had quitted cut the sky like an edge of night; then Elgro snorted disgustedly, and delivered his opinion. 'Giants I cannot speak of, or Gods,' he said. 'But I have had some small experience of demons. And demons it was beyond a doubt that shaped that place, to be their own.'

Beyond their resting place a track led through a little wood. Bluebells hazed the grass. It was as if the tree boles rose from a vivid lake; between them shone the sunlit flank of a hill. They climbed, slowly. At the crest they turned, saw the place they had left lie black and shimmering like a miles-long scab of pitch.

That night they came on a scattered flock of sheep, grazing untended at the head of a tree-filled valley. At the base of a rocky outcrop showed the mouths of several caves. They built a fire in the largest, slept comfortably for the first time in weeks, and with full bellies.

Elgro roused his master early next morning. Rand sat up, grunting and rubbing his face. Outside the cave mouth, sun-light dazzled through a screen of leaves. The morning was golden, and still. Somewhere a bird piped; close at hand was the tinkle of running water. Rand turned, frowning; and the Dancing Man tilted his head, laid a finger to his lips. He heard it then, distant but clear; a high fluting, mixed with the steady thudding of a drum.

The others were already awake; they stood chafing their hands and frowning. The noise faded, eddied closer. The Dancing Man ducked under the cave mouth, cautiously parted the bushes. He stiffened then and wriggled back, beckoning the others to join him.

Along the valley bottom moved an odd procession. First came the musicians, leaping and gyrating; then a little knot of white-robed men; then a cart drawn by oxen, an elegant affair with slender gilded wheels. On it, bound upright to a post, stood a black-haired, bare-legged girl in a short yellow tunic. She was wrenching at the cords that held her, trying to break free. Cymbal men followed, and more dancers and priests; bringing up the rear was a procession of folk in multicoloured trews and tunics, for the most part carrying bows or spears.

The Sealanders watched in silence. The procession passed not much more than a stone's throw away, moved on up the little coombe. At the head of the valley the track climbed steeply. The cart was halted, the girl released. She was bundled roughly forward; and the whole group of people vanished from sight over the crest.

Rand, staring, met Elgro's puzzled frown. He ran stooping, along the high side of the valley, darting cautiously from rock to rock. The others followed, keeping below the skyline.

Beyond the ridge the land sloped with unexpected steepness. Hills ringed the horizon, blue and grand; closer, immediately below their vantage point, was a great tongue-shaped depression, its sides thickly overgrown. In it a lake lay black and utterly still.

The procession was once more visible, descending the last few yards of a rocky path. At the water's edge grew a stout, gnarled tree. The strangers clustered round it, with much shouting and gesticulating. A wait; and horns blew across the water, their voices clear and glittering. The party began to retreat, it seemed with more haste than dignity; behind them, tethered at the lake edge, they left the girl. The cart was turned, the oxen prodded into a trot; and the procession headed back the way it had come, vanishing finally between the sloping shoulders of the hills.

Elgro watched it go, and shrugged. 'This,' he said, 'is extremely odd. Either these folk are mad, which seems most likely, or my eyes have been deceiving me.' He rose; and there drifted from below a single piercing cry.

'Eyes and ears both,' said Elgro dryly. 'Now that I cannot have. *My Lord …*'

He was too late. Rand had risen without a word, set off down the hillside at a fast run. Elgro swore his loudest and loped in pursuit, waving to the rest to follow.

By the time they gained the lip of the depression their leader was halfway to the water, running with great leaps. Elgro pulled up, panting; and Matt gripped his shoulder, pointed silently. Across the loch, speeding toward the opposite bank, ran a smooth vee-shaped ripple. For an instant, a pale bulk might have showed behind it; then it was gone. The water swirled, and was still again.

Elgro tackled the descent, still cursing. When he reached the tree, Rand had already slashed through the cords. The girl sagged forward, knee-deep in water; the Dancing Man caught her roughly, pulled her to the bank.

'What is your tribe?' he demanded. 'This is my Lord Rand, a King of Sealand. What is this place called?'

She could only shake, and whimper.

Galbritt said, 'Something was in the fjord.'

They stared at the water, gripping their sword hilts. Orms were not unknown in Sealand. Egrith said apprehensively, 'Perhaps we should have left her where she was. The monster will be angry.'

Elgro snorted derisively. He said, 'The water horse eats no maiden's flesh. Salmon he will take in season, and browse among the deep weed. These people are fools. In any case, better use can be made of this.' He shoved the girl's kilt up with his foot, stared appraisingly, then hauled her to her feet. He said, 'To ease a sickness, we would all risk much.'

Galbritt said, frowning, 'What sickness, Dancing Man?'

Elgro inclined his head, and grinned. He said beneath his breath, 'The sickness of our Lord the King.'

From above came a high-pitched shout. Elgro jerked his head up; and something bright and rushing flicked past his eyes. A thud; and Galbritt staggered. He said, 'Our Lord the King.' Then he dropped to his knees, sagged forward. From his neck protruded six inches of gaily-feathered shaft.

Elgro took his captive's wrist, and ran. Missiles hummed past him. Another man flung his arms up with a shriek, toppled into the lake.

Ahead, the valley side steepened. A great rock thrust out above the water. The Dancing Man ducked underneath, Rand at his elbow. A yell from behind; the Sealanders turned, stared back appalled.

The figure, howling defiance, was running swiftly up the steep path to where a fringe of heads above the valley rim marked the attacks. They saw an arrow strike it, and another. It staggered; and a volley of shafts hissed down the cliff. Ensor rolled, fell headlong. The body struck the sloping ground behind the path, rolled again with a flailing of arms and legs, lay still. Silence fell; and Egrith groaned, beating his fists on rock. 'King Rand,' he said, 'you have killed us all.'

The path was filling now with jostling men. Thirty or forty were visible, and others still crowding to the brink. The Sealanders backed, frowning; and Rand exclaimed. Beneath the overhang, what had seemed a dense shadow was in fact the mouth of a considerable cave. He rolled sideways, wriggled; they heard him thump down inside. His voice called again, hollowly, from the ground.

Elgro followed, shoving the girl ahead of him. The others crowded after, straightened staring. They were in the shaft of a ragged tunnel. It sloped down steeply, into blackness. Somewhere close could be heard the splashing of water.

There were voices at the cave mouth. They edged back instinctively, further into the dark. The voices jabbered excitedly. A spear glanced from the rock wall; but none of the pursuers made to enter.

The girl was dragging back, desperately. Elgro shook her, like a dog with a rat. 'Be still, you little idiot,' he said. 'Or I shall put my sword into you.'

Rand frowned behind him at the darkness. He said, 'Elgro, where could this lead?'

Elgro shook his victim again. He said, 'To all the Hells, for all I know.'

Egrith said shakily, 'I would not care to go down into Hell.'

Elgro nodded at the cave mouth. 'Go back the way you came then,' he said, 'and take the quicker route.' He ducked into the gloom, towing the girl behind him.

The passage wound and twisted, in places barely an armspan wide. Fifty paces from the entrance the darkness was complete; the air was filled with a sharp, fishy stench that caught Rand's throat, making him cough and gag. The girl moaned, wordlessly.

Elgro grunted, prodding with a spear tip, setting each foot carefully. For a while the rock trended steeply down in blackness; then the passage widened. He straightened, and blinked. From somewhere ahead came ghostly grey light.

The light increased. They emerged in a little round chamber, like a room hewn from stone. In the far wall the tunnel plunged down again, gaping like a throat; above, a shaft rose to a circle of pale sky. Rand, staring up, saw translucent fronds of bracken; as he watched, the lip was eclipsed by a sailing edge of white. He said, 'Elgro, we could climb.'

The Dancing Man frowned, nostrils dilated. He said, 'Listen.'

At first there was nothing but the omnipresent splash and drip of water. Then they heard a far-off gurgling, ending in a noise like a great sucking gasp. It came again; and with it a slithering and rasping, as of some huge weight dragging itself over rock. The girl screamed. In the enclosed space, the sound was deafening.

Elgro grabbed Rand's elbow. He said urgently, 'Up …'

A yard or more above the cavern floor ran a rock ledge, green with algae. The party scrambled hastily, stood tensed on the insecure footing; and Rand, staring, saw the opposing tunnel fill and bulge. A pale mass rose into the chamber, grew a great glistening tip that waved and quested. He saw liver-coloured rings of muscle, a raw mouth that opened, snapped.

Instantly the place was full of din. The girl cried out again, scrabbling at him. Rubble showered, crashing; Egrith, brushed from his perch, vanished with a despairing shout. The mass swelled, ballooning to fill the chamber; and Elgro raised his sword double-handed, struck.

The effect was appalling. The keen blade, with all the Dancing Man's strength behind it, sheared cleanly through the horror. The body-tip fell, mouth still gaping. The monster writhed, geysering foam and blood; then the whole great bulk subsided. The thing extended itself, weaving in blind pain; and as slowly began to stream past, yard after yard, groping into the tunnel they had quitted. They stared down, eyes bulging, and saw it clearly for what it was. It was obscene, gigantic; and it was a worm.

Egrith lay still at the bottom of the pit. Elgro, his face contorted, stepped down, turned the body with the butt of a spear. What flesh the slime had touched was white and scalded, as if by boiling water; the head lolled grotesquely to one side. The Dancing Man stared up. He said, 'He broke his neck.'

Rand turned to the rock wall, shuddering, and began to climb.

That night as they lay in the heather the Dancing Man crawled to where the girl was huddled, pulled the cloak they had given her roughly aside. She began to writhe and mew; and he clapped a hand impatiently across her mouth. 'Be still, little Rat,' he said. 'And for the sake of all the Gods, be quiet. I mean no harm, but to keep you from a chill. Now lie close, and stop your snivelling; for you are for my Lord the King.'

2

His dog's sense roused him at first light. He frowned, sniffed and was instantly awake. His hands, groping beside him, touched nothing but grass. He sat up, with an oath. There was no sign of her. The little dell in which they had slept lay empty and still, mist-streaks drifting between the trunks of trees.

He stared round him, narrowing his eyes; then rose, buckling his sword belt. A path wound through the copse; he followed it, stepping silently, and paused. Somewhere ahead, a twig snapped; and again.

He flattened himself to the bole of a tree, stayed waiting. The figure came cautiously, muffled in its cloak, a silhouette in the early light. It stepped past; and Elgro pounced, knife in hand. The blade was poised when a muffled squeak checked the stroke. He half-overbalanced, grunting.

She said furiously, 'Let me go, you Sealand oaf. You'll make me drop the eggs.'

Elgro said, 'Eh? What?'

She said, 'These.' Beneath the cloak she held a wicker basket. The Dancing Man, staring, saw it was filled to the brim. Beside the eggs were a loaf of bread, a pitcher of milk, a great round of cheese. He frowned at them. He said, 'Where did you get these?'

She sniffed. She said, 'That's my affair. In any case they're not for you. They're for the Prince.'

He fell into step with her. He said, 'He's not a Prince. He's the King of Crabland.'

She tossed her head. She said, 'If I am a Rat, I will call you what I choose. Are you his servant?'

Elgro drew himself up. He said quietly, 'I am his Dancing Man.'

She looked at him curiously, from black-rimmed hazel eyes. She said, 'I have heard of such people. Can you raise the dead?'

He snapped, 'If needs be, child.'

She sniffed again. She said, 'I doubt it. If last night was an example, you cannot raise the living. I thought you Sealanders boasted of your prowess.'

He stopped, staring; and she glanced up at him amusedly. 'Go on,' she said. 'Now beat me, to prove your manhood. And make me drop your Lord's breakfast.'

'Last night,' he said grimly, 'when you were whimpering with fright, you were glad enough of company.'

'Last night,' she said, 'I whimpered with the cold. I needed a man to warm me.'

He growled. He said, 'You were warmed.'

'Aye,' she said composedly. 'By your cloak.'

She turned aside; and he gripped her arm. He said, 'This is the way we came.'

She pulled away, disdainfully. She said, 'And this is the way I go.' She laughed. 'Sealander, if I were to run, you and your great feet would never catch me.'

He said tartly, 'Why don't you?'

'Because my folk live far away,' she said. 'And you at least, as I have seen, can use a sword.' She pushed aside an overhanging branch, let it spring back. He caught it, and swore.

The path wound down to a little glade, hazed with the blue flowers. The sun, striking between the tall saplings that lined it, made shafts of misty light. A brook chattered over stones, ran clear and deep between overhanging banks.

She thrust the basket into his arms. She said, 'Orm killer, with that great weapon of yours, do you think you can guard my eggs?' She walked to the middle of the stream, stood fiddling with the neck of her dress, raised it quickly over her head. She said, 'I have a certain odour clinging to me. I think it's Sealand sweat.'

The tunic thumped into his arms. She walked forward to where the water deepened. She knelt, panting, began splashing herself vigorously. She said, 'Why are you so far from your homeland? You and your fine King?'

He stared. Her body was slender, with high, firm breasts. Beneath her arms were crisp curls of black hair.

She looked over her shoulder. She said, 'I asked a question, Dancing Man.'

He shrugged. He said, 'It's a long tale. Not one you would understand.'

She said sharply, 'What makes you so sure?'

He stayed silent.

She ducked her head; then rose, flinging water drops from her hair. She said, 'If you have seen enough, put your eyes back in your head and undo that bundle. Also, give me back my tunic.'

The bundle contained trews and a woollen jerkin; the clothes a sheep-herder might use, up in the hills. The tunic she employed to dry herself. She waded to the bank, dressed quickly. She said, 'In Sealand, do the women wear fine clothes?'

He frowned, remembering a certain Queen. He said, 'It has been known.'

She examined herself, critically. She said, 'You sound gruff. I think you are displeased.'

He smiled, and made no answer.

In the clearing, Rand sat quietly on a rock. Beside him was Matt. There was no sign of the others.

Elgro ran to him. He said, 'What happened, my Lord?'

Rand withdrew his eyes from a high tree branch, where a lone bird sat and piped. He said, 'They found me unworthy to be their King. So I released them.'

Elgro flushed deep red, pulling his lips back from his teeth. In his rage he ran a little way up the side of the coombe, and back. He said, 'Had I been with you, this would not have happened.'

Rand shook his head mildly. He said, 'It was their choice. Also they came honourably, when they could have killed me as I slept. Who was I to tell them no?'

Elgro snarled, and turned on the one-time Navigator. He said, 'You could have prevented them.'

Matt, whittling at a stick, stared up with his little black wide-spaced eyes. 'Use your head, Dancing Man,' he said bluntly. 'What could I have done, against six? As things stand, at least I spared one pair of hands to serve the King.'

Elgro stood glaring at the empty hillside, clenching and unclenching his fists; but the girl shrugged. 'Good,' she said. 'There will be that much more for us. Dancing Man, if I gather sticks, will your powers extend to the kindling of a flame?'

Elgro stared at her darkly, pulling at his badger-striped hair; but Rand smiled. He said, 'Can this be the little thing we stole from the Worm?'

Elgro grunted. He said shortly, 'It is.'

She walked quickly to the King, knelt with unexpected humility and reached to touch his wrists. She said, 'These hands saved my life. Now it is yours, to do with as you choose.'

Rand shook his head, and pushed her hair back gently. He said, 'Your life is your own, child. And my Champion struck the blow, not I. How are you called?'

She hung her head. 'Rat,' she said meekly.

He frowned, and rubbed his mouth. He said, 'That is no sort of name.'

She blushed. 'If it please you,' she said, 'it will serve, till my Lord bestows another on what he owns.'

Rand looked up, surprised. 'She speaks well, Elgro,' he said. 'Also, see these shapely hands. She is a pretty child; she will make someone a fine wife one day.'

But the Dancing Man was still too angry to answer.

A fire was built; and the girl prepared a meal, quickly and deftly. When they had eaten, and the pots were scoured and packed, she ventured a question. Elgro answered curtly that they had come from the north, from the country of the Hare People; and she frowned. 'Then you crossed the Black Rock,' she said. 'How long did you spend on it?'

Elgro, more soothed by a good breakfast than he would have cared to admit, shrugged. 'A night,' he said carelessly. 'And parts of two days.'

She frowned again, biting her lip. 'That was badly done,' she said. 'As you love your King, do not be so foolish again. I would not have the devils rot his teeth.'

Elgro sniffed. 'We saw no devils,' he said. 'Or if we had, I have powers to overcome them. I do not fear your stories, child; the Rock is empty.'

'Oh, la,' said the Rat, turning up her short nose. 'Then do you return there, friend of ghosts, and sit a week with them. Come back to me blind and hairless, and tell these things again.' She stared intently, eyes glowing beneath her thick brows; and Elgro grunted and turned away, impressed despite himself.

Later the question of a direction was raised. Rat was once more informative. 'All this land,' she said, waving a slim arm, 'the Land of the Hundred Lakes, was taken by the Horse Warriors in my grandfather's time. Their great castle lies to the south. Beyond is the sea, and my father's country. Where people sit in safety, and are not fed to Worms.'

Rand said quickly, 'Do you have strong Gods?'

She pulled at her lip. 'We have Gods,' she said. 'But I cannot answer for their strength. Every year the Horse Warriors oppress us worse, raiding for slaves and sacrifices.' She brightened. 'We do have a Cunning Man though,' she said. 'He lives in a cave in a mountain, and is older than the trees. They say he remembers the Fire Giants, and fighting-ships like iron islands. If my Lord pleases, I will take you to him.'

So the matter was settled; and the diminished party struck south, through a land of purple hills and bitter blue waters. They travelled by night, hiding during the day. Villages there were in plenty; and farms and stockaded Towers, stony roads that carried a traffic of lumbering ox carts. Everywhere too were soldiers; dark faced, steel-capped men riding proud, tall horses. Left to themselves, the Sealanders would have fared badly; but mornings and evenings the girl flitted away, invariably returning loaded with provisions. Salt fish she brought and flour, eggs, goat cheese, milk. At Elgro's questionings she merely tossed her head. 'Rats live by stealth,' she said, 'and are accomplished thieves. Would you expect less of me?'

On the fourth morning they saw on the horizon a remembered band of pearly light. They pressed on swiftly, crossing great fells, always in sight of the sea. Evening found them once more clear of the hills; and by dusk they reached the coast. The sun, sinking in a yellow blaze, showed the outlines of a huge earthwork, brooding humpbacked over a shadowy foreland. Nearer stretched a desolate beach. Sand dunes were laced with wiry grass, through which the wind sang mournfully.

Rat walked to the water's edge and pointed. 'That is the castle I told you of,' she said. 'The Lake King sits there, with a thousand men to guard him. Beyond is Long Spit.' She chewed a knuckle thoughtfully. 'I was captured on a fishing boat,' she said. 'There are villages somewhere to the west here. We are too few to man a warship, even if we could steal one; a fishing boat it must be.' She glanced up sidelong at Elgro. 'Unless your magic can grow us fins and tails,' she said, 'and swim us home in comfort.'

They walked some distance before coming on signs of habitation. The villages they finally reached were ramshackle and dirty. Boats there were, certainly; but all were drawn up firmly, and watchfires burned close by. Also dogs set up a shrill chorus at the party's approach. They saw what they wanted finally; a chubby, unhandy-looking little vessel, beached by herself in saltings a mile or so from the castle mound. Close by, smoke rose from a low hovel built of turves. There were no other signs of life.

Elgro circled away, pressing a finger to his lips. They saw him flit across the mud; moments later, straining ears might have caught a dull thump, the faintest of splashes. Then the Dancing Man was back. He squatted, driving his knife-blade into the ground to clean it. He said, 'She has a sail and oars, and water in the casks.'

Launching the vessel proved nearly beyond their strength. They strained and splashed, panting. A rising tide helped them; eventually, the boat slid clear. They sculled cautiously half an hour or more before hoisting the sail. A light breeze blew, steady to the south. Matt took the tiller; Long Spit, and the castle with its torchlit walls, faded in the gloom astern. The boat rolled, water chuckling and slapping under her blunt bows; and Elgro felt his spirits rise at the tang of salt.

He stood in the bows, muffled in his cloak, Rand at his side. 'My Lord,' he said softly, 'you have seen by now, surely, how the world goes. The crops spring, fish swim in the sea, there are men and women and towns. As in our own country, so in this; there is no Land of Ghosts. Also' – he jerked his head amidships, to where Rat dutifully tended the sail – 'you have, to my eyes at least, replaced all you have lost. Let us stand further from the coast. Smaller ships than this have sailed to Sealand.'

But Rand turned a shocked face in the gloom. 'Elgro,' he said, 'that would be a shameful thing. She is no more than a child; also my word is given. What sort of men would we be, to save her from a Worm then bring her to more grief?'

Elgro opened his mouth again, closed it with a snap. He groaned inwardly, and held his peace.

They made good time. In the dawn they saw, stretching to the left, a great steely estuary; and Rat, crowing, called for Matt to alter course to the west. They sailed through the morning, closing slowly with the land. At midday she pointed again. Blue hills rose inland; beyond, ghost-pale against the sky, was a great massif. 'Snow Mountain,' she said. 'The highest hill in our country. My Lord, you will very soon be safe.'

Rand turned absentmindedly, and squeezed her shoulder.

They stood in once more toward the coast. To the right and left, bobbing specks resolved themselves into fishing boats. The Lakeland vessel creamed between them, Rat capering and shouting in the bow. Shouts answered her, from every little ship.

They rounded a great snake-like promontory. Beyond was a narrowing estuary. Rat pointed excitedly. 'The Old Ones had a castle there,' she said. 'Then the Fire Giants came, blasting the land. Only we survived. We are the People of the Dragon, the oldest folk in the world.'

They passed the ruins, rising amid a green tide of trees. Beyond was a well-built town. A harbour was guarded by watchtowers and high earth walls; above, on the hill, reared a white-painted Hall. Boats were tied up at the quays, and great-ships of unfamiliar design. Elgro, frowning, nudged his Lord's arm. He said, 'They have no trusses. How can that be?'

She turned to him scornfully. 'It is our secret,' she said. 'Our scribes wrote many secrets, hiding them in magic caves.' Then to Matt, 'Hold the centre of the channel, Sealander; the water shoals fast here.'

The sail came down at the run. The vessel rolled, bumped alongside the quay. Ropes were thrown and caught; and a surge of men came running, some with swords in their hands, some with spears. Elgro clawed at his belt, cursing; but the Rat jumped ashore, shouting delightedly. 'Dyserth, Cilcain,' she said. 'Put your weapons down this instant, and help my friends; or my father will have your ears.'

Consternation, on the quay. A man prostrated himself; others leaped to steady the boat. The noise spread; a crowd began to form, jostling and shoving. Elgro sheathed his sword, stood staring up. 'Rat,' he said gravely, 'who might your father be?'

She turned jauntily, hands on her ragged hips. 'Talsarno King,' she said. 'Lord of the Western Hills.'

Lines of torches lit the Hall with a warm orange glow. The light gleamed from glassware and brooches, costly silver plate. Board after board was piled with delicacies; trays of spiced meat, pastry, fresh-baked fish. Sucking pigs smoked, garnished with herbs and apples; lobsters reared blood-red, their claws locked in mock battle. Musicians played and jangled on a gallery; servingpeople moved among the many guests, replenishing horns and drinking cups from jar after jar of yellow Midsea wine. Sweet-smelling rushes covered the floor of the place; on the walls tapestries, heavy with golden thread, showed dogs and fishes and dragons. Mer-things swam and dolphins; the Great Orm reared its fearsome bulk, in a shower of glistening spray.

It was a feast such as the Sealanders had never seen. They lolled at ease, winepots in their hands, while a minstrel sang the tale of the great fight, repeated already a dozen times or more. Men roared their approval, banging cups and goblets; but Rand shook his head. 'It was a sad thing, living underground,' he said. 'I think it meant no harm.'

The song ended; and Talsarno clapped his hands. He sat at the head of the great table, the Rat beside him in a dress of blue and green, her hair bound with flowers and silver leaves.

'Now, King Rand,' he said, 'Name what gift you choose. A woman here or there is nothing much; but a daughter is a different thing, more so as one grows old.'

Rand smiled. 'Honour my men,' he said, 'and it will please me well, my Lord. Elgro here struck the blow; and the Navigator brought us safely through our many troubles.'

'This is true,' said the Rat brightly. 'Also the Magician guarded me very well, taking me under his cloak to shield me from the cold. Yet for the love he bears our House, he offered me no harm.'

Rand toyed with his cup. 'I seek nothing save wisdom,' he said. 'Among ourselves we call these lands the Isles of Ghosts. If the dead in their country can be visited, then I must journey there; or know no rest.'

The King pulled at his beard. 'It saddens me to hear of such a wish,' he said. He lowered his voice. 'If I may counsel you,' he said, 'from greater years if not from greater wisdom, then I say this; that sorrows pass. All sorrows. King Rand, you are still young. Nothing endures.'

Rand said gravely, 'This will endure.'

Talsarno shrugged, and drained his cup. 'I have no skill in these matters,' he said. 'But there is a Sage, of whom my daughter spoke. For forty years and more he has shunned the light, communing only with the Gods. Old he was in my father's time; and his father before him, so they say. My seal will part his lips, if this is truly what you desire; but my spirits tell me no joy will come of it.' He laid a hand earnestly on Rand's arm. 'My Lord,' he said. 'Let me equip a greatship, to carry you to your homeland. Gold you can have in plenty, and wine and cloth; a dowry, for my daughter's life. You will sit in your own high Hall again; and the years will bring you peace.'

But Rand stayed silent, staring down; and the other sighed. 'More wine,' he said. 'In the morning, my daughter will guide you to the Sage. For the rest, we have no cause to love your countrymen; but between my house and the people of the Crab shall be eternal friendship. This my scribes will write and this I swear; by the White Hill and the Dragon, by Talgarrec and the Sons of Osin, who founded this kingdom when the Giants died and Time began afresh.'

The party was lodged for the night, richly enough; but Rand turned and tossed, waiting for the dawn. In another part of the place Rat too lay sleepless, wetting the new silk sheets with tears.

The track led up through a green valley, set thickly with lilac and tall spikes of delphinium. Higher, the hill slopes flamed with gorse and poppies. Rat led the way, astride a shaggy, goat-footed little pony. Myrnith, chief priest of the Dragon, followed; Rand and his Sealanders brought up the rear, with a file of Talsarno's soldiers. From time to time the Dancing Man swore, slapping at his arms and neck. The heat was intense; above each rider buzzed a cloud of stinging flies.

Beyond the treeline the air was cooler. They crossed screes of naked grey rock. The sun shone from a deep blue sky; a buzzard circled, a doe in the vast emptiness. Ahead were peaks and rock-walls, drenched in light. A breeze blew, lifting Rand's hair, bringing the scents of summer from the rich valleys below.

The girl reined. Beside the path was set a tall square post, outlandishly carved and painted. The party halted, uncertainly; and Myrnith turned, his round dark face impassive. 'Your men will wait here,' he said, in his lilting voice. 'The ground beyond is holy; only priests may enter.'

Elgro dismounted awkwardly, hitching at his belt. 'I am holy too,' he said, 'having danced away greater ghosts than any in this country. Also, I serve the King. Where he goes, I go.'

The soldiers muttered, frowning; and Myrnith shook his head. He said stonily, 'It is forbidden. It is the Law of the Dragon.'

The Dancing Man dropped a hand to his sword hilt. 'When one Law meets another,' he said equably, 'a test of strength is customary. Which of you will discuss the matter with me?'

A pause, that lengthened; then the priest shrugged. 'Defy the Gods if you choose,' he said. 'On your head be it, friend.'

Rat swung her legs from the pony, hitched his reins to the totem. 'I also claim my right,' she said. 'I am a priest, by privilege of birth.'

Myrnith stared down at her gravely. He said, 'You will not like what you see.'

They climbed again. The path steepened, angling across a great slope of granite. Above, the shoulder of the mountain rose in soaring buttresses. The priest stepped to the cliff face, raised a hand. 'Wait here,' he said. 'Perhaps the Old One will speak, perhaps not.' He moved forward, vanished behind a projecting spur of rock. He was gone some time. 'The Gods favour you,' he said when he returned. 'Also he knows your errand, by some skill of his own. Listen, but do not question. If you question him, he will not answer.'

Rand stepped forward, the girl at his elbow, the Dancing Man close behind. The spur concealed a cleft in the apparently solid rock. Within it, the air struck chill. The cliff walls closed, gleaming with damp. A dozen paces, and the way widened again. The King stopped involuntarily, the girl clinging to his arm.

It was as if at some time gigantic forces had split the entire mountain. The walls of the fissure in which he stood soared to an unguessed height. Above, all that was left of the sky was a ragged silver thread. What light reached the floor of the place was grey and dim. The wind bawled, over the distant peak; the chasm responded, uttering a single note that shook the rock, passed to silence.

Some fifty paces ahead the walls of the place swept together. He made out a flight of rough-hewn steps, bowls piled with rotted offerings. Above, the rock was pierced by a single hole, no more than a handspan wide. A heavy stench came from it; round it roughly mortared blocks showed where the anchorite had been sealed alive. They were stained and blotched, as if over the years the thing had become a filthy throat.

His stomach rebelled. He choked, and would have turned away; but a voice spoke from the cell, thin and reedy as a ghost.

'In the old times,' it said, 'the Giants came. Elwin Mydroylin was King in the west. The warboats came, the boats of floating iron. Forests grew on their decks. Others sailed beneath the water, hurling javelins that scorched the earth. The crops were withered, and trees in the passes next the sea. The cities of the Giants were destroyed. Elwin Mydroylin went down to night, and his sons who killed the Dragon on Brondin Mere. The Wanderer came to the White Hill. He saw the love of women, and it was false. He saw the love of men, and it was false. The Dragons came in the north. The hills were shaken.'

Elgro's voice rang in the cleft. '*Seer, where is the Land of Ghosts?*' The rock-walls caught the words, flinging them mockingly forward and back; and the wind roared, playing the place like a gigantic pitch-pipe.

The noise faded. The voice went on, inexorably. 'Elwin went down to night. The House of Mydroylin was extinguished. Haern came, and Morfa, and Amlwych Penoleu. The Dragons fought in the north, and the sea was let in. The indivisible was divided.'

The stink gusted. Rand swayed, feeling sweat start out on him coldly. The voice came again. 'The Mere People took the south, loosing the Devils of the Fen. Beyond, the Forest grew. The seeker after Gods must pass it. None succeeds. After the realm of Gods, there may be Ghosts.'

A pause; and a scrabbling, at the hole. A hand appeared, and forearm; mired with filth, streaked with bright sores. The sores moved and throbbed. The voice rose in a shout of laughter. 'Approach, Sealander,' it said. 'Receive my blessing.'

Rand's sight flickered. He reeled, felt the Dancing Man grip his arms. He turned, hands to his face; when he could see again the sun was hot on his back. Above rose the cliff; below, a great distance away, were the horses and waiting men. He panted, shuddering; and Elgro took his shoulders. 'Now we have seen wisdom,' said the Dancing Man between his teeth. 'Where to next, my Lord?'

The guide reined, pointing. 'Follow the track,' he said. 'The way is clear enough. Beyond the woods, the Mere People have their towns. No Kermi deals with them; they are a jealous folk, not to be trusted. The Horse Warriors hold the south, from the Great Plain to the sea. If you must journey in their lands, journey by night. They love no strangers.'

He turned his horse. 'I have brought you as the King ordered me,' he said. 'Here, Talsarno's writ ends. Trust no man beyond the woods; and the Gods be with you.' He raised his arm briefly in salute; and the Dragon staffs wheeled, the little escort clattered back the way it had come.

Rand clicked to his mount, moved on down the winding track. Matt followed, slumped unhandily in the painted saddle; Elgro, grumbling, brought up the rear.

They were leaving the high hills now. They crossed long slopes bright with speedwell, set with heather tufts and clumps of bilberry. Beyond, pines rose from thickets of rhododendron. There were no apparent signs of life; but twice Elgro turned, watching back fixedly at the skyline.

On the lower ground the pines gave way to a dense forest of beech. They rode an hour or more, through tilted green glades; it was early evening before they reached the forest edge, and reined. A last slope led to a meandering, shallow stream; beyond, a blue plain lifted to the horizon.

Elgro ranged his horse beside his lord. Rand turned, enquiringly; and the Dancing Man smiled. 'We should camp there, by the stream,' he said, pointing. He glanced once more over his shoulder. 'I saw some mushrooms a little way back,' he said, 'that will make a tasty supper. I will be with you presently.'

He drove his heels at his pony's sides, jogged back the way he had come. Rand stared after him with troubled eyes, but made no comment. He walked his horse forward, to the stream.

The Dancing Man waited, eyes narrowed, till his companions were out of sight. He turned his mount then, at an angle from the path, crashed into the undergrowth.

The rider came slowly, letting the pony pick its own way. To either side, the forest was still and warm; the late sun, slanting through the leaves, spread a canopy of gold.

At one point the track angled sharply beside a massive smooth trunk. A branch as thick as a man's body hung above the way. The pony passed beneath; and a figure dropped with a swift thud. The animal squealed, kicking its heels with fright. Its rider, borne from the saddle, rolled threshing. She tried to rise; but the weight of the attacker kept her pinned. She writhed, desperate; and a broad-bladed dagger was pushed between her teeth. 'Answer me quickly,' hissed Elgro, 'and tell no lies. Are you alone?'

She nodded, whimpering; and he twined his fingers in her short hair. 'Now know,' he said, 'women are my bane. A Fairy woman it was that cursed my Lord, making him the child he is. Twice you have shamed me, and many more than twice times mocked my words. Now in your silliness you follow us again. Is it to mock?'

She moaned, terrified, and tried to shake her head.

'Oh, la,' said Elgro, 'This is a different song. Who sent you, Rat? Was it your father, to spy?'

The merest headshake. She closed her eyes, panting.

'Why then,' said the Dancing Man, 'perhaps you love the King. Is that the tale?'

She tried to cough, and choked.

'I have seen this business of love,' said Elgro. 'And a curse and plague it is, when women get their hands on it. Love there is, as we Magicians know; it leaps between the stars, and drives the whole green world. Yet foolish men pine for a face or thigh, with bone beneath no prettier than their own, swearing for lack of them the sun will fade; and this you know full well. So you run to one and to the next, saying "Oh la, behold and worship me"; or, "You are a King, and this your Dancing Man; how quaint he seems".' He groped for her, with his free hand; and she groaned. 'Now hear a Mystery,' he said. 'That these, and this, and this beneath your kilt, were given you by God. Yet women, who are bags of blood, are vain as little babes, and price the shape that Heaven only lent. So kingdoms fall, and men run mad, because you squat to piss.'

The knife-blade shook. 'No man followed me, in all my life, and lived,' he said. 'Yet for my lord's sake, I bear with you. This perhaps is love; and high above your understanding.' He flung her from him, with a great heave. She rolled across the leaves, lay shaking. He sheathed the dagger, walked to stand over her. 'You chose the road,' he said. 'Now follow it. Be faithful to my lord; or my ghost will find you, if I no longer breathe.'

She got to her knees, wearily; hung her head, and was very sick. When she had finished she raised an ashen face. She said in a low voice, 'Dancing Man, now may I catch my horse?'

He stepped aside, impassively. She walked to where the animal stood; mounted and rode with icy dignity, down toward the Plain.

The sun rose, and set. They walked to the south, steadily. Rand led, his chin sunk on his chest; after him came Matt, jogging stolidly, gripping the saddle horns in front of him. The girl led the packhorses; Elgro Dancing Man brought up the rear. Duck and heron rose at their approach, honking and wheeling. They forded shallow streams, paced by the hour beside desolate fens, flecked all over with the fluffy white of marsh grass. Sometimes they passed rough settlements, once an entire lake city, built from the shore on a forest of stiltlike legs. The inhabitants of the region were numerous; but they neither approached nor offered harm. One and all seemed content to watch from a distance, standing in sullen little knots as the Sealanders passed.

The girl rode for the most part silently, bearing the discomforts of the journey without complaint. Each night she boiled the party's drinking water, setting the pannikins carefully aside to cool. A pouch at her belt contained delicate bone hooks. She set traps for the water birds, tying the baited hooks to wooden floats; and once she stole some little wicker pots, with them caught a yard-long eel. The Sealanders wouldn't touch it, to a man; she cleaned the fish and ate a part herself, sitting a little distance away, her dark eyes fixed on Rand.

The following day they came on an ancient road, its surface cracked and broken. In places chunks had been levered up entire by the springing of bushes and weeds. They were of stone chips set in a black, tarry matrix. Such roads existed here and there in Sealand, though the art of making them had long been lost. To Rand it seemed strange to come upon one here; but it ran south, straight as an arrow, vanishing into distance. He turned his horse on to it, calling to the others to follow.

The road dipped and rose, flooded for much of its length. The horses splashed knee-deep, sidling and snorting. Ahead the lake stretched to the horizon, dotted by clumps of reed, islands crowned with stunted, unhealthy-looking trees. The party rode in silence, eyes screwed against the dazzle of sunlight; till at midday the girl reined. Rand, glancing back, saw she sat the pony rigidly, staring down.

He walked his mount back, and stared in turn. Beside the road, the water was crystal clear. In it, pinned to the drowned grass, lay the body of a girl. She was naked, her flesh white as Midsea marble. Her eyes were open, watching up with a curious intentness; her hair, dark and long, flowed slowly round her face, graceful as fern. At knees and elbows, forked stakes had been driven into the earth to hold her firm.

Twice the King spoke, gently; but Rat, it seemed, could no longer hear. He took the pony's bridle finally, led her away. She came unprotesting, staring back at the death place as it receded. He spoke twice more, receiving no answer. He shook his head, and let her be.

They camped, unhappily, on the driest part of a swampy islet. Rat moved about her duties quietly, cleaning and preparing the game they had brought with them, setting out her baited lines. Later she slipped away, walked to the water's edge. She sat awhile, rocking dully on her heels, staring to the north while the sunset flared and faded. Then she reached to her belt, took out the little knife she carried. She laid her hand on the ground, pressed the blade without fuss into her palm, dragged it down her forearm.

It was Rand who missed her from the camp. He walked, frowning, to where she still sat huddled. He stopped then with a cry, tried to take her arm; but she wrenched away. 'Leave me alone,' she said unsteadily. 'It's my blood; I can drop it where I choose.'

He scooped her up despite her struggles, blundered back shouting for Elgro and Matt. A linen shirt, her father's gift, was brought from one of the packs, torn into strips for bandages. He washed the long wound carefully, binding her arm and wrist; when it was done, and the fire stoked and blazing, he regarded her sternly. 'Why did you do it?' he demanded. 'Have we become so terrible to you, that you must creep off and take your life?'

She sat shivering, huddled in a blanket. 'It wasn't for me,' she said bitterly. 'It was to quiet a ghost. Myrnith would have known the proper way; but all I had was blood.'

'Whose ghost?'

'Bethan,' she said. 'Whom the Marsh Gods took.'

He stared, in dawning understanding. He said, 'Was she a Kermi?'

She grimaced, cradling the injured arm. 'We played together,' she said. 'Afterwards, we were in love. She vanished a month ago. We thought it was a wolf.' She swallowed. 'There was a storm,' she said. 'I took a boat. I hoped

I would be drowned. But the Gods didn't want me. The Horse Warriors caught me instead.'

She stared at the fire. 'If we go north,' she said, 'they take us to feed to Worms. If we go south, the Marsh is always hungry. The Sealanders raid from the west and the people from Green Island, who drink seal blood and cut their fingers off when their chieftains die. And all the time the Horsemen want our land. Soon, if my father doesn't stop singing and being wise, there will be no more Kermi. The world will be at peace again.' She turned to stare at Elgro, for the first time in days. 'She did not ask to be nailed into a bog,' she said. 'But doubtless as a woman she deserved it.'

Rand frowned at her, shaking his head; and the Dancing Man rose, stalked off into the dark.

That night she lay beside the King, wrapped in his blankets. Twice in the still watches he woke to hear her sobbing. He drew her to him finally, stroking her hair. 'You should not have followed us,' he said gently. 'Your debt was paid already; I go to the Land of Ghosts, where there is nothing but sorrow.'

In time her head grew heavy against his shoulder. He lay till dawn, watching the white mists crawl, hearing the sighs and gurglings of the marsh. He dozed at first light, woke bleary-eyed and heavy. The party saddled up and mounted, headed once more south. Rat looked as blenched as the water girl, while the usually silent Matt complained of pains in the head and back. Only the Dancing Man, splashing grimly in the rear, seemed unaffected.

By late afternoon they were clear of the marsh; but the Navigator's condition was worse. He rode wild-eyed, ranting and muttering, breaking into snatches of song. They camped before nightfall, improvised a couch for him from the packs and their contents. The girl sat beside him, raising his head from time to time to drink. He moaned and shouted far into the night, talking nonsense about Crabland, and fishing, and drinking Midsea wine. A very little wine they had with them, brought from Talsarno's Hall; they gave it him, and it seemed he dozed at last. To Rand's anxious questionings, the girl shook her head. 'He has a marsh fever,' she said. 'Twice I saw him drink bad water, in spite of what I asked; this has come of it.' She stared at Elgro, with her disturbing eyes. 'The time has come for your skill, Dancing Man,' she said. 'You who know the secrets of the stars.'

But Elgro turned away, his face set darkly. Later, while the girl slept, he spoke bitterly to Rand. 'In Crabland,' he said, 'when I was your father's man, I danced more fevers than my body has bones. I danced you into the world, though the midwives doubted your life. Now the power has gone. My legs no longer seem to belong to me, I see things several times over.' He spread his hands, regarded them gloomily. 'The Gods do this for shame, or mockery,' he said. 'Or this business of enchantment is more widespread than I thought.' He spoke as if to himself, frowning at the fire. 'What I said was true,' he muttered. 'And is true, through the world. And yet I sinned. How can this be?'

Rand reached to grip his shoulder. 'It will come back,' he said, 'When we are out of this place, and breathe clean air again.'

But Elgro shook his head, his eyes opaque. 'The times are altering,' he said. 'My Lord, I have the oddest thought; that one day Sealanders will own this country too. There will be no ghosts then, or need of Dancing Men.' He rubbed his face, wearily. 'It's my conceit,' he said. 'We think as we grow old, the world is ageing with us. Get yourself some rest, my Lord; I will watch for now.'

By morning, Matt had fallen into a slumber from which none of their efforts could rouse him. They talked together, anxiously; then Elgro cut two saplings, lashed them to the harness of the packhorse, wove branches for a makeshift stretcher. On it the Navigator was tied, still breathing stertorously; and the grim march was resumed. They climbed steadily, into rolling green hills. By midday the sick man was awake, wrestling with the straps that held him, calling on all manner of Gods and spirits. When they stopped, to give him water and breathe the horses, he barely recognized them.

Deep in the hills, they came on the Black Rock again.

Rand would have ridden forward; but the girl clung to his arm. 'My Lord,' she said, 'there is death there. No one goes twice on the Rock, and lives.' She appealed to Elgro. 'Dancing Man,' she said, 'this isn't for myself. But if you go on, then think of a promise you made. I would as soon rest here and sleep, as see the King with the flesh boiled off his bones.'

Elgro stared at her for a time, setting his mouth and pulling his hair; then he turned his horse. 'My spirits tell me she is right, my Lord,' he said. 'Many demons live on the rock. We must pass it by.'

They turned east, thinking that offered the easier route. For most of the day the black band shimmered on the horizon. Finally it curved away, ending in a great ragged crest. They turned the horses thankfully, riding due south.

The land to which they came was the strangest they had seen. For mile after mile, the little hills were coated with hectic green. The grass grew limp and brilliant, the stems pulpy, the leaf blades a handspan broad. Crowning the hills were trees of proportionate vastness. Their shapes were bizarre. Some flung their branches straight as spearshafts, a hundred feet and more into the sky; others writhed and twisted, springing in great knots and curves, thrusting out fists of root wherever they touched the ground. The horses shied and snorted; and the Rat looked concerned. 'I think,' she said, 'we should go east again, my Lord. This is bad land too; the winds from the Black Rock make these things happen. I have heard it said that men grow monstrous too.'

But Rand shook his head. 'We will go south till nightfall,' he said. 'If the taint is in the air as you believe, then we have breathed enough already. We shall take no greater harm.'

Toward evening Matt, who had quietened, began to sing and shout once more. His bawling floated into the sky, among the appalling trunks and limbs; and the Dancing Man pulled at his lip. 'I wish the Gods would take him,' he said frankly. 'At least he would be at rest; here it seems he lives in Hell.'

The sun dropped toward the horizon. They topped a hill and bunched, instinctively. Facing them across the intervening slope was the strangest monster of all that strange land. Its limbs, bone white and stripped, raged and squirmed for yard after yard, stooping to brush the grass, flinging out roots thicker than the body of a man. The light struck through the sea of branches, luridly; and Elgro jerked a hand from beneath his cloak, fingers circled in the sign that wards off death. They sat the horses, staring; and a voice beside them made them leap with shock.

It was Matt. He stood swaying wildly, his face suffused. 'Behold,' he said. 'I see the World Tree, that stands at the end of Time. Under its roots the sea-Orms sit, and the Wolf that will eat the sun; and there are the Gods all in a row, with their eyes on fire and their pricks like a greatship's truss. Can you not see them?'

Rat cringed, hands to her mouth; and the others turned, climbing quietly from their horses. 'Matt, old friend,' said Elgro gently, 'we will let these matters be. We will sit down now, and eat; for these Gods, whom I see very clearly, are tired and do not want to chatter. In the morning, you can talk to them; meanwhile tell me about the Great Storm again, when we rowed King Cedda to Blue Fen and saw the water snake. That is a better tale.' He nodded to Rand; and they leaped.

The other hunched his shoulders with surprising speed, and thrust out his arms. He had always been noted for his strength; now it seemed redoubled. Rand, for all his bulk, was hurled across the grass; Elgro rolled cursing between the horses' feet. He was up in an instant, but the Navigator was quicker; he cried out, raising his arms, set off toward the monster calling at the top of his voice. They fled after him, appalled.

The branches were overhead, swooping and curving. Matt howled at the trunk, beating his fists. They reached him, and were flung away again. Red marks appeared before him, on the blenched white wood; then he fell, arcing his body. They grabbed him, hauled him back somehow the way they had come. They laid him on the grass, prized at the locked jaws; but it was too late. His tongue was in his throat, and he was dead.

Rand straightened slowly. 'We will put him back in the harness,' he said. 'We will not leave him here; his ghost would never rest.'

They walked the horses silently, circling well clear of the great tree. In the last of the light, the girl reined. Beneath the pony's hooves was normal grass; they had passed the Forest.

Next day the sun was hidden. Cloud masses drove low overhead; it seemed they trapped the heat close to the earth, so that they sweated as they rode. Thunder shook and muttered, but no rain fell. Toward evening they reached the edge of a great plain. It soared away in the dull light, its ridges crowned by wind-smoothed crests of trees. To right and left tall posts were planted in the grass. They rode to the nearest. Plumes of dark hair moved in the rising wind; topping the thing was a great bleached skull. Lightning flickered, above the clouds; and Rand turned. 'This is the place they spoke of,' he said. 'The edge of the Horse Warriors' land.' He walked his mount forward, into the emptiness.

The storm broke toward nightfall. Rain fell in torrents; the blazing and din were continuous. They were far from shelter; they plodded grimly, cloaks flapping, hair and leggings streaming. An hour after dark they reached a village, huddled in a fold of downs. It was a poor enough looking place; but fires were burning here and there, there was a watchtower of sorts. They rode to the stockade, too weary for caution. Their hammerings finally produced a response. Questions were shouted, and answered; the gates creaked back. It seemed the Dragon's name carried some force, even in the south.

The huts were miserable affairs for the most part, mere holes scraped in the ground and thatched with reed. In one they were lodged, and Rat saw to the stabling of the horses. They lay restlessly, huddled in damp cloaks, while the storm grumbled into silence. Rand dozed eventually, only to be visited by monstrous dreams. It seemed the Orm-child floated to him, time and again, holding out her white arms. He lifted his own arms to her; and the whiteness changed on the instant to another thing, that woke him shaking in the first light of dawn.

He rose, stood swaying. Her breasts rose and fell in the dimness; the lashes brushed her cheeks. She slept quietly, as though her ghost had made no journeyings. Beside her, the Dancing Man's face looked pale and drawn as a corpse. He left the hut, walked to the southern stockade. Hills showed on the horizon; the air was cold, and sweet.

Later they took counsel with the headman of the place; a grey-headed, embittered old creature, frail and much bent. 'The horses we will keep,' he said. 'Also their packs, to pay the trouble we have been to. The Horsemen do not like strangers in their country; heads have rolled, and villages been burned, for less than we have done. If you go south, and I say you are mad to think of it, you must go as slaves; for we are all slaves here. The Horsemen own the land.'

Rand said slowly, 'What do you know of their Gods?'

The other spat. 'Gods they have in plenty,' he said. 'Some ask for grain, and so they steal our crops. Others call for blood, and then they take our children. There is a great God in the south, or so I hear. His Priestess came of our people; but so holy was she that they let her be. And once she visited the Land of Ghosts, wandering there some time.'

Rand gripped his shoulder. 'Chief,' he said, 'is this the truth?'

The other shrugged tiredly. 'What should I know of truth?' he said. 'Once we were free, to farm our grain and feed our flocks in the valleys. Now we are slaves, and kiss the ground if a Horseman happens by. These are truths. If there are Gods, they have no thought for us. More than this I neither know nor care.'

Clothes were found for them; trews and coarse tunics of unbleached cloth. 'Now, surely, your heart's desire is achieved,' said Elgro grimly to the King. 'Lands you had, and they are gone. A Tower, that you left behind; a ship, and men to follow you. A ransom was in our saddlebags; and that we paid to lodge a night in a wet hole in the earth. Now we must bend our necks, wear cloth that stinks of farmers' sweat. If this is wisdom, then the world is on its head; and time enough for me to leave it.' He stared at his swordbelt lovingly, laid it aside. He hung the weapon from a lanyard round his neck, arranging the folds of his cloak to hide the blade. 'Some dirt on our faces would not I suppose come amiss,' he said. 'And while the thought is on me, my nose tells me there are pigs herded close by. I think I will go and roll in one of their sties; if I am to play a part, I must play it well.'

They left the village, tramping along a stony white road. A final slope took the place from sight. At the crest the girl turned, tears shining on her face. Rand, approaching awkwardly, laid a hand on her shoulder. He said, 'What is it?'

She pulled away, brushing her lashes with the back of her knuckles. 'It's nothing,' she said. 'It's only for my pony. They can't sell him; it would be dangerous.'

He frowned. He said, 'What will they do?'

She shrugged. 'Kill him and eat him, I suppose,' she said. 'My Lord, we must go on.'

The land was populous. They passed lines of ox carts, file after file of the dark-faced, steel-capped soldiers. Here and there were ramshackle villages like the one in which they had lodged, and chequer-patterns of small square fields. Between them, palisaded towns clustered beneath Towers not unlike the castles of Sealand. Suspicious looks were cast at them a score of times; but they passed unmolested. In time the villages became less frequent. The road climbed and climbed again, crossing the great chalk backbone of the country. Hills reared in the emptiness, topped by the gaunt shapes of beacons; farmhouses huddled in the valleys, cattle no bigger than toys cropped the sparse grey grass. At one such place they bargained for their supper, paying with the last of the gold from Rand's belt. They slept the night in a rustling, hay-filled barn. In the morning a troop of soldiers passed, in charge of a dozen heavily loaded carts. Behind the tailboard of the last staggered four or five weary-looking men. Rand, frowning, saw one of the prisoners fall. The cart rumbled on indifferently, towing him in the dust.

They were nearing the sea. They entered an area of heath-land, a flat, sour expanse laced by little watercourses, splashed with bogs. Pine trees rose in clumps above the endless rhododendron thickets. Across the horizon ran a curving line of hills; closer, chalk headlands showed eroded rivers of white. They left the road, striking directly across the heath.

The sun climbed, gathering intensity; the bracken shimmered and swam. They rested through the heat of the day, crawling into the heart of one of the bright-flowered clumps. Toward evening they moved off once more, striking the road again where it swung back toward the hills. Along it they plodded, thirsty and footsore, till the girl stopped, gripping Rand's arm. Beside the road lay the body of a man, one of the prisoners they had seen pass. A gaping wound showed in his back; round him the magpies were working already, scolding and flapping on the stained grass. They passed the spot grim-faced, and hurried on.

The sun was levelling when the Dancing Man turned. He narrowed his eyes, staring back the way they had come. Along the road behind them galloped a troop of men. The pouring light struck sparks from harness and weapons, the riders' bright steel caps.

To either side the heath stretched empty and flat; there was nowhere to run. They drew to one side, humbly, stood heads bowed for the column to pass. Instead, it reined; and the leader a strapping, hook-nosed man with flowing hair and beard, rode forward. 'You, I think, are the people we seek,' he said without preamble. 'Which of you is the Sealand Lord?'

Rand shook his head. 'I don't understand you, sir,' he said. 'We came from the coast to the villages by the Great Plain, to sell sheep for our master. Now our task is finished, and we are on our way home. Please let us go on; for it is late already, we shall be beaten.'

A man rode forward from the column, smiling. He wore a gaily-patterned surcoat; and his long fair hair was carefully dressed and tied. 'Well spoken, King of the Crab,' he said. 'But you must put aside your modesty this once. We are honest folk here in the south, and anxious to entertain you.'

The Dancing Man's hand flew to his neck, but for once he was too slow; a swordtip was already pricking his throat. The Horseman spoke gutturally. He said, 'Let your weapons fall.'

He did as he was bidden slowly, his grey eyes hard as stone. 'Why, Dendril,' he said, 'this is a strange affair. In Lakeland I killed a Worm; it seems a lesser escaped me, to dress in fine clothes and speak ill of its betters.'

The Sealander swung from his horse, unconcerned. 'When I raise me in my Tower of the Crab,' he said, 'with these my friends to help me, my dress will be finer yet. But you will not be there to see it.' He stooped to retrieve the sword, and turned away. 'Kill him,' he said. 'The others will give no trouble.'

Rand stepped forward quickly. 'Hear me,' he said. 'We came in peace, with white cloths on our ship. We would have sailed to your great towns, bringing gifts; but our boat was wrecked, as our friend here can tell. We brought no harm; we came to worship your Gods, and learn wisdom from your priests.'

Dendril walked forward. 'No harm?' he said. 'No harm? Then where is Cultrinn? Where is Egril? Where are Galbritt, and Ensor, and all the rest?' He weighed the weapon in his hands, swung it viciously. The crosspiece, heavy and rough, caught Rand across the temples. Light burst, inside his head; when he could see again, he was staring at a horse's feet. He made to rise; and the warrior spoke distantly. 'On your knees to a Horseman, Sealander,' he said. 'Or I will cut your heels.'

He put a hand to his forehead, It came away red and wet. The Rat knelt by him, pressed a cloth to his face.

Elgro had crouched, eyes blazing; now he relaxed. 'Well,' he said, 'so much for Kings. When they fall, the time has come to seek new masters.' He turned to the Horsemen, spreading his arms. 'My Lords,' he said, 'you need have no concern for me. I have no wish to die before my time. Also, I have powers undreamed of. In my own land, I was a notable Magician.'

Dendril said narrowly, 'Kill him.'

A sword was raised; but Elgro lifted a hand. 'Wait,' he said. He turned to the black-bearded leader. 'Kill me and you make a great mistake,' he said. 'I could serve you well. When I dance men grow big with vigour, taking twenty maidens in a night, and still demanding more. Others pine and falter, developing great pains. My enemies sit down and groan, sending quickly for a priest. All this I bring about, by steps in the dust.'

Dendril said, 'Do not trust him.' But the leader frowned, eyes narrowed curiously. 'I have heard of these Dancing Men,' he said. 'Let him show his skill.' He stared at Elgro. 'Dance a pain, pirate,' he said. 'Fling it from distance, and perhaps I will let you live. Fail, and you die this minute.'

Elgro bowed his head. 'Lord,' he said humbly, 'it will be as you wish.'

The Horsemen circled, grinning. He stepped into the ring made for him, and began to dance. He danced such a dance as had surely never been seen. He howled and roared, twisting his supple body into knot after knot. He bent till his forehead touched the ground between his heels; he leaped and capered and spun cartwheels. Dust rose round him; and the smiles of the

Horsemen turned to laughter. 'Do your magic quickly, Sealander,' shouted the leader. 'This leaping is for children.'

Elgro climaxed his performance with a dozen gigantic standing somersaults. The last brought him alongside the Horseman's mount. By his knee hung a dagger in a decorated sheath. The Dancing Man snatched it, quick as a snake, and threw. A thud; and Dendril stared down appalled. His face turned grey, and then a blazing white. His legs gave way; he sat in the dust, hands gripped to his stomach, and began to shriek.

Elgro straightened, snarling. 'There is your pain,' he said. 'Is it enough, for one small Dance?'

A frozen moment; then the ring of Horsemen closed in.

The column trotted slowly, in the gathering dusk. Rand stared up, swaying with weariness. Ahead, the hills swept down to a pass carved through the chalk. In the pass rose a great steep-sided mound, its summit crowned with nubs and spikes of stone. High on the crest stood a fantastic Hall. Its windows blazed with light; on its ridge pole, dim against the night, monstrous shapes of rushes clambered and loomed. Round it torches burned, and many fires; the terraces thronged with figures that were cloaked and horned.

There was a gatehouse, built of crumbling stone. The horse to which he was tied clattered through. Inside were more soldiers. Challenges were shouted, and answered. The bridle was seized, the lashings cut from his ankles. Beside him the girl was dragged from the saddle; he saw the Dancing Man dumped on the ground like a sack of grain. Hands gripped him; he swung his legs clumsily, and the grass rose to meet his knees. He rolled sideways, felt the hill sway. The hands came again and faces, mouthing red-lit. He closed his eyes, and sank away from them.

The crash and rumble of wheels shook the ground. The tip of the great ram swayed and lurched; beyond, the face of the Tower was brightly lit. Flames rose, above the rampart walk; he saw arrows fly blazing, strike the wooden walls. A man plunged, screaming. Water cascaded; the twinkling spots of light were extinguished.

The wheels pounded. He pressed his chest to the axle, driving his feet at the packed earth of the compound. A roar from the Crablanders; and the pace increased. Something rang on his shield, bounded into the dark. In front of him a man shrieked and fell, hands to his face. He stumbled and ran on.

Another shout; and the engine brought up against the Tower door, with a jerk that fetched him to his knees. Missiles rained on the roof of stout stitched hides; beneath it the Sealanders, stripped to the waist, frantically cast the lashings from the great shaft. He stared, through the slits of his battle helmet. Arrows hissed overhead once more. Frantic activity, on Engor's battlements; and a leather mattress began to jerk and sway down the Tower front.

Men scrambled to lay hands on the ram. Something smashed and patterned on the hides. Fire ran, streaming; and the chanting began. '*Way … and ho … Way … and ho …*' He leaned his weight with the rest; and the ram swung. The head, wedge-shaped and shod with iron, struck the door with a noise of thunder; and again. Creaks and snappings sounded; the mattress danced and leaped.

Flamelight showed through cracks that broadened. He let go the shaft and ran, sword in hand, shield held slanting above his head.

'*Way … and ho … Way … and ho …*'

Light poured from the Tower. The door crashed inward, torn bodily from its hinges. The ram swung free; he ducked beneath it, leaped. A spear glanced from his shoulder armour; he gripped the shaft, drove with the blade, wrenched it free, struck again. His voice roared in the mask; behind him the Crablanders burst into the Hall like a flood.

There were steps, of sounding wood. He bounded at them, swung his sword again. A man shrieked, toppled past him. There was a remembered door. He drove at it, shoulder and shield; and the latch-thongs parted. Beyond were crying women. He flung them aside, strode to the bedchamber. The couch was tousled, and the room empty.

There was a further door. He wrenched at it, reeled back. Night air moved against his skin; below was the flame-lit compound.

It seemed the nightmare was continued. The masks pressed closer, jostling; and the hands were on him again, gripping shoulders and arms. The hill-top was a great confused mass of building, roofs and chambers clustering round the high central Hall. He was dragged through room after room, orange-lit by torches, full of a pungent, sweetish scent that made his brain spin. The masks whirled and bobbed; masks of stone and wood, masks of metal and bone, masks of feathers glimmering on girls who wore nothing else at all. The torches swayed; somewhere drums pounded, mixed with the pounding in his ears.

In the Hall a great fire burned. He saw, in darts and flashes, the trestles laid for a feast, the rush-strewn floor, walls hung with trophies of the God; his lances and spears and swords, his axes and chariot wheels and bolts of silk. He was hustled to a place, the girl banged down beside him. Weals showed on her face and neck. The bandage had been pulled from her arm; the cuts had bled again, spattering her clothes.

His wrists had been bound with a rawhide strip. He placed his hands on the trestle, palms together; and a cup was jammed against his teeth. He drank perforce, feeling the stuff flood across his chest. The wine woke new and burning images; the long room spun once more.

Horns sounded, close and harsh. The doors were flung back; and a procession debouched into the Hall. First came dancers and Hornmen, girls with cymbals and bells; next creatures in rustling costumes of straw; and finally a covered, gaily-decked chair, borne on the shoulders of four burly priests. Above it rose nodding heads of maize and wheat; and the Sign of the God, a phallus of bound green rushes. The horns blared; the chair was set down and silence fell, broken only by the crackle of the flames.

A voice spoke querulously from behind the drapes. 'Bring me closer,' it said. 'How can I see them, from here?'

The bearers hurried, deferentially. The chair was raised again, the curtains parted; and Rand stared, trying to stop the spinning in his head. He saw what at first seemed nothing more than a mound of brilliant feathers; then the cape moved, rustling. Black eyes glittered through the mask slits; and the voice spoke again. 'Why did you come to my land, and to my House?' it asked. 'Do you bring the Touch that Heals? For this, I saved you from my Horsemen.'

He swallowed, shaping his lips round words. 'Where is my Dancing Man?' he said. 'Is he alive, or dead?'

The mask quivered. 'What is life?' it said. 'What is death? I, who died on the hill, knew both.' The voice wavered, seeming to lose the thread of its thoughts. 'What has happened?' it asked plaintively. 'Where is the God? For seven times seven years, I was his Bride. Never did he fail me … Sealander, where are the years? Can you answer?'

He lowered his eyes. He said, 'I came seeking wisdom, not to give it.'

The mask bobbed again. The crone said abruptly, 'Is this your woman?'

He shook his head, in pain. 'Do not harm her,' he said. 'Her father is a King in the west. He will give the God rich gifts.'

It seemed he went unheard. 'How red her blood runs,' said the priestess. 'The blood of the young … Show me, child, there is no shame. Show me and I will tell you how the God went with me, seven times seven years …' The voice sank to a mutter, rose again. 'Where is the God?' it asked. 'What has happened to me?' Then in a thin shout, 'I burn …'

Rand groaned, bringing his fists down on the table. 'Mother,' he said, 'this is age …'

She shrieked, 'The Favoured cannot age …' She snatched at the mask, with a thin brown hand; and he turned away. The face had withered, falling in round the smashed nose, the cicatrice of a great scar. 'We have searched,' said the creature. 'First we sought the touch that heals all ills; but no man brought it to my Hall. Now, we search again. For the soul lives in the flesh, like a silver worm. Who finds that worm, and swallows, will be young; but it is quick, and shy.' She called, rattling the feathered cape; and a great wooden wheel was carried into the Hall, set down.

The King rose slowly, arms extended, face like a man suddenly blind. He swayed; then the thing before him spoke. Little enough remained, to show that it was Elgro; but the voice was the Dancing Man's. *'My Lord,'* it whispered slowly, *'I think now, your penance is done.'*

In Engor's Tower, the noise had died away. He ran, feet pounding, back the way he had come. He took a woman by the throat, shouting for the Queen; but she could only wail. He hurled her from him, ran again.

In the Great Hall, the dead lay sprawled and heaped. Blood mapped the flags with brilliant traceries. A man sat on the door edge, patiently, holding up the remnant of a hand; beyond, in a silent semicircle, stood the Crablanders. In their midst the leather mattress swung, still cradled in its web of ropes. Bulging it was, and sodden; and its corner as it moved traced a thin pattern on the sill.

He was unaware that he slashed and screamed; but the leather parted, before his face. He turned away, hands to his skull; but not before he had seen, above the red and white, the coils of ash-pale hair.

The cry that came from him was the noise of a wolf. He raised his arms, the fingers crooked; and the bonds that held him snapped. The trestle barred his way; he laid a great hand to it, flung it aside. Screams sounded; the masks swirled and fell. He seized the wheel and raised it, ran staggering to jam it at the flames. Logs spilled and rolled, blazing; and Elgro's ghost fled from him, with a shriek.

A sword was in his hands. Foam flecked his mouth; he struck, not knowing that he swung the blade. He struck for Egril and Cultrinn, Calbritt and Ensor and Matt. He struck for Cedda, and Engor, and Deandi the Fay; and each blow was a life. The fight swayed round him, surging; the noise doubled and redoubled, till the rafters rang. Then it seemed there were none to oppose him; so he struck the trestles and chairs, the drapes on the walls, the rushes, the jars of wine. Lastly, he struck the litter of the priestess. The gilded grasses flew, and tatters of drenched silk. He stamped and trampled, screaming; and a thin wail rose. Then the thing inside was young again.

The redness faded. He ran to where the girl was crouched, seized her arm. He raised her; and the doors of the Hall burst inward. Faces poured forward, shouting; and the bronze strapped shields of Sealand, swords, the tips of spears.

He ran again, crouching. Behind him the Hall was hazed with smoke. The flames spread swiftly, licking at the drapes, leaping to the roof. Thatch fell, blazing; the smoke swirled, thicker than before.

There was a low door, iron-barred. He smashed his foot against it. Night air blew round him; he stumbled, dragging the girl behind him across a slope of grass.

The blazing thatch of the God House lit the hill-top with an orange glare. He ran swerving, between tall pillars of stone. A roof section caved in; the flames roared up, brightening. Yells sounded from where the raiding party engaged fresh troops of Horsemen. There was a crumbling wall; he tumbled the girl over it, heard her land with a crackling of branches. A man was close behind him. He turned, parried the mace-swing, drove upward. The blade passed below the God-mask, burst out through the skull. The body convulsed; he tore the weapon free, vaulted to the wall-top and dropped into the dark.

The side of the mound was thickly overgrown with bushes and young trees. He half-ran, half-skidded down a cliff of grass, still towing the girl. The slope steepened. He tripped, rolled. The girl yelped; he landed in a smother of bushes, lay staring up. High above, over the great shoulder of the mound, the Hall roared like a furnace.

There was a stream, running cool and swift between tall fern-hung banks. He stepped into it, pulling her after him. Trees arched overhead, velvet-black in the night; he waded groaning, hands to his temples, and heard her cry.

He turned back, floundering. She was crouched below the bank, head down, arm gripped across her chest. He glared, face working; then he stooped. He raised her carefully, feeling her shake and sob; and waded on again, into the dark.

The two figures moved slowly, down the long rough slope of grass. Beyond was the sea. The dawn was in the sky, washing the land with pale grey light.

Bushes fringed the edge of a low cliff. Rand crouched, parted the branches carefully. Below, greatships were drawn up on the beach. Fires burned at intervals; closer, tall standards were thrust into the grass. He stared, narrowing his eyes; and let his held breath escape. 'Ulm of the Fishguard,' he said. 'Crenlec, from Long Fen. Friends of the Crab.'

She sat staring dully at the water, still gripping her arm. He turned her wrist gently, pulled her fingers away. 'They are all gone,' he said. 'Matt, and Egrith, and Egril and his sons. If she is in Hell, she knows I tried to follow. I sent my best before, to tell her so.'

He scooped his arms beneath the girl, raised her once more. She laid her head on his shoulder wearily, eyes closed. 'We are all dead,' he said. 'The Rat is dead. Child, how are you called?'

The lips moved, in the drawn face. 'Mavri,' she said. 'Of the White Rock.'

He frowned. 'There is a Tower, in my country,' he said. 'If I sit there again, I will try to be a King.'

She made no answer; and he stepped forward heavily, climbing the zigzag path down to the ships.

The greatships crash back into silence; and Potts is well content. He's been through a bit of a patch, certainly; but the crisis has passed. He feels convalescent; you can always tell. Like after a bad go of asthma. He used to enjoy his convalescences; walking to the park in the thin spring sunshine, and school a week away.

She'll be with him soon now. He wonders how he'll look. Maybe not too bad. He's lost a lot of weight; a canteen of water stands at his elbow, but he hasn't eaten in days. When she comes he'll speak to her, simply and sincerely. He wonders why he didn't understand before how easy it all was. This business of love.

He feels he ought to make some sort of effort. Maybe go out and start the Champ. She'll need running, her battery must be down. But in a little while. Not yet.

He looks round the little room. He sees the camp stove, the cups and plates, the tins of grub. Have to get that lot tidied as well. Near his hand is the pistol. He's surprised to see it's coated with thin rust. Once that would have appalled him; but now he can afford to smile. It's served its turn, after all. He's won, beaten them all. They didn't think he would, but he has.

Sunlight is reaching into the little room from the window above his head. The beams enter at an acute angle, striking the rough wall in patches of pinkish gold. It's evening then. The serene light lies across hills and headlands, heath and sea; all his western world.

He lies back. He sees, now, tall and majestic towers topping those hills. Strange towers of whitened wood, with barbicans and complex outworks, baileys of rich green grass. He smiles, and closes his eyes. Once more the Wheel is turning; rushing summer into winter, winter into golden spring …

SEVEN

Usk the Jokeman

1

Once more the year had turned. A spring breeze blew, drying the harsh earth, swaying twiglets in their haze of golden-green. The same wind pressed against the tower in the high chalk pass, as against a sail; and the tower responded, with a medley of squeaks and groans. Other sounds rose from the complex of buildings that surrounded it; clank and scrape of pails, clatter of churns from the buttery, heavier grumble of the cornmill from the lower ward. A herdboy yodelled, whacking the flanks of his sway-bellied charges; the heifers bellowed mournfully, cramming their way through the narrow entrance with its jettied wooden gatehouse.

From the Great Chamber atop the rustling edifice King Marck stared vaguely down. The casements, ajar to the bright sky, admitted sunlight that striped the rough floor with gold; but the King seemed unaware. In one hand he gripped a sheaf of parchments; in his other he held a fine goose quill, the tip of which he employed alternately to scratch forehead and nose. He noted, unseeing, the progress of the little herd; then turned back, frowning, to the trestle table on which his work was spread. He drew his shabby gown about him, scotched on his stiff-backed chair. 'The Devils take our ancestors for their wandering ways,' he said, half to himself. 'Here, clear enough, is the tale of Rand, son of Cedda, son of Ceorn; the same who was Rand Wolfkiller in the Saga of Usgeard. This much is plain; that he fought with Fenricca, whose clan bears the Wolf-staff to this day. But what of this other tale, that he sailed to the lands of the dead and met with ghosts? Also he saved a Princess from a dragon of the Northern Fens. "Sea Worm" is given in the Usgeard. Now the Sea Worm was the Mark of the Fishgard tribes; what are we to make of this?'

'That the Devils already have thy ancestors for their own.' said a dry voice over his head. 'For their minds surely wandered farther than their feet; and their tongues' wanderings were such as to put both to shame.'

Marck looked up, his frown deepening to a scowl. Usk, Jokeman to the House of the Gate, was a strangely fashioned creature; thick in the body and spindly in the shanks, with a swarthy, slab-sided face fixed now in an elaborate leer. His eyes were deep-set and black, his nose imposingly hooked. His cap, with its swastikas and bells, was as usual rammed slantwise on his cropped head; he tweaked it in mock obeisance before swinging by one leg from the beam on which he perched, to swipe the air above his master. Golden motes rained thickly; and he sneezed and cackled. 'Library dust, my King,' he said. 'Thick it lies, where learning most abounds; and thickest of all' – he fielded a missile hurled up from below – 'thickest of all, I say, round genealogists of Sealand.' He regained his perch, seemingly without effort. 'But what's the matter, Lord?' he said. 'What is so sore amiss, that thou repayest thy Fool, who ever honoured thee, with naught but brickbats?' He spoke winningly, offsetting by his tone the malice of the words; for the Old Tongue was little pleasing to those who boasted Sealand blood.

His estimation of his master's mood was sound. The bright morning, it seemed, had lightened even Marck; the royal scribe merely smiled, and began ticking points on his fingers. 'Rand it was who came south, through the Narrow Sea to the Land of Rocks,' he said. 'With him he brought the Mark of the Crab, which my house still bears; the blood lines are clear enough. Arco was Rock King then, Arco the White, whose folk also had been kings in Sealand. This Arco gave in mockery the land a hide might cover; but Rand and his women – Rand the Cunning, he is called in the Edva Rigg – sliced the hide so finely, the thong they made circled a mighty hill. This is the part of the tale that likes me best.'

Usk, who had sunk his head between his hands, heaved his most lugubrious sigh; but his master, once embarked, was not to be checked by trifles. Marck rose, running his fingers through his unkempt yellow-grey hair. 'Daughters Rand had in plenty, but no sons,' he said. 'So Crab Hold passed to Renlac, by marriage to Ellean the Fair. This Renlac fathered Bralt, my great grandsire, taking the Mark in honour of his wife. When Arco came here with a mighty host, Renlac was his Shiplord. Arco honoured him, after the Battle of the Sandhills where the Midsea power broke; and so the Crab was restored to its ancient place. Renlac took the Southguard where we sit, holding it for Arco and his sons; after which …' A thought struck him, and he paused. 'I have heard in jugglers' stories,' he said, 'that this land, and the Misty Isles, were once the Islands of Ghosts. Could that mean …' He scrabbled among the papers with which the trestle was strewn. 'Could that mean merely this, that Rand Wolfkiller came here for his bride? Is the old tale true?'

Usk dropped neatly from the beam. He swung his feet on the table edge, watching their pointed shadows flit across the boards. 'There was a People of the Dragon in the west,' he said. 'Or so I heard my father tell. These the Horsemen broke in foolish pride, before they bowed the proper knee to Sealand.'

The gibe, if gibe it was, went unremarked. Marck chewed the quill tip, frowning again. 'If that were true,' he said musingly. 'Ellean, Rand's daughter, did take a Dragon for her Mark. Why, that would mean …' He glanced up, sharply; but the Jokeman, with a return to his former mood, interrupted him. 'That thou mightst stretch thy hand to western hills,' he said. 'Yet there thou sittest, Marck of the Gate, like breathing stone or a statue of thyself, blotting a fair day with ink. These dusty things with which thou strivest will be thy death.' He ran to bound at the windowsill, checked dangerously on the lip of the sheer drop. 'The air trembles, every live thing stirs,' he said. 'Fowls in the frith, the fishes in the flood … Why sittest thou there, my King? Up, and ride …'

For a moment a curious expression, almost of yearning, might have flitted across Marck's drawn face; then he shook his head. 'Be silent, fool,' he said. 'Soon, under Atha King, all these lands will be one. There will be need then for libraries; and books to fill them, telling how we came by greatness. If you cannot be silent, at least be still.'

The other swung a carrot-coloured shank across the sill, and pulled a face. 'My Lord,' he said. 'Out of thy wisdom, what makes a man a fool?'

Marck raised his head, with a grimace. 'Ceaseless babbling,' he said.

'Then answer this,' said Usk. 'An I babble not, how may I show myself a fool, and worthy of my keep? Speak, sir; for when a fool babbles, wise men from their charity answer him. Else are they not wise, and he no fool.'

He caught the coin the other flung him, nimbly. 'Also I have heard, that wise men live for ever,' he said. 'Pray tell me, master, if thou think'st this true?'

The King stared thoughtfully. 'No man lives for ever,' he said. 'Neither King nor commoner. Which is well enough known, even to fools. What is your meaning?'

'For that you must excuse me,' said Usk, equally grave. 'For a fool can have no meaning. I say but this; that two doors, both as dark, stand close upon each other. That we must pass between them, it being the will of certain Gods. That fish swim in streams, and birds call close to palaces; that kingdoms of linen are but chilly lands, an they be desert.' He bit the coin insultingly, stowed it in his belt. 'A fool's words have no wit,' he said. 'Or I might further ask; who follows thee, King, in thy high chair? For whom are coffers stacked? This little matter of the flesh stands between thee, and immortality.' He skipped to the door. 'I leave thee to thy labours,' he said. 'Perhaps the birds will quiet their song, in honour of thy wit; but that I doubt.'

The door thudded behind him. Marck once more ran his fingers through his hair; he turned the papers on the table, made to write, threw down the quill. He rose, seemingly with irritation, stood at the window. The breeze gusted, bringing with it the scents of earth and fresh grass. The tower creaked; and he saw, as if for the first time, the clear blue sky, dotted with puffy clouds that sailed like ships.

The spring night was chilly; so that fires crackled in the kitchens and lower halls of the place, throwing orange reflections on ceilings of limewashed wood. Above, the Tower stood austere and dark; save for a glimmer, faint as a marsh spirit, where the Lord of the Gate still busied himself at his tasks.

Round the largest of the fires, and sweating a little from its heat, sat a varied group of retainers: a Serjeant of the Wardrobe, a couple of handlers from the royal mews, a soldier of the standing garrison; and a plump-faced kitchen maid, black hair straggling beneath her grubby cap. Beside her, lolling at ease, reposed the great bulk of Thoma, Marck's seneschal. At his feet squatted the Jokeman. He was prodding at the fire with a long metal spit, and as usual talking with some animation. 'Why, man,' he said, 'a hair will turn the matter, one way or the next; as thou shalt see.'

Thoma, whose thoughts never ran far from food, had possessed himself of the part-carved carcass of a chicken. He sucked a legbone noisily, and licked his wrist. 'A hair is a poor thing on which to hang our fates,' he said. 'I for one would not see a Mistress of the Gate. I hold we get by well enough, and keep our state, without a woman to oversee our lives.'

'No woman, surely, would care to see much of thine,' said Usk tartly. 'As for hairs; they are very potent, and oft enough hath answered for folk's lives. With hairs I would attempt this Tower; aye, and hear the wailing for the dead ere dawn.'

Thoma laughed rumbling, and belched. 'Thy tongue could ever turn my wits,' he said good-naturedly. 'But this once I will dispute with you. Make that good.

The Jokeman sprang to his feet with curious elation, danced a step in the ashes. 'For shame, good captain,' he said. 'Thoma, thou bladder of valiance, did'st thou not sit outboasting the cocks not three nights since, about thy service with King Atha's train?'

'That I did,' said Thoma. 'At Long Creek, and Great Grange, and Morwenton when we put down the pretender Astrid. Aye, and burned his Hall.'

'What breached that Hall, to let in thy sweaty feet?' asked the Jokeman sardonically.

'The catapulta, certainly,' said Thoma. 'But this is from the point.'

'The Gods forgive,' said Usk. 'Thy wit grows short in breath.' He danced another jig. 'What, bound among its ropes, gives an engine strength? What lends power to its skein, that else would burst? I hear Queen Maert was first to shear her locks, to give great Atha victory.'

The soldier spat at the fire. 'Your wit is hollow, Jokeman,' he said. 'It rings like a cracked pot.'

'And yours is earth,' muttered the other, forgetting in his annoyance his habitual mode of speech. He turned back to Thoma. 'Was not thy grandsire of Horseman stock?'

Thoma waved a large hand. 'These things are long gone,' he said. 'Long dead.'

'And well dead,' said the soldier, rising. 'The Sealanders own this country, Jokeman; as you had best remember.' He turned on his heel, and stalked away.

Usk watched him go with narrowed eyes. 'Well,' he said lightly. 'Those who make heart's matter of the babble of a fool are fools indeed.' He sat back beside Thoma, securing a portion of the chicken. 'Yet this is true,' he said, watching up. 'Our fathers took this land; took it and were lords of it, before the sea-folk came.'

Thoma shrugged. 'What's gone is gone,' he said philosophically. 'And I for one have no complaints. But tell me these thoughts you have of the king.'

The other nodded, his dark face sombre. 'Many years have I served him, seneschal,' he said. 'Wishing naught but his good, as do we all. Yet still it grieves me to see him solitary; the rareness of his person cries out for a mate. So I have wound my skein, hair by hair; a twist here and a tweak, to win him to my thought. Now I must seek thy help; for married he must be, and that ere further winters fall.'

'And to whom would you marry him, rogue?' asked the kitchen girl, yawning. 'Or is such high policy not for common ears?'

'Not for thine, certes,' snapped the Jokeman. He pushed his cap further to the back of his head, and smirked. 'I know a Maid, not of this common earth,' he said. 'Of high blood, and most ancient line; most fitting, for a King.'

The kitchenwoman, and the others, attempted to draw him further; but Usk, for once, held his peace. He twirled his cap, jangling the bells, and smiled again; till one by one they sought their beds, and let him be.

Sometime in the night a contraption of ropes and levers, set high on the wall of the little hall, moved briefly. A bell jangled, and again. The Jokeman, still sitting beside the barely glowing embers, stared up, eyes white in the gloom. 'Ring till thou burst,' he muttered balefully. 'Call Demons or the Gods, for all I care; for Usk is with his ancestors ...' He stretched, curled himself in the corner farthest from the fire, and was quiet. In time, the bell ceased to move.

Marck could not have been said to wake. Rather, he became aware; of the dim light diffusing through the high chamber, the brighter grey of the single window-slit, stark as cut lead. The air of the room was cold, and still.

He turned his head, listening. The silence seemed to suggest by its completeness the immensity of the sleeping land. No bird, no voice. No snore. The grey light, he knew, lay across heath and tillage, forest and sea; across the Great Plain with its crests of wind-carved trees, across the marshes far to the north where the unknown country stretched out for ever. His mind, free-ranging, saw the villages huddled beneath their thatch, hill-tops crowned with their ramparts. On each a stockade, pale gate houses criss-crossed with timbering; crowning each a Tower, ragged in the early light. Gaunt-eyed, and still. Utterly still.

Increasingly it seemed his life was lived in these dawn watches. Almost it was as if his days, the activity, the petty irritations that filled them, were in reality brief as dreams, meaningless interruptions of a vigil that was in itself endless. He wondered at this vigil; and at the Fate that, creeping by still degrees, had placed him so apart from life. Once, surely, there had been wine and warmth, laughter and good company. When had these things ceased to be?

As ever, there was no answer. It seemed he had grown to silence, like an ageing tree.

There were many dreams. Once – not he, surely, but another – had sat in Midsea palaces, at the feet of learned men. There also had been women, veiled, swaying creatures with the eyes of deer; and a fire in the blood, long cold, that marred his studies of the wheeling stars. He remembered these women, like creatures from another world; and the palaces, their towers bright in sunlight, topped by domes like sharp-tipped onions, red and yellow and green. The dry voices scraped, down the years; while his hands made the dots and squirls, the runes and flowing curves, that are the Midsea tongue.

The dream was interrupted by another. This echoed with battle noise, the thunder of siege trains, the roar of flames. Altred was overlord when his father's death called Marck from his studies, back to a troubled land; Altred who took his brother's wife, and split a new-found kingdom to its roots. In that great war the Crab Shield followed the gonfalon of Atha, from the Marshes to the eastern fens, Southguard to the Great Black Rock where remnants of the Horsemen lingered out their lives in wind-scorched keeps. Towns burned, ringed by the lesser spots of siege fires; battles were fought on parching plains, amid reddened winter wheat. Finally, in a river valley hemmed by endless woods, the last great siege was laid; and Altred died, his life the price of peace.

And there were the Towers on their hills, the great Hall Marck's father raised in a chalk gap next the sea; quietness, and armour hanging dusty on the walls, the martens nesting under the high eaves.

Yet the war-sounds still clamoured in his dreams; so to buy his rest Marck wrote the tale of battles, the Shields that had gathered to Altred and to the House of the White Horse. Those who had lived, and those who had died. Later – and this was an unheard-of-thing – scribes were summoned to copy out the work. Few enough there were, in all the White Island; but the word spread, first to the Land of Rocks, later to the Middle Sea itself. So the clerks came flocking, to sit in lines in the Great Hall of Marck's Tower while the royal writing-master strode forward and back, intoning the story that had come to him. A scroll was sent to Atha King, in his palace by the narrow sea; and Atha, delighted, heaped honours on the scholar of the Gate. Fine horses came to Southguard; hunting dogs, a brace of white sea-eagles and a purse of gold. Marck, moved by such royal favour, redoubled his efforts. His fame grew; so that minstrels and wandering sages took to calling at his Hall, in hope of refreshment and reward. They were seldom disappointed; and the King found new material constantly to hand. He traced the wanderings of the Horse Warriors from their Midsea home, penning the epics the minstrels carried in their heads. The Horsemen too brought with them Gods and ghosts, peopling the Mound on which Marck's Tower was raised; the Mound that was blood and flesh and standing stones, bones of old folk from the start of time. Magic obsessed him; trolls and Marsh monsters, reed-women haunting the noonday pools and red-eared phantom hares. Behind them all, discernible yet, stalked a vast golden shade. From his Tower the King looked out on a bulging hill of chalk; at certain times, in summer evenings and at dawn, lines might be discerned on its surface. Sometimes one saw an upraised club, sometimes the head and shoulders of a great Man; the marks a God himself might make, rusting on the grass. Marck, in learned argument, dismissed the fables that were told; yet still from time to time the hill drew his curious gaze. Chalk carvings were unknown to his Sealand forebears; he produced a monograph on the subject nonetheless, verifying by experiment the ease with which the green skin of grass might be stripped away. Atha, sensing the means for a fresh demonstration of his power, ordered that his Mark be inscribed on all his boundaries, wherever suitable subsoil could be found; so white horses, and sometimes red and brown, once more came to inhabit the land.

It was at this point that a strange malaise gripped Marck, born of the laughter of a carter's child. The shout, vibrant and innocent, came winging up to the Tower one bright day, sending him mumbling from his work to stare into a mirror, pull at the straggling hair the years had turned to grey. The child's voice pierced him; he knew that he was old, and the Tower rooms were chill, and his audience was a jester with cap and bells. The days of joy were done; now he saw the passing of the seasons, snow and fresh spring, the world turning its strange circles under moon and sun. He was oppressed by futility; his food was soured, and his rest destroyed.

He had begun his greatest project, a history of the conquests and journeyings of all the Sealand tribes. Once the tales would have joined beneath his fingers to make patterns undreamed-of; now, the work was stale. Days and nights he spent in sightless staring, a pen in his fingers, the pages spread before him. He took to riding, sometimes at curious hours; a shabby, restless King in breeches and homespun, muttering and dull-eyed. Those of his subjects who met with him bowed the knee, wondering and a little fearful; but Marck was unaware. He brooded by high woods, in lightning flash and summer rain; smelled the wet earth, uncaring.

In time, the sickness passed. A fragment of the former joy returned, buoyed by returning skill; but the shadow that had swept down that bright day was never wholly lifted. Scholars came to the Southguard, some with gifts, some from the Middle Sea itself. Marck received them courteously, as of old, delighting in learned talk; but constantly his eyes and mind would wander. It was at this time that Usk began his wheedling; and strange thoughts flickered in the mind of the King.

The sky was brighter now; and sleep had fled, for yet another day. Marck pushed back his blankets, felt the washing of cold against his skin. A drain, ill-smelling, projected from the wall; he used it, sighing. Over his breechcloth he hung a knee-length riding tunic; he buckled the heavy leather belt, and stamped into his boots. He took down his thickest woollen cloak, and eased open the chamber door.

The guards on duty at the gatehouse clashed to attention, grounding their spears on the turf. A Serjeant, still bleary with sleep, began bawling for an escort; but the King stilled him with an upraised hand. 'Leave me,' he said simply. 'I ride but a little way; none will molest me.'

The other eyed him dubiously; but he was used by now to his master's queerish habits. The gates creaked back; and Marck passed through with a muffled stamping of hooves, the champ and jangle of the charger's bit.

At the foot of the Mound a village had grown up over the years. He paced silently before the white-walled dwellings with their roofs of heavy thatch. Once a dog yapped briefly; a child wailed, and was quieted. Beyond the sleeping houses a steepening way led to a little brook, arched over by tall trees. Mist moved round the belly of the horse; the water-scent was powerful and cold. Beyond the brook the path once more began to rise, climbing the shoulder of the flanking hill. Marck urged his mount, impatiently. When at length he reined, the Tower was small with distance. Below him the mist stretched out like a sea, hiding the real sea beyond. Over its surface ran ripples and fading flashes of light, now here, now gone; and the whole, he saw, was in stealthy, steady motion, flowing inland to the great chalk pass. The sight arrested him. It was as if he, and he alone, had glimpsed a Mystery; the ancient, inscrutable life of the hills themselves.

He rode on, engrossed with the fancy; and feeling too the rise of an excitement he had thought stilled for ever. Once before, in another lifetime, he had ridden thus. Then as now, the chill air lanced at face and arms; then as now some Presence, older than the wandering lanterns, older it seemed than the ghosts that thronged the Southguard, moved before him. The hills stretched westward, shadowy still, humped rampart-like against the sea. The hidden waves seethed to his left; the track rose, fell and rose again. He clicked to the horse, shaking the broad rein, feeling the creature's swaying, hearing the creak of harness, the snort of breath. He knew himself at one with the land, the land that itself was awake and watchful. The spirit, the very essence of the place breathed out some message in a tongue as powerful as it was strange; and he saw, or sensed, all the folk who had known the hills since time began. The Giants, still unforgotten, with their glistening engines; after them the growers of corn, the spinners of wool, the makers of butter and beer. The Horsemen, spreading like a stain; and the New Men, the Sealanders, threshing the water in their many-legged ships. Last of all his own folk, Altred Brothercutter and Atha whom he loved, who set him on his own great chair and placed the sword across his knees, the ring of ancient yellow on his head. All this there was and more, much more; a tale that, could it but be told, would be the greatest in the world.

The slope he climbed was easing. Before him glowed a cloud of light; he panted, driving in his heels. The warhorse scrambled the last yard to the crest; and King Marck blinked, rubbing dazzled eyes.

He had come miles; much farther than he had intended. He stood now on a broad, smooth ridge of chalk. To his left, a marker rose above a tall cairn of stones; the sun, mounting the sea's rim, touched the rough iron with gold. The shadow of the Crab was flung across the mist; the land to westward was a haze of brightness, in which shapes of fancy moved.

He dismounted, walking to the cairn. The horse, left to itself, wandered a pace or two, dropped its head to crop the close-knit grass. Marck drew the cloak more tightly, laid his head against the great piled stones and closed his eyes. Somewhere a sea bird called; the light, refracted by the mist, burned at his lids. In more prosaic mood, he might have said he slept; but certainly the strangest vision came to him.

It seemed the spirit of the place, the Thing that had plagued him on the way, once more returned. Her limbs, he saw, were the creamy brown of tide-washed sand. Her hair shone rich and dark as jet; her eyes, deep pools, reflected headlands and seas. She towered, all-encompassing; yet the hands she placed in his were slight and warm as the hands of the carter's child. He wondered how such things might be; and she laughed, knowing his thought. '*I am she you sought*,' she said. '*I am the land and sea, snow on far hills;*

summer mist, the hot bright grain. I am the reed-pool woman, sun on green water ...'

Warmth coursed through him then, the blood raced in his veins. He would have risen, joyful and light; but the Spirit laughed, pressing a finger to his lips. She spoke much, of many things, and later showed him Mysteries; cities and towers beyond imagining, great roads that thronged with folk, ships of floating iron. For there too she had lived, in the time of the Giants; and worn bright short clothes and laughed, and served men beer in a room of amber light where a stone fish swam in a case of priceless glass. And once she lay on a hillside, and wore a kilt of doeskin and a necklace of coral and jet. She who died in silk and flames was born again a Princess of the West; while Dragons fought, and the magic ships roared, and Gods and cities fell and rose. '*And once*,' she said, '*I lay in a house with round white towers. I walked in a deep green marsh, and wonderful things were done. These things you shall do, for a need; for a King must wed his land. Once I was Mata. Then I was the Reborn. Now my name is ...*'

But Marck, rousing with a great start, already knew.

At times during the long ride back, he sang snatches of song. At others fear and guilt came on him, so that he wrung his hands. He addressed arguments to the rocks, colloquies to the wheeling gulls. Once, hands to his temples, he cried, 'It is not fitting ...' Then the warmth her touch had brought once more flooded him. Riding a green stretch of turf, his mind was eased; crossing a tumbled scree he roared that a King could feel no desire. He pulled at his hair and beard, plucked his sleeves; then he laughed again and said, 'Thoma is my man, and will perform my offices.' He also wept; but by the time his Tower once more came into sight, gleaming in the early sun, he was calm again. The hooves of his horse rang hollow on the outer bridge; as the Serjeant ran to grip the rein, he raised his head. He said, 'It will be for my people.'

'And that,' said Thoma heavily, 'is the tale of it. Or as near as man may judge. So Scatha take all smooth-tongued schemers, all wearers of motley, all dabblers in matters of high estate; and above all Usk, who I verily believe has turned our good King's head with his prattle. Were there such times, in memory? Once, in faith, we were content enough; now we must wear ... *ahh* ... fineries that chafe the skin, constrict our persons to the shape of ... village wenchels, on the word of some Godforsworn tailor, whom the Nightrunners may as willingly keep.' He wrenched at the collar of his tunic, and groaned with relief. 'As for the rest,' he said, 'we must take what comfort remains ...' He swigged deeply from a pot-bellied flagon, and wiped his mouth with the back of his hand.

His companion, a strapping young Captain of the Royal Guard, stared round him dubiously. Certainly the chamber in which they were lodged, and in which for a week they had waited the pleasure of King Odann of the Plain, seemed little calculated to promote cheerfulness. Apart from the two narrow beds it was empty of furniture, and its gloomy walls were unrelieved by paint or drapery. A single arrowslit, unshuttered, admitted grey light and the piercing wind of the Plain. The door was massive, studded with iron and barred, ominously, from the outside. From beyond it now came the tramp of feet, a shouted order. The wind rose again, with a sigh and rumble; and the Captain grinned, turning back to his companion.

No finery, certainly, could have constricted the seneschal's ample person to the dimensions of which he complained; but if the thought crossed the other's mind he forbore comment. Instead he shrugged. 'By the Gods, Thoma,' he said, 'but when Jokemen control Kings, the world is upside down. Or we should all wear motley, and make our fortunes presently. But what was this other tale you spoke of, that the King met with a Fairy woman who promised him great riches?'

Thoma scowled, and made a sign with his fingers. 'As for that,' he said, 'I'd as lief be ruled by our lord Usk. His scrawny neck I could at least take between my hands.' He shuddered, and readdressed himself to the flagon. 'If it was true,' he said, 'and our lord not touched in his wits with riding in sea mists, then there was power there; more than Usk and all his marshalled ancestors might command. But witchcrafts are for priests, Briand, not for us. Talk no more of it.'

The other frowned in turn, rubbing at his lip. 'But did he say aught else?' he persisted. 'What were these prophecies she made him?'

'Aught else,' groaned Thoma. 'What did he not say ...' He shook his head, running blunt fingers through his thatch; then it seemed the desire for confidence overcame his instinct for caution. 'All night I sat with him,' he said, 'and on into the dawn. The half of what he spoke, I own, has gone out of my head; for much of the time I dozed. Something there was of Gods most certainly, and a Great One reborn as a carter's child; but the manner of that is past the telling. In this much the Jokeman spoke truth; that fuddling with old books, and older stories, waters a man's brains, an he hold to it enough. For my part I could wish us home again, out of this stinking place. And this whole business ended, or not begun.'

But the other rose and punched him cheerfully. 'For shame, Thoma,' he said. 'What, a courtier of thy proved mettle to leave the game half played? Thou hast worked mightily for our Lord in this matter, and will ere yet bring him handsome winnings. Though I must own, if Goddesses are in question he has perhaps sent thee to shop in the wrong market ...'

Almost certainly he would have said more; but the sudden sideways glint of Thoma's eye warned him to silence.

An hour passed, draggingly. Thoma had emptied the flagon, and begun once more to complain, when the doorbolts were withdrawn with heavy creaks. Both men rose, hands to their sword hilts. The door swung inward; and a cowled priest faced them in the gloom. 'My Lord Odann bids me tell you his decision is reached,' he muttered. 'He requests you to attend him.'

They followed the other's flapping gown down ill-lit steps. The Great Hall was as dank and gloomy as the rest of the place. The windowslits, deep-set between massive timbers, were muffled with smoke-stained cloth. Lamps burned here and there in niches, crude wicks floating in saucers of stinking oil. At the end of the high chamber, on a dais flanked by torchbearers, sat Odann King. In one hand he held the great staff of his house, with its snarling wolf's head; his other was hidden amid the dark folds of his robe, but it seemed he gripped himself as if to ease a pain. Round him clustered priests and nobles. Bronzed skin was much in evidence, and hooked noses, black-browed eyes; for the Horseman blood was strong here on the Plain.

To the King's right stood a cloaked and hooded woman. Little could be seen of her face save the dark eyes, the finely arched brows; but her figure was slender and desirably formed. Behind her and a little to one side stood Dendra, brother to the King. His feet were set apart on the rushes, his thumbs hooked in his belt; and he scowled at the ambassadors with little favour. Round him lounged some dozen heavily armed men. They made no move to salute the newcomers, but stared like their leader in silence.

Thoma sensed well enough the tension in the Hall. He stepped forward, sweating slightly, grounded his staff and began to speak. 'Greetings,' he said, 'to Odann of the Plain and to his House, from his brother Marck of the Gate, Keeper of the Southguard, Lord of the Seaward Hills.'

The raised hand of the King cut short the formal speech. A spasm crossed his face. He arched his back, pressing with his elbows against the arms of the throne. The moment passed; and he turned to stare at the girl beside him. A wait; then she put the hood back, with a quick movement. Her hair was black, they saw, her skin clear and brown, her arms and shoulders gracefully made.

'This,' said Odann, 'is my daughter, much beloved. What does the Gate King give, for such a prize?'

Thoma's eyes moved round the company, finding little comfort. He cleared his throat, and smiled. 'My master is a simple man,' he said. 'Yet his coffers are rich, and for this blessing he has opened them. He offers thirty horses, each strong-backed and trained for war. Also a chest of gold, such as two strong men might carry; three of silks and yet another of spice. A waggon of fine wine from the Midsea lands, both yellow and red ...'

Dendra swore, loudly. Odann once more raised his hand; but the other went on unchecked.

'Silks,' he said. 'And spices. The Gate insults us, brother.' Then to Thoma, 'We have no use, here on the Plain, for women's toys. Go home, chalkdweller, while yet thy legs can bear thee.'

A burst of laughter from the soldiery; and Thoma stepped forward, neck reddening. The glances that passed between Dendra and his brother, and between Odann and the girl, were lost on him; for the Plainsman had spoken in the Old Tongue, in which 'chalkdweller' and 'barbarian' are one. He would have drawn, regardless of his mission; but Odann had risen, stood racked and swaying. His daughter clung to him; but he put her gently aside. 'You will forgive my brother's words,' he said wearily. 'When he sits here on this throne he will speak as he chooses; then if you wish, you may answer him.' He turned back to the girl, staring a great time; then he raised his voice. 'Hear me,' he said. 'All you within this Hall. The gold we will take, and the spices. Also fifty horses, sound in wind and limb, with their saddles and all trappings of war. This, and nothing less; I do not barter, Hill Men, for what is without price. Will you answer for your King?'

Thoma, dry-mouthed, gifted his master's stable. The girl turned on him a blazing white face; then drew the hood about her and hurried from the Hall. The King stepped from the dais, taking the arm of a priest; and Dendra turned with a final glare and stalked from the place, his followers at his heels. Servingmen scurried with the trestles for a feast; and Thoma, slowly relaxing, grimly caught the Captain's eye.

From a chamber high in the Tower the girl stared down. Beyond the outworks of the place, the baileys and barbican with its steps and gantries, clustered the banners of the Crab. The stamp of horses carried to her and a bawled order from Thoma, bulky in a cape of fur. The little column formed itself, turned and trotted away, vague in the early light; became a darker smudge that receded against the vast blurred greyness of the Plain.

She turned, her face pale and set, and gripped the wrap tighter round her shoulders. She said in a small voice, 'I will not go to him.'

Beside the royal bed a flask of wine stood on an inlaid table. Odann reached clumsily and poured, held the cup to his lips. He drank, and sighed. 'Miri,' he said, 'sit with me. Come here.' She did as she was bidden, silently. His fingers touched her hair, where it lay coiled against her shoulder; then he pulled his hand away. 'Listen,' he said, 'and hear me well. Soon, Dendra will sit in my chair. There is no place for you here.'

She had turned, lips parted; and he took her hand. His sight blurred; and a part of him was nearly glad of the pain that made her increasingly remote. 'Miri,' he said gently, 'try to understand. This man, this Marck, will use you honourably. Once, many years ago, I knew him well; and he you. A child, at your mother's knee ...' He drew his breath, sharply; grimaced, and went on. 'There is no place for you,' he said again. 'The Southguard lands are richer than our own; his Tower is well-founded, and he stands high with Atha King. In one month, you will go. You must take the chests of cloth, and the things that were your mother's ...'

She threw herself down abruptly, hiding her face. She began to sob; and his hand once more found her hair. 'My child,' he said, 'do this for me. Do not make my pain the worse.'

She said in a muffled voice, 'I will never serve him.'

The King lay awhile watching up at the ceiling, his face drawn and grey. 'Do as you will,' he said finally. 'If you cannot honour him as a husband, perhaps you will learn to love him as ... a father.'

She raised her head then slowly, staring at him with her great dark eyes.

Throughout the day, Thoma refused to slacken pace. The party muttered, Briand complained more loudly; but the seneschal pressed on grimly, his face to the south. At last, toward nightfall, the desolation of the Great Plain was left behind; and a village showed ahead, a well-found place with high watchtowers and a stockade on which torches burned at intervals. Only then did the leader rein, to stare back narroweyed at the heights still visible in the growing dark. The Captain, his spirits rising at the prospect of warmth and food, ranged up beside him. 'Well, my Lord,' he said, 'in spite of thy complaints, thou hast discharged thy duty fairly. And gained for the King a most comely bride.'

But Thoma was not to be soothed. 'A devil, from a place of devils,' he said. He touched heels to his exhausted horse. 'Worse is to come of this,' he growled. 'Mark me, my friend.'

Yet later to the King he said, 'She is a pretty brown child.'

Then began a house-cleaning such as the folk of the Gate had never known; for Marck, the most industrious of clerks, had ever been the most indulgent of rulers. Now, all was changed; and men stared to see their liege lord resplendent in scarlet and gold, stepping briskly about his affairs. Small whirlwinds swept the kitchens of the Tower; and its pantries and buttery, its stables, dormitories and mews. In their wake they left stone flags gleaming, cooking vessels scoured and bright. Cartload after cartload of rushes, scraped from the floors, made their way down the Mound, to be dumped in heaps on the banks of the little brook; in their place, floors were strewn with precious hay. It became a commonplace to see Marck perched dangerously on a tottering stool, personally supervising the removal of some high cobweb that had offended the royal eye; for the King brought to his new preoccupation the same meticulousness that had earned him fame as a scholar, and many a night the household got to its rest with groans and aching backs. Nor was this all; for craftsmen were summoned, some from as far off as Great Grange, to beautify the chambers and Hall. The walls of the Tower dazzled white in the sun before they were through, while the Great Hall acquired a ceiling of vivid green, pricked all over with golden stars. It was in fact, as Thoma heavily remarked, no longer a fit place to drink in; he took refuge in the farthest and meanest of the kitchens, only to be evicted in turn by a small army of limewash-wielding work-men.

Meanwhile the formal business of the marriage must be attended to. Clerks drew up the contract, working under the direction of the sorely-baffled seneschal; for Marck, in a state of high alarm, refused to bring his scholarly wits to bear on the matter in any way. A messenger despatched to Atha's court returned not merely with the royal assent but with a rich gift, a furlined robe and necklet of gold, fit wearing for a Queen. The following day an armed contingent of Plainsmen presented itself at Marck's gate; when the warriors left it was with twentyfive mares and stud animals, and a massive chest of plate. After which the tailors reappeared, to fit the housefolk with fresh livery. Everyone, from the meanest turnspit to the most dignified Serjeant, became resplendent in yellow and green; such expense was unheard-of, hitherto unimagined. Usk, it seemed, profited from the changed circumstances most of all; so that plump Maia, coming upon him one day in the inner courtyard of the Tower, stood and stared. The Jokeman had discarded the motley of his calling; his jerkin gleamed with thread of gold, while his shanks were clad in richly coloured silk.

'Now Scatha take all misbelievers,' said Maia. 'For if as I hear the King sees wonders, no less do we all. Is this some new jest, Jokeman? For Usk turned courtier is the greatest wonder yet.'

But the Jokeman merely regarded her disdainfully. 'The King has put away his books,' he said, 'I my foolishness, and thou thy greasy cap. But an ill grace, it seems, is not so ready hid.' He brushed past, his head held high, and left the woman staring.

Messengers rode again; for the lands of the Crab were wide, extending east to the Black Rock villages, west to the borders of the wild lands where the Sea Kings have their halls, paying no taxes and owing allegiance to none. Marck's summons was handsomely couched; and headmen and priests from all the vassalage, together with their families, began to converge on the Tower by the Gate. All brought gifts; oxen and sheep, beer by the barrel and the tun, horses to make good the bridefee. Though none existed in all the Southguard to match the animals that had been lost. Or so at least claimed the stable-master, who added hard words on the bargain struck by Thoma for his lord. But the stablemaster was a simple soul, whose fat wife boiled his broth and clothed his children, and who looked for nothing more.

At last all things were in readiness; and a great day came when outriders, who had scoured the Heath since dawn, flew back to Marck's Tower with news of a procession that wound its cautious way among the green bogs of the coastland. A fine procession it was too that finally drew in sight of the Gate. First came priests and spaewives, blowing on gold-bound horns and waving green branches of peace; then a troupe of acrobats and jugglers, dressed in the motley Usk so recently disdained; then a cart drawn by lumbering oxen with the going-gifts of Miri, Princess of the Plain, her silks and dresses, the draperies and Sealand tapestry that had been her mother's pride. Lastly came soldiers from the household of Odann, footmen and helmeted cavalry, their breastplates winking back the morning sun; and a closed carriage drawn by further oxen, its sides wreathed with sprays of flowers and leaves. Its appearance threw Marck, if possible, into greater confusion than before. His hair and beard, once carefully combed, he had scrabbled to disarray; he danced on the roof of the Tower, staring beneath his hand, before turning to shout for his aides.

'Thoma,' he said, 'to the gate, to welcome her. No, to horse; take a troop, go welcome her from me. Take her this ring.'

'My Lord,' said Thoma, 'my place is at the gate.'

'Yes, yes to be sure. Thoma, is it she? Where are my Captains, where is Briand?'

Here, my Lord,' said Briand. He too had profited from the transactions at Odann's Tower. His tunic and leggings were of richest cloth; his yellow hair and sweeping moustaches gleamed like silk.

'Good Briand, go to her,' said his master. 'And Usk, where is Usk? Let him also ride.'

'My Lord,' said Thoma, shocked. 'To send a Jokeman ...'

'He sends no Jokeman,' said a sour voice at his side.

The seneschal turned, staring; for Usk was no less resplendent than the rest. His tunic was of green silk, well stitched with precious thread, his cloak lined with red and trimmed with snow-white fur. Rings glittered on his fingers, a jewelled dagger hung at his hip. 'See to your offices about the Tower, friend,' he said loftily. 'I with my lord's permission, will bear his greetings.' He took the ring, bowing, and skipped for the stairs, calling for soldiers to attend him; and Thoma favoured his retreating back with a glance that was both foreboding and dire.

'Now,' said King Marck, all unaware. 'The bride-price, Thoma; is the balance prepared?'

'It is, my Lord,' said the seneschal heavily, and turned to follow his King.

*

Every window of the Tower shone with light. The noise of the feast, the shouting and laughter, rang across the baileys; so that the gate guards turned from eyeing the crawling mists to stare up with longing and resentment. Pigs and oxen, roasting whole, dripped and sizzled over blazing courtyard fires while in the Great Hall every available inch was taken up by trestles and the diners. Serving men and girls threaded their way between as best they might, bearing aloft steaming dishes; in the winestores cask after cask was broached, bowl after bowl filled sparkling to the brim.

On the Royal dais, set high above the heads of the commoners, gleamed the greatest wonder of all: candles of priceless beeswax, filling the air with a golden scent. At one end of the long table was placed the painted chair of Marck. Flanking the King, in strictest order, sat the officers of his household; Thoma and Briand, the Captains of Infantry and Horse, the Serjeants with their wives. At the far end of the board, between two women of the Plain, sat Miri. Her black hair glittered with dustings of gold; her eyes in the candlelight looked dark and huge, her face and faultlessly modelled arms seemed brown and warm as the honey wax. She wore a simple dress of green, embroidered at the throat with golden thread; and on her breast, glinting, hung the great Gift of Atha. She sat unsmiling, eating little, drinking occasionally from the cup at her side; and Marck, his head spinning with the heat and wine, gripped the seneschal's elbow urgently.

'It is she,' he whispered. 'The Fairy-girl of the hills. Thoma, *it is she …*'

But Thoma, sweating heavily and hampered by an unaccustomed fork and knife, answered with little more than a grunt.

The moon was sinking to the rim of hills, and the mists floating high amid the trees that lined the brook, before the last of the feasters sought his bed. The bride had long since retired to her chamber; below in the Great Hall, yawning kitchen staff scraped up the last of the leavings, extinguished the rushlights that had burned in profusion along the walls, squabbled at the High Table for the drippings of scented wax. In the courtyard the remnants of the fires pulsed sullenly, sending up columns of smoke that mingled with the mist. Between them, close to the great inner wall, stood the Jokeman. The collar of his fine tunic was soiled with food, and he had been a little sick; but he stared up fixedly at the massive pale face of the Tower, the light that glowed softly from its upper chamber into the dark.

In the chamber, Marck stood at the foot of the Royal bed. On it, heaped in profusion, lay creamy fleeces and the skins of spotted cats the Midsea traders brought. Above it hung a drape of yellow silk; and among the skins nestled the Lady. The eyepaint she still wore made her look fierce as some forest creature; and her face was set like stone. Round her neck she wore a delicately worked gold torque, and below it a shift of fine green silk, through which her breasts showed with their firm, high buds.

The King rumpled the linen at his hips, helplessly. The vision had uplifted him; faced with its reality, he was all but dumb. It seemed her very stare drained his strength from him; the room spun a little, and he attempted to smile. 'But my dear,' he said meekly, 'I am your husband now. You are bound to obey.'

Her nostrils widened. 'You are my purchaser, King Marck,' she said, 'and that is all. Obedience may not be bought, as you yourself should know. Like love, it must be earned.'

Marck took a half-step, shuffling his feet. He said, 'Then tell me … what may I …'

Her eyes with their heavy lashes drifted closed. She said tiredly. 'Restore me to my home, and King Odann. Is this within your power?'

He twined his fingers. 'My child, the gifts are given …'

She snapped at him. '*Then leave me …*' She rolled her head miserably against the furs. 'Oh why did I come here, why did I let him persuade me … No!' That to Marck, who had once more moved toward the bed. He stopped, mouth working; her eyes blazed at him, then softened. She smiled, and patted the skins. 'My Lord,' she said, 'do not alarm yourself. Here, come sit with me. For a little while.'

He scotched, hesitantly, on the side of the bed. A scent came from her that set his pulses racing; yet it seemed he dare not raise his eyes. A silence; then she spoke again more kindly. 'This you must understand,' she said. 'My father sold me, for fifty horses; like a … chattel, or a dog. I cannot so quickly … give myself afresh.'

He gripped her hand impulsively, and kissed. She stiffened, for an instant it seemed she might pull away; then she relaxed once more. Her fingers were brown and slender, the nails flat like the nails of a boy. He marvelled at her, feeling a great surge of joy; and she squeezed his hand, as if protectively. 'Of course,' she said, 'since as I say you own me, my will is yours. And you will find me dutiful. If you … force me I will not resist, for my father's sake with whom I still keep faith. But my Lord, to force would be a dreadful thing, with Athlinn's green knot still about my waist. For the first night belongs to the Gods who made us all. Also, and this you surely know, women who are tired, as I am tired, cannot love well, or truly.'

'I …' he said. 'I …'

'My Lord,' she said. She squeezed his hand again, and drew away. She wriggled, where she lay among the fleeces. 'How welcome you have made me,' she said. 'And what a fine bed you prepared, I never saw a finer. Or slept therein.' She lay with her great eyes fixed on him, solemnly. 'King Marck,' she said, 'grant me one wish. And make me truly happy.'

'My dear,' he said, moved. 'Anything. Anything ...'

She gave him a tiny smile, that barely curved the corners of her lips. Her eyes searched his face, moving in little shifts and changes of direction. 'Give me ... a little time,' she said. 'Just a little. And I will come to love you truly, as a friend.'

She saw the shadow that crossed his face. He wrestled, it seemed, with some compulsion; then he nodded, inarticulate. He said, 'It will be ... as you say.'

She sighed. 'Oh,' she said, 'how I regret my sharp words now. For I can see in your face, that you would never bring me harm. Now, this is what we will do. Are you listening?'

'Yes,' he said. 'Yes, my dear.'

'You will come to me,' she said, 'each day. And we will talk. Perhaps many times each day. You shall instruct me; for on the Plain they say you are the greatest scholar in the land. Also I wish to see your realm of Southguard; for my father told me many wonderful things. Then when I know your country, and know its people, and truly feel it to be my home ...' She let the sentence hang delicately in air, and smiled once more.

The heart of King Marck was lightened by the words; and he rose. 'My dear,' he said, 'all this will be done. Now you must rest, for I see you are very tired.'

'Yes,' she said. 'Thank you.' Then as he turned, 'My Lord ...'

'Kiss me good night,' she said.

He stooped to her. She raised her hands modestly, covering her breasts. His lips brushed, lightly, her hot, dry brow; he smelled the perfume of her hair, and rose. 'My dear,' he said, 'if you should need ... the housepeople ...'

She shook her head, eyes sleepy and warm. 'Nothing, King Marck,' she said. 'Good night. And ... the Gods attend your sleep.' The smile curved her lips once more; it stayed fixed there long after he had taken the lamp, and the chamber was dark.

Toward dawn the Jokeman hemmed in his sleep, and coughed. Thoma groaned, champing his lips like a dog; and Briand turned, and dreamed a certain dream. While in the highest chamber, lit by its marsh-sprite lamp, a strange sound might have been heard; dry and repetitive, like an old shoe scuffed endlessly against a plank. It came from the Royal couch; where Marck of the Gate, great vassal of Atha the Good, wept in expiation for an uncommitted sin.

Spring deepened to summer. Once more the martens nested under the high eaves of the Tower, raising their broods of squeaking young; skies gleamed blue and faultless, while white dust rose behind the waggons that toiled down to the great gap in the chalk. They came from Long Creek, and the sea-haunted lands of the west; from Great Grange and the Hundred Lakes and Morwenton itself, the sprawling metropolis where Atha had his Hall. Silks they brought and linen of marvellous fineness, jet and amber from the north, mirrors of burnished bronze; and once a tub of honey from the Misty Isles, brown and rich and smelling of the heather from which it had been won. Nothing it seemed was too much, no expense too great, for the Lady of the Gate; and the Queen fulfilled her bargain faithfully, delighting her lord in many different ways. From him she learned the great tales of his people, their sieges and battles and wanderings; and the King never found a more willing audience. Also she rode the length and breadth of the Southguard, by litter or on horseback, speaking to all not as great lady or Queen but as an equal. For this and for her beauty, she was much beloved; so that children would run to bring her flowers, or field-gifts of cider and beer.

Marck for his part showed her his kingdom with joy; the swaying, rolling uplands of the chalk, dotted by gravemounds old when Time began; the tree-lined coombes, drowsy with bee-sound, each with its nestling village and chuckling stream; the Great Heath, empty and vast, rhododendrons blazing beneath dark-topped clumps of pine. He showed her fishing villages, clinging limpet-like between sky and sea; headlands that strode each beyond the next, hazed with sunlight against the brilliant blue; ragged saw-edges of cliff, where the mist whirls up in summer and the wind comes in. He showed her the Ledges, where stone groins slope into the water and the sea sucks down and up, and no boat can live; and there she swam, for her Lord's delight, in a great rock pool among green and dark-red fern.

At length it seemed he saw, reflected in her eyes, a dream that had been his own. He spoke of this, one morning in high summer. She heard him through, not frowning; but when he had finished she shook her head. 'My Lord,' she said, 'half of what you have said I admit I have not understood; but it seems you do me too much honour. Lord, women are not Goddesses. This you must know. We eat like you, and sleep like you, we have needs of the body and … functions; in truth, no Goddess lives in me. I would not see you so sorely disappointed.'

'But you do not understand,' said Marck. 'You have not listened. I knew you, you see, so many years ago.'

'As a baby, yes,' she said. 'My father told me.'

'No,' he said. 'No, no, no …'

She knelt, and took his hands. She was wearing a new white dress, and her hair smelled of summer grass. 'My Lord,' she said, 'you have been kinder to me than I would have believed. Kinder than my own father, who once was all I had; and I am your Queen, so I can speak frankly. Do not make me a Goddess, King Marck, or think in such terms again. Goddesses are for worshipping; and I … am not worthy.'

He touched her hair. 'You do not understand,' he said. 'But why should you? Miri, if a Goddess is in you, she may not choose to reveal herself. But... listen, Miri,' he said earnestly. 'You have brought me great joy. My dear, have you heard the people? Have you heard what they say? They say, "King Marck laughs. King Marck is happy." And Miri, this is true. Listen to me now.'

She sat beside him, hands in her lap, and smiled.

'This was my dream,' he said. 'But words are not enough. Have you seen ... the grass, the greenness of it? Green, and soft ... And the grain, standing against the sky? And the sea mist, how it stripes the hills? And with the sun behind it, *gold* ...'

She said, puzzled, 'My Lord?'

He flexed his hands, stammering in his eagerness. 'This was my dream,' he said. 'That I *was* the grain, and earth, and creeping things upon it. And mist and sky, the stones the Giants placed between the hills. I was the land, Miri, and the land was me. In the dream I found a woman, who was also the land; and we made children who would ... know the land, and live out golden times. And ... this too was the dream. That we died, returning to earth; but we *were* our children, and their children's children, and the golden grain again. It seemed a ... Mystery, a worthy thing.'

She stared at him, with troubled eyes; then took his hand, and laid her head against his shoulder. 'I cannot say,' she said. 'But ... perhaps, some day, these things will be.'

Nothing further passed between them at that time; but it seemed the notion of the Mystery remained with the Queen. She spoke of it some weeks later, to a servingmaid. Autumn was on the land; a calm, mild autumn of gold and blue. In the Tower rooms the first fires had been lit, crackling with sweet-scented cones. Before one such hearth Miri lay, amid piles of fleeces. She wore a skirt of pleated green linen, held closely to her hips by a splendid belt broidered with gold. Between her breasts hung the Gift of Atha; but she was otherwise bare. The girl, a daughter of a Sea King's thrall, knelt beside her. Something of the sea seemed to have marked her wide-spaced eyes, which were blue as Miri's were brown; they sparkled now with amusement as she laughed. She took up a little vial of scented oil, poured a few spots between the shoulders of the Queen and began to massage gently.

'Why do you laugh?' asked Miri. 'This I have on no less a word than that of my lord the King, who is the wisest man in Southguard. And probably the world.'

The girl giggled again. She said, 'Yes, my Lady.'

'Then may it not be true?' demanded the Queen. 'I have the parts of a Goddess, Atta, as you may perhaps have noticed. It follows I have something of her power.' She sighed. 'Lower, Atta, lower,' she said. 'Just there I'm *very* sore ...'

The girl poured more oil.

'What would you have me do, in earnest of my power?' asked Miri. 'Shall I call up a demon?' She propped her chin in her hands, eyes vague. 'Perhaps I shall raise a tempest,' she said. 'Like the ghost-wizards did in our fathers' time. Do you not tremble?'

Atta grinned, but made no answer.

Miri pouted. 'I have it,' she said after a while. 'Since I am not believed, and would have you worship me, I shall bring the lightning. Will you love me then, Atta? When you see the hilltops smoking, and every Tower split?'

For the first time a trace of uneasiness showed in the outlander's face. 'My Lady,' she said in an unsure voice, 'these things should not be mocked.'

The Queen rolled over into her lap and seized her wrist, watching up with glowing eyes. She said, '*I do not mock.*' A little pause; then she lowered her lids sleepily, and smiled. 'Kiss me, Atta,' she said. She pulled the other's head down, slowly; then took the sea girl's lip between her teeth, biting until she pulled back with a gasp. She laughed then, composedly; sprinkled oil, and guided the other's hand. 'I shall do as I choose,' she said. 'And you will serve me; for a Goddess can do no wrong.'

2

The weather worsened toward the end of the year. First came gales from the south; winter gales, hissing and filled with sleet. They turned the sea to a smoking plain of grey, flung great waves crashing at the battered cliffs. Boats drawn high on the foreshore were smashed or swept away, thatch and tiles torn from cottage roofs. Later came torrential rain. It beat the last leaves from the trees, mashing them to brown pulp. The brook that flowed below the Mound became a racing flood while night after night Marck's house-people lay awake, feeling their beds shift under them and creak, hearing the boom and roar as the wind fought with the Tower. Shutters burst and the fastenings of doors, the oiled silk panes from the windows of the Great Hall. Torches streamed beards of flame, till they were extinguished in fear. Then the wind died away. It left the Tower dripping, silent, and fearful still. For a rumour had run, from the Serjeants to the gateporters, the porters to the grooms, the grooms to the mews servants and their wives. None knew how it began; but all took to walking carefully, and speaking in low tones. No fear, however, sustains itself for long; so that when nothing further chanced the bolder or less reverent members of the household began to do a much worse thing than huddle and talk. They began to laugh.

Of all these happenings, one man seemed unaware; and that man was King Marck. Through the wild weeks of storm, and through the dark, calm days that followed, he worked incessantly, copying out sheet after sheet in his angular, precise hand. At last, after so much heartsearching, his mind was calm again; and a new subject had come to him. He was writing, for his Queen, the tale of all the Sealand Gods; Athlinn and Devu Spearwielder, Gelt who forges the lightning and Scatha who sends the Runners of the Night.

It was on one such gloomy afternoon, soon after the turn of the year, that the royal scribe heard above him a familiar cough. He stared up, amazed; and on the beam, his thin legs swinging as of old, sat Usk. Rich living had fattened him, so that his tunic stretched tight across his belly; but he wore his cap and bells, and had twisted his face into his most unpleasant leer. 'Now, King,' he said, 'I see a well-accustomed sight. What occupies thy royal wits now?'

'Nothing,' said Marck, troubled. 'Nothing that concerns you, friend. Usk, why have you done this? You know it was my wish that, having no need of Jokemen, you should not humble yourself for me.'

Usk ignored the question. 'Nothing?' he said. He flung his heels up, cackling. '*Nothing concerns the King*,' he mocked. 'Well hast thou spoken, Lord; with Nothing hast thou concerned thyself, this many a day. And Nothing will be thy reward ...'

'Come down from there,' said Marck with some asperity. 'Also, explain this nonsense. Or take it somewhere else; already I have heard enough.'

'*Come down from there*,' said the Jokeman. 'Kings may come down from thrones, Gods from the sky; scholars may take leave of truth, and wise men of their wits. But Usk, in all this jangling, holds his place.'

Marck flushed. 'I said come down ...'

'Would that I might,' said the other mournfully. 'But I am bound here, Lord. Within the shadow of a greater, the Jokeman's, folly goes unseen ...' He craned his head. 'What writest thou?'

'You know very well,' said his master angrily. 'I finish my book; with the tale of Devu, and the singing bird of Midgard.'

'Singing birds,' said Usk. 'Lord, of thy goodness, tell me another tale.'

'What tale is that?' snapped Marck.

'Of Athlinn and the nymph Goieda,' said the Jokeman. 'That is a better story.'

'You know it as well as I,' said the King shortly. 'The jongleur from Morwenton sang it, not two months since in Hall.'

'Yet would I hear it from thy lips,' said Usk winningly. A favour, Lord ...'

'*Hmmph*,' said Marck. He turned the pages before him, grumpily, casting suspicious glances at the other. 'Athlinn, who was lord of Heaven, wooed the nymph,' he said. 'But Goieda refused him in her pride, cherishing the love of Basta, a Midgard King.' Then it seemed that despite his annoyance the scholar in him gained the upper hand. 'This is the version I have written,' he said. 'So it is set down in the Saga of Ennys, who was Arco's bard. But in the Usgeard Goieda becomes a mortal girl and daughter of King Renlac, my great-kinsman. Which makes me wonder if…'

Usk coughed, 'My Lord,' he said, 'the tale…'

'Be still,' snapped Marck. 'Is there no pleasing you?' But the thread of his discourse was lost; he frowned, scratched his head and resumed the story. 'Athlinn carried the nymph to his great Hall,' he said, 'and there plied her with gifts. But Goieda mocked him, putting scorn on him, calling him grey-beard and old man…'

He stopped abruptly, as if realizing for the first time the Jokeman's drift. He scowled; then his face cleared, and he shook his head. 'This tale was told in Sealand in the times of Rand the Wise,' he said. 'Those days are done.'

'Till on a day,' said Usk, 'the patience of the High One was exhausted. Those are thy words, my King. So Athlinn took a spear butt, and with it beat the nymph. Then when he wearied of the sport, he knew her. Then her blood flowed, even to Middle Earth; then the crops sprang; summer came, and the tribes of men rejoiced.'

'Peace,' said Marck wearily. 'Peace, my friend. You do not understand.'

'Then was Athlinn stricken in his heart,' said Usk remorselessly. 'Then for a year and a day the sun was hid; and the doors of Heaven gaped, for Goieda to go or stay as she might choose…'

'At the end of which time,' said Marck, 'Athlinn returned. And Goieda washed his hands and brought him bread, repentant. And on her Athlinn fathered all the Gods…' He raised his hands, half-laughing. 'Usk,' he said, 'I am not King of Heaven, nor desire to be higher than I am. Under Atha I hold this country, between the hills and sea, and rule as justly as I may. What Gods might do is not in question.'

'No,' said the Jokeman bitterly, 'but honour is. If thou put on thy cap and bells, King Marck, can Usk do less?'

The King's eyes flashed. His colour rose; but his voice remained calm. 'Enough,' he said. 'Usk, I have heard you for the love I know you bear me. Now say no more, but listen. I saw a Goddess, surely, in the hills; and she as surely spoke to me. But perhaps I did not hear her words aright. Later, when I thought I saw her in my Hall… but she is a child, my friend. A child who hourly brings me joy. One day she will hold this place and all it owns, my daughter under the Gods. As for this other; before you talk of honour, think on this. Rather men had stayed in darkness; rather the Earth itself remained unformed, than that one drop of innocent blood be spilled.'

'To that I bow,' said Usk. 'For it is rightly said of Gods and men, to spill the blood of the innocent is a crime.'

His tone, and the look that accompanied the words, arrested Marck. He turned slowly, his eyes blue and bright. 'What do you mean?' he said.

'Nay, remember,' said Usk. 'A Jokeman can have no meaning. And such as attach great import to his words are needs more witless than he.' He lolled composedly on the beam; took off his cap, spun it and whistled a tune.

The King rose, frowning. 'None the less you will speak,' he said. 'You have said too much, or not enough.'

'I will *say* nothing,' returned the other. 'But for a token, I will jest with thee.' He caught the coin Marck flung him, bit it as was his custom and stowed it away. 'Gold it was that brought King Altred down,' he said, 'more than the blow that joined his brother to the Gods. Life is an evil thing.' He shook his head mournfully. 'For that love I bear thee,' he said, 'I will tell another tale; of Scatha One-eye, Lord of Night, and Sceola, and the Horseman of Devu.'

Marck's frown deepened. He said, 'I have not heard of this.'

'Then do thou compose thyself, Lord,' said Usk. 'And a Fool shall increase the tally of thy wisdom.' He cocked his head, gravely. 'Sceola, you must know, walked ever on her master's right,' he said. 'This being the side that Scatha King was blind. Till one day Methleu came, who was Athlann's dwarf and the Jokeman of the Gods. "Scatha," said he, "tell me the tale of how you lost your eye." So Scatha told of the winning of the Sword, by whose power the Night Hounds are held in check, or made to run at bidding. "That is a good tale," said Methleu when he had done. "Yet I say this, Lord; that glory and defeat are like death and life, the two sides of one coin. The Hounds give thee safety in the night, and power over giants and shadows; yet on thy right side thou art blind. Who guards thee there?"

'Then Scatha said, "The Horsemen given by my Lord Devu; and their Captain, whom I greatly honour." Then he remembered how his wife walked to his right. Then he remembered …'

He said no more; for an alarming change had come over Marck. He raised his hands, the fingers crooked; then his eyes, glaring round, lighted on a heavy knife that lay before him on the trestle. He snatched it up, and threw. A thud; and Usk stared down in turn, face paling. Then he reached with shaking fingers to free the slack of his sleeve, where the blade held it pinned fast to the beam. He waited for nothing further; but scuttled to the floor, and ran.

Nothing more was heard from the King's high chamber all that day. The folk of the household moved about their affairs, casting troubled glances upward to the Tower, the slitted windows set beneath the eaves. But they remained dark; and the food that was sent, by a trembling servingwoman, was left untouched. But long after the last lamps were extinguished, and the Tower got to its uneasy rest, a listener at Marck's door would have heard, mixed with his groans, one endlessly repeated word.

'Briand …'

The dawn light lay grey across the Heath when the King rode to the outer gate. He returned no answer to the muttered greetings of the guards but sat hunched and still, his pale face shadowed by a heavy cloak. The hooves of the horse clattered on the bridge, drummed on the turf beyond; and he was gone. An hour later a second rider passed beneath the towering gantries of the gatehouse. Like his lord, he was muffled in a cloak; and he too set his horse at the Heath, not looking back. The guards exchanged glances, but spoke no word. Nor were many to be found bold enough to voice their thoughts. The day passed gloomily; and by nightfall Marck had not returned.

The fire roared brightly, fed by fresh billets; and round it a ribald company had assembled. Two stablehands, in the grubby green and yellow of the House, seemed somewhat the worse for beer; beside them a porter fondled the youngest and least prepossessing of the kitchenmaids. But the most drunken of the group, by far, was Maia. As ever, her hair straggled from beneath her cap; she stood swaying and giggling, her plump legs spread, her feet bare on the flags. Her bodice was unlaced; and over her ample breasts she gripped two cups. 'Why, thus it would be,' she said, 'were I a Goddess, and thou a noble Captain.'

The stable boy thus addressed guffawed with pleasure; the kitchenmaid shrieked.

'Marry no, good Captain,' said Maia. 'Not till my will permits. For as thou knowest, I am a Goddess. Not till my will permits.' She attempted a curtsey, and all but overtoppled. 'For if thou *force* me, Captain,' she said, 'thy fingers will drop from thy hands. Or some other part …!' She screamed with merriment; then became aware, by degrees, of the appalled stares directed past her. She turned, slowly, her own face blenching; and the cups fell and shattered. She put her hands before her, and began to whimper.

In the doorway stood the master of the Gate. He wore a robe of dull homespun; such a garment as his people had once grown used to when he rode abroad. His face was white; his eyes glared, it seemed with all the wildness of his Sealand forebears. His tongue-tip ran across his lips before he spoke. He said, '*You mocked her …*'

Somebody whispered, 'My Lord …' But the words were cut short by the scream of Marck. The hand he jerked into sight held a knotted flail. He raised it, struck; and the screaming was redoubled. The first blow fell across the woman's forehead, the second on her upflung arms. She scuttled, wetting herself in terror, for the shelter of a table; but Marck laid his hand to it, and the table was flung aside.

It was Thoma, dragged to the place by the incoherent porter, who took the weapon from his master, Thoma who gripped him till the thin shoulders ceased their jerking. The seneschal stared down then, unbelieving. 'My Lord,' he said heavily, 'what have you done?'

The King also stared. Spittle flecked his beard; but the blindness, that had made him a red man striking shadows, was gone. He saw the maimed eye, the blood that brightened the grubby dress, the fingers from which the torn flesh stood in spikes. The woman crouched, quivering; and he turned, hands to his skull, and blundered from the kitchen. They heard his long cry fall and rise as he climbed the Tower stairs.

The Queen was waiting for him in a dress of blue, decorated with silver thread. Her hands were clenched at her sides, and her voice when she spoke was low. 'I heard ... cries,' she said. 'What has happened, my Lord?'

Marck stared at her. 'I have been riding,' he said. 'I rode to the beach. But it was empty. The hills were empty, and the sea. You emptied them.'

She said, 'My Lord ...' But he cut her off.

'In all my life,' he said, 'I lived here at the Gate as a King should live. When the poor cried, I heeded them. Where other hands fell heavy, mine was stayed. Now I face the Gods with a sin of blood. An evil has come to us. You brought it.'

'*I?*' she said. 'My Lord, I ... do not understand ...'

'I waited,' he said. 'Waited, and watched. Then I returned, to punish. But he had gone ...'

'King Marck,' she said, 'hear me ...'

He shouted at her. *Why did you not ask?*'

'What?' she said. *What?*'

'I would have given,' said Marck. 'Anything. Do you not understand? Him, anything ... To keep you here, and happy ...'

She stared a shocked instant; then a change come over her face. She said, 'So it has come to this.' She walked forward, eyes blazing. 'All my life,' she said, 'I have been plagued by men. Old men, and fat men, and men who bought and sold. For *these*, and *this* ... Can I help them?'

'Why?' he said. *Why?*'

'I asked nothing,' she said. 'Nothing of anybody. To ... smell the air, and see the summers come, and lie in peace. But no. No, no, no ... By the Gods, I could be sick. Yes, throw up all the mess and filth men brought me ...'

She faced him, fists clenched; and he moaned, pressing his hands to his head. He said, 'I brought you love ...'

'And I gave it,' she shouted. 'All there was to give ...' She caught her breath; then her expression altered once more. 'What else did you expect?' she hissed. 'Caging me here like a Midsea bird, with none but loutish girls for company, in a room that stinks of old men's piss ... *What did you expect?*'

He lowered his hands, slowly.

'And now he's gone,' she said. 'You drove him away. So you can lie in peace again. It's over.'

But Marck shook his head. He said, 'It will never be over.'

She tried then to dart past him to the door. He caught her, flinging her back. She fought with him; and he struck her. She fell across the bed; and he leaped upon her, gripping with his knees. First he tore away the gift of Atha King, then her belt and dress, raking her shoulders with his nails. He crushed her to the fleeces, but she kicked and cried; so he beat her again. After which he took her, with the vigour of his rage. She lay quiet when he had finished, trembling a little and with her eyes tightly closed. And so he left her, reeling to his chamber. He closed the door behind him, dropping the heavy bar, and sank to the floor.

Through the Tower and all its rooms, silence prevailed. Torches burned, lighting empty corridors; but no man stirred. Across the baileys, moon-whitened, stretched ragged shadows of gatehouse and wall; and the gates themselves stood open to the empty Heath. An enemy could have crept in from the misty trees; but no enemy came.

It was dawn before one stirred. There came the click of the stable gate, the creak of harness. A horse snorted, stamping. The hooves sounded again, by the gate and on the trackway beyond; then the noise was swallowed up. The morning was silent once more.

From the shadows by the outer gate, one man kept vigil. Spindly he was of shank; and the furs with which his body was swathed accentuated its curious bulkiness. For a time he watched the empty Heath to the north, lips parted; then he turned away, staring up at the high face of the Tower. 'Now I have thee, King, and all thy tribe,' he muttered. 'For this is no minstrel's tale …'

Dendra lounged on the high chair of King Odann. His long legs sprawled indolently across the dais; his hair, braided and greased with butter, hung to his shoulders; and he gripped a heavy winecup in a hand that gleamed with rings. Round him clustered his fighting men; and below him on the littered floor of the Hall stood Miri. The cloak she wore hung open; her dress was splashed with mud to the hips, and the pallor of her face accentuated the great bruise that had spread across her cheek.

'I have left him,' she said in a low voice, 'and that is enough. Now I seek shelter of a kinsman, as all our laws demand.'

Dendra swilled the wine in his cup. 'Your kinsman is dead,' he said at length. 'I mean, your father.'

A shout of laughter greeted the words. She swayed, closing her eyes. 'Then justice and mercy are likewise dead,' she said. 'I see that now.' She swallowed, and moistened her lips. 'What is your will,' she said, 'King Dendra?'

Another smothered laugh; and Dendra scowled, raising a hand for quiet. 'Not my will,' he said, 'but the Gods. You come here, to my Hall, asking for justice. Perhaps you will receive it.' He drained the cup, and set it aside. 'Why did you leave the Tower of the Gate?'

She stared round, in the torchlit gloom; then drew herself erect. She said, 'Its lord put shame on me.'

'Shame?' said Dendra. 'Shame?' He raised himself on the throne, gripping its arms, and peered about him. 'Friends,' he said, 'hear a wonder. The daughter of King Odann talks of shame ...'

When the noise was done he leaned toward her. 'Here is the justice you came so far to seek,' he said. 'Your crime we will not name; but you will be taken from this place, and heavy stones laid on you. Also, here is my mercy. Your veins will be cut, so that life will run out quickly.'

She shrank at that, as though struck afresh; but when the priests moved forward she rallied. 'Does my uncle,' she said above the rising clamour, 'pass sentence for the Gods, or for himself? My uncle who came to me, a child, the very night my mother died?' She flung away the hands that were laid on her. 'Ever after that,' she said, 'I slept beside the King. And ever after that you raged and wondered. But you will never know ...'

Uproar, in the Hall. Dendra leaped forward, his face suffused; and she shouted him down again. 'Nor may you take my life,' she said. 'The life I carry is not yours to claim.'

The King had halted, fist raised; now he scowled. 'What?' he said. 'What is this? What life?'

She stared back, mocking. She said, 'The Heir of the Gate.'

He stared in turn; at her heaving breasts, the faces of his followers. Then, slowly, he remounted the steps of the throne. He snapped his fingers, and the winecup was recharged. He drank; and when he put the thing aside none there could read his eyes. He said, 'What say my priests?'

A hurried muttering; and a withered, grey-robed man piped up. 'This is true, by all our Sealand laws,' he said falteringly. 'You may not harm her.'

The King sat back, still with the unfathomable stare. 'Then to these laws I bow,' he said. 'Ruling justly, and mindful of the Gods. No man of the Plain shall injure her.'

Miri pulled the cloak about her throat. She said, 'And the child?'

Dendra put his head back then and laughed. 'The child will be born,' he said. 'My subjects will wish to meet him.' He signed, impatiently, to the men about her; and she was hustled from the Hall.

The winter that followed was bad, as bad as any in memory. For weeks the sun stayed hidden, while bitter winds scythed across the Plain and through the great gap in the chalk. The lengthening days brought no relief; instead snow fell, great silent shining hills that clogged the narrow ways a spearshaft deep. Wolves came down, howling night after night round the scattered villages of the Southguard. Horses stamped and snorted in their quarters, children wailed; men peered from gatehouses and walls, pulling their beards and frowning into the dark. The Towers were cheerless; but none more so than the Tower of the Gate.

The King was now seldom seen. Servants carried food to the door of his high chamber; but as often as not the platters were left untouched. From the courtyards Marck might sometimes be descried, a vague, hunched shape staring out across the speckled waste to the north; but what the thoughts were that possessed him no man could say.

The summer was cold, with gale after gale sweeping in from the sea. Grain rotted in the square fields clustering round the village walls; what little grew was flattened by the wind. Only autumn brought relief. Then, curiously, the land smiled once more. Flowers bloomed, on the banks of the little brook; reeds were cut for winter flooring, what remained of the harvest gathered under cloudless skies. Days were warm, nights misty and mild. The storm-battered Hall was repaired and patched; but the gloom that had gripped the household remained. For a rumour had come, brought first by a travelling tinker; that round the Tower of Odann were many crows.

The sun was setting in long banners of red when a stranger rode to the Tower. The gate guards marked him far off on the Heath; a Serjeant was summoned and the walls fresh-manned, so that when he came within hail many curious heads regarded him. He turned his horse casually, in the dusty road beyond the outer bridge. His hair, which was fair and long, blew round his face. He wore greaves and a cuirass of Midsea workmanship; heavy gold bangles circled his arms, a long cutting-sword hung at his hip. But what attracted the onlookers' eyes was none of these things. Round his waist, and hanging to the knee, was knotted a thick scarlet sash. It glowed in the sunset light; the war-lanyard of the Sealand Kings, unseen now for a generation.

The warrior was hailed from the gate, and bidden enter; but he shook his head arrogantly, setting his long hair flying. 'Here I remain, chalkdwellers,' he said. 'I bear a message for your master.'

The Serjeant flushed at that, fingering his beard. 'Our King receives no strangers,' he said finally. 'Neither are messages welcome, save from the Gods. Tell it to me.'

The stranger spat. 'The first is this,' he said. 'A son was born to Marck, Lord of the Gate. The rest is for his ears.'

If the consternation caused by the words reached him he gave no sign. He sat the horse calmly, staring past the Tower at the brilliant light, while men ran back across the turf of the outer bailey. A further wait, a stirring by the inner court; and Marck himself appeared, with Thoma in attendance.

All were shocked by the gauntness of the King. His eyes gleamed bird-bright in his sunken face; a soiled robe flapped round his calves and he walked as if with difficulty, clinging to the seneschal's arm. He climbed the steps to the gate parapet hesitantly; but when he spoke his voice, though thin, was clear. 'What is this news you bring?' he asked. 'Say what you must; then come inside, and we will find refreshment.'

The other shook his head again. He stared up, eyes pale.

'These are the words of Dendra of the Plain,' he said. 'Hear, and mark him well. That shame was put on him by the Gate, blood of his House being bartered for unworthy gold. That he will have a window on the sea, as fits his Line; that he will seat him in your Chair, as penance for his shame; and that his arm is strong. For the horses of chalkdwellers breed faster than their Kings.'

A hubbub rose at once from the watching men. More than one soldier dropped a hand to his side, nocked an arrow to his bowstring; while round Marck Tower and gatehouse seemed suddenly to spin. Thoma gripped him; but he shook his head, pushing the other away. He raised his arms; and by degrees the noise was stilled. 'All this is strange to me,' he said, when he could once more make himself heard. 'I seek no war with Dendra; nor with any man in all the world, having given my life to penitence for great crimes. But tell me of my son, if this was the message you brought. Tell me and I will pay you well, with gold.'

The other turned his horse contemptuously. 'No Chalk King pays a Plainman save with blood,' he said. 'As for your son, this also my master bade me say. The child was born high, according to his station; *and there were many midwives.*' He waited for nothing further but drove his heels at the horse, with a long yell.

The watchers saw the Gate King reel; but next instant his hand was up. They heard his voice rise cracked and high.

'*Take that man ...*'

Arrows flew, hissing. It seemed the messenger swayed in the saddle; but he collected himself, spurring the horse and bending low. Feet pounded on the gantries and wooden steps, the gates squealed back; and a stream of cavalry thundered in pursuit, fanned out across the Heath.

It was midnight before they returned. They brought back a man blinded and two others ashen and groaning, their limbs wrapped with makeshift dressings; for the Plainman, though wounded, had fought well. The messenger, or what remained of him, they dragged behind a horse. They hauled him to the gatehouse; and from its wall they hung him, by the heels.

A Sealand war-drum is a vast affair, big as two wine barrels and with a skin of tight-stretched hide. Its throbbing in still weather carries many miles;

and it was such a drum that spoke, all night and all next day, from King Marck's Tower. Everywhere throughout the Southguard the beat was taken up; till the weary drummers, resting beside their great instrument, heard the answers thudding back like echoes in the hills. The Sea Kings heard them far to the west, and turned uneasy in their beds; the lands beyond the Black Rock heard them, and the Marsh Folk to the north. But fast as the summons spread, the news spread faster; that the Queen was dead, the Heir of the Gate given to the crows. Cressets blazed, on walls and watch-towers, till it seemed the Southguard was aflame. Men marched and rode, armed and grim-faced, converging on Marck's Tower. Two days passed, and a third; then from the hills an army poured, like wasps from a shaken hive.

The winter that followed lived long in minstrels' stories. The Plain was wasted, from south to north; for what the hill folk happened on, they slew. Everywhere across the land, from Long Creek to the marshes of the west, went the red lanyard; behind it followed terror, fire and death. Atha's messengers rode in vain; Towers were sacked, whole vassalages destroyed. Dendra's wild horsemen fought like devils; but the men of the hills fought better. The Plainmen were forced back, raging; and every step was a life. Till there came a day, in an unwanted spring, when King Marck once more entered Odann's Hall.

A great time he stood, in his armour that was battered and stained. He saw the light that flooded the place, pouring through shattered walls. He saw the piled dead, the blood that marked the flags, the women who wailed and crouched. He smelled the fresh, raw stink, perhaps smelled the fear. He spoke then, to his followers. His words were few; but those that heard them grew paler than before.

It was Thoma who, in an upper chamber of the place, came on the Jokeman. In his arms, still stained from the morning's work, Usk gripped a great bundle of spoil. His tongue-tip ran across his lips; and his eyes flickered nervously, past Thoma to the stairhead. For a time neither spoke; then the seneschal latched the door closed behind him, and set down the basket he carried. 'Now, friend Jokeman,' he said, 'we have a reckoning to make, you and I.'

'Reckoning?' said Usk. 'Art thou mad?' He licked his mouth again; then with a return to something like his former manner, 'Thoma, thou bladder, warm work and a very little exercise have cooked thy remaining wits. Let me pass ...'

But the other caught him, hurling him back. The bundle dropped and spilled; Usk groaned, and the stout wall shook. Silence fell; a silence in which both heard, mixed with the crackle of flames from the outer court, the wails of the condemned.

'Old friend,' said Usk, 'for that I used thee haughtily, I confess my fault …'

'Used me, turd?' snarled Thoma. 'What care I for the bearing of a Jokeman, good or ill? It is not for that you answer.'

'Thoma,' said the other, 'by all the Gods …' But the seneschal raised an arm, striking backhanded. 'Who,' he said, 'against all use, prompted our King to wooing? Turning his wits with rubbish, and talk of Gods?' He struck again, and Usk fell and grovelled. 'Who brought to the Gate, of all he might have wed, a Great Plain whore?' said Thoma. 'For Crab and Wolf were ever enemies, as well you knew. And who then brought the tale all others kept from him? *Answer …*'

'What I told, I told in love,' whimpered Usk. 'Desiring that no shame come to his House. And see how I was requited. Banned from his sight …'

'No shame?' said Thoma. 'But for you we might be sitting at the gate this hour, and King Marck with us. And all this work undone.' Then as the Jokeman gripped his knees, 'Off me, I say …'

But the other clung with the strength of desperation. 'Thoma, hear me,' he said. 'I ever loved the King. And thee …'

The seneschal flung him away. 'Stop your mouth,' he said disgustedly. 'Your foolishness will not avail you now.'

'Foolishness?' said Usk He glared up, panting. 'The Towers of the Plain were few,' he said. 'Now they are fewer. Who burned them? A God, with his thunderbolts; or Usk, the Jokeman? Now the Long Creek Kings will come, they who were bound by treaty to Odann. And Morwenton, great Atha … now these Kings of ours will waste themselves. And you, a Horseman, wish a tithe undone …'

Thoma said, frowning, 'You are mad.'

'Aye,' said Usk. 'Mad to serve a Sealander; I, whose fathers owned this country. And you are mad, we are all mad. But now the wild pigs fight, now we will live on bacon …'

Thoma heard no more but closed with him, gripping his jerkin front. 'But my last jest was the greatest,' shouted Usk. 'Who made the rumours fly? Who wound his skein, for a Sealand Queen? Perhaps she was unfaithful, perhaps a certain Captain went to her by night. Perhaps the King was just to take revenge. *Even as I …*' His hand flashed up, gripping the jewelled dagger. He drove the blade with all his force at the seneschal's side, into the crack where breastplate and backplate met.

A silence, that lengthened. Thoma stared down, amazed; then he put his fingers to his side; and then he smiled. He took the other's wrist, squeezing; a crack, and Usk once more began to shriek. Then Thoma raised his mailed fist, striking down; then stamped, once and again, with his booted feet. He raised the sagging body to the sill of the one tall window, heaved, leaned out to see it fall. He saw the arms flail, heard the great thud as it struck the courtyard flags. Dizziness came then, and flickerings across his sight. He leaned against the chamber wall, hand to his side, and groaned. He said between his teeth, 'Now he will never know...'

He took up the basket he had carried, heavily. On the stairs, he staggered; and a flicker of movement shot past his feet. He closed his eyes, breathing harshly; then he shook his head. 'A vow is a vow,' he said. 'That we should come to this...' He moved forward painfully, gripping the basket. 'Kitty,' he called. 'Name of the Gods... here, kitty. Kitty-kit-kit...'

The heights of the Plain rose vague and sweeping in the early light; and the endless wind blew, shivering the manes of horses, stirring the many flags. The Tower of Odann, and the stockades that surrounded it, stood silhouetted and stark. Round about, from where the army had encamped, rose the smoke of many cooking fires. Oxen grumbled in the baggage lines; but from the great dim flock of men who stood with upturned faces came no sound at all.

From point after point on the Tower projected the massive arms of gallows. Now a signal was given; and on the nearest, ropes and pulleys creaked to tautness. An animal bellowed, in fear and pain; then the carcass, huge and misshapen, swayed swiftly up the Tower wall, hung black and twisting. Another followed it, and another. First they hung the stockade cattle, then what horses remained; then the remnants of the garrison, then every living creature within the walls. And of them all, the tiny furry things on their gibbets of twigs took longest to die.

Later, when all was still, fire was brought. The flames ran swiftly, small at first but spreading and brightening, till the, whole great place roared like a furnace, a beacon visible for twenty miles. The fire burned for two days fed by sweating men who tumbled into the glowing embers all that remained of gatehouse and gantries, bridges and palisades. At the end of that time the hillock stood bare, and the Tower and all it had contained were gone; but Marck's vengeance was not ended. Waggons were drawn forward and back over the still-hot ash while others toiled in long lines across the Plain, each with a glistening load. Only when their cargoes had been spread, and the hill and its surroundings coated ankle-deep with salt, did the King retire, to his Tower in the pass.

In the spring of the following year, a small party of horsemen rode swiftly along a lane bordered with hawthorn and elder. The day was bright and warm, puffy clouds chasing each other across a sky of deepest blue. Birds sang from the bushes fringing the rutted path; once a magpie started up and winged away, in dipping flashes of white and black.

The leader of the little group seemed by no means unaware of the sweetness of the morning. He glanced round him as he rode, at the Heath that stretched shimmering in the distance, the pines lifting their dark heads above the rhododendron thickets. Once he sniffed, appreciatively, the rich scent of the may; but at a bend of the track he reined.

Ahead, in its chalk gap, stood the Tower. Even from distance, its aspect was unwelcoming. He saw the stained walls, weather-worn and grim; marked the shuttered face of the keep, with its strapwork of timbering, the heavy outer works that fronted it, the village that straggled at the foot of the Mound. He glanced back to his escort, but gave no further sign; instead he touched heels to his horse, rode jingling down the narrow way between the dusty houses. Children ran from their scrabbling in the dirt, women stared up open-mouthed at the party and the devices it bore; the pennants with their white horses and the gilded staves, each topped by a four-spoked wheel.

The Tower gates stood open; the traveller had half expected them barred. He rode beneath the portal with its massive wooden groins, nodded curtly to the men within. A page ran to take his reins; he dismounted stiffly, walked forward. To the stout knight who confronted him he said, 'The lord of this place, the greatvassal Marck of the Gate; has he been informed?'

'My Lord,' said the other, fidgeting under his keen stare, 'your message was passed.'

'Good. Then bring me to him.'

'My Lord,' said the knight uncomfortably, 'I am Thoma, seneschal of the Gate. Will you take wine?'

The Great Hall, airy and cool, belied to some extent the grim exterior of the place. Cups and a mixing bowl were set out on a low table; a serving maid in green and yellow hurried forward, but the newcomer waved her aside. 'Present me to King Marck, I pray you,' he said. 'And make no delay. I have journeyed far, and have many miles to travel before nightfall.'

Thoma wiped his face. He said, 'It is not possible.'

The other's voice rang sharply. 'What? Am I denied?'

'You are not denied,' said the seneschal. 'He ... sees no one.'

The herald drew a sealed packet from his riding tunic. 'Then,' he said, 'I will see *him*. I am charged by Atha King to deliver this into his hand. His, and no other. Where is his chamber?'

He turned for the curtained stairway; and Thoma stepped before him, arms spread. He said pleadingly, 'My Lord ...' Then he stopped; for the other had raised his knuckles level with his eyes. On the middle finger, carved in a dull-green stone, he saw the prancing horse.

'Yes,' said the herald sharply. 'His great Seal. Who denies me, denies him. Now, take me to your lord.'

Thoma turned with a gesture of despair, tramped before him up the broad wooden steps.

At the head of the third flight an open door gave a glimpse of a sparsely furnished chamber; but the seneschal did not check. The other followed, frowning. A further climb, and Thoma stooped to fiddle with a catch. A trap swung back, letting in a flood of air and light. The messenger stepped through, and stared.

They had emerged on the roof of the Tower. Below him huddled the village. To either side the flanking hills rose clear in the bright air, crossed by their sheeptracks, dotted with clumps of scrub; while from the great height the sea was visible, an endless plain of cobalt stretching to the south. These things he saw at a glance; then his attention was concentrated on the sunlit space before him.

Everywhere, pinned to the steeply pitched central gable, on poles set above the breast-high parapets, meat lures swung and rotted in the wind. To one side, their feathers stirring idly, were; heaped the fresh carcasses of a dozen crows, while in the far corner of the place stood a hide of weather-beaten canvas. Slits in its sides provided loopholes; from one he saw the tip of a slim arrow withdrawn. 'What is it?' asked a thin voice querulously. 'What is it now? You have spoiled my sport …'

Thoma stepped heavily to the door of the hide, and raised the flap. He said, 'My lord, King Marck of the Gate.'

For days before the arrival of the army, the hill folk knew of its progress. By night its campfires glowed for many miles; by day the dust rose towering in its wake, a cloud visible from far off across the Plain. The foragers it sent before it scoured the country, paying good gold for grain; and the noise of its passing shook the ground. Here were infantry in rank on rank, bright-cuirassed with their pikes and spears; here cavalry in gaudy cloaks, each troop with its banners and pennants. Here were war engines of every shape and size; catapults and trebuchets, their great arms lashed, ballistas with their massive hempen skeins; mantlets and scaling towers, the Cat and the Tortoise, the Mouse and the Ram. And here too were Midsea weapons, the legendary firetubes no White Islanders had ever seen, the tubes that spit out thunder and bring the lightning down. They rumbled past on their squat, iron-bound wheels, each drawn by a dozen plodding oxen, each with its contingent of turbanned, white-robed engineers. Behind them came slingers and archers; and behind again rode Sealand chiefs with their war bands, massive men in bright-checked cloaks and leggings. At the head of each troop jolted the sign of the Wheel; and over all, cracking and rippling, reared the White Horse of Morwenton, the Mark of Atha's house.

The Gate heard of his coming, on a grey morning when the clouds rolled low over the seaward-facing hills and spatters of rain drove like slingshots across the empty Heath. Then was the faith of Thoma sorely tried; but after half a day the drums began their pounding, and once more the lines of men and horses crept out blackly from the fortress in the pass. A mile from the Tower the seneschal deployed, in a crescent straddling the road; and here the Royal vanguard found him. To his right, bogland stretched to saltings where the sea birds wheeled; to his left, half-seen behind veils of rain, were the hills.

From his position near the centre of the line, Thoma watched the King's outriders fall back. The main body rolled on, to halt two hundred paces from his men. The cavalry checked, swinging to either flank; then the ranks of infantry parted. Between them lumbered the firetubes. The teams, unyoked, were herded to one side, and the pieces trained. Some were shaped like monstrous fish; others, the greatest, took the form of dragons. But all opened black mouths to gape at the opposing force; and beside each stood a dark-skinned man, a torch smoking in his hand. A silence fell, in which the sough and hiss of the rain could be clearly heard; and the seneschal glanced grim-lipped at the man beside him. 'Flagbearer,' he said briefly. 'I will speak with them.'

A page rode forward with the Mark of the House, the red crab on a field of yellow silk. Thoma nodded to his Captains of infantry and horse, and cantered forward. Halfway to the King's ranks he halted, bareheaded in the rain. A stirring, among the infantry; and a man moved out alone. A gasp from beside the seneschal, a swift uncovering; and the other reined, sitting his horse coldly. Like Thoma, he wore no helmet. His mane of hair, once yellow, was badger-grey, and the years had marked his face with weariness; but he had held himself stiffly in the heavy war saddle, and he was armoured from neck to feet. 'This is a sorry thing to see,' he said at length. 'My subjects come to war with me, breaking the fealty they owe.'

The seneschal swallowed. 'We break no oaths, Lord Atha,' he said. 'Nor do we war, save with those who war on us. My Lord, why do you come? If it is to punish, then we must resist. For the word of each man here is given to the Gate.'

Atha nodded grimly. 'Loyalty I respect,' he said, 'though I see little enough of it. But loyalty is not in question.' He raised an arm, pointing. 'One word from me,' he said, 'and you are swept away. You and your army, like chaff before a wind. Now answer me, will you hold the path? Will you speak, for all these peoples' lives?'

A voice behind them said, 'He has no need.'

Thoma turned, slowly. Marck wore his battered armour, and a sword. A hillboy led his horse, a shock-haired lad of maybe some ten summers. The eyes of the King shone brightly, tears mingling with the rain that soaked his cheeks, plastered the thinning hair close to his scalp. 'They are all my people,' he said. 'My good people, whom I lead …' He halted some six feet from the King, regarded the ranks behind him and shook his head. 'This is Thoma, seneschal of the Gate,' he said, 'and my true and faithful man. Deal justly with him …' He peered again, shortsightedly 'Why do you come before me with such array?' he asked. 'We were not prepared, we would have prepared. It is not knightly, not done like a King. You sent no word …'

'I sent you word,' said Atha grimly. 'But none returned. Who spurns my messenger, sent under my Seal, spurns me.'

Marck shook his head again. 'I saw no messenger,' he said. 'The castle folk … but they are good people. I have been … much engaged. It has not been … easy, keeping your peace in the west.'

'Of that,' said Atha dryly, 'I was made aware' He leaned forward. 'King Marck,' he said, 'it is not good to sit here, in the rain. And my patience is an old boar's patience; short. Will you fight with me, or no?'

The wandering attention of the King was riveted. 'Fight?' he said. 'Who spoke of fighting? Was it Thoma? He was most remiss …' He scrambled from the saddle; and the boy hastened to take his arm. 'We came to do you honour, as your subjects …' He was on his knees, gripping the hem of the King's rich saddlecloth; and Atha, stooping from the horse, endeavouring to raise him. 'My Lord,' said Marck, sobbing, 'great evil came. I was its author. And now, at night; I cannot rest, there is no rest. But you, with your great army … deal justly with them. And you will sit in judgement on me; I am content …'

Atha signed to the column; and priests ran forward, dark-habited, each with the wheel sign topping a golden staff.

'I am well content,' said Marck. 'But, Lord, this child, born of a forester. His father died, his mother cannot support him. I commend him to you, take him to your care. I did great wrong …'

'Old friend,' said Atha gently, 'go with these Brothers. And be calm. All is well; later, I will speak with you.' He waved again, and an officer spurred forward. 'Tell the firetube masters to stand down,' he said. 'And send my Captains to me.' Then to Thoma, 'Lead the way, good seneschal. This … greeting does you honour. Ride with me, and tell me of your lord; for I sup with you tonight.'

The dawn had not yet broken over the Heath. Above the tall trees that fringed the Mound the sky showed a broadening smudge of silver; but the brook with its tangled banks still lay in velvet dark. The Tower reared its brooding height against the scarcely paler west; and all round, twinkling and dim, gleamed the campfires of the waking army.

Atha paused in the lower bailey, sniffing the ancient chill of the brook air. Then he turned to the man at his side. 'Some say I leave a madman in my path,' he said quietly, 'and some a traitor. Whom do I leave, King Marck?'

Marck chafed his thin hands together. 'A loyal subject,' he said in his tired voice, 'who would fain ride with you to this war.'

But the other shook his head. 'No,' he said. 'No, Marck, I have another need of you. Sit here, and be strong for me; hold the Gate till I return, and I shall be well satisfied.' He gestured to where, a pace or so away, two priests stood like shadows in the night. 'For the rest,' he said, 'I leave you these good Brothers, who are men of God and strong in wisdom. They will bring you comfort.'

Marck said dully, 'There are no Gods. This much wisdom has taught.'

'No Gods,' said Atha vibrantly. 'But one God, merciful and just. Who came to us, a man among men, in Sealand; who was broken on the Wheel and yet raised up, to bring eternal life. This was taught me by his priests; and this I believe.' He circled his hand, forefinger raised. 'See this sign,' he said. 'By it I have sworn to make these islands one; to raise up the weak and lowly, bringing mercy to every man. For this, I ride west. The north we have subdued, to the shore that fronts the Misty Isles. Six Long Creek Towers burn; foes to the Crab, on whom I put my heel.' He made the Sign again. 'One people,' he said. 'Worshipping one God, and walking without fear. They will be a proud people, and a great. In this, as in all things, I need your skills.'

But Marck shook his head. 'I have been through a long valley,' he said. 'Even now its darkness calls me. And she calls me, at night from all the hills. She who was so little.'

Atha's hand was on his shoulder; he felt the trembling start, and tightened his grip. 'No,' he said gently, 'you have not understood. You have played with madness, King Marck. But play is for children; and you are not a child. It is over.'

Marck bowed his head. 'I am not worthy, Lord,' he said. 'Take the Tower from me. Give it to another, and let me end my days.'

He felt the other's answer in his silence. Finally Atha shook his head. 'No,' he said. 'Neither may you escape in death. It is not his will, whom I serve.'

Marck said in a muffled voice, 'But what remains …'

'Remains?' said Atha vaguely. He stared round him, at the dark expanse of the Heath. 'The stars,' he said, 'the empty hills. We are all alone; it is a Mystery the Brothers will explain.' He shook the gaunt man gently. 'I, to bring wisdom to the Scholar of the Gate,' he said. 'You sought to own her, buying her with gold. Old friend, *you own her now …*'

He turned to gaze up at the Tower with its looming face. 'Another thing you will do,' he said. 'Get out your books, and find the way. Build me a Hall of stone, such as the Giants knew. Strong founded, gripped to rock, proof against arrows and the firetube darts. Build it to Heaven; and let it stand for her, if not for me.'

Marck licked his mouth. He said, 'I cannot.'

Atha shook his head once more. 'You have still not understood,' he said. 'The Brothers teach, and I believe, that death is a beginning, not an end. That on a certain day we all shall rise, in glory before the Lord. Then she will see it, if her bones have now no place. Will she not know it was made for her?'

He turned away, pulling on his steel-banded gloves. 'Other men will come, from other parts,' he said. 'To marvel, and to learn. So Towers of stone will guard the realm, and its folk will be free from fear. Fine Towers they will be, King Marck; but none finer than yours, the first.'

A horse was led forward, with a stamp and jingle. He mounted, and turned. 'Build the Tower,' he said. 'Keep this place for me; and may the great God guard you.' His hoofbeats thudded on the sloping turf; they heard his voice at the outer gate and the quick laugh of a guard, surprised as if by some jest.

Marck had made no answer. He stood now staring up; and it was as if he saw, sketched against the night, the walls of a mighty Hall. His mind, despite itself, was busied afresh. It saw already patterns of joists and stairs; the slings they would use to hoist the blocks, the scaffoldings on which masons would work. He saw, finally, the sun burn on the cliff of new white stone; and the flags that topped it, proud against the blue. The Crab of Sealand, the Horse of Atha and the Wheel of God. It seemed his heart was lightened; so that he called to the priests, ran to the gatehouse steps. He saw the looming figure of the King pass into dawn dusk; he saw the clustered roofs and moving mists. Then it seemed the new God entered him so that he saw other things, too many for remembrance or the telling. Flowers broke free and sailed the sky, clouds sailed like flowers; and a great Deer rose and shook his smoky head, down there below Corfe Gate.

The traffic ahead has ground to a halt again. The line of stalled vehicles stretches into distance, twinkling in the heat-haze. An hour back the mirages started forming, breaking and splitting like pools of quicksilver. Now the sun beats down on the Champ's canvas hood. There's a smell of exhaust fumes and dust.

The patrol car is moving, slowly. Its loudhailer is working, the words come crackling and flat. Stan Potts watches the blue flasher revolve and wipes his face and swears. He wants to pee, and has wanted to pee for an hour or more, and dull pain has grown to sharper pain and then to all-consuming need. He hasn't dared leave the vehicle, hasn't dared turn off the road. He slicks the gearstick forward and back and stares through the blotched windscreen and tries to think of nothing, nothing at all.

The observer has left the car, is working his way from vehicle to vehicle along the jam. Uproar breaks out somewhere, hoots and shouting. Stan wipes his face again with the back of his hand and gropes behind him. There's an old bait tin; he finds it, works it down behind his heels.

The observer leans on the windowsill. He's in his shirtsleeves; sweat makes a dark patch under his arm. He says, 'Wareham's restricted; they won't let you in. Best turn round.'

All Stan wants in the world is for him to go away. He says, 'I have to try. My father's very old.' It's as if the words came from somebody else, unasked. He swallows, stares at the chipped paint along the top of the dash. But the policeman has gone on anyway. He isn't really interested.

He grips the can between his knees, pulls at his flies. His head spins a little; but the relief is momentary. The other thing reasserts itself; he remembers the miles he still has to go and what must happen at the other end, what he has to do. It seems he can't think straight any more. He must be mad; mad to have started, mad to be sitting here among all these shouting cars.

He lies back, in pain. He knows he's not going to make it.

KITEWORLD

[illegible]

server; but that was to be expected [illegible] of his [illegible] knows, as the Church herself knows, the value of the proper form of things. He would present himself upon his [illegible] but not before [illegible] and earth as the ritual dictated [illegible]

[illegible]

1

Kitemaster

The ground crew had all but finished their litany. They stood in line, heads bowed, silhouetted against the last dull flaring from the west; below me the Launch Vehicle seethed gently to itself, water sizzling round a rusted boiler rivet. A gust of warmth blew up toward the gantry, bringing scents of steam and oil to mingle with the ever-present smell of dope. At my side the Kite-captain snorted, it seemed impatiently; shuffled his feet, sank his bull head even further between his shoulders.

I glanced round the darkening hangar, taking in the remembered scene; the spools of cable, head-high on their trolleys, bright blades of the anchor rigs, fathom on fathom of the complex lifting train. In the centre of the place, above the Observer's wickerwork basket, the mellow light of oil lamps grew to stealthy prominence; it showed the spidery crisscrossings of girders, the faces of the windspeed telltales, each hanging from its jumble of struts. The black needles vibrated, edging erratically up and down the scales; beyond, scarcely visible in the gloom, was the complex bulk of the Manlifter itself, its dark, spread wings jutting to either side.

The young priest turned a page of his book, half glanced toward the gantry. He wore the full purple of a Base Chaplain; but his worried face looked very young. I guessed him to be not long from his novitiate; the presence of a Kitemaster was a heavy weight to bear. His voice reached up to me, a thread of sound mixed with the blustering of the wind outside. '*Therefore we beseech thee, Lord, to add Thy vigilance to ours throughout the coming night; that the Land may be preserved, according to Thy covenant ...*' The final response was muttered; and he stepped back, closing the breviary with evident relief.

I descended the metal-latticed steps to the hangar floor, paced unhurriedly to the wicker basket. As yet there was no sign of Canwen, the Observer; but that was to be expected. A Flier of his seniority knows, as the Church herself knows, the value of the proper form of things. He would present himself upon his cue; but not before. I sprinkled oil and earth as the ritual dictates, murmured my blessing, clamped the Great Seal of the Church Variant to the basket rim and stepped away. I said, 'Let the Watching begin.'

At once the hangar became a scene of ordered confusion. Tungsten arcs came to buzzing life, casting their harsher and less sympathetic glare; orders were shouted, and Cadets ran to the high end doors, began to roll them back. The wind roared in at once, causing the canvas sides of the structure to boom and crack; the arc globes swung, sending shadows leaping on the curving walls. The valve gear of the truck set up its fussing; I climbed back to the gantry as the heavy vehicle nosed into the open air. I restored the sacred vessels to their valise, clicked the lock and straightened.

The Kitecaptain glanced at me sidelong, and back to the telltales. 'Wind-speed's too high, by eight or ten knots,' he growled. 'And mark that gusting. It's no night for flying.'

I inclined my head. 'The Observer will decide,' I said.

He snorted. 'Canwen will fly,' he said. 'Canwen will always fly ...' He turned on his heel. 'Come into the office,' he said. 'You'll observe as well from there. In any case, there's little to see as yet.' I took a last glance through the line of rain-spattered windows, and followed him.

The room in which I found myself was small, and as spartan as the rest of the establishment. An oil lamp burned in a niche; a shelf held manuals and dogeared textbooks, another was piled with bulky box files. A wall radiator provided the semblance at least of comfort; there was a square steel strongbox, beside it a battered metal desk. On it stood a silver-mounted photograph; a line of youths stood stiffly before a massive, old-pattern Launch Vehicle.

The Captain glanced at it and laughed, without particular humour. 'Graduation day,' he said. 'I don't know why I keep it. All the rest have been dead and gone for years. I'm the last; but I was the lucky one of course.' He limped to a corner cabinet, opened it and took down glasses and a bottle. He poured, looked over his shoulder. He said, 'It's been a long time, Helman.'

I considered. Kitecaptains, by tradition, are a strangely-tempered breed of men. Spending the best part of their lives on the Frontier as they do, they come to have scant regard for the social niceties most of us would take for granted; yet the safety of the Realm depends on their vigilance, and that they know full well. It gives them, if not a real, at least a moral superiority; and he seemed determined to use, or abuse, his position to the hilt. However if he chose to ignore our relative status, there was little I could do. In public, I might rebuke him; in private, I would merely risk a further loss of face. I accordingly remained impassive, and took the glass he proffered. 'Yes,' I agreed calmly, 'it has, as you say, been a very long time.'

He was still watching me narrowly. 'Well at least,' he said, 'one of us did all right for himself. I've little enough to show for twenty years' service; save one leg two inches shorter than the other.' He nodded at my robes. 'They reckon,' he said, 'you'll be in line for the Grand Mastership one day. Oh yes, we hear the chat; even stuck out in a rotting hole like this.'

'All things,' I said, 'are within the will of God.' I sipped, cautiously. Outback liquor has never been renowned for subtlety, and this was no exception; raw spirit as near as I could judge, probably brewed in one of the tumbledown villages through which I had lately passed.

He gave his short, barking laugh once more. 'Plus a little help from Variant politics,' he said. 'But you always had a smooth tongue when it suited. And knew how to make the proper friends.'

'We are not all Called,' I said sharply. There are limits in all things; and he was pushing me perilously close to mine. It came to me that he was already more than a little drunk. I walked forward to the window, peered; but nothing was visible. The glass gave me back an image of a bright Cap of Maintenance, the great clasp at my throat, my own sombre and preoccupied face.

I sensed him shrug. 'We aren't all touched in the head,' he said bitterly. 'You won't believe it, I find it hard myself; but I once had a chance at the scarlet as well. And I turned it down. Do you know, there was actually a time when I believed in all of this?' He paused. 'What I'd give, for my life back just once more,' he said. 'I wouldn't make the same mistakes again. A palace on the Middlemarch, that's what I'd have; servants round me, and decent wine to drink. Not the rotgut we get here ...'

I frowned. Rough though his manner was, he had a way with him that tugged at memory; laughter and scents of other years, touches of hands. We all have our sacrifices to make; it's the Lord's way to demand them. There was a summer palace certainly, with flowering trees around it in the spring; but it was a palace that was empty.

I turned back. 'What do you mean?' I said. 'Believed in all of what?'

He waved a hand. 'The Corps,' he said. 'The sort of crap you teach. I thought the Realm really needed us. It seems crazy now. Even to me.' He drained the glass at a swallow, and refilled it. 'You're not drinking,' he said.

I set my cup aside. 'I think,' I said, 'I'd best watch from the outer gallery.'

'No need,' he said. 'No need, I'll shade the lamp.' He swung down before the light a species of burlap screen; then arcs flared on the apron down below, and all was once more clear as day. Anchors, I saw, had been run out in a half circle from the rear of the Launch Vehicle. 'We've never needed them yet,' said the Kitecaptain at my elbow. 'But on a night like this, who can tell?'

A ball of bright fire sailed into the air, arced swiftly to the east. At the signal Cadets surged forward, bearing the first of the Kites shoulder-high. They flung it from them; and the line tightened and strummed. The thing hung trembling, a few feet above their heads; then insensibly began to rise. Steerable arc lamps followed it; within seconds it was lost in the scudding overcast. The shafts of light showed nothing but sparkling drifts of rain.

'The Pilot,' said the Captain curtly; then glanced sidelong once more. 'But I needn't tell a Kitemaster a thing like that,' he said.

I clasped my hands behind me. I said, 'Refresh my memory.'

He considered for a while; then it seemed he came to a decision. 'Flying a Cody rig isn't an easy business,' he snapped. 'Those bloody fools back home think it's like an afternoon in Middle Park.' He rubbed his face, the iron-grey stubble of beard. 'The Pilot takes up five hundred foot of line,' he said. 'Less, if we can find stable air. The Lifter Kites come next. Three on a good day, four; though at a need we can mount more. The Lifter's job is to carry the main cable; the cable's job is to steady the Lifters. It's all to do with balance. Everything's to do with balance.' He glanced sidelong once more; but if he expected a comment on his truism, he was disappointed.

Steam jetted from the Launch Vehicle, to be instantly whirled away. The Launchmaster squatted atop the big, hunched shape, one hand to the straining thread of cable, the other gesturing swiftly to the Winchman; paying out, drawing in, as the Pilot clawed for altitude. Others of the team stood ready to clamp the bronze cones to the Trace. The cone diameters increase progressively, allowing the Lifters to ride each to its proper station; and therein lies the skill. All must be judged beforehand; there is no room for error, no time for second thoughts.

An extra-heavy buffet shook the hangar's sides, set the Kitecaptain once more to scowling. Mixed with the hollow boom I thought I heard a growl of thunder. The Trace paid out steadily though, checked for the addition of the first of the vital cones. A second followed, and a third; and the Kitecaptain unconsciously gripped my arm. 'They're bringing the Lifters,' he said, and pointed.

How they controlled the monstrous, flapping things at all was a mystery to me; but control them they did, hauling at the boxlike structures that seemed at any moment about to fling the men themselves into the air. The tail ring of the first was clipped about the line; orders echoed across the field, the Kite sailed up smoothly into the murk. Its sisters followed it without a hitch; and the Captain visibly relaxed. 'Good,' he said. 'That was neatly done. You'll find no better team this side of the Salient.' He poured more spirit from the bottle, swallowed. 'Arms and legs enough have been broken at that game,' he said. 'Aye, and necks; in gentler blows than this.'

I restrained a smile. Despite his sourness, the quality of the man showed clear in the remark; the pride he still felt, justifiably, in a job well done. The Rigs might look well enough in high summer, the lines of them floating lazy against the blue, as far as the eye could reach; or at the Air Fairs of the Middle Lands, flying, beribboned, for the delectation of the Master and his aides. It was here though, in the blustering dark, that the mettle of the Captains and their crews was truly tested.

All now depended on the Launchmaster atop the Launcher. I saw him turn, straining his eyes up into the night, stretch a gauntleted hand to the

Trace. Five hundred feet and more above, the Pilot flew invisible; below, the Lifters spread out in their line, straining at their bridles of steel rope. The Rig was aloft; but the slightest failure, the parting of a shackle, the slipping of an ill-secured clamp, could still spell disaster. All was well however; the Launchmaster pulled at the Trace again, gauging the angle and tension of the cable, and the final signal was given. I craned forward, intrigued despite myself, brushed with a glove at the cloudy glass.

Quite suddenly, or so it seemed, the Observer was on the apron. A white-robed acolyte, his fair hair streaming, took from his shoulders his brilliant cloak of office. Beneath it he was dressed from head to foot in stout black leather; kneeboots, tunic and trews, close-fitting helmet. He turned once to stare up at the hangar front. I made out the pale blur of his face, the hard, high cheekbones; his eyes though were invisible, protected by massive goggles. He saluted, formally yet it seemed with an indefinable air of derision, turned on his heel and strode toward the Launch Vehicle. I doubt though that he could have made out either the Kitecaptain or myself.

The Ground Crew scurried again. Moving with practised, almost military precision, they wheeled the basket forward; the Observer climbed aboard, and the rest was a matter of skilled, split-second timing. The Manlifter, shielded at first by the hangar from the full force of the wind, swayed wildly, wrenching at its restraining ropes. Men ran back across the grass; the steam winch clattered and the whole equipage was rising into the night, the Observer already working at the tail-down tackle that would give him extra height. The winch settled to a steady, gentle clanking; and the Captain wiped his face. I turned to him. 'Congratulations,' I said. 'A splendid launch.'

Somewhere, distantly, a bell began to clang.

'They're all launched,' he said. 'Right up to the high G numbers; and south, down through the Easthold. The whole Sector's flying; for what good it'll serve.' He glowered at me. 'You understand, of course, the principles involved?' he said sarcastically.

'Assuredly,' I said. 'Air flows above the Manlifter's surfaces faster than beneath them, thus becoming rarified. The good Lord abhors a vacuum; so any wing may be induced to rise.'

He seemed determined not to be mollified. 'Excellent,' he said. 'I see you've swallowed a textbook or two. There's a bit more to it than that though. If you'd ever flown yourself, you wouldn't be so glib.'

I lowered my eyes. I knew, well enough, the dip and surge of a Cody basket; but it was no part of my intention to engage him in a game of apologetics. Instead I said, 'Tell me about Canwen.'

He stared at me, then nodded to the valise. He said, 'You've got his file.'

'Files don't say everything,' I said. 'I asked you, Kitecaptain.'

He turned away, stood hands on hips and stared down at the Launcher.

'He's a Flier,' he said at length. 'The finest we've got left. What else is there to say?'

I persisted. 'You've known him long?'

'Since I first joined the Corps,' he said. 'We were Cadets together.' He swung back, suddenly. 'Where's all this leading, Helman?'

'Who knows?' I said. 'Perhaps to understanding.'

He brought his palm down flat upon the desk. 'Understanding?' he shouted. 'Who in all the Hells needs understanding? It's explanations we're after, man ...'

'Me too,' I said pointedly. 'That's why I'm here.'

He flung an arm out. 'Up in G7,' he said, 'an Observer slipped his own Trace one fine night, floated off into the Badlands. I knew him too; and they don't come any better. Another sawed his wrists apart, up there on his own; and he'd been flying thirty years. Last week we lost three more; while you and all the rest sit trying to understand ...'

A tapping sounded at the door. It opened to his shout; a nervous-looking Cadet stood framed, his eyes on the floor. 'The Quartermaster sends his compliments,' he stammered, 'and begs to know if the Kitemaster – I mean My Lord – wishes some refreshment ...'

I shook my head; but the Captain picked the bottle up, tossed it across the room. 'Yes,' he said, 'get me some more of this muck. Break it out of stores, if you have to; I'll sign the chitty later.' The lad scurried away on his errand; the other stood silent and brooding till he returned. Below, on the apron, the ratchet of the winch clattered suddenly; a pause, and the smooth upward flight was continued. The Captain stared out moodily, screwed the cap from the fresh bottle and drank. 'You'll be telling me next,' he said, 'they've fallen foul of Demons.'

I turned, sharply. For a moment I wondered if he had taken leave of his senses; he seemed however fully in command of himself. 'Yes,' he said, 'you heard me right first time.' He filled the glass again. 'How long has it really been,' he said, 'since the Corps was formed? Since the very first Kite flew?'

'The Corps has always been,' I said, 'and always will be. It is the Way ...'

He waved a hand dismissively. 'Save it for those who need it,' he said brutally. 'Don't start preaching your sermons in here.' He leaned on the desk. 'Tell me,' he said, 'what was the real idea? Who dreamed it up?'

I suppose I could have remained silent, or quit his company; but it seemed that beneath the bluster there lay something else. A questioning, almost a species of appeal. It was as if something in him yet needed confirmation of his heresy; the confirmation, perhaps, of argument. Certainly I understood his dilemma, in part at least; it was a predicament that in truth was by no means new to me. 'The Corps was formed,' I said, 'to guard the Realm, and keep its borders safe.'

'From Demons,' he said bitterly. 'From Demons and night walkers, all spirits that bring harm …' He quoted, savagely, from the Litany. '*Some plunge, invisible, from highest realms of air; some have the shapes of fishes, flying; some, and these be hardest to descry, cling close upon the hills and very treetops …*' I raised a hand, but he rushed on regardless. '*These last be deadliest of all,*' he snarled. '*For to these the Evil One hath given semblance of a Will, to seek out and destroy their prey …* Crap!' He pounded the desk again. 'All crap,' he said. 'Every last syllable. The Corps fell for it though, every man jack of us. You crook your little fingers, and we run; we float up there like fools, with a pistol in one hand and a prayerbook in the other, waiting to shoot down bogles, while you live off the fat of the land …'

I turned away from the window and sat down. 'Enough,' I said tiredly. 'Enough, I pray you …'

'We're not the only ones of course,' he said. He struck an attitude. '*Some burst from the salt ocean,*' he mocked, '*clad overall in living flame …* So the Seaguard ride out there by night and day, with magic potions ready to stop the storms …' He choked, and steadied himself. 'Now I'll tell you, Helman,' he said, breathing hard. 'I'll tell you, and you'll listen. There are no Demons; not in the sky, not on the land, not in the sea …'

I looked away. 'I envy,' I said slowly, 'the sureness of your knowledge.'

He walked up to me. 'Is that all you've got to say?' he shouted. 'You hypocritical bastard …' He leaned forward. 'Good men have died in plenty,' he said, 'to keep the folk in fear, and you in your proper state. Twenty years I flew, till I got this; and I'll say it again, as loud and clear as you like. *There are no Demons …*' He swung away. 'There's something for your report,' he said. 'There's a titbit for you …'

I am not readily moved to anger. Enraged, we lose awareness; and awareness is our only gift from God. His last remark though irritated me beyond measure. He'd already said more than enough to be relieved of his command; enough, indeed, to warrant a court martial in Middlemarch itself. And a conviction, were I to place the information before the proper authorities. The sneer reduced me to the level of a Variant spy, peeping at keyholes, prying into ledgers. 'You fool,' I said. 'You arrogant, unreasoning fool.'

He stared, fists clenched. 'Arrogant?' he said. 'You call me arrogant? *You …?*'

I stood up, paced back to the window. 'Aye, arrogant,' I said. 'Beyond all measure, and beyond all sense.' I swung back. 'Will you be chastised,' I said bitterly, 'like a first year Chaplain, stumbling in the Litany? If that's the height of your desire, it can readily be accomplished …'

He sat back at the desk, spread his hands on its dull-painted top. 'What do you want of me?' he said.

'The courtesy with which you're being used,' I said. 'For the sake of Heaven, man, act your age …'

He drained the glass slowly, and set it down. He stretched his hand toward the bottle, changed his mind. Finally he looked up, under lowering brows. 'You take a lot on yourself, Helman,' he said. 'If any other spoke to me like that, I'd kill him.'

'Another easy option,' I said shortly. 'You're fuller of them than a beggar's dog of fleas.' I shook my head. 'You alone, of all the Lord's creation,' I said. 'You alone, beg leave to doubt your faith. And claim it as a novel sentiment …'

He frowned again. 'If you'd ever flown …'

'I've flown,' I said.

He looked up. 'You've seen the Badlands?' he asked sharply.

I nodded. 'Yes,' I said. 'I have.'

He took the bottle anyway, poured another drink. 'It changes you,' he said. 'For all time.' He picked the glass up, toyed with it. 'Folk reckon nothing lives out there,' he said grimly. 'Only Demons. I could wish they were right.' He paused. 'Sometimes of a clear day, flying low, you see … more than a man should see. But they're not Demons. I think once, they were folk as well. Like us …'

I folded my arms. I too was seeing the Badlands, in my mind; the shining vista of them spread by night, as far as the eye could reach. The hills and valleys twinkling, like a bed of coals; but all a ghastly blue.

It seemed he read my thoughts. 'Yes,' he said, 'it's something to look at all right …' He drank, suddenly, as if to erase the memory. 'It's strange,' he said. 'But over the years, I wonder if a Flier doesn't get to see with more than his normal eyes.' He rubbed his face. 'Sometimes,' he said, 'I'd see them stretching out farther and farther, all round the world; and nothing left at all, except the Realm. One little corner of a little land. That wasn't Demons either though. I think men did it, to each other.' He laughed. 'But I'm forgetting, aren't I?' he said bitterly. 'While the Watching goes on, it can never happen here …'

I touched my lip. I wasn't going to be drawn back into an area of barren cant. 'I sometimes wonder,' I said carefully, 'if it's not all merely a form of words. Does it matter, finally, how we describe an agent of Hell? Does it make it any more real? Or less?'

'Why, there you go,' he cried, with a return to something of his former manner. 'Can't beat a good Church training, that's what I always say. A little bit here, a little bit there, clawing back the ground you've lost. Nothing ever alters for you, does it? Face you with reality though; that's when you start to wriggle …'

'And why not?' I said calmly. 'It's all that's left to do. Reality is the strangest thing any of us will ever encounter; the one thing, certainly, that we'll never understand. Wriggle though we may.'

He waved his glass. 'I tell you what I'll do,' he said. 'I'll propose a small experiment. You say the Watching keeps us from all harm …'

I shook my head. 'I say the Realm is healthy, and that its fields are green.'

He narrowed his eyes for a moment. 'Well then,' he said. 'For a month, we'll ground the Cody rigs. And call in all the Seaguard. That would prove it, wouldn't it? One way or the other …'

'Perhaps,' I said. 'You might pay dearly for the knowledge though.'

He slammed the glass down. 'And what,' he said, 'if your precious fields stayed green? Would you concede the point?'

'I would concede,' I said gently, 'that Hell had been inactive for a span.'

He flung his head back and guffawed. The laughter was not altogether of a pleasant kind. 'Helman,' he said, 'you're bloody priceless.' He uncapped the bottle, poured. 'I'll tell you a little story,' he said. 'We were well off, when I was a youngster. Big place out in the Westmarch; you'd better believe it. Only we lost the lot. My father went off his head. Not in a nasty way, you understand; he never hurt a fly, right through his life. But every hour on the hour, for the last ten years, he waved a kerchief from the tower window, to scare off little green men. And you know what? We never saw a sign of one, not all the time he lived.' He sat back. 'What do you say to that?'

I smiled. 'I'd say that he had rediscovered Innocence. And taught you all a lesson; though at the time, maybe you didn't see.'

He swore, with some violence. 'Lesson?' he cried. 'What lesson lies in that?'

'That logic may have circular propensities,' I said. 'Or approach the condition of a sphere; the ultimate, incompressible form.'

He pushed the bottle away, staring; and I burst out laughing at the expression on his face. 'Man,' I said, 'you can't put Faith into a test tube, prove it with a piece of litmus paper …'

A flash of brilliance burst in through the windows. It was followed by a long and velvet growl. A bell began to sound, closer than before. I glanced across to the Kitecaptain; but he shook his head. He said harshly, 'Observation altitude …'

I lifted the valise on to the desk edge, unlocked it once more. I assembled the receiver, set up the shallow repeater cone with its delicate central reed. The other stared, eyes widening. 'What're you doing?' he croaked.

'My function is to listen,' I said curtly. 'And as I told you, maybe to understand. I've heard you; now we'll see what Canwen has to say.' I advanced the probe to the crystal; the cone vibrated instantly, filling the room with the rushing of the wind, the high, musical thrumming of the Cody rig.

The Captain sprang away, face working. 'Necromancy,' he said hoarsely. 'I'll not have it; not on my Base ...'

'Be quiet,' I snapped. 'You impress me not at all; you have more wit than that.' I touched a control; and the Observer roared with laughter. 'The tail-down rig of course,' he said. 'New since your day ...'

The other stared at the receiver; then through the window at the Launch Vehicle, the thread of cable stretching into the dark. 'Who's he talking to?' he whispered.

I glanced up. 'His father was a Flier, was he not?'

The Kitecaptain moistened his lips. 'His father died over the Salient,' he said. 'Twenty years ago.'

I nodded. 'Yes,' I said, 'I know.' Rain spattered sudden against the panes; I adjusted the control and the wind shrilled again, louder than before. Mixed as it was with the singing of the cables, there was an eerie quality to the sound; almost it was as if a voice called, thin and distant at first then circling closer. Canwen's answer was a great shout of joy. 'Quickly, Pater, help me,' he cried urgently. 'Don't let her go again ...' Gasps sounded; the basket-work creaked in protest and there was a close thump, as if some person, or some thing, had indeed been hauled aboard. The Observer began to laugh. 'Melissa,' he said. 'Melissa, oh my love ...'

'His wife,' I supplied. 'A most beautiful and gracious lady. Died of child-bed fever, ten years ago in Middlemarch ...'

'What?' cried Canwen. '*What?*' Then, 'Yes, I see it ...' A snapping sounded, as he tore the Great Seal from the basket; and he began to laugh again. 'They honour us, beloved,' he cried. 'The Church employs thaumaturgy against us ...'

The Kitecaptain gave a wild shout. 'No,' he cried, 'I'll hear no more of it ...' I wrestled with him, but I was too late. He snatched the receiver, held it on high and dashed it to the floor. The delicate components shattered; and the room fell silent, but for the close sound of the wind.

The pause was of brief duration. Lightning flared again; then instantly the storm was all around us. Crash succeeded crash, shaking the very floor on which I stood; the purple flaring became continuous.

The Captain started convulsively; then it seemed he collected himself. 'Down rig,' he shouted hoarsely. 'We must fetch him down ...'

'No,' I cried. 'No ...' I barred his way; for a moment my upflung arm, the sudden glitter of the Master's Staff, served to check him, then he had barged me aside. I tripped and fell, heavily. His feet clattered on the gantry steps; by the time I had regained my own his thick voice was already echoing through the hangar. '*Down rig ... Down rig, for your lives ...*'

I followed a little dazedly, ran across the cluttered floor of the place. The great end doors had been closed; I groped for the wicket, and the wind snatched it from my hand. My robes flogged round me; I pressed my back to the high metal, offered up a brief and fervent prayer. Before me the main winch of the Launcher already screamed, the great drum spun; smoke or steam rose from where the wildly-driven cable snaked through its fairleads. Men ran to the threatened points with water buckets, white-robed Medics scurried; Cadets, hair streaming, stood by with hatchets in their hands, to cut the rigging at a need. I stared up, shielding my face against the glaring arcs; and a cry of '*View-ho*' arose. Although I could not myself descry it, sharper eyes than mine had made out the descending basket. I started forward; next instant the field was lit by an immense white flash.

For a moment, it was as if Time itself was slowed. I saw a man, his arms flung out, hurled headlong from the Launcher; fragments of superstructure, blown outward by the force of the concussion, arced into the air; the vehicle's cab, its wheels, the tautened anchor cables, each seemed lit with individual fire. The lightning bolt sped upward, haloing the main Trace with its vivid glare; then it was as if the breath had been snatched from my lungs. I crashed to the ground again half-stunned, saw through floating spots of colour how a young Cadet, blood on his face, ran forward to the winch gear. He flung his weight against the tallest of the levers, and the screaming stopped. The Manlifter, arrested within its last few feet of travel, crashed sideways, spilling the Observer unceremoniously on to the grass. A shackle parted somewhere, dimly heard through the ringing in my ears; the axes flashed, a cable end lashed viciously above my head. The Lifter train whirled off into the dark, and was gone.

I got to my feet, staggered toward Canwen. By the time I reached him, the Medics were already busy. They raised him on to the stretcher they wheeled forward; his head lolled, but at sight of me he rallied. He raised an arm, eyes blazing, made as if to speak; then he collapsed, lying still as death, and was borne rapidly away.

The eastern sky was lightening as I packed the valise for the final time. I closed the lock hasp, clicked it shut; and the door was tapped. A fair-haired Cadet entered, bearing steaming mugs on a tray. I smiled at him. A fresh white bandage circled his brow, and he was a little pale; but he looked uncommon proud.

I turned to the Base Medic, a square-set, ruddy-faced man. I said, 'So you think Canwen will live?'

'Good God, yes,' he said cheerfully. 'Be up and about in a day or two at the latest. He's survived half a dozen calls like that already; I think this gives him the record ...' The door closed behind him.

I sipped. The brew was dark and bitter; but at least it was hot. 'Well,' I said, 'I must be on my way. Thank you for your hospitality, Kitecaptain; and my compliments to all concerned for their handling of last night's emergency.'

He rubbed his face uncertainly. 'Will you not stay,' he said, 'and break your fast with us properly?'

I shook my head. 'Out of the question I'm afraid,' I said. 'I'm due at G15 by zero nine hundred. But I thank you all the same.' I hefted the valise, and smiled again. 'Its Captain, I've no doubt, will have had too much to drink,' I said. 'I shall probably hear some very interesting heresy.'

He preceded me through the now-silent hangar. To one side a group of men was engaged in laying out long wire traces; but there were few other signs of activity. Outside, the air struck chill and sweet after the storm; by the main gate my transport waited, in charge of a smartly uniformed chauffeur/acolyte. I began to walk toward it; the Captain paced beside me, his chin sunk on his chest, still it seemed deep in thought. 'What's your conclusion?' he asked abruptly.

'About the recent loss rate?' I said. I shook my head. 'An all round lessening of morale, leading to a certain slackness; all except here of course,' I added as his mouth began to open. It's a lonely and thankless life for all the Cody teams; nobody is more aware of it than I.

He stopped, and turned toward me. 'What's to do about it then?' he said.

'Do?' I shrugged. 'Send Canwen to have a chat with them. He'll tell them he's seen the face of God. If he doesn't, go yourself…'

He frowned. 'About the thaumaturgy. The things we heard…'

I began to walk again. 'I've heard them often enough before,' I said. 'I don't place all that much importance on them. It's a strange world, in the sky; we must all come to terms with it as best we may.' Which is true enough; sometimes, to preserve one's sanity, it's best to become just a little mad.

He frowned again. 'Then the report…'

'Has already been made,' I said. 'You gave it yourself, last night. I don't think I really have very much to add.' I glanced across to him. 'You'd have been best advised,' I said, 'to leave him flying, not draw him down through the eye of the storm. But you'd have seen that for yourself, had you not been under a certain strain at the time.'

'You mean if I hadn't been drunk,' he said bluntly. 'And all the time I thought…' He squared his shoulders. 'It won't happen again, Kitemaster; I'll guarantee you that.'

'No,' I said softly, 'I don't suppose it will.'

He shook his head. 'I thought for a moment,' he said, 'it was a judgement on me. I'd certainly been asking for it…'

This time I hid the smile behind my hand. That's the whole trouble, of course, with your amateur theologians. Always expecting God to peer down from the height, His fingers to His nose, for their especial benefit.

We had reached the vehicle. The acolyte saluted briskly, opened the rear door with its brightly blazoned crest. I stooped inside, and turned to button down the window. 'Goodbye, Kitecaptain,' I said.

He stuck his hand out. 'God go with you,' he said gruffly. He hesitated. 'Someday,' he said, 'I'll come and visit you. At that bloody summer palace ...'

'Do,' I said. 'You'll be honourably received; as is your due. And Captain ...'

He leaned close.

'Do something for me in the meantime,' I said. 'Keep the Codys flying; till something better comes along ...'

He stepped back, saluting stiffly; then put his hands on his hips, stared after the vehicle. He was still staring when a bend of the green, rutted track took it from sight.

I leaned back against the cushioning, squeezed the bridge of my nose and closed my eyes. I felt oddly cheered. On the morrow, my tour of duty would be ended. They would crown a new May Queen, in Middlemarch; children would run to me, their hair bedecked with flowers, and I would touch their hands.

I sat up, opened the file on Kitebase G15. A mile or so farther on though I tapped the glass screen in front of me and the chauffeur drew obediently to a halt. I watched back to where, above the shoulders of the hills, a Cody rig rose slowly, etched against the flaring yellow dawn.

2

Kitecadet

He had been up before first light, as had all the leavemen. Now the long, barrel-vaulted bath house echoed as usual with the shouts and high jinks of his classmates. He stood at the urinal, naked as the rest; the ritual created in him its usual strange sensation, half floating, half exhilarated. Olsen, as ever, was noisily displaying his morning excitement to all and sundry. Something warm splashed his ankle; he swore, would perhaps have lashed out, but the other's mouthing was lost suddenly in the huge banging of the steam pipes. The yelps redoubled; he grabbed for soap, the semester's last issue, ran for the shower stalls. He had no intention of being caught for long behind a giggling, shoving queue.

Despite the brightening days, the big stoves in the barrack blocks had been allowed alight; beside each stood a blank-faced Sector servant, fanning warmth up steadily from the glowing grille. He fetched the spare towel hoarded in his. locker, and was hailed. 'Hey, Raoul, after you . . .!' He grinned and shook his head, already busy. He was proud of his hair; it was long and thick, the colour of dark corn. He snapped at the Centre man, relaxed, preened himself in warmth.

The breakfast hooter took him by surprise; he was barely halfway through. He hesitated, then drew his hair up quickly into the double ponytail that had recently become the rage. Others, he knew, would do the same; on this morning of mornings, such minor affectations were invariably winked at. It looked well, he decided; nonetheless he felt a vague unease. Almost a guilt. He kept a sharp lookout for the omnipresent Olsen. On Feast Days, a certain ebullience was likewise tolerated; it was time, he had decided, for the other to receive a small memento of his displeasure, possibly in the form of a well-blacked eye. But the stocky youth averted his gaze, seeming mightily preoccupied with the texture of the limewashed refectory wall. Which Raoul decided was just possibly a point to him.

By zero eight hundred he was through. His uniform, fresh-pressed by the Sector domestics – Base Rats they called them, though never to their faces – felt warm and comfortable; his tunic buttons had been polished till they gleamed. He adjusted the new brassard lovingly; the loop of silver cord, worn over the shoulder, that represents the main Trace of a Cody rig. In strict truth, he had no right to it as yet; he'd done his training flights, all ten of them, but that had been over the flat fields surrounding Base Camp, well behind the lines. He'd missed out on his first Operational, one of the vicious little fevers that stalk the low ground of the Salient had laid him low; but the T.O. in charge of Cadet messes, in most respects a hard and uncompromising man, had shown an unexpected flash of charity. His term's work had been good; and not all Frontier men go strictly by the book. So when the lists of Cadet Fliers had gone up on the noticeboards his name had been with the rest. He drew the new badge gleefully from Stores, and laughed at Kil Olsen's face; because for some reason the other had been pegged.

One duty remained to be performed, before leave properly began. He flicked a final time at his boots, hefted his duffel and presented himself at the office of Warrantman Keaning. He was kept waiting a considerable while; but that was part of the ritual, and accepted. He stood arms folded, staring out across the Base. The sky was bright now, on that mild spring morning; the early sun gleamed on the low lines of barrack blocks, the taller, gaunt shapes of the Kitehangars. G15, biggest of all the Stations on the Salient, would be working for the next few days at much reduced capacity; she would still man four Cody rigs though, round the clock.

The Night Observers (Blackbirds they called them, in Base slang) were coming in; he watched with approval the neat handling of the rigs, Lifter after Lifter sailing down to be detached by the ground crews, hurried into the safety of the great canvas-sided sheds. He'd heard that in the low Gs, up round Streanling way, they didn't even draw a String for shiftchange; the Observers simply swapped places in the basket, and up she went again. He curled his lip. They were all bog-happy up there anyway. At G15 each rig was drawn for checking, every time, and a new Trace flown. But G15 was the showplace of the Frontier; the best Station, he thought privately, in the Corps.

The Launch Vehicles jetted their plumes of steam; and he touched his arm again. Very soon now, he'd be a full-fledged Flier; one of the elite. The thought served to straighten his shoulders fractionally. He was tall, taller by a head than the Salient lads from whom the Corps was mostly staffed; and though Olsen had jeered often enough, asking how many extra Lifters he'd need for a Force Three Stable, awareness of physical superiority still brought a degree of pleasure.

The opening of the door behind him interrupted the train of thought. He turned, saluted. Warrant Keaning was a grey-haired, seamed-faced man; the longest serving of all the Base personnel, if the tale was true. His eyes flicked, from the habit of a lifetime, over the young Cadet's uniform; finally it seemed he was satisfied. He gestured, briefly; Raoul followed him into the inner sanctum, stood stiffly before the desk.

'At ease,' said the other mildly. He took from his uniform a pair of curious half-round glasses, adjusted them on his nose. He said, 'Ready for the off? You'll have a fine day for it.'

Raoul suppressed a smile. Expecting some such comment, he'd taken careful note of the telltales on Hangar Six. 'Force Three and a Half sir, gusting Four,' he said. 'Sou-sou-west, steady. I'd rather be flying.'

'*Hmmph*,' said the other. He spread papers on the desk, studied them. He said, 'Seen your family recently?'

'No, sir. Not this term.'

'I see. You didn't think of travelling up to Hyeway then?'

Raoul swallowed. The thought of the little Northland farmhouse didn't appeal; his mother clattering in the kitchen baking the dry May cakes, his father sway-backed from the years he'd spent trudging his land. 'Sower's arse', they called it, and there was no cure. Though they had machine spreaders now for the horse-drawn rigs, there was even talk of investing in an old tractor. A Kitecadet might not earn much, by Middle Lands standards; but in the economy of the Salient, the wages he sent home were critical. 'I've never been to Middlemarch,' he said. 'I felt it was too good a chance to miss.'

The Warrantman grunted again. 'So when will you be thinking of going?'

Raoul opened his mouth, and closed it quickly. The words 'First Air Leave' had all but slipped out; but at least he'd avoided the trap. You don't count those sort of chickens, if you're wise, at least not while you're still a Cadet. He said formally, 'At the next opportunity, sir.' The affair of the brassard rankled with Keaning, he knew; the old man at least was a stickler for regulations. He'd been expecting some sort of grilling; it was a small enough price to pay though.

It seemed the other still had not finished. 'I see you were in line for a Church scholarship once,' he said. 'What made you change your mind?'

Raoul thought quickly. The Corps paperwork he could handle well enough, the trig, met and all the rest; but theology was another matter. The other knew that well enough of course; but he wasn't going to make the admission. Not at least till it was forced out of him. He raised his head. 'It was my mother's ambition really,' he said. 'I didn't feel I had a vocation; I thought I might perhaps be more use here.'

Keaning stared over his glasses. 'Probably just as well,' he said. 'They don't give too many of those things out. Not in the Salient at least.' So the point was made anyway; but he wasn't a long term Warrantman for nothing. He stared at the papers a final time, and shuffled them together. 'Very good,' he said. 'These seem to be in order.' He handed them over. Base Pass and ID, security clearances, the little wallet of credits; exchangeable, Raoul knew, at any counting house of the Church Variant. Or at Main Bank, in Middlemarch. He took them, saluted again smartly. The other removed his glasses, tucked them back in his pocket. 'Enjoy your leave, Cadet,' he said. 'And keep your nose clean, won't you? You know what I mean.'

The Warrantman sat for a while after the door had closed, staring into space. He wondered how many boys like that he'd seen come and go now, over the years. He glanced through the long, metal-framed windows at the Rigs; bright sails of the Lifters steady in the high blue, thin cobweb-lines of Traces. He sighed, rubbed his face and busied himself with other tasks.

The Transports were waiting, up by Main Gate; most of the other leavemen and Cadets had already clustered round them. Raoul took deep breaths of suddenly wine-sweet air, and resisted the temptation to break into a run. Good enough for a First Year maybe, or one of the Base Rats; but not when you'd got your Trace up. He strode out smartly instead, saluting the Controllers on Three and Four Rigs as he passed. Then two pilots soared simultaneously ahead, and he stopped to watch. He'd wondered vaguely why the shiftchange had been delayed; now it became clear. Hangars One and Two were racing, for the benefit of the assembled crowd.

The little Kites rose swiftly, dragging their light lines, clawing for altitude; and the singing of the winch gears checked for the addition of the first trace cones. The Lifters followed, climbing each to its appointed place as the winches paid out again; in what seemed a startlingly short time the black Manlifters were run out from the hangars. The Observers appeared, goggled and helmeted even on that bright day. The handlers stepped back; and the Rigs were climbing once more, steadily, into the blue. He stared up, shading his eyes. The pilots were all but invisible now, mere dots against the glowing sky; and still the lines paid out. The traces angled, steadied; altitude bells pealed faintly from the hangars, and the winches were locked at last. The Rigs hung, watchful, over the low hills of the Frontier.

Orderly Meggs was jubilant. 'Five fifty two,' he said. 'Five bloody fifty two, we cracked six minutes. Beat that, for a Force Three launch …' The G15 Cadets cheered lustily; the lads from Twelve and Fourteen, who'd be travelling with them, looked more glum. Raoul smiled. It was a smart enough stringup, certainly; but by the normal standards of the Base, the Launchers had been double-manned.

He climbed aboard the first of the gaunt, high-sided vehicles, slung his duffel in the baggage net and hurried for the back. He was long-legged, the seating centres fixed for Salient personnel; he had no intention of suffering the best part of a day of bruised kneecaps. The rest piled after him, with much pushing and shoving; the old hands grabbed the front compartment, set up a card game almost at once. Meggs checked his clipboard, yelling for quiet; and at last they were away, jolting down the rugged track that led to the first of the ramshackle Salient villages. He stared back at the Base, the Kitestrings tiny already against the eastern sky. He felt again the rise of an intense pleasure. The pleasure was anticipation. Quite what to expect, he had no idea. But he was looking good, his uniform looked good; and this was his first real furlough.

Two hours later, he was feeling bemused. He'd received an impression, his first, of the sheer size of the land the Corps protected. The Transports shook and clattered, solid tyres bouncing over potholes; and this was still the Salient, the country he'd known from a child. Dotted with little farms, the occasional small hamlet; broken here and there by the low rise of a hill, but for the most part deadly flat. Little traffic either, and few signs of life; just the odd cart, sometimes a peasant leaning at the wayside, scowling suspiciously at the small convoy. Though once they passed through a slightly bigger settlement; nearly large enough, he supposed, to be called a town. In its centre, placed at the crossing of four roads, were the twin buildings he'd come to expect from his odd trips to the Easthold; the arrogant, thrusting spire of the Church Variant, fronting the whitewashed barn of the milder Middle Doctrine.

His fellow Cadets had fallen quiet as well. Once Olsen, typically, had begun to bawl a vulgar ditty; something about how far you could get up, with a fifty-lifter string. Meggs snarled at him finally to shut up, and Raoul was vaguely glad. There was a sombreness about the place that matched his altered mood.

A brief stop, at an inn that looked as decrepit as the rest, and the land finally began to change. They were climbing now, into lush green hills. The road surface was better too; the wheels of the Transports crunched on fresh-laid gravel. This country was prosperous, more prosperous than any he'd seen; there were well-stocked fields, neatly fenced paddocks in which fine horses ran. He essayed a question, and Meggs nodded. 'Yes,' he said. 'It's the Middle Lands.'

They rounded a bend; and Raoul gasped. Ahead lay the biggest house he'd ever seen. It dominated a tree-lined combe; a high stone frontage, embellished with corner towers, set with line on line of elegant windows. Above it, over the low-pitched roofs, flew massive Kitestrings. The streamers flapped, gaudy and graceful; on them he made out the cabalistic signs that protected the Realm from harm. The Seeing Eye, the clenched fist of the Church; and the Vestibule, the ancient leaf-shape that forever distracts the attention of the Evil One. He remembered the shock he had received as a small child, when its use and meaning were first explained to him.

Stev Marden called a question; and once again the Orderly was ready with an answer. 'Kitemaster,' he said, and sniffed.

Raoul pondered. Kitemasters were the high churchmen who controlled the Corps itself, shaped its policies, ran each detail of its daily functioning. Always, to him, they'd been semi-legendary beings; now he understood why, if they lived in palaces fit for kings. But his attention was rapidly distracted. Ahead, and closing fast, was a private transport vehicle, one of the very few he had seen. Its sides were blazoned with the insignia of the Church Variant; so it was bound, perhaps, for the great place they had passed. Beyond it was another, and another; soon the road was dotted with them. There were more of the fine buildings too, glimpsed briefly; though none, he thought, as grand as the very first of all.

The hills rose steeper now, coated with heather and gorse. At the highest point of all the rock of which they were formed broke through the grass, showing in weathered outcrops, in rounded domes like the old, patched skulls of giants. A final wheezing climb, and the view ahead abruptly opened out.

Even Olsen, it seemed, was momentarily stunned to silence. Far off, the mountains of the Westguard loomed in silhouette, like pale holes knocked in the sky. To right and left, as far as the eye could reach, the land rose to other heights; while below, dwarfed by the vast bowl in which it lay yet still it seemed stretching endlessly, lay Middlemarch, greatest city in all the Realm.

Somebody whooped; and abruptly the spell was broken. The Cadets fell to chattering like magpies as the Transports began their slow, cautious descent. Raoul joined in, pointing to this and that wonder; the Middle Lake, the great central parkland where on the morrow the Air Fair would begin, the pale needle-spires of Godpath, Metropolitan Cathedral of the Variants. The sprawling building beside it, he knew from his books and lectures, was the Corps headquarters; beyond was the Mercy Hospital, the Middle Doctrine's chief establishment. Beyond again loomed other towers, too numerous to count; while in every direction, spreading into distance, were the squares and avenues, the baths and libraries and palaces of that amazing town. To the south, Holand, the industrial suburb, spread a faint, polluting haze, but all the rest was sparkling; clear and white, like a place seen in a dream.

The road, the ribbon of gravel, decreased its slope by slow degrees; perspectives became more normal. Middlemarch sank from sight behind the curtain of its own outlying trees. Half an hour later the Transports were bowling along a wide boulevard, fringed with fine houses. From each, for this greatest Festival of the year, flew the strings of sacred Kites; and the Orderly prodded Raoul in the ribs. 'Nice number, that,' he said, nodding. 'If you ever get tired of the Codys. Kiteman to one of the Masters; you'd be made for life.'

The Cadet dragged his mind back from distance. He was bemused, it seemed, by the giddying whirl of traffic. 'Yes,' he said. 'Yes, I suppose I would.' He'd been a million miles from the Base; from the stink of dope in the hangars, the scents of oil and steam, harsh roar of the roof arcs on winter nights of wind. But leave the Codys? The thought was insupportable. The great Rigs were his life; they would be his life for ever.

They passed the massive pile of the Cathedral, folk thronging its steps already for the pre-Feast service; and the Transports swung right, and right again. Then left, beneath a high stone arch. They drew up in a courtyard, windows staring down all round; and the throbbing of the engines stopped at last. 'All right, lads,' said Meggs, swinging himself to his feet. 'Get your gear together. Reception on the right . . .'

The hostel was a massive, echoing place; but the room into which he was finally decanted was sufficiently like his old dorm on the Base to make him feel almost at home. The same brown, highly-polished floor; the same identically-spaced beds, each with its blanket cube deposited neatly at the foot; even the same tall, potbellied stoves, surrounded by their thin, well-polished rails. He slung his kit down next to Stev Marden, and grinned. 'Well,' he said, 'we made it.' Suddenly, the words seemed curiously trite; but the other didn't seem to notice. 'At least,' he said, 'we got rid of that little fucker Olsen. I can't wait to get out on the town.'

Raoul grinned again. 'Me too,' he said. 'Thank Heaven for small mercies.' He started laying out his gear.

Passes were issued; but the curfew was at twenty-two hundred. Lights Out twenty-two thirty. Stev moaned a little; privately, the other was pleased. The long day, the excitement, had taken more out of him than he'd realized. He was glad to hit the sack; he was asleep almost as soon as his head touched the pillow.

It seemed he had barely closed his eyes before the reveille hooters were blaring. The Cadets rose, grumbling noisily; but Raoul for one ran to the high windows, stared up anxiously. Light clouds were scudding, but the day was fine.

The Section was herded to Ablutions, then to Early Service. It seemed the chaplain droned on for an age; but at last they were free to leave. A hasty breakfast, an even hastier Dorm Fatigue; and they debouched in threes and fours, on to the city streets.

Middlemarch, that brilliant morning, presented a spectacle Raoul thought he would never forget. The hordes of people, hooting of the flower-decked Transporters; here, he decided, must be all the folk in the world. Everywhere, the dark blue of the Corps; and priests in plenty, grey and sage green of the Middle Doctrine, white, black and purple of the Church Variant. Even, here and there, the vivid scarlet of a Master and his aides. There were startling girls too, in robes the like of which he'd never seen. They too had decked themselves with flowers; they passed in chattering, laughing groups, down with all the rest. Toward the park, the great Air Fair.

He'd been separated from Stev and the others; but finding his way presented no difficulty. It seemed he was swept along, as by a tide. Within minutes, he saw the place ahead; the tall stands erected for the visiting dignitaries, the hangars that housed the score on score of Show Strings. Decorative Kite trains already flew, outlining the whole ground with spots of vivid colour.

The proceedings were opened by the Grand Master himself, from a dais higher than all the rest. Raoul wasn't near enough to catch the words; he doubted privately though if anybody heard much. The cheering was too intense. The Master raised his arms, in a final blessing; and the first of the Launch Vehicles swept on to the field. A gust of vapour whirled above the crowd; the stink of hot oil mingled with the sweetness of crushed grass. Raoul grinned, in pure excitement; and his arm was caught.

He turned. It was a boy a year or two older than himself, a tall lad in the pale blue of a Middlemarch Cadet. He took in the other's uniform, eyes twinkling, glanced at the shoulder tags. 'G15,' he said. 'You're a long way from home. Well, Outlander, have you come to find out how to fly a Rig?'

Raoul hesitated; but there was no malice in the words. He grinned again. 'I doubt I shall learn very much,' he said, and turned back to the field.

Five pilots soared together; within seconds it seemed, their Lifters were airborne too. Privately, he was amazed. He'd seen some fast stringing up, but never anything like this. 'There's a trick to it of course,' said the other. 'They strip the fairleads, the cones are ready-spaced.'

'We wouldn't have that, not where I come from,' growled Raoul. 'Cable warp on the drums.' But the other laughed outright. 'New cables,' he said. 'They're only used the once. No expense spared, in Middlemarch.'

The Fliers worked their tail-down tackles; the Strings swung dangerously together, lapped somehow each over each. Three hundred feet above, the baskets all but touched; and from them burst a storm of pink and yellow petals. The crowd roared its delight; and Raoul's new friend grabbed his sleeve again. 'That's it for half an hour,' he said. 'Come on, quick. I've got a pal in the cider tent; get a move on, or we shall never get a drink.'

It was the start of a hectic, exhilarating week. There were formal tours of the hangar complexes, a banquet for all the Cadets presided over by no less a personage than Kitemaster Helman himself. By accident or design, G15 drew the top table; the preparatory spitting and polishing went on for most of the day. It promised to be a prickly affair; but by the end of the evening Raoul had all but lost his awe. The old man sat beaming happily, surrounded by Variant children in their new Confirmation robes; later he shook hands, it seemed with everyone in the hall. Meanwhile, the displays went on. Girls in tiny costumes performed feats of aerial daring; Raoul gasped, but only partly at their skill. There was even a demonstration of the new-fangled hydrogen balloons; the city had been buzzing with the news for days. Research had been known to be proceeding, but the Church had hitherto released the slimmest of details. Raoul attended with the rest; he was however curiously unimpressed. The silver blimps rose slowly, above the gaggle of gas bowsers; and he shook his head. They would never replace the elegance and flexibility of the Codys.

The Festival reached its climax. On the final afternoon Canwen, senior Flier of the Salient, was to attempt a new height record. Stev was enthusiastic; but Raoul once more pulled a face. A Cody basket at three thousand feet? There'd be no air to breathe, no air at all. He'd seen the Rig designed for the attempt; the Traces looked no thicker than a pilot line, even the Lifter frames were of some new lightweight alloy. The Lifters themselves were massive, twice the span of anything they had at Base. He brooded. There were Fliers and Fliers of course; but there had only ever been, there would only ever be, one Canwen.

The day closed with a massed display. Again, he knew he was seeing something he would probably never see again; fifty Rigs, all taking to the air at once. He stared up. The Lifter strings glowed oddly bright against the clouds massing overhead; the hissing of the wind through the forest of struts was deep in his skull, like tinnitus. The crowd roared; and from every basket shot trails and loops of fire, white and scarlet and green. Aerial bombs exploded, a cannonade; as if in answer, the heavens finally opened. He ran, laughing, with the rest. It was for all the world as if the good Lord had deliberately stayed His hand; that was probably Canwen's doing though. 'He's always been like it,' puffed a fat priest, jogging at his side. 'Born in God's arse pocket . . .'

He realized there were two Festivals in Middlemarch; the second was just beginning. Great bands of folk, young men and girls, pranced through the streets regardless of the deluge; every window blazed, the city's many inns and taverns roared. Tonight, it seemed nobody would sleep.

He tacked from pub to pub, drank cup after cup of the rich yellow wine, juice of the miles of orchards for which the Middle Lands were famed. His pockets jingled with cash; but nowhere would they take his money. For a Kiteman, everything was free. He laughed, his arm round the waist of a serving girl. She swung to peck his cheek, her hair brushed at him; he thought it was her scent that made him giddy.

Where he found the other, he could never afterwards remember. Nor could he recall with clarity whether she first spoke to him, or he to her. She was small and neat and rounded, and her skin was brown; he thought he'd never seen so many freckles. She was barefooted, in the short skirt of a serving maid; but that was all to the good. He admired her slim legs, her sturdy little knees. She curled on his lap, feather-light, in a room where a band played jigs, where waitresses circled between the many tables with more decanters of the vivid wine. She reached up, stroked his hair; he bent his head to kiss. 'It must be marvellous,' she said. 'What's it really like? To be a Flier?'

He pulled a face. Much sooner concentrate on rubbing her behind. 'It's all right,' he said. He nuzzled at her again; but she chuckled, pushed away. 'Tell me,' she said. 'I want to know it all. You must have an awful lot to learn. Who teaches you, the Kitecaptains?'

'No,' he said, 'they'd never . . .' He stopped. To a Kitecaptain, Cadets were the lowest form of life; but it wouldn't do to admit that. 'They're usually pretty busy,' he said. 'So we have special people. We call them T.O.s. Training Officers.'

She toyed with the brassard on his shoulder. 'You've really flown,' she said. 'Right out across the Frontier. Weren't you very scared?'

He hesitated. He'd have liked to turn the conversation, but there seemed to be no way. 'A bit,' he said modestly. 'But everybody is of course. The first time.'

'The first time,' she said. 'How many times have you done it then?'

'Oh,' he said, 'a few.'

Her eyes were very big and dark. 'Are the Badlands really like they say? Do they really shine at night?'

He checked again; but the lie must be maintained now, he'd gone too far to stop. He launched into a description, of a place he'd never seen. He'd heard about it though, often enough; the hills and ridges of that drear expanse, treeless and desolate, stretching as far as the eye could reach, twinkling in darkness with their own blue fire.

'Gosh,' she said. 'Gosh, you're so brave. I'd never dare ...' She shivered, deliciously. 'And are there people there as well? People like us?'

'There are people,' he said. 'You don't see much of them as a rule. They're not like us though.'

'What ... are they like?'

He touched the little curl beside her ear. 'You wouldn't want to know.'

She glanced up quickly. 'Have you ever seen a Demon?'

'Ah,' he said. 'Now that would be telling.'

'No, honestly ...'

He frowned. 'No,' he said after a moment. 'No, I haven't.'

'Some of you have though.'

'Yes,' he said. 'I expect some of us have.'

She frowned in turn. 'I've never understood about them,' she said. 'What do they look like? Really?'

'You know the Litany.'

'Yes,' she said. 'But it's never seemed to make much sense. I mean, it's difficult to believe in them. All that about fishes, flying in the air. And the flames all coming out. Fish can't fly.'

He said, 'They made the Badlands though.' He smiled. 'Don't worry, perhaps there aren't any left. But we've still got to be ready. In case they ever come back.'

'What would you do if you saw one?'

He said easily, 'Get rid of it, of course.'

She looked at him solemnly. 'Would it work?' she said. 'Just saying words? What do you call it, exorcising ... Would it really turn round and fly away?'

He made a face. Once more he seemed to be getting out of his depth. He said, 'That's what we're there for.' He signalled to one of the waitresses. The girl grabbed the cup from him, drank. Wine trickled on her chin, ran down inside her dress. He said, 'Messy thing.' He kissed her. The sweetness of the drink was on her mouth.

The street door opened abruptly. 'Oh, no,' he said. 'Oh, no ...' It seemed he'd been tracked down by his entire Mess. They set up a cheer at the sight of him, and Stev Marden called across. 'Save some for me ...'

They crowded round. Olsen was drunker than the rest. He crashed against a table, wine was spilled. A Middlemarcher shouted; Stev said anxiously, 'Cool it ...'

The girl had tensed. Olsen grabbed for her wrist. She snatched it back, and Raoul said, 'That's enough.'

'Enough?' said the other thickly. 'Wha' y' mean, enough? Wha's she then, private property?' He pawed at her again; she jumped up, eeled away, and Raoul was on his feet. *'I said pack it in ...'*

The other's mood changed instantly. 'An' who the Hell are you?' he said. 'Jus' who the Hell are you?' He snatched at the brassard. 'You don' even have the ri—' He got no further; because Raoul hit him in the mouth.

He was off balance; and the blow had been delivered with all the other's strength. He reeled back, sprawled across two tables. Uproar arose; instantly he was up, arms flailing.

To Raoul, it was as if events were curiously slowed. There was time for regret, even horror, at what he had done; also for fear to grow, because it seemed he was fighting a madman. The air was full of flying fists; his lips split, numbingly, a blow on the cheek sent him crashing against the wall. He all but fell; then suddenly the objects round about seemed oddly tinged with red. He launched himself at his opponent, in a berserk rage.

There was no memory, later, of physical contact; and certainly none of pain. He was aware, dimly, of the blows he rained, of the other's contorted face; then it seemed his sight was wholly swamped. He wrestled with the arms that held him back; and Stev's voice reached him faintly. 'For God's sake,' he said, 'you'll bloody kill him ...'

His vision cleared, abruptly. Olsen had rolled on to his side; he lay whimpering, hands to his reddened face. A dozen separate scuffles had already broken out; and the girl was tugging desperately at his arm. 'Quick,' she said, 'quick. Before the Vars get here ...'

It registered, dimly. He'd seen the Variant police in action once or twice before. He ran with her, half-leaning. He felt giddy now and sick, disoriented. 'Come on,' she said. 'Come on. It isn't far ...'

The street outside was crowded still. They turned and twisted, desperate; and there was an archway, closed off by iron-studded doors. She pushed at a wicket, ducked through, slammed. He saw treegrown grounds, a drive; beyond, lines of tall lit windows. She turned aside though, to a stable block. 'Up here,' she said, 'up here. You'll be all right ...'

He negotiated, with difficulty, a steep wooden ladder. Round about was a powerful, sweet scent that in his dazed condition he couldn't place. A match flared, in the dark; by the light of the lamp she lit he saw they were in a hayloft. He sat down, shakily. His cheek was stinging now; he put his fingers to it. They came away red. He stared at them, surprised.

'It's all right,' she said again. 'It isn't much, I'll get some things.' She swung quickly down the ladder.

She was back in minutes with a bowl and cloths, a towel. She knelt beside him, wiping gently. She said, 'He caught you an awful whack,' and he said dully, 'I nearly killed him, didn't I?' She paused then in what she was doing. She said, 'I wish you had.' She finished finally, sat back. 'There,' she said, 'it's not too bad at all. How do you feel?'

'Fine,' he said. 'I'm all right now, honestly.'

She drew her knees up, linked her arms around them. In the dim light, her eyes were unfathomable. He watched back; and suddenly he knew why he was there, what the end of it must be. His heart gave a great leap and bound; like the surge of a Cody basket almost, caught in a squall.

She saw he'd understood; she rose, unhurriedly, undid her frock and let it fall. He thought he'd never seen anything as beautiful. She knelt before him again, began to work at his tunic. He licked his lips; and when his voice came it was little more than a croak. He said, 'What about the others?' and she smiled. 'They'll be out all night,' she said serenely. 'Nobody will come here.' She pressed her mouth to his, twined fingers behind his neck. He tasted salt again, and didn't care.

It was over far too quickly, the first time. 'Sorry,' he said, 'I didn't mean …' But she merely chuckled. 'You should have played with me first,' she said. 'Don't worry, it'll be better soon.' Later, he fell into a deep and dreamless sleep.

She roused him at first light. He was disoriented for a moment; then memory returned. He lay blinking sleepily. He said, 'I've been to Heaven,' and she smiled. She said, 'Where's Heaven?' and he said, 'Between your legs.' She rolled on to him then, bottom pumping rhythmically, thrusting sweetness at him.

Zero nine-thirty was Departure Time. Walking back through the city, he had leisure to feel scared. He needn't have worried though. Most of the Mess had failed to make the previous night's curfew; they were still staggering in, in bedraggled twos and threes. It was well after ten hundred before they finally got on the road.

Stev greeted him enthusiastically. It seemed he'd had quite a night as well. One eye was decorated in festive green and purple, and there was an angry-looking weal across his forehead. That was nothing though, or so he proclaimed. 'You should see Olsen, K.,' he said. 'We really ought to get a picture. Before the swelling goes.'

Raoul said nervously, 'Is he … was he badly hurt?' But the other shook his head. 'Take more than that to kill the little bastard,' he said. 'More's the pity …' He nodded at the broken brassard. 'Anyway, that's a Charge to start with. If you wanted to make it stick. And we'd all back you …'

Raoul was silent, while the Transports ground through the city. As they climbed the long road to the hills, he found himself staring back. Middlemarch lay as he had seen it first, basking in mild sunlight; but infinitely, secretly, more lovely now. He touched his tunic pocket, where he'd tucked the locket she'd given him. In it a scrap of paper, with her name and Postcode; and a tiny curl of hair.

'What's that?' he said. 'I'm sorry,' and Meggs laughed. 'I know what's wrong with him,' he said. 'He found himself a groupie. What was she, Landy Street? They mostly hang out there. Work in the big houses.' He dug Raoul in the ribs. 'First one was it, youngster?' He grinned. 'Nothing like the first time, eh? Nearly makes me wish I was your age again ...'

Raoul smiled. For a moment, there'd been a flash of rage; but it was quickly gone. In its place was almost a species of compassion. Because the other had got it so wrong; nobody could know what he'd known, or share. He lay back, felt himself sliding toward sleep; and the Transports turned due east, to the high and glowing pass.

He opened his eyes. The city still stretched into haze, the sun still shone; but lacking now in warmth. The land was altered, subtly; the leaves of trees hung still and golden, or stirred uneasy in the puffs of western wind, harbingers of the first gales. Bad weather, for the Kitemen; soon, winter would be here.

He stared round the Transport. No faces he knew, this trip; not a single one. Secretly, he was glad. He'd no desire to chatter; too much was still going on, in his mind.

He checked in at the hostel. He thought they looked at him a little oddly. He shouldn't be here of course; he should have been in the Northlands. But that was his affair, not theirs.

He walked to Middle Park. The place was deserted, in the early dusk. The stands still stood, skeletally. From one hung tatters of cloth; fragments of banners that had flown there, half a life ago.

The lamplighters were about, when he got back to city centre; tramping the streets, giving their high, yodelling cries. He tipped one, absently, and found himself a bar. A woman came to him, and smiled. He looked at her, and she went away.

The city quietened, by degrees. At twenty-two hundred, he paid up and left. He walked to Landy Street. He found the remembered archway; beyond it, strands of some creeper swayed from the high wall. He tapped the wicket softly, and it opened. She drew him inside quickly, kissed him with all her body. She said, 'I didn't think you'd come. I didn't think I'd ever see you again.' He stroked her hair, smelling the fragrance of her. He said, 'I promised.'

No lights showing, from the big house; the shadows by the stable block were velvet-dark. She took his hand. 'Careful,' she said. 'There's a step there. And another.'

She lit the lamp, stood looking at him. The place seemed oddly cold. She said, 'You've grown, Raoul.' He shook his head. She smiled a little quirky smile. She said, 'A bit different from last time.' He said, 'Yes.'

She took his hands. Her eyes were troubled. Dark. She said, 'Have you eaten? I could get you something.' But he shook his head again. He said, 'It's all right.'

'Raoul,' she said, 'what's the matter?'

'Nothing,' he said. 'It's nothing.'

She was still unsure. She stared up again, eyes moving in little shifts and changes of direction. She said, 'Do you still want me?' and suddenly his own eyes stung. 'You don't know how much,' he said. 'God, you don't know how much.' He clung to her; and she drew him down, into the hay. She said, 'Undress me.'

He felt self-conscious, walking for the first time in a Flier's stiff red cloak. Stev Marden drew it from him, face carefully expressionless; though as he stooped to lay the thing aside he took the chance to mutter, 'Good luck, Raoul.'

He stared round the field. He'd been up two hours or more; but he still felt curiously lightheaded. It took a moment for details to sink in. There was the Launcher of course with its battered, maroon-painted sides, streaked here and there with rust; beside it stood Warrant Keaning, and both Adjutants. A little farther back was Captain Goldensoul himself; hands as ever clasped behind him, feet a little apart on the tarmac of the apron. That was an honour he certainly hadn't expected.

He squared his shoulders consciously, stepped out. Zero eight hundred, on a fine June morning; and the Rig already streamed of course, angled up steady into the blue. He saw they'd flown five Lifters; so Olsen's jibe had in part come true. Olsen himself, pilot-rigger for the day, stared down from the top of the high truck. His face was as inscrutable as the rest.

The Launchmaster nodded curtly. 'Your Uptime will be one hour,' he said. 'You shouldn't have any problems. Wind's Three, gusting Four; stable barometer.' Raoul nodded in turn. He said, 'Thank you, sir.'

The Manlifter rocked slightly, restrained still by half a dozen Cadets. He climbed into the creaking wicker basket, checked his pistol, the breviary he carried, checked the angle of the tail gear. He remembered at the last instant to turn, salute the Base Commander. Goldensoul acknowledged, it seemed absently; and the Launch-master snapped, 'Clear Rig …'

As ever, there was no sensation of leaving the ground. The briefest of bumps, a lurching of the cradle; and he was rising smoothly, drawn behind the immense string of Kites. He stared back, and down. Already, the hangar roofs had changed perspective; the big numbers painted on them showed clear, white against corrugated grey. The group round the Launcher had spread out, foreshortened on the grass. The peri fence slid underneath, swayed gently as he gained in altitude; ahead lay the border, the low hills of the Badlands.

At three hundred feet he primed the pistol, slipped the copper cap over the nipple. He checked his harness, the snap-releases that held him to the basket. The rule had only just come in, he'd heard a lot of the older Fliers wouldn't use them. He tugged them anyway, conscientiously. Because rules are rules, they're there to be obeyed. And this was his first Op.

The wind was keen already, slicing at him; he was glad of the protection of the leather suit. 'The Breath of God' they called it, in those endless early sermons. On the ground, the words seemed trite; up here though, as ever, they made sense. He marvelled, as he had marvelled before, at the sheer silent power of a Cody rig. He peered up at the String. The trace snaked, gracefully, gave him a glimpse of his first Lifter; beyond, the vivid dot that was the pilot. The wind-flaw caught the basket; he lost altitude, worked at the tail-down tackle. The train steadied again.

He guessed he was at operational height. Downstairs the hangar bells would be pealing, the Launchmaster setting the safeties on the big winch. He looked back, to the grey rectangles of sheds. Westward the land stretched into haze. Somewhere beyond the bright horizon lay Middlemarch. He stared straight down. High though he was, the low, humped bushes showed clear; it seemed he could have numbered the individual blades of grass.

There was a ringing snap. The thrill lashed back through the train; instantly the Rig began to snake again, more wildly than before. He stared up, appalled. He had lost his pilot.

The Cody was now hopelessly unbalanced. The basket dipped sickeningly, soared; he grabbed for the main trace, felt the vibration of the winch. Below, he knew, binoculars would have been trained; they'd have seen, at the same instant. A Lifter boomed and flapped; at once, the line tension eased. Somewhere, a deadly calculation was going on. Too slow, and his lift was gone; too fast, and they'd crack a strut. Then he'd be done for good.

He glared back at the boundary fence; the long thin line of it, stretching into distance. So near, and yet so far. Then there was time, it seemed, for one strange thought. He remembered Olsen's face, the lack of expression there. One slip, a badly-adjusted tackle; but accident or design, it made no difference now. Olsen was through. He stared at the fence again, regauged his height. He'd realized he had more pressing problems; he'd just received an aerial lesson in trigonometry.

The basket struck, rebounded. Had it not been for the harness he'd have been thrown out, on to the sick grass of the Badlands. He worked the tail-down tackle; and the wind gusted suddenly. It made him another hundred yards; but the fence looked as far away as ever.

The shouts carried to him. '*The basket, the basket* ...' He understood, at last; it was tilted to one side, carrying far too much weight. He grabbed the pistol from its wicker holster, but he was too late; the thing that had boarded him already had his wrist. It was no bigger, perhaps, than a three or four years child, and its skin was an odd, almost translucent blue. It was mature though, evidently; he saw that it was female. Dreadfully, appallingly female.

The gun went off, wildly; then it was jerked from his hand. The basket rebounded again; but the other didn't relax its grip. He stared, in terror. What he saw now in the eyes was not the hate he'd read about, but love; a horrifying, eternal love. She stroked his arm, and gurgled; gurgled and pleaded, even while he took the line axe, and struck, and struck, and struck ...

He flung the girl away from him. She fell back, panting, in the hay. 'Raoul,' she said, 'what is it? What have I done ...' He couldn't answer though; he was grabbing for his clothes. He ran, for the tall ladder; and she screamed again. 'Raoul, no ... no, please ...'

The city was round about him. He ran again, through Landy Street, into Main Drag, past the huge bulk of Godpath. The Middle Park was ahead; his breath was labouring, lungs burning, but he knew he would never stop now. 'I'm sorry,' he screamed, to the sky that didn't care. '*I'm sorry, I'm sorry, I'm sorry* ...'

3

Kitemistress

The room was as spartan as the rest of the camp buildings; bare walls, a radiator, the statutory filing cabinets. The only touch of elegance was the broad, polished desk. Its top was bare save for a blotting pad and inkwell. Beside the inkwell lay a pearl-handled quill sharpener.

He stood stiffly to attention while Captain Goldensoul reread the paper in his hands. Finally he laid it down. A brief silence; then he took off his *pince-nez*, slipped the little lenses into a case of soft leather. He said, 'I see.' He looked up. He said, 'Why do you wish to leave the Corps, Cadet?'

He swallowed. He said, 'It's in the resignation, sir.'

Goldensoul smiled faintly. He said, 'The resignation tells me very little.

You merely state you no longer wish to fly the Codys. I think I deserve a fraction more than that.'

The other didn't answer. Goldensoul glanced up at him again. He'd seen the Kites break enough men in his time; Fliers of many years' seniority sometimes. The strain, the endless danger, finally became too much. But this boy's nerve hadn't broken. Not if he was any judge. He pursed his lips. He said, 'Stand easy, Cadet.'

He turned back to the little sheaf of reports. In the main, an excellent record. The odd small escapade certainly; but those he both expected and allowed for. As did any Base Commander worth his salt. What mattered, finally, were the Codys. And his flew well. It had always been his belief that good Kitemen were born, not made. And this lad was a Flier. He drummed his fingers. He said, 'It has cost the Corps, and therefore the Realm, a great deal to train you, Josen. A great deal of money, and a great deal of time. Have you considered that?'

'Yes, sir. I'm sorry.'

He pushed the papers together. 'You say you no longer wish to fly the Codys. Have you thought about switching to Ground Duties? These things can be arranged, you know.'

The boy was still staring past him. He said, 'Yes, sir.'

'And your decision?'

Raoul swallowed. He said, 'I wish to leave the Corps.' He couldn't explain; but to see the Codys, to be close, and not to fly … The thought was insupportable. He said, 'I've thought about it a long time, sir. I've thought about it all.'

The other nodded. He said, 'I'm sure you have.'

He rose, stared through the windows; at the neat grass of the outfield, the Kites flying in their immaculate line. He knew well enough what was troubling the youngster; he'd presided perforce at the court martial that had followed the wretched affair. One Cadet dismissed with ignominy was bad enough; but he hadn't thought at the time it would lead to this. But what boy, or indeed what man, ever did stop to consider where jealousy and hatred might lead? 'Cadet,' he said, 'you saved both yourself and your String. You showed coolness, and considerable courage.' He paused. 'You are here, we are all here, to protect the Realm. You did your duty. I see no shame in that.'

But he'd been neither cool nor courageous. He'd been terrified. He'd seized the first weapon that came to hand, killed a defenceless creature with it. He said, 'Have you ever cut a baby's head off with a hatchet?' His back stiffened instantly. He said, 'Sorry, sir. Beg pardon.'

The Captain waved a hand, mildly. He stared a moment longer, then sat back at the desk. He said, 'You didn't kill a baby. You killed nothing human. You destroyed an alien. An enemy of the Realm.'

Raoul moistened his lips with his tongue. 'It was human,' he said. 'And it wasn't our enemy.'

Goldensoul nodded. He said, 'So you see yourself as a murderer.' He steepled his fingers, looked pensive. 'Your concern does you credit,' he said. 'I can share neither your sentiments nor your conclusions; but I respect them.' He considered. 'An attempt was made on your life,' he said. 'What motives the wretched young man had, I neither know nor care. He failed; but ask yourself this. Are you now going to allow him to ruin your career by proxy?'

No answer; and the Captain shrugged. 'Very well,' he said. 'At the end, the decision can only be yours.' He tapped the papers. 'I'm not forwarding your resignation,' he said. 'Instead I'm giving you a conditional discharge. It's a privilege allowed me under certain circumstances. In view of your past conduct, and your excellent service record, I judge these warrant it. In effect, you're on twelve months unpaid leave. If at the end of that time you've reconsidered, come back and see me.' He glanced at the papers again. He said, 'Your people are in Hyeway, are they not?'

Raoul said, 'Yes, sir.'

'There's a Transport leaving in the morning,' said Goldensoul. 'It should pass quite close. I can arrange travel, if you choose.'

He stood to attention again. 'No thank you, sir,' he said.

'Then where will you go?'

'I don't know, sir.'

'What will you do?'

'I'm sorry,' said the Cadet again. 'I don't know.'

The Captain sighed. He said, 'I see.' He rose, and held his hand out. He said, 'Good luck, Raoul.'

He said, 'Thank you, sir.' He unclipped the silver Trace from his shoulder, laid it on the desk. He stepped back, saluted smartly. He closed the door behind him.

The Captain Goldensoul put his hands on his knees. Difficult to recall the passions and emotions of one so young. Easy to remember, but difficult to recall. One thing only was certain; the Corps had lost a good man. He unlocked one of the desk drawers, slipped the papers away. He supposed over the years he'd done a fairish job. Certainly he'd done his best; nobody could do more.

It was a shallow comfort.

Raoul strode across the Base. He ignored the Codys. There was no longer any need to salute; his Trace was down. Once he knuckled his eyes, furious with himself. Because he knew once clear, he would never come back. Nobody saw though.

It was evening already, the sun setting in long swathes of crimson. He'd put the resignation in at zero nine hundred, after yet another sleepless night;

but Goldensoul had been off Base, he'd had to kick his heels most of the day.

He headed for the refectory block. Seventeen thirty; the bar should be open by now. He walked into the long, high room, with its chequered flooring of black and white tiles. As ever, it was cool. The Fliers used it; to a man, they professed to dislike warmth. He paid for a pint of beer, downed it and ordered a second. It seemed like an evening for getting drunk.

A harsh, quiet voice said, 'Kitecadet…'

He started. He hadn't even seen the man sitting in the far corner. He turned, and swallowed. Canwen, senior Flier on the Salient; and one of the most respected in the Corps. He said, 'Good evening, Master.'

The other gestured, curtly. Raoul hesitated, walked across to join him. Canwen had never spoken to him before; never, it seemed, deigned to notice his existence. Despite himself, he felt the rise of awe.

The Flier produced a black, stubby pipe. He lit it, unhurriedly. He smoked a while in silence; then he said, 'So you've resigned the Corps.'

He looked back; at the hard, high-cheekboned face, the icy, almost colourless eyes. He said reluctantly, 'Yes, sir.' He wondered how he had known. But Canwen, it seemed, knew everything.

The Flier lit the pipe again. 'Good,' he said. 'Then perhaps your training will begin.'

He frowned. He said, 'I'm sorry, sir?'

'Like all young men,' said Canwen, 'you wish to run before you can walk. You wish to fly before you can crawl. You wish to rise, before you have known the depths.'

He shook his head. 'I'm sorry, sir,' he said again. 'I don't understand.'

Canwen looked vague. He said, 'I don't suppose you do.' He laid the pipe down. 'What do you think of?' he said. 'When you're aloft?'

'I … nothing,' he said. 'Well, the job I suppose.'

The other shook his head. 'You don't,' he said. 'You think how fine the String looks. You think how fine you look yourself. You think of the yarns you'll spin, later on. You think of how you'll boast, next time you lay a Middle Lands tart.'

He lowered his eyes. The words were uncomfortably near the truth.

Canwen sipped ale. 'I consider the Void,' he said. 'I enter it, become a part of it. And the Void becomes a part of me. I join a third State, in which there is no scale. No large and small, no life and death. The reflection of a greater, perhaps. But that State may not be gained by idle wishing. It must be earned, with pain and sacrifice.' He set his glass down. 'Wallow in mud, and then the stars come close,' he said. 'Because you have earned the right to see their glory.' He nodded, curtly. He said, 'Drink.'

He obeyed, wonderingly.

The other waved his hand at the bar. The steward served him, quickly.

Canwen took a pad and stylus from his jerkin pocket. 'Go to the Middle Lands,' he said. 'Go to Barida. Do you know the town?'

He shook his head. 'No, sir,' he said. 'Only Middlemarch.'

Canwen smiled, thinly. He said, 'You soon will.' He scribbled. 'Go and see this man,' he said. 'The Master Halpert. My name will open his door. He'll find you a position.'

He said, 'A position?'

Canwen nodded impatiently. 'He supplies household Kitemen to most of the Middle Lands,' he said. 'The Salient too.' He rose abruptly. He said, 'You must find the Way.'

Raoul had half-risen himself. He called after the Flier, falteringly. 'Master,' he said, 'What is the Way?'

Canwen turned back. 'That is for each of us to discover,' he said sardonically. 'To each of us it presents a different face. Which is why some claim, there is no Way at all.' He pushed through the door, and was gone.

Raoul woke next morning fuzzy-headed. The evening had turned into a party after all. His fellow Cadets had been reticent at first, unsure how to react; for the rumour had spread round the camp like wildfire. 'Wish I could do the same,' said one, a freckle-faced lad called Hanti. 'Fuck the Codys, I say. Only I need the money ...' There was a general laugh. He joined in, but he still felt pained. He wished Stev Marden could have been there. He'd have understood. Possibly guessed his real reason for quitting. But Stev, to his intense disgust, had been posted to the Easthold only a week before.

He breakfasted – the final time on a Kitebase – checked the last of his kit back into Stores. He collected his arrears of pay, withdrew his savings from the Adjutant's Fund; by midday he was free. He shouldered his duffel bag, tramped toward the gates. The Duty Corporal opened them for him, silently. He nodded curtly, feeling his eyes sting again. A few yards down the lane he turned, defiantly. He saluted the Codys, one final time.

He had no illusions as to the size of the Salient. He trudged steadily, across the featureless land. Though it was still early in the year, the day was warm. He pulled his jerkin undone, later devised a strap to hang it from the duffel. He saw no vehicles, not even a farm cart. No signs of life at all. But this was the Empty Quarter; sparsely inhabited even by Salient standards. He walked a further hour. For a time the G15 Kites, and those of the flanking Stations, had been visible, tiny dots against the eastern horizon; but when he finally turned again they were out of sight.

He swung the duffel bag down. He sat on the grassy bank and stared at nothing. The full enormity of what he'd done hit him quite suddenly. He put his face in his hands and cried. He got up finally, tramped on.

The old green lane turned north. Which wasn't the direction he wanted. But it soon met up with a broader, gravelled road. There, he had more luck.

A farm lad overtook him, on a tractor. He thumbed experimentally, and the other slowed. He called down. 'Where do you want?'

He said, 'Barida,' and the driver grinned. 'Bit out of my way,' he said. 'I can take you a mile or two though.' He jerked his thumb. The tractor was hauling a cart loaded with swedes. But of course the grass wasn't rich enough yet, the spring flush had hardly begun; they'd still be opening the clamps for cattle feed. Raoul said, 'Thanks a lot.' He scrambled up.

The other dropped him a few miles farther on. He dusted himself down, shouldered the bag again. He walked till nightfall. By then his feet were aching abominably. He reached a village; one of the tumbledown hamlets in which the Salient seemed to specialize. There was an inn of sorts. He shrugged, and stepped through the doorway. With luck, the beds would be merely flea-ridden. He had a horror of lice.

He was on the road early next morning. To his surprise, the linen had been tolerably clean; though the refreshment offered had left much to be desired.

It seemed his luck had changed. Within a couple of minutes a private vehicle drew up beside him. It was mudstained and elderly, but still one of the very few in the Salient. The driver, obviously a farmer of some means, asked where he was headed. He said, 'Barida,' and his benefactor jerked his head. 'Hop in,' he said. 'I can take you part the way. I'm going down to Crossways.'

In fact he took him the best part of forty miles. Raoul stood and waved as the vehicle lurched off to the south. He started walking again.

At least the land was more populous here; and what villages he passed through looked better kept. In one though he was threatened by a pack of scrawny dogs. He caught the leader a smart kick in the chest, more by luck than judgement. The animal yelped, and fled. The others followed it. Nobody came to his aid; but then, the Salient had never been overfond of strangers. A mile or so on he came across a pile of ash poles, dumped on the side of the road awaiting collection. He selected the stoutest, spent an hour haggling it to a usable length. At first he felt faintly ridiculous, stumping along like some Middle Way pilgrim; but the staff came in useful on more than one occasion.

The good fortune of the morning wasn't repeated. Night found him seemingly miles from anywhere. He climbed on to a partly demolished hayrick. He emptied the duffel, spread the contents as some sort of covering. He pulled the bag up round his legs. He still thought he'd never been so cold. He slept finally, woke frozen and stiff. Also he'd made up for the night before, he'd been bitten from head to foot. What the creatures had been he had no idea; but his back felt as if it had been peppered with shot. He wondered if it was the beginning of the penance the Master Canwen had ordained.

The day that followed was much the same; and the day after that. Though at least he managed to find himself accommodation. On the fifth morning he was overtaken by a Corps Transport. He flagged it, but it rattled past unconcerned. He set his mouth. Of course, he was a civilian now; and scruffy to boot, he had no doubt. He rubbed his stubble of beard, and hefted the stick. He tramped on again.

He neared the Salient boundary, finally. The ground trended steadily upward; ahead were the hills that fringed the Middle Lands.

The villages were more frequent now, and inns relatively numerous. But the better-looking refused him at a glance; he had to make do with their less salubrious counterparts. At least he managed a shave, and a change of clothes. After which he was picked up by a lorry loaded with milk churns. It rattled through the hills, decanted him some twenty miles from his destination.

He was fortunate again. A private vehicle pulled up almost at once. He stared. He thought he'd never seen such a resplendent motor. Its coachwork glittered, coats of arms were emblazoned on its doorpanels; on its wings pennants displayed the Vestibule, gold thread against a scarlet ground. The private carriage of a Master, evidently. The chauffeur buttoned down the window on his side. He leaned across. He said, 'Where you want, lad?'

He said, 'Barida.'

The other grinned. 'You're in luck,' he said. 'I'm going through.' He nodded. 'Get rid of that thing though. You look like a mendicant bloody friar.' Raoul threw the ashplant regretfully into the hedge. He'd become quite fond of it.

He leaned back, against luxurious upholstery. He was still amazed that the thing had stopped at all. He said curiously, 'Who are you with?'

The other said, 'I serve the Master Helman.' There was a species of pride in his voice.

He frowned. He still didn't understand. He said, 'But why did you stop for me?'

The driver glanced across. He said, 'The Master would have.' He lapsed into silence.

He nodded. It explained a lot.

He sniffed, appreciatively. Even the air of the Middle Lands smelled different. Softer somehow, and warm. In summer he knew it was heavy with the scent of flowers. He looked round. They were passing a big stone-built house, set back from the road on a little rise of ground. Codys were streamed, the first he'd seen for days. He said, 'Do you know the Master Halpert?'

The other glanced at him again. 'Sure,' he said. 'Bishop of Barida. What are you after, a Kiteman's job?'

He nodded, and the driver chuckled. 'You'll need a deep pocket then,' he said. 'Even if he condescends to see you. I've known people wait months, just for the chance to grease his palm.'

He said, 'Canwen sent me,' and the other whistled. 'Nice one,' he said. 'Nice one indeed.'

Barida reminded him very much of Easthope; he'd spent the odd furlough there. The same smart lines of shops, same bustling, well-dressed crowds. But of course this was the Middle Lands. He should have expected nothing else.

The big car dropped him at the crossroads in the centre of town. There was the Variant church, with its soaring spire; as ever, the white barn of the Middle Men faced it calmly. He walked into the church. An altarservant told him the Bishop was at the Palace. He chuckled. 'He don't see the likes o' you though,' he said. 'You've got no chance.'

He walked up the gravelled drive of the place, with little hope. The Official Residence was smaller than he'd expected, but excellently maintained. Above it flew a spectacular Cody String; round it, velvet-smooth lawns were dotted with bushes sculpted into the shapes of animals and birds. He raised the knocker of the big, iron-studded door, and again. His rappings finally produced a response. A small grille opened; a servant peered out suspiciously.

It seemed the name of Canwen was magic. A wait; then bolts were shot back, he was ushered into the Bishop's study.

In fact the great man was small and somewhat gnomelike. His eyes flickered constantly, never dwelling on his face for long. There was almost a furtiveness about him. Raoul decided he didn't care for him overmuch; but he hadn't come here to make bosom pals of Churchmen. He showed him Canwen's note, and the other beamed. 'Well, well, young man,' he said, 'we must see what we can do. Yes, indeed …' He rubbed his hands. 'Have you broken your fast today?'

Two hours later he was feeling almost human again. He'd bathed and washed his hair, changed into his one clean suit. It had been rumpled from the travelling; but a kitchenmaid had pressed it for him. The cook, a sturdy girl with a mass of auburn ringlets, served him an excellent lunch; and he felt his spirits rise a little, for the first time in many days. He glanced at the address the Bishop had given him. He said, 'Who is this Master Kerosin?'

The cook sniffed. 'Big place out on the Middlemarch road,' she said. 'About a mile. Richest bloke in the Realm, some reckons. Ain't a tractor nowhere what don't run on 'is fuel.' She banged a big metal heater. 'These things an' all,' she said. 'We gets through gallons of it, there's a big tank out the back. Lorry comes every week, in winter.' She sniffed. 'Ain't 'im you gotta watch though,' she said. 'It's 'er Ladyship.'

He said, 'Her Ladyship?'

She said, 'The Lady Kerosina.'

'What's wrong with her?'

She began to scrape plates. She said, 'You'll find out soon enough.' She would add nothing more.

He walked down in the afternoon. His first sight of the place took his breath. It was big; as big, he decided, as the Palace of a Master. Its stone front, hung in parts with some bright creeper, was crenellated in the Middle Lands style. Cody Strings flew to either side, but not from the roof; there were custom-built towers, as impressive as the house and topping it by a storey. On their fronts and sides leafshaped embrasures repeated the motif of the Vestibule. They were edged with bright red mosaic; the tops of the towers were similarly decorated. He realized with a species of faint shock that each was a multiple phallic emblem. He shrugged. After all, it was sound Var theology. Perhaps this was an extra-religious household. Somehow though he doubted it.

The Master Kerosin was a slim, balding man, brownskinned and bland-faced. He too wore a pair of gold-rimmed *pince-nez.* He was poring over a ledger when Raoul was shown in; he didn't trouble to rise. He presented his credentials; but it seemed the name of Canwen carried less weight here. The Master shrugged. His voice was flat, with a hint of sibilance, and as expressionless as his face. 'These seem to be in order,' he said. 'But you must see the Mistress Kerosina. She has to do with the housefolk.'

He said, 'Thank you, Master.' He inclined his head; but the other had again immersed himself in his work.

The Lady Kerosina was lounging in a chair of silvery Holand fibre. Behind her, long glass doors gave a view of landscaped grounds. A glass was at her side, and a bowl of some confection. He stared. Her hair was dark, shot with bronze highlights. It tumbled to her shoulders and below. Her cheekbones were high and perfectly modelled, her eyes huge and of no definable colour, her nose delicately tip-tilted. She wore a simple white dress; the neckline plunged deeply at the front. She wore ankle-high sandals, again of some silvery material. He saw they were uppers only; the soles of her feet were bare.

She inclined her head, graciously. 'Good afternoon, Mr Josen,' she said. 'Sit down, and tell me about yourself.'

He took a chair, hesitantly. She crossed her knees. Her skirt was split to the top of her thigh. Her legs were long, and exquisite. He blinked. He'd seen some daring fashions in Middlemarch odd times, but nothing to compare with that. He rested his eyes carefully on the middle distance. He was aware she smiled.

He began to talk, haltingly at first, about his training, early career; but she interrupted him. 'Who,' she said in her well-modulated, slightly husky voice, 'was your Captain, in the Salient?'

'Goldensoul, Mistress,' he said. 'He gave me an excellent testimonial.'

'Dear old Goldensoul,' she said. 'Always the do-gooder.' She selected a sweet, bit into it deliberately. Displayed even, pearly teeth. 'And what brought you to Barida?'

He swallowed. He said, 'I was sent by the Master Canwen.'

'Ah,' she said, 'I begin to understand. I was wondering how you breached our good Bishop's defences. Tell me, is the Master still as mad as ever?'

He frowned. He said. 'He's one of the most respected Fliers in the Realm.'

She looked amused. She said, 'No doubt.'

He risked another glance at her. She wore no jewellery of any kind; but round her neck was a slender leather collar. The sort of thing you might put on a dog. It seemed oddly out of sorts with the rest of her *ensemble*; he wondered what its purpose could be. He hesitated, held out the papers he carried. He said, 'If the Mistress would care to see ...'

She waved a hand. She said, 'I'm sure they're perfectly adequate.' She selected another of the little comfits. 'You must see the tailor,' she said. 'I like my housefolk to be liveried. Can you drive a motor vehicle?'

'I'm sorry, Mistress,' he said. 'I'm afraid I can't.'

She shrugged. She said, 'It's of no importance.' She picked a book up, began to turn the pages.

The interview seemed to be over. He rose. He said, 'Thank you, Mistress. Thank you very much.' He walked toward the door; but as he opened it she looked up. She said, 'I hope you'll be happy with us.'

He said, 'I'm sure I shall.' He walked off feeling in some way reprieved.

He found the retiring Kiteman. He was a grizzled, time-expired Corps Sergeant; he'd been putting in a few more years before, as he said, finally taking to the rocking chair. He showed Raoul over the Towers. They were immaculately kept, and seemed to be well equipped. But at that the Kiteman shook his head. 'We're all right for cable,' he said. 'Should last you a season or two at least. Bit low on frames and fabric. No point me stocking up; every Kiteman has his own ideas.'

Raoul took a tracecone from a rack, looked at it ruefully. It was a toy compared to what he'd trained on. He shook his head. He said, 'I'm new to this game I'm afraid. Have to learn as I go.'

The Sergeant shrugged. 'It's a piece of cake,' he said. 'Nothing to it really.' He glanced sidelong. He said, 'Better than eight hour watches over the Badlands, eh?'

'Yes,' he said. 'Better than that.'

They climbed to the roof. He was surprised to see a small hand winch. The Codys were deceptive though. Even this size of String could develop considerable lift; streaming by hand could be hazardous, particularly in a blow.

The Kiteman chuckled. 'No expense spared,' he said. 'Nothing but the best, for Kerosin.' He glanced at Raoul quickly. He said, 'I assume you've met the Mistress.'

'Yes,' he said. He paused. He said, 'A very beautiful lady.'

The other chuckled again. 'She's all of that,' he said. 'Even give me ideas, if I was a decade or two younger. As it is, it's just as well I'm not. She's not interested in old stagers.'

He frowned. Surely it couldn't be as bad as that. Not with her husband home.

It seemed the other read his thoughts. 'Old Kerosin ain't here once in a blue moon,' he said. 'Too busy making his fortune. He don't give a damn what she does. She's windowdressing for him. Same as these.' He patted the little winch. 'Watch yourself with her, boy,' he said. 'Just watch yourself.'

He set his lips. 'I fly Kites,' he said. 'Nothing more.'

'Yes,' said the other grimly. 'So does she.'

He picked his kit up from the Palace, stowed it in the room allotted to him and went in search of the tailor. His little workroom was on the ground floor at the back. He sat crosslegged, stitching away contentedly. He was surrounded by ceiling-high bolts of material. Raoul narrowed his eyes. He said, 'That's Kitecloth.'

The other jumped down, got busy with a tape. 'That's right,' he said. 'Dresses all her housepeople in it.'

He frowned. 'I didn't think that was allowed.'

The tailor looked up. He was a smallish man; baldheaded and with thick, hornrimmed glasses. 'If you're a Kerosin, anything's allowed,' he said. 'Dress on the left, sir?'

He said, 'Er ... yes.' He frowned again. This was a standard of tailoring he likewise hadn't seen.

The uniform – for uniform it was – was ready in a couple of days. He reported to the Mistress Kerosina. She was sitting in a little summerhouse. It faced the south, the distant pale blue hills that ringed Middlemarch. She eyed him critically, told him to turn round. 'Yes, excellent,' she said. 'Where's your Trace?'

'I'm sorry, Mistress,' he said. 'I may not wear a Trace. I've rejected Flier status.'

She glanced at him with her great, tilted eyes. 'How very honourable,' she said. 'Kneel down.'

'I beg your pardon, Madam?'

'Kneel down, Kiteman,' she said. 'Just here.'

He did as he was told; and she ran her fingers through his hair. 'What a mane,' she said. 'There's girls who would be proud of it. If I were younger, I'd probably be bowled over.' She lifted it, bunched it into the double ponytail favoured by the Cadets. She turned his head, considered. 'Yes,' she said, 'it suits you. Wear it like that.' She patted the chair beside her. 'Sit with me awhile,' she said, 'and have a glass of wine.'

'By your leave, Mistress,' he said, 'I have urgent work to do.' He hesitated. He said, 'Permission to draw Strings?'

She raised her eyebrows. 'Do what you like,' she said. 'You're in charge now.' She watched him walk away, again with an amused expression.

He met the household, over the next few days. In the main they seemed friendly enough. The cook, around whom so many establishments seemed to revolve, was a cheerful, bustling person in her fifties. It was said in season, her apple pies were the finest in the Midlands. There were numerous dairy and chamber maids, a cobbler; the Mistress even retained the services of a full time dressmaker, though most of her creations she designed herself. Sometimes, as he had seen, with startling effect. There was also a considerable stable, though the horses seemed to be kept solely for the amusement of guests. The Kerosins owned most of the land around them, but they didn't farm; it was all rented out. When Kerosina went abroad it was invariably in a closed carriage, drawn by a pair of highstepping greys. The coachman, he discovered, was from the Salient; as a boy, he'd known Raoul's father. He even kept some of the dreadful Northland spirit. Raoul took to dropping into the coachhouse occasionally for a chat; but when the dark brown bottle was produced he always smilingly declined.

The only sour note was struck by the head horseman. Aine Martland was a swarthy, bow-legged man; a head shorter than Raoul, but powerfully built. His face too was powerful rather than handsome; broad across the cheekbones, with a thick-lipped mouth and brilliant light-green eyes. His thatch of dark blond hair was tousled and unkempt; he wore ruffed, old-fashioned shirts, usually stained from the horses, knee breeches of heavy corduroy. His hose were as suspect as the rest. The household were more than a little afraid of him. It was rumoured he had the Frog's Bone; certainly at his touch the most nervous horse was calmed, the unruly instantly became manageable. Perhaps that was why he was tolerated.

To Raoul's surprise he was often to be seen about the house itself. Once a young boy was with him; once he had the arm of a nervous, pixie-like girl. She couldn't have been more than nine. Raoul frowned; but after all, it wasn't his affair. His job was to fly the Kites.

At first downhaul he saw what the Sergeant had told him was true. The fabric of the Lifters was stained, beginning to fray; a refurbishing was called for, through both Strings. For that he went to Middlemarch. He requisitioned a horse from the stables. If he couldn't drive, he'd been riding since before he could walk. Martland offered him a wall-eyed bay; but he shook his head. 'No thanks,' he said. 'I'll take her.' He indicated a fine, big-boned chestnut. The other growled – his habitual mode of communication – but made no further demur. He saddled the creature; an hour later Raoul trotted through the yard gates, turned the mare south on the Middlemarch road.

He found himself enjoying the ride. The weather was fine, trees bursting into their first spring green; and after all he was travelling in style. A bit different from the way he arrived. Also he found the flashes on his shoulders, the Kerosina insignia, commanded great respect. They ensured good service, the choicest rooms, the best place at table. He took his time, rode into Middlemarch early on the morning of the third day.

He hadn't approached the town from this direction. At first everything looked strange; but then he was on Main Drag, the great bulk of Godpath rearing ahead. He was surprised at the pang it brought; riding past Landy Street, he looked the other way. He stabled the horse at the 'Cap of Maintenance', the best hotel in town. He booked a room and freshened up, walked round to the big shop that had supplied all College wants. To his surprise, one of the assistants recognized him. He outlined his requirements, and the other nodded. 'Yes,' he said, 'we can supply all that. How will you get it back?'

He frowned. That was the one point he hadn't been sure of. He'd supposed the spares would have to come by carrier; he'd been hoping his sails would last till they arrived. But the other shook his head. 'We can supply a packhorse,' he said. 'No extra charge. You can return it when you next come down.' He was surprised, momentarily; then he remembered again. Now, he wore the livery of the House of Kerosin.

The other looked thoughtful. 'I was wondering, sir,' he said. 'Have you considered fantailing your Traces?'

He frowned again. He said, 'Sorry?'

'They've only just come out,' said the assistant. 'But we've had considerable success with them. Would you come with me?' He led the way into a back room, almost as big as the shop itself. A dozen men were hard at work repairing Pilots, building Lifter frames. The assistant showed him a complicated Kite. Its span was eight feet or more, but it was obviously feather-light. He said, 'How does it work?'

The assistant set the thing back on the table. 'Rather like a tail-down tackle,' he said. 'You fly a double Trace. The second cable's very light of course.' He waggled a control. The tail of the Kite moved obediently up and down. 'Runs through fairleads on the Main,' he said. 'Bit of a nuisance when you're downing; but then, you shouldn't have to very much. They come rather expensive at the moment, but . . .' He left the rest unsaid.

He narrowed his eyes. He said, 'Can you give me a demonstration?

'Certainly,' said the other. 'One moment.' He called, and two lads appeared. They dismantled the assembly quickly. He followed them up the stairs.

There was a Tower, bolted centrally to the flat roof. A Pilot was already flying, on a light line. They paid out, released the fantail. It sailed up to its cone, and the assistant took the thin wire trace it had trailed. 'We find we can vary up to five degrees each side of Force Three Norm,' he said. 'A considerable gaining in flexibility.'

He tried for himself. He found it was true. It was a fascinating toy.

He made his mind up. 'Right,' he said, 'can you supply three? Two operational, and a spare.'

'No problem,' said the other urbanely.

He had one other commission to fulfil. There was a little studio, behind the Mercy Hospital. The Mistress Kerosina also designed her own Godkites. Some of the symbols were startlingly explicit; but he was growing used to them already. The studio kept the tracings; he ordered fresh paintings prepared, went back to the hotel. He ate well, got an early night. For once, his sleep was undisturbed.

Leaving Middlemarch, he found himself heaving a sigh of relief. There was a certain person he hadn't wished to see. The thought of her brought the pang afresh; but for him women were ended. They ended with a Cody basket bumping over Badlands grass. He clicked to the packhorse, urged the mare into a trot. Climbing the first of the hills, he looked at the city spread beneath him. 'Rye,' he whispered. 'Rye …'

Rounding the last bend before the Kerosin mansion, he held his breath a little. After all, this was his first big test as Kiteman to the household; the Codys had been flying unattended for five days. They'd come through well though; both Strings were still streamed, at not far short of optimum angle.

He set to that same evening; downhauled from the western Tower, got to work on the Lifters. He reskinned the first, and doped it. At twenty-one hundred though a message came for him. The Mistress Kerosina required his presence in the dining room.

He swore, and washed his hands. He put his tunic on, hurried to the house. She was seated in solitary state, at the end of the long table. The candlelight made her eyes seem very dark. She said, 'Good evening, Kiteman. You've worked well; so I've invited you to dinner.'

'Thank you, Mistress,' he said. 'But I've already eaten.'

She looked at him. She said, 'Then you'll eat again.'

He sat. There seemed nothing else to do.

She poured wine, handed the glass across. She rang a little bell. She said, 'How was Middlemarch?'

He answered, as best he could. Her dress top was diaphanous; her breasts with their high, firm buds showed clearly. She might as well have been naked to the waist. He stared at the wine; and the first course was produced. She applied herself to it, delicately. She said, 'Why did you leave the Kites?'

'I haven't, Mistress,' he said. 'Not exactly.'

She said, 'You know what I mean.'

He hesitated. He said, 'It's difficult to explain.'

'Was it to do with a woman?'

'No,' he said. 'It wasn't.' You couldn't call it a woman, could you? Two feet long, translucent and blue?

She looked up at him. She said, 'Don't you have girlfriends? A fine young man like you?'

He said, 'I had one once.'

'And where was that?'

He said, 'In Middlemarch.'

She smiled. 'You're a very secretive young man as well,' she said. 'I think you have hidden depths.' She poured more wine. She said, 'Did you see her the last trip?'

He shook his head. He said, 'I didn't look for her.'

'Did you fall out?'

'No, Mistress,' he said. 'We didn't fall out.'

She rang the bell again, for the first plates to be cleared. 'Sometimes,' she said, 'I could be angry with you, Raoul. Would you like me to be angry?'

He looked at his hands. He said, 'I hope I have given the Mistress no cause.'

She laughed. 'Always so formal,' she said. 'Always so very correct. Don't you ever relax?'

He said, 'It's hardly my place to.'

'What do you mean?'

He said, 'My father was a farmer.'

She stared at him. 'And what do you think mine was?' she said. 'I know about Sower's Arse as well.'

He didn't answer; and she drank, refilled the glasses yet again. 'Raoul,' she said, 'I decided one thing, a long time ago. That we only have one life. I know the Church says this and that, but I've got no proof.' She linked her fingers under her chin. 'We must live each day as fully as we can,' she said. 'Ideally, they should be filled with love. But if that's not possible, there are compensations. Why did you leave the Kites?'

He said, 'It's a long story.' He looked back at her. Her fingers gleamed with rings. The candlelight woke fire from them; blue, and gold, and red. She saw the direction of his glance. 'I often decorate myself,' she said. 'Or perhaps you hadn't noticed.'

It must have been the wine. He said, 'The Mistress needs no ornament.'

'You say the nicest things,' she said. 'You are the sweetest boy.' She addressed herself to her plate. 'I'll tell you why you left,' she said. 'Your eyes are the wrong colour.' She waved a hand. 'They should be the blue of the midsummer zenith,' she said. 'But they're not. They're a sort of muddy green.'

He didn't look up. He said, 'I'm sorry they displease you.'

She said, 'They don't displease me.' She reached to touch his wrist. 'I'm putting too much pressure on you,' she said. 'I'll take it off.' Amazingly, she did.

Later – the plates had been cleared away – she said, 'What did the Master Canwen say?'

'What about, Mistress?'

'About you leaving.'

Again, he didn't answer; and she laughed. 'Young men wish to run before they can walk,' she said. 'They wish to fly, before they have known the depths.' He looked up, startled; and she laughed again. She said, 'I've known him a very long while.' She gestured; and a serving girl came forward. She proffered a polished, inlaid box; the Mistress Kerosina selected a long black cheroot. 'I always like to smoke after a meal,' she said. 'It's the only time I really enjoy it.' She bit the end off the cigar, spat it across the room. She said, 'I really do have some disgusting habits.'

The girl offered the box to him. He shook his head. He said, 'No thank you, Mistress.'

Kerosina raised her eyebrows. 'Mistress?' she said. 'She's not your Mistress. I am.' He didn't answer; and she stroked ash into a tray. She said, 'Don't you ever smoke?'

He shook his head. He said, 'Not very often.' He glanced at the chronometer on his wrist. He said, 'Will you excuse me, Madam?'

'For what reason?'

'We're only streaming from the eastern Tower,' he said. 'I have to check the String.'

'Of course,' she said. 'Otherwise the Demons might get in.' She nodded. She said, 'Go and fly your Kites.' She sat a long time after the door had closed, staring at nothing in the dim-lit room.

He found he couldn't sleep. He dozed from time to time; but images of her intruded constantly. Her eyes, her hair; her breasts, her long, slim legs. He groaned and tossed, restlessly. He was angry with himself; but that didn't help the case. He sat up finally, clasped his arms round his knees. How could someone like her have sprung from the background she claimed? From earth? He shrugged. All folk sprang from earth. As they returned to it. Where was the difference then?

He rose, and lit the lamp. It was zero two hundred. He let himself out by the servants' door, locked it behind him. He climbed the stairs of the western Tower to the workshop. He got busy on the Lifters. By dawn, the String was aloft again.

Summer came, the ripening of the crops. He was amazed at them. Never had he seen wheat grow so tall. But the soil was black, and rich. He began to see why the Middle Lands were wealthy.

Kerosina drew up fresh designs; Godkites to be flown for Harvest Home. At least they were more conventional than the last. He rode to Middlemarch with them, took the first week of his leave. He'd learned to trust his fantails. Barring a Force Ten, they would fly. He walked the streets more boldly now. At first, he'd been afraid of meeting her; but he'd realized he wouldn't. Because people never come back. He walked to Middle Park, sat half a day watching gangs of workmen prepare the stands. The big Air Show was due; he'd miss it by two days. He was glad. The basket Codys were no longer his concern; he was a private Kiteman now.

He wondered why Kerosina haunted him so. He was beyond emotion, beyond love; yet day and night he couldn't rid himself of her image. Each turn of the head, each nuance of her voice; her hair, her hands, her feet. He imagined kissing her; privately, as he had once kissed Rye. The Vestibule had gaped then, leafshaped as the Kites. Demanding, and pathetic. He stared up at the Codys. The answer was there, the answer was in the sky; but the Strings were mute.

He rode back, when the new designs were finished. The studio lent him a horse as well. Aine Martland wasn't pleased. He walked round it, hands on hips. 'What?' he said. 'You expect me to feed a spavined nag like that?'

He shrugged. He said, 'Take it up with the Lady Kerosina.'

The other mimicked him. '*Take it up with the Lady Kerosina*,' he said. He picked up a short hayfork. Take it up with her yourself,' he said. 'You're more qualified than me, you longhaired pretty.' He turned, and lunged.

Raoul was appalled. He'd been standing by the stable wall; now he was pinned to it, the tines each side of his neck. He realized he'd missed death by half an inch. His knees were shaking; but the rage still boiled and bubbled. 'I saw you driving Charm the other day,' he said. 'I know where you put your hands to keep them warm.'

Expressions chased themselves across the Horseman's face. Finally he wrenched the tines from the wood. He flung the implement away, walked off. He looked back once; then he clicked to the horse. He said, 'Come on, girl.' The old mare whickered, and followed him.

The Master Kerosin was home. He was surprised at the pang of disappointment he felt. Two days later though she sent for him. She was sitting alone as ever, at one end of the great dining room. This time he took his place without argument. She said, 'Wine?' and he shook his head. He said, 'As a matter of fact I prefer beer.'

She rang the bell. A serving girl appeared. She said, 'Beer for the Kiteman.' The other curtsied, reappeared with a foaming tankard. He said, 'Thank you.'

The Mistress Kerosina followed the girl with her eyes. She said, 'You'd prefer her to me, wouldn't you?'

'I beg your pardon, Madam?'

'For fucking,' she said irritably. 'She's younger.'

He looked at the table. So much to say; yet there was nothing to say at all. He said, 'The Mistress realizes I cannot answer.'

'Of course you can,' she said. 'It's very simple. Yes or no.'

He looked up. He said, 'If there is no answer, there cannot be a question.'

'So you're Middle Doctrine,' she said. 'I wouldn't have believed it.' She shook her head. 'Now I shall never know,' she said. 'It's such an unfair world. But then, you're still living in it. So you wouldn't understand.' She toyed with a richly-decorated coaster. 'What I'd like,' she said. 'But there's so many things I'd like. I'd like to be you. Then I could run after Maia, and catch her in the kitchen. I'd screw her arse off for her.' She smiled, crookedly. 'I'll tell you what I'd like,' she said. 'I'd like to see a little Cody rig. About so long.' She spread her arms. 'I'd like to see it anchored that end of the table,' she said. 'And I'd like to see it streamed. So the Demons in the room couldn't spoil the food. Could you fix that for me?'

He set his lips. He said, 'No, Madam.'

'No,' she said. 'I didn't expect you could. It's still a nice idea though.' She considered. 'What would have happened, if I'd been born rich?' she said. 'Would I have been satisfied then? I know I'm beautiful; but it doesn't seem to matter.'

He said, 'I don't understand you, Mistress.'

She shook her head. 'Raoul,' she said, 'sometimes you disappoint me.' She drank wine. 'I've got servants by the score,' she said. 'I snap my fingers, and they run. But it doesn't really give me any pleasure.' She brightened. She said, 'Will you be my servant?'

He said, 'I am your servant, Mistress.'

'In a way,' she said. 'Should I make you my body servant though? You'd have to stand behind me. Massage my neck, every time it got sore. And move my chair, whenever I wanted to get up. Would you do that for me?'

He knew, meltingly, that he would do it all. But he still shook his head. He said, 'I fly her Ladyship's Kites.'

The weather broke, with wind and floods of rain. He drew both Strings, spent time on more refurbishing. He reorganized the stores, made a complete inventory. After that there was little else to do. He sat in the eastern

Tower day after day, staring through one of the leafshaped apertures. Out there, somewhere beyond the veils of grey, was the Salient. The Salient, and all his folk. He felt he should write; but his father could scarcely read, and his mother wouldn't try. It would just embarrass them. He wrote to Stev Marden instead. He hardly expected an answer; nonetheless, one came. He deciphered the scrawl, with difficulty.

'Ray, you old bastard. How crafty can you get? Here's me stuck down on an F Base, and you living off the fat of the land. How do you manage it?

'They double-man the Codys here. Which means eight Lifters, even for a Five. The local Vars were sure we were in for an invasion. Haven't seen any signs of it yet though …

'How's that little girl of yours in Middlemarch? You still scoring with her? There's not much talent down this way. Mostly, they're broader than they're tall …

'We've got these new six-shooters. It gives you a better chance. I can't shoot worth fuck, I never could. But I reckon I could just about get the Adj …'

He sniffed the envelope. It was absurd of course, it was all in his mind; but it seemed even the paper smelled of Cody hangers. The oil and dope and steam. He shook his head. 'If only you knew,' he said. 'Stev, if only you knew …'

The skies cleared. He streamed his Kites instantly. The following day a letter came from his folks. Ill-spelled, but at least they'd made the effort. Which was more than he had done. There was another communication with it. On Corps notepaper. It was from Goldensoul. Stev Marden had been lost, from F16. The Captain tendered his condolences.

He showed it to the Mistress Kerosina. She read it quickly, shrugged. She said, 'You'd better have a drink.'

For once, he felt like it. It led to several more. She matched him glass for glass. She was lounging on a settle in the drawing room, the room in which he'd first been interviewed. Her dress was negligently buttoned; from time to time he saw the quick flash of a nipple. He said, 'He was a good friend.'

'Yes,' she said. 'I'm sure he was. Come on.' She took his hand. It was a major shock. He'd forgotten how warm a woman's fingers are.

He followed her. Things were spinning, he was no longer sure of his surroundings. She led him down a flight of steps, unlocked a door.

It was a part of the house he'd never seen before. A basement, lit by the electric light. She pushed a further door. She said, 'Are you fussy about smells?' He shook his head.

She clicked a switch. He was surprised to see the little room was ankle deep in mud. Thick, and blue-black. The sort of harbour sludge he'd seen once in the Southold. She said, 'My private beauty parlour.' She slipped out of the dress. She wore nothing beneath it. 'I told you I'd make you my body servant,' she said. 'Massage me. Don't get your uniform dirty though.' She walked into the mud, lay on her back. She grabbed a handful, smoothed it between her legs. 'It's wonderful for the skin,' she said. 'It tones it up like nothing else.'

The world collapsed. He took her twice, harsh and desperate. Finally he staggered to his feet. He said, 'I've got to go somewhere.' He'd seen a further chamber; a shower, and a loo. She said, 'No …'

'Kero,' he said, 'I must.' He wasn't really conscious of the words. He said, 'I've got to have a pee …'

She clung to his knees, and kissed him. She tightened her grip. She said, '*I'm not stopping you …*'

He woke at first light. The shame woke with him. He packed his clothes carefully, shouldered the duffel. Walking down the drive, he glanced back at the Towers. No need for checking though; both Rigs streamed at optimum angle. Both would fly, his fantails would fly; until they found themselves another Kiteman.

He turned south. Life, he supposed, was a series of ups and downs. Like the switchbacks he'd seen odd times, at Middle Lands fairs. He wondered which direction he was headed in right now. Hard to decide; but then, nothing was ever simple. He wondered how many people actually lived inside each human skin. The boy who'd known Rye in Middlemarch, the boy who'd used the hatchet, the boy who'd tendered his resignation from the Corps; none of them were him. Last night's ravening creature hadn't been him.

She'd trapped him of course, he realized that vaguely. Chosen her moment well. To him, Stev Marden had still been flying, high up in the blue. To her though it had been vital to win. By any means at hand. He frowned. Were there other people inside her too? Was there a little child, who wanted model Codys streamed above the table?

He eased the strap of the duffel bag. He'd caught himself trying to blame her. No use in that though. He'd been in love with her, he realized now. In love from day one. Had a part of her been in love with him? The words of the Master Canwen returned, with almost shocking force. '*Wallow in mud, and then the stars come close. Because you have earned the right to see their glory …*' He shook his head. How could he have known? How could he possibly have told? At least he knew now where his own star hung. There was a tart, in Middlemarch; freckled and short-skirted, with sturdy little knees. She loved him without question, without demand; and that was good enough. He said, 'I'm doing it for her.' He meant the Lady Kerosina.

The sun rose, steadily. He'd entered an area of scrubland. He'd marked it briefly, on his rides to town; now though it seemed endless.

He walked two hours; finally he turned. There was a horseman behind him, moving fast. He recognized the chestnut. He flung the bag away, ran on to the heath. It was useless of course, the other rode him down. He rose, tried to run again; but Martland had already launched himself from the horse. He tackled him round the knees, fetched him headlong. 'Well, my pretty,' he said. 'Here's a different tale. Well now, my pretty ...'

He tried to defend himself; but it was equally vain. For a time, he thought Martland had been sent by Kerosina; but after the first few blows it seemed Raoul entered a new state of awareness. The Mistress wouldn't do a thing like that; she'd been in love with him. This was a private revenge. The horseman might procure for her; but he would never know her favours.

He rolled on to his side finally, raised his arms to cover his face. So Aine Martland used his boots. When he had finished he stood over him. 'I shan't kill you, my pretty,' he said. 'I'll leave that to the Land. It'll be slower.' He whistled to the mare. She trotted to him; he mounted, and rode away.

Raoul began to crawl, on hands and knees. Once he rose to his feet; but the pain in his side was too intense, he soon returned to the proper mode of locomotion. He reached a brooklet, finally. He slithered down the bank and bathed his face. He traced the damage with his fingertips. One thing was certain; he'd never be pretty again. So if that had been his only crime, he'd been well paid. He crawled back to the grass, and fainted.

He woke some hours later, pushed himself up on his hands. The sky was dark, which meant it was the night. He must go on though. He had to get to Middlemarch. He tried to stand; but the world spun, he collapsed again.

There were many voices in his brain. Rye, the Mistress Kerosina. One seemed more persistent. It was thick and bubbling; it sounded very close. '*Man thtay to water,*' it lisped. '*Man not go away.*'

'What?' he said vaguely. 'What?'

'*Man thtay to water,*' said the voice again. '*Water good ...*' He sensed a rustling round him, in the dark. '*No-man help Man,*' gurgled the voice. '*No-man hand poithon. But no-man not touch food. Food good ...*'

'Food?' he said. 'What food?' There was no answer. The creatures, whatever they had been, had fled.

He collapsed again. He woke at dawn. For a time, the things round about were shadowy. Then they returned to focus. In front of him, a couple of feet away, lay an old cracked plate. It had blue flowers round the edges. On it were what looked like rabbit haunches. A small, mouselike creature was working at one of them; nibbling nervously, scrabbling at the food with its paws. It stared at him a moment, with huge black eyes; then it turned, and bolted.

He overcame his revulsion. He crammed the food at his mouth, regardless of the pain. Later he drank again, from the brook. He crawled into a stand of bushes, went to sleep.

They brought him food again; and again the third night. By then his brain was clearer. He thought, 'So they're even here. In the Middle Lands.' So much for the Kites then. Once he thought he saw one of the creatures humping away. On all fours; smaller than a dog, and blue. He pushed himself up on his hands. 'Come back,' he called. 'Come back, I want to talk to you …' But the bushes stayed still.

He wiped his cheeks. He'd met its sister once, and killed her. This was how they were repaying him. With Life.

On the fifth morning there was no food. He understood that he was better. He got up, staggered off toward the road.

He was still lightheaded. Sometime in the day he saw a Cody string. He intoned to it. '*For that our brother in God hath felt the call; for that he, in answering the Most High, hath taken to himself the sacred duty …*

'*For that he hath from henceforth pledged his life … to the protection of the Realm, of all that we hold dear …*

'*From the authority vested in us, we do appoint him … Kitecadet, and Guardian of the Way …*'

He was appalled. As he'd been appalled lying in the mud. The things he'd done, and said. He decided he was going mad. Later, it seemed a fresh awareness was vouchsafed him. The Demons, Badlanders; all were irrelevancies. He'd flown the Kites simply because he loved them. He built a Cody string, in his mind. He streamed the Pilot, on its slender line; he attached the cones, and saw the Lifters rise. He climbed atop the Launch Vehicle, felt the great Trace thrill. She lay under the Kites. The Mistress Kerosina. But they all lay under the Kites. Even the Badlanders.

The sky flickered again. 'Kitecadet,' he said. He rolled into the ditch.

He came round toward evening. A group of folk were moving up the road. Tinkers, if he was any judge. Dam-makers. They haunted the Middle Lands as well. But there was no harm in them. They mended pots and pans, and paid no tax. They were the Free Folk; free as the Fliers. He got to his knees. He said, 'How far to Middlemarch?'

They clustered round him, stood staring down. Then one of them pulled at his jerkin. He resisted, feebly. It was no use of course. It was dragged from him; and another grabbed his shirt. It tore.

'Look at that,' said the Tink disgustedly. 'Bad times, we're livin' in. No use even robbin' beggars.' He put his foot against Raoul's chest, and shoved. He rolled back, into the muddy water.

The great Air Show had come and gone; the visitors had left; Middlemarch was settling down, preparing for the winter. Though the streets were still crowded, the inns doing a good trade. Better to collect while you could though; these were the last pickings.

All steered clear of the creature on the path. It was ragged, and dirty; it veered from side to side, seemingly half blind. '*Innocent*,' said one woman. She made a certain sign, and hurried on. Later, a child said, 'Mummy, what's *wrong* with him?'

'He's drunk,' said the other. 'I'll tell you when you're older. You wouldn't understand, not yet.' She steered well clear. 'Come on,' she said. The child stared back, wide-eyed.

The Vars strode purposefully across Main Drag. 'We got another one,' said the Sergeant. 'Must be the season for 'em.' He approached the derelict, dragged at his hair. He said, 'Where you from, my friend?'

The other whispered something. He leaned closer. 'Sorry,' he said. 'Din' quite catch it, sir …'

The scarecrow whispered again.

'Kiteman,' said the policeman. 'Kiteman. The things you people do get in your heads.' He hauled the other to his feet, and hit him. He fell down again.

'Oh, look,' said the Constable. 'Run straight into your hand. What clumsy blokes they are.'

'Yes,' said the other, 'aren't they? Comes from all the booze.' He unslung the automatic from his shoulder, administered a few desultory whacks. The derelict got to his hands and knees, eventually; but there was no more fun in him. He hung his head and panted, dropped bloodspots on the path.

'Don't be here in the morning,' said the Sergeant. 'You might be in trouble else.' He nodded to his partner; and they strolled away.

It seemed his life had focused to a point. He staggered on, reached his objective finally. The Church of the Moving Clouds. The steps proved an obstacle; he climbed them on hands and knees. There was an iron-studded door; in its centre, a great bronze ring. He grabbed it. It moved downward, slightly; and a bell tolled, deep within the building. 'Sanctuary,' he said. 'Sanctuary …'

There was a Var patrolman. He sauntered up. He was already unslinging his gun. He said, 'What?'

'Sanctuary,' whispered the fugitive. 'Give me peace …'

'I'll give you peace,' said the Var. 'All the peace you could want.' He swung the weapon by the barrel; and his wrist was caught.

He looked round, startled. The priest was tall, and gaunt; he was dressed, of course, in the sage green of the Middlers. His face was calm; but the deep-set eyes were blazing. 'Sanctuary has been claimed,' he said. 'Sanctuary is granted.' He relaxed his grip. He said, 'About your business, Master.'

The other's face mottled. He opened his mouth; and the priest held a great looped cross before his eyes. Golden, and plain; the Life Symbol of the Middle Church. 'By all Laws, this is just,' he said. 'Uphold the Law ...'

The Var backed off, unwillingly. He shouldered the gun. He said, 'You're welcome. We need more garbage collectors anyway.' He adjusted the sling, walked huffily away along the path.

The priest looked down pityingly. 'Sanctuary has been claimed,' he said. 'It is yours, my son. Come ...' He reached to raise the other's arm; but the derelict shoved him away. He snatched something from round his neck. A locket, on a thin gold chain. 'Her name is Rye,' he said. 'Her name is Rye ...' He lost his grip on the door, rolled down the steps. He landed on the pavement, lay on his back unmoving.

The girl walked swiftly. A shawl was across her shoulders, a scarf over her head. She reached the steps of the Mercy Hospital, hesitated. She made her mind up finally, and entered. Inside, she was once more bemused; at the noise and bustle, clattering of utensils, trolleys. The air had a faint, sharp tang; young women scurried in long white robes, neat caps. She stepped back, all but ran away. 'The Master Trenchingham,' she said. 'The Master Trenchingham. He sent for me. Where is he?'

'I am here,' he said. 'Have no fear, sister. Come with me.' He proffered his arm; she took it, sensed the strength in him.

There was a side ward. A little room, one-bedded. She ran to him. Saw the poor, broken face. She dropped to her knees. 'Why?' she whispered. 'Why, Raoul? Was it because of me?'

He brushed her cheeks, feebly. 'You mustn't blame yourself,' he said. 'It wasn't to do with you.' He stroked her hair. 'Rye,' he said. 'Rye of Middlemarch.' He took her hand.

4

Kitecaptain

The bawling noise he made was that of an animal in pain. He ran from the house, hands clutched to his head, and reeled across the yard. 'Ruined,' he moaned. Then, 'Why ... why her ...' Then, 'No ...' And again, in desperation, '*No, no, no ...*'

Although so early, little after zero four hundred, the long house and the buildings clustered round it were already astir. Folk hurried, attracted by the din; all stopped at sight of him. They backed away; and a buttery maid bit her wrist and began to whimper. This was a Justin Manning they'd never seen before.

He wrenched at the doors of the barn, dragged them back. Their iron-shod leading edges screeched on cobbles. The early sunlight shafted on to the motor inside; gleamed from the coachwork that had been his pride and joy, the smart brass rad. He advanced the spark, twisted the hand throttle; desperate, scarcely aware of what he did. He swung the handle, and again. The engine sputtered, caught. 'Why her,' he moaned. '*Why* ...' The pain was acute now, torturing; like a poison swallowed, burning at his vitals.

A hand was on his shoulder. Rik Butard, his Manager. He was unaware of what was shouted, what he answered; but the other's face changed abruptly. He set off toward the house, at a run.

Quickly, because of the poison. The pain. The air would blow it away. *Must.* He careered across the stackyard, past the tall, glinting silos. He couldn't see them for the tears that starred his vision. '*Tan*,' he whispered. '*Tan, my little Tanny. Tan, Tan, Tan* ...'

He jolted down the lane. A mile to the main road; he swung left, still unaware. The road beyond was rutted too, rank grass growing between the wheel tracks, weeds showing through the hardcore with which it was sporadically patched. But metalled roads were rare, throughout the Eastern Sector; in the Salient, they were almost nonexistent.

His foot was to the boards. The Swallow whined and crashed, protesting. Old when he bought her, she'd always been cosseted; he'd never punished her like this. But what came of cosseting? Blood came from cosseting. Blood, and agony. The pain he felt now.

His hands were slippery on the wheelrim. He looked at them. Over the right knuckles, thick caps of skin stood on edge. He didn't know how that had happened. It was fitting though. His blood mingled with hers.

There was a village. Better kept than the rest of the Salient hamlets; neat cottages in pink and white and blue. And garden fences, the occasional patch of flowers. But the Manning Estate had always cared for the welfare of its tenants; as three generations had taken pride in the great farm. Grandfather Manning it was who'd really built up the spread, laid the foundations of the family fortune. But he'd left the money entailed. His own mother would have spent it; as a Landy Street groupie would, it had once been whispered. But she'd never had the chance. Middlemarch held the purse strings, his grandfather's solicitors; and they held them tight. An implement, an outbuilding, a machine part; wire for a broken fence, the silos of which they'd been so proud; all had to be fought for, justified. So she'd worked instead; at the scrubbing and mending and baking and buttermaking, the thousand and one tasks of a farmer's wife. It had aged her prematurely; helped her to an early grave perhaps. Partially, it was seeing that happen that had made him break away;

that and the burning ambition he'd owned for as long as he could remember. He would be a Kiteman; there was nothing else in the world.

Through the village, up the long slope beyond; the big car wheezing now, complaining. But her use was almost done. As everything was done. The sun shone; but there was no light. Only the pain.

He crested the rise, racketed down the farther hill. One of the few hilly parts of the Salient; for the most part it was deadly flat. G9 to his right, two Codys streamed; and the dawn wind blowing stronger, as it always did. A part of his mind realized the Launchers would be paying out as the Observers clawed for altitude. The gateman saluted him, surprised. He didn't respond.

Another Cody, tiny in the distance. That was G7; the others in the chain were out of sight. They crawled out in a great curve, protecting the huge bight of land. Winter and summer, day and night; untiring, loyal and useless. He groaned, tears coursing down his face. He said, 'The Demons are already here.'

Another hamlet, straggling this time and sullen. Coldmarsh. He scattered chickens; they squawked, erupting. One flew into the screen, left excrement and feathers. He didn't use the washers. He could see enough for his needs. He'd seen enough already.

A villager shouted, a dog ran yapping after the car. He swung right. The lane narrowed at once. Tall hedges, thick with the lush weeds of summer; poppy and speedwell, foolflowers with their stinking creamy heads. He stamped the brake, hauled right again. G8 gatehouse flashed by. The guard, equally taken aback, hurried to salute; but he was too late.

He left the car door swinging, ran across the compound. The single string was being drawn; he waved his arms, crossed them above his head. 'Belay,' he shouted hoarsely. 'Belay …' The Launchmaster hesitated, surprised. Stared up at the Observer's basket. It hung at sixty feet, rocking and vibrating. He snapped an order. Steam jetted; the clanking of the winch ceased abruptly. The Rig began to climb again, into safer air.

He ran into the hangar, stared at the wind telltales. 'Sergeant,' he said. 'Rig for high flight.'

If the other was surprised he didn't show it. It's the privilege of any Base Captain to schedule Stringups as he chooses; and he knew Manning for a conscientious Commander. He'd high-flown enough before, on hunches; and doubled, sometimes even trebled the Watching. But the enemy had never been found. The Sergeant saluted, briskly. He said, 'Three cables, sir?'

'Six,' said the other. 'Six …'

This time, the shock registered. Nobody, except the great Canwen himself, had ever flown six cables. And those height trials had been in Middlemarch, in air more stable than any to be found here. In the Salient the manoeuvre was unheard of. He wondered for an instant if his ears weren't playing him tricks.

Vital to leave the Earth. Fly far, far off. He shouted again, '*Six* …' and the Sergeant jumped. He said, 'Six cables, sir.' He ran off, bellowing orders. Whistles blew; within seconds Manning heard the bugles from the gatehouse. The call for All Personnel.

He couldn't wait; he grabbed the first of the spools, began to heave it forward. Gashing his already lacerated hands. Some fragment of remaining sense made him pause, snatch up a pair of the ground crew's heavy gauntlets. Nobody can man a Cody with fingers cut to the bone.

The place was filling now. Cadets scurried, half of them still bleary with sleep; two Corporals were hastily assembling the extra Lifters they would need while the Riggingmaster, with a set face of disgust, was laying out the great bronze spliceblocks that would link the cables end to end. Riggingmasters as a breed detested altitude flying. Fine if you could bring the Cody back in steady, detach each union, clamp off and respool; but in practice that seldom happened. Height meant danger, emergencies; reel in fast, lump the spliceblocks on to the drum, and you were in trouble. Five blocks meant six warped cables; and that meant a report to Middlemarch.

The Launchmaster was at his elbow. He said, 'Permission to draw the String, sir?' He glanced at his wrist. 'Well overdue,' he said. 'Forty-five minutes.'

Justin nodded, vaguely. Eight hours in a Cody basket, even on a summer night, is enough for the most hardened Observer. And he was a kindly man; or had been, in other times. 'Yes,' he said. 'Bring him in.'

His ears were buzzing; and the pain coming again in waves. He could barely hear the voices round him, although they shouted close. He said, 'Prepare Launcher Two.' No, wait. That would take time; and time was running out. 'Belay,' he said. 'I'll fly from No. 1.' Heads turned sharply at that. Within seconds the news would be across the Base; a Captain flying watch? That was unheard-of too.

The bowser was already bumping across the field. Hoses were slung; men scrambled to turn the massive stopcocks. Water splashed; the Launcher replenished herself as she worked.

The Manlifter was grounded, on the back of the huge truck; two Cadets were holding it, wrestling with the struts as the wind gusts tried to lift the great black wings. 'Sergeant,' he said again, 'belay. Don't draw the String. Just give me two more Lifters.'

This time the other looked aghast. The Launchmaster had turned too, was staring down as if unable to credit his ears. He glanced at the hangar, back to his Commander. It was contrary to every rule in the book. Once only had he heard of such a thing; in G12, on a wild night of storm. But he'd never expected, in all his life, to receive such an order himself.

For a moment, sanity returned to Manning. He understood the other's dilemma well enough. The splicedrums must be hoisted in sequence to the Launcher's back; to do that she would use her own steam derrick. The operation was simple enough; back tail-first into the hangar entrance, reanchor there. But she'd have to down rig first. To move a Launcher with a Cody streamed was tantamount to heresy. Then the roaring was back, threatening to block out sense entirely. 'Do it,' he groaned. 'Do it, in the name of God...'

The Sergeant waited no longer. He picked up one of the electric megaphones just coming into use. '*Clear anchor tackles*,' he said. '*Secure basket*.' He swung the trumpet-mouth of the machine toward the hangar. '*Attention*,' he said. '*Launcher movement. Live String*.' The disgust was patent, even in the distorted metal voice.

The machine thundered, began to edge cautiously back. The Sergeant walked beside it, one hand to the maroon side, the other signalling the driver. Down left, and straighten; right. The Launcher clattered steadily; above it the Kitestring flapped and dipped. The cable thrummed; and the Sergeant dropped his hand, palm flat. A hissing; and the brake was set. He said with evident relief, 'Re-anchor.' Cables were run out smartly to the mooring rings halfway down the bay; and the tension eased a little. The Captain leaned against the truck's side, rubbed a hand over his eyes. He said, '*Why? Why?*'

The Base Medic was touching his arm. He said anxiously, 'You all right sir?' Don't look too good to me.'

He opened his mouth to send the man packing; but the words were lost anyway. The Launcher's donkey engine clattered, deafening in the confined space. More steam gusted; the first of the spare drums was slung aboard, spindle already rigged. Cadets guided it to its sockets, snapped the keepers shut.

'Two Lifters,' said the Sergeant. 'Unship basket.' Cable paid out; the first of the extra trace cones was attached. He said, '*Hurry. Hurry*...' The wind telltales vibrated, rose again and steadied.

'Lifter clear,' said the Launchmaster. 'Pay out.' The great Kite sailed up the line to join its sisters; the angle of the Trace altered at once.

The Base Chaplain was there, with his stole and book. He handed across the breviary and pistol. He said, '*For those who watch as for those who wait we pray; honouring Thee, Lord, begging our vigilance receive reward*...'

'Enough of that,' he said. '*Enough* ...' The other glanced at him keenly, pursed his lips. He turned and walked away.

The second Lifter flew. The Launchmaster said, 'Clear fairleads.' His face was set as well. The fairleads with their curving arms were geared to the main winch drive; through downhaul they moved from side to side, disposing the cable neatly on the drum. But the spliceblocks wouldn't pass them. The cable would rise now straight from the drum itself; and to the drum return. It was an offence to his tidy mind.

The Manlifter was reattached. He climbed in, clicked the harness straps. He said, 'Clear basket,' and at last he was rising smoothly, up into the wide blue sky. The din behind him faded, replaced by the singing of the wind. A wave of sickness came, and passed.

He slipped the pistol into the holster in the basket side, tucked the book into the pouch by his left hand. He stared at his fingers. The blood had dried now, in ragged brown stripes. Her blood, that had been so vivid. It was as if she herself had faded, become already a creature of the long-dead past. He felt true madness flicker at the thought.

He looked around him. The horizon was half lost in pearly haze. Somewhere to the southwest, miles away, lay Mannings; Mannings, and everything he loved. Had loved, he told himself. Because nothing remained. A knife had been drawn, across memory. Across his brain and heart. He stared up, past the great wings of the Lifters. The Pilot was a tiny dot, against the deeper blue of zenith. He rubbed his face.

Flying had always calmed him. He felt its influence, even in his present desperate state. The tumbling thoughts had slowed, allowing him at least to put them in order. An old fantasy had come to him. The Kites were in some way conscious, sentient. Knowing his need, they drew him upward smoothly; away from the realm of despair, to where he needed to be. The sky was unsullied, spotless. The sky could not bleed.

Operational height; the climb continued through it. Five minutes, and he sensed that he had checked. He stared down. Already the buildings of the Base, the hangar from which he had flown, seemed small as matchboxes. They lay almost in plan; he could see the big numbers painted on the roofs, white against corrugated grey. G8, and SAL for Salient. Down there they would be attaching the first of the big splices, tightening the cable nuts, checking and double-checking; the Riggingmaster fuming no doubt, the launch crew watching impassive. He could imagine the excitement among the Cadets, the whispers and flutterings; for they were seeing something they'd never seen before. Would probably never see again.

The faintest of jerks; and the upward flight continued. He stared at the String again, shading his eyes. The Lifters pulled steady, barely rocking. He'd found stable air, as he'd known he must. The sun, climbing now and strengthening, struck thin reflections from the distant dural spars. Some of the Salient Stations were still rigged with wood; but he'd insisted, years back now, that G8 receive the up-to-date equipment. Pestered and pestered till Middlemarch had given in; more in self defence he'd thought, than out of special love for him. After all, G8 wasn't a showplace. Not like Middlemarch, or even G15. Just a cluster of huts, the hangars and workshops, little parade ground where the Cadets worked out each morning under the eagle eye of an irascible PTI. A workaday Salient Station.

He squared his shoulders fractionally. Workaday or not, the safety of his men had always come first. They'd had a bad blow a year or two ago, the worst in memory. G10 had lost an Observer, G11 two. All for the same reason; collapse of the wood-framed Lifters. His people, mercifully, had escaped; but that had been when the barrage of letters had started. And continued, until he got his way. He'd known he must finally win; because he'd always had recourse to a second threat. Unspoken, but still real. If a Captain could order the flying of all Traces, he could also order their grounding, for the safety of his men; and that would leave a gap in the defences through which the enemy might swarm. So Middlemarch acceded, gracefully; though he'd had no doubt Admin had damned him black. He'd shrugged. He'd done his best for the people he commanded; as he'd tried to do his best by everybody. Though that had still ended in ruin and failure.

He checked the pistol. One of the new-fangled revolving arms; something else he'd badgered Middlemarch into supplying. Copper caps in place over the nipples, fronts of the chambers smeared with grease to ward off flashround. G8 carried no armourer, none of the smaller Bases did; but priests were usually experts. Previss certainly was an old hand, and a crack shot as well; he would have allowed no-one else to arm him. A pyrotechnic expert too. He'd granted Previss a weekly firework levy from the pay of all personnel; and though there'd been some grumblings here and there, come Foundation Day no Station on the Frontier boasted a better show. He'd wondered with amusement, in the old life when he'd been sane, if all priests just liked bangs, if that was the true attraction of the Cloth.

A Lifter flapped slightly in a flaw of wind. Dipped, steadied again. He watched it; but the String was stable, balanced. He had a good team. It ought to be; he'd trained most of them himself. Cadets had asked often enough to transfer back after their tours; to volunteer for the Salient was no small accolade to him. So he couldn't in the main have done too bad a job. A hard man certainly, when need arose; because you couldn't run a Cody station on softness. Fair though. He'd always tried to be fair.

The notion of sentience remained. The Codys had been a part of his life now for more years than he cared to count; but their fascination had never faded. He remembered, vividly, the first time he'd ever seen a streamed Trace. He'd been a tiny child, little more than a babe in arms. He'd forgotten the occasion; some Fair or other in the Middle Lands, he supposed. Certainly it had been his first long trip away from home, in the old carriage his father had owned. And his father before him. It still rested in the carthouse; a beautiful wagonette with curving strakes and deep-dished yellow wheels.

Varnished and lined with gold, the name of the farm displayed proudly on the sides. It had been drawn by two high-stepping greys, their harness agleam with brass; and he and his mother, the housefolk, sitting high, well muffled against the winds that swept in clear from Southguard. That had all been exciting enough; but when they'd rounded a bend he'd seen the great Kites rise majestically, strung half across the sky, and all else had faded. He'd held his arms out; as if he could catch the bright wings, draw them down to him. 'What are they?' he'd said, again and again. '*What are they?*' They'd answered as best they could; in the main the country folk knew little, and truth to tell cared less, about the Corps that guarded the land. His mother knew, for she had lived in Middlemarch; later she came to regret the knowledge she imparted. It would have made no difference though had she held her peace. He'd stared behind, as the strange, lovely things receded; but soon of course there were more. Many more. Their sisters, he decided; sisters of green and blue, orange and scarlet and bronze. For it was a Feast Day; every Station they passed – and there were many, along the route they took – was dressed overall. He'd chattered about them the rest of the day, and all the long drive home, till his family no doubt got sick and tired of hearing. They humoured him, expecting the fad to dissipate; but it did no such thing. He badgered and badgered; till on one glorious, never-to-be-forgotten day his father had put him into the car – they owned a little automobile by then, an almost unheard-of thing in the Salient – and driven him off, to a secret destination. They jolted down a lane, rounded a bend; and before him was the neat white fencing, the small square guardhouse just inside the gate. He could read and letter well enough by then – his family had never stinted on tutors – he had no difficulty making out the letters on the big white board. G8.

They'd passed through unhindered – the name of Manning carried weight, even with the Corps – into a magic world. He saw a Launcher close up for the first time; the great truck with its high maroon sides, its drums and winches and derricks, its hoses and big, spoked wheels. Cables ran back from it to anchor points in the grass; and a rig was flying high, almost invisible in the blue. He stared and stared, squinting, till when he walked into the hangar he could see nothing at all for the spots of colour floating before his eyes. His other senses though seemed preternaturally acute. He heard the talk and laughter of the Cadets, smelled the scents of steam and oil, heavier sweetness of dope from where they repaired and refurbished the great wings of a Lifter. Up close, he was amazed by the sheer size of the Kites. Though here were no gaudy colours. This was a working Station, an outpost of the Realm; its rigs were sober, matching its sober task.

He was lifted into an Observer's basket, stood on tiptoe to peer over the edge. He crouched in the bottom of it; and in imagination he was already flying, the keen air round him and the endless, flawless blue. He watched a String drawn, saw the new Trace streamed; and his ambition, already fixed, became unalterable. There was only one thing to do, in all the world; he would be a Kiteman.

His father at first had been inclined to scoff. Certainly his mother shook her head. The life was dangerous, hard and thankless. None knew better than she; her father had been a Flier, two of her brothers had joined the Corps. Only to be lost together, in the same disaster; a Southguard Kite-ship dragged her anchors, swept helpless onto the murderous lee shore. She chided, telling him his place was here, working at his books, learning to run the farm that would one day be his; but the words had no effect. She saw in his eyes that he would never change; she wept, privately, but after that she let him be.

Things might not have fared so well had it not been for his grandfather. Curt Manning was ailing then, well into his eighties and long past useful work; but his mind was as sharp as ever, he was still a force to be reckoned with. Justin remembered being summoned to his presence, one day in early autumn. The old man regarded him sternly, hands clasped round the head of his great gnarled stick. His hands were gnarled as well; the skin brown and wrinkled, marked with the frecklings of age. He considered for a while before he spoke; then he began. He questioned Justin in detail on his knowledge of the Codys, of the Corps, the Church to whom they owed allegiance. He answered, stammering a little; the old man's eyes were still a piercing blue, their gaze unnerved him. But he didn't falter. Sensing real interest, tutor after tutor had brought him books; he had his own library upstairs, well thumbed, and knew them from cover to cover. He could reel off the Stations of the Salient, their complements, supply depots, even their duty rosters. While as for the Kites, he knew the different patterns of Lifter, height and endurance records, configurations for each windforce. He'd flown a Cody trace so often, in his mind, he felt he could do it blindfold. The old man nodded finally, sat quiet again awhile. He watched down at the carpet, still unsure, listened to the faint crackle of the fire in the grate. Then the other nodded. 'Well, Jus,' he said – he seldom used his forename, even less often its diminutive – 'I think I can probably help you. As you know, we're by no means badly connected. I know a couple of Masters; I think old Helman would probably be the one. If you're going to do it, and it seems you've made your mind up, there's nothing like starting at the top.'

There'd been a sudden great leap in his chest; but he'd shaken his head. 'Please, sir,' he said falteringly. 'If you please … I'd like to do it like everybody else. Start as an Apprentice. Then I'd know …' He stopped. He didn't know how to finish the thought.

Surprisingly, the old man chuckled. Then he reached out, slapped him on the shoulder. 'Hoped you'd say that,' he said. 'Spoken like a Manning. That's the way it will be then.' He leaned back. 'You've a year or two to wait of course,' he said. 'Work as hard as you can. Remember you can't ever learn enough. The Kites aren't the only thing in the world. But you'll find that out from the Corps, soon enough.'

Next year, Tan was born.

The Trace had checked again. He peered down. He was well over the Badlands now, the Station buildings all but vanished in the haze. Below and behind was the cobweb line of the Boundary, the broader scar of the ditch they'd dug to keep at bay the crawling things that lived there. Not that they'd attempted infiltration for years now; perhaps they'd all died off. He himself only remembered one attack; that had been in the Easthold, miles away, when he'd been a mere Cadet. The Border Guards intercepted rapidly enough. One they shot dead; the others fled, wailing and splashing what passed with them for blood. Curiosity – the curiosity of the young and brash – had made him peer close at the thing on the grass. He'd shuddered, and wished he hadn't. He'd walked away, and been very sick. In the morning, there'd been no sign of the invaders; save that where the body fluids had touched it, the grass was yellow and dying.

Time enough now for them to have fixed the splice. Time and to spare. He leaned from the basket, held out the signal pistol all Observers carried. A bright green ball arced upwards, drifted down slowly toward the half-visible ground. The flight was resumed.

He'd resented her birth, as an only child will. At first, when his mother had told him formally she was carrying, he'd been confused. He'd said, 'Carrying what?' and looked round him. She'd laughed then, and patted her body. 'A child,' she said. 'A brother for you, Justin. Or a sister.'

'Oh, no,' he said. 'You can't, mother, you *can't* . . .' He'd fled to his room and cried, thrown himself on the bed, kicked out in sheer frustration. This was the end of it then. The end of it all. He hated babies; nasty, sticky things that crawled about and spoiled your books and stole all the attention so you sat in the corner and sulked, because nobody had any time for you any more. He'd seen it happen often enough, or thought he had. He was silent for a week; then, slowly, it seemed acceptance grew. And with it a certain curiosity. He thought how strange it was that one human being should make themselves inside another; and how they managed to pop out. On that matter he was wholly unsure, and far too shy to ask. He wondered if the other thing was true after all, that they were found under certain bushes or that the fairies brought them. It had always seemed far more likely.

His tutor helped him, gently. He supposed with hindsight it had been at his parents' suggestion. He sat frowning. The facts seemed bizarre. Later he began to worry. He was a dutiful child, and loved his folk; but especially his mother. What he had learned seemed painful and dangerous. He found resentment of the unborn child beginning to rise again. Nor would it go away. His mother was worried, his father downright vexed. Finally he tearfully confessed his fears to her; and she laughed, and hugged him. 'Jus, don't be so silly,' she said. 'Hundreds of women have babies, every day. In the Salient, and Middlemarch, and Southguard; all over the Realm. There's nothing to it at all, you'll see.' She smoothed his hair. Think how nice it will be,' she said. 'Someone for you to play with, and talk to. Your father and I have wanted another child for years; but we were thinking of you as well.'

He stuck his lip out. He wouldn't be consoled. He said, 'You can't talk to *babies.*'

She sighed. 'I know,' she said. 'You're being one yourself. Now run along, and find something to do. And put a better face on at dinner, young man; you're getting your father really annoyed.'

He went and read his Kitebooks; but for once, they brought no comfort.

A midwife was hired, and a wetnurse – he had to have that explained as well – and the great day finally arrived. He hadn't seen his mother for nearly a week; she'd taken to her bed, and there were whispers in the household that things weren't as they should be. Cook had definite information, and the parlourmaids went round with knowing looks in their eyes. He tried to pump them of course, but it was no use. He felt more shut away than ever.

He was allowed to see her briefly, the last morning. He'd wondered how on earth she could tell just when the baby would come; but that was a mystery as well. He puzzled over it for a while and gave it up; he'd become tired of the inexplicable.

He was shocked at how white and tired she looked: but by that time he'd learned just a little. He held his tears back, talked cheerfully till the nurse rose to usher him from the room. Mav took his hand then. 'Go and see your father,' she said. 'I think he's got a surprise for you. Then you can come back later.'

'Yes, mother,' he said. 'I will.' He leaned over and kissed her. Her forehead was dry and hot.

His father was genial; in a better mood than he'd seen him for days. 'Now, young man,' he said, 'come with me.' He followed, puzzled, to one of the outhouses, stared at the big flat packing crate. The lid had been prized up; he rummaged in the woodwool that filled it, gave a cry. For a moment, words failed him. 'It's,' he said. 'It's . . . I . . .' He rushed to his father. There were tears in his eyes again; but they were tears of gratitude. 'Thank you,' he said.

'It's not just for you,' said Tange Manning. 'It's for the house. I'm putting you in charge though; you're the expert.' He smiled. 'I'll lend you Aniken for the day,' he said. 'We shall want a good strong anchor point. Where would you suggest?'

'Middle of the west front,' he said instantly. 'There's access from both boxrooms. Good liftpath too. No obstructions.' Which was true of course. The great main stacks were toward each end of Mannings; the Trace could fly between.

His father grinned again. 'You're the boss,' he said once more. 'I'll leave you to it. Tell Ani when you're ready.'

Left to himself, he lifted out the great bright Kites with reverence. A personal Cody rig; wealthy families often bought air rights from the Church, streamed them to ensure protection and prosperity. Some, he knew, even had their own Kiteman; and certainly all the Masters. They were respected members of the household staff. He assembled the String, almost with the ease of practice; his books, pored over for so long, made actions nearly automatic. Then he hared in search of Aniken. The old man left his work grumbling. No Manning had ever flown a Cody; he'd never thought he'd live to see the day. In his opinion, it was downright superstition.

He bullied him. 'It isn't, Ani,' he said. 'It *isn't*. It's vital ...' He'd realized that every second was precious. His mother lay in labour, in an unprotected house; his scalp crawled at the thought of what might happen. 'Aniken,' he said, 'hurry. Please, hurry ...'

The old man grumbled more at all the stairs; while the final spidery ladder all but defeated him. He hauled himself through eventually; stood blinking, looking round.

The roof was steep-pitched; but round the edge ran a narrow walkway. Flat-bottomed, lined with lead, protected by a waist-high parapet. Justin ran to the spot selected. He held up a streamer – supplied with the pack – saw he had chosen rightly. The little ribbon fluttered bravely, marking the wind direction. So if the fixing was *here*, just by his hand, the Trace would fly up well, above the houses and the stackyards, straight toward the Badlands. A warning and a threat, to every Demon that flew. They'd veer aside, invisible, and leave the place in peace. 'Quick, Ani,' he said again. 'Just *here* ...' The old man sniffed; but he set to work.

The job took longer than he'd realized. Much longer. Aniken was thorough, nobody more thorough on the farm; but he was slow. It was lunchtime and past before he pronounced himself satisfied.

Justin went back to the boxroom. He cleated the Pilot to the line, measured and marked the cable at the recommended intervals. He frowned. He realized he could have been doing this while the old man fixed the mooring. Somehow though he hadn't been able to tear himself away. It seemed he had to see every part of the procedure; make sure in his own mind it was good. Now, he had to hurry.

You couldn't hurry though. That was the first rule of any Kiteman. Hurry, and you made mistakes. That would be disaster. He went back to the booklet, reread parts to make sure he'd got it right.

He positioned the little bronze cones, checking their diameters with care. The fixings were strange to him. Instead of heads, the bolts had octagonal indents; and there weren't any spanners. Instead there were little metal rods, right-angled at one end. He supposed they'd just come in; some of the books he'd read had been quite old. He took care not to over-tighten; he knew about stripping threads. Then he remembered he was only a boy, and gave all the bolts another half turn. He sat back. He was sure that would be right.

One of the housemaids called, from the corridor outside. 'Justin … Master Justin …' He frowned. Hoped she wouldn't open the door. He couldn't stop to *eat*. She didn't. She gave a little snort of exasperation, went away.

He coiled the line, carried the Pilot to the roof. It began to flap and pluck, a live thing already. He slipped the line through the upper mooring ring, and then the lower. He held the little Kite above his head, released it. He paid out, heart in his mouth. It hung uncertain for a moment, then began to climb. Sure, and sweet. He whooped.

He tied off with a hitch he'd learned, went back for the first of the Lifters. He paid out till all cones were clear, clipped the tail ring to the line, released. The Lifter climbed sweetly as well, checking and clicking, to its proper place. So did the rest.

The Trace angle looked good. He tested its power, tying off carefully first. He was surprised at the generated lift. Pull back on the tautness and it was as if you held a live thing, trembling and shaking, tugging at your arm. The rig would certainly fly a rabbit, or a small dog. Perhaps even him.

He fetched the Godkite, the big pale oval with its Seeing Eye and the other symbols he couldn't understand. Bold and black, but picked out beautifully in gold. He streamed it, and paid out. Tied the fall off with a jamming hitch. Then another, to make sure. The Trace hung proudly, far out over the pastures, shimmering in sunlight; he put his hands on his hips, and smiled with joy.

There was a distant noise. He stared round, puzzled. People were cheering; from the barns, the stackyard, everywhere. His father among them. He waved; and they waved back.

There was a closer sound. Muffled, but coming from inside the house. He frowned, cocking his head; and it came again. A scream.

He dropped to his knees, started confusedly to pray. He prayed to God, to Father Andri, to the Cody trace. It dipped at once, and swung. As if it understood.

The rig had checked. He waited, frowning. Had they come for him already? He leaned from the basket, fired the pistol. The ascent was resumed.

*

First thing next morning he rushed outside. He was appalled. The Trace was at negative angle, all but brushing the farmland. He pelted upstairs and drew the Rig. He squatted, puzzling. Breeze lighter, and a little flawed; but it shouldn't be doing that. He rebalanced the Lifters. Present more face to the wind, that was the answer.

He frowned, biting his lip. No. It wasn't the answer. Windspeed was the answer. Create more flow, more vacuum … He rebalanced the other way. He streamed the Cody, again with trepidation.

He couldn't believe his eyes. Even in that light breeze, it rose and rose. Why, it must be … it must be making more than forty degrees! He shouted with joy. He felt it was the best moment of his life. Then he remembered his mother, and felt instantly guilty.

It was a week before he saw her again. And much longer than that before she was allowed to get up. When she finally came downstairs she looked if possible even more pale and haggard than before. Her hair was lustreless, and there were great dark marks under her eyes. He ran to her, appalled; but she pushed him gently away. 'Don't be silly, Justin,' she said. 'I'm better now. I shall get stronger every day.' She wasn't better though; she paused frequently as she walked, and sometimes had to hold on to the backs of chairs.

He stared curiously at the tiny thing in the cot; the cot they always kept by the sitting room hearth, where a fire burned night and day. Its skin, he saw, was red and wrinkled-looking, its eyes a strange pale colour he could not determine. It lay solemnly, staring up; but there seemed to be no focus in the gaze. He said, 'It's funny,' and his mother smiled. 'Not "it", Jus,' she said. 'She's your baby sister.'

He returned again and again, to stare. It didn't cry, like other babies do; nor did it move about much, wave its legs and arms. It seemed content to lie there, and be still. Though sometimes it made little mewing noises. Like a kitten, he thought. Or a very young puppy. The wetnurse would come then, and shoo him from the room; once as he closed the door he saw her unfastening the top of her dress. He understood better by then; he knew the damp patches he sometimes saw on her clothes were milk.

He shook his head, in the privacy of his own room. He thought, with one of those strange flashes of wisdom that often come to children, 'At least there'll be no more babies.'

Nor were there of course; and as his mother promised, she gained in strength. Though she was never quite the same again. His earliest memories were of her working with the maids or buttery girls; swabbing the stone-flagged floors, turning the handles of the great wooden churns. Now she sat quietly by the fire, and was easily tired.

A winter came and went. Another summer. Tan lay in her cot and didn't move. He thought his mother sometimes looked at her with worried eyes. He streamed his Kites, and prayed; early, in the high green dawns, last thing when the rain was falling, snow and sleet flurries swirled about the big house. He mended the spars the buffeting spring winds snapped – he learned the skills from the village carpenter – replaced the fabric as it wore and rotted. He learned to know when a Lifter could be spared, without endangering the Trace; because at all times the Cody must stay flying. His former notion seemed strengthened. The Kites had saved his mother, of that he had no doubt; so they were sacred things.

Eighteen months after her birth, Grandfather Manning sent for the child. Justin of course was banned from the discussion; he heard about it later, from a chambermaid. Though how she knew so much he was never sure; perhaps his mother had confided in her. The old man took the silent little bundle, stared long and carefully into its face; the eyes that focused now, but in which there was no awareness. He was silent for a while, as was his wont; then he shook his head. He handed Tan back, gently. 'There is no spirit,' he said. 'Give her to the Church.'

Mav had started up, appalled. 'No,' she said. 'No, *no* ... She is a creature of God.'

The old man looked at her pityingly. 'Then to God she must return,' he said. 'For she is no Manning. She is no human child.'

He'd winced, as the girl prattled on; because for once he'd known precisely what was meant. Though 'euphemism' had not been part of his vocabulary then. Fear stalked the Realm; it always had. Year in, year out, the westerlies blew; but just occasionally, they failed. Then the Codys streamed backward, into the Salient, the Easthold; and the people quailed, slammed their windows and doors. Because the Badlands were exhaling, and their breath was doom. The churches closed, field beasts were hurried into their byres. Let man or woman breathe the vapours, or a mother big with child; the results could not be guessed. Or dreamed of, save in nightmare.

Mav shook her head, violently. 'No,' she said again. 'No, *no* ...' She cradled the little bundle, rocking and crooning. She knew as well as the other what the priest would do. He would examine his conscience, commend himself to God; then he would take a small, leaf-bladed knife, and with it gently sever the baby's head. 'It wasn't the Badlands,' she cried. 'No winds blew from them, the Kites streamed every day. Justin saw to it. He is my loyal son; and she my daughter, grandfather.'

Curt Manning shook his head. 'It may not be,' he said. 'My decision is made.'

The eyes were burning, in her wasted face. 'Then I will leave this house,' she said. 'Barefoot if needs be, no coat to my back. Or die myself, by the same priestly blade. She is my own, old man; nobody takes her from me.'

A silence, that lengthened. Her husband stepped forward, alarmed. He touched her shoulder, and she pulled away. Then she relented, reached to grip his hand. She spoke more quietly. 'Under the Kites we live,' she said. 'Under the Kites she was born. No Dark Thing reached to her; so if she is afflicted, and I do not own she is, then the affliction comes from God. Not from a Demon.'

Silence again; then suddenly the old man lay back. 'No joy will come of it,' he said tiredly. 'Let my words be heard. Let them be written down.'

'No curses, grandfather,' she said. 'Grant me the one boon.'

He closed his eyes. 'So be it,' he said faintly. He waved his hand, in a gesture of dismissal.

Curt Manning died in the autumn of that year; and a great entourage arrived to take him to the dour Variant church that stood apart from the village on a knoll of ground. The cars and traps, the carriages, drove back to the house, passing the silent knots of fieldpeople; and Justin worked with the kitchen staff, circulating through the big old rooms, handing out food and beer. His mother told him afterwards how good he had been; but it hadn't been like that. It was the first death he had known; he hadn't realized what the effect on him would be. It seemed he still heard the old man's deep, slow voice, the rap of his stick as he called to the kitchen to bring him ale. Or for the nurse to come, adjust the pillow behind his head. His shape still occupied the old chair in the morning room; nonexistent, and yet visible. It was many months before it began to fade.

At four years old, Tan suddenly began to walk. Her first efforts were extraordinary; wild, blundering rushes, accompanied by much flailing of her arms. She fell continuously, cutting herself, bruising her face; but once aroused her will seemed indomitable. Always she would get up, stagger on; only to collide with something else, a chair, a table, a wall. She never cried; instead would come the little mewings that were the only sounds she ever made, and that he realized – though he didn't formulate the thought at the time – were expressions of frustration. Or despair. He ran to help a hundred times; but she would shove him away, and her face would flush with rage. This was something she would conquer on her own, or die.

She'd changed by then. Her hair and eyes had darkened, to a wonderful browny-gold. He saw that she was well-named Tan. She was still tiny, almost frail-looking, and for a long time she was insecure. But she rapidly gained in confidence. It almost proved her undoing. Once she fell headlong, from top to bottom of the great main flight of stairs; he rushed to her appalled, but she was already struggling up. She pushed him off, again with her mewing cry. He thought her unhurt; then he saw the blood welling from the long gash on her arm. He carried her to the kitchen despite her struggles, and Cook helped him to bind it. Tan watched the process carefully, making no demur. When they had finished she looked at the bandage, touched it. She turned to him, looked back again at her arm. His heart leaped, because he thought for a moment she was aware; but there was still nothing at the backs of the great eyes. Nothing, at least, that he could understand.

Cook told his mother; and she said how well he'd done. He frowned, staring at the fire. Something he needed to say; but he couldn't find the words. 'I didn't really,' he said. 'She was hurt. I tried to help.' He bit his lip, fell silent. How explain further? The pain he'd felt, seeing the blood stream from her skin, was a new experience to him.

She smiled. 'You're a good boy, Justin,' she said. 'You've learned to look after her so well. Better than I do sometimes. I saw you in the garden yesterday. She'd fallen asleep; and you fixed a sunshade for her. So she wouldn't be burned.'

He looked at the carpet, embarrassed. He hadn't thought anyone had noticed. 'That wasn't anything,' he said. 'You would have done the same. Or father.'

She shook her head. 'Tange wouldn't have thought of it,' she said. 'He's a fine man, I've got so much to thank him for; but he wouldn't have done that.' She smiled again. 'Do you remember how angry you were?' she said. 'When I told you I was pregnant again?'

He frowned. The word was newly-learned; he still felt faintly embarrassed by it. He said, 'I'm sorry. I was only small then.'

She said, 'And now you're a grown-up man.' She saw the hurt in his eyes, saw him tense; and laid a hand quickly on his arm. 'I'm only joking, Jus,' she said. 'A man can take a joke. One day I shall be very proud of you.'

He worked hard at his lessons. It seemed one year blended with the next. The leaves fell, grew again fresh and new; the days lengthened and closed in. There were trips with his father, on business for the farm; to Easthold, the Middle Lands, on one occasion Middlemarch itself. He learned the complex affairs of Mannings; the sowing and harvesting and ploughing, building of ricks and clamps, ordering of cattlecake and seedcorn, the endless accounts and bills. In between he studied; maths and history, what history of the Realm was known, logic, theology. It seemed his brain was a sponge, soaking up knowledge almost despite itself. He realized dimly it was a time that would never come again.

He was sixteen when the revelation finally came. Master Holand, who he'd never cared for overmuch, had been cramming him without mercy. He sat in the morning room, in the big old chair his grandfather once used, and rapped out answers to the dominie as fast as he could fire the questions. In just a week he would travel to Middlemarch, sit his exams for entrance to the Kitecorps College; he was beginning to feel supremely confident of the result.

The door opened, and Tan ran in. She was lithe now, and brown. She wore a dress that left her slim legs bare, and there were flowers in her hair. He guessed her mother had put them there, or one of the maids. She would never have thought of such a thing for herself. She crossed to him, ignoring the dominie. She put her arms round his neck, and kissed. Her lips were frank, and sweet.

He disengaged her, gently. He said, 'Not now, Tan. Go and see Meri. Or find one of the Trandon boys, I bet they're in the cartshed. I'll be finished soon.' He ushered her to the door, closed it. From the corridor came one of her mewing wails.

He rose again instantly, and the dominie looked annoyed. 'Let the wretched child be,' he said. 'I'm tired of hearing her.'

Justin knew his face had darkened. He was quite unable to explain the sudden gust of rage. He looked down. He'd broadened a lot; and he was tall for his age, he all but topped his father. He didn't speak; instead he walked to the door, opened it. He scooped her up, walked back. 'It's all right, Tan,' he said. 'Hush now.' He brushed her cheek with his finger; and she snuggled contentedly.

It was like a burst of light. He thought, 'I love her. And she loves me.' It came as a considerable shock; he wondered why it had taken so long to understand.

He thought about it later, sitting in his room. He hadn't thought himself capable of the emotion; or rather, it had never crossed his mind. He tried to analyze his feelings. Was it because of her beauty? Or because she needed him? Or was it both? He frowned. There was no answer; least, none that he could see. He wished there was someone he could ask. Someone cleverer. Older perhaps. But there was not. His last thought, just before he slept, was strange. Maybe there would be, in Middlemarch.

The Corps ran coaches to the College. One picked up round the southern Salient, passed almost by his door. He could have taken a horse, his father would have loaned him one, and ridden there in style; but he didn't ask. He had no doubt it would be frowned on. Horses were for the gentry; there was propriety to be observed in all things. He was going as a tyro, as a tyro he would arrive. And prosper, the good Lord willing.

He streamed a new Trace, early on the day he left. He thought vaguely it was for himself as well. He watched the Cody critically, as it climbed in the light puffs of breeze. The angle was good; it would fly awhile. He said softly, 'Look after Tan for me.' As ever, the Kites seemed to curtsey an acknowledgement.

He made his farewells to his parents and the housepeople. He saw there had been a reversal of roles; now the tears stood in his mother's eyes. His father too was gruff; but in any case he had few words now. He seemed to have sunk further into himself since the birth of his second child. Justin sometimes vaguely wondered why.

Lastly he ran to find his sister. She was in the little orchard behind the house, sitting on a swing. He whirled her for a while, till she mewed with pleasure. He was sure now he could detect the different meanings in the cries. He stopped the swing finally, knelt on the grass in front of her. 'Tan,' he said, 'I've got to go away.'

She frowned. Joggled hopefully, trying to make him swing her again. He touched her knees, shook gently. 'No, Tan,' he said. 'Please listen.'

At least her eyes returned to his face. Though whether she could actually hear words he'd never quite decided. He said again, 'I've got to go away. I'm going to learn to be a Kiteman. Do you understand?'

She watched him. Then suddenly flung her arms about his neck. She began to sob. He'd never ever heard her cry before.

'Tan,' he said. 'Oh, Tan. Don't make it worse.' He rubbed her back; then gently pushed her away. He took her hands. 'Listen,' he said. 'And try to understand. I've got to go, but it won't be very long. I'm going to Middlemarch. There are trees there and Kites, and a park with a great big lake.' He pointed, over the roof of the house. 'That's a Kite,' he said. 'Only they're bigger, and they fly much higher. You can go right up in the sky. Do you understand?' He shook her again. 'Listen,' he said. 'When I've been to College, and learned to be very clever, and got to be a Captain, I'll take you there as well. I'll buy you lovely clothes, and look after you. That's all I'm going for really. So I shall be able to look after you. And it won't be very long. Will you wait for me? And be good?' Strange words; he wondered why he was saying them at all.

She put her arms round his neck again, and solemnly kissed him.

He stared round, from the basket. Four Traces; higher than he'd ever flown before. The sun was a white-hot ball; he could feel its heat even through the searing of the wind. He looked down. The horizon was clearer now, the dawn mist boiling away. The Badlands showed in stark detail; outcrops of rock, vast scarrings where it seemed the land itself had flowed, frozen into ripples like glass or burning iron. The occasional stunted trees, clinging precariously to life; and far off on the horizon, still cloud-dim, a hitherto-unsuspected range of hills. He worked the tail down-tackle, felt the basket begin to rise again. The movement was all but undetectable; it was only his Kiteman's senses, developed over many years, that told him it was taking place at all.

*

His awareness had seemed sharpened. Tan rode with him, on the coach. He remembered a time she'd pirouetted across the lawn. Spinning and twirling, poising on her toes. He thought he'd never seen anything so lovely. He clapped his hands. She paid no heed; so he clapped again, in front of her face, and finally drew her eyes. 'That's dancing, Tan,' he said. 'It's beautiful. Do it again.' She still paid no attention; so he imitated, clumsily. 'Dancing,' he said. 'Dancing . . .' She'd already lost interest though. Her eyes were blank again; she walked off, back into the house.

Another time he'd tried to take her on a trip. Down to the Easthold, with his father. Tange had hummed and hawed; Justin had realized he was unwilling. He'd persisted, and finally the other had given in. She'd climbed into the motor obediently enough. He sat her on his lap; he'd thought it would please her. Before they reached the main road though she'd begun to writhe, emit the mewing cries. They became more piercing; and his father looked across grimly. 'It's no use, Jus,' he said. 'Not when she's in this mood. I knew it was wrong from the start.' He pulled on to the rough, bumped round in a circle. Headed back the way he had come.

He'd been blackly disappointed. He said, 'What's wrong with her, father? What's *wrong*?' But the other merely shrugged. 'You tell me, son,' he said. 'You see more of her than I do.'

The mood had persisted. That evening though she'd come to sit by his feet. She put her chin in her hands, stared up. She didn't take her eyes off him all night. He'd tried to ignore her at first; finally, he stroked her hair. He couldn't be angry with her. He wondered if she knew it as well.

The Transport slowed for a bend. One of the brakes made a funny little sound. Like a kitten. He wondered where he'd heard it before.

Middlemarch nearly defeated him. His first view of the town took his breath, as it had the time before; the avenues, the buildings, stately lines of houses, palaces of the Masters in their elegant landscaped grounds. The coach was old and ramshackle; but at least its slabsided height gave him a good view. He was decanted with a dozen more into an annexe of the Central College; and then of course the round of fatigues began. He'd thought, with critical exams coming up, they'd be given a breathing space at least; but not a bit of it. He polished and scrubbed with the rest; and slowly the anger built. He realized, or thought he realized, they were testing him; testing his will, to see if he would break. Though there were times when he even doubted that. These Corporals and Lancejacks, jumped-up Orderlies; they seemed to take real pleasure in the infliction of indignity, the handing out of pointless and banal tasks. He bore it nonetheless. He scraped and painted, blackleaded already gleaming stoves, washed windows by the yard; first light till dusk, for the best part of a fortnight. Finally, when he was thoroughly jaded, when everything he'd thought he had by heart had vanished from his mind, they sat him in a hall with half a hundred more. A dour Kitecaptain saw to the issuing of papers, and the examination began. He dashed his answers off with contempt, disinterested in whether he gained admittance or not; and was mortified to see, a week or ten days later, how close he had come to failing. He steadied down – a conscious effort, his temper still tended to get the better of him – and wrote to his folks. To Tan, he sent a line of big red crosses. Knowing she wouldn't understand. He still found the exercise oddly comforting.

The mortification continued. His work was wrong he discovered, from first to last; his maths suspect, his theology gravely wanting. He studied in a species of cold fury, and over the first term his marks began to improve. It was then he received his greatest shock to date. Term breaks existed, he'd been counting off the days; but not for First Years. No let-ups for them; it would be winter before he saw his folks again.

His group protested, in no uncertain terms. Their tutor was unimpressed. 'What?' he said mildly. 'A year in Middlemarch? Folk pay good money for that. You're getting it for nothing.'

Somebody said sullenly, 'It isn't fair.'

'Fair?' said the tutor. 'You'll be telling me life's fair next.' He shook his head. 'So you want to be Kitemen,' he said. 'But you can't stand a semester in the biggest city in the world. How'd you get on with a twelve month posting to the Salient?'

He said abruptly, 'I was born there.'

The other turned to him. 'Then perhaps you'd better go back,' he said. 'Nobody's stopping you. There's just one thing. Don't try to come back here.'

He set his mouth. He didn't understand, they'd none of them understand. Tan wouldn't have expected this. She'd think he'd let her down. Or forget him altogether. But perhaps she had already.

He wished he hadn't had the thought. But it was too late. It was there, and nothing would drive it away. He experienced a time of desolation. He was sure that it was ended, he would leave. He wondered what Curt Manning would have thought.

She came to him in the night, and mewed. She said, '*I haven't forgotten. I shall never forget.*' But that was just the dream.

He opened his eyes. It was still pitch dark. He started to cry. The sobs got louder, he couldn't control them. Later he was appalled. What if they had heard? But the dorm snored on, regardless. Maybe they were used to it.

His other trial came in the second term. He'd worked hard, topped his set in logic and science. Then he encountered Master Atwill.

For the first time, the syllabus included theology. But he'd never heard theology like Master Atwill taught. His questions were illogical, his choice of topics baffling in the extreme. Demons existed; of that there was no doubt. Very well. Granted their reality, could one deny the presence of angels? Excellent. Granted then their co-existence, how big were they? How many might one pile into the basket of a Cody? He suggested various formulae by which an answer could be reached, and left them to it.

He answered, as best he could; yet it was his paper on which the dominie chose to heap his scorn. What, and he a logic First? Come now, an error surely had been made. The little man rubbed his hands. He would take the matter up with the Master Geen, at the first available chance. Meanwhile, would he condescend to try again?

His temper snapped. He said deliberately, 'I know nothing of angels, Master. But I have been flying Codys since I was ten.'

'Flying Codys,' said the other. 'Hmm ...' He looked up, over his little half-spectacles. 'Repeat your statement,' he said.

He sensed another trap. But he was unsure in which direction it lay. He said, 'I've been flying Codys since I was ten.'

'Hmm,' said the other again. He seemed lost in thought. 'Come out here a moment, will you?'

He rose, puzzled. Walked up to the desk. It was placed on a low dais. Master Atwill perused a pile of exercise books. 'Closer,' he said. 'Closer, Mr Manning. A strange thing.'

'What?' he said. He leaned forward, thinking his attention drawn; and the other's fist flashed out. The blow took him in the ear.

It wasn't the force of it; it was little more than a push. It was the unexpectedness. He was off balance; he ended sitting on the floor. The set rocked with laughter, then was suddenly still.

He got up, slowly. He was seeing the world through a thin haze of red. Nobody – not his father, not anyone else – had ever struck him. Not since he had been a tiny child. He took a step forward, fists bunched; then suddenly a strange thing happened. He was icy cold.

'That's better,' said the dominie. He regarded him mildly over his glasses. 'You come here to learn, young man,' he said. 'Not to boast. You may sit down.'

He returned to his place in silence. He should have felt humiliated, less than an inch high; and yet he didn't. An image had come to him, in that frozen moment; Tan, swinging in her little orchard. He felt her arms, almost with physical strength, felt the pressure of her lips. He'd told her once, he was doing it all for her; and he'd forgotten. Now, she'd reminded him.

He walked the town, when he was finally released. Stared at the troops of folk thronging Main Drag and Centre Parade, stared into the bright-lit windows of shops. He bought her a dress; pretty, beribboned, the sort of thing a child would wear in Middlemarch. He'd never done such a thing before;

but again, there was no embarrassment. He discussed her measurements solemnly with the assistant; he found her most helpful. He had it packed, walked on and found a carter who admitted trading with the Salient. He haggled, came to an agreement. He paid the man – the whole transaction would leave him short for a time, but that was of no importance – and wandered back to his dorm. He took supper with the rest, washed his plate and cup with care. Later, after Lights Out, Dav Sollen – one of the few friends he'd made – spoke thoughtfully. 'Why didn't you kill the little runt?' he said. 'I would have.'

He shrugged, in the darkness. He said, 'I'm here to learn the Codys. He doesn't really matter.'

The other didn't speak again; but Justin sensed his bafflement.

The basket was halted again, he assumed for the addition of the fifth trace. At this height even his Kiteman's sense was becoming confused. The shocks and little thrills that normally ran through a cable were absent; also the sag and droop of it, the extra trailing weight, induced strange behaviour in the train. Despite the extra Lifters. The tail-down tackle, semi-automatic, adopted unexpected angles; also a swaying motion had begun, a libration for which he was unable to account. He trimmed the tackle fractionally. The motion eased.

He stared back and down. Far off, in the grey smudge that was G8, keen glasses would be trained. He doubted he was visible at all; he fired a green regardless, and another. Later he detected further movement by the slow creep of the land beneath. He trimmed the tackle again. This time his Kite senses once more aided him. He'd doubted further lift was possible; but he was rising again. Quite fast. He swallowed to equalize pressure. He'd heard it claimed, with all solemnity, that above three hundred feet there was no air to breathe. In that case he was dead; he'd already entered God's realm. It was an eerie place. Round him, above, below, nothing but blue. Blue, and an intense silence; a silence almost of expectancy. He rubbed his face. It was as if the air itself was becoming visible; an azure fluid, seeping to fill the basket, flowing and ebbing through the interstices of its sides. Though that was absurd of course; the defect was in his sight.

He swallowed again. He'd thought, for a whirling instant, he might see God Himself; a great calm figure, seated on His glowing throne. What would he beg Him, from his earthbound speck of a Cody? To turn the clock back by a day? Two hours? It seemed such a little thing to ask, for the world to live again. His world; after all, He'd made it.

He groaned. It wasn't for him, a sinner, to ask favours. Pray then that his crimes be visited on him? 'It was me,' he cried to the empty sky. 'It was me. *Why*...' The punishment had been visited on another. It had been monstrous.

That first year at College was bad. The Corps didn't believe in leaving its Apprentices any illusions. The life of a Kiteman, as his mother had warned, was hard and thankless. A few, the favoured ones, would be posted to Middlemarch itself; there, their duties would be largely ceremonial. Though the spitting and polishing would be awesome. For the rest it would be the Salient, the bleak lands of the Easthold; or the Kiteships of the south, the barren northwest coast. Three weeks or so of journeying, just to reach their Station. He shrugged. He didn't want the Middle Lands, they weren't why he'd joined. The folk were fat and prosperous, their Stations a mere second defence. In case the Salient failed. He no longer cared where he was posted. After all, his job was to fly the Codys. Nothing more. He gave no further thought to quitting; though many of his fellows did in fact give up. Even his hatred of Atwill ebbed in time, settled to a cold and steady contempt. The little man didn't brave him again; though had he done so the result would have been the same. To strike a dominie, even to raise a hand, was instant dismissal. It would take more than Atwill to destroy what he had planned.

There were girls of course, girls in plenty; the bright cloaks of the Apprentices drew them like moths to candles. Though for his part he could never see what they hoped to gain. He was hard-put to make ends meet; and the bulk of the students were much worse off than he. He sampled the high life occasionally, when his allowance had come through; worked the city centre pubs with Dav, sometimes the others. But after the first experiments it seemed his interest waned. See one of the squawking creatures and you'd seen them all. He'd have liked to say there was nothing behind their eyes; but there was far too much. Dav pulled his leg a bit, once chided outright; but Justin merely smiled. He bought a pair of summer sandals for Tan; tiny white things, held by a single strap between the toes. Despatched them by the carrier.

A letter came from home; an ill-spelled note from of all people, Aniken. They'd had a storm; three Kitestruts had been snapped, he was running short of spares. Also the fabric of the Lifters stood in need of repair, he urgently needed more. '*Bleu*,' he suggested, or '*grin*.' Nearest supply was in Easthope, two day's journey away; and at this time of year no-one could be spared for the ride.

Tange had increased his allowance; he had more than enough for present needs. He bought the supplies on Main, in the big shop that catered for the College; and the carter was pressed into service again. '*Keep the Trace flying, Ani*,' he wrote. '*As you love Mannings, and me, never let it fail. May God bless everyone; but most of all, may He bless you ...*'

His mother's letter he opened with more care. '*All is well*,' she had written. '*Mannings looks lovely now. The crops are good, the best I've ever known. We shall get fat, this wintertide.*

'Tan is growing fast. When you come home you'll hardly recognize her. She's very brown. She should be; she spends all day in the garden. Except when it rains of course. She'd even go out then, we have to stop her. She made a fuss at first; but she's much better now. It's just as well, because she's got so strong. I can hardly hold her any more. When she's naughty, I tell her you'll be cross. I read your letters to her, and say your name. Over and over. It always quietens her; I'm sure she understands.

'It's strange, but she spends most of her time in the orchard. Where you left her that last day. I'm sure she thinks if she waits, you'll come back to her there.

'Thank you for sending the shoes. She hasn't worn them yet, though she keeps them in her room. She won't wear shoes any more, she hasn't since you left. Father Andri says it's a sort of penance; but I don't know.

'He's come round a lot. You know he wanted to take her when your grandfather Condemned her. But he visits regularly now to see that she's all right. I think everyone loves her. I'd like to think Grandfather would too, if he could see her now. She'll be a beautiful woman one day.

'Keep well my dear, and all my love. I'm sending you some warm things by the carrier. You'll need them, with the winter coming on. I know Main Drag in leaf-fall; only too well . . .'

She didn't mention the dress.

Autumn was another trying time. After the Air Show, the lure of the great Kites redoubled; but no First Year would ever touch a Cody. Or even be allowed nearby. Instead he was seconded for duty in Godpath, the great Cathedral of the Variants. He spent his days in purple-carpeted gloom, serving at the altar, swinging a censer while they chanted the endless prayers. At first, bored, he would allow his attention to wander; float in the clouds, at the end of a mighty Trace. It took several cuffs from the Master of Novices – himself a one-time Flier, and no man to be trifled with – to remind him of his duties. Later, there were compensations to the humdrum days. As he learned its secrets, the building came to intrigue him. The endless dim-lit corridors, the shuffling monks that thronged them; the plaques and statuary, busts of old Fliers draped with more purple for the Festival to come; the lines of lancet windows admitting their dull, rich light. The great East Window in particular fascinated. It showed Cody rigs, train after train of them in complex, crossing patterns. They flew above a town, or city, that had surely never existed; plain square buildings, flat-roofed, jumbled on a hillside. Beyond were towers, topped by curious domes; onion-shaped, and pointed. Above them, the sky was a rich and jewel-like blue. Master Anton assured him there had indeed been such a place; in the Old Time, before the Demons came. But its name had been forgotten.

The Demons were his study subject now; their habits, their natures, their infinite maliciousness. He'd learned the Litany of course, as a good Variant child; here though were complexities undreamed of. The bodies of some were striped, he learned, others were chequered. Some were blind; others had eyes in their foreheads, many eyes, and spinning brains behind them bent on death. Some swam wholly beneath water, striking at ships. The wounds they made tore outwards, in some way he couldn't grasp, so that their victims sank swiftly. Some spawned in midair, tearing themselves apart; the children they released in swarms were deadly too. There had even once on a time been friendly Demons, whose very glance would eat up all the others; but the art of controlling them had been lost. Justin wrestled with the complexities; but for each fact learned there seemed to be half a hundred more. He committed it all to memory, grimly, as he had committed the rest; and his winter paper earned top marks in his intake. It even carried a prize; a model of a Cody rig in silver and gold, flying from a base of polished wood. There was a plaque, inscribed with the names of winners from previous years. He could keep it for a twelvemonth; after which his name would be added to the list, and it would be awarded to another. He asked to be allowed to take it home with him for the holiday, and permission was granted. He packed the tiny thing with care, locked it away.

The last week was one of continual services, dawn to dusk. He'd discovered a fairly pleasant tenor voice. He'd never make a soloist or cantor; but it passed muster well enough with the rest. He sang in the clerestory choir; at least it saved him from the chore of incense-swinging.

Candles were lit, for the last service of all; Godpath discovered a new, ethereal beauty. Then it was over, and the drudgery of the first year finally ended. Next term he would start his proper training. A bus had been laid on, thirteen hundred tomorrow; in just a day he would see Mannings again. His parents, the staff, old Ani. He would see Tan. The rush of feeling the thought brought in its train left him nearly giddy.

He felt giddier later. He drank wine, with Dav Sollen and a dozen more, in one of the city centre taverns; legally at last, though they'd drunk wine enough through the year. They smuggled it into the dorms for late night parties; the practice was known to go on, but it was generally winked at. Unless of course there was too much noise, or a boy was late on parade, or a tunic button was dirty; then, all Hell would break loose. He'd thought odd times a full scale visitation of Demons could scarcely have been worse. Tonight was different though. This one night of the year, there were no rules.

He left the others carousing finally, slipped away. He had his packing to finish; and he wanted a clear head for the morning. He laid out his parade tunic and slacks, buffed shoes that already gleamed; by that time the rest of the dorm had begun to drift, or stagger, in. The talk was desultory, soon ended; after a very few minutes the place resounded with snores.

He had one surprise. After refectory next morning. He bumped into

Master Atwill. He bowed, as the rules of the place dictated, stepped to one side; but the other also stopped. He regarded Justin brightly, head on one side. 'Ah, Manning,' he said. 'You've worked and studied well. I've made a good report on you to the Master Devine; and I have seen your other assessments. They are uniformly excellent. Congratulations.'

He inclined his head again. He said formally, 'Thank you, Master.' He wondered what the other could be getting at. There was something else, he was sure.

Atwill was still watching him thoughtfully. He said, 'There are some things I would like to discuss with you. Can you spare me a few minutes of your time?'

He havered. He half-glanced at the big clock on the corridor wall; and the dominie smiled. 'Your Transport is not for three hours,' he said. He touched Justin's arm. 'Come,' he said. 'I shan't keep you long.'

He followed, wondering. The little Master led the way out of the College, stepping briskly. They emerged into bright winter sunlight. Atwill turned right and left, into Main Drag, crossed the wide road in front of Godpath. Beside it stood a smaller building; squarish, and as plain as Godpath was ornate. The Church of the Moving Clouds.

He hesitated again. He'd known for a long time of course that Atwill was of the Middle Doctrine; but he'd never set foot in one of their places of worship. Though his mother had told him a little, his father had always been strict Variant; and he was nothing if not loyal. But the other urged him, still with a faint smile. 'Come,' he said. 'You are not here to pray.' He led the way. Inside the big street door was another, lined with thick green cloth. He stepped through. It swished to gently behind him.

The inside of the place was as spartan as the exterior. No statuary, no inscriptions; just limewashed walls, relieved at intervals by the slim grey shafts of pillars. Only in the roof was there complexity; curved wooden beams supported others that rose in tiers below the high gable. The glass too was plain; lamps burned here and there in coloured bowls, although the day was bright. In the pews were scattered groups of people, heads bent in meditation. He saw Brothers of the Order, some of the female priests that only the Middle Doctrine allowed. He frowned, would have spoken; but the dominie touched his arm again. He said, 'Come with me.'

He led the way quietly, down a side aisle, toward the rear of the place. He pushed open another door. He said, 'My little hidey-hole. A sanctum the Brothers allow me to maintain. I sometimes think it preserves my sanity.'

Justin looked round. He saw a desk and chair, a bunk bed, a leather-padded easy. Above the desk hung a complex model; a six lift Cody rig, in flight. The other followed the direction of his glance and nodded. 'Yes,' he said. 'I had my dreams too, once. I wanted to be a Flier. But I was never thought robust enough. I was prone to a nervous disability, a stammer I later managed to cure; and my eyesight was too weak. In short, I was a failure; you will achieve what I could not.' He crossed to a wall cupboard, took down a decanter and glasses. He said. 'Wine?'

He nodded, wondering. He said, 'Thank you, Master.'

'Be seated,' said the old man. 'Be at ease.' He handed one of the glasses to him. Justin took it. Delicately cut crystal. The wine inside, a Middle Lands vintage, seemed to glow with its own yellow fire.

Atwill scotched down at the desk. Flicked his cloak across his knees. He said, 'This will perhaps sound unusual. But I feel I owe you an explanation. Maybe even an apology.'

He looked up, sharply. He said, 'That is not necessary, Master.'

'I think it is,' said the dominie. He pursed his lips. 'I have seen many Apprentices come and go,' he said, 'I know their minds; to a certain extent, their dreams. I knew your father, many years ago; and your mother, when she came to Middlemarch. She was a member of this congregation.' He shook his head. 'We take the Middle Way,' he said. 'Punishment forms no part of our doctrine. Though we can be stern when occasion demands.' He smiled, fleetingly. 'As stern as our brothers of Godpath. Sometimes I think sterner.' He swirled the wine in his glass. 'A building is a concept,' he said. 'To decorate it with spire and pinnacles, to grace it with rich fabrics and many-coloured glass; that is to make it gorgeous to the eye. But to say, "This is a roof," and, "These are walls. This is a doorway; these are windows, by which light may enter." I sometimes wonder if that does not take more courage.'

Atwill set the glass down. 'It was necessary,' he said. 'Not as a corrective, but to focus your attention. You had become complacent; from complacency springs arrogance. You had embellished a simple fact – your desire to be a Flier – with figures of your own conceit. And so your mind had wandered and become vague; although at the time you were unaware of it. You would have failed.'

He picked the glass up, sipped. 'By the mercy of the Lord, I was saved from your anger,' he said. 'For which I thank Him. I am in no sense a brave man. You were saved from the ruination of your life; by self denial, and your own intelligence. That very moment, my hopes for you began. Now you must go on. There will be distractions; tragedies perhaps, disasters. You must see them for what they are, and not allow yourself to become diverted again. That way you will perhaps become a fine Flier. As fine as the Master Canwen; who can say?' He considered again. 'Who is the girl,' he said, 'who so fills your waking thoughts?'

Justin jerked, startled. All but dropped the glass. For a moment he couldn't speak; he was almost sure his jaw had sagged. Then, quickly, anger flared. So they rifled student lockers. He'd thought better of the College.

It seemed Atwill read his mind. He raised a hand, gently. 'No,' he said. 'Your privacy has been respected. The Corps does not employ spies.'

He said slowly, 'Then how did you know?'

The other said simply, 'Because I saw her, reflected in your eyes. I saw her on the day of the rebuke. I think her hands reached out, to comfort you.'

He said impulsively, 'It's not as you think, Master. It's not like that at all.'

'Nothing is quite as one thinks,' said the dominie. 'No life is like the next. Even the lives of the dullest people have secrets.' He drank again. He said, 'Would you like to tell me about her?'

He hesitated; then it all came, with a rush. How his mother had saved her from the knife; how she'd grown and changed, how she'd become a person. Real, somehow, to him; more real than the five-sensed folk who talked and prattled everywhere. Atwill heard him through, not interrupting; when he finally stopped, he smiled. 'There is much love in you, Justin,' he said. 'And it is strong and true. But be counselled by me. All things have their other side; as a coin must bear two faces. And if one of those is bright, the other must needs be dark. There must be night; else how could we know the splendour of the day? There must be winter; or how could we cleave to the spring? This is a belief we hold, that the Variants abhor.

'Go to your little girl, who I've no doubt loves you too. Though she cannot in our terms express that love. She is a child in a cage; a cage not of her making, but the Lord's. Why these things must be, we cannot tell; nor may we question His will. Once, He allowed Demons to punish all the world. Another Mystery; the answer lies beyond our little understandings. Go to her, pour out your love; it does you naught but credit. Stint not, nor fear; for love, true love, is the only well that never can be drained. But at the same time, tread with caution. There are pits in every pathway; this pathway most of all. They are deep; and their bottoms are cruel-lined with spikes.'

He frowned. He said, 'What are they, Master? These pits?'

The other shook his head. 'That I cannot tell,' he said. 'It is not given to me to know the future. Any more than to you.'

There was more. The dominie talked of his own young life, in the Middle Lands. His Ordination, his first ministry; a mission for seamen, far off in the Southguard. He questioned Justin about the farm; its running, maintenance, the number of servants and field folk it employed. Justin tended to lose track of time. He felt wholly at rest; more at rest than he'd been in years. He realized for the first time in his life he'd talked about the matters closest to his heart; and in the process he had made a friend.

The little man rose finally. 'Consider this refuge yours as well,' he said. 'When things become too much. As they sometimes do for us all. I make no claim to wisdom; but a sympathetic listener is perhaps worth more. Talking, we hold a mirror to ourselves; discover our own natures.' He held his hand out. 'Go with God,' he said. 'Tread boldly, but with care. Remember we must all walk down a street; but every street has sides. We may choose the sunshine, or the shadows.'

Justin felt his eyes sting, suddenly. He dropped to his knees. 'It's I who must apologize to you,' he said. 'Give me your blessing, Master.'

The dominie laid a hand lightly on his head. 'You have it already,' he said. 'It has never been withheld.' He gripped his arm, gently. 'Come, Justin,' he said. 'Your friends will all be waiting.'

The restlessness returned, on the long coach journey home. The others laughed and chattered, roared out bawdy songs, engaged in rumbustious games of cards. He sat apart, turning over in his mind what the dominie had said. Was it then possible to decorate a concept? Pile spires and pinnacles on it, till it towered in the mind as Godpath towered over Middlemarch? And a simple, obvious truth was lost? There seemed to be some relevance to him; to his feelings for Mannings, for the Kites. For Tan. But the link, if link there was, eluded him. He grappled with the notion; but try as he might, it endlessly slipped away.

The Transport, even older than the one on which he had arrived, wheezed and rattled, pulled in time after time to cool its overheated engine. Night had fallen long before he reached the Salient; and still two hours to run. His mind outpaced the ancient vehicle, time and again; seeing the old house decked with solstice greenery, hearing the chattering and laughter, seeing the blazing hearths, the great range sizzling in the stone-flagged kitchen. Cook would be bellowing instructions, ordering this, countermanding that, setting the parlourmaids and spitboys scampering; rolling out pastries with her sturdy, powerful hands, setting the puddings boiling, drawing the trays out golden and smoking from the stoves. And old Ani swearing under his breath, staggering in with the baskets of logs, almost certainly a little the worse for wear. He had his own private liquor store in the house, he'd had it for years; the raw spirit brewed in the local villages, that only he could drink. Justin's mother knew about it he was sure, probably his father too; but nothing had ever been said. Nor would it be. He was their oldest and most loyal retainer; he had served them well, and his father's folk before that. Ani would never change.

He debussed finally, waved to the few Apprentices remaining. He hefted his duffel bag, set out to walk the two miles to the farm. A hundred yards on he was hailed. He stopped, made out the dim shape of a pony and trap. He said uncertainly, 'Ani?'

He scrambled up. He said, 'It's good to see you, Ani. Have you been waiting long?'

'Not long, Master,' said the old man; but he was blowing his hands with the cold.

'You are a fool,' he said. 'You could have caught your death. Then where would we have been?' He leaned to light the sidelamps. 'Move across,' he said. 'Get yourself under a rug. I'll drive.' He grinned. 'Best get that bottle out as well. I'll join you.'

The other hesitated, then groped under the seat. He took a swig, wiped the neck and handed it across. For once Justin took a mouthful. It was even more vile than he remembered. He managed not to spit it out, swallowed it somehow. It left his mouth and throat feeling they were on fire. 'Good stuff,' he said, when he could get his breath. Later though the warmth spread stealthily right through him.

He thought his mother looked frailer than before; though she greeted him happily enough. His father too was greying; it was as if much more than a year had passed. There was awkwardness for a while; then Tange fetched drinks, set bottles and glasses on the table. The gesture was a silent one; but it warmed him as the spirit had done. It meant, subtly, that he'd matured; now, he could drink like a man. He knew his progress had been reported to them; and that they were pleased. Later he fetched the trophy from his pack, set it on the sideboard. His mother touched it, wonderingly. She said, 'What a beautiful thing.'

Tan was the only disappointment. He ran to her, when she walked into the room. He would have hugged her; he tried to take her hands, but she snatched them back. Her eyes were dead, expressionless. She stared as if she looked right through him; as if he were glass, invisible. He experienced a moment of desolation. 'Tan,' he said. 'Tan, please ...'

Mav touched his arm, gently. 'Leave her,' she said. 'She'll come round; but it will take a little time.' She smiled. 'Come and sit down,' she said. 'Tell me about College.'

The girl walked away. She sat in the far corner of the room, her back turned to him. He saw she wore no shoes. The words of Master Atwill, still so fresh, came back with doubled force. '*There are pits. They are deep; and their bottoms cruel-lined with spikes* ...' He said, 'Did she like the dress I sent?'

Mav glanced at his father, set her lips. 'She tore it,' she said. 'I did my best; but it will never be the same.' She touched his wrist. 'Don't blame her,' she said. 'She was very upset.'

'I don't blame her,' he said. 'I don't blame her at all.'

He sat with Tange until the early hours, discussing this and that; his schooling, Middlemarch, the running of the farm. The executors had finally agreed to the erection of two of the new-fangled silos; the senior Manning hoped to ensile for neighbouring farms as well, sell to the millers in bulk. It would be a handy source of extra income. Also he had at long last bought a tractor. Elderly perhaps, and a little decrepit; but a tractor nonetheless, something he'd set his heart on years ago. It seemed the lawyers had finally relented a little; but so they should of course, the profits from last year alone would more than cover the outlay. Ani had complained loud and long at its arrival, and still took every opportunity to revile these modern methods; but it had become his secret pride and joy. Nobody could handle it as he could; he'd talk to it on cold mornings like a recalcitrant horse, and somehow it always started. Tange smiled, poured more of the Middle Lands brandy. He touched on the possibility of increasing Justin's allowance, but he shook his head. 'I can get by,' he said. 'You've done enough already. Wait till I've earned it.'

He got to bed eventually; lay and tossed for a while and thought about Tan. He slept finally, only to be haunted by dreams. She came to him, with her little mewing cries; knelt before him, tried to kiss his hands. The image shocked him; he jerked awake, saw grey light was already in the room. He rose hastily, began to dress.

His first act was to climb to the roof, check the Godkite and its Lifters. He drew the String – easier now than for the child who had first flown it – but the Cody was in fine shape. He streamed it again, stared round him in the biting wind. He saw the tractor move far-off across a dark hogback of land; a gaunt, skeletal machine, Ani perched on high like a well-muffled doll. Justin examined it later in the shed, admiring the massive frame, the great rear wheels with their spiked iron rims. Ani shrugged, said it was all right for them as liked new ways; but he grinned. The brightwork, what little it possessed, was gleaming; and the engine had that sleek, well cared-for look that only constant attention will achieve. The old man was in his element.

Tan took a week to forgive him. He ignored her, following Mav's advice, though it was a constant pain to do so. Finally, her mood changed. She ran to him; he heard the mewing again. She glanced down, drawing his attention; and he saw she was wearing the shoes he'd sent. The summer sandals, with their pretty thongs. Absurd of course, on an icy winter day; but not for worlds would he have tried to make her change them. He hugged her and she cried, dabbing her eyes. He saw she'd learned to blow her nose as well. She did it clumsily, left a wet smear on her lip. He wiped it for her, gently. At least the effort was there. She sat by him afterwards, her hands in her lap. He knew her eyes were seeing him again. 'Tan,' he said, 'I've got to back to College. Not yet, but in a little while. I'm learning to fly the Kites. The Codys, like we have on the roof. Do you understand?'

No response.

'The Kites,' he said. 'The Kites that keep us safe. The Codys.' He crossed to the sideboard, picked the trophy up. 'These,' he said.

She mewed. For a moment he feared she would snatch at it, but the hand she extended was gentle. She touched it with a finger, as she touched everything that interested her. Stroked the slender golden Trace, the spread wings of the Lifters. She mewed again, it seemed with pleasure.

He returned the prize to its place of safety. He sat down, took her hands. 'Tan,' he said, 'you must promise. You mustn't be unhappy again. Because this time I shan't be long. We get term breaks now, do you understand? It's only the first year you have to stay away.'

She looked worried; and he rubbed her fingers. Raised them gently, and kissed. 'You understand,' he said. He stared into the blank, lovely eyes. They were tilted, almond-shaped, the lashes long and dark. 'What do you think about, Tan?' he said. 'What goes on, inside you?' The worry increased; and he hugged her instantly, laughing. 'It doesn't matter,' he said. 'Because you're Tan; and I love you. At least you know that much. I sometimes wonder if the rest matters anyway.' Later, in the quiet of his room, he shook his head. The answer had made itself; perhaps it had always been there. It didn't matter. Nothing else mattered at all.

She sat with him at dinner, refused to be parted again. Later she curled up by him, on the settle. Snuggled. He let her. It was good to feel the closeness of her again, even to smell her. The freshness of her linen, faint scent of her hair. She was clean, clean as one of the cats that sat blinking sleepily by the hearth. Though there had been a time when the reverse was true. He'd taught her patiently, over the years; by persuasion, by example. He'd taught her the use of a potty, later the privy. Blushing furiously, hating himself, biting his lip till it bled. And that was something not even his mother knew. It had been a desperate, last-ditch attempt. But he'd persevered. Because it seemed wrong; wrong that she lived in worse state than an animal. She who was so beautiful. He'd come close to despair; then suddenly, when hope had all but gone, she'd understood. And life for the household had changed. It had changed for him.

He looked up, caught his mother's eyes. She was smiling. She knew how much he'd done for Tan. Most of it anyway. Maybe she'd even guessed the rest.

The Rig was stationary again, in its world of biting blue. A part of him realized he was chilled to the bone. It didn't seem to matter.

Strange that he was still tethered to G8. Almost impossible to believe it any more. There was no Kitestation, no Salient. No Earth. He brought his mind to bear, with difficulty. Down there, in that world he had left for ever, he knew what they would be doing. The line clamped off, over the great drum; and the derrick chuffing, lifting the last spool into place. The Riggingmaster would be waiting, to fix the final splice; and the Launchman standing anxious, gauntleted hand to the cable, feeling the throb and thrill. The tension. They'd have doubled up the anchors; because with that weight aloft there was a chance the Trace could drag even a Launch Truck. A chance, but that was all; none of them could tell. Because nobody, not the Rigging-master, not the oldest hand on Base, had ever flown such a string. Nor would they again.

He frowned. Because climb as he might, he could not escape. The link, though tenuous, was real. Soon, the last cable streamed, they would begin to draw him down. To the world he knew he could no longer bear. If orders didn't reach them before. He glanced above him, to the Trace. He could sever it, sail off into the blue for ever. The cutters were there, part of the emergency gear every Cody carried. He shook his head. That wasn't the way. Do that, and every man on Base would feel the consequences; because the enquiries would be endless. He'd no intention of allowing the innocent to suffer; there'd been enough of that already. He lowered his eyes to the horizon. There were other heights beyond the first. Mountains, infinitely distant; like pale holes knocked in the sky. He thought he saw on one the gleam of snow. He thought how she would have liked them.

He shook his head again. He knew, with a strange certainty, that he would not return. One of Master Atwill's pits would open; but it would reach upward. Into the sun.

Clouds were sailing. The puffy white clouds of summer. One passed around him; the others floated beneath. When the sky cleared; the Rig was rising again.

He experienced a hope, as faint as it was fleeting. Maybe the air would thin, eventually. He would sleep then. Sleep, and not wake up. He knew in his heart though, that was not going to happen.

The Lifters pulled steadily, climbing even higher.

That holiday, the first, had passed swiftly. Far too swiftly for his liking. It seemed impossible; but the last morning arrived, and the packing of his bags. He folded the new clothes carefully, the clothes they'd given him, stowed them in the duffel. Then it was goodbye time; and Ani waiting with the trap, to take him to the Transport. He made his farewells quickly, kissed Mav, shook his father's hand. Lastly he turned to Tan. She was standing empty-faced, still wearing the shoes. She hugged him. He kissed her, and was startled. She opened her mouth as wide as it would go, pushed her tongue between his teeth. He stepped back instantly. 'Tan,' he said, 'that's wrong. It's very naughty. You must never do it again.' She stared at him, uncomprehending; and he took her shoulders. 'Tan,' he said, 'do you remember what I told you? You mustn't be unhappy. It upsets Mummy and Daddy. I shan't be away long. Not this time. I shall come back to see you as soon as I ever can.' He kissed her again, trying to be gentle; but that was one lesson she would never learn. He shook his head, and turned away. As he walked through the doors, she deliberately kicked off her shoes.

He reflected wryly, as the coach rolled west, that any Middle Lands tart could learn from his kid sister. But what they learned they could never put into effect. One cannot copy innocence; either it exists, or it is gone.

The year that followed was bad. The worst, he decided, of his life. Spring term was bearable, even enjoyable in parts; but early in the summer came horrendous news. He slit the flap of the envelope with foreboding, recognizing his father's hand. Tange Manning was a reluctant correspondent; it was a serious matter that could induce him to put pen to paper.

There had been an accident, at Mannings. The tractor had run away; and Aniken, who'd served it well and loyally, had been its victim. Nobody seemed too sure how it had happened. The headland had been steep, the brake had failed; or maybe the old man, for the first and only time, had neglected to set it properly. He'd been in front; and he had had no chance.

Justin applied for, and was granted, compassion leave. He made the long haul back once more. It bit into his savings; the trip was unofficial, the College made him pay. His father reimbursed him. For once he accepted the gift.

He talked to a fieldman who'd seen it happen. Seen it, but been helpless to intervene. The front wheels veered evilly, caught in a rut; so one of the great spiked rims … The body had been whirled, he said. Again and again. Under the high mudguard, passing back to earth. Till the machine had come to rest, a hundred yards away. Displaying its trophy for all the world to see. It had been sold for scrap, and what was left of Ani buried; but the farm would never be the same again.

He walked, past the big shiny silos. He stared up at them. The sunlight reflected from their silver sides. He was confused; appalled at the shortness of life, its inconsequentiality. He wondered why they flew the Codys; day after day, night after night, year after year. What were they protecting? A fragileness, that was doomed as it was born.

Tan came to him shyly, took his hand. He touched her cheek with one finger. 'I'm protecting you, Tan,' he said. 'Do you understand? You're all that matters. I don't know why; but there isn't anything else.' She mewed, and pressed herself to him.

He talked to his father, late that night. 'I don't know,' he said. 'I haven't graduated; but I think I've lost my faith already.'

The other took his time about answering. Just as his grandfather had done. 'You're not thinking straight, Just,' he said finally. 'He was an old man. He'd had his life; a good one. And it was quick; I don't suppose he knew a thing about it. Better than lying for years, wasting away from some disease or other. You know him; he'd have preferred it the way it was.'

Justin shook his head. 'It isn't that,' he said. 'He loved that damned machine. Kept it going when nobody else would have bothered. And see what it did to him.'

His father poured more of the rich, dark brandy. 'You think it knew what it was doing then?' he said. 'You believe that machines are alive?'

He looked up under his brows. Recognized the trap, and refused to be drawn. 'All I shall ever do is fly big Kites,' he said. 'You can't help questioning, sometimes.'

The other didn't answer.

'It's pointless,' he said irritably. 'I'll come and work the farm. Work for you. It's what you always wanted anyway.'

Tange sipped the brandy, carefully. Set the glass down. 'Listen,' he said. 'I'm going to tell you something you don't know. Remember that day you streamed the Cody? The first day of all?'

He put his hands round the glass. He said, 'I was a little child.'

'That's not the point,' said his father. He leaned forward. 'The midwife saw the Trace through the bedroom window,' he said. 'She raised Mav to look. She told me later she'd just about given up hope. It was all it needed. Her faith is very strong.'

He looked up again, sharply. 'But she screamed,' he said. 'I heard it. She screamed ...'

'She screamed because it was over,' said Tange Manning. 'It happens like that sometimes.' He looked down at the table. 'I don't want to get drawn in,' he said. 'I know as much theology as you could write on the head of a pin. But if you hadn't flown that Trace, I wouldn't have a wife. And you wouldn't have Tan.' He reached across, gripped his arm briefly. 'She's all right, Justin,' he said. 'She understands. I don't know how, but she understands. And you've gone too far to pull out now. Go and fly your Kites.'

Only he wasn't flying Kites. That magic was still to come. He was learning the intricacies of the Launchers, spending long days in the classroom, others elbow-deep in blackened grease. Crossheads and cylinder cocks, water lifts and steam outlets, valve chests, differentials. His notebooks filled, became a half-inch thick apiece; and still there was more to know. Some nights he got to bed dog-tired; but he was grateful for that. It took his mind from a careering tractor, a tattered body whirled on a great wheel.

The other news came the day before he was due to break up for summer. Brought by a Variant policeman. The black-edged envelope had arrived by special courier; so he knew the worst had happened. He read it, uncomprehending. Then again. Mav Manning had passed away; peacefully, in her sleep. Her health had been failing for months; years probably, though she'd never complained. In its way, it had been a merciful release.

No chance of transport, so near end of term. He had to wait for the morning. He went to Middle Park, sat staring at the lake, the big stands round the Air Show ground. He flicked stones at the water. And thought of nothing at all.

Dav Sollen found him. He squatted beside him for a while, not speaking. Then he said, 'Come and have a drink.'

'No, thanks,' said Justin. His mind was far away. Now, if ever, he needed Master Atwill. But the old man had retired last term, on a sudden whim. Gone to the little cottage he'd bought, in Southguard. Where he could see the sea. 'I'll be okay,' he said.

The other put a hand on his arm. 'You won't,' he said. 'It's all right, I shan't talk. I shan't say a word.' So he'd gone with him, sat in a pub off Landy Street, listened to the din; watched the tarts working the leavemen, barmaidens circling with their trays of wine. Later, as he'd lain sleepless, one horrendous thought had come. He tried to block it; but it was useless, it was already there. As he read the letter, his heart had given a bound. He'd thought it might be Tan.

She came with him, to the funeral. She wore a summer dress; white, with embroidery of roses and pretty leaves. And the white sandals. He'd tried at the last minute to persuade her into something more suitable; but she'd begun to squall and cry. And so he'd let her be. She clung to his arm, stared down at the raw hole in the earth. He wondered if she understood. She mewed once, and pointed. But it wasn't at the grave; it was a Cody rig, rising tiny above a distant line of hills.

The summer was long, and hot. He studied the books he'd brought home with him, talked to Tan. Played with her; for sometimes she would play. Once she threw a ball to him, for nearly a whole hour. Her aim wasn't very good; but he sensed she was trying hard. Was it to make up? Usually though she sat and watched him solemnly. And sucked her thumb.

Her favourite place was still the little orchard. She'd swing there half the day, she never seemed to tire. Once she mewed, and took her shoes off; he looked alarmed, and she smiled. She put them back on.

His father engaged a full time nurse for her. She seemed pleasant enough; a bustling, homely woman from the village, widow of one of his tenants. Tan seemed to like her, as far as he could tell; which was the most important thing. Mav, of course, would always be a part of him; but his concern now was for the living. He sensed that she agreed. She came to him one night, and blessed him. He had heard of such things before.

He flew, and graduated. Looking down from the swaying basket, his sole thoughts were of Tan. He wondered if she'd like to ride a Cody. He forgot to be afraid; but he didn't forget his drill.

He wrote to Master Atwill, telling him the news. He felt he already knew what the old man would say. '*A coin must bear two faces. And if one of them is bright, the other must needs be dark. There must be night; else how could we know the splendour of the day?*' He wasn't far wrong.

He put the letter down, smiling. Tan was the day, to him; the dark had gone.

He received his first posting. As he'd feared, it was to the far northwest. A six month tour. He wrote a long letter to his father, another to be read to Tan. Stupid perhaps; but she would know it was from him. He sent her clothes, even a picture book. Horses and ships, the lazy Middle Lands cattle. She kept it in her room, even learned to turn the pages; but she never understood it. As often as not, she would hold it upside down.

The years passed. One day he realized with a shock she was sixteen. He'd made Lancejack a long time back, then Corporal; served his time on the Southguard ships, done a tour of the Easthold. He'd been faced with a choice then. Go for full Flier status, or switch to Ground Duties. Sergeant, then try for his commission.

Once, the decision would have been easy. Now, it wasn't. He talked it over with his skipper, a grizzled Major on the point of retiring. He'd seen too many good men lost in his time; to squalls, to fatigued rigs, to Groundcrew error. The sky was a dangerous place to be. Even Dav Sollen came a cropper, high over the Salient. Smashed a leg so badly it had taken months to heal; there was still some doubt if he would continue in the service.

The Major agreed. 'It's a young man's game,' he said, pulling at a tankard of beer. 'We can't all be Canwen …' So the choice was made. Justin hadn't told the other the whole truth though. Tugging the other way, and mewing, had been a slender, bronze-haired wraith. Tan needed him; and she had won.

Always, during and between his tours, he'd taken every chance to travel back to Mannings. Always, the big house welcomed him; it was still his home. He'd sit with Tange far into the night; puff his pipe and sip his brandy, pore over the books. Father Andri would visit or the local medic, bigwigs sometimes from the Easthold, the Middle Lands. Always, Tan would be there. Suggestions were made of course, insinuations that her presence was less than helpful to the smooth transaction of business; but that was just too bad. Try to shut her out and she'd mew and kick. And that he would not bide. So Tange gave in; and the rest could take their choice.

She ran to him wailing, when he came from Easthold. Tugged his arm in distress. 'Tan,' he said, 'what is it? You can tell me. Tell me now …' She wouldn't though; just pulled him even harder. He gave in, followed her. He knew, with a strange certainty, where she'd head. Toward the orchard. 'All right,' he said. 'What is it?'

She mewed, glared right and left. Grabbed her frock hem, hauled it to her waist.

He stared. Then he slowly shook his head. 'Poor little creature,' he said. 'So it's only just happened. It took you a long time to walk as well.' He pushed her shoulders gently, made her sit on the swing. 'Tan,' he said, 'it's not your fault, you haven't done anything wrong. It happens all the while, to everyone.' He fetched towels, a bowl. He cleaned her, gently; showed her what she had to do next time. 'Change dress,' he said. He gestured. 'Change your dress. Then we can go out. Would you like to go out?'

She smiled. She was comfortable again, and reassured. She flitted into the house.

He sat on the swing himself. Pushed with his toes, made it move in little arcs. He thought, not for the first time, that it was a strange relationship. It wasn't really though. Things like that don't matter. Because love is a bottomless well.

They strolled nearly to the village. On the way he gathered posies for her; buttercups and scabious, dandelions with shaggy sunburst heads. She didn't seem interested; so he threw them away again. 'I agree,' he said. 'They're not half as lovely as you.'

His father was away, on business in the Easthold. He sat her in the study, fetched her food. May cakes – she seemed to prefer them to anything else, though he'd always found them dry – a carafe of Cook's rich, biting lemonade. Later he shook his head. 'You poor little creature,' he said again. 'They thought you couldn't understand. Even Mother, sometimes. She was wrong though. You were so afraid, you daren't even show Nurse.' He took her hands. 'You needn't be scared,' he said. 'Not any more. It's just you're grown-up now. So nothing else will happen.' He looked her up and down. The lovely, vacant eyes, the mane of hair from which the sun woke long bronze streaks; the perfect breasts, slight under the thin white dress, long legs that tapered to the slender ankles. 'Tan,' he said. He sighed. 'Will you ever know how beautiful you are?'

Later, in his bunk, he lay and tossed sleepless. Because another thought had come, unwanted but not to be driven away. He wasn't sorry, he'd never been sorry. Because her beauty belonged to him. To him and no-one else. Master Atwill had counselled once against the onset of pride. There were worse sins though. Dishonesty, hypocrisy ... He wasn't sorry. Did that mean he was glad?

He whispered to the dark, 'I'm sorry, Master ...'

The years seemed crowded on him. Posting after posting; the Southguard again, Middlemarch, the North, even a stint in the mansion of a Master. A part of him still longed for the dip and surge of a Cody; he supposed it always would. He performed his duties conscientiously, and in time diligence was rewarded. He was commissioned in Middlemarch, received the precious *bulla* from the hands of the Kitemaster Helman himself. The old man smiled as he slipped the silver chain round Justin's neck. 'Go with God,' he murmured conventionally, 'and fly for Him. Congratulations, Captain.'

For a moment, he couldn't believe his ears. They'd skipped two ranks; he hadn't realized they valued him so highly. Bad form though, to let elation show. He stepped back, saluted stiffly. He said, 'Thank you, My Lord.' He strode out feeling he was walking on air. He wished Dav Sollen could be with him, right this minute. Because he knew exactly what the other would say. 'Well done, old boy. Tell you what, let's go out on the toot ...'

There were women of course; older now and more responsible. Some he loved dearly; one he sat with all one warm spring night, in a big house on the outskirts of Kiteport, the great town in the Southguard. But with the dawn she smiled, and shook her head. 'It's no use,' she said. 'I've just been fooling myself. You don't want me, do you? I don't think you want anybody.'

He shook his head. It seemed he was already in thrall. To a pair of tilted, longlashed eyes, a mane of bronzy hair. A girl who could never be his; yet could never belong to anyone else. 'I don't know,' he said. 'I just don't know, Shani.' He rose, abruptly. He said, 'Forgive me ...'

He wangled himself a three day pass, commandeered Base Transport. He drove to the Salient; and Mannings, the great stone house on its hill. Again he felt himself tugged in differing directions. His father was far from well; the weight was dropping off him, he was unable any longer to work the fields with his men. It distressed him; he saw it as a failing of his duty. Justin tried to reassure him; but Tange Manning shook his head. Hair white now, eyes tired behind his steel-framed specs. 'It isn't right, son,' he said. 'It isn't right. I'd like to have seen you settled.'

'I am settled,' he said. 'I've got Mannings. And you.'

The other looked up sharply. His lips parted; but whatever he'd meant to say was left unspoken. He carried the secret to his grave.

Justin's career thrived. Staff Officer at G12; then a Section at G15. Where he might have gone, with singlemindedness, was an open question; because his loyalties were still divided. He travelled home time and again; spent long hours in his father's study, poring over his accounts. Increasingly it seemed, the running of the estate devolved on him. He saw to the hiring of extra hands for harvest, motored to the Easthold to haggle with the millers for the ensiled grain. He whirled Tan on the orchard swing, and brooded. She was twenty-two, coming twenty-three. She still looked a bare sixteen.

It was his father's last year at Mannings. He died in the autumn, as Grandad Curt had done; and once more Tan watched empty-faced. The horses came, black-plumed; and the motors with their sombre bonnet ribbons, their railed toploads of flowers. He took her back to the house, sat down to take some sort of stock.

The Corps were good to him. Six months' leave of absence, with full pay.

The pay he refused; he had no need of cash. It could go to the Fliers' Fund; God knew there were enough deserving cases. He summoned the executors from Middlemarch. Later he travelled there himself, in the old Swallow he'd bought. Bought with his own cash; the entailment of Estate funds still caused irritating problems. He took Tan with him, packed her things himself. Her nurse fretted, worried for her charge; but he merely smiled. If he couldn't look after her by now, it was time he learned.

There were harnesses fitted to the front seats of the Swallow. Most newer vehicles had dispensed with them, but these old motors still had built-in luxuries. He slipped the straps over her shoulders, clicked the belt round her waist. She looked alarmed at once, began to pluck and complain. 'It's all right,' he said. 'Tan, it's only so you'll be safe. I don't want you to be hurt. Please trust me.' She frowned, but made no further protest.

He drove down the track from Mannings, pointed the bonnet west. 'It's funny, Tan,' he said. 'Do you remember, years ago? I said when I was very clever, I'd be a Captain. Well, I did it. I said I'd take you to Middlemarch then, and buy you pretty things. We're doing that as well. I didn't really believe it when I said it. But it's all come true.'

She glanced at him sidelong with her tilted eyes. Pulled at the straps again.

He drove past Station after Station. Always with a faint but definite pang. Sometimes she smiled, pointing to the Codys; once clapped her hands and laughed, seemingly with pleasure. At other times her eyes became opaque. Blank, yet with a quality of wariness. He wondered if new impressions were flooding in.

It was a long run. Even in the Swallow. He stopped halfway, at an inn deep in the Middle Lands. He knew its owners to be kindly folk. The landlady took Tan under her wing at once. She trotted after her happily enough. Later though she ran back into the bar, flung herself wailing into his arms. Mistress Lanting followed at once, apologetically. 'I'm sorry,' she said. 'I think it was the horse. We rented the paddock, she didn't know it was there.'

'She's seen enough horses,' he said. 'She's just being silly. Aren't you, Tan? You're just showing off a bit. New people to impress.'

The other diners were watching the scene curiously. He glanced at them, and they instantly dropped their eyes. The tinkle of cutlery was resumed.

Driving into Middlemarch, down the long slope of the eastern hill, he waved a hand. 'We're here, Tan,' he said. 'Isn't it a big place? Don't you think it's beautiful?' But the great vista failed to evoke a response.

There was an inn he knew. A little way from the Drag. A quiet place, unpretentious but clean. He left her in the car, hoping she wouldn't panic. But she didn't seem concerned. She'd brought the picture book with her, she was looking at it. The right way up for once.

He knew they had a double room. He hoped it was free. He was in luck.

He put her in the little inner chamber. To reach the landing she would have to pass his bed. She didn't try.

He got a good night's sleep. When he woke she was already up and dressed. She was sitting on the bed, trying to comb her hair.

'Here,' he said. 'Let me. Your fingers are all thumbs.' He took the comb away. Once she would have mewed indignantly; but now she seemed content.

He took her to the outfitters the College people used. They had a lady's section. He knew the manageress; she was the wife of one of his old tutors. She clucked at sight of Tan.

'Fix her a wardrobe,' he said. 'It doesn't matter what it costs.' He paused. He said, 'Her mother's dead.'

She clucked again. 'Poor soul,' she said. 'You'll be all right with me. It's all right, Daddy won't go away.' Tan went, not without a backward glance.

He rubbed his face, a little ruefully. So she'd forgotten him. Or had he changed that much?

They were gone a considerable time. There were no problems though. When they came back their arms were full of clothes. Tan was mewing continuously, with pleasure or excitement. He said, 'Was it all right?' and the older woman smiled. She said, 'She was as good as gold.' He thought there were tears in her eyes.

Tan demurred when the other started to pack the things. He had to take her wrists, shake gently to make her attend. 'It's just to keep them clean,' he said. 'They still belong to you. We're taking them with us, Tan. Look, here's the first.'

She gave him a fashion show in his room. Dashing through each time to change. She'd never done a thing like that before. He lay on the bed, a pillow at his back, and applauded each appearance. Strangely, despite his father, he felt at peace.

The last dress was the prettiest of all. Plain white, with a skirt slit to the thigh. And a deep vee neckline, closed by a little lace. 'Tan,' he said, 'that's naughty. Really naughty …'

She smiled at him.

She wore the dress at dinner. Despite his protests. She turned heads, in the dining room. She was unaware. He tucked a napkin round her carefully; but no disasters ensued. Later they walked, down to Middle Park. Codys were flying, gay streamers fluttering from each Lifter and strings of little coloured lamps. She tucked her arm in his. She was lissome, elegant. He felt the defocused happiness again. He decided it was sheer pleasure in her. Perfection of face and figure, hair, the flawless amber skin. She *was* perfection, he realized it quite suddenly. The First Woman of the myth, from whom sprang all the world.

*

Apogee. The Lifters hung unmoving, in an endless dream of blue. He leaned back in the basket, wearily. Clenched and unclenched his clumsy, numbed fingers. There can only be perfection once. It can never come again.

Somewhere, the faintest of jolts. The basket swayed fractionally. He glanced down, unwilling, and the drifting clouds were closer. They were reeling him in, like a bulky skyborne fish.

A Staff Major visited, to discuss his future prospects. Justin sat in the morning room, long unoccupied, and talked. Waving his hands to the windows, the rolling spread of farmland. Tan curled on the corner settle, watching with her gold-brown eyes. More than once the other's glance strayed to her worriedly. He said, 'So you're leaving the Corps.'

He'd shaken his head. 'I don't want to,' he said. 'It's the last thing I want to do. I've made it my life.' He offered more brandy; the Kiteman declined, with a smile.

Justin's glance strayed to the corner too. 'You can see the responsibilities,' he said. 'I can't evade those either. It's the hardest decision I ever had to make.'

The Major said, 'Hmm.' He riffled papers, thoughtfully. He drummed his knee, stroked at his little clipped moustache. Then it seemed he came to a decision. 'I'm maybe overreaching myself,' he said, 'and I certainly don't want to raise false hopes. But … between you and me, G8 is coming up. Old Lowndes is retiring at last. I could put in a recommendation. How would that appeal?'

It was like a burst of light. G8, the Station he'd first seen as a tiny boy. It had always been a special place to him. 'Could you?' he said. 'Could you do that for me?'

'Don't see why not,' said the other. 'Have to go to Middlemarch of course. So don't rely on a thing. But they have started a local staffing policy; and with a record like yours I'd say you stand as good a chance as the next.' He slipped the papers into a briefcase. 'Consider it done,' he said. He pulled a face, and rose. 'Got to get on the road,' he said. 'Due in the Easthold at some ghastly hour tomorrow. Court martial. Some fool of a Lancejack slugged a Sergeant Rigger …' He shook hands. 'Good luck, Captain,' he said.

The posting came through. There followed the happiest time of his life. He put in a Farm Manager, fetched him from the Middle Lands. Later he installed a housekeeper; a greying, hardfaced woman, Mrs Brand. He didn't care for her overmuch; but there was no doubting her efficiency. And her references were irreproachable. He gave her very special instructions, particularly with regard to Tan. She smiled thinly, clipped the keys to her belt. She said, 'I shall try to give every satisfaction, sir.'

He said, 'I'm sure you will.'

Tan disliked the new arrangement at first. Twice she wandered, searching for him perhaps, got nearly as far as the village; but she was brought back gently enough. Finally she seemed to grow accustomed to the routine. Off at zero nine hundred, generally back by seventeen hundred latest. The evenings he spent with her were long and rich. Particularly in summer. She could go to her beloved orchard, swing and suck her thumb.

Straightforwardly, G8 was in a mess. Lowndes had been long past retirement, things had been let to slide badly. The Corps had let him stay on out of kindness; but it was obvious nobody at Headquarters had known the true state of affairs. Justin got rid of a couple of Corporals, had them posted. Then a new contingent of Cadets arrived, and things began to look up. He started out with them the way he meant to go on. Kantmer the Rigger and Holbeck the Launchmaster were old hands of course. Stalwarts. He had the beginnings of a team.

He bullied Middlemarch for the new Lifters. Then the special pistols. There was less hassle over them; they were getting used to his stubbornness. There followed a spot inspection. The brass descended in droves; but he merely smiled. He'd known it would come; his people had been spitting and polishing for days. Even a kerchief rubbed on the guardroom floor disclosed no speck of dirt. Three Rigs were streamed; his maximum capacity. The launch times compared quite well with G15. And they had a double manning capacity. After that he was left in peace.

Mannings prospered. Beyond his father's dreams. He added a third silo, took on four more men. The Salient folk were pleased. Work had always been scarce; traditionally, it was a depressed area. They'd been suspicious of him at first; he sensed his stock had risen considerably.

Dav Sollen visited. At first Justin barely recognized him. He was burly now and bearded, sporting a wife and a brace of fair-haired kids. He carried a stick, and walked with a heavy limp. The leg had healed better than the medics had thought; though it still gave him Hell in wet weather. He'd left the service; he was a civilian contractor now, supplying anything from cable drums to logbooks and tide tables. So he was still in touch with the world of the great Kites.

Tan charmed them all. The children in particular took to her. She showed them her toys, one after the next, winding up the little, squeaking dogs, the green tin frogs that hopped along the carpet. Later she even let them use her swing; a signal honour, that.

His first harvest in, the work piled up again. He couldn't expect Butard the Manager to cope with the wholesale/retail side as well. There just weren't enough hours in the day. He needed an outside man, somebody free to travel, make the contacts for him. He found one in Easthope, courtesy of an acquaintance of his father's. He'd been a stocktaker once, worked for the Corps. Mal Trander. He looked to be in his thirties. Rakishly handsome, curly chestnut hair. He said he'd been married once, given it up as the bad job. Which was all to the good. Nothing to distract him.

He rolled his head from side to side, and groaned. 'How could I have known?' he whispered. 'How could I have guessed …'

As ever, he studied Tan's reaction carefully. He'd hired and fired accordingly, and never been wrong. She'd become his voiceless partner, though nobody else knew that. Sometimes it took her a while to make up her mind; but this time she seemed to have no doubts. She ran to the stocktaker at once, giving her little mewing cry. Within the hour she brought him her picture book. She held it out to him, upside down. He turned it round for her. 'That way, my love,' he said, eyes twinkling. 'Gee-gees aren't very good at standing on their heads.' He looked at her appraisingly. She was wearing denims, figure-hugging, and a new top Justin had bought; stripy, and with a wide scooped collar. They'd told him the style was called boat-necked. Later Mal Trander said, 'What a pretty kid. Nice with it too.'

The Captain glanced up briefly. 'Yes,' he said. 'She's sweet.' He consulted the notes he'd made. 'What say we start with Ransams in Condar Street? I've never sold to them yet; they'd be a good outlet to have.'

He'd never have known anything was wrong. Never suspected. Had it not been for a stray whisper, overheard on Base. He brooded about it; then he sent for Kantmer. He havered a bit, staring through the long windows of the office while the Riggingmaster waited. He'd never been one for confiding in inferiors. It was a weakness; led to slackness, indiscipline. But Kantmer was an old hand. And anyway, a Lineman of his experience could scarcely be termined inferior to a Captain of three years' seniority. He turned from contemplation of his No. 1 String, hanging steady against the blue. 'This character Mal Trander,' he said. 'What do you know about him, Bend?'

The other was ready with his answers. His marriage, reasons for breaking with the Corps; he was terse, and to the point. Justin felt his mouth set in a harder line. Finally he nodded. 'Thank you, Riggingmaster,' he said. 'Thank you very much.' He inclined his head toward the cupboard, 'Drink?'

'No thank you, sir,' said Kantmer steadily. 'Got to get that shackle fixed on Three. She's due to stream at seventeen hundred …'

When the other had gone he sat and brooded again. Drummed his fingers on the desk top. Certainly Trander had worked well enough for him. He'd no cause for complaint; the contrary in fact. And his past was his own affair. To an extent at least.

By fifteen-thirty he'd made his mind up. The other was due back that afternoon, from a trip to the Middle Lands. Best face him with what he'd heard. Give him a chance to put his side of things. He left the Base abruptly, drove the Swallow home.

The stackyard was wide; he knew the engine sound would be inaudible from the house. He left the car by the silos anyway, walked the last two hundred yards. Trander's old jalopy was parked beside the main door.

He let himself in, silently. The place seemed oddly quiet. He checked the lower rooms. Nobody. But of course the nurse was having one of her rare days off. The rest would be in the dairy, Mrs Brand taking her afternoon nap.

He walked upstairs. The door of Tan's room was ajar. He pushed it with his foot, walked in.

Her skirt was round her waist, her ankles locked about Trander's hips. He was panting, driving into her hard; and there was blood. A lot of blood, spattering the sheet. So it was the first time. She was clawing at him, giving the little mewing cries.

He put his hand to the other's shoulder, heaved. He was a powerful man; but he'd never used his strength in anger before. The stocktaker landed on the floor. He tried to scuttle away; and Justin caught him, hauled him up by the shirt. He slammed him against the wall. The room shook. He used his knees and boots. Then started with his hands. When the other fell he picked him up. He knocked him down again. His vision had narrowed; what sight remained was tinged with red.

He stepped back. Trander was on his hands and knees. His breathing sounded harsh. He retched; and there were teeth, bright spatterings. He hauled himself up by the doorframe, staggered. He began to work his way along the landing; gripping the banister, his other hand to his groin. He didn't turn. From somewhere came a scream. Mrs Brand would give her notice now. Refuse to work in an unruly house.

She'd pulled her skirt down. She was huddled in the corner of the bed, her knuckles to her mouth. He yanked her toward him, hit her across the face. Then again. She whimpered, tried to cling to him. He flung her away. She rolled over, lay face down. He tugged at his belt buckle. He beat her with all his strength, across her back, her thighs, her bottom. In time the mewings stopped. She lay silent, shaking. He walked out, closed the door. He went downstairs. Walked into the morning room, opened the drinks cabinet. He took down brandy and a glass.

The house seemed muted still. There were shufflings, whisperings; but nobody came near him. He drank, and watched the light begin to fade. He'd never beaten a living thing like that before. Not a human, not an animal.

He lost track of time. The afterglow was flaring when there was a scratching at the door. She opened it. She stared a moment; then she dropped to her knees. She worked her way toward him slowly, skirt brushing the polished parquet. She reached the chair, stared up. He saw the swollen lips, the teart-racks on her poor bruised face. He thought, 'If I touch her now, I know what the end will be. At last, I understand.' There was a sense of doom, the yawning of a pit; but also a curious rightness. Who but himself anyway? He who knew her every cry, the meaning of each whimper. He stared a moment longer; then reached out gently, began to stroke her hair.

He'd entered cloud again. As he'd entered cloud before. The greyness swirled, obscuring. He wondered why he'd never understood.

He supposed in a way he had. He'd crowned a simple Fact with pinnacles and spires, not wanting to see it as it was. '*This is a roof . . . and these are walls, and windows . . .*' The meaning of the parable came clear at last.

The moral issues ceased to trouble him. It was right to hold her, right to love. Right to bathe her, comb her beautiful hair. He encircled her; as she encircled him. She was Dawn Woman; and she needed him. As surely woman never needed man before. He was complete; he existed in her aura.

Days came and went; the seasons followed their course. He trimmed her nails; an hour of chuckling, playing, for each hand and foot. Her fingernails were shell-pink, shapely. When they showed signs of splitting he varnished them, with dope from the Lifter sheds. He sent for dresses; from the Southguard, Easthope, Middlemarch. Each one she greeted now with cries of delight. She'd pull open the tall doors of her wardrobe; run her fingers along the hangers, make a wooden clatter. 'Yours,' he'd say. 'All yours,' and she would crow and chuckle. She'd try them on, one after the next, and prance and pirouette; and then she'd take them off. Sometimes she'd dance in the stackyards, in the garden; shake fruit from the orchard trees, the blossoms in their season. She was destructive, mischievous; like a bird, a squirrel. Other times the mewings would return. She'd huddle close then, in his great bed; draw herself down beneath the covers, into dark. He'd huddle with her, rub till she was warm, the tremblings stopped. She'd kiss him then and whisper; tiny broken sounds that were nearly words. He understood in time what each breath intake meant. 'Tan,' he'd say. 'Oh, Tan . . .' By day, the Codys flew.

Mrs Brand didn't leave. He should have been warned; but he was deaf and blind. She went about her duties, calmly and efficiently. Checking the household lists, supervising the laundry that bubbled in the great brick coppers. She announced his visitors, as and when they came. One morning – he was taking a rare day's leave – she ushered in the village priest.

He was working in his study at the time. 'Father Andri,' he said. 'You're welcome. Please be seated.' Then came the shock, the dreadful pang. The other was in his formal robes; the blazing scarlet, Cap of Maintenance, of the great Church Variant itself.

The Father waited till the housekeeper had rustled from the room. And closed the door behind her. He said without preamble, 'You know why I am here.'

His throat had dried; for a moment his vision flickered. 'No,' he said. 'No, I don't.'

'Captain,' said the priest, 'Don't make it harder for yourself. Harder than it has to be.' He still waited; and finally the other sighed. 'A sin has been committed,' he said. 'A vile and grievous crime, for which there can be neither pity nor forgiveness.'

Justin looked through the window, to where Tan kicked high on the orchard swing. Crowing, showing her legs. Her little yelps of pleasure sounded through the glass. He put his face in his hands. They were shaking. 'Father,' he said, 'tell me one thing. If there is no awareness, where is sin?'

'Awareness?' said the other. 'The Demons sinned, by wasting all the world. Were they aware?'

He said, 'She is a child.'

'She is a woman,' said the priest. 'And with a woman's parts. Chop me no logic, Captain.'

He laid his hands flat on the desk top. He already saw, dimly, the way the thing must go. He wondered how he could have shut it from his mind. The consequences of actions. It had been madness. And yet ... mad? Mad to love beauty, wherever it is found? Mad to love the Ultimate? He said, 'She's everything. Mother, daughter, wife. A child of God. But you wouldn't understand that, would you?'

The other looked up, under his brows. 'A child of God?' he said. 'She was Condemned once. As you know very well.'

He was finding it difficult to make words. He said, 'But she has done no harm.' The other's expression didn't change.

He raised his hands, the fingers crooked. 'She is an Innocent,' he said. 'Can you not understand? Will you not try?'

'She was Condemned once,' said the priest. 'It can be done again. There are larger knives. For tougher little necks.'

Justin found he could no longer see. Also his hearing was impaired. There was a buzzing, roaring. When vision returned he was standing over the Father, fingers still crooked. And the other watching him calmly. 'Kill me then,' he said. 'Do you suppose your secret will be safe? Do you imagine I'm the sole repository?'

Once before, he had experienced an icy calm. He experienced it now. He walked away, stood staring through the window. Watching Tan on the swing. He said, 'It's hatred, isn't it? Hatred of beauty. Freedom. Hatred of love. You, who profess to peddle love of God.' He turned back. Nodded toward the farther wall. 'Out there,' he said, 'is a place they call the Badlands. Have you seen them? Have you seen the things they spawn?'

Father Andri didn't answer.

'Their flesh is blue,' he said. 'Their lips are made of blubber. Their inner workings can be seen quite plain; and you cannot meet their eyes. Once they were men. And women.'

He sat back at the desk. 'We were spared,' he said. 'This one little Realm. We praised God for it. For His mercy. Then what did we do? We spawned you. To sit among us, dispense burning fluids. When your blood drops on to grass, it dies.' He pointed. 'Leave this house,' he said. 'Leave, while you can walk.'

The Father didn't move.

He rose again; but it was useless. The rage had gone, as quickly as it had arisen. He remembered the hold the Church had on the land. Every city, village, town; always the Scarlet, always needle-pointed spires. Nowhere would she be safe. They would find her; and out would come a shining, leafshaped knife.

He'd seen, just once, the ruin of a Cody string. Snapping of struts, the sagging of the Trace; then the other Lifters, folding under too much stress. Till what had been proud and lovely lay a shambles on the grass. He knew he was destroyed himself. He turned back to the window. The swing still moved; but empty. She had run away. He said dully, 'Can you save her?'

The priest said, 'Yes.'

He moistened his lips. He said, 'I suppose you have conditions.'

The other nodded. He said, 'You know what they are.'

'Yes,' he said. 'Of course.'

The door opened. Tan came in. She hesitated when she saw the priest. Then she ran forward with a little mew. Tried to grasp his robe. He twitched it away. She stood back, puzzled and a little hurt.

Justin stood up. He said, 'I shall do as you require.'

Father Andri rose in turn. 'See to it, Captain,' he said. 'For her sake, if not for yours.' He paused at the door. 'If you love her as you claim,' he said, 'then it should be a joy.' The door closed behind him.

She was still looking concerned. He smiled. 'It's nothing, Tan,' he said. 'Come out and play.'

He swung her, the rest of the afternoon. Later they sat on the grass. 'Tan,' he said, 'I want to talk to you. Very seriously indeed.'

She linked her arms round her knees, put her head on one side. He pushed her legs down, gently. She smiled a little, troubled smile.

'Tan,' he said, 'I love you more than all the world. Because you are the world. That's why I have to go away.'

He pulled a stem of grass. 'You see,' he said, 'there are certain things that are wrong. I don't think they are, not really. Not with someone like you. But other people think they are. And we've been doing them.' He looked up at the sky. 'Some people think that everything is wrong,' he said. 'I think they believe it's wrong to love at all.'

She didn't respond.

'You see,' he said, 'It's not us. You and I. That isn't what matters. It's the Church.'

She frowned, looked partly over her shoulder.

'Yes,' he said. 'That's right. People like Father Andri. Maybe they think what they're doing is right. I don't know any more. I think we made our own Church. Just the two of us.'

She reached out, grasped his hand. He pushed her away, gently. 'Tan,' he said, 'if I go on loving you, they'll cut your head off.'

She put her fingers slowly to her neck.

'Yes,' he said again. 'That's right.' He looked at the grass stem, tossed it away. 'It's all a question of priorities,' he said. 'Getting things in order. The most important first, and then the rest.' He thought a moment. 'I was told that once,' he said, 'by a very wise old man. That was when I was at College, learning to be clever. Only I didn't learn. Not properly. I'm still learning now.' He looked round. 'I shall have to sell this place,' he said. 'Father Andri wouldn't want me to stay. But that will be all right. I shall be able to find you a really lovely home. In the Middle Lands, perhaps. He'll help, if he knows we're both sincere.'

She looked round the orchard, troubled. He smiled; he almost took her hands. Then he remembered. 'Don't worry,' he said. 'There are trees all over the Realm. I can buy you swings. And send you letters, and more dresses.' He swallowed. 'That's the way it's got to be,' he said. 'There isn't another answer. I've known it for a long time now.'

He glanced round him again. 'I did it all for you,' he said. 'Learned to fly the Codys. So you would be safe. Well, this is for you too. You can be safe again.' He stared at his hands. 'A lovely home,' he said. 'There'll be others just like you. You'll be able to talk to them, and play. And you'll be safe for ever.'

No response. He tried another tack. 'Do you remember, all that time ago?' he said. 'I beat you, dreadfully. You should never hurt anyone like that. Whatever they've done. Well, this is my punishment. Because when you do something bad you have to pay for it sooner or later. And I've been bad to you. You see I'm not really a very nice person at all. I love the Kites; there isn't room for anything else. No room for you; not a teeny little place.' He swallowed again. 'You think I'm being hard,' he said. 'Well, that's the way it is. You see, life is hard. Flying the Codys is hard. You can't let feelings get in the way of that.'

She stared at him; then for the first time in her life she slowly nodded.

'My angel,' he said gently. He leaned forward, kissed her carefully on the forehead.

He'd thought she'd understood. But at bedtime she began to squall. She clung to him, desperate; and he pushed her away. 'No,' he said, 'it's over. Tan, *it's over* ...'

There was a rustling, at the door of the room. Mrs Brand glided forward, lamp in hand. 'You may leave her, Captain Manning,' she said calmly. 'I will see to her.'

He ran for the door, slammed it behind him blindly.

Blind? He was no longer blind. He was below the clouds, Earth taking shape again. Sunlight struck from above; made ragged silver edges, dazzling against the blue. He fell back in the basket. 'No,' he groaned. 'Please, no ...'

There was brandy in the morning room. He finished one bottle, started on another. He lost track of time. Perhaps he slept; if he did, he was roused by the chirpings of birds. It seemed her voice mixed with it; the trilling, and the mewing.

Always, the rustling of that dress. She shook his shoulder. He started, stared round wildly. 'Captain,' she said, 'you must come with me.'

'What is it?' he said hoarsely. 'What is it, Mrs Brand? Is it Tan?' She didn't answer directly. She said, 'You must come with me.'

He followed, reeling on the stairs. The bedroom door was open. He ran in. She lay head turned, hair wild on the pillows. He'd thought she was asleep; but she wasn't. Because her teeth were clenched. 'Tan,' he said again. 'Tan, what is it ...' But the housekeeper forestalled him, snatched back the covers with a quick, contemptuous flick. His eyes dilated. He saw the dreadful brightness of the sheets, the lake that was her blood; the knife still gripped, her leg vibrating with shock. On it from knee to ankle, crudely carved in quarter inch vee gouges, was his own name; JUSTIN. He'd always known, one day she'd speak to him. She'd spoken now.

The bawling noise he made was that of an animal in pain. He ran from the house, hands clutched to his head, and reeled across the yard. '*Ruined*' he moaned. His lovely temple ruined. Then, '*Why ... Why her ...*' Then, 'No ...' And again, in desperation, '*No, no, no ...*'

*

The noise in his ears was thunderous, drowning the wind. He sat up, stared. He rose, stood in the rocking basket. He gripped the Cody sides, while the colour left his face.

It moved forward slowly, sharp-cut against the silver clouds above. And it was big, bigger than he could have dreamed. He saw the sun glint from its silver flanks. He saw the fins, the markings on its sides. He saw the scarlet rings that tipped its nose.

He grabbed for the pistol, cocked. *'Accursed Demon,'* he said. *'Messenger from Hell. Thou sooty spirit, get thee gone. Avaunt ...'* He fired; and the thing vanished, in a dazzling burst of light.

There was another, and another. He fired, and fired again. Pushed at the barrel release, flung the smoking cylinder away. He grabbed a second, rammed it home.

They were flying beneath him now. They had the shapes of fishes, just as in the Litany. Below were others and still more; the Cunning Ones, clinging to the land. None passed; because his aim was true. Spots swam before his eyes; he grabbed for the third cylinder, the fourth. Skin tore from his fingers; but still he rammed the red-hot barrel home. He laughed; because his life had been fulfilled. This was the point toward which all had been directed. At last he was protecting her; really protecting her. His lovely, wounded angel. The Demon-shoal scattered, panic-stricken, diving. Flicking their vile shadows on the land. The yellow fins, the black, the red. They turned back, angry, desperate, roared at the Rig. Those too he atomized; and suddenly, the sky was clear.

He dropped to his knees. He knew now – why had he not seen before – that all had not been lost. It was so easy; he would go back, he would take her away. Far away. And heal and minister, till she was whole again.

The gun fell from his hand. He hung his head. The roaring was back; but louder than before. He coughed, desperately; then darkness overtook him.

They'd heard the fusillade of shots. Coming it seemed from miles away. The winch was yelling; atop the Launcher Cadets stood in pairs, steel crowbars in their hands, guiding the snaking cable on to the drum. A desperate manoeuvre; hands had been lost and arms, playing that game. The Winchman yelled; and at last the cable, sloping impossibly into the blue, became the cable of a Cody rig. They saw the swaying basket, beyond it the great train of wings. Snaking and dipping from the crazy speed.

The Winchman threw his lever. Squeals from the brakeblocks, and the Trace was close. The Cadets flung themselves away. He worked the lever again, head turned, gentling the train in. The Launchmaster raised an arm; suddenly the Observer's basket filled the sky. A dozen pairs of hands grabbed, lowered down; and silence fell, broken only by the seething of the truck.

Slowly, the Base personnel crowded round. They peered into the basket; and more than one Apprentice blenched. Their Captain lay curled up in the bottom of the Cody. The blood he had voided soaked his chin and tunic, spattered the wicker sides. His hands were clenched; and his eyes still glared at the sky. In triumph or in terror, none could tell. Lastly the Chaplain approached. He stared down calmly; then reached with a finger and thumb to close the lids.

Across the field stood a massive scarlet vehicle. Almost the size of a Launcher, but totally enclosed; and with a vicious ram jutting from between its wheels. By it stood a little knot of men, also robed in red. To one side, Rik Butard still sat a lathered horse. The priests paced forward; and their leader folded his arms. 'So die all heretics,' he said. 'All sinners, who seek to evade the Lord.'

The Chaplain faced him mildly. 'Perhaps,' he said, 'he didn't choose to escape. He flew to meet Him.'

The Hunter-Bishop waved a hand dismissively. 'We will take the corpse,' he said. 'It will be disposed of, in a fitting manner.'

'You will not,' said the other, still quiet. 'Last rites are for the Corps to organize.'

The Bishop's colour flared immediately. 'Out of my way,' he said. 'His goods and property are forfeit. Also there is another sinner to attend.' He pointed. 'Clear that Rig.'

An axe flashed, contemptuously. The Trace leaped, snaked up into the sky. Whirled out over the Badlands, and was lost from sight.

The Bishop stared, as if unable to credit the evidence of his senses. 'For that,' he said, 'your head will roll, Launchmaster.' He groped beneath his robes; and behind him there was a click. He froze, turned slowly. He and his group were surrounded by a ring of armed men.

He swallowed, and the flush faded quick as it had risen. Was replaced by pallor. 'This,' he said, 'is heresy. Heresy, and insurrection.'

The Chaplain shook his head. 'No,' he said, 'it is justice. The Corps ministers its own. For all your trumpeting.'

The other opened his mouth, and closed it.

'Where is your authority?' said the Chaplain. 'Where is your warrant, from Middlemarch? Your power wears thin, my friend.'

The other felt, cautiously, under his robes. 'This is my power,' he said. He held out a Staff of Office.

'And this is mine,' said the slim man. He held out in turn a small looped cross; the symbol of the Middle Doctrine. He jerked his head. 'Hold them, during my pleasure,' he said. 'Later, they will answer to their own.' The Variants were hustled away; and he turned to the great rig. 'Launchmaster,' he said, 'you are in command. Secure the Base; post guards, until another authority comes.' He turned again. Glanced at the scarlet truck, back to the Launcher. He smiled, thinly. Because the Base was angry at last; angry at useless sacrifice. The Variants had stirred a hornets' nest; and found that hornets can sting. 'Doctor,' he said, 'a hurt child needs your urgent skill.

Will you come with us?' But the Medic was already there, carrying his black tin box. He swung into the Launcher's cab; armed Cadets ran forward at once, clustered the top of the great truck, its running boards. The Chaplain followed; and the cables snaked away. The massive machine bellowed, lurched toward the gate. The last the others heard was the roaring of its engine, building speed along the lane.

5

Kiteservant

He'd been awake by zero three-thirty, on the road by four hundred. Though that hadn't been much of a trick of course. His things were laid out for the morning, and his bags all packed; the two big grips he'd bought the day before, the valise Rone had lent him for allegedly important papers. Though it contained little of significance at the moment.

He glanced behind him, into the body of the Buckley. Two oval windows in the rear doors, giving light; and the dark red paint, same as the outside. The doors would never shut properly, however he tried to pad them. They'd always squeaked. They were squeaking now.

Rand looked round him. At first the morning had been misty, cool; great shapes of trees hanging to either side of the road, each a still shadow of bluey-green. By Garnord though the heat of the day had been beginning to make itself felt. Sky clearing to a vivid blue, the dust starting to rise. The little van trailed a whitish cloud behind it; a cloud that dissipated slowly in the almost windless air.

At Garnord he encountered a metalled road; one of the very few, in truth, he'd ever seen. Streanling, where he'd been born and where he'd lived his first quarter century, was the acknowledged capital of the Northwest; and though Garnordians – Garnordites some called them, though that was an invitation to instant battle – were traditionally fond of quibbling the fact there'd never been much doubt in his mind. After all, it was in Streanling the Variants held greatest sway; apart from Middlemarch itself of course. There was Skyway, second Cathedral of the Realm; and the Civil College, at which he'd toiled four long and sometimes wearisome years. But Streanling still didn't have paved roads. Somehow they'd never felt the need of them.

Though he had heard rumours the Vars were losing ground even in Middlemarch. Why, he'd never been too sure. The Middle Doctrine that opposed them had always seemed to his mind vague and bumbling by comparison;

while those of its priests he'd met had an irritating habit of answering questions with others. Thus:

'What is the Middle Way?'

'The Middle Way is what you decide it is.'

'Is it a religion?'

'If you wish it to be.'

'But all religions are Ways.'

'Perhaps. Then are all Ways religions?'

That had been years ago though, with Father Alkin; when he'd had an argumentative, perhaps more enquiring mind.

He glanced at his fuel gauge. Then the bright new chronometer on his wrist. That last a present from Rone; unexpected, and to tell the truth unwanted. The fuel gauge was of little help either. As with all these old Buckleys, the needle flickered continually across the little yellow dial; full to empty, empty to full. Dipping the tank was the only real answer; but even that was difficult. Somebody had rebuilt the Buck from a pair of wrecks. Overall he'd done a fairish job; but he'd neglected to allow for a proper fall in the gas hose. It made filling a slight difficulty too.

He remembered an incident up in Seahold, on the ragged Northwest coast. One of the first trips he'd taken when he'd acquired the van. A little filling station, set on its own beside a dusty track that seemed to lead to nowhere; and a striking girl, elegant and tall, with a mane of tumbling auburn hair. He'd already put a notice on the Buckley's side; CAUTION, SLOW FILLER. She'd been impatient though. Maybe there'd been a reason; her beautiful and miles from anywhere, the day too hot. But three pulls on the big old handpump and the nozzle had still blown back, left her soaked to the knees and the tarmac of the little forecourt glistening. She'd abused him roundly; old crocks on the road, wasting her time and his own. The words stung; after all the Buckley was a new possession. He paid her, curtly, told her to keep the change; and then she'd tried to walk away. He'd seen the soles of her smart new shoes had glued themselves to the matrix of gravel. He'd laughed, and started up the little van. Later though he'd streamed a new train for her, from the house roof. The Godkite carried a vestibule in gold; cost him a fortune in the Skyways shop. He wondered why he'd bothered. That night the wind got up; and the whole thing blew away. So maybe the Lord had noticed too.

He set his lips. He'd realized deep inside him he was scared.

He set himself to analyze the feeling, with some care. So he was taking up his first appointment as a Servant. Internal audits on the Easthold Bases, later a tour into the Salient. His first long trip from home; and in the first motor vehicle he'd ever owned. New experiences all; but were they in themselves a cause for fear? Emotion was burned from him; so he could know neither joy nor apprehension. He grimaced. Because he knew, or could guess, what the Master Sprinling would have said. '*Fear, like pain, is a gift from God. Both have a purpose, as all things in life have a purpose. Against them we test ourselves. As the Church has been tested, and will be tested again. We must not be found wanting . . .*'

He shook his head. It didn't really help. Because Father Alkin was in his mind as well.

'What is fear, Father?'

'Fear is what you decide it is.'

'Why does it come?'

'That, my son, you must discover for yourself.'

'Is there a reason for it?'

'Perhaps, perhaps not. One day, you will decide . . .'

He rubbed his face. He was remembering a time when he cowered in the corner of his room all night and whimpered, wanting the impossible; that all the folk he knew, all the folk he'd ever met in the world, could somehow be with him, crowding round, holding back the dark. The dark that seemed to crawl, encroach, flood through him. Because he'd realized for the first time, he was mortal too. He wondered why it had taken so long. But of course that was after Janni.

He pushed the thought away, as he'd pushed it away before. He'd risen from where he crouched, walked to the window. The simple act had taken all his willpower. He sat and watched a green dawn brighten round the spires of Skyway. He'd washed and shaved then, changed as required into the robes of an acolyte; and walked to College, to sit the first of his finals.

He looked at his wrist again. He'd made good time, better than he'd hoped for; coming zero six-thirty, and the rounded hills that encircled Garnord already behind him. The Buckley had chuffed a little, climbing them; he'd pulled in twice to rest her and cool the little engine, but she hadn't boiled. Which had been the first blessing of the day; he'd been afraid of the rad leak starting up again. He'd cured it two days before, with the additive Master Bone had supplied him; but he'd been warned the respite would only be temporary. He'd have liked to install a new core, but funds were scarce; and in any case such things had to come from Middlemarch, there'd been no time to order. So here he was, with a suspect cooling system and a diff that as ever bonked and clattered, crossing the Realm from one side to the other.

He wondered why he'd set himself the task. After all he could have made it easily enough by College coach; first stage to Middlemarch, second to the Crossways, third curving down into Easthold. He suspected it had to do with Janni; though what the exact connection was eluded him. One certain fact was that whether he succeeded or failed, she wouldn't care. Why should she? She'd already made her views plain, on that and other matters.

Rone then, or Shand, his sister? She would have been no help either though. The dark eyes would have watched, from the slim brown face; she'd have stroked ash sideways, from one of the rank-smelling tubes she always insisted on smoking, and shrugged. He could even hear her voice. 'You'll have to make your own mind up. I can't live your life for you. Nobody can.'

No. He'd never tried to live hers. Despite the accusation she once made.

He took a bend. There was a further vista of trees. More, he imagined, than you'd find in the whole of Northguard. He supposed he'd entered the Middle Lands; though there'd been nothing to announce the fact. The rest of the country looked the same as the land he'd been driving through the last hour or so. Low, rolling hills fringeing the horizon; broad fields yellow with crops, others under grass. Fat cattle grazed the pastures, the occasional donkey or horse. No people moving, no other vehicles; and a good half hour since he'd passed as much as a village. He was beginning to appreciate, if he hadn't known before, the sheer size of the Realm.

He narrowed his eyes. Ahead, far off, was the bright string of a Cody. That was also the first Rig he'd seen since Garnord. In the town the Kites, even the great string on the Tower that was their pride and joy, had all been trailing; at negative angle in the nearly windless air. He saw the new train was no exception.

He changed gear, more to relieve boredom than for any real reason. He allowed the Buckley to build up speed a little. The clanking from the rear warned him at once; he returned to his former sedate pace.

He thought about the Master Bone. How he'd have laughed at Rand's new-found excess of caution. He supposed he'd been a bit headstrong then, when he first started working for him; though he'd known plenty worse. The job still supported him most of the way through College, supplemented the pittance that was all the Church allowed. Evenings and weekends, in the little tin-roofed shed at the back of the manse, the shed that reeked of oil and gasoline and hand cleaner, that was baking hot in summer, burning cold in the long Northwest winters. He supposed the old man had taught him a lot, one way and another. He remembered one occasion vividly. Wrestling overhead in the half-dark trying to dismantle the spring assembly of an ancient, rusty Swallow; sweat running into his eyes, the wrench slipping, grease stinging the cuts on his knuckles. He's lost his temper finally, beat at the thing; and instantly a hand was on his shoulder. He turned, and caught the old mechanic's eyes. The Master gestured curtly; Rand thought for the first time since he'd known him he looked angry. He wriggled aside; the other stared again, and took the adjustable. He showed him, silently, how the thing should be done. The nut turned sweetly; the Master handed the spanner back, and walked away. The silent rebuke had more effect than a volume of abuse.

Later, in the little pub they sometimes used after work, the Master condescended to discuss the matter. 'A vehicle, any vehicle, is a machine,' he said. 'A machine assembled by men. What has been assembled can be disassembled.' He puffed at his old, stubby pipe. 'Never let me see you lose your temper again,' he said. 'If you do, you know where the yard gate is. Walk through it, and don't come back . . .' He smiled, glanced across with his vivid blue eyes. 'Tip up, young Rand,' he said. 'Your turn for a round . . .' He bought the drinks, thoughtfully. He was wondering, not for the first time, if the Master was of the Middle Doctrine too.

He supposed he'd learned more than engineering. He'd thought about it sometimes, when the hot nights made him restless. A human being, he decided finally, was a machine assembled by God. Any human being. So they too were to be gentled, understood; not abused, coerced by bad Mechanics. He'd thought his feet were on the Way; though finally he'd been disabused of that as well. Once more, he'd failed.

The land was flatter now, the vistas wider. Also the road was trending upward steadily. Which meant he was closing with the place he privately dreaded. He'd been cocky enough, making his farewells to the few chums he'd made during his twelve month stint in Streanling Supply. But over the horizon, not too far off now, lay Middlemarch, greatest city of the Realm. His first and sternest test of driving skill. Roads existed to the south and north, the maps he carried showed them well enough; but he'd elected, again for obscure reasons, to route himself through the city. He wondered what Father Alkin would have thought. Applauded his courage, determination? Or merely raised his eyebrows, shaken his head a little?

Father Alkin. He'd gone to him the night of the great shock. When he'd finally realized what Shand had done. How long ago had that been? He winded as he remembered. Nine years. Long years, and for the most part full of pain. And Father Alkin had smiled, and made no comment. He'd given him a glass of wine – it had made his head spin a little, you're not used to such things at sixteen – and sat and talked. About animals and people, the Northwest and the Kites and cars; he'd known already they were a passion with Rand. He'd been appalled; he'd thought the old man didn't know what drove him, what he had come to say. He nearly interrupted, blurted out the angry words; then he saw the priest's eyes. What Father Alkin was doing he couldn't understand; not at the time at least. But he'd held his peace; and when he finally rose to leave the other smiled again. 'Life is long, Rand,' he said gently. 'It consists of many lessons; one follows hard upon the next. As for you, so for us all. You are still learning; so am I. Never will the whole truth become clear. Knowledge is for the One we worship; He of the Kites. So make no judgements; hold yourself in peace. Judging, we betray ourselves; against the day the Lord will judge us too.'

Walking home he'd felt uplifted, almost cheerful. He'd thought again it was the beginning of maturity; but the road, like all roads, was long and hard. What he'd felt was not forgiveness, but the rising of contempt.

He'd gone to the old man's cottage many times after that; the cottage that winter and summer he managed to surround with colour. Flowers, or bright-leaved shrubs. But that of course was part of Alkin's special magic. He loved Life and the folk who lived it; fervently, and with candour. Always there would be Middle Lands wine for him; and the Maycakes the Father embellished, even on Holy Days, with helpings of cream and fragrant home-made jam. Cherry, and wild strawberry. He'd questioned him once on that, greatly daring; but the priest had merely shrugged. 'God made them,' he said gently. 'As He made the flowers of the field. Who are we to refuse His gifts? It would be ingratitude ...' He'd realized then the old man took the sternest view of all; he saw things for what they were. Sweetmeats were for the eating, wine was to be drunk. A spring shackle wasn't to be shed blood on, to be cursed and hammered; it was an assembly, to be dismantled.

He shook his head. He'd wondered, often enough, what Rone had thought; but his stepfather, wisely perhaps, had remained silent. The peace wrought by the Father was real enough; but it was tenuous. A volcano still seethed, waiting to erupt; the Variant disciplines they had all professed sat ill now on the house.

A Kitestation was on his right. One of the first big Stations of the Middleguard. He'd seen it coming up ahead for a mile or more; long shapes of the hangars, the stubby control tower, cluster of low huts that he knew would be the barracks, workshops, refectories. He stared as he passed, through gaps in the boundary hedge. He saw a Cody string had grounded. The basket was tethered safely enough atop the Launcher; beside the big maroon truck a group of men stood disgustedly. The Observer was among them; goggles pushed up to his forehead, hands on hips. Others were running, across the open ground in front; he saw two Cadets heft a massive Lifter, stagger back towards the sheds with it. He shook his head. There'd be bills to the Church for sure; for flattened crops, damage to boundary hedges. He should know; he'd served his time in Accounts. There'd be a reprimand for the Captain too; loss of pay increments, perhaps the pegging of his career. God's vagaries were one thing; but the Vars had never acknowledged human error.

All the same, there was something disquieting in the sight. Shocking almost. He'd never thought himself particularly devout; but an image had come to him, unbidden. All across the Realm, on this stifling, airless day, the Codys would be grounded; lying like bright confetti across the pastures, hills. So the sky, the empty, burning vault, was open to anything that might choose to come. He shivered, despite the heat. He'd wondered, as a tiny child, just what a Demon looked like. The answer had come in the form of a recurring dream. It was always tiny at first; he'd see it winging from the distance, an inkblot against just such an infinity of blue. It would land and fold its wings, spread its long talons on the grass; and somehow in the dream he always found his voice. He'd speak to it, ask its name and what it wanted; and it would turn. Then the screaming would start. Because it had no form; it was a black shape merely, a hole in reality through which one might see the ultimate Void. It had no eyes; but he always knew it stared.

He shuddered again, briskly. He was giving himself the horrors; as if there hadn't already been horrors enough. He wiped the wheelrim with the cloth he carried in the dash. He topped the rise; and Middlemarch was spread before him, detailed in the brilliant light, seeming to stretch for ever. He swallowed, made a conscious effort to clear his mind.

An hour later, he was feeling slightly better. The traffic of course had been heavy, even at that still-early time. Coaches and lorries, the private cars of the wealthy - more than once he saw, flying from a high mudguard, the scarlet and gold pennant of a Master – even the odd jalopy like his own. Plus horses and carts of course, dashing two-wheelers drawn by high-stepping greys, the closed carriages of ladies, lumbering waggons piled with the rich produce of the Middle Lands. At each junction stood a Var policeman, resplendent in white and gold. Pistols were strapped to their hips; they blew whistles from their little railed podiums, waved and gestured imperiously, made half-comprehensible signs. He observed them carefully, trying to give no offence; he'd heard a little about their methods from the Middlemarchers at College. A couple of bad moments, when he felt himself hopelessly lost; but in the main the road ran straight and true. He oriented himself on the great bulk of Godpath, daunting with its immensity, saw beside it the square white barn of the Middlemen. Leastways that was what his Variant colleagues always dubbed them. It nestled close, almost companionably, by the side of its vast companion; arrogance, it seemed, was answered by quiet assurance. He'd liked to have stopped and entered; but there was no chance, no chance at all. He drove on instead, following a battered grey coach routed for the Salient; lads waved through the high rear window, one brandishing a bottle. Corps Apprentices no doubt, fresh from a Central College course. They at least didn't seem concerned at the grounding of the Codys. Or maybe they hadn't noticed.

Another swirling confusion of traffic; and it seemed the worst was finally behind him. He drove along a wide boulevard, straight and tree-lined. To his left he saw the Palaces of the Masters. Each massive building stood in its own grounds; and beside each rose a high, latticed Tower. But no Codys flew.

He nodded. The Strings would have been drawn. Disaster to let a Pilot touch the grass; but far worse, loss of face. The population, even in Middlemarch, were by no means universally convinced of the efficacy of Faith. Less so than ever, as the years went on. The Kiteman of each household would have been up since before dawn; if he'd gone to bed at all. He'd heard that *in extremis* some of them would even wet the Lifter sails, to catch what fragment of breeze remained; but tricks like that wouldn't avail today. Windspeed was zero.

Climbing the great hill to the east of the city he fancied the air lightened fractionally. But the engine still began to overheat. The Buckley carried no temperature gauge of course; but some sixth sense still warned him. A change of note perhaps, harder rattle of the splash-fed bearings. He pulled in and switched off. The engine clanked awhile before condescending to stop. He set his lips, prepared himself for a long wait. He wiped his face, sat in the shade of the van and stared back at the city.

An hour later he saw how lucky he'd been. The rubber filler cap had jolted from the tube atop the block, lodged by some miracle in the inlet manifold. He frowned, and checked the sump. The dipstick barely touched oil. He got a gallon from the back, poured in three pints. He checked the water; but curiously that seemed fine. He swung the crank by hand. It turned freely enough. He got in, pulled the starter. The engine caught first time.

Over the hill, the treelined vistas returned. Here though the land was more populous. He passed cart after cart, each drawn by a burly shire. Some of the drivers sat stolidly, staring ahead; but mostly they waved. He acknowledged them curtly, checked the chronometer again. Not midday yet; and the trip already nearly half done. He wished now for one of the devices the Variants used, the little machines the commoners thought devil-possessed but that he knew were wireless telegraphs. Then he could call Streanling, speak to his home. Tell them he was on course, that the Buck was running sweet, that Middlemarch was behind him.

His face clouded at once. Tell them? Tell whom? Rone, and Shand? What would they say, would they truly care? Yes, he decided sourly. They'd care, and they'd rejoice. Because of the miles between. Now, perhaps, they were safe.

Stupid too to feel a yearning for the place. After all, it wasn't his home. Not any more. It hadn't been for years. In a way he'd known that all along. He'd been a supernumerary, surplus to requirements. An embarrassment perhaps. He frowned again. It was still the house he'd been brought up in. Most of his life at least. He'd known every brick of it, every bough of the orchard trees. In part, it had seemed to belong to him. Stupid of course, nothing belonged to him. But maybe the notion was unavoidable.

He pulled in to consult the map. Realized he was a bare ten miles from Crossways. He decided he'd earned a break. So had the Buckley of course. He drove on, keeping an eye open for a likely-looking inn.

He saw one almost at once; a pleasant, white-walled building, low and thatched, set back a little from the main road. Obviously it served some local village; he could see a scatter of house roofs, lost among further trees. He pulled in, tyres scrunching on gravel, turned the key. This time the engine stopped without complaint.

Rand stretched, took his glasses off and rubbed his face. Normally he didn't wear the spectacles except for office work; some lingering trace of vanity perhaps. But on a drive like this it was better to be safe than sorry. He closed the van and locked her, walked towards the pub. He saw by its sign it was the 'Kiteman'. Must be a base nearby. He couldn't remember offhand; and the Civil maps were locked in his case. He ducked through the doorway, turned left into a wide, stoneflagged bar. The place was refreshingly cool; but the thick stone walls saw to that.

There was just one other customer. Launchmaster by his shoulder tags, in off-duty drab. He nodded pleasantly, gestured for Rand to join him. He bought a beer, sat down. The other produced a much-battered pipe, glanced at him keenly. He said, 'Kites?'

He was vaguely surprised. He said, 'To do with,' and the other chuckled. He nodded to the window, answered Rand's unspoken question. 'Saw you pull up,' he said. 'Not a farmer's truck; and the local yokels don't get round to gasoline.' He puffed the pipe alight. 'What are you, Civil?'

Rand nodded. 'Audit,' he said. 'Easthold, part of the Salient.'

The Launchman laughed again. He said, 'They'll love you like a brother. This your first tour?'

He shook his head. 'No,' he said. 'I did a year in Streanling.'

'Dead and alive hole,' said the Corps man. 'Did a stint there myself. Glad when they shipped me out.'

He was irritated for a moment. Then he realized how absurd that was. After all he'd knocked the Garnorders enough. He said, 'You zeroed as well?'

The other nodded. He said, 'With a vengeance. I got out. Before some smartarse found me a spit and polish job. Come far?'

'Yes,' he said. 'Streanling.'

The older man glanced up again. But if he realized he'd made a gaffe he wasn't concerned. His eyes twinkled slightly. He said, 'What's it like farther over?'

'Flat,' he said. 'Everything down.' He described the grounded String he'd seen, and the Launchmaster grinned. 'That'll be West Four,' he said. 'Always did fancy themselves. They'll have their heads on spikes.'

'You have any trouble?'

He lit the pipe again, and shook his head. 'No way,' he said. 'We downed at zero two thirty. Skipper's like that. Doesn't take that sort of risk. He'll down for anything. Force Six and he starts getting the trots.'

'Your place close?'

The other jerked his thumb. 'Just through the woods. Five Stringer. Supply depot too. You'd have fun with us.'

He said, 'Lucky it's not my patch then.'

Some other personnel came in. The Launchmaster excused himself, ambled over to join them. Rand was vaguely glad. Something about the clipped slang of the Corps always got to him. Took him back. Too far, sometimes. His father had been a Flier. One of the best in Northguard. Till a wild night of storm, nearly twenty years ago. He'd seen the squalls come lashing across the sea and shuddered, though he was still a tiny boy. He found out later his father had seen them too, and known instinctively the Cody wouldn't live. He'd given Ground a red; they'd downrigged, but they hadn't been fast enough. He'd been a year in hospital, half his bones shattered, some beyond repair; and never walked again, except with massive sticks. They pensioned him well enough; it kept his children clothed and fed, but for him life had lost meaning. He hung on till Rand was ten, his sister twelve. He'd taken to his bed then; worn out, Rand realized now. By grief, frustration, by the endless pain. Something in the boy had known he wouldn't last long; but he'd suppressed the thought. Until the night his father called him to his room. He lay propped up by pillows; cordial beside him on the table, his pipe and baccy case, a box of lucifers. He wasn't smoking though; he stayed quiet for a while, gazing through the window, blueing now with dusk. Far off a Cody flew, tiny with distance, graceful against the deepening sky. He talked then, inconsequentially it seemed; about his own young life, the many postings he'd had, the close calls he'd survived. Finally he gripped the boy's wrist. 'Rand,' he said, 'I'm going to ask you something.' He frowned, seeming to search for words. 'The Codys cost me your mother,' he said. 'Soon after Shand was born. She couldn't stand the strain. Not any more. She gave me a clear choice; so I've got no complaint. And then they gave me this.' He glanced down at the bedclothes. 'I was a good Flier,' he said. 'One of the best. But they still gave me this. You see, it isn't a case of whether it's going to happen. It's a case of when.' He looked back to the boy's face. 'Don't do it, Rand,' he said. 'Don't be a Flier. Your life's worth more to you. And me.'

For a moment the room seemed to spin. He hadn't realized his father understood his secret dream; because in all the years since the accident he'd never spoken of it. He swallowed; when he could speak again he said, 'I promise. I'll get the Book.'

The other shook his head. 'No,' he said, 'I don't need any Book. Your word's good enough.' He lay back tiredly, and closed his eyes.

Rand made a private pact with God, later that night; but God, it seemed, had not seen fit to listen.

So Rone had come quietly to the grieving house; Rone silver-haired and dignified, even then. But he'd been silver-haired from youth. He spoke quietly, to the aunt who was the only relative, the priest, the Corps Chaplain who had organized the service. He'd borne the children away with him, to the sprawling house on the hill; Rand and the dark, hollow-eyed girl. And there they lived till the boy became a man, and Shand a graceful woman.

The house looked down on the town. Behind it, over the orchard and the garden wall, the Codys streamed; the wind sang in their Traces. He'd watch them by the hour, in between schoolwork, the chores Rone found for him. Rone, who had become his legal guardian. Sometimes he thought he'd learned to hate the Strings; but the emotion didn't last. Only the promise held. Break it, and his father would be truly dead. He pondered, sitting alone in his room; and finally his decision was made. He knew he couldn't keep away from the Codys, not for ever; so if he couldn't be their master, he would be their servant. He broached the matter, at dinner that same evening; but Rone as ever was brusque. 'Do what you choose,' he said. 'It's your life; only you can lead it.' He wiped his mouth with a napkin, readdressed himself to his wine.

He frowned. Shand was the one of course, the apple of the old man's eye. Shand with her whisperings, her snufflings, her instant stamping tempers. He'd have slapped her; in fact he often did. She'd scurry to Rone for comfort then and he'd take her on his knee; sit and let her cry against his shoulder, soothe her, stroke her hair.

He rose, abruptly. He'd been meaning to eat; but now he couldn't face it. He strode out to the Buckley, started up and drove away.

They made Rone a Freeman, for his services to the State. He became more dignified than ever. The official scroll hung framed above the dining table; the chain and medallion he wore whenever possible. Rand frowned again. Was it petulant of him, to doubt the other's virtue? Behind Skyway loomed a high, dour building, the Northwest Hospital. Though hospital, he felt, was a misnomer. There they sent the castoffs of society; Corps men who had been broken by the Kites, the other unfortunates whom the good Lord had seen fit to bereave of wit. Rone had worked there all his life, risen from the humblest of positions to be Chief Administrator, finally Head Warden. It was his domain; there, his word was law. For the happiness of others he had given up his own; refused marriage offers, the chance of a family. His devotion was patent; and in his field he was the acknowledged master. He travelled extensively when his other duties allowed, to the Middle Lands, the Southguard; lectured in church after church, to congregations that hung on every word. Always he would tell them what they needed to hear; that the power of God was infinite, the Variant Church His one true mouthpiece; that the Law was paramount, because it meant normality. The preservation of the order of things. And after all, who was better equipped than he to preach the *status quo*? He'd seen the reverse of the Lord's coin, the horrendous results of tolerance.

Rand frowned. He'd visited the hospital just once. He'd seen the shambling oldsters, blank-eyed children, the girls with filthy, matted hair. He'd heard the howls that came from barred rooms. He saw that on their uniforms the inmates wore at front and back a florid, circled initial. 'I' for Innocent.

He tackled his guardian about it the same evening. 'Father,' he said – he'd called him that for years, perforce, though it still irked him – 'what's normality?'

The other looked surprised. He gestured with his pipestem, waved a hand at the quietly elegant surroundings. 'This is,' he said. 'Books to read, and flowers on the table. Wine in the cellar, good silver. Sometimes I don't understand you, Rand.'

He considered. He said, 'But all folk don't have things like this. Some of them are poor.'

'Of course,' said Rone comfortably. 'So what they have is normal for them.'

He pursed his lips. 'Then normalities are different,' he said. 'Perhaps there's a different one for everybody.'

The other narrowed his eyes, looked suddenly cautious. 'Normality is normality,' he said. 'That's plain and obvious.'

'But you've just said it varies.'

Rone glared at him. 'I gave my life to that place. My life and more. Don't presume to question me, young man ...'

He shouted back. 'Then what are they doing there? Who decides they have to be locked up?'

The other shook his head. 'It had to come,' he said wearily. 'I suppose it was inevitable.' He slung his napkin away. 'Have you ever gone hungry?' he said. 'Have you ever been ill-clothed? Have the Realm, the ideals it stands for, not supported you? Have I failed so badly? Answer me, my son.'

He looked up, under his brows. He said, 'I am not your son.'

Rone Dalgeth sighed. 'That too I should have expected,' he said. 'The ingratitude of the young. Perhaps it was no more than my due.'

He said, 'You pompous charlatan.'

The other nodded. 'I know you aspire to the Middle Faith,' he said. 'And so I try to understand it. Difficult though it might be. It preaches logic. Or pretends to. So we should burn this house. What would that achieve? How would it help those wretches down in Skyway?'

It was no use though. The volcano was bubbling, forcing at its cone. He said, 'Tell me, why do they cry?'

'Why do who cry?'

'The inmates. The ones you lock in cells.'

His guardian shook his head. He said, 'They are not cells.'

'They looked like it to me.'

'They are placed there for their own protection,' said the Warden. He sighed. 'Very well. They see them as a prison.'

'Why are they put into prison? Because they cry?'

The other said, 'I am becoming tired of this conversation.'

Rand ignored him. He rubbed the dark wood of the dining table, almost wonderingly. 'I think,' he said, 'this should be made of bones. The bones of other people.'

Rone Dalgeth rose, stood leaning on his knuckles. He said, 'Go to your room.'

He'd risen in his turn. His face was white; but a red anger-spot glowed on either cheek. 'So you're the arbiter,' he said. 'You choose normality for all the rest. That rather lets you off the hook, doesn't it?' He smiled. 'She's my sister,' he said gently. 'Tell me, does she call you Father too?'

The old man's hand flashed out. The blow was heavy; but he made no attempt to avoid it. He felt a trickle of blood start, run to his chin. He bowed his head. 'I could kill you of course,' he said. 'But I won't. I want my hands to stay clean.'

Rone was breathing heavily. 'You will leave this house,' he said. 'As soon as possible tomorrow. You will beg my forgiveness before you ever return.'

He shook his head. 'Not tomorrow,' he said. 'I'll go tonight.' He turned and walked from the room.

He was startled, momentarily. Ahead was a great intersection. More vehicles moving on it, more of the lumbering carts. Crossways; he hadn't realized his attention had wandered so far. He'd driven the last few miles automatically.

He slowed behind the little line of waiting traffic. A heavy private car, probably a farmer's, two smartly turned out traps; one of the big, gaunt tractors he'd heard were coming into use. He edged forward, slowed again. Finally his turn came. He glanced to either side. The other road ran southwest to northeast; Southguard to the Salient. His route lay straight across; later it would curve down, into the Easthold. He waited for a farm cart, another private carriage, eased the Buckley carefully across. He built up speed again.

He'd stayed that night with friends. He lay a long time sleepless, trying to make the anger drain away. He remembered that first dread revelation. He'd been sleepless then as well; turning and tossing, sheets sticky with the summer heat. At zero four hundred he'd given up the attempt. He rose and dressed, padded to the kitchen for a drink of water. On his way back up the stairs he froze. He'd heard, quite clearly, the click of a bedroom door. His guardian's. It was followed by the creak of a floorboard. He'd heard such things before, in waking dreams; but his mind, half-dazed, had refused to understand.

He stood in shadow, in an angle of the stair. He saw her clearly though. Her flimsy night-things shimmered in dawn dusk; through them her body gleamed pale. He took her wrist, heard the quick intake of breath. Her eyes blazed with fear, became opaque again. She said, 'Let go my arm.'

For a moment he couldn't speak. Finally he whispered, 'Why? Why, Shand, why …'

She snatched free quickly, drew the little shawl she wore closer about her shoulders. 'My life is my own,' she said. 'I do with it as I choose. Find your own solace, brother.' She raised her chin, stared at him a final time; moved away, and was gone.

He couldn't remember how he got through the next few days. Or weeks. He visited the Father, ate May cakes and drank his wine. Walked aimlessly through Streanling, out to the Northern Road, sat for hours at a time and stared at distant hills. It seemed his world was shattered. That she, that she … His mind balked, circling, refused even to finish the thought. He'd felt his life foursquare; rooted to rock, well-bastioned and safe. Now a corner-stone had suddenly been wrenched away. Sometimes the rage came; rage such as he wouldn't have believed. Because each night he lay on her and grunted. *Her* … He realized, belatedly, he'd loved her. As had her own father. The thought brought floods of hot and bitter tears. He'd wipe his eyes, stare up; and the Cody rigs were flying all around. Keeping the Realm from harm.

The Codys haunted him; by day, and in his dreams. Sometimes they bore symbols he couldn't understand; sometimes the Godkites had faces of people on them. Some were folk he thought he knew; but they changed and melted even as he stared. Others were people he'd never seen before; so maybe the future had its ghosts as well.

He was saved, finally, by something Father Alkin said. 'Actions are actions, Rand. Each has its purpose, each its allotted place. Though purposes are things we cannot grasp. But if you are dressing, you are dressing. If you are brushing your shoes, you are brushing your shoes. Perform each as is proper; and do not search for meanings. In that way, meanings will one day become plain …' So he began; and in time he found the doctrine easier. Breakfasts were breakfasts, school was school; the night time was for sleeping. He discovered courtesy, as a secondary effect; he was grave and quiet, till even Shand began to look at him with puzzled eyes. He affected not to notice, finally took pride. Though pride had its own dangers, as he realized later.

*

The land was changing, with surprising speed. The hills had gone; round him flat country stretched to the horizon. The villages were more numerous; he passed through half a dozen in as many miles, each visible from the next. In the last he found a little gasoline station. He filled up, pulled two wheels of the Buckley on to the kerb to ease the flow to the tank. The attendant seemed amused at the manoeuvre.

More of the flat emptiness, through which the road ran for the most part arrow-straight. Finally he came to a great arch of rusted iron. It spanned the carriageway; in its centre it bore a medallion, once gilded. He couldn't make out the device. Below though were the ragged letters EASTHOLD. He pulled in for a while, sat staring. For some reason he found it an oddly touching sight.

He started up again, drove through. It seemed with the simple act he put his life behind him, began afresh.

Today, the day of the grounded Kites, seemed a time for introspection. He found himself remembering the pumpmaid, with curious vividness. Her slimness, lovely legs in their blue cloth, the sunlight sparking from her hair. He wondered what she was doing, at this exact time. What everyone was doing, all the folk he'd ever known. And what about the others, the ones he would one day meet? The notion of future ghosts returned to him. After all, if the past had its shades it stood to reason the future must own them too. He felt a curious thrill, almost of anticipation.

He'd moved into College accommodation, the first available chance. The Church cavilled, cautious as ever of its funds. Eventually, Middlemarch grudgingly agreed. He expected letters had been exchanged with Rone Dalgeth. He wondered what had been said.

His studies came hard at first. He attended to them assiduously; Father Alkin's advice was once more a blessing. The opening of a folder, the closing of a textbook, became small Actions in themselves. He thought his tutors looked on him with favour; though at least once the Master Sprinling frowned. He wondered if the Middle Teaching was discernible from acts as well.

In time the work began to pall. He realized just what he was committed to; the endless totting of figures, counting of parts, spares, supplies. Cable drums and spliceblocks, Lifter stays and cones, crossheads and valve assemblies, grommets, bolts and screws. Cane for the baskets; though 'cane' was a word he hadn't come across. The substance was manufactured by extrusion in the industrial suburb of Middlemarch; in fact there was a move afoot to call it Holand fibre.

He struggled nonetheless, toiling at his books, huddled in blankets sometimes when his stipend wouldn't run to coal. He scraped his grades the first two years, groaned at the thought of the rest. He would have given up at any time; but he'd burned his boats. Or had them burned for him. He set his lip. He would succeed because he had to. And then get out of Northguard. For good.

Janni Nesson changed his life. In more ways than one. Though at first she was a greater distraction than the rest. He'd known girls enough of course. He cultivated them, when he got the chance; and found that skill became easier too. In fact Brad Hoyland, one of the few chums he'd made, commented on it one night. They were sitting in a bar – one of his rare binges, his grant had just come through – and the other shook his head. 'Wish I knew how you did it,' he said dolefully. 'Round you like flies, they are; and you don't even put any effort into it.'

He was genuinely puzzled. 'I just talk to them,' he said. 'I don't know anything about the rest.'

'That's just the point,' said the other. 'I try that, they want to see my grant statements ...'

Janni was different though. To start with she'd applied for, and won, college entrance. An almost unheard-of thing for the Vars; the Church had fixed views about the role of women. It didn't seem to trouble her though. She buckled down, worked hard; by the end of that first term she was heading her section. He'd noticed her of course, in refectory and elsewhere; you couldn't really miss her. The mane of dark hair, the broad-cheekboned face, the candid violet eyes. She wasn't particularly tall; but then she didn't need to be. The students danced attendance to a man; but she didn't seem impressed. She'd treat each one the same, gravely and politely. She'd come to study Civil Administration; and that was what she was going to do. There were rumours naturally, whisperings; stirrings of jealousy, even the odd dormitory fight. He was glad, not for the first time, he wasn't living in. He'd seen the results of that sort of thing before. An iron wall existed, in his mind.

One day she sat opposite him at table. The long Refectory was more than usually full. It was about the last vacant place. She said, 'Mind?' and he shook his head. He said, 'Of course not.' He passed the condiments.

She talked as she ate. As if she'd known him for years. Who had done what in class, who had said that or this. Student chatter, inconsequential enough; but he still found himself intrigued. Her voice was low, with a trace of huskiness; but beautifully modulated. She'd had a good education; but that was a matter of common knowledge. Her folk were well-to-do, farmers in the Middle Lands who ran a livery stable on the side. He found himself watching her hands. They were sinewy, slim-fingered but broad across the knuckles; more like the hands of a boy. There was a preciseness too, an economy of movement. He wondered if it came from the years of training.

It seemed she divined his thoughts. She said, 'Do you ride?'

He shook his head. 'The original ignoramus,' he said. 'Don't know one end of a horse from the other.'

Janni grinned. 'That's easy,' she said. 'One end kicks.' She pulled her sleeve up, showed him a big scar on her arm. Curving, and deep. He said, 'Good Lord. You mean it didn't put you off?'

She shrugged. She said, 'These things happen.' She glanced up again. She said, 'You're Rone Dalgeth's son, aren't you?'

Rand looked at his plate. 'No,' he said. 'I'm not.'

She waved a hand. 'Oh, I know about that,' she said. She considered. 'My father knew yours,' she said. 'There was a big Station near us. On our land in fact. Shame when they pulled out. Nice little source of income.'

He steered the conversation on to safer ground. She chuckled at his tales, once wrinkled her nose at a mention of Master Sprinling. He found the gesture enchanting. Finally she pushed her plate away. He said, 'Like a sweet?' but she shook her head. 'Sorry,' she said, 'got to dash.' She grinned. 'In any case, they reckon I'm sweet enough already. See you around.'

On the way out another student nudged him in the ribs. 'Hands off, Rand,' he said. 'She's spoken for.'

'Who by?' he said. 'You?' He put his hands in his pockets, and sauntered away.

He thought about her a lot after that. Behind the banter there was high intelligence; of that he had no doubt. But in any case it wasn't in dispute. Something extraordinary must have induced the Vars to admit a girl student; social influence existed of course, but there were limits to what it could achieve. Also there was something he hadn't met before; an openness, a candour he found intriguing. She could have pulled rank on him, boasted about her family, their holdings; any other Midlander would. But she'd done no such thing.

He grimaced, faintly. She was also very lovely. He grudged the thought at first, later admitted it more freely. He wondered what Father Alkin would have said. He remembered the jam and cream on Holy Days, and had little doubt.

The engine of the Buckley died. He swore, and steered on to the rough. Though he needn't have bothered; the long straight road ahead was empty. He opened the bonnet, tapped the little fuel pump with the handle of the jack. Nothing. He frowned. Then reached into the cab, turned the ignition switch he'd cancelled. The pump began to tick at once. He drove on again.

Mid-afternoon; and the heat at its most intense. Mirages floated over the road ahead. Each silver lake dissipated as he approached. The blue sky was still unmarked. No Cody strings; but of course there were no Stations here. The Easthold was much like the Salient. There, they fringed the Badlands; here, they ringed the coast. The inland folk weren't rich enough to matter.

He passed through another village. Bigger this time, but curiously deserted. Maybe they were all sleeping through the heat. A tractor stood outside a filling station. So there was at least one wealthy farmer round about. Hard to credit, seeing the barren fields. Even the livestock seemed scarce.

Gaven was the first town of any note. Then Killbeggar, and Fishgard. His destination. Though there was little enough fishing these days. In this Sector at least. Sometimes the sea was bad. 'Urination of Demons', the Master Sprinling had said; and he'd frowned. The image wouldn't form; it didn't sort with his view of physics. He shrugged. The Master was the College's top theologian; so he ought to know. It hadn't troubled him overmuch. He'd been deep into duplex bookkeeping at the time.

In Gaven he noticed something he'd seen before. To the right of the High Street rose the thin spire of a Variant church; facing it, opposing almost, was the square barn of the Middlemen. The juxtaposition recurred on the eastern edge of the town; and again in the hamlet beyond. It was visual proof of what he had felt before; in the Salient, the Easthold, the power of the Vars was challenged. Gently, peacefully; but challenged nonetheless. He frowned. The Demons, in their squabblings with God, once ruined all the world. Would the last Men one day finish their task for them?

Beyond Killbeggar the road surface deteriorated sharply. The Buckley slewed and bounced, wheels dropping into potholes. He was vaguely surprised. After all, Fishgard was the capital of Easthold. But then, Streanling had never found a use for paving either.

His thirst was rising, his mind running on thoughts of a glass of ale. An inn showed to the right; before it was a parking area lined by stunted, dusty bushes. He almost pulled across; but the place had a shabby, ramshackle look. And even if he could rouse them, they'd be grumpy; they'd certainly be having their siesta. He drove on.

She did see him around. Quite a lot in fact. He resisted for a while the notion that she was seeking him out; finally it became patent. It didn't improve his stock with his fellow students; once he thought he was in for a major fight. She laughed when he mentioned it to her. 'Oh, Giggleguts,' she said – she meant an urbane youth called Giller. 'He thinks whenever he whistles, the girls should come running. It doesn't work with me though.'

He frowned. Somehow it seemed she'd become a special person to him. 'I don't whistle,' he said.

She looked at him. 'I know,' she said. 'That's why I'm here.' Unexpectedly, she tucked her arm through his. 'Come on,' she said. 'Let's go and have a drink.'

She had strange views about the role of women. Heretical at first, to his mind. He pondered them. If a woman did a man's job, she should get a man's pay. He supposed that was morally right. Indeed, it couldn't be gainsaid. But women *didn't* do men's jobs. Janni did though. Or would one day.

Her views on marriage were even more bizarre. Women should have the right to choose their partners, the same as men. After all, marriage was a business like any other; it should be run on business lines.

'Fair enough,' he said. 'But every firm still has to have a boss.'

She punched him. 'Yes,' she said. 'And that's you, isn't it?' She was only being playful; but he still rubbed his arm. He hadn't realized just how strong she was. He reflected ruefully that he wouldn't want her to hit at him in anger. There was more in this equality of the sexes than he'd realized.

The evenings with her ate into his slender reserve. Her notions of equality, it seemed, didn't extend to the sharing of bills. Not at first anyway. He examined his finances carefully, considered. He went to see the Master Bone. Things were a little easier after, though keeping abreast of his College work meant studying far into the night; till zero four hundred sometimes. He'd stagger to bed dog-tired, catch a bare three hours sleep; because First Session started at zero eight.

Surprisingly, the College work didn't suffer. In fact his grades steadily improved. He topped his set in his third year, again in the early fourth. It seemed she'd become a source of inspiration to him. Certainly a source of energy. She drained it from him; but always it was mysteriously replaced. The emptiness he'd felt before had gone. Life had a purpose again; though what that purpose was he didn't for a time admit.

Vacations were more difficult. He'd see her to the coach, watch it set out on the long drive to her home; and subtly the world would change. He'd wander aimlessly, on those days when Master Bone had no need of him, scuffing at pebbles, staring up at the high, bright shapes of the Codys. The old fantasies returned. He decided he'd like to fly one, higher and higher, till he could see the Middle Lands themselves. He was sure the place she lived in would have a glow to it. An aura. He decided he was in love. He'd wonder what she was doing, every minute of the day; riding perhaps, or mucking out the stables, cleaning tack. Or out with friends; she had a lot of friends, she'd chattered about them often enough. Perhaps of course there was a special friend. One she hadn't mentioned.

The thought was like a dagger in the heart. He was faintly ashamed of himself; but it was no use trying to deny what had flashed through his mind.

Perhaps she was just using him, whiling away the evenings of the long terms; so when she had finished College …

He shook his head. There were plenty of students better off than he; she could have chosen from a hundred. He reminded himself he was a lucky man, told himself not to question the Lord's bounty. After all he had been tested, tested to the hilt; and he had not broken. Could it be she was his reward?

It seemed the question was answered instantly. Almost as if she had known. There was a letter waiting for him when he got home. He recognized the strong, sloping hand; unfeminine, yet so typical of her. He tore the flap, his fingers trembling with excitement.

It's been beautiful here, she'd written. The weather's perfect, there hasn't been rain for weeks. How has it been with you?

Centus is coming on wonderfully. I think he's the best horse we've bred. I take him out nearly every day. Daddy says he's going to enter him for the Yearling Stakes in Middlemarch. He's absolutely sure he'll win. Isn't it marvellous?

I think of you a lot, working on those greasy old cars. Do you think of me? I bet you've got a girlfriend I don't know about. Probably loads. I'm sure you could take your pick …

I'm going to the races myself tomorrow, we're all going down. Daddy has got a fortune on a horse called Blue Equality. It's going to be Blue Murder if he loses; but I think he'll still be running when we get back home.

What I want to know is, why can't there be women jockeys? I'd beat any of the boys I know; sidesaddle too. I think I shall have to start a campaign …

'Bye for now. Rand. Write if you get a minute, I'd love to hear from you. If not, I'll see you next term. I'm looking forward to it.

Much love,

Janni

PS. We had a Cody land here yesterday. All the way from Streanling. I looked to see if there was a message from you on it. I could imagine you dashing about with a hacksaw …

He tucked the note under his pillow that night. He got the best sleep he'd had in weeks.

He met the coach when it jolted in, the day before the start of summer term. She ran to him at once, and kissed. Put her arms round his neck. He swung her, laughing, set her back on her feet; to the envy of some, and the fury of quite a few. That didn't matter though; nothing mattered, except that she was back. He walked her to her digs, she chattering all the way;

about the races, and the farm, and the new foal. She insisted he come in and wait while she bathed and changed. 'I'm all grot,' she said. 'Dead yucky. Look at this.' She pulled her skirt hem up, exposing a vista of bronzed thigh, frowned at the dirt that marked the creases. 'Those coaches are filthy,' she said. 'I'm going to write to College. Suggest they clean them at least once a year. Maybe Foundation Day. Shan't be long.' She dashed for the stairs.

In fact she was gone an hour or more. He didn't mind. He sat and sipped at the wine she'd left him and pondered. There was a change in her, something he couldn't place. She had always been vivacious; now she was electric. Poised somehow, like a dancer. As if some inner excitement was about to burst through.

She came back looking radiant in white. Twirled to make the skirt fly out again. He said, 'How do you get so brown?'

'There's this barn,' she said. 'You can get out on the roof. I lie up there all day with nothing on.'

He thought his heart was going into spasm.

She grinned at him. 'Where shall we go?' she said.

He kissed her. 'I don't mind,' he said. 'As long as it's with you.'

She took his hand. 'Let's go and have something to eat,' she said. 'Then I feel like getting drunk. Just to celebrate.' She waved a wad of notes. 'Don't worry, Daddy put my allowance up. It's all on me ...' For once, he didn't argue.

They walked past Master Bone's on the way into town. She glanced through the gates and turned her nose up. 'You can chuck that grotty old place soon,' she said. 'You won't need it any more. Anyway you'll have to when you get your posting.'

Again the little pang; and once more it seemed she read his thoughts. 'Don't worry,' she said. 'It's still a term away. And a term's a lifetime. I should know: I have to live through them too.'

'Perhaps I might fail the Finals,' he said. 'Deliberately, just to stay with you.'

She looked solemn. She said, 'You say the nicest things.' She took his arm. 'How about the "Twisted Trace"?' she said. 'Then we can go on to the "Master of Streanling". The lobster there's divine ...'

She did get drunk. Not raucously so, it wouldn't have been her style. But very definitely tipsy. He walked back with her finally, saw her to the door of the little cottage. She kissed, in the shadow of the porch; and he all but gasped. She'd kissed often enough before; but never like that. Mouth opened wide, tongue pushing. He reacted; and his hand, instinctively it seemed, cupped her breast. Began to squeeze and fondle.

She pushed away. 'Not here,' she said. 'Not here ...' He thought for a desolate moment she was dismissing him. He stepped back; and she instantly took his wrist. 'Don't be a clot,' she said. She fiddled in her handbag, still swaying a little, found the key. Climbing the stairs, she took his wrist again. 'Careful,' she whispered. 'That one creaks a bit.'

They kissed again, in her room. She touched him between the legs, and chuckled. She said, 'You are a naughty boy.' She reached behind her. The dress slid down without fuss. She said, 'You can take the rest off. Part of your job.'

She twitched the covers aside, lay back on the bed. She sighed; then she sat up again, took something from a little jar. She popped it into herself; the movement of her hand was almost too quick to follow. 'Sweetie,' she said. 'The sort I like the best.'

He was fumbling with his shirt. 'Janni,' he said. Or croaked. 'Janni, are you sure? Are you really sure?'

'Why?' she said. 'Don't I look as if I am? Come on, slowcoach …'

Ahead, unexpectedly, was a low range of hills. The road angled toward them. He changed down, tackled the first incline. He glanced at his rear view mirror. He'd thought a haze was spreading from the west; now he saw for the first time a blue-grey edge of cloud.

Another bend; he changed gear again, breasted the final slope. Beyond was a straggling village. He saw the style of architecture had changed. The houses were of stone, narrow-windowed and dour. He stared. Jutting from each chimney stack was a narrow ledge. A Demon seat. Night horrors could rest there before flying on. They'd be grateful, and not trouble the folk beneath. He shook his head. He'd heard of such things, but never quite believed them.

He stared again. Ahead was a second range of hills; above them, faint but unmistakable, a pearly glower. The reflection of the sea.

He qualified, passed out in the top ten. His posting came with commendable speed. He read the flimsy twice; the first time he hadn't believed his eyes. His first tour was in Streanling.

He took Janni out, to celebrate. Events tended to repeat themselves. He was more skilled by now of course. He tucked his forearms under the pillow. That way he could kiss her, and not muss her hair. They slept awhile; he woke in the wee small, saw she was awake too. She sighed. She said, 'It's such a pity.'

'What do you mean?'

'That you have to go. I'd like to wake up in the morning with you. Then we could do it again.'

'You,' he said, 'are without doubt the sexiest girl I know.'

She eyed him sleepily. 'I was the first, wasn't I?' she said.

'The first what?'

She refused to be drawn. 'You can always tell,' she said. 'Don't go for a minute.'

He cuddled her again. Finally he pushed himself away. 'Janni,' he said, 'I *must*.' He swung his legs from the bed, started to dress. 'We may have a place of our own,' he said. 'One day …'

No answer; and he turned. She had drifted back to sleep. He covered her, gently, and tiptoed from the room.

He rented a little flat. It left him short; but the first year with the Corps was traditionally difficult. In time he found he could supplement his income by private jobs; stocktaking for the local shopkeepers and such. The work bored him; but money was money. By careful budgeting he found he could even save a little each week. A few months later he went to see the Master Bone. The Buckley was standing in the corner of the workshop. The other eyed her appraisingly. 'Not much to look at I grant,' he said. 'In need of a little love. But I've checked her through, basically she's sound. She'll do you a turn for a year or two.' He twinkled at him. 'No racetrack stuff though,' he said. 'Or you'll soon regret it. She's not a young lady any more.'

Rand glanced up sharply. He wondered if the other had heard rumours. But the old engineer's face remained bland.

He started the little van up. She rattled. But she was dirt cheap. He paid the Master on the spot, and drove her home. He stripped her interior, scrubbed through. He paid special attention to the seats; because she would be carrying a queen.

Janni came round in the evening. He stared. She was wearing a pair of the figure-hugging blue trousers favoured by working girls. He kissed her, rubbed her bottom; and she grinned. She said, 'You like them?' and he smiled back. He said, 'I like what's inside better.'

She pushed him away. 'Later,' she said. 'We've got work to do.'

They carried on till nightfall. He managed to get the first coat of paint on. He stood back finally, hands on his hips. The Buckley was already starting to look spick and span. He said. 'She really is a pretty little motor.'

She turned her nose up. She said, 'I'm jealous.'

'Why?'

'I think you love her more than me.'

He said, 'We can work that out tonight.'

He took her to his local pub. Over glasses of beer he said, 'How did you manage to get those things so tight?'

'What things?'

'Those things you're nearly wearing.'

She glanced down, smoothed at her thighs. 'Sat in the bath,' she said. 'Then let them dry on me.'

He'd never heard anything like it. He said, 'That's immoral!'

'Yes,' she said. 'Nice, isn't it?'

She should have gone down at the end of the summer term. But she was taking a postgrad course, she'd already booked for it. She'd finish up better qualified than him. She sat her Finals, came through with flying colours.

She invited him to the Middle Lands, to her parents' home. 'Come the last week of the hols,' she said. 'Then you can bring me back. Save me going on that ghastly coach.'

He havered. Unsure of the reception he would get. After all, they were way out of his class. But the prospect of a whole week with her was irresistible. He said, 'I'd love to ...'

She'd been pestering him to get in touch with Rone Dalgeth. He'd set his mouth at first, refused to discuss the matter. She didn't know of course what the cause of the quarrel had been; nor would he tell her. But she could be winsome when she chose. 'I know it must have been bad,' she said, time and again. 'But whatever it was, you're big enough to take it. We're a long time dead; and anyway, he could be useful to you one day.' She'd dimple at him then. 'Won't you?' she'd say. 'Not even for me?'

He gave in, finally. He couldn't refuse her; and anyway, guardian or not, they weren't of the same blood. So no crime had been committed. Except perhaps the omission of the banns. Also – and here of course was the nub of the whole thing – he'd got Janni now. The Lord had been good to him; it was time he gave a little on his side.

He hardly expected an answer to his letter. Nonetheless one came, couched in stiffly formal terms. It invited him and his young friend to dinner in two days' time.

It was end of term; Janni was a little sloshed from the breaking-up party. He wondered what the old man would make of that. He held the van door for her. She climbed in, albeit unsteadily. But in sight of the house she clapped her hands with delight. 'It's beautiful,' she said. 'It's beautiful. You never said ...'

'Yes,' he said. 'It is rather fine, isn't it?'

He'd asked her once, what he ought to call the Buckley. She'd been ready with an answer. 'Janni,' she said. 'I'm not having any competition.'

He stroked the wheel rim. 'Janni,' he whispered. 'Janni ...'

Strange to walk into his old home after so long. See the furniture still in the same positions, nothing changed. He paused in the hall, half-involuntarily; and she instantly took his hand. Gave it a little squeeze. His heart leaped, for sheer pleasure of her. She understood.

The dining room looked smaller somehow than memory painted it.

Smaller, and darker. But Rone Dalgeth was the same; sitting in the high-backed chair beside the empty fireplace. Shand hovered uncertainly at his elbow. She'd filled out, matured; but she was still a beautiful woman. She came forward, unsure; and he took her hands. He said, 'It's good to see you.'

She said, 'Me too.' She pecked him on the cheek. He returned the gesture, carefully. She hugged him then, with something like a sob. She said, 'It's been a long time.'

'Yes,' he said. 'It has.'

The conversation was stilted to begin with. He spoke carefully, avoiding delicate topics. He talked about the Kites, his career so far, his chances of promotion. Janni kept her side going with skill and tact. He wondered how he'd have fared without her.

At least the meal was excellent. But Shand had always been a superb cook. Janni greeted the main dish with cries of delight. Middle Land venison, marinaded to perfection and served with simple vegetables. 'It's wonderful,' she said. 'Nobody – sorry – can grow it like us.'

He smiled. In excitement, she often spoke with her mouth too full. In another, it would have been an annoyance; with her, tiny blemishes merely underlined perfection. Like the scar on her arm, the mole an inch below her navel. The thought sent a thrill through him at once.

Rone Dalgeth seemed intrigued by her. He listened attentively to her descriptions of her parents' home. But then, property had always been a major interest. Or why would he have acquired so much, scattered throughout Streanling? And for all Rand knew, the rest of the Northguard.

The meal over, Janni was borne off to see the house. It was obviously prearranged. Silence fell for a moment; then his guardian coughed. He said, 'A very lovely girl. You're most fortunate.'

He swilled the wine in his glass. 'I know what you're waiting for, Father,' he said. He hesitated, set his lips. 'I apologize for speaking harshly,' he said. 'No-one should speak harshly, whatever the circumstances. But my opinions are my own. They have not changed.'

The other rose, stood staring through the window at the tree-grown grounds, blueing now with dusk. Finally he turned. 'That must suffice then,' he said. 'You're of an age now to make your own judgements. For right or wrong.' His manner seemed to soften fractionally. 'There's still a room here for you,' he said, 'If you choose. Pour yourself some more wine.'

'Thanks,' he said, 'It's appreciated. But I think I'll stay where I am for the moment. I shall have a posting coming through in a month or two anyway.'

The other nodded curtly. He said again, 'As you choose.' Later though, when he and Janni were leaving, he shook his hand. 'Visit us again,' he said. 'Don't leave it too long this time. None of us are getting younger you know.'

He smiled. 'And bring your young lady with you. Or this time you won't be forgiven ...'

Janni left for home. Walking back to the flat he felt better than he had in years. At last, everything in his world seemed to be coming right. He was overdue for leave. He booked a fortnight of it, got into the Buckley and just drove. He quartered the Northguard, stopping off at inns, wandering the little hill villages as fancy took him. He called at most of the Kitestations he passed, and sent his card in. Each time he took care to write across the bottom ON LEAVE. He was made welcome at them all; he began to wonder if the horror stories he'd heard about audit tours really were just that. He learned a lot about the manning of the Frontier Codys; more, he thought, than he'd learned in all his studying. Field courses had been part of training; he'd done his trips to Garnord and Settering, once Middlemarch itself. It was good to smell the hangar scents again; oil and dope, hot steam. These Stations were different though. Optimum Lifter rigs, terminal speeds for downing, all existed in the standard manuals; here he found in practice they varied widely from Base to Base. In the hills the winds could be cranky; while conditions changed with lightning speed, sometimes it seemed from minute to minute. One and all, the Launchmasters were long-service men; and a good spattering of them local. It was they, and not the Captains, who had the final say; they who really ran the Bases.

The Frontier could cause other problems too. He found out quickly what salt air could do to cable. 'Look at this lot,' said one dour Riggingmaster. He kicked disgustedly at a corroded pile in the corner of a hangar. 'Never tell a Seabase they're carrying too many spares,' he said. 'You're liable to have a drum wrapped round your ears.' Rand nodded thoughtfully. He felt instinctively that was a piece of advice that would prove more than useful.

At All, set high on the cliffs above a place called Dancing Bay, they even half-jokingly offered him a flight. His heart leaped; for a moment he was minded to accept. Then he smiled, looked out to sea. Purple clouds were lowering and massing; the horizon was a brilliant, glowing band. 'No thanks,' he said. 'I think it's coming on to rain.' The Winchman looked down. 'If it rains,' he said, 'I'll lend you my coat.'

The Launchmaster, a grizzled man who must be close to retirement, glanced at him keenly. 'You're old Del Panington's son, aren't you?' he said.

He nodded, surprised. 'How did you know?'

'Oh,' said the other, 'the word gets around.' He shook his head. 'I knew him,' he said. 'One of the best. Launched for him more times than I've had hot breakfasts. It was a downright piece of luck.' He glanced up at the pair of Codys already streamed, and pursed his lips. Rand wondered how much of the rest he had guessed.

He watched a Stringchange. The sea breeze was keen and capricious, gusting up over the cliffs. They still handled the great Kites smoothly, it seemed easily. He knew that last was deceptive. The fresh Trace was streamed, the Lifters sailed to their places; '*Clear basket*' was ordered, and the winch ratchet began to clank as the Cody rose to operational height.

It was a big Base, the biggest he'd seen so far; they had good mess facilities and a first-rate bar. He made a night of it, got fairly tipsy in the end. They gave him a bunk in one of the ground crew huts. The place resounded with snores; but he was used to that. He slept quickly and well.

Two Cadets were going on furlough. He took them back a few miles towards Streanling, dropped them where they were sure to pick up another lift. Everybody stopped for Kitemen. He turned west again; and there came a day when he stood on the farthest promontory of the Realm. Behind him and to the south the cliffs marched into distance, ragged and grand, the sunlight on their faces; while a mile or two offshore was a low, mounded island. From it, barely visible in the haze, flew a solitary Cody rig, its wings bright against the blue-grey crawl of the sea. The Realm protected itself, at every point.

He turned for home; reached Streanling by early evening, left the Buckley with Master Bone for a check. He was pleased with her; she'd run all the way with scarcely a hiccup. He still wanted her in top condition though, for his trip to the Middle Lands.

He let himself into the flat. On the carpet was a little pile of letters. Four or five of them, all addressed in the same hand. The hand he knew so well. He took them through to the kitchen, put the kettle on. He arranged them in date order, sat and smiled at them. Finally he slit the flap of the first. He more or less knew what he would read. Janni had a way with words that would curl the hair. 'Loin language,' he'd called it once; and she chuckled. 'Women aren't supposed to like that sort of talk,' she said. 'I do though, I always have. It turns me on.' As it was turning him on now. 'You naughty girl,' he said. 'Oh, you naughty little girl …' He smoothed the second sheet. The kettle had almost boiled dry before he remembered. He sat down later to answer. His phrasing was more careful. Quite sedate in fact. But they'd developed a private language of their own. She would know what he meant.

The visit to her folk went better than he'd dared to hope. Her mother was a bustling, friendly woman, quite different from what he'd thought, her father amiably vague; though Rand suspected the studied absentmindedness concealed a sharp enough brain. They were both considerably older than he'd realized; but then she had two married brothers, both with families of their own. He guessed she must have been lonely as a child; nobody of her age at all.

They placed him in a big, comfortable room in one of the wings of the house, itself a building of considerable extent though in typical Middle Lands style; stone-faced, the shallow-pitched roof half hidden by a decorative parapet. Driving to it, he'd seen at the south west corner an anchor point for a Cody rig; but nothing was streamed at the moment. He bathed and shaved, looked down later from the tall windows. The paddocks stretched to the horizon. He smiled. He'd decided, to his surprise, he was going to enjoy himself.

His behaviour, of course, had to be equally sedate. Though there were ways and means. On the second day she surreptitiously piled blankets and pillows into the Buckley, directed him to a place she knew on the far edge of the estate; a little wooded knoll, bright now with summer light. He nosed the van into the trees, switched off. He looked round. Not a building, not a farmworker for miles. 'Nobody ever comes here,' she said. 'When I was small I used to call it my castle.' She kissed him; then pulled with urgency, at the fastening of her skirt.

For the first time, he loved her half-clothed. He found the experience curiously exciting. When she wanted to go again though he undid her blouse. Wrong to hide her glory, even for a second. Finally she lay back with a sigh. 'Nobody does it like you,' she said. 'It's like fireworks going off, all the time. With a great big cracker at the end.' She snuggled against him. 'I couldn't have waited any longer,' she said. 'It was terrible. I nearly got dairy elbow keeping myself going.'

She slept. He lay listening for footfalls, the sound of an engine. None came. Finally he felt dozy himself. But that was dangerous. He kissed her awake and she sat up. 'I told you they wouldn't,' she said vaguely. She started pawing for her clothes. 'Look,' she said. 'Somebody made these knickers back to front.'

She showed him the stables, proudly, and the new young racer. Later she tried to get him on a horse; but at that he demurred. He said, 'I'll leave it to the experts.'

She pushed her hair back, laughing. 'Coward,' she said. 'It's easy.'

'It might be for you,' he said. 'I need an ignition switch. I know what I'm doing then.'

He watched her ride. Even to his unpractised eye she seemed superb. There was a grace to her, a fluidness; she and the animal seemed in perfect unison. Also it was unnervingly erotic. He'd never seen a woman ride astride before. But she merely laughed. She said, 'One day it will be the normal thing. Just wait and see.'

He gave in to her, finally. She chose a big old gelding for him. 'He's so docile,' she said, 'If you let him stand still too long, he goes to sleep.'

He stared at the saddle. He said, 'What do you call that?'

She said, 'Even you know what *that* is.' He said, 'It's more like an armchair.'

He mounted, gingerly. He didn't make too bad a fist of it. In fact she said he did it quite well. 'Very professional,' she said. 'You're facing the wrong way of course.'

'This,' he said firmly, 'is the front. It's sharper.'

'So it is,' she said. 'I never noticed.' She led the way into the yard.

'One thing,' he said. 'I'm not going to jump.'

She looked over her shoulder scornfully. 'It's not a jumping saddle. It would kill him.'

'It would kill me.'

She said, 'It would probably be mutual.'

He found the experience more pleasant than he'd thought. In fact towards the end of the morning he was positively enjoying it. She rode to a little pub, a gnomelike building set deep among woodlands. Other horses were tethered to a rail outside. She knew all their owners of course; but they seemed friendly enough as well. 'You see,' she said later, 'We're not all like you think. Us Midlanders.'

He said, 'You're not like I thought. There isn't another like you in all the Realm. That means the world of course.'

She glanced across. She said, 'You haven't seen the world.' To his surprise, her eyes were bright with tears.

The week ended far too quickly. He drove her back to Streanling. Work came hard; she said it did for her as well. But there were still weekends and evenings. They were better than before. If that was possible.

A message came, from Middlemarch. He opened it with trepidation. He knew well enough what it contained; advance warning of his new posting. Again he had to read the thing twice. The Northguard tour was extended by six months; his new patch would be Garnord. Central was apologetic. A mixup over postings; plus a temporary shortage of trained men. He whooped; and that night they went out on the town.

He was bidden home for the winter celebrations. The invitation included Janni. She accepted with alacrity, and he frowned. He said, 'But you'll be with your folks.'

'As a matter of fact, I won't,' she said. 'I'm a big girl now, I can stay away from home if I like.' She simpered. 'I can stay up after twenty-four hundred too,' she said.

He grabbed her. He said, 'Not if I have anything to do with it.' Later he said, 'But what will you do, Jan? You can't stay at the cottage. College digs close down, I always had to move out.'

She looked troubled. 'Yes,' she said, 'it *is* a problem. If only I knew someone with a little flat . . .'

He hugged her. He thought life had never been more perfect.

Shand fixed them rooms with a communicating door. So that was just right too.

He saw more of his guardian, as the year wore on. Janni came with him each time; the old man wouldn't hear to the contrary. He seemed to have taken a genuine liking to her. Sometimes, if it got too late, they'd stay the night; the twin rooms were always there. As the days lengthened once more he'd walk with her on the hill, where the great Kites swooped and rustled. A score of times he turned to her, and the question that was uppermost in his mind all but popped out; he couldn't imagine life without her now, didn't even want to try. But always for some reason he held his tongue.

The posting came through. The Easthold. He rushed to tell her; but she seemed curiously withdrawn. 'You'll have to go then,' she said. 'After all it's a good number. You'll get Frontier allowance; it'll mean a lot more pay.'

'But what will you do?'

'Finish my course I expect,' she said. 'It's almost finished anyway.'

He felt the rise of desperation. 'But Janni, it's only ten days!'

'That's all right,' she said. 'You'll have plenty of time to pack.'

He took her shoulders. 'Janni,' he said, 'Janni …' He tried to kiss her; and for the first time ever she turned her face away. 'I'm tired,' she said. 'Not now …'

Rand left her, stunned. Sat in the flat and brooded till dawn was in the sky. Finally his decision was made. He'd realized why she'd been so cold. It should have been sorted out before. A long time ago. Despite her vaunted liberality she had her areas of reticence; he'd known that well enough. She'd been waiting for him to ask, waiting for months; and he hadn't. So she'd thought she was being taken for granted.

He rummaged in the sideboard drawer. Took out a little leather-covered box. Inside it was the ring his mother once returned to Del Panington; a delicate thing crafted in pale gold. It bore an oval plaque; on it was the leafshape of the Vestibule. Outlined in gold, carnelian against turquoise. A proper ring, the only ring for Janni; a ring for a Kiteman's bride. He put it into his pocket.

The day dragged. He thought it would never end. He hurried to the cottage, banged the door. She answered. He said, 'Janni, I've got to see you. I've got something important to say.'

She looked dull and pale. Defeated, somehow. She said, 'I've got something to say as well. You'd better hear me first.'

She led the way into the little morning room. Stood back turned for a moment. Then she clenched her fists, 'I can't see you any more, Rand,' she said. 'I can't see you after this.'

'What?' he said. '*What?*'

'I can't see you,' she said. 'It's as simple as that. It's over. It's been nice, but it's over. That is all there is to it ...'

His mind was whirling. 'But,' he said. 'But Jan, Jan ...' The things they'd done, the places they'd been, how they'd mattered to each other; the horses, the farm, the driving ... All blown away, as if they hadn't existed. It was impossible. Simply and straight-forwardly impossible. He said stupidly, 'But you can't mean it. You can't. Why ...'

She swung to face him. There were tear-tracks on her cheeks, but her face was like stone. 'Because I've found somebody else,' she said, 'who can look after me better than you. It's as easy as that. It happens all the time.'

'Janni,' he said. 'Jan ...'

She shouted at him. 'Go. Just go. And never come back ...'

He found a pub, and drank. He drank all night as well. Somehow he got to work the following morning. Two days later he closed the audit abruptly; left a Streanling Kitecaptain whistling with surprise. And maybe heaving sighs of relief. He despatched the papers; after which he was free to drink again.

One day blended with the next. She was gone. It was over. His mind, circling, came back again and again to the single monstrous fact. Like a rudderless ship smashing into rocks. Assimilation was impossible. It couldn't have happened; and yet it had. It was like the gigantic pain of toothache. But this tooth could not be drawn.

Brad Hoyland found him. Brad on furlough, revisiting his old stamping grounds. Rand found he couldn't talk to him either. What could you say? The other went away.

He sobered a little, finally; and a notion came to him. He'd go to see his guardian. Once they'd fallen out, certainly; but the mess he'd made since of his life had left him wondering which of them was truly wise. This time the apology would be complete. Sincere. And the old man would advise him. Tell him what to do.

He got the Buckley, drove up out of town. He made a detour to avoid the place she lived. Dusk was falling by the time he reached the hill; although it was high summer. He hadn't realized how late it had got. Perhaps the Warden would be in bed.

There were lights on in the house though. As he pulled up, the front door opened. A figure slipped away. It shielded its face; but there was no mistaking. He even caught the dark sheen of her hair.

He drove again. When he finally stopped he was lost. Even the hills around him looked strange. He sat awhile and watched a Cody rise, dark against the afterglow. 'One wasn't enough,' he said. 'One wasn't enough.' He screamed, at the sky. '*One wasn't enough* ...' He found himself lying on the ground. His fists were bloody. Sometime, somehow, he got back to Streanling.

His room was warm. He still kindled a fire. He took everything of hers;

her letters, clothes, the little trinkets she'd given, and burned them. It was as if the flames were eating along his veins. Lastly he picked up the valise. He stared at it, and put it down again. He could dispose of that later.

Dawn was in the sky by the time he finished. The early pubs round the marketplace would be open already. He got some more money, staggered from the house.

Two days from departure his brain suddenly cleared. It was as if he'd drunk himself back to a state of sanity. He'd heard of such things happening, but hadn't believed it possible. He wanted no more beer; the very thought of it made him gag. The rage had gone; in its place was an icy, deadly calm. He saw now that he existed for revenge; revenge on both of them. And sometime, somewhere, that revenge would be exacted. He piled his things into the Buckley, looked back a final time and drove away.

He topped the last rise, pulled in. For the first time in the day, a breeze was blowing. Strong and cool, steady from the west. Before him, detailed in the bright air, lay the town and port of Fishgard; huddle of stone roofs stretching into distance, darker spires of churches, bland faces of the occasional taller buildings. Beyond, silver-blue and vast, was the sea.

He started up, and let the clutch in. As he rolled down the slope he saw a Cody rise, bright against the pale shield of the water.

6

Kitewaif

Velvet couldn't sleep because of the heat. She tossed and grumbled, in her little room. The room was built into the side of the great stone arch that spanned Fishgard High Street. It was cluttered with nests of old unwanted tables, folding chairs, garden furniture and the rest; because it wasn't really an arch at all, although it crossed the road. It was the sign of the 'Dolphin', the biggest hotel in town; and a feature of which the owners were very proud. It was sturdily built of stone; it rose from massive buttressed pillars, pillars so broad that on the pavement side there was barely room to squeeze between the foundation and the long front of the inn. Above it was a writhing crown of carvings. At its centre rose the great fish itself; a creature of legend surely, for none existed now. There were tales of course that they had been seen sporting themselves, by mariners far out in the ocean; but nobody in their right mind gave credence to the yarns of seamen. Not at least after a night spent in the taverns with which the town abounded. There were many other oddities; serpents with pretty, waving fins, strange creatures half-fish, half-man. Some with mitres on their heads, some holding three-pronged spears. Like the fish spears Velvet remembered seeing as a tiny child. But that must have been in another part of the Realm.

One of the creatures she particularly liked. She was a girl, also with a great fish tail. Her hair was long and flowing, her breasts well-formed and slight. She was very naughty at the front, you could see the lot; but her face was sweet. In one hand she held a glass, in the other a comb; and her lips were parted, as if she was singing. Velvet would have liked to climb up and touch her, but there was no way. The arch was high, and at that point its side was smooth and sheer.

Round the rest of the sides were Demons. The inevitable Demons that clustered and crawled on nearly every roof in Fishgard. And most of the Easthold; or so she'd been told. Why they put them there she had never been sure. After all, a real Demon flying by would be more tempted to stop and look if he thought he saw a friend. They even put seats on chimneystacks for them. The priests said they were grateful for the rest, and wouldn't harm the people in the house beneath. It had always seemed dubious to her; though so far it had seemed to work. She'd certainly never seen a Demon. She wouldn't particularly want to.

One of the beasts on the arch side was particularly bad. He was clinging to a buttress right by the stair to her little room. At first the thought of him outside all night had prevented her from sleeping; also she never liked to open the door first thing, see him staring in. Till one day she had become angry, and hit him with the handle of her parasol. To her amazement his great hooked nose broke off, and flew across the street. It made him look so funny she began to laugh. Now she was quite fond of him. After all, a Demon without a nose can't hurt anybody.

She was proud of the parasol. It had been given her last year at one of the big houses on the edge of town. She'd gone there with her truck, selling cordwood for lighting fires. It had been raining, and she was very wet. The person who opened the door of the servants' wing had seemed upset to see her. She'd turned away, but the other had taken her arm. She made Velvet go inside, into a great kitchen. She'd sat her by the fire and dried her hair, given her a bowl of soup. It had been very good. Later the lady of the house bought all the wood. Gave her a good price too. After which she had made the place a regular call. They were good customers, for other things apart from kindling.

When she left, the cook had hugged her unexpectedly. 'You poor little waif,' she said. 'Here, take you this. And don't get wet again.' She'd put the parasol into Velvet's hand, and she'd gasped. After all, people didn't give things away for nothing. It didn't make sense. She'd grabbed it and fled, before the other changed her mind. Later she'd wondered at the word she'd used. What was a waif? She was sure it was nothing to do with collecting wood.

The parasol became her prize possession. She carried it everywhere with her, winter and summer; though she seldom opened it, save in the privacy of her room. It was very gay, all white and pink stripes, and little tassels she was sure were made of gold. It was very old though, because the colours were faded. She was afraid the rain might harm it; and she wouldn't want to be without it now.

She guessed by the brightness of the sky it was zero five hundred. She couldn't understand chronometers, they'd always baffled her; but her sense of time was nonetheless acute. She got up, muttering to herself, began to put her dress on. Beneath it she wore voluminous petticoats, layer on layer. Got a bit hot in summer, but it was only sense. She always wore as many of her clothes as she could. After all, somebody might get in while her back was turned and nick them. Where would she be then?

She scuffed at her hair, in the fragment of mirror she owned. It was nice hair, it hung right down her back. She tied it with a fresh piece of string, and put her hat on. It was made of black straw, with ribbons and flowers to one side. Though they were getting faded as well now. She'd found it in a rubbish bin on the Ridge. That was where the really well-off people lived. She wondered why they threw such things away. She supposed they could afford to, being rich.

She adjusted the hat to what she thought a cheeky angle, slipped a big pin through it to keep it firm. She couldn't remember how she'd got the pin. It seemed she'd always had it. It was another of her treasures; it went everywhere with her. Which was why she always wore a hat. You couldn't just put a pin through your hair; it would look silly. Besides, it wouldn't stay put.

She picked the parasol up. Her feet she left bare. She had a pair of shoes, very smart, with pointed fronts and little inch-high heels. Though the leather was cracked a bit. She'd thought they made her look very grown-up. But the only time she'd worn them they worked big blisters on several of her toes. Now she left them behind. She didn't care if they did get nicked.

She opened the little round-topped door, grinned at the Demon outside. She padded down the flight of worn stone steps, stood staring up. It was still early; but the air felt even hotter. It was going to be a scorcher, she could tell. No breeze at all to clear it.

Which was one good thing of course. Without the wind, the Codys couldn't fly. Normally they streamed a big Trace from the Tower near the church, it flew right over the High Street. Fishgarders were proud of it, they said how fine it looked. She'd never shared their enthusiasm. She hated the idea of it hanging over her head. After all, she hadn't asked them to put it there.

Though even the Kites could be useful. She remembered finding a great String once, caught up in trees a long way from the town. A place she always went to, to get mushrooms. She'd scurried back, gone straight to the church; though the man she'd seen, when they finally let her in, had been less than sympathetic. He'd shaken her and said, 'Where is it then?' And when she'd refused to tell, started to beat her. She yelled; and the other man had come, the one in bright red clothes. He'd said, '*Leave her.*' He'd sounded really angry. He'd taken her to a little side room, sat and smiled. He said, 'Won't you tell me? Please?'

She'd glowered at him. She knew there was a reward. She said, 'I wants my money first.'

He'd sighed. 'You'll get it,' he said. He'd taken her in a car – the first time ever – and paid her for the find. All in a big brown envelope. She hadn't dared to open it, not then; but later on she'd gasped. More money than she'd ever seen; up to that time at least. She'd been looking for broken traces ever since. But she'd never found another.

Crows were working in the street, big shiny flocks of them. She stumped toward them. Some flew away, cawing indignantly; the rest just shuffled to one side. Carried on squabbling over gutter scraps. She swung the parasol, tapping as she walked. She'd seen rich people do that, though she didn't do it often. It tended to wear the tip away.

She paused outside the 'Anchor', stared. She couldn't believe her luck. They'd left some crates of empties in the yard; and nobody was about. She hurried back to the 'Dolphin', undid the small door at the foot of the arch and got her truck. She collected the spoils, watching round her cautiously. She hid them in the arch. It was one of the advantages of early rising. There was good money in bottles; and the crates as well. She'd take them to Master Lorning later on. He always paid her without argument.

She frowned a little. She had a nasty feeling he knew where they were coming from. And that when she took his crates back to the 'Anchor', they knew as well. It piqued her slightly. She liked to earn her keep; she'd always rather resented charity.

She thought about Master Lorning. His family had owned the 'Dolphin' now for three generations. She didn't know how long that was; she supposed it must be hundreds of years. He'd been very good to her though. She'd been sleeping behind one of the houses on the Ridge, in a little hut she'd found. She'd thought it would be all right, but they chased her away. They had a dog with them too, it tore her dress. Though she'd mended it, you couldn't really see it now. She'd scampered back with the truck, sat awhile and brooded on the waste ground opposite the 'Dolphin'. For once, she was feeling a bit depressed. She hadn't been doing any harm. Not that she could see. She'd have gone away without the dog. She examined the torn dress mournfully. It was her best as well. Finally she had a walk about the town. She did her usual trick with the bottles, went round the back as soon as the 'Dolphin' opened. She knew they didn't like her in the bars; that was where the well-off people went. After he'd paid her, Master Lorning said, 'Where are you sleeping now? Haven't seen much of you this last few days.'

She shrugged. She never liked to give too much away.

He'd stared at her keenly. Too keenly for her taste. He said, 'What's the matter? They booted you out up top?'

She looked at the ground and pouted, scuffed her toes on the cobbles of the yard. He was a big man, huge to her, with masses of iron-grey hair.

A little silence; then he stopped out, and closed the door. He said, 'Come with me, Velvet. Don't worry, you'll be all right.'

He walked across the dusty, rutted road, up the steps on the far side of the arch. He unlocked the little door – she'd always wondered where it led – and ushered her inside. 'I know it isn't much,' he said. 'But it's all I can do.' He looked a bit helpless. Funny, for a grown-up. 'It's the wife,' he said. 'She's difficult. Otherwise … you know what I mean.'

She didn't know what he meant, she hadn't the faintest idea. Nor did she care; because she'd fallen in love with the place at once. It was like a house, a real house of her own. She couldn't believe it. She even started to cry. She knuckled her nose, furious, and he touched her shoulder. 'Here,' he said. 'No need for that. Here …' He looked helpless again. 'You'll be all right,' he said. 'I can send some grub across. If we're busy, nobody will notice.' She wondered if it would matter if they did.

She brought her things up from the truck. Lucky she'd already had it packed. But then, she'd always had a funny feeling about that shed. She spent a happy hour arranging them. The place was thick with dust. But that was normal, wasn't it? You got dust everywhere.

There was even a little cupboard at the back. She put her shoes in it, and the other bits and pieces she didn't care about. Then she arranged her driftwood. She was an experienced beachcomber, she'd been doing it for years. And driftwood fetched good value, it made pretty-looking fires. The Mistress Kerosina told her once the flames came blue and green. Some of the bits she kept though. They reminded her of things. Animals mostly, though she wasn't sure such creatures had ever existed. There was one with about twelve legs, and all sorts of eyes, and its mouth open like a cow when it was lowing. And another like the dolphin on the arch, and another like the lady with the tail. Least, if you looked at it certain ways. She placed it in the middle of the sill; stepped back, and was quite pleased. Then she set about the bed. It stood upright against the farther wall; she lugged it into position with a bit of puffing, spread the blankets she'd fetched from the truck. She lay down to try it out. She thought she'd never been so comfortable. Later in the day she took a walk about the town. Some of the harbour boys laughed at her; but she merely raised her chin. She was a lady now, she had a home of her own. Which was more than they could say.

She wandered down the High Street; but the pickings weren't too good. Even the tailors' rubbish bins were empty; she could usually find cloth scraps to sell to Tinka. Though to tell the truth she was half afraid of him. He'd always spit on the coins before he paid her. She'd take them, gingerly; but she never felt right till she'd washed them in the sea. She tried the back of the forge; old horseshoes were worth money, she sold them on the Ridge. Some nailed them with the points upright, so the luck wouldn't run out; but most put them upside down, in case the Demons saw them and were annoyed. That way they attracted lightning too. Master Billings usually kept them for her; but this time he hadn't put any out. She went back, got the truck again. She squeaked down to the harbour, turned along the Quay. Beyond the mole a track led to the beach. She plodded stolidly, steering the truck through clumps of wiry grass. At the bottom of the incline she looked up and scowled. A Kiteship was lying at anchor. You could always tell them, they had a tower thing in front. She scowled again. She didn't like the Codys, though she'd never been too sure why. Something about her father, the Master Lorning said he'd had to do with them. But then, he said all sorts of things. For instance, he always reckoned she was twelve. But she knew – no way to explain it, she just knew – she was fourteen.

No driftwood; but a lot of seacoal had been washed up. Not much use this time of year; but it could always be stored. Though the bin the Master Lorning let her use was getting really full, there wouldn't be space for much more. She'd have to start storing it in her room; though somehow she didn't like the idea of that. She collected it anyway, spent an hour or more. By then it was getting really hot. She pushed the truck back up, trundled it to the 'Dolphin'. She unloaded it – just managed to get all the coal in – and put the truck away. She went upstairs, and bolted the door of her room. She saw she hadn't got much water left. Enough to soak the May cakes though. This lot were stale, and hard. But they were better after she'd left them for a bit. When she'd eaten, she lay back on the bed. She was feeling sleepy. She closed her eyes; her breathing steadied, and became deep. It was afternoon before she woke. She was really quite surprised.

The heat lay like a blanket on the town. It seemed it even muffled sound as well; so that the jingle of a passing cart, the desultory clip-clop of a brewer's horse, were flattened somehow. Stray noises came from the little boatyard; clang of a hammer on metal, sudden scream of some machinery. The gulls wheeled, circling; but they were muted too. Everything endured, waiting for the dusk.

The silting had been bad, this last few years. Even fishing boats had trouble with the quay; you had to know the marks to aim for, to stand a chance at all. The big stuff – coasters, Kiteships – had to anchor offshore, or tie up to the buoys. The Church had been appealed to, times enough; but they never seemed to care. All right for the farmers well inland, over the Doomview Hills; they were looked after. But then of course, they could still pay their dues. Fishgard grumbled, discontentedly; or drooped its shoulders, settled for its lot. The place was dying. Slow maybe, but sure. Perhaps it suited Central policies.

Not that there was much fishing any more. The boats that landed catches still had to run the gauntlet of the Vars. They were always present, on the quay; day or night, the news of an offing brought them down in droves. And with a scarlet Hunter Truck to back them. They'd hold strange instruments above the fish; black, shiny things that clicked and rattled. Sometimes they'd nod, and the baskets would be hurried ashore; at others they'd shake their heads. Then, at gunpoint if needs be, livings would be thrown back to the water. Never an explanation, never a by-your-leave. The town seethed, quietly.

Between the quay and boatyard stretched a long spit of mud. On it, half submerged when the tide was in, lay the shell of an old boat. Most of her planks had gone; her ribs rose gaunt and blackened, Within her, cooled by the mix of sea and mud, lay half a dozen harbour boys, sons of the fishermen whose cottages crowded the straggling lanes above. 'Littluns', they were known as; the Biguns, when they troubled to appear, used the other wreck, the hulk that lay close beside the boatyard wall. The Littluns would have resented the description; but the distinction, though undefined, was curiously precise. From time to time one of them moved lazily, flipped water on himself; but for the most part they lay eyes closed, too tired by the heat to talk.

'No Kites,' said Tol Vaney indolently. He was a slender, long-shanked lad, half a head taller than the rest. He nodded at the flawless sky.

'Fuck the Kites,' said somebody succinctly.

The slim boy shook his head. 'Likes to see 'em,' he said. 'Gets used to 'em. What if the Demons come?'

'Fuck Demons,' said Rik Dru belligerently. 'I ain't never seen none. An' the Kites ain't never done nothin' for me.'

'They ain't supposed to.'

'Then why ain't my ol' man got no work?'

'That ain't to do wi' the Kites.'

'Still likes to see 'em,' said Tol. 'What you then, a bloody Middler?'

'I ain't nothin',' said the lad who'd spoken. 'No more than you. Don't matter what we are anyway. It's only for the toffs.'

'What toffs?'

'The Ridge lot. You can afford it then.'

'What you know about 'em?' said a small lad who'd not yet spoken. He splashed water on his hair.

'I knows though,' said Tol. 'Wait till you get wi' the Biguns. Find out then.'

There was a ripple of laughter.

'Oh, Kerosin's *ol'* sow,' said Rik. 'I could do 'er a turn.'

'You couldn't do nobody a turn.'

'Like to bet?'

Nobody seemed to want to. Silence fell again.

'I reckon we stands more chance 'ere,' said Dil Hardin. He was a thoughtful boy; generally left the others standing. They all agreed, privately, he was a bit round the twist.

'More chance o' what?'

'You know.'

'I don't! I don't!' A chorus of denials.

Dil leaned back. 'Don't think she's what you said,' he opined. 'I think she's pretty.'

'Garn!'

''Andsome is as 'andsome does,' said the small boy.

'What's that mean?'

'I dunno. My Ma's always sayin' it.' He scooped a handful of mud, plopped it contentedly on his head. Runnels began to trickle down his face. He stuck his tongue out. 'Dirty sod,' said Tol.

'She bin back 'ere in that coach of 'ers?'

'Last week, they reckoned.'

'Ought to get the priests to try them Demon detectors on 'er,' said Dil.

'Why's that?'

'She takes enough out the sea.'

'I'm piddling',' said the small boy. 'Anybody feel it?'

'Long as it ain't the other. Stinks enough already.'

'Who says it ain't?'

'We'll chuck you out the boat!'

'It ain't a boat. It's a wreck.'

A tussling. Water flew, and mud. The small boy vanished over the side. He climbed back, cautiously. 'I was only jokin',' he said plaintively.

A Church patrol came along the quay. They cheered, derisively. The big van slowed; they tensed, ready to dive in different directions. It moved off, turned the corner out of sight. They relaxed again.

The afternoon wore on. The heat abated slightly. To the west, over the town, the sky veiled itself. Tol cocked an eye. 'Won't last,' he said.

Nobody argued. They were all weather-wise.

The men knocked off from the boatyard. They tramped along the quay, carrying their kit. A cloud grew, over the chimney tops. 'Breeze gettin' up,' said Tol.

The small boy squeezed his chest. He said, 'Why do we 'ave tits?'

'Why do girls 'ave pricks?' said somebody.

'They don't!'

'My sister 'as! She let me feel it! So there!'

'Don't be stupid.'

'I ain't!'

'They ain't as big as ours,' said Tol magisterially. 'But they do got 'em.'

The Littluns pondered the information, carefully.

'What about this?' said Rik. A pink-tipped column rose, from the mud between his legs. He stroked it affectionately. ''Ave anybody, that would,' he said.

'Dirty bastard,' said Tol. 'Go blind, you will.'

There was a clicking of heels. A small figure hove into sight along the quay. It was dumpy and foursquare, and wore a long and grubby dress. Beneath it showed the hems of several equally suspect petticoats. It wore a ribboned hat; and over its shoulder, rather like a rifle, it carried a furled parasol. Velvet, for once, had decided to wear her shoes. She observed the boatload coldly, raised her chin. Crossed to the other side, and turned the corner out of sight.

'Orlright,' said the small boy. 'You're all chops. Let's see 'ow you go on about that.'

Rik jumped from the boat with surprising speed, ran up the steps to the quay. He mugged at them, leaped in the air. He loped across the road, vanished in pursuit. Silence for a moment; then they all distinctly heard a thwack and yelp. He came back looking dejected. There was a general laugh.

'Look,' said somebody. 'There's a Cody.'

'Fuck the Codys,' said Rik. He nursed himself, beneath the soothing water, and scowled.

A car drove across the quay. It screeched to a halt, and a tall man with black hair ran across. 'Hey,' he called. 'Hey …'

There was a hasty exodus.

He sat in his room. It was a small room, square and plain. But there was a wash-stand, water in a jug; towels, and a bed. He needed nothing more.

He turned the valise in his hands. It had a cheap brass lock. In fact he hadn't realized before just how tawdry the whole thing was. There was a relationship to Rone somewhere. Though he couldn't quite see it.

He opened the case. Took out the photograph inside. The precious contents. He laid it face down on the little table. Finally he turned it over. Janni smiled at him. The eyes, the lovely hair. Across the corner she'd written, '*To Rand, with love.*' There followed a line of little crosses.

He put it back in the valise. Love was what she was surrounded by now. Well, that was what she'd wanted.

He lay on the bed, stared at the ceiling. Fishgard had been a shock, there was no denying that. Even in his dulled state. He'd heard the tales of course, hadn't they all? But ... the narrow-slitted windows, streets that crisscrossed and meandered, the endless goblins scrambling on the roofs. They clung to chimney breasts, to eaves, to cornices. They stared down as he passed; each face seemed more malevolent than the last.

The place was haunted surely, possessed. Needing a mighty blast of wind, something to blow it clean. He wondered what Janni would have said, and instantly choked off the thought. There was no Janni. She had never existed.

He'd stopped off at the big Var church. But they'd known nothing; hadn't heard of him, didn't know of the posting. And the Civil Headquarters had been locked up. His banging finally produced a grumpy caretaker. He advised him to come back at zero nine hundred, slammed the door. He drove away, feeling the anger mount. This was all he needed. He'd crossed the Realm; and this was his reward. But that was wrong of course. He'd had his reward before.

He drove through the fishermen's quarter. He was appalled by the hovels that leaned and clustered, each staying upright it seemed by the support of its neighbour; by the narrow, garbage-choked lanes, by the evidence of poverty on every hand. Groups of men lounged in doorways; they turned as the Buckley approached, watched it go by. Their faces were blank; though once an old woman, rocking under a stone-roofed porch, took a pipe from her mouth and spat.

He reached a little market, finally. The oddest he had seen. A cobbled square stretched to a low stone wall; beyond was the sea. The lines of stalls looked as ramshackle as the rest, their awnings bleached and ragged, their wooden trestles decayed. Some were selling fish. Beside each stood a red-robed priest, Counter in hand, demonstrating their harmlessness. Other stalls sold fruit and vegetables, clothing, churchware. He saw a well-dressed woman haggling with a trader. Above his head hung a faded Vestibule.

A gaggle of boy-children dashed up from the beach. They were naked. Others, equally bare, were serving behind stalls. Nobody seemed to bother.

At least there was a Variant policeman. He asked where he could get accommodation for the night. He gave Rand complicated instructions. He tried to follow them, got lost in another maze of lanes. He gave up, headed back toward the sea.

He saw an attempted rape. At the other end of a street of leaning houses. He blew his hooter, careered toward the combatants. The girl vanished into an alley; the other – unclothed as seemed to be the norm – took to his heels in the direction of the quay.

He wasted several minutes looking for her, drove down himself. He hailed a group of children in an old, decaying boat. They ran like hares.

He drove past more of the shabby stone-roofed cottages. Interspersed with them were pubs and warehouses. He turned left, into the High Street. A stone arch spanned the road. Beneath it hung a sign. *The Dolphin Tavern.* He swung into a cobbled yard, parked the Buckley by a creeper-hung wall. And yes, they had a room. Payment would be in advance.

He walked to the window, studied the great arch with its fantastic top-load. Malevolence, it seemed, was concentrated here. Above it, plumb down the High Street, flew a massive Cody string. Six lifters. He wondered why they needed them; there was no Observer's basket.

He craned his head. He saw the Trace was anchored to a Tower not unlike the Tower of Garnord. Buttressed, and castellated. He looked back to the arch. The juxtaposition seemed extraordinary. He took the valise, walked down to the quay. More folk about now, in the growing dusk; they strolled in groups and pairs, enjoying the cool of the day. The offshore breeze blew steadily; he saw a Kiteship was anchored, a half mile from the curving bight of land. She was streaming too.

There was a sandy path. It wound to the beach, through waist-high tussocks of grass. He followed it, walked to the water's edge. He watched the wavelets cream and lap awhile; then he flung the case as far as he could, into the sea. He hunched his shoulders, climbed back to the quay. Despite himself, he hadn't been able to dispose of all of her at once. But there was nothing left now. Not even memory.

Fatigue hit him, suddenly. He walked to the 'Dolphin', let himself into his room. To his surprise, he slept.

Headquarters were apologetic, next morning. Some mixup with the postings, they'd thought they were taking an Officer from the Southguard. Then when his cancellation had come through …

He shrugged. It was of no significance.

An office had been made available to him. Somewhere to prepare reports. He even had the partial use of a secretary. He seemed to be a rather partial young man himself. Willowy, and languid. He waved a hand, apologetically. 'Not much of a place,' he said. 'But remember, this *is* Fishgard …'

He looked round. The building seemed as cranky as the rest of the town. Smart enough facade, stone-lined and set back from the street; but the rest was evidently much older. Walls of wavy plaster, erratic black-painted beams. Door architrave at one angle, window-frames at others. But there was a desk, and filing cabinets. Even a little loo. He said, 'It'll serve.'

Digs had been fixed for him. A Mistress Goldstar, just back from the quay. He picked the van up from the 'Dolphin', drove it round. He was beginning to know the town a little now. The morning was bright and sunny; but the heat of the day before had gone. He pulled up briefly on the quay, glanced left and right. Four Codys streamed to the north, three visible to the south. It seemed he was in for a busy time.

Mistress Goldstar seemed a pleasant enough person, cheerful and capable; the widow of a fisherman lost in the Great Storm, the storm that had wasted half the Easthold. Later, the little boarding house he'd bought for her had been a boon. 'Don't know what I'd 'a' done without it,' she said. ''E were like that though. Always thinkin' ahead.' She sighed. 'Trouble was, the Kites were down,' she said. ''Ad to, see? Not as I blames 'em for that. Wouldn't 'ave 'appened else though …' She took a saucepan from the stove, poured. He accepted the cup, mind busy. This was a level of faith he hadn't seen in years; he certainly hadn't expected to encounter it in Easthold.

They were sitting in her little kitchen. Neat curtains, polished red-tiled floor. 'We runs a decent 'ouse,' she'd said as she showed him his room. 'Not like some I could mention. Bawlin', comin' in all hours … 'Cept for you,' she added hastily. 'You comes and goes as you chooses, Kites is Kites. Can't do no special meals though. You know, funny times.'

He'd smiled, in spite of himself. 'That won't be necessary,' he said. 'I don't suppose I shall be in all that much. Got a lot of work to get through …'

They'd given him a schedule. He saw his first audit was the Tower. He called that afternoon, sent in his card as protocol dictated. Unembellished this time. He was shown into a pleasant little office, well lined with books. All the standard manuals plus Corps histories, biographies; even a few he hadn't seen. He took one down. And Canwen. *The Flier and his God.*

The door opened. The man who entered was tall and well set, blond hair drawn into a double ponytail. He had what he'd heard called a lived-in sort of face. A scar across his forehead, another on his cheek. Also his nose had been broken at some time, and badly reset; or not reset at all. He seemed pleasant enough though. 'Raoul Josen,' he said. 'Controller, Fishgard Tower.' He held his hand out. 'Pleased to meet you, like a glass of something?'

Rand said, 'I wouldn't say no.' The Basket Bases, as they called them, warranted a Captain, or a Major at least. Town Stations didn't. Josen was a noncom; but Rand sensed he was a good one. After all, the noncoms were the mainstay of the Corps; he'd found that out already.

The other handed him a drink, glanced at the book he'd laid down. He said, 'Ever meet him?'

'No,' he said. 'Did you?'

The Controller looked reflective. 'Yes,' he said. 'Flew with him for a bit.' He smiled. 'He was Senior, G15,' he said. 'I was a singularly snotty-nosed Cadet.'

Rand said, 'What's he like?'

The other shrugged. 'Strange man,' he said. 'Don't think anybody ever understood him. I certainly didn't. You know he lives round here?'

He shook his head.

'Got a place up on the Ridge,' said the Controller. 'Posh end of the town. You get some funny people, on the Ridge.' He put the glass down. 'Doubt you'll meet him though,' he said. 'Bit of a recluse. But then, he always was. Never used to start below a thousand feet.' He riffled through the book. 'You can borrow it sometime if you like,' he said. 'Put down the day and the date though.'

'Maybe,' said Rand. 'Let's clear the junk first though.'

They got down to work. The Tower, like most Bases of its grading, carried a standing complement of twelve. Plus Launch- and Riggingmasters, and a Painter and Apprentice. They supplied Godkites to half the Southern Sector, sometimes as far as the Salient. It was a lucrative sideline. Supply Depot F12, immediate superior F4. At which Raoul Josen pulled a face. 'Watch the Skipper there,' he said. 'Real Taildowner. Eats Controllers regularly, on toast. Audit people too.'

'Thanks a lot,' he said. 'That's my next trip.' He made the last of his notes, and closed the folder. The Controller said, 'Like a look round while you're here?'

Rand nodded. He said, 'Fine.' The other's manner had been guarded at first; but he'd rapidly thawed. Seemed to accept him as another Kiteman, though he couldn't really see why. He followed the blond man from floor to floor; workshops and rest areas, the Kiteflat where they refurbished the great gay Lifters; a Studio where a tall, cadaverous man in paint-smudged robes meticulously applied gold leaf to a big cartouche. They emerged finally on the launch platform, where a bored-looking Cadet leaned on the parapet and stared moodily down into the street. He saluted smartly enough though, at sight of his Controller.

'Something you haven't seen,' said Raoul. 'Maybe you have though. Ever come across twin stringing before?'

Rand shook his head. The fixed winch carried two drums. The cables were cinched at intervals by slim brass coupling tubes; he could see the first half dozen winking in the sunlight. He said, 'What the Hell's the idea of that?'

'Search me,' said the Controller. 'Local regulations; overflying a built-up area. Easthold is a law unto itself.'

Rand stared up at the great curve of the Trace. The Lifter wings showed one above the next; the Pilot was little more than a bright speck. 'That's crazy,' he said. 'Wondered why you were six-flying without a basket. If one goes, the other's bound to part. You'd ditch in the sea anyway.'

'Try telling 'em,' said Raoul. He picked up a coupler that lay on the parapet. 'Don't ask me to account for these things either. Fine on a normal down; but if you're in a hurry you don't have time to clamp. They go like snot off a doorknob. We get 'em brought back occasionally; record's three hundred yards.'

A thought occurred to him. He said, 'Do the Lifters override okay?'

'Sometimes,' said the Controller. 'Sometimes not. Depends on your luck.'

He made another note. 'I shan't query your cable backup then,' he said. 'Leaving aside corrosion.'

The other glanced sidelong. He said, 'You've been here before.' He looked round him. 'Good view, ain't it?' he said.

Rand nodded. Heightwise, they topped all but the church steeple. The grey roofs of the town, with their misshapen population, stretched in every direction. Beyond were the quays, beyond again the huge expanse of water. He saw the Kiteship still rode at anchor.

He peered down into the street. Almost directly below, a small figure ambled along. It was pushing an old wooden truck. He touched the Controller's sleeve, and pointed. He said, 'Who's that?'

Raoul shrugged. 'One of the local denizens. They call her Velvet. Funny little kid, don't know much about her. Asked a couple of times, but nobody seems to want to let on. Why?'

He shrugged. 'No reason,' he said. 'Just thought I'd seen her before.'

The audit went well. He prepared his report, left it for the secretary to transcribe. He walked back to the Tower, smiled at the Controller's enquiring look. 'No problems,' he said. 'You run a tight Base, Raoul.' He steepled his fingers. 'Look,' he said, 'I can't guarantee a thing. I can only advise. We're toothless really, it's one of the hazards of the job. But I'm recommending we scrap the twinning, go to single cable. It'll nearly halve the rig costs. That should appeal to Central if nothing else does.'

The other fetched a bottle and two glasses. 'To that I will drink,' he said solemnly. 'Let's hope they see the light ...'

They drank again that evening, in one of the town centre pubs. Later he went on to the Controller's house, a pleasant little cottage on the outskirts of town. He met Raoul's wife, a slender, dark-haired woman, and a brace of cheerful kids. The meal she prepared was excellent. They chatted afterwards about old times; Middlemarch, the Northguard, the Salient he had yet to see. It was only later, sitting alone in his room, that the ghost returned to plague him.

He saw the girl again a few days later, stumping along the High Street.

Minus her truck this time; but there was no mistaking. The rakish little hat, the dress, the froth of grubby petticoats. 'Hi,' he shouted. 'Hi …' She hesitated, turned; and he called, 'Velvet …' She stopped at that, appalled; then took to her heels.

It was a market day, the town was crowded. He jinked and swerved, cursing; dodged round one farm cart, was almost run down by another. But by the time he reached the opposite sidewalk she had vanished again.

He raised the matter with the secretary. 'Denning,' he said, 'that kid who goes round town. The one who pushes the truck. Know anything about her?'

The other shrugged, studying a file. 'Couldn't say, I'm sure …'

'But who are her folks? What's her other name?'

The secretary looked vague. 'Hell,' he said. 'That's what they call her anyway.'

'*What?*'

Denning said, 'Hell …'

Rand spread his hands on the desk. 'Do you know what you just said?'

The other looked surprised. 'Just told you what her name was,' he said. 'Sorry, I'm sure …'

He gritted his teeth. He said, 'Forget it.' Next morning he drove to Base F4.

Velvet had had a good day. The Flaxtons were away, she'd got it from the maid. She rose at first light, pushed the truck to the Ridge. The property was surrounded by a high stone wall, topped along its length by broken glass; but there were ways and means. And the orchard was out of sight from the house. She'd equipped herself with a massive basket, woven of Holand fibre. She filled it to overflowing with cherries, spent the morning hawking the wares round town. By lunchtime she'd disposed of the lot; she repaired to the back door of the 'Dolphin', tapped. She waved the bundle of grubby notes, demanded ale. But Master Lorning smiled. 'I'll bring you some over in a mo',' he said. 'Got a job for you.'

She frowned. 'Can't do it till tomorrer,' she said.

He shook his head. 'Customer o' mine,' he said. 'It's got to be tonight.'

'A'right,' she said. 'Expect I can fit it in. Don't be too long though, will yer?'

He came over to her room in minutes, with a crate. He outlined his requirements, and she nodded. 'Yeah,' she said. 'I can fix that up all right.'

'Good,' he said. 'I'm relying on you. Twenty?'

She opened her mouth. It was on the tip of her tongue to say twenty-five; then she remembered he'd given her her house for free. 'I don't want nothin', Master,' she said. 'You knows that.'

'Don't be daft,' he said. 'I makes good money, why not you?' He rose to leave; but on the steps he paused, stared at the Demon with his smashed-off nose. 'Look at that,' he said. 'Nothin's safe no more.'

She shook her head. 'Terrible, ennit?' she said. 'Shockin', what some folk'll do.'

She ate a handful of cherries, drank one of the beers. She hurried round to Transon, the fishermen's quarter that lay behind the boatyard. Mo Sprindri was at home; sitting in the little front parlour, sucking at his pipe. Velvet laid the deal out briskly, and he nodded. 'All right,' he said. 'I'll send Hol round tonight.'

A wild-haired child was watching, from the inner room. Sucking her thumb, staring with big smoky eyes. She wore a ragged singlet, full of holes. It stopped at her waist; the rest of her was bare. Velvet looked her up and down appraisingly. She put her age at nine. 'Sorry,' she said. 'Send Rye.'

He twitched at that, and clenched his fists. He set them on the table. '*No,*' he said hoarsely. '*No* …'

She mentioned a figure, saw his face begin to crumble. After all, he hadn't worked in years. He was quiet for a while; finally he spoke. 'All right,' he said. 'I'll see she gets cleaned up.'

She shook her head. 'No,' she said. 'Send 'er as she is.' She rose to leave; and he looked up. There were tears in his eyes. 'I don't blame you, Velvet,' he said. 'It isn't you I blame.'

She hurried back into town, vaguely puzzled. She couldn't work out what he'd meant. After all, it would bring him in good money. Better than the days he'd been employed. No blame in that. Walking up the High Street, she glowered at the Codys.

She climbed the hill to the Mistress Kerosina's home. Privately she thought her the most beautiful person in the world, with her lovely clothes and her huge green eyes and her long slim legs. She wished hers were the same. She tolled the bell and waited, leaning on the parasol. She looked round at the garden. The Mistress was also very good for trade; there was no denying that. With Velvet, affection was keyed perforce to practical considerations.

The carriage was waiting, the newest one her Ladyship had bought. All curtained, just with little chinks to peep through. She changed her carriages constantly, but people always got to know. There'd even been whispers about this one, and she'd only had it a few weeks. She'd have to tell her soon, but she'd been putting it off. The Mistress Kerosina wouldn't be best pleased.

They jogged back into town, turned on to the quay. The Littluns were mudlarking as ever; her employer parted the drapes with the little fan she carried. She stared awhile, and pointed. 'The tall one,' she said huskily. 'The tall one with the long fair hair.'

Velvet waited her moment, hopped down. She ambled to the quayside, gestured. Tol Vaney came across, unwillingly. A bartering; and she held up a handful of notes. He swallowed at that, waited his chance and ran for the steps. He glanced to either side as she had done, bundled in. She followed. He crouched in the carriage shivering and dripping mud. The horses clopped away.

The Mistress Kerosina crooned at him. Her eyes were glowing. She liked them bare; because then they were wholly in her power. She pulled his head back, kissed him savagely; then she did something else. Velvet cupped her hands round the parasol. Tomorrow he'd have to go to the other boat.

It was late before she got back to the arch. Well, lateish anyway. She wondered whether to drink more beer, decided not. She settled for cherries and a damp May cake. She thought about the man who'd called to her, the tall man with the glasses and dark hair. Quite good looking, he was. He'd been there the other night as well, the night old Rikki tried it on. She'd thought he was Church at first; they always reckoned they used plainclothes Vars. But now she wasn't sure.

She reached under the bed, pulled out a black valise. She opened it, looked at the picture inside. She was really pretty, she wondered who she was. Pity the damp had spoiled it a bit. It had gone wavy now, and the writing down the side had got all smudged. Not that it would have made much difference if it hadn't. She'd watched him throw it in the sea, waited for the tide to bring it back to land. She'd known whereabouts it would drift in. She'd been disappointed at first; but she'd kept it anyway. Everything had potential.

She made her mind up. One thing was sure; he certainly wasn't a Var. They'd never do a thing like that. She swung her legs from the bed. She grabbed the parasol and headed for the door. 'Never spoil a winnin' streak,' she said.

G4 was as bad as he'd been warned. They started giving him a hard time from day one. He retaliated in the only way he could. You didn't count each nut and bolt, not on Frontier audit; it was a matter of give and take. He counted them twice. Then he turned to the books. Discrepancies showed at once; they hadn't even been cleverly disguised. Nothing much in themselves; but after a while, they totalled. And they hadn't had an audit for five years. He put the fear of God into a Quartermaster and a Rigging Corporal, made an unofficial visit to a local farmer. He gave equally short shrift to him. After all, what sort of fool fences his pastures with Cody wire? He repaired to the office of Captain Helworth. He presented his views; and the other stroked his moustache. While he didn't accept the findings, he nonetheless found them interesting. Surely though an arrangement could be reached?

Rand looked up, under his brows. 'Transfer them, Captain,' he said. 'Transfer with reprimand, pegged promotion. These things can be arranged.' He saw the other's face begin to mottle, and forestalled him. 'You fly the Codys,' he said. 'I serve them. We both serve the Corps.'

The Captain blustered anyway. 'You Central people,' he said. 'Time-servers, the pack of you. A penny here, a shilling there; why this, why that? Poking your fingers into things you don't understand, things that don't concern you … We're the people who do the work, we're the ones who take the risks. To keep you folk in comfort. You and the bloody Church …'

He shouted back. Stung into retaliation for once. 'My father understood. He understood enough to give his life. I give what I can; and may the Lord forgive me if it's not enough.' He slammed the folder on the desk and rose. 'It's not wire they're selling,' he said. 'It's blood. Men's lives …'

The other looked up, startled. A silence; then he slowly shook his head. He said, 'You're a funny sort of audit clerk.' He spread his hands on the desk top, frowned. He said, 'Who was your father?'

He said, 'Del Panington.'

Helworth appeared to wrestle with himself. Then he got up, walked to a side cupboard. He took down glasses, and a bottle. He said, 'I didn't know. I didn't have any idea.'

'I know that, sir,' said Rand. 'I'm not questioning your honour. But you know now.'

The other nodded tiredly. 'Yes,' he said. 'I shall comply with your suggestion. Have you any other recommendations for me?'

He thought the matter over, on the short drive back to Fishgard. He wondered if he'd discovered a new source of strength. He decided no. After all, what had they tried to do? Frighten him with bogles; he who lived with Demons.

He took a few days break. He felt he needed them. He wandered the town, got to know it better. The quayside taverns were best avoided, at all times; but there were others, tucked away in sidestreets, where you could get a peaceful beer. He seldom went near the water anyway. Invariably, he put the mudlarks to flight; like firing a maroon into a cloud of gulls. He'd no wish to alarm them; but there seemed no cure for it. He wondered who on earth they thought he was.

Mistress Goldstar had laid supper for him in the kitchen. He often ate with her now, away from the other lodgers. He found her company pleasant, undemanding; presumably she felt the same of his. She'd talk about the old days; the hauls they'd made, the catches they'd brought in. Though that had been before the Vars had taken over. Spoiling the town's prosperity, ruining honest folk's trade. He'd frown a bit at that, though he wouldn't contradict. He knew a little about the instruments the priests carried; and though the notion of Demon piss had never suited his vocabulary he knew they'd saved the people from themselves. Time and again. The Church guarded the Realm; and the Codys were its offspring. Yet in her mind the great Kites were discrete, an entity. He began to see how complex the whole issue was.

He pushed the plate away. 'Mistress, that was delicious,' he said. 'Thank you very much.' She made to speak; and a rapping came at the door. She clicked her tongue. 'Who on earth?' she said. 'This time o' night, an' all … 'Scuse, my dear …' She bustled from the room; he heard a low exchange, the sudden flurry of her voice. 'That I shan't do, Mistress Minion,' she said. 'That I will *not*. The gentleman's at supper; an' I knows your kind …' He frowned; and she raised her voice again. 'Off you go, Miss Velvet; an' don't you come back. I runs a decent 'ouse …'

'Mistress Goldstar,' he said. 'Please …' The short figure was already receding along the path. 'Velvet,' he called, 'Come here …'

She returned, uncertainly. 'You was the gentleman what called me,' she said. 'Come to see what you wanted.'

'I'm sorry, Mistress,' he said. 'She is right. Do you mind?'

The other's face froze. 'I wouldn't 'ave thought it of you, sir,' she said. 'Straight I wouldn't.' She hesitated a moment; then she stalked away. After all, she was a Fishgarder; and the Corps were her best customers. 'No noise,' she said over her shoulder. 'An' it's lights out twenty-four hundred.' She slammed the kitchen door.

He looked after her; then he touched the small girl's arm. 'Come on,' he said. 'This way.'

She sat warily on his bed, the parasol gripped between her knees. She still wore the black straw bonnet; he wondered if she slept in it as well. 'All right,' he said. 'You wanted to see me, and you have. Now, what did you really want?'

She looked up, guardedly. Till then he hadn't realized the full beauty of her face; broad cheekbones, the great tilted eyes, the stubborn, perfect little chin. The candles woke reddish highlights from her hair; wisps hung beside her ears, the rest draggled nearly to her waist. It looked greasy though, he was sure it probably stank; the rest of her he'd already become aware of. He smiled. 'You're very lovely,' he said. 'But God, you could use a bath.' She turned her nose up, instantly. 'Baths is fer kids,' she said.

He smiled again. 'And what do you think you are?'

She bridled. She said, 'I can take care o' myself.'

He said, 'That wasn't what I asked.' He rose carefully, poured a glass of wine. He offered it to her; but she shook her head. Also the tension of her knuckles warned him she was poised for flight. He sat back, well away from the door. She seemed to relax fractionally. 'When I shouted, you ran away,' he said. 'Why did you come back? And how did you know where I lived?'

No answer. He tried another tack. 'Where do you live?' he said.

'Close,' she said. 'Not far.'

'Close, not far,' he said. 'Sounds like a riddle. Only I'm not very good at them. Is Velvet your proper name?'

She stuck her lip out.

'Do you have parents? Do you live with them?'

Velvet risked another glance at him. He really was good-looking, even with his glasses. Funny way of talking as well. Sort of soft. There was something else though. She knew he wouldn't hurt her. She didn't know how, but she could tell. For a moment, strange thoughts stirred. She couldn't for the life of her have said what they were.

He was still watching. He said, 'It was you that first night, wasn't it?'

'What night?'

'When I came down in the van.'

Her silence was eloquent.

He said, 'What was happening?'

She shrugged. She said, 'That wadn't nothin'. Wadn't nothin' at all. 'Appens all the while.'

'It happens all the while,' he said. 'I see.'

She gripped the parasol afresh. She was wondering if he might be a Var after all. She looked round her. 'Ain't ever bin in 'ere before,' she said. 'It's nice.'

'Why haven't you been in?'

She shot a baleful glance at the door. 'She won't never let me,' she said. 'She says …' But it didn't matter what she said. What anybody said. Not really.

He was still gentle. He said, 'She let you in tonight.'

She looked up, and away again. He realized what had been troubling him. The face was young, and tender; but he thought he'd never seen a pair of wiser eyes. She said, 'That was 'cos o' you. She likes you. Gettin' on all right.' She stared at her hands. The meeting wasn't going well. Not well at all. She'd thought … well, there were many things she'd thought. She'd thought she'd known what he wanted. When she found out he wasn't a Var. Now though she wasn't so sure. Normally, half a dozen pitches would have sprung to mind. She thought about Rye Spindri. She'd be upset for a day or two, they always were. But they soon got over it. She'd be all right; till somebody ruined her of course. Then there were the mudlarks, if he was the other way. Rik was coming on nicely, he'd be quite useful soon. She frowned. It wasn't right, none of it was right; she knew instinctively. Everybody was the same; and yet he wasn't. It was all very puzzling.

She looked up. He was still watching her. He said, 'What do you do for a living, Velvet?'

She grasped the straw. 'Things,' she said. 'I do things fer people.'

'What sort of things?'

'Anythin',' she said. 'I can do anythin'.'

'What do you mean?'

She waved a hand impatiently. 'The usual,' she said. 'You know. I ain't on offer though,' she said. 'I ain't in the deal.' She considered. 'Well, p'raps fer special rates.'

He said, 'You poor little girl.' He smiled. He said, 'You should have some cards printed. What would you call yourself though? Procuress?'

She looked baffled. She said, 'What's cards?'

He reached into his pocket. He said, 'This is a card.' She took it, frowning, stared at it. Turned it the other way, handed it back no wiser. She said, ''Course, you needs stuff like that. You're a toff.'

Rand laughed. 'I'm not a toff,' he said. 'I work for the Kites. None of us are toffs.'

Her face clouded instantly. He said, 'What's the matter, Velvet? Don't you like the Codys?'

No answer.

'They're nothing really,' he said. 'I think they're rather fine. They keep us safe, keep all the Demons away. What's wrong with them?'

She shivered slightly. ''Angin' over yer 'ead,' she said. 'There all the time. Can't never get away.'

He looked quizzical. He said, 'You're not afraid of them …'

She blazed at him. 'I ain't afraid o' nothin' …!'

He'd stepped on delicate ground. He changed the subject. 'What else do you do? Apart from what you said?'

'Anythin',' she said. 'Anythin' that comes along.' She brightened. 'Bin pickin' cherries this morning. Whole lot. Flogged 'em as well.'

'That was very good. Were they your cherries?'

Velvet stuck her lip out. She said, 'They wadn't 'ome. Bin away fer a week.'

'It still wasn't very honest.'

'They wouldn't 'ave eaten 'em,' she said. 'They never do. There's too many.'

'The Demons will get you,' he said. 'They'll pinch your nose.'

She said, 'Garn.' She grinned, suddenly. It lit her face up, like a little lamp. 'I knocked a Demon's nose orf once,' she said. 'Wi' this.' She brandished the parasol.

'That wasn't very kind. Where was he?'

'Up on the arch. It went fer miles.'

'What went for miles?'

She said, ''Is nose.'

'I can imagine. Why did you do it?'

'Din' like 'im,' she said. ''E was right outside my h—' She stopped dead. Realized she'd gone too far.

He said, 'So you live near the arch.'

No answer.

He remembered the carvings clustering the columns. He said, '*In* the arch? Are there rooms *inside* it, Velvet?'

She bit her lip. Wished she hadn't spoken. But she supposed it didn't really matter. He could have found out easy enough by asking someone else. 'It was Master Lornin',' she said. ''E was ever so good to me. 'E don't charge me no money.'

'No,' he said. 'I suppose you render services instead.' He shook his head. 'This town's rotten,' he said. 'Rotten through and through. It stinks …'

She looked indignant. 'It don't,' she said. 'Well, maybe a bit when the tide's out …'

He started to laugh. 'Velvet,' he said, 'you are priceless. Absolutely priceless …'

She scowled. She thought he was laughing at her. Then she realized he wasn't. She joined in, though she didn't know what was funny; and a door slammed on the landing. She jumped up at once. 'I gotta go,' she said. 'She's comin' …'

'She's not. Anyway, you're all right. You're with me.'

'I'm not,' she said. 'You know what she said. It's twenty-four hundred.'

He looked at the chronometer. It was indeed a minute to. He said, 'How did you know?' but she was already scrabbling at the door. 'All right,' he said, 'Go steady. You'll wake the house up else. You'll need a light.' He grabbed a candle, turned with his hand on the knob. 'You don't have to go at all,' he said. 'You can stay here if you like. You'll be all right, I can sleep in the chair.'

She considered. Nice to curl up for once, and just be safe. It wasn't on though, the old sow would come. He'd get in trouble as well. Also her own little house was calling. This place was all right, it was done up nice. But it wasn't like the arch. She shook her head. She said, 'I gotta go …' She hesitated. She said, 'Thank you, sir.'

'What for?' he said. 'I haven't done a thing.'

Velvet frowned. She supposed he hadn't. Not really, when you thought about it. She'd even forgotten what she'd come to say. There was a moment when she felt she'd like to kiss him. But that was funny too. She couldn't remember kissing anybody ever. She'd seen other people do it, but she didn't know what it was like. She supposed it must be all right. Else they wouldn't bother.

It seemed he understood. He put his hand on her shoulder. He said, 'Come on, Littlun.' He kept his hand there all the way down the stairs. It was nice.

He shot the front door bolts. He said, 'You be all right?'

''Course,' she said. She was always all right.

He opened the door. 'My name's Rand Panington,' he said. 'And Velvet …'

She turned.

He said, 'Thanks for coming to see me. I enjoyed it.'

She walked off, baffled; and he called again. Softly. 'I'll be away four days,' he said. 'But then … I'll buy some cherries from you. Don't get into trouble though.'

She looked over her shoulder scornfully. 'I don't get inter trouble,' she said. 'See yer …' She turned the corner, and was gone.

Rand didn't feel like going to bed. He walked down to the quay, sat on the sea wall. The tide was making; the old wreck the mudlarks used was already part-submerged. The moon was high, riding a clear sky; he watched the long reflections move and dance. Beyond was the vast horizon of the sea. He imagined he could see the curving of the earth. He shook his head. He'd thought himself beyond the realm of feeling; but it seemed it wasn't so. He set himself to analyse his mood. So she was on the game. Or worse, controlling it. He shook his head again. Despite what Mistress Goldstar had said, despite what he'd said himself, he'd been talking to a child. A child who didn't realize her own needs. He wondered what Janni would have said, and closed the thought away. Janni didn't exist; because she wasn't here. There was only the moon, and the sea.

He shrugged. Wrong to seek for meanings; stop looking, and they made themselves plain. She hadn't known herself why she had come. Because people were people; and they made demands. Sometimes they didn't know themselves what the demands were; but as long as folk existed, they would flow. If you acknowledged them, you paid. One way or another. If you didn't …

If you didn't, what? Became less than human, he supposed. Though he wasn't wholly sure that mattered. One thing was certain; you'd get on a whole sight better.

He got up, walked back to the digs. On the way he watched the Codys; rig after rig receding into distance, the moonlight glinting silver from their sails.

He woke early, shaved and dressed. He considered; then he walked through to the kitchen. After all he hadn't been told not to. Breakfast was distinctly fraught. Mistress Goldstar wielded pots and pans, her lips set into a line; finally he spoke. He said, 'I think there's something you need to understand.'

She kept her back turned to him. She said, 'I understands enough, sir.'

'No,' he said, 'You don't. You haven't even started.' He rubbed his lip. 'I didn't ask her to call,' he said. 'That was a lie. But neither could I turn her away.'

She said, 'I'm sure you knows your own business best.'

Things flickered for a moment. He remembered something Father Alkin said once, something from an old book. What it would have been he had no idea. *Whosoever causeth one of these little ones to stumble ...*'

She banged a pot.

'*It were better for him, if a millstone be hanged about his neck ...*'

She banged another.

'*And he be cast into the depths of the sea ...*'

He stood up, leaning on his knuckles. He hadn't been as angry for a long time. 'Mistress,' he said, 'there are many people in this Realm. Some take their pleasures one way, some another.' He spoke very quietly. He said, 'I do not take sexual advantage of children.'

Mistress Goldstar was turning, with a saucepan. She dropped it. Soup spilled across the tiles. He rose, fetched the mop. He didn't hurry; because if you are talking to a child, you are talking to a child. And if you are swabbing the floor, you are swabbing the floor. When he looked up she was wringing her hands. He'd never actually seen that done before. 'She's not a child, sir,' she said. 'She's not a child.'

He said, 'That was all I saw.' He put the mop away.

She served his breakfast. Later she said, 'I'm sorry, sir.'

Rand looked up, vaguely surprised. He said, 'Sorry for what?'

She seemed uncertain. 'You knows the Kites,' she said. 'So you knows more than I.'

He shook his head. 'I know very little,' he said. 'I know the Kites are flying, and that the bacon is good. There's no call for apologies, Mistress.'

He took himself round to the Middle Doctrine church. The big one, opposite the Tower; fronting the Vars as usual. The incumbent was pottering about replacing candles; the little lamps they kept burning night and day. 'Ah, yes,' he said, 'the little girl. The one who pushes the truck. Lives somewhere by the 'Dolphin' I believe.' He coaxed another flame alight with the long taper he carried. 'A sad case,' he said. 'Very sad indeed. Her father was a Flier. Lost at sea, some years ago now. Her mother ...' He clicked his tongue. 'A fickle creature,' he said. 'Lacking responsibility. Still, she was as the good Lord made her.'

'So the child was deserted. Left to fend for herself.'

'In a manner of speaking,' said the priest. 'Yes, I suppose that's correct.'

'And nobody took her in. Nobody helped her, gave her shelter ...'

The other faced him blandly. 'She seems to be self sufficient,' he said. 'Remarkably so in one so young.'

'Self sufficient,' he said. 'Living like a rat in a skirting. What if she's taken ill? What if she dies?'

The priest smiled. 'All,' he said, 'is within the will of the Lord.'

Rand walked out. He'd realized, not for the first time, that any discipline, however noble, is only as strong as its adherents.

He drove to F5. His first sight of the place was a shock. Weeds round the guardhouse, the ill-kept buildings; paint flaking, windows unwashed. Beside the gate stood a broken-down, rusty Launcher. Bird droppings streaked its sides; and a low String was flying, on a three-lift. He stared. They had a basket aloft; but there was no Observer.

He tackled the Commander, a tired-looking middle-aged Major. The other shrugged. 'No relief,' he said. 'Poor chap has to have a day off sometimes.'

He said, 'But this Section is unguarded. That's a court martial offence.' The other merely shrugged. 'Then break us,' he said. 'Central have been informed, we can't do more. You'll find the books are in order though.'

Amazingly, they were. And the spares, what there were of them, well-kept. He finished sooner than he'd estimated, sat in his room and brooded. His responsibilities, after all, were clearly enough delineated. To take stock, and examine the accounts. Finally he began his report. After he'd finished he sat and drummed his fingers. He added a terse observation that morale seemed low, more positive support would be an asset. He closed the file, walked round to the local inn. He was introduced to Downstringers. He'd heard wild tales of Frontier hooch. He found they were understatements.

Velvet rose early, at first light. She pushed the truck to the beach. There wasn't much in. A few knobs of coal, not worth the picking up, the odd bit of wood. She collected them anyway, trudged on.

The path descended to the sea. Pushing the truck was hard; but she persevered, rattling over the shingle. She passed under the Strings of the first big Station, glowering at them. She found the path again.

The way curved left. There was a little inlet. She'd always thought of it as her private bay. This time she found some bottles though, strewn about on the grass. So other people knew about it as well. She was disappointed. She retrieved the rubbish anyway, put it in the truck. It would be worth a few coppers from Master Lorning.

She looked back. The town was out of sight of course, the Station hidden by a rise of ground. She edged the truck to the water. The sea-kale grew here in profusion; Master Lorning wouldn't buy it, but the 'Anchor' usually gave her a good price. She collected a dozen bunches; then she sat on the beach and brooded. 'Reckons I stink,' she muttered. 'More or less said as much. Cheek …'

She looked back again. The Codys were still close; but both were well out over the sea, and rising. She hoped the Observers would have more important things to look at. She took her top off, pulled her skirt undone. The various petticoats fell one after the next. Finally she tugged at the hatpin. She half withdrew it, then set her lip. She pushed it back firmly. You had to keep some sort of decency.

She walked into the water, waded a long way. When she stopped the sea was only to her thighs. She looked down. She didn't really like herself all that much. Her breasts were coming, but they weren't like Kerosina's; she imagined they were floppy already. Also her fur was growing, downy and fine. She didn't like that either, she'd be like one of the Biguns before you knew where you were. But there didn't seem to be anything to do.

She sat down. It brought the water nearly to her shoulders. It was even colder than she'd thought. She began to rub herself desultorily. She'd never seen much point in it. If you carried on long enough you only got sore. Later though she piddled contentedly.

A long weed worked itself between her legs. Round, like dark brown grass. She was frightened for a moment, she thought it was a worm. She pulled it by the roots. It floated away.

She splashed back to the beach, used one of the petticoats to dry herself. She looked at the rest and shrugged. If she was dirty she supposed her clothes were dirty too. She didn't know what to do about that though, the problem was far too complex. She dressed, and wriggled. She wondered if she felt cleaner. She decided she did, a bit.

She headed into town. There was a hubbub on the quay. A fishing boat was in, from Mattingale; the Vars were clearing the catch. She liberated three baskets from a warehouse loading bay. She swaggered back with them, pushed into the crowd. She'd found if she swung her hips, people didn't argue with her.

She'd taken a handful of money. She disliked actually parting with it, but sometimes there was no choice. She piled the baskets on to the truck and wobbled away. The load was a bit top-heavy, but she knew she could manage. After all she'd done it often enough before. She wheeled the truck to the High Street, pushed it onto the waste ground the other side of the arch. She stopped where a stand of bushes hid her from public gaze. She scratched her head and considered. There was a new fishmonger, a Master Finling. She was sure he'd be pleased to buy the local produce; after all he probably hadn't made good contacts yet.

She fetched the cherry basket. She lined it with paper, emptied two of the creels. Big square stones were lying about; she wondered if they'd once fallen off the arch. She weighted the baskets, redisposed part of the catch. She stumped up the High, turned down toward the Transon.

Master Finling was suspicious. Unnecessarily so she thought. She was quite hurt. He insisted on tipping the contents of the first creel out, examining them in person. The price he offered wasn't good; but she supposed she could have done worse. She staggered in with the others, dumped them gratefully round the back.

He called as she was hurrying from the shop. ''Ere. What about the baskets?'

'It's all right,' she said. 'I'll pick 'em up later. Ta …' She wheeled the truck hastily away.

As soon as she woke next morning she knew she wasn't well. She felt dull, and had the beginnings of a headache. She lay awhile watching the sky brighten through the one pointed window. She'd have liked to stay where she was. It was no use though, the day was wasting. She sat up, and there was an instant twinge. She felt her behind, and groaned. 'Oh, no,' she muttered. 'No' again …' Another boil was coming, she'd had some terrible ones lately. Lasted for weeks sometimes. So that was what came of hygiene. Limping up to Master Billings' forge, she glared at the Codys. 'If you was any good,' she said bitterly, 'these sort o' things wouldn't 'appen …'

It was worse next day, worse than ever the day after. On the fourth morning she didn't think she'd be able to walk. She had to though, there was a contract to fulfil. The Kiteman needed cherries.

On the way back from F5, his fuel pump failed again. Terminally, or so it seemed. He banged and sputtered three or four miles; finally he coasted into a village. Pleasant-looking place, stone-built and set with trees. Ducks floated on a railed-off pond; beyond, the Vars and the Middle Doctrine opposed each other across a cobbled square.

He fiddled with the pump, but it seemed beyond his skill. It clacked desultorily a few times, packed up once more. He stood back, scratched his head.

A cottage door opened. A red-haired man came out. He said, 'Do you have trouble? Can I help at all?' So they weren't all surly, in the Easthold.

Rand explained the problem briefly, and the other smiled. He pointed. 'Can you make it across to Aro?' he said. 'He'll sort you out.'

'Suppose so,' he said. 'Thanks a lot.' The engine sputtered, and caught.

The garage reminded him of Master Bone's; a dark, junk-piled cave, smelling richly of oil. Old cars stood about and farm equipment, even one of the obsolete steam tractors. The man who met him was short and bandy-legged; brilliant-eyed, and with a great aquiline nose. Rand began to tell him what was wrong, but the other waved his arms. '*Nah*,' he said hoarsely. '*Nah* …' He ran out to the Buckley, raised the bonnet. He checked the ignition, went straight to the fuel pump. '*Dia-phra*,' he said. '*Dia-phra* …' He fitted a new diaphragm, quickly. The engine started at a touch. He laid fingers to the bonnet, tested the vibration and smiled. '*A-ri*,' he said.

Rand took his wallet from his pocket. He said, 'Thanks a lot. How much?' But the other shook his head. '*Ki*,' he said. '*Ki* …' He patted the symbol on Rand's shoulder, steepled his hands. He pointed to where, distantly, a Cody string was flying. He said again, '*A-ri* …'

Rand drove away. It seemed responsibilities were loaded on to him. Whether he wished it or no.

*

It was lunchtime before he reached the digs. Mistress Goldstar met him. 'That young gel come round,' she said. 'Twice, already. Got some stuff for you. Wouldn't leave it though.'

He said, 'Stuff?' He was vague; then he remembered the cherries. 'That'll be all right,' he said. 'I'll sort it out.' He wondered why he'd asked her to bring them. He wasn't even particularly fond of them. He decided it had probably been to help her out.

She was back at fourteen hundred. He took the basket from her. 'They're the Whites,' she said. 'Don't look so good; but they eats better.'

It seemed she had trouble with the stairs. Couldn't walk too well. He said, 'Velvet, what's the matter?'

Unexpectedly, she started to cry. He held her. Had a bit of bother with her hat brim. 'It's all right,' he said. 'Velvet, what is it?' He rubbed her back. Later he patted her bottom. She shrieked.

He moved faster than she'd have thought possible. He whipped her clouts up. The lot. She stood for a moment paralysed with shock. He stared; then he said, 'Right. Come on.'

She started to squall at once. It was no use though, he'd already got her wrist. He put her in the van. She had to sit sideways a bit.

They drove up the High Street. He stopped outside the Tower. She started to yell again. 'No,' she said. 'Not there …'

'Shut up,' he said. 'Shut up …' He hauled her inside, by main force. There wasn't a Base Medic; but they had first call on one of the local doctors. Rand summoned him, in no uncertain terms.

Once through the doorway she fell curiously quiet. Compliant almost. Till the doc appeared. She started to kick up a fuss again then; but he took her hand. 'It's all right,' he said. 'Don't worry, I'll come with you …'

She lay face down, whimpering. Though whether with fright or shame he couldn't say. The doctor boiled a kettle on a little hob. He filled a wine-glass, tipped it away and filled again. He said, 'I thought you'd lance it,' but the other shook his head. 'Cause her less trouble afterwards,' he said. 'Old-fashioned, but effective.'

He watched, with a species of fascinated horror. He'd never seen cupping before. The first application didn't work. The doctor frowned, boiled the kettle again. He took the steaming glass, pressed it to the girl's behind.

There was a pop. Velvet shrieked. The doctor held the glass up. 'Look at that,' he said. 'Drop of the best. We got the core as well.' He pointed to something that looked like parcel string.

Rand turned away and swallowed. He was feeling very sick.

The other busied himself with dressings. Once he looked up, keenly. He said, 'I didn't know she was Kites.'

He hesitated. He said. 'They owed her this.'

'*Hmmph*,' said the doctor. He pulled the grubby skirt down. 'There you are, young lady,' he said. 'Feels better already, doesn't it?' Velvet didn't answer.

He shook his head. Stood up, and washed his hands. 'For God's sake get her cleaned up,' he said. 'She gets an infection in that sore, I wouldn't like to answer. Get some proper food into her as well. Ninety per cent of this is malnutrition.' He packed his bag, and left.

Raoul was hovering. 'Take her up to the house,' he said. 'Rye will look after her.'

Rand shook her shoulder. 'Come on,' he said. 'You're all right now.' She gave him a smouldering glance.

Rye clucked when she saw her. She said, 'Poor love.' She bore her away. He sat and drank a glass of wine. He expected ructions; but in the event none came. He thought how peaceful life had suddenly become.

Velvet did demur at first. She said, 'I can't get in that. I got a dressin' on.' But the dark woman merely smiled. She said, 'Then I can change it for you later.'

She gave up, climbed into the bath. She stuck her lip out; but in fact she thoroughly enjoyed the process. She'd never bathed in warm water before. She lay back, luxuriated. Later the other even washed her hair. The stuff she used felt soft. Quite different from washing in the sea.

She got upset when she couldn't have her clothes. Rye just smiled though. 'Tough luck,' she said. 'They're in the copper, boiling.' She held out a sort of little gown. She said, 'You can wear this.'

Velvet recoiled. She said, 'I can't go inter town in *that*,' and Rye smiled again. 'You're not going to,' she said. 'You're staying here tonight. You can have your things back in the morning. Don't worry, Rand's staying too.'

Raoul turned up at eighteen-thirty hours. They ate a meal. It was somewhat punctuated. The shampoo had discovered a wavy, dark red mane; and Velvet was inordinately proud. She ran to Rand several times, flung her arms round his neck. Finally she whispered, 'Sorry ...'

'Velvet,' he hissed. 'Sit down. Or I am going to get extremely cross.' She only chuckled though. She knew he didn't mean it.

It seemed Raoul read his mind. They escaped to the local pub. The other set the beers up, sat awhile in silence. Finally he said, 'You do make problems for yourself, don't you?'

He said, 'Perhaps.' He glanced up. He said, 'What's with the pony tails?'

The other grinned, and flicked at his hair. 'Reminds Rye of her misspent youth,' he said. 'Little word of warning for you; never marry a fruity woman.'

Rand said, 'It seems to have suited you.' He considered, staring at his glass. He said, 'It's funny.'

'What?'

'Problems,' he said. 'Responsibilities.' He considered. 'The car broke down, on the way back from F5,' he said. 'A deaf-mute fixed it for me. He wouldn't charge. Because we fly the Kites.' He smiled, ruefully. 'Least, you fly the Kites,' he said. 'I just make myself a nuisance round the edges.' He paused again. 'I sometimes wonder if we're doing any good,' he said. 'The whole pack of us.' He took a swig of beer. 'They were all Grounded when I came across,' he said. 'We had a Zero, right across the Realm. You're still here though. So am I.'

Raoul looked at him. 'I tried to duck out once,' he said. 'It didn't work. That's why I'm doing what I'm doing.' He paused. 'You can only do what you're given,' he said. 'And do your best.'

'Yes,' he said. 'Even though you're being taken for a sucker.'

The noncom glanced up again. He said, 'She isn't taking you for a sucker.'

Rand said, 'I wasn't talking about her.'

He replenished the beers. Raoul produced a stubby pipe. He said, 'How'd you go on F4?'

'So-so. F5 was worse.'

The Kiteman rubbed his lip. 'Yes,' he said. 'Poor old Silverton. Lost his wife a couple of years ago. Been trying to lose himself ever since.'

He said, 'I didn't know,' and the other shook his head. 'No,' he said. 'I don't expect you did.'

'Raoul,' he said, 'it seems to be a night for getting drunk.'

They did no such thing of course. They had another and then headed back. Velvet had gone to bed. Or been put there, firmly. He looked in on her. She was asleep, cuddling a big woolly toy. It had been lent to her by one of the kids. He stared for a moment. 'So that's a whoremistress,' he said. 'Just as well they told me.' He closed the door quietly, and walked away.

She was chirpy, on the drive back into town. 'I wants some cards,' she said.

'What sort of cards?'

'Cards. You know. Like the one you showed me.'

He glanced sidelong. 'What good would that be?' he said. 'You can't even read 'em.'

She looked indignant. 'I could learn,' she said. 'Anyway, don't matter if I can't. Other people can.'

He said, 'I'll think about it.' He dropped her by the arch. He said, 'Will you be all right?'

''Course,' she said. 'Ta-ta …'

She decided just for once it wasn't a working day. She took a stroll round town instead. Paused on the quay, and watched the mudlarks playing. She leaned on the parasol, and stuck her backside out. Rik gave her a bit of cheek; she lipped him back, and he ran for the harbour steps. She wagged the parasol, and he thought better of it. She walked back to the High, head in the air. From time to time she couldn't help sniffing her dress. Because it smelled so good.

*

Rand made his first tour of the Salient. Bases G4 through 7. He found a strange, green land. Humpy and hillocky in parts; yet even the hills looked wrong. As if the Lord had not created them, they were the work of lower hands. He remembered his theology. This too was where the Demons fought. Once, in the long-ago. The grass had spread, vivid and persistent; yet here and there vast patches were still bald. He shook his head. Was it true then, after all? What the Master Sprinling had said? Was this where they had voided their dirt?

He reached the Frontier, finally. Stood and gripped the wire, saw the great fence stretching into distance. He turned to the Launchmaster at his side. He said, 'I can't believe there's people still out there.'

The other shrugged. 'Probably not,' he said. 'Haven't been seen for years. They weren't people anyway.'

He looked at the older man curiously. 'You ever see one?'

The Kiteman nodded. 'Years ago,' he said. 'Just the once. Wouldn't want to again.' He held his arm out, thumb and finger circled. Made a little tent-shape above his head. He said, 'All dead and gone by now. The good Lord willing.'

Rand stared at the Codys rising to either side. String after String, each at the same perfect angle. Reaching into distance, like the fence. A line from the Exorcism came to him. '*Go back. Go back into the night. Into the Blue Shining* ...' He said, 'I don't think it was their fault.'

The Launchmaster shook his head. 'Nobody said it was ...'

He drove on to Easthope. Unusually for the Salient, it was a pleasant, bustling little town. Most of the rest were mounded, humped and sullen; eyeless to the east, in case the Bad Winds blew. In Easthope though were shops, lines and arcades of them; more, he thought, than he'd seen since Middlemarch. He sauntered past them, smiling. He'd always been bad at shopping, or so it had been alleged; but that had been when he was a tiny child. He saw what he wanted, finally; a black straw boater, trimmed with velvet roses. He went in. Once again the Kite tags on his shoulders worked their charm; the assistants were more than helpful. How old was his little girl? How tall was she? They conferred busily, finally fixed on a size. If it wasn't right of course it could be changed. They packed it for him, in a smart round box. It even had a knot of ribbons on the top. He paid them, and walked out. It had been too complex to explain; and so he hadn't tried. But the assumption they'd made stayed with him. She'd never had a father of her own; by the same token, he'd never had a daughter.

He finished at G7; wrote the last of his reports, and packed his bags. He headed back to Fishgard. The town had seemed strange at first; now there was almost a feeling of coming home.

Master Finling was incensed. After all, he was an honest trader. Like his father, and his father before him. And he'd been cheated. By this ... whatever she was. Urchin certainly, foundling; and worse, if the tales were true. He'd been on the lookout for her for days; but she'd always given him the slip. Now though she couldn't escape. He shook her by the wrist, holding her arm high in case she tried to bite. 'Wot about them fish then?' he said. 'Wot about them fish?'

Velvet howled, trying ineffectually to wriggle free. 'I can't 'elp it,' she said. 'So they picks up bits o' grit. It ain't my fault.'

'Bits o' grit,' he said. 'You're a bit o' grit.' He hit her across the face, raised his arm again.

His wrist was caught. He looked round, startled. The stranger was tall, well-built. Black, curly hair, a handsome, strong-boned face. But he thought he'd never seen a pair of colder eyes. He hadn't registered the squeal of brakes; he registered it now. He saw the shoulder tags. The other said, 'What seems to be the trouble, Master?'

He embarked on an explanation; but the Kiteman cut him short. He said, 'What does she owe?'

He estimated, rapidly; but again the other didn't let him finish. He flung a wad of notes on to the path. He said, 'I think that should cover.'

The passers-by had hesitated; now, being Fishgarders, they streamed past unconcerned. Finling retrieved the money, cautiously. 'I'm sorry, sir,' he said. 'I didn't know. Didn't know she was under the Kites.'

'We're all under the Kites,' said the stranger. 'Don't forget again. Now, go and run your shop.'

The fishmonger made his escape. Later, when he checked the money, he whistled. Triple the value, at least; it had been a profitable transaction. And he'd still got the baskets.

Velvet was clinging to him. Rand put her into the Buckley, drove down to the march. She only spoke once. 'Bin chasin' me all over,' she said. 'Lucky you come by.' She rubbed her face, resentfully, 'Belted my ear'ole,' she said. 'Nasty ol' git ...'

He glanced sidelong. 'If it had been me,' he said, 'I'd have taken a strap to you.' He pulled the Buckley into the kerb, and set the brake. He said, 'Are you all right?'

'Yeah, fine,' she said. She hesitated. Then she nodded. 'Want ter come in?'

'Ah,' he said. 'The *maison* Velvet. At last.' He considered in turn. 'You don't deserve it,' he said, 'you naughty little girl. But all right. Just for a minute.'

She tramped up the steps, flung the door wide. The last month had seen a transformation; though of course he wouldn't realize that, not having been before. She'd scrubbed through, with salt and vinegar; later she scurried all the junk into what cupboards she owned. She'd even acquired herself a bowl of flowers; though Mistress Gellern's garden wouldn't look the same for days. He still sucked his breath though, stood staring round amazed. 'What's the matter?' she said. 'Don' you like it?' She felt a bit disappointed.

'Of course,' he said. 'It's fine.' But he didn't sound convinced.

She scotched on the bed, crossed her ankles under her dress. She tucked it round her toes. She'd noticed she'd got tidemarks again. This cleanliness could get to you, after a bit.

He was looking past her. She gasped. It was too late though, he'd already seen the valise. She should have put it away. He said, 'Where did you get that?'

She avoided his eyes. 'I seen you throw it in the sea,' she said. 'Sorry …' She held it out to him, but he shook his head. 'It's yours now,' he said. 'You found it.'

She hesitated. 'Who is it?' she said. 'She's pretty.'

He said, 'Someone I used to know.'

She fingered the brass catch. It had gone all green now; but that was the salt of course. She said, 'She looks nice.'

'Yes,' he said. 'I used to think she was.'

She sensed danger. She laid the case aside, quickly. For a moment she couldn't think of what to say. It was all right though, he changed the subject for her. He nodded to the windowsill. He said, 'What's that?'

'What's what? she said. 'Oh, 'im.' She picked the creature up. 'That's Bruno,' she said. ''E's got twelve legs. Well, more or less.' She hugged him. 'Don't know why I calls 'im that,' she said. 'Just seems ter suit.'

He said, 'It's a bit of driftwood,' but she shook her head. 'No it's not,' she said. 'It's Bruno.'

'Velvet,' he said, 'you are the most extraordinary girl.'

She pouted slightly. She couldn't decide whether it was a compliment or not. 'Where you bin?' she said. 'You bin away fer ages.'

'Oh,' he said, 'here and there.' He settled back, took out a pipe and lucifers. 'So what have you been doing?' he said. 'Apart from cheating fishmongers?'

'Earnin' me keep,' she said. She put Bruno back on the window ledge, haughtily. Sat back on the bed, and covered her feet again. She decided it was time for a bit of an attack. 'More than you do,' she said. 'Least, that's what Master Lorning reckons.'

He nodded. 'I know how he earns his,' he said. 'He's still probably right though.' He shifted his position. He said, 'Do you remember your parents, Velvet?'

Her face set at once. 'A bit,' she said. 'I was only a kid though.' She nodded at the window. 'They took my Dad,' she said. 'The Kites …'

He shook his head, gently. 'They didn't take him,' he said. 'They don't take anybody. He gave himself to them. That's a bit different.'

She brooded. Then she brightened. 'I seen a Dragonfly today,' she said.

'A what?'

'Dragonfly,' she said. 'They're always goin' about. Least, that's what people call 'em.'

His attention was wholly engaged. He'd heard the stories before of course, most folk had; but he'd never talked about them. 'What do they look like?' he said.

'Big,' she said. 'They only comes over the sea though. Big silver wings,' she said. 'You can see 'em miles an' miles.'

He considered. It didn't make sense. Big silver animals, that used the sky. He said, 'Velvet, are you pulling my leg?'

'No,' she said. 'Why should I?'

'Are they Kites?'

'No,' she said. 'They're not Kites.'

'You say they don't come close.'

'No,' she said. 'Well, not usually.'

'Have you seen one close?'

'Once,' she said. 'Long time ago, that was.'

'Do they make a noise?'

'Sometimes,' she said. 'It depends.'

'What sort of noise?'

She shrugged. 'Just a noise,' she said. 'Noises is noises.' She was looking wary again.

'What do you think they are?'

'Dragonflies,' she said. She pointed, over his shoulder. 'Would you like some beer? I got a bottle or two.'

There was a curtained alcove. He pushed the drape aside, looked at the head-high stack of crates. 'Velvet,' he said, 'you haven't got a bottle or two. You've got a brewery.'

He was quite whistled by the time he left. He ran down to the van, and groaned. He'd seen the hat box. He hurried back. He thought she looked startled when she opened the door. 'Sorry, I forgot,' he said. 'Little pressie for you. Hope it'll be all right.'

She crowed. Sat on the bed and stared at it, turned it in her hands. Finally the strain became too much. He said, 'Well, try it on.' It fitted.

She ran the big pin through it. 'I'm goin' out,' she said.

'That's all right,' he said. 'I shan't hold you up.'

After he'd gone she looked up at the Codys. They didn't seem quite so menacing now. After all, a Kiteman had bought her a hat. Nobody had ever bought her a hat before.

There was a letter waiting, at the digs. He turned it over, curiously. It was faintly scented. Astringent, but haunting. The stationery was good too. He slit the flap. He was bidden forth to dinner that evening, at the home of the Mistress Kerosina.

He drove up in the Buckley. He'd seen the Ridge of course, but never visited any of the properties. The house he finally reached was spectacular. He scrunched up the drive, sat a moment and stared. At the great south-facing mullions, the battlemented eaves. Kitemasts were rigged on both wings. The western Trace was streaming. The symbols were unusually explicit; The Tower Master had enjoyed himself; or maybe his Apprentice.

Mistress Kerosina met him personally. He was surprised at that. Though the notion of surprise soon left him. He half glanced at the drive. Realized he should have left the Buckley round the back. It seemed she read his mind. With alarming accuracy too. 'That's quite all right,' she said. 'You're not a tradesman. You're from the Kites.'

She led the way into an elegant sitting room. She gave him a perfumed drink, in a tall slim glass. A transparent dragon snarled, clutching the stem. It was climbing from an egg.

On the side table was a bowl of sweets. Rose petals, coated in some way with sugar. She took one, ate it slowly. She said, 'I always like to meet new people in the town.'

He looked at her. Decided he'd never seen a such a startling woman. Huge tilted eyes, no colour he could define; a mane of hair; long legs, very much in evidence now. 'Catlike' was a phrase he'd heard applied; he realized it occasionally had relevance. He stared carefully through the window. He said, 'Is the Master Kerosin at home?'

She took another sweet, and shook her head. She said, 'He very seldom is.' She glanced round her. 'All done on tractor fuel,' she said. 'Amazing isn't it?'

He set the glass down. He said, 'Do you have the Kitefaith?' and she shrugged. He wished at once she hadn't. She said, 'It comforts the servants.'

A gong called them to dinner. He was the only guest. As he'd expected, the meal was superb. He'd thought it might be served by naked children. It wasn't though. Perhaps she kept them round the back.

She called for liqueurs, smoked a long cheroot. He was having trouble with her nipples. Either one was showing, or the other; sometimes both at once. She said, 'I believe you know my little helpmate.'

He brought himself back from distance. 'Velvet,' he said. 'I think she's rather sweet.' He knew why he was there of course. But then, he'd known before he arrived. For all its vagaries, Fishgard was a small town.

It seemed the remark amused her. 'She's invaluable,' she said. 'I couldn't do without her.'

He set the glass down. He said, 'A lady needs her servants.'

Her eyes burned at him. Those incredible eyes. She said, 'Don't give me fucking shit.' She stubbed the cigar. She said, 'Will you walk me? In the garden?'

He complied. His mind was curiously busy. He was remembering the small girl's tale. About the Dragonflies. He supposed he should report it. After all, things that lived in the air were the province of the Corps. But it had been reported often enough before. He frowned. He'd have to have a word with Raoul sometime.

She was clinging to his arm. She said, 'You weren't there for a minute, were you? You were miles away.'

He looked down. 'Lady,' he said. 'Adjust your dress.'

'I'm not a lady,' she said. 'The whole town knows what I am. You know.'

'Lady,' he said. 'Adjust your dress.'

She looked up at him wonderingly. She said, 'You mean it, don't you?'

'Yes,' he said. 'I do.'

She brushed at her cheek with a knuckle. 'I'm a funny old soul,' she said. 'Things get to me sometimes. I'm sorry.'

He set his lips. He'd expected the whoring; he hadn't expected this. He thought, *So it begins again.*

There were strange trees in the orchard. Medlars. He hadn't seen them since he was small. She snatched fruit from them. 'You eat them when they're rotten,' she said. 'I like things when they're rotten. But some I prefer fresh.'

There was a little summerhouse. She sat and stared at him. She pushed the dress down to her hips. Then to her thighs. She said, 'It's adjusted now. Do you like it better?'

He didn't answer; and she took one of the medlars, squeezed. He watched the liquid trickle to her fur. She lay back. She said, 'Do you like fruit juice?'

Velvet was picking pears. It being the season. She fell out of the tree. She used a very rude word, on the way down to earth. She sat up rubbing her behind. She'd turned her ankle as well. But the windows of the house stayed blind.

She got up, still swearing faintly. Grafted on to the wrong stock, those trees were. You'd need a Cody basket to get to the top. She wondered how the Gellerns coped. Maybe they didn't bother though. Like the cherries.

She walked round to the Kiteman's digs. Mistress Goldstar met her. 'He ain't up,' she said; but she'd already ducked under her arm. 'Rand,' she said, 'it's me. Got a pressie for yer ...'

He was lying face-down in the bed. 'Rand,' she said, 'it's me. Rand ...' She shook his shoulders, and he opened one eye blearily. 'There's some money on the mantel,' he said tiredly. 'For God's sake go away, Velvet. Come back later on ...'

She limped for the stairs. 'Cuntstruck,' she said sagely. 'Bin goin' on fer weeks. Still, it was bound to 'appen. But then,' she soliloquized, ''e wouldn't want me. Short legs,' she whispered.

Mistress Goldstar caught her in the hall. ''Ow is 'e?' she said. 'I gets worried about 'im. Goin' up the 'ill all the while. 'E ain't eatin' proper neither ...'

Velvet repeated her diagnosis, with some vigour. Mistress Goldstar picked up a broom. She fled, as fast as her injured ankle would allow. Later she put the truck away. She locked the little iron-barred door with pride. Master Billings had given her the lock. It was very fine, and made of brass. Nobody would get in there.

They walked in the garden again, the last fine day of the year. She'd put a leather collar on, and given him the lead. 'Snatch it if I misbehave,' she said. 'I like being made to mind.'

He sat in the summerhouse with her. He said, 'What's the Master Kerosin like?'

She looked at him. 'He pays the bills,' she said. 'It's what he's there for.'

'And doesn't he care?'

'Care about what?'

'Me,' he said. 'And all the rest.'

'There aren't any rest,' she said. 'I've rather gone for you.'

He smiled. He said, 'Can you hear the clock?'

'What clock?'

'The big one, in the house.'

'Of course not,' she said. 'Not from here.'

'It's a machine,' he said. 'It measures the seconds, and the minutes. Then the days, and years.'

She considered. She said, 'You think I'm a machine as well.'

'No,' he said. 'I didn't say that.'

She brooded. 'I ought to throw you out of course,' she said. 'I shan't. But you knew that anyway.'

He said, 'Perhaps.'

She got up, suddenly. She said, 'Let's go to bed.'

He glanced at the sky. He said, 'It's early yet.'

She said, 'The earlier the better.' Later she lay face-down, and talked to him. She said, 'You're a strange man, Rand.'

'How do you mean?'

'I don't know,' she said. 'Just strange.'

He said, 'Most people are strange.'

She shook her head. He saw it in the half-light. It was still barely dark. She said, 'Most people are very ordinary. The more you know them, the more ordinary they get.' She pushed herself up on her elbows. 'Don't fall in love with me,' she said. 'If you do, I shall destroy you.'

'You're destroying yourself,' he said. 'You might take one or two with you.'

'But you won't be among them?'

'No,' he said. 'I don't aim to be anyway.'

She traced a little pattern on the pillow. She said, 'You were badly hurt once, weren't you?'

He said, 'Perhaps.'

She traced the pattern again. She said, 'Maybe she had her reasons. Most of us do.'

He said, 'I expect she had.'

She half rolled over. 'I ought to let you have me when I'm dry,' she said. 'You'd get more feeling from it.'

'But you never are.'

'That's your fault,' she said. 'You can't blame me for that.'

He said, 'I don't blame you for anything.' He looked up at the sky. He said, 'It's the most important thing.'

'What is?'

'The thing between your legs.'

'That's not very nice.'

'Yes,' he said. 'It's proper, for a Lady.'

'I'm not a Lady,' she said. 'I told you once before. Don't call me that.'

'There are many sorts of Lady,' he said. 'You're the best.'

She said, 'An animal.'

He nuzzled at her. 'Yes,' he said. 'That's right.'

Unexpectedly, she started to cry. He kissed her till the tears stopped. He said, 'You're not being fair of course. '

She rolled on to her back, lay looking up. She said, 'What's fair?'

He said, 'Very little.'

She was quiet awhile. Finally she said, 'I suppose it comes from the Kites.'

'What comes from the Kites?'

'It changes your attitude,' she said. 'I could never really understand it.'

'I don't fly the Kites.'

'You fly them all the while,' she said. 'Every day the good Lord sends.'

He considered. He said, 'Do you have a family?'

She lay quite still. 'What do you think?' she said.

'I don't know. That was why I asked.'

'Three,' she said finally. 'Why do you think I'm slack?'

'Where are they?'

She said, 'A long way from here.' She brooded again. She said, 'Even unto the seventh generation.'

'What?'

She turned, impatiently. 'We've married, in and out. To keep the money in the Clan. The stock weakens, eventually.' She rubbed him. 'I wouldn't want a great big thing like that,' she said. 'Flopping about between my legs. It would feel untidy.'

He said, 'You're just jealous.'

She said, 'A lot of us are. I've read about it.' She dragged him on to her, dug her nails into his back. 'Quick,' she said. 'I can't wait any longer …' Later, when he pulled away, she gasped. He said, 'I'm sorry. Did I hurt you?' and she laughed. She said, 'You are a silly boy.'

He went to G8. He'd heard some curious stories about the Station. He found it much the same as any other. Two hangars, with a standby; normal for the Salient. The Kites were streamed in good order, and the books were neat. He thought a lot about the Lady Kerosina. However they appeared, there was a human being underneath. Or was there? He remembered Janni, and instantly closed his mind. There was no Janni, he'd told himself that before.

He walked to the Perimeter. The Base Captain was with him. He stared at the Badlands. They were blueish even in daylight. He turned to him. He said, 'Was there a Captain Manning here once?'

The other's face changed instantly. He said, 'Are the books in order, Kiteservant?'

'Of course,' he said. Later he said, 'I'm sorry, sir.'

The other shrugged. He said, 'It doesn't matter. Get your rumours from somewhere else though. If you please.'

They were walking back across the Base. Under the high strings of the Codys. He shivered. The winter winds were striking early. He said, 'Are there any people still out there?'

'Out where?'

'Beyond the Frontier.'

The other glanced at him. 'There was one a year ago,' he said. He held his hands a little apart. 'It was about that long.'

'What did it do?'

'Crawled under the wire,' said the Kiteman.

'What did you do with it?'

'Nothing,' said the other. 'Stood and watched it die. Then we buried it.' He pointed. He said, 'It's just over there.'

Rand shook his head. Somehow there seemed to be a relationship with

Velvet and the Mistress Kerosina. But for the life of him he couldn't decide what it was.

He found out what an Easthold winter was like. It was grey, and howling. Waves smashed over the sea walls; a mile or more from land, the water boiled like yeast. The town closed in on itself, barricaded its windows and doors. He fixed the shutters for the Mistress Goldstar personally. She heaved a sigh of relief when he had finished. 'My 'usband used ter do it,' she said. 'I can still manage; but I ain't so young ner more.' She touched his arm. 'You're good to me, sir,' she said.

He was surprised. He said, 'But anybody would have done that for you.'

She shook her head. 'No, sir,' she said. 'Not necessarily …'

Kites were lost of course, and their Observers. Replacements were rushed from Middlemarch. Men, and *matériel.* Because Demons love the storms. The skies glowed, over Easthold and the Salient. Flier after Flier discharged his flares, into the wild night. He found the sight oddly moving. '*We're here,*' they seemed to be saying. '*We're ready, and we're waiting …*' No Demons came.

The Master Kerosin returned to Fishgard. Which meant a month without his Lady's company. To his surprise, he found he missed her. He set himself to analyse the feeling. You could buy what she was offering, in any pub in town. Yet he felt no inclination. It was her, he decided finally. She herself. Something inside her, burning like silver fire. Something he had accessed. He shook his head. The trap was honeyed, obvious; yet also it was multilevelled.

She wrote a letter to him. '*It's boring without you,*' she said. '*I went for a walk yesterday. I kissed a sheep. It was only because he looked fed up as well. We were both soaking wet.*

'*I asked the Master Kerosin to kiss my navel. He was quite disgusted. Yet you kiss me everywhere.*

'*I'd like you to fuck me again. I like to feel it squirt up in my tummy. Women aren't supposed to say things like that. I do though. Did she say them as well? The other one? I think I love you.*

'*Did I tell you my husband was bald? It's supposed to make men sexier. It doesn't seem to work with him though. But since he's given me three children I suppose he thinks he's done his duty …*

'*You know the sort of things I really like. You're different though. I keep trying to tell you, but you never listen. I'll let you know when it's all right to come back. You probably won't want to though. I'm an old lady now; I've got a big fat bottom.*

'*Did I tell you Thoma plays the sitar? It's a great help to him, it stops him getting involved. He was playing it when my third was due: I was bleeding quite a lot, but he stayed upstairs. But after all he is an artist. He's very sensitive …*'

He put the letter down. He thought, *One day, I shall probably kill somebody …*'

The Master Lorning's trade was definitely seasonal. From the solstice celebrations onwards, he progressively laid off his staff. They complained, with varying degrees of bitterness. But Velvet merely shrugged. 'It always 'appens,' she said. 'Bound to, ennit? Stands ter reason …'

There was a village a mile or two out on the Easthope road. She waited for the weather to set in hard and took the truck. There was a pond there where the ice got really thick. And Kerosina had an ice house. There was a pond in Fishgard, but it was nowhere near as good. The ice from it was full of little worms; they woke up in the summer, started wriggling. All right for the Gellerns maybe; but not for the Ridge. Besides, she wouldn't cheat the Mistress. It wouldn't be fair; apart from that, she'd lose her best source of trade.

She heard the honking quite a long way back. She steered into the side of the road and scowled. Always somebody shoving people about. She turned, saw it was the Buckley. It pulled up beside her. The Kiteman slid the window back. He said, 'Want a lift, young lady?'

'Can't,' she said. 'I got the truck.'

He said, 'And I've got an empty van.' He got out, opened the back doors. It wasn't empty really. There was a stack of little Kitesails to one side; he was bringing them back to the Tower for mending. There was plenty of room for the truck though. He swung it on board. It didn't seem to cause him any effort. She realized he was much stronger than she'd thought. He lashed it into place. Kitemen were a bit like sailors; they knew all sorts of funny knots. He said, 'Where are you taking it?'

Velvet said, 'The Mistress Kerosina.' She wished at once she hadn't told him. He didn't seem to mind though. He said, 'Good. I can drop you then. I'm going past.'

She glanced at him sidelong. 'Better not,' she said. ''E ain't gone back yet.' Her teeth started to chatter.

He looked across at her. He said, 'Are you all right?'

She nodded. Rubbed her arms. 'Funny, ennit,' she said. 'You gets in somewhere warmer, then you starts feelin' the cold.'

He compressed his lips. 'No shoes on,' he said. 'And that silly hat …'

'It ain't a silly 'at,' she said. 'You bought it for me.'

He shook his head. 'Velvet,' he said, 'you're a summer creature.'

She frowned. She wasn't sure she understood. 'It ain't the summer,' she said.

'No,' he said. 'It's not the summer.' He changed gear for a bend. 'I'll drop you at the end of the drive,' he said. 'Then I'll wait for you.'

'Wait for me?' she said. 'What for?'

'Shoes,' he said succinctly. 'And a hat.'

'I can't wear shoes,' she said. 'They pinches.'

He said, 'Not if they fit your feet.'

Fishgard showed ahead. She couldn't believe they were nearly back already. He coasted down a hill. Climbing the last slope to the Ridge, the van began to cough and splutter. She said, 'What's the matter with it?'

'Getting old,' he said. 'Like me.'

She glanced at him again. There always seemed to be things she wanted to say to him. But she could never really decide what they were. She didn't expect she'd know the words anyway. Words were difficult. Especially when you hadn't been to school. She expected he'd been to all sorts of schools. You had to, to know about the Kites. She said, 'You wants ter buy Master Lornin's car.'

He was surprised. He said, 'The Falcon? He wouldn't part with that.'

'Garn,' she said. ''E 'as to, every winter. Then 'e buys it back when 'e's got a bit o' trade. Be lorst without doin' that.'

He looked thoughtful. 'What does he ask for it?'

She told him. It sounded astronomical.

'And what does he expect to get?'

That seemed much more reasonable.

'I dunno,' he said. 'I should have to get somebody to look at it.'

'It's all right,' she said quickly. 'They're a bit 'ard on bearin's. But 'e 'ad 'em done last year. Keep the oil well up, you shouldn't 'ave no bother. External pump,' she explained.

He started to laugh. 'Velvet,' he said, 'is there anything you don't know?'

She was surprised in turn. 'I don't know 'ardly nothin',' she said. 'That's the 'ole trouble.'

They weren't shoes really. More sort of boots. Nearly like the Kitemen wore; and lined too, really thick. She hadn't seen a hat like that though. Furry, and with bits that even covered her ears. She walked round town in it, for the sheer pleasure of feeling warm.

Cook had given her a big box of goodies. Honey cakes, all sorts. She took some round to the Kiteman as a thank-you present. She thought he was looking moody; but he brightened when he saw her. She kissed him. She said, 'Thanks ever so much.' He held on to her. Anybody else and she'd have pushed away; but he was different somehow. She said, 'I think I love you.'

He smiled. He said, 'I know I love you.' She did stiffen fractionally at that; and he laughed outright. 'Velvet, Velvet,' he said. 'There's many sorts of love.'

She frowned. She didn't know really what he'd thought was funny. She hoped it wasn't her. She supposed it would be fair enough though. After all it wouldn't be the first time she'd been laughed at. 'I ain't worth lovin',' she said bitterly. 'I ain't no good. I'm a procure – procure – what you called me.'

He held her by the shoulders. Looked down and shook his head. He said, 'You procure cherries too. They're always very good.' He led her to the window. He said, 'Have you seen the new Cody?'

She could just make it out against the dusk. The string of oval plaques below the last of the Lifters. They were twisting gently as it flew. 'Yeah,' she said. 'Ain't seen one like that though.'

'No,' he said. 'Neither has anybody else.' He opened a book. It was full of coloured symbols. He traced them with his finger. 'V, E and L,' he said. 'V and E again; then a T. It's your string, Velvet; I had it streamed for you.'

She knuckled her cheek. She said, 'You goin' ter buy that car?'

He shook his head again. 'He wouldn't sell to me. He doesn't like the Kites either. And I'm not all that fond of him.'

'That's all right,' she said. 'I'll soften 'im up.'

'Velvet,' he said. 'Velvet ...' It was too late though, she'd already dashed for the stairs. Letting herself out, she wiped her face again. She always hated crying in front of people. It made you look a baby.

The Master Lorning wasn't enthusiastic. Quite the reverse in fact. But she happened to know he was unusually strapped for cash. She hinted as much, delicately, but it brought no result. She considered, and leaned forward. She also knew the Mistress Lorning visited her sister this time of the year; otherwise she wouldn't have dared walk into the 'Dolphin' to start with. She murmured a certain suggestion; but he merely looked more irritable. 'What's the good o' that?' he said. 'I ain't got no PGs.'

'I wadn't thinkin' o' the guests,' she said. 'It was fer you. An' it wouldn't cost.'

She saw his eyes change. He said, 'Could you fix it up?'

''Course,' she said airily. 'No problem.' She only hoped she was right.

She headed up the hill, to the big school on the Ridge. She knew they were back, they'd come back the day before. On the way she glanced up at the Cody string. Too dark to see it properly; but she still felt a little rising of pride. Also the lump was back in her throat. She set her jaw and stumped on.

An orchestra was playing, in the big hall. She peered through a crack in the curtains. Winter and summer, the girls were always in white. She thought how smart they looked. She always fancied she'd have liked to go to a place like that. But you had to have rich folks. To start with of course you had to have folks. She listened to the music. She supposed it was very clever, but there never seemed much tune in it. She waited till they stopped, risked a sharp tap on the glass. The Mistress Hollan looked across at once. She'd been standing at the front, wagging a sort of stick.

She ducked out of sight. The other would know who it was. She waited. In time a side door opened, let out a yellow gleam of light. She hurried over.

The Mistress Hollan was blonde, and tall; nearly as tall as Kerosina. Looked a bit like her too. She outlined her requirements, and the other considered. She said, 'You'd better come in for a minute. I can't be long though, I'm taking Prep tonight.' Velvet followed her down a corridor floored with shiny wooden tiles. It always smelled of lavender.

She laid out cash. A lot of cash. Even more than the hat and shoes. Though not so much, she supposed, as it would cost to fly a Cody. The Mistress considered, tapping her fingers. Finally she nodded. 'All right,' she said. 'Let's make it next weekend.'

She said, 'Who else shall we use?' and the tall woman's eyes gleamed. 'Who else?' she said. 'Do you mean we need three?' She pulled her forward. She said, 'We'll have to practice first though.'

Velvet groaned, and shut her eyes. She nodded, set her teeth; and Miss Hollan lifted her skirt.

The deaf-mute ran his fingers along the car's block. He raised the throttle linkages, tested the vibration again. He concentrated, screwing his face up. He rocked the front wheels, crawled beneath the chassis. There were unidentifiable sounds from the direction of the steering assembly. He sat in, waved for the Kiteman to follow. He checked the movement of the gearstick, drove across the yard. He circled the town, drove as far as the Ridge. He frowned finally, pulled in. He opened the bonnet, made some small adjustment. '*Be—er*,' he said. '*Be—er. How Mu*'?' Rand knew a little of the hand talk. He gestured, and the other nodded. '*A—ri*',' he said. '*A—ri*'.' He nodded again, vigorously.

He paid the Master Lorning cash, drove the sleek black motor away.

'Well,' said Kerosina. 'Gone up in the world, haven't we?' He turned his head. The Falcon was visible, through the tall windows of the bedroom. It gleamed. He'd worked solidly on it the last two days, cutting the layer of road film that had been allowed to collect. 'Yes,' he said, 'I think so.' He rolled over, lazily. He said, 'I was surprised he sold it to me.'

'You shouldn't have been,' she said. 'I know how it was arranged.'

He said curiously, 'What do you mean?' But she shook her head. She would say no more.

He fondled her, and kissed. 'As a matter of fact I've fallen in love with her. She goes like a bird.'

She shook her head, eyes closed. 'No,' she said. 'It's just the ego thing. It's the long bonnet that does it. It reminds you of this.' She squeezed him. He stiffened again instantly, and she began to pant. Later she sighed. 'I'd love to go with you,' she said. 'Get in your big black car and drive and drive. And never stop.'

Rand shook his head. He said, 'I doubt it.'

She sighed again, dreamily. 'Can't you just imagine,' she said. 'If I was on my own. Say I was a Kitebase secretary, or that I worked at the school. And you'd just come to town.'

He pushed himself up on his elbows. 'Yes,' he said, 'I can. You'd be looking for someone like the Master Kerosin to marry, and someone like me to fill the time in with.'

She opened her huge eyes. She said, 'You can be so cruel.'

'And you,' he said, 'can be so dishonest.' He stared at the pillow. 'I live in the real world, Mistress,' he said. 'Because I have to. Black's black, white's white; and red's red.' He saw a tear form, trickle. He brushed it; but she pushed his hand away. She said, 'You never loved me, did you? You never loved me at all.'

He considered. He said, 'That's a very difficult question.'

'It isn't,' she said. 'It's a very easy one. Black's black, and white's white. So the answer's yes or no.'

He smiled a little sadly. 'Caught,' he said. 'I asked for that though, didn't I?' He lay down, attempted to pull her to him. She arched her back, pushing at his shoulders. 'No,' he said. 'Don't do that. Don't do that Mistress, please.' She relaxed.

He lay quiet. He was thinking about what she'd asked. And the impossibility of making a true answer. He was wondering why he'd gone to her in the first place. After all, her household was notorious; a byword, even in that town of rumours. Curiosity perhaps, curiosity that turned to lust? Or had it been simple desire for revenge, the need to take from someone else what had been taken from him? That was where the vivid boundaries ceased, the colours began to blur. You couldn't know someone as he had known her and remain disengaged. He knew the scar on her hand, where she'd cut it on glass as a child; he knew two toes of her left foot were crooked, because she'd been stepped on by a horse; he knew the foot hurt sometimes in the wet. He knew her back muscles knotted when she was fatigued, that her neck often gave her pain. He knew she sometimes voided blood. Between periods, and from the wrong outlet. He knew it frightened her. It frightened him as well. She'd ceased to be a puppet, become a human being; when she cried, her tears were as salt as his.

He put his mouth close to her ear. 'Listen,' he said, 'I love you. I love each hair of your head; I love your breasts, I love your tummy, I love your fur. I love what's underneath it. I love your legs, I love your toes, I love your fingers. I love *you*. Is that white enough? Or black?'

She clung to him. 'Don't go away,' she said. 'Stay, just for tonight. It will be all right.'

He frowned. He said, 'I don't know if I should.'

'Please,' she said. 'Please, Rand.'

'What's so special about tonight?'

She said, 'I'm frightened.'

He stroked her. He said, 'What are you frightened of?'

'I don't know,' she said. 'I think I'm frightened of being afraid.'

'It's all right,' he said. 'Hush there, hush. Shhh …'

The Falcon waited, patient in the drive.

She was cool to him when he visited next. And again the time after. 'The boys are coming home,' she said. 'It's going to get very difficult, Rand.'

'No,' he said gently. 'It's going to get very easy.' He took himself off to the G Bases. This was the dripping tap routine; he thought it had come about on cue. He didn't bother to return to Fishgard between calls; there was always somewhere or other he could stay.

The days lengthened. The spring came early and warm. Velvet called again and again at the house of Mistress Goldstar. But the Kiteman was never home. She realized she'd probably never see him again. But then, there was no reason why she should. ''E's got what 'e wanted,' she whispered. ''E's got 'is car …' She wept a small and private storm. When it was over she washed her face. She took her parasol, headed for the quay. She was summoned forth to the big house on the hill. Rik Dru went with her. When he came back he joined the Biguns' boat.

His duty tour ended, finally. The recall reached him at G12. A month's refresher course in Middlemarch, some leave, and then another posting. He made his formal farewells at the big Base, headed back. The Falcon, as ever, ran well. Soon she'd be on the smooth roads of the Middle Lands. The roads she'd been designed for.

He called at the house of Kerosina. After all they purchased air rights from the Church, it was on his official list of visits. He saw it was shuttered, empty. He met a disgruntled gardener. He said, 'Where have they gone?'

The other shrugged. ''Ow should I know?' he said. 'Don't tell the likes o' me. New people comin' in next week. Least, I bin paid till then.'

Rand got back in the car and drove away.

The fall of Velvet was brief and parabolic. She was stumping along the quay, parasol as ever at the ready, when her skirt was snagged. She spun round, alarmed. She'd forgotten she was passing the Biguns' headquarters. Rik Dru though had a longer memory; and he was experienced now. He twisted the boathook, and yanked. '*Eeee*,' said Velvet. '*Aaaiiieee* …' There was a splash, and silence.

*

He packed his things at the digs, said goodbye to Mistress Goldstar. He left her a cash present, and the biggest bunch of flowers he could find. He called in at the Tower, but Raoul was away on leave. He drove down to the arch, and parked the Falcon. He ran up the steps, tapped the door. There was no answer.

He tapped again, waited a moment frowning. He tried the handle. The door was unlocked.

The curtains were drawn, across the single window. He had to wait a moment for his eyes to adjust to the gloom. Then he saw her. She was lying on the bed. A bowl of water was beside her; it was tinged with pink. So was the compress she'd laid across her forehead. He knelt, appalled. 'Velvet,' he said, 'what is it? What's happened?'

She looked at him dully. 'Gang-banged,' she said faintly. 'Thought they would one day. Allus somethin', ain't there?' She dabbled the cloth in the bowl, laid it back. 'I don't know,' she said vaguely. 'I don't know at all. 'Ad a good trip?'

He was holding her, stroking her hair. Then before she realized he'd scooped the bedclothes round her, lifted her. She struggled feebly. 'What you doin'?' she said. '*Rand*, what you doin'?'

She thought she'd never seen him look as angry. He said, 'I'm leaving. And you're not stopping here.'

'I can't,' she wailed. 'I got me livin' to earn. *Rand*, no …' She jammed her feet violently against the doorframe. She said, 'Me 'at …'

'Oh, blow your hat,' he said. 'I'll buy you another.' He backed anyway, scooped it up somehow and plonked it on her head. He left the door swinging. Master Lorning could shut it at his leisure. He put her in the Falcon, tucked the blankets round. He started up; and she began to squall again. 'The truck,' she said. 'The truck …'

'You don't need the truck.'

She said, 'But all the money's in it …'

He looked at her. Pulled up beside the arch. He took the key from round her neck, unlocked the little door. He hauled the handcart into the light, pulled up the false bottom. He stared at the inch-thick layer of notes. He said, 'You crazy little creature …' He grabbed them up in bundles, stuffed them into the Falcon's boot. He sat back in and wiped her face. He pushed her hair back and kissed her. He swung under the arch, headed up the High. She said feebly, 'Where we goin', Rand?'

He glanced across at her, his lips still compressed. 'You're a summer person,' he said. 'We're going to the summer.'

7
Kitemariner

He walked into town, in the early evening. The housebirds were squealing and trilling, swooping under the high eaves, making their last flights of the day. Nath glanced at them, vaguely. There were many types of housebird; he knew none of them. But then, there was no reason why he should. He was a mariner.

He looked up at the sky. Still clear, but with the faint greenish cast that always seemed to come at the end of summer. He saw clouds were massing, low in the west. A front was coming in; could be a blow by morning.

He headed down the steep, cobbled High Street. It was so steep the cottages and shops were set on little platforms, each stepped below the next. Six courses of bricks on the downhill side, zero at the other. In sight of the harbour, he paused. As ever, perspective made the sea appear to climb a reciprocal slope. He saw the occasional whitecap form, a long way out; precursors of the coming wind. Beyond, the first of the Inshore Units rode at their buoys; *Holdfast*, *Windwrack*, *The Lady Guardian*. He could recognize them by their silhouettes, even at this distance. They'd all be streaming of course; but the Codys weren't detectable in this light. Not even to his keen eyes. A pair of glasses would have brought them in clear enough; but he had brought none with him. He had no need of them.

He turned right, along the quay. *Kitestrength* was still at her moorings; but she wasn't due to slip till twenty-three hundred. He stared at the tall gantry on her bow. The Cadets would be aboard already, checking the Cody strings. The Pilots and the Lifters, the baskets and mancarriers. The priests of course wouldn't board till later; and by tradition the Fliers would come last of all. This time though she'd sail without her Second Engineer.

He saluted her vaguely, but there was no response. Old Toma would be on the bridge by now, probably enjoying the odd sip of the skipper's gin. Or fast asleep already. As a watchman, he was a joke; but he was coming up for retirement, and even the Vars could be generous on occasions. In any case there was little need for high security in the Southguard. Not as yet, anyway. There'd been rumours of unrest in other parts of the Realm; Militia called out in the Salient, and several times up north. There'd even been some nasty reports from Middlemarch. He shrugged. Things like that worried him sometimes; though he'd never essentially thought of himself as a thinking man. The Church held the Realm not by force, but fear. Fear of the grounding of the Codys, a sudden inrush of Demons. But the Codys had been grounded, time and again. And nothing had happened. So if that fear ceased ...

He twitched the jacket back round his shoulders. He'd been forced to wear it like that because of the sling. He hadn't really needed it, the evening was still warm; but he'd probably be glad of the dark blue reefer later on. He eased his wrist. His left hand was paining him, under the heavy dressing. But then, he only had himself to thank for that. He grimaced. About the stupidest accident he could think of; and him a Second.

Yesterday morning it had been. Preparing for his shift. He'd clamped the work to the drill bed, securely as he'd thought; checked his centring, brought the big handle down. Like a fool, he'd steadied the job; and the casting had lashed round, carried his hand between the bed and centrepost. He'd wrenched back somehow, stood and stared; then he'd called. 'Denzi ... Denzi ...'

The Apprentice had paled. 'My God,' he said, 'What have you done?'

'Been a damned fool,' Nath said between his teeth. 'Will you get the Mate?' He gripped his wrist and stared; at the white bone showing, the squibbing blood. His third finger was shattered; he thought, 'That's gone for certain.'

The Mate was there in a flash. He always liked to be first on the scene if there was news. He said, 'Don't worry, I'll sort you out.' He came back grinning. 'There you are,' he said. 'Drip into that.' He slung a filthy bucket down, on the iron-ribbed deck.

Nath's sight had flickered fractionally; and to his surprise, sounds had become dim. When his vision returned they'd wrapped his hand in some sort of dressing. It looked like engineroom rags; but by then he'd lost interest. They put his jacket round his shoulders, took him ashore. He lay on a couch, somewhere in the Kiteport Tower, while a Medic attended to him. He clicked his tongue a bit. 'I'll try and save the finger,' he said. 'But I can't guarantee a thing.'

He turned his face away. He was feeling a little ashamed. There was a girl in the room; a nurse, in a long white gown. Only the richer Towers could afford them. 'It'll be all right,' he said. 'Why don't you cut it off?' She approached, and wiped his forehead. 'Don't worry, Mariner,' she said. 'You'll be fine.'

He gritted his teeth again. He said, 'Just get on with it.' After which the clickings and the little scrapes were one. As were the twangs and stabs of pain. They could have been the effects of knives and scissors, could have been the antiseptic they used from time to time. 'I don't think the guides are damaged,' said the Medic. 'We'll try it, Sister.' He felt his finger being bound. Later they swathed his hand in a bulky, chalk-white dressing. They called a car for him, and took him home. For which he was privately grateful.

Kari was cold, when she opened the door to him. She said, 'What is it this time?' Then she saw the sling, and shook her head. 'Ah, the Kitetoll,' she said. 'Getting quite used to it, aren't we?'

'It wasn't the Kites,' he said. 'It was something I did myself. In the machine shop.'

'What happened?'

'I hurt my finger,' he said. 'Nobody to blame but me.'

She looked at him. She said, 'You'd better come and sit down.'

He swayed a little. 'I think,' he said, 'I'd better go to bed.'

A little wait. Then she said, 'Do you need a hand?'

He shook his head. 'No, thanks,' he said. 'I've still got one left.'

She brought him a meal, later on. He was half-dozing. He managed part of it, to show willing. Then he slept, with relative soundness. Though when he woke at zero seven hundred his hand was throbbing like the Devil. His arm as well. He wondered if the wrench had been transmitted through the nerves.

He slept again. To his surprise, he was feeling better when he woke next time. He'd expected delayed shock.

The storm broke in the afternoon. As he'd known it would. She said, 'How long must this go on?'

'How long must what go on?'

She didn't answer. Just set her lips, wielded a breadknife with unusual vigour. 'Better be careful,' he said. 'You might cut yourself.'

She threw the thing down, ran to him. 'Nath,' she said, 'I can't stand it. Not any more.'

'Stand what?'

'Not knowing,' she said. 'Not knowing what's out there.' She swallowed. 'When you go,' she said, 'I have to wait and wait. And wonder if you'll come back …'

He said, 'I always come back.' He pushed her away, with his one good arm. 'I'll be all right,' he said.

She shook her head. 'One day,' she said. 'One day, you'll go like all the rest. And where shall I be, then?'

'Kari,' he said, 'I hurt my hand, in harbour. It was a silly thing to do.'

She looked up at him. The tearstained eyes, shoulder-length yellow hair. 'You hurt your hand in harbour,' she said. 'The rest will happen later …'

He took her chin. 'Kari,' he said, 'do you remember? In the Northguard?'

She shook her head, confused.

'You married me for what I was,' he said. 'A Mariner.' He pulled her to him. She was wearing bright blue trousers, like a fishergirl. They roused desire in him. The old desire. He pushed his fingers underneath the waistband, reached to twitch at her belt. She wrenched back. 'You'll have to choose,' she said. 'Between me and the sea.'

'Kari,' he said, 'you are the sea ...'

'Not to you,' she said. Later though she touched the dressing, gently. She said, 'Can I look? I might be able to help ...'

'No,' he said, 'Best leave it alone for now. They knew what they were doing.' He gripped her shoulder. 'Kari,' he said, 'it's nothing.'

'I'm nothing,' she said, bitterly. 'I can see that now.'

He glanced up. He'd decided years ago the Southguard wasn't like the rest of the Realm. Not even the Middle Lands. There were the Yards of course farther along the quay, the Yards where they built the ocean-going ships; Kitevessels, the occasional small freighter. The other way, out of sight from here, were the pits and foundries. You could smell the stink from them way out at sea. But the westerlies carried the smoke away, so the villas on the ridge of hills weren't troubled. He stared at them; the roofs cluttering the treegrown slopes, as far as the eye could reach. Kites flew from almost every one; but that was understandable. For years now, money had been streaming steadily to the south. Why, he was not so sure. Except that the Middle Lands seemed less secure than they once might have been. He shook his head. He'd seen mobs shouting Middle Doctrine slogans. The last thing, surely, that mild Order would have desired. Or was it? He looked back to the harbour. The sea was calm tonight. But it still concealed a lethal fury.

He decided he was getting depressed. He glanced again at the endless plain of water. He was remembering a night with Kari, the first night ever. They'd sat and stared at the ocean; another ocean, stretching out for ever. 'Look at it,' she'd said. 'What colour would you call it?'

'I don't know,' he'd said. 'It hasn't got a colour. There's not a word in the Realm, that would describe that.'

He touched his wrist again. There was a word, of course. He'd realized, over the years. The sea was red.

They'd lit the lamps, along the front of the 'Mermaid'. Although it wasn't really dark as yet. He glanced at the pale, high frontage. Lights showed, in several of the rooms; and a sleek black car stood at the kerb. A Falcon. He walked to it. He'd fancied owning one himself, one time; but the chance had never come. They were getting scarcer now; this was well maintained though. He pushed open the big door of the pub, walked in.

The front bar was empty save for one other customer. He was tall and slim-faced; he sported a neatly-trimmed beard, a mass of curly black hair. He was leaning on the bar, studying a thick manual. It was bound in blue, heavy metal rings through the spine. He glanced up, nodded briefly. He said, 'Evening, Mariner.' He looked at the sling. He said, 'Been in the wars?'

'You could say that,' said Nath curtly. Ale was brought him; he swigged, set the cup down and wiped his lip.

The stranger looked up again. Then he closed the manual, set it aside. 'Sorry,' he said. 'What happened?'

He shrugged. 'A bloody silly cockup. Simple machining job. Nearly took a finger off. Don't know whether I have or not yet.'

The bearded man sipped his ale. He said, 'These things happen. That your line then?'

He nodded. He said, 'Second Engineer. *Kitestrength*.'

The other glanced at the windows. He said, 'She's sailing tonight, isn't she?'

'Yes,' he said. 'Twenty-three hundred.'

'Tough luck.'

Nath stared at his beer. He was tempted to drain it and go. But somehow he wanted to talk. He said, 'That your Falcon out the front?'

'Aye.'

He considered. You needed a bit behind you to run a motor like that. He said, 'What are you in then?'

The other smiled. He took a card from his pocket. He said, 'Panvet-Hoyling. Chandlers extraordinary. Used to be Gib and Crossey.'

He handed the card back. He said, 'The one thing that gives me the shivers is the sight of a foul anchor.'

The chandler grinned. 'It's bread and butter to us,' he said. 'Anyway, we inherited it. Had to pay for it, thought we might as well keep it.'

Nath knew the shop of course. Big handsome premises next to D7. The Kiteport Tower. Even had its own Cody mast; they streamed the foul anchor from that as well. It was a sort of permanent flying insult. Or a warning. He said, 'I've never seen you in there.'

The bearded man shook his head. 'You probably saw my partner,' he said. 'I'm generally out the back. I fly a desk these days.'

The Mariner glanced up quickly. He said, 'Were you Kites?' That would explain a lot.

The tall man nodded. 'On the civvy side,' he said. 'Came out about eighteen months ago.'

'Why'd you jack it in?'

'It's a long story,' said the other. He drank ale. 'You get tired of counting spares for other people,' he said. 'Makes more sense to do it for yourself.' He nodded. 'Like another in there?'

The Mariner considered. Finally he said, 'Don't mind if I do.' He eased his position with a little frown.

'Look,' said the Kiteman, 'you want to have a seat? You don't look too happy where you are.'

'Wouldn't say no,' said the Mariner gruffly. He picked the ale up. He said, 'Thanks a lot.'

There was a corner table. He eased himself down, took his cap off and laid it on the side. He was a broad-shouldered young man with a shock of dark brown hair. He sported a full, luxuriant moustache. The other held his hand out. 'Rand Panington, by the way,' he said. 'That first name's a bit of a mixture.'

He said, 'Nath Ostman.' He looked thoughtful. He said, 'I've heard of you.'

The dark man shook his head. 'No,' he said. 'You heard of the generation back. Where do you hail from yourself?'

'The Northguard, originally,' said the Mariner. 'Then all over. Just spent a season on the Easthold Station.'

The other pursed his lips. He said, 'That was my last posting. You know Josen? Commandant, Fishgard Tower?'

'God, yes,' said the Mariner. 'He was a drinking buddy. Helped make up for the rest. Bit of a dump, Fishgard.'

The Kiteman nodded. He said, 'In more ways than one.'

'What do you chandler?'

'Anything that's called for,' said Rand. 'We do quite well out of the Kite-bases actually. Easier to come to us than send all the way to Fronting.' He patted the book. 'Been trying to get to grips with that Seaking quad-expander. But I think I shall have to give it best. Leave it to the professionals.'

Nath leaned back. His mood seemed suddenly to have improved. 'A rich source of mechanical vitamin,' he said. 'Otherwise known as a plumber's paradise.'

'You ever work on them?'

The Mariner nodded. 'Aye,' he said. 'In the Northguard. They build 'em here; but then they're all exported. Which is the first sensible idea they have.'

'You ever stream Dancing Bay?'

The other nodded. 'Many a time. With a Seaking rig, that just plain isn't funny.' He grinned. 'Still, I was only a Third then. If we'd gone aground, it wouldn't have been my fault.'

'That,' said the Kiteman, 'was no doubt a great comfort.'

There was an irruption. Nath stared at the newcomer with faint disbelief. She was short; stocky, one might almost say. He put her age at somewhere in the early teens. She wore an elegant hat of black-glazed straw, its rim decorated with artificial flowers. It was attached at a rakish angle; he saw the head of a spectacular pin. Her hair was long and lustrous, hanging to her waist. Her dress reached to her ankles; from beneath peeped bare and somewhat grubby toes. 'Thought I'd find you 'ere,' she said. 'I can't get in.'

The Kiteman pointed. 'Where,' he said wrathfully, 'are your shoes? How many times do I have to tell you?'

She leaned on her parasol composedly. 'Can't wear 'em on the quay,' she said. 'They bin unloadin' fertilizer. It spoils 'em.'

'What were you doing on the quay?'

'Just lookin',' she said in an injured tone. ''Ain't no 'arm in that.'

Rand sighed, and took a key from his pocket. 'Go straight home,' he said. 'And don't stay up all hours. When I get back I shall expect you in bed, my girl.'

'Ta,' said the urchin. 'See yer. G'night, sir,' she added winsomely.

The Mariner watched her retreat. He said, 'Does she belong to you?'

The other smiled. 'In a manner of speaking,' he said. 'As a matter of fact, she's one of my partners.'

'Your *what*?'

'Three of us put up equal shares,' said the tall man. 'So she gets equal profits. Got quite a little nest-egg already.' He smiled again. 'She's got a strong-box up in her room,' he said. 'Spends half the night counting it. At least it's taught her to count beyond ten.'

'But how the Hell could she put up money for a chandlery? How old is she?'

'She reckons she's fifteen now,' said the Kiteman. 'But I don't reckon she's anywhere near it. As for how she got it; well, that really is a complicated story. I don't know the half of it myself.' He considered. 'Fancy some grub?' he said. 'The lobster's pretty good here. Guaranteed all caught by P and H pots.'

The Mariner frowned. Kari would be looking at the clock already. Sighing, and setting her lip. He felt the first stirrings of anger. After all he hadn't asked to have his hand trapped in a machine. He'd still got the rough end of her tongue though.

'All right,' he said. 'So what the Hell …'

*

Velvet let herself into the chandlery, went through to the back. She emerged from the yard gate a few minutes later, pushing a little handcart. You couldn't get as much in it as in her old truck, but it was rather fine. It had large spoked wheels, and paintings on the sides; anchors, with ropes twisted round them. She passed the first of the boatyards, turned up Groping Lane. The name was suggestive, but there didn't seem to be much of that sort of thing these days. She pushed the truck on to waste ground, hid it behind some bushes. There was another chandlers, run by a Master Fishley. The name suited him somehow. They had a delivery from Holand, always the same day of the week. It never arrived till late though. The driver had gate keys, but you couldn't lock the wicket from outside. She ducked through, made a quick inspection. She found a pile of new wooden blocks. Three-sheavers. The fishing boats used them, they were always good stock to carry. Farther on were some bottle screws. Small; but they'd stay a Kiteship's jigger. Or go for jury spares. You couldn't take too many though; Rand had more than once queried what seemed to be surplus stock. She shrugged. She couldn't sell them herself; after all she was in proper business now, they had to go through the books. She still didn't think he'd be happy though. He had funny ideas about that sort of thing.

On the way back she pushed the truck more brazenly. After all, that was what it was for. It had been made to carry things like rigging blocks. She dumped her finds into the storehouse bins and put the truck away. She got some milk and biscuits and went up to her room. She took her hat off, shook her hair out. She got to her knees, unlocked the strongbox. She got out the first wad of notes, began to count it contentedly.

The Mariner took to calling in at the Stores. At first he feared he might be in the way; but they didn't seem to mind. On the contrary, his knowledge came in very useful. Who for example knew that the valve gear on a Seaking quad was identical to that on a Dayle Marine unit? Or that both sets fitted some of the larger trawlers? The makers denied it strenuously; but they all came from Saltways in the Holand, and they only marketed one pattern. Spares were frequently hard to come by, even the boatyards sometimes sent round. Hardly a normal line in chandlery; but then, Kiteport was hardly a normal town. Rand commented on it one night, and the Mariner grinned. 'You can say that again,' he said. 'But at least it's better than Fishgard. Those bloody dragons on the roofs gave me the creeps. I'd have taken a mallet to the lot.'

Rand brooded. 'Yes,' he said. 'It's a funny place all right.' He glanced down. 'How's the hand?'

The other frowned. 'Coming on,' he said. 'At least it's out of that blasted sling. Don't think I shall ever bend the finger again. I suppose I'm lucky in a way though. At least I've still got it.'

They were in the bar of the 'Mermaid'. Nath drained his beer, and ordered another round. He said, 'Does your partner live in too?'

The Kiteman shook his head. 'No,' he said. 'Just me and the brat. Cheers.' He drank, and set the glass down. 'I've got a lot to thank you for, Nath,' he said. 'You've brought us in a lot of trade. We'll be making you a partner next.'

The other shrugged. 'Glad to help,' he said. 'It gets me out of the house.'

Rand didn't comment. The Mariner had hinted at tension before; but if he wanted to talk about it he would. In his own good time. He said, 'You been at sea long?'

'All my life,' said Nath. 'Such as it is. All I ever wanted to do. Funny, I was born inland. My folk were farmers. Still are.' He shook his head. 'That's not really going to sea though,' he said. 'Streaming the Codys. That's coasting. Except you're not going anywhere. You can see Kiteport with a decent glass, even from the Outstations.'

Rand smiled. He said, 'I can imagine it could get tedious.'

The engineer drummed his fingers on the bar. 'That's the whole trouble,' he said. 'It isn't even that. All right if you get the Vars; but if you get the Ultras you've got problems.'

He said, 'Why's that?'

'They bring an armoury with them. You've never seen anything like it. I swear to God one day they'll ship a cannon.'

'Why?'

Nath shrugged. 'Who knows? In case of mutiny I expect.'

He considered. No Middle Church in Kiteport of course; the wealthy didn't need them, and it didn't matter what the yards and foundries thought. But two churches still opposed each other. The Vars, and the Ultras. He hadn't had experience of the latter. He'd seen them strutting the quays though, guns strapped to their waists over their scarlet robes. He'd decided they were best steered clear of; he hadn't realized they ran the Kiteships too. He said, 'They certainly don't look good news.'

'No,' said the Mariner darkly. 'Best keep away from 'em. Keep your little girl away too.' He lit a stubby pipe. 'I used to do the Island run,' he said. 'That's a bit more like it.'

Rand was intrigued. He'd heard about the Islands; as a trader he'd even handled some their produce. Matting, some turned goods – they did a nice line in belay pins – coils of curious-looking rope. In the main the fishing fraternity distrusted it; but he knew from experiment it had enormous strength. He'd never seen a map of them though. Maps of the Southguard were rare enough, and wholly denied to commoners. The Corps had to have them of course, as the Mariners had to have their charts; but they were closely guarded, classified Top Secret. The reason the Church gave was that they would be of benefit to Demons; though he suspected there were other, darker motives. It wouldn't do to have the ordinary folk find out too much about the land they lived in; knowledge is dangerous, except of course in the proper hands. He said, 'What are the Islands like?'

The other looked far-away. 'You wouldn't believe 'em,' he said. 'You just wouldn't believe 'em ...' He drank ale. 'The Warm Stream splits round Tremarest,' he said. 'That's the biggest of the group. Gives 'em a lot of fog, some seasons of the year. The rest of the time ... There's plants you just don't see on the mainland. Big spiky things, they call 'em palms. You get some pretty funny animals too. Nothing very big though, and none of them dangerous.' He considered. 'There's no industry,' he said. 'Only the ropemaking, bits and pieces like that. And they don't bother with those unless they feel in the mood. Don't need to, they can live from the sea. The Warm Stream never varies; so the fish are safe.'

He said, 'Do they fly the Codys?'

Nath looked amused. 'What for?' he said. 'They'd laugh at you.'

'You make it sound a bit like paradise.'

'It is,' said the Mariner. 'Sometimes I think …' He drummed his fingers on the bar again. 'The people are brown,' he said. 'Much browner than us. Should be, they spend all day in the sun. As for the women …' He drank more beer. 'There's a mountain on Tremarest that spits out fire and smoke. It blows up sometimes. The rock runs down the sides. Like red-hot rivers.'

It sounded like a traveller's tale. Rand said, 'Come on,' and the other looked at him. He said, 'I've seen it.'

Nath's eyed veiled themselves again. 'I'd like to have been an explorer,' he said. 'It's the schoolboy in me. Just take a ship, and go. Follow the dolphins.'

'You mean they exist?'

'Of course they exist. Did you think they didn't?'

'You'll be telling me there's mermaids next.'

Nath Ostman looked at him, amused. He said, 'You should know. You've got a captive one at home.' He looked thoughtful. 'I'd like to find out where the Dragonflies live,' he said. 'That'd be worth doing.'

Rand looked up sharply. He said, 'Dragonflies?'

The other shrugged. 'Something else nobody believes in,' he said. 'So we don't bother to talk.'

'Velvet told me she used to see them,' he said slowly. 'I thought she was pulling my leg. Or making up fancy tales. She's very good at that.' He drank ale. 'What are they like?' he said.

'If she's seen them, you already know,' said the Mariner. 'Big. Long silver wings.'

'Have you ever seen one close?'

The other shook his head. 'They keep well clear of shipping. I still think they're watching us though.'

'Have they ever done any harm?'

'No. They just watch.'

'What are they?'

Nath shook his head. 'I don't know,' he said. 'But I think … I think they're machines.' He drained his beer. 'There's another island to the south anyway. Beyond the Tremarest group. A day's sail at least. Big 'un too.'

'How do you know?'

'Because we got blown off course once. That was in the old *Sea Trader.* I saw it in the distance.'

'Did you make landfall?'

The Mariner grimaced. 'Did we Hell', he said. 'The skipper was a good

Var. Put his helm up, went for Fishgard as if the Devil was behind him.'

Rand finished his own beer. 'Look,' he said, 'you want to step round for a bite to eat? There isn't much; but there is fresh crab. Velvet got it this morning. Said it was cheap as well. Which I wouldn't wonder at. *Very* cheap,' he added.

'Fine,' said the other. 'Don't mind if I do.' Two men brushed by them as they were walking out. He thought both gave them hardish looks. The Mariner quickened his pace. 'Watch that pair,' he said.

'Why so?'

'Ultras,' said Nath. 'They're not all in fancy dress.'

There was a big sitting room over the shop. Its windows faced the sea. It was curiously furnished in parts; Velvet had started her driftwood collection again. She was sitting on the sideboard, barefooted as usual, drinking a glass of milk. ''Ello,' she said.

'Fix yourself some wine,' said Rand. 'I'll see what I can rake up.' He vanished into the kitchen.

'I'll do it,' she said. She jumped down, padded across the room. 'Somethin' I bin meanin' to ask,' she said. 'When you'd got a minute …'

Nath all but dropped the glass. It had been a very basic question, about seamen on shore leave. He said, 'How do you know about things like that?'

'Well,' she said, 'stands ter reason, don' it? An' it don't 'appen in Gropin' Lane, I checked.'

'No,' he said faintly. 'It doesn't happen in Groping Lane.'

Rand came back with a tray. Big dressed crabs, a pile of salad on the side. Fresh, crusty bread. Later they smoked a pipe in companionable silence. Finally Rand spoke. 'I always say there's nothing to beat fresh crab,' he said. 'I wonder where they get all that flavour from.'

'Dead sailors,' said Velvet instantly. She looked guilty at once. 'Sorry,' she said.

The Mariner smiled. He said, 'You're probably right.' He tapped the pipe. 'I'm not just paying back a compliment,' he said. 'I was going to ask the other day, and I forgot. How about coming up to our place for a meal? Kari's a damned good cook; and you could bring the littl'un.'

Rand shook his head solemnly. 'I couldn't do that,' he said. 'She wouldn't behave herself.'

Velvet jumped up, instantly defensive. She clenched her fists. 'I *would*,' she said. 'I *would* …' She turned to the Mariner, appealingly. 'I'd be as good as gold,' she said.

The Kiteman laughed. 'I'd love to,' he said. 'When?'

'Tomorrow,' said the other. 'Never spoil a good mind.' He considered. 'Tell you what,' he said. 'Why don't you stop the night? Save you the hassle of driving back. The Vars can get a bit stroppy after twenty-four.'

'Right, you're on,' said Rand. 'Hear that, Velvet?' He snapped his fingers. He said, 'Bath, young lady.'

'Oh,' she said airily, 'there's plenty o' time fer that.'

'No there isn't,' he said. 'I don't want any of your last minute jobs. I mean now.'

Her composure sagged a little. 'I was talkin' to the Mariner,' she said.

'You can talk to him tomorrow,' he said. 'All evening, unless he gets fed up with you. Go on, scat.'

She looked at his face, and decided he meant it. She stalked out with her nose in the air, slammed the bathroom door. He called after her. 'There's some clean towels in the cupboard. Mistress Dolkin brought them in.'

Her voice floated through the panels, plaintively. 'Do I 'ave ter take my clothes off?'

He said, 'It is customary when bathing.' The Mariner chuckled.

Rand fetched more glasses of wine. 'Thanks,' said the other. 'Can't be too long though. Got to soften Kari up for tomorrow. She's out at the moment; that's why I came round.' He sipped. He said, 'That's the oddest little girl I ever met.'

'Who, Velvet?' said the Kiteman. 'Yes, she has her moments.'

Nath lit his pipe again. He said, 'I can imagine that.'

Rand looked at him, eyes narrowed. 'What's she been saying?'

'Nothing,' said the seaman. There was a silence, that lengthened. He shrugged. He said, 'She was asking about the Gropings. Wouldn't have thought she'd have known about things like that.'

'She knows,' said Rand. He sighed. 'I'm not exactly surprised.'

The Mariner looked troubled. He said, 'I probably shouldn't have mentioned it.'

'It's all right,' said the tall man. 'I'm glad you did.' He hesitated; then he began to talk. Nath heard him through. 'I see,' he said. 'So you brought her back here. Did you adopt her formally?'

The Kiteman shook his head. 'How could I?' he said. 'She didn't belong to anybody, nobody wanted her. She was a piece of flotsam.'

Nath looked thoughtful. 'Still might have been best to check up,' he said.

He was surprised at the change that came over the other's face. 'Why?' Rand said. 'She's an Innocent. They'd have sent her to Skyways.'

Velvet was back. Wearing a large, ill-fitting bath robe. She eyed her protector balefully. 'I'm goin' ter bed,' she said. ''Case I gets mucky again.'

'Not with soaking wet hair,' said Rand. 'Come here, minx.' He took the towel from her, rubbed vigorously. 'All right,' he said finally. 'That'll do. Go on, I'll come and see you later.' He slapped her bottom.

She stalked away. She paused by the Mariner. 'Goodnight, sir,' she said. She kissed him.

Rand walked as far as the 'Mermaid' when the other left, went in for a nightcap. He looked in on Velvet as promised. The bedclothes were pulled to her chin, and her eyes tight closed. But he knew she wasn't asleep. He scotched on the bed. 'Velvet,' he said, 'are you on the game again?'

She sat up, startled. 'No,' she said. 'No, Rand. I promised …'

'Then why are you asking funny questions?'

'What about?'

'The Gropings.'

She pouted. ''E tol' on me. The Mariner. I din' think 'e would.'

'No,' he said, 'he didn't. It was someone else.'

She traced a pattern on the blankets with her finger. 'I just likes ter know,' she said. 'Force of 'abit. I ain't done nothin', honest …' She hesitated. 'I did nick them crabs,' she said. 'But they'd left 'em all just laid there, it were their fault reely.' She looked up, hopefully. 'Good though, wadn't they?' she said.

'Velvet,' he said, 'you're beyond redemption. One of these days I shall take a great big stick to you. Come on.' He tucked the covers round her, kissed her forehead lightly. 'Go to sleep,' he said. 'Or I shan't let you come tomorrow after all.'

She lay awake for a while after he closed the door. He didn't trust her, that was what. She turned on her side, and snuffled a bit. She didn't like not being trusted. She rubbed her nose with the back of her hand. She'd show him one day. She'd run away to sea with that nice Mr Ostman. She was sure he'd be kind to her. She felt better in the morning though.

He drove up in the Falcon. Climbed up the steep High Street, and turned left. Velvet was feeling very grand. She was wearing a new white dress with roses on it, and a little matching hat. Though they were ribbons really, rather than flowers. She sat up very straight, staring down her nose at everybody they passed. Finally she pointed. She said, 'It's up there.'

Rand glanced at her. He said, 'How did you know?' and she shrugged. She said, 'I gets about.'

She was right of course; though he'd have found the place anyway, the Mariner had given him clear directions. He was surprised at the size of the house; an elegant, stone-fronted mansion, set in its own grounds and with Codys streamed from Towers at either end. He wouldn't have thought a Second could have run to that. Though Nath explained the paradox later on. 'It belongs to the Master Helman,' he said. 'He's got property right through Southguard. Most of the Middle Lands too. He lets an awful lot to newlyweds.' He grinned. 'Very advantageous rates too.'

Rand nodded. He said, 'He must be quite a character.'

'Yes,' said the Mariner, 'I suppose he is. Getting on a bit now though.'

He handed Velvet from the car. She curtsied. He threatened her with a backhand. She grinned at him.

They had a ground floor flat. Rand pressed the bell. While he was waiting he looked out to sea. The panorama was spectacular. The whole of Kiteport spread out like a map, the quays and harbour, yards. Above it the Kites, flying like bright confetti; beyond, the great blue rising shield of water. Nath had told him from this height the nearest of the Islands was visible on a good day. Rand screwed his eyes up, but the horizon appeared unbroken. He'd probably meant with a glass.

Kari was much as he'd imagined; a slight, quiet girl, blue-eyed and with soft fair hair. She chattered readily enough, acting the hostess to perfection. She talked about her early life in the Salient, as the daughter of a moderately well-to-do farmer; her travels through the Realm, as secretary to this or that tycoon. She'd finished up in Middlemarch, where she'd finally met Nath. She'd journeyed to the Northguard with him for his first Kiteposting, spent two years in a cottage overlooking Dancing Bay. From her windows she could see the A-ships. She'd always known when it was him on duty, because he'd stream a special Cody for her. 'It cost him a fortune,' she said. 'I kept telling him he was a fool; but he never listens to me.' She turned to Velvet. 'Where are you from, love?' she said.

'Oh, the Easthold,' said Velvet in her poshest voice. 'Fishgard, in fact.' She toyed with her fork. 'Not much of a place,' she said. 'Rather rough and ready down there I'm afraid. But I think I might be beginning to live it down.' She shot a look at Rand. 'You won't believe it,' she said, 'but in our house we didn't even have a bathroom.' He addressed himself to his food, studiously. Reminded himself to clip her ear for her later.

It was all very pleasant and relaxed, and the meal was excellent. Yet underneath he sensed a certain tension. Mistress Ostman excused herself soon after dinner was over; to his surprise, Velvet went to bed soon after. She said she was feeling tired, and for once she looked it. Perhaps it was the strain of all that good behaviour. She stood on tiptoe to kiss him. He hugged her; and she whispered, 'Sorry …'

'That's all right,' he said. 'I'll beat you in the morning.' He rubbed her bottom. He said, 'Sleep well.'

Nath crossed to a corner cupboard, came back carrying glasses and a bottle. He said, 'Have a drop of the real stuff.'

Rand eyed it. 'If that's Kiteship liquor,' he said, 'no thanks. I've heard it's even worse than Salient sockrot.' But the other merely grinned. He said, 'Don't drink with your eyes.'

He sipped. 'My God,' he said. 'What's this?'

'Middle Lands,' said Nath. 'Even we get the odd perk. Dig in; I've got a few more bottles stashed away.'

There was a long, glassed-in conservatory. They sat awhile and looked at the sea. Finally Nath shook his head. 'It's the one thing I'm afraid of,' he said. 'Maybe that's why I keep going back. I sometimes think it's like having a tooth pulled out. It hurts to poke your tongue in the hole; but you keep on doing it.'

Rand sipped. 'Yes,' he said. 'My father told me once he felt that way about the Kites. We're a pretty cross-grained species, after all.'

The Mariner nodded. 'That's what's wrong with Kari of course,' he said.

He waited.

The Mariner put his glass down. He sat forward, hands between his knees. He said, 'I think we're going to split up. We can't go on like this.'

Rand said quietly, 'Is there nothing to be done?'

The other shrugged. 'I don't know what. She wants me to come ashore. For good.'

'But you don't want to.'

For answer, Nath waved a hand to the horizon. He said, 'Would you?'

'I'm not a Mariner.'

'There's more to it than that of course,' said Nath. 'She wants to start a family. You know what women are like.'

He wasn't sure he did.

The seaman leaned back. 'It isn't that I don't love her,' he said. 'I feel the same about her as the day we met. But I just don't feel I'm ready.' He smiled. He said, 'I think I'd make a lousy father.'

'I think you'd make a very good one.'

The other glanced at him. He said, 'You should know.'

Rand said, 'I'm not her father.'

Nath reached to top his glass up. He said, 'Well, if you're not I don't know who is.' He replenished his own drink. He said, 'She's a very lucky little girl. I hope she appreciates it. I've never seen a child surrounded by so much love.'

He was vaguely startled. He'd never looked at it like that. He said, 'It's strange. If you just think you've been hurt, you hate the world. If the knife's really gone in, you think more of people as a result.' He took out his little tobacco pipe, struck a lucifer. He said, 'I do what I can.'

'You do a sight more than that,' said the Mariner. 'You wouldn't see a hair of her head harmed, would you? For all she deserves a tanning now and then.'

Rand said slowly, 'I wouldn't like to see any child harmed.'

'I'm afraid you're going to,' said the other. 'Before too long as well. Did you hear about the riots in Middlemarch?'

'A bit.'

'They tried to burn Godpath,' said Nath. 'Which wouldn't in itself have been a loss. The Vars are out in force, the Militia are armed from Fronting to the Northguard. I was talking to a guy the other day who'd just come down. He reckoned there's over two hundred dead to date.' He shook his head. 'They can't hold it much longer,' he said. 'Once it really starts, it'll spread like wildfire; everything will be up for grabs. The Realm will be a shambles; nobody will be safe.' He slammed the glass down. 'We were saved,' he said. 'Just us, out of all the world. What for? I sometimes wonder whether we were worth it.'

Rand was silent. The fear had been in him of course a long time now; but he hadn't suspected the other of harbouring such notions. Somehow, hearing them from Nath's lips made them all the more the chilling. He summoned a mental image of the Realm. The hills and valleys, towns; sour heaths of the Easthold, rich fields of the Middle Lands. Over it all, the bright flags of the Codys. Proud, defiant, watchful. But what if all the time they'd been watching the skies for nothing? No Demons would plunge from the zenith; shouldn't they rather turn, and look into each other's eyes?

He pushed the thought away. He said, 'Who are these Ultras, Nath? What sort of people are they?'

The other looked sardonic. He said, 'I'd have thought you'd know more about that.'

'I've heard of them,' he said. 'But you've had dealings with them.'

The Mariner snorted. 'You don't deal with them,' he said. 'Largely because they're mad.'

Nath considered. 'They're Vars I suppose, basically,' he said. 'But they've taken it to the limit. And the Vars are bad enough. You know what they say; a Church like nothing ever seen before. Which is why they're Variants of course. Though personally I doubt it. I don't think there's anything new.'

He swilled the drink in his glass. 'They've got some funny ideas,' he said. 'There's one rest day a week, you can't lift a finger. I've seen a man shot for landing a tub of fish. That was down in Stanway. They'd like to enforce it through the Realm, but they can't. They've only got a real grip in the Southguard.' He glanced across. 'Their big depot's near Stanway,' he said. 'Few miles along the coast. Hunter Trucks and Battle Waggons. Where they get the money from beats me. Extortion mainly, I expect. You mean you haven't had a call?'

Rand frowned. 'We had a couple of odd characters in a few days after we took over. Wouldn't come out with what they wanted. I sent 'em packing.'

'And you've had no trouble since?'

'No, not a thing.'

'You're lucky,' said the Mariner. 'You supply the Kites though. They're Kiteworshippers to a man. But if they come back again, pay them.' He heaved himself from the Holand fibre chair, walked into the lounge. He came back carrying a lamp. Under his arm was a big leather-bound book. Looked like a ship's log. He said, 'You might be interested in this.'

Rand turned the pages, carefully. He said, 'I didn't realize you had to keep these.'

'We don't,' said Nath. 'Skipper and First Mate only. Except that our First Mate can't read. This is for private interest.'

He said, 'Good God …' Between the entries were sketches. Rough, but vigorous. The dolphins of legend, arcing through the waves; strange fish that almost seemed to have wings; great creatures blowing jets of water from their heads. He said, 'How big are these?'

'They vary,' said the Mariner. 'Biggest I saw was twice the length of a Kiteship.'

He said, 'That's impossible.' Nath shrugged. He said, 'I must have been drunk then.' He pointed. 'There's some sightings of Dragonflies. Six days on the trot. They must have been busy that year.'

Rand studied the neatly-written entries. Bearings accompanied each, notes on weather conditions. He said, 'It always seems to be fine when they come. And always daylight.'

'Seems to be,' said the Mariner. 'Couldn't really say though. If it was dark you wouldn't see 'em anyway.'

'But you never tried to draw one?'

The other shook his head. 'I can't,' he said. 'I don't know what they look like, when it comes down to it. They're just a twinkle in the sky. Your little girl's seen one closer than me.'

Something swooshed out of the book. Rand retrieved it; and the other looked faintly rueful. 'Shouldn't really have seen that,' he said. 'That's why I keep this thing locked up. Ought to get rid of it really; but I haven't got the heart.'

He stared at the photograph. The girl stood arms akimbo, legs braced apart. She wore a little kilt of patterned cloth. It scarcely covered her loins. The rest of her was bare. Her hair was long and dark; and there were flowers twined. He said, 'Who's this?'

The Mariner said, 'Addi.'

'Where's she from?'

'Tremarest. She's waiting for me.' Nath jerked his head. 'I could go to her tomorrow. Leave all this. There's ways and means.'

'Why don't you?'

The other hesitated. He said, 'Because I don't duck out of my responsibilities.'

Rand sought his rest, finally. The room they'd given him was large, again with windows looking on the sea. Before them, on a tripod, stood a great brass telescope. He frowned. He'd heard the Ultras worshipped a female principle. God-mother, dream-woman, he'd never been too sure. He swung the great barrel, peered through the eyepiece. He shook his head. It must be the Midland hooch. He'd expected to see Addi of Tremarest; but the field was dark.

Velvet was excited, in the morning. She dashed through carrying what looked like a piece of shaped stone. 'What's this?' she said. 'It floats ...'

The Mariner smiled. 'It's from the Islands,' he said. 'You can have it if you like, we've got plenty more. It keeps your skin smooth.'

She stuffed it into her pocket instantly.

Rand took the Ostmans for a drive. Velvet for once was constrained to the back seat. He struck out west along the ridge, turned inland. He found a wooded village. There was a long, half-timbered pub. The food was excellent, the beer less so. Nath ambled to the bar to complain; but the landlord was unsympathetic. 'What's wrong wi' that?' he asked, holding the cloudy glass to the light. '"Saint's Bathwater", we calls that.'

The Mariner leaned on the counter. 'Then,' he said easily, 'I suggest Her Holiness stops cutting her toenails in it ...'

The beer was changed.

They both seemed more cheerful, when he finally took his leave. Kari hugged Velvet, and gave her a little present. Yet another hat. She said to come again. Driving back through Kiteport, he wondered cautiously if he had at last done a little good.

The weather remained fine. It was only the shortening of the days that reminded him the season was drawing to a close. That, and the absence of the Housebirds. He wondered if they migrated to the Islands.

Velvet took to watching the ships. Very interesting things, ships. She'd never actually been on one, though she'd been born by the sea. Least, she thought she'd been born by the sea. She'd certainly lived there most of her life. She strolled the quays, parasol at the ready; but Kiteport wasn't like the Easthold, there was never a real need of it. She did have one nasty moment; but that was on Quay Four, the place she found the crabs. There were girls there, who worked the fishing boats; most of them younger than she was, she'd decided. One of them approached one day. 'Fuck orf,' she said forthrightly. 'This is my bleedin' patch.'

Velvet regarded her coldly. Her dress hardly came to her knees, and it was full of holes at that. 'I am a businesswoman of this borough,' she said. 'If I chooses ter take the air, it ain't no concern o' your'n.'

'Businesswoman,' sneered the other. 'I knows what you are. It's writ all over yer ...'

Velvet gripped the parasol. 'You won't like what's goin' ter be writ orl over you,' she said. She advanced. The other fled, precipitately; but there was a little knot of them farther along the quay, they were waving their arms and pointing. Velvet retreated. She'd found out long ago, discretion was invariably the better part.

She returned to her contemplation of the Kiteships. She knew all their names by now; *Holdfast* and *Windwrack*, *Spindrift*, *Guardian*, *The Lady.* Plus the others that had come round from the Northguard; *Demongroom* and *Demonbride.* They were sister ships, somebody had told her; though she wasn't too sure what that meant. All the people on board seemed to be men. They were the only two it was hard to tell apart. She couldn't read the lettering on their fronts, not as yet; it was annoying to have to ask. But she was beginning to recognize the shapes. As she knew the shapes of the ships.

Also of course there was *Kitestrength.* She was Velvet's favourite. She wasn't too sure why; except that Mariner Ostman had once sailed on her. Would do again very shortly, if what she'd heard was true. She watched her comings and goings with particular interest. Her crew always debarked to a man, as soon as she docked. Left just one old watchman, and he was usually asleep. She observed them, counting carefully. It was useful being able to number. One day when she knew there was nobody aboard she tiptoed to the gangplank. She glanced quickly to left and right, and hurried up it. She jumped down with a scuff and thump, looked round her awed. At last she was standing on an actual, real ship.

She padded along the deck. Somehow *Kitestrength* seemed so much bigger than when she had been standing on the quay. She stared up at the great masts with their complication of rigging, the spars with their brown furled canvas. There was so much; she couldn't work out what half the things were supposed to do. By the mainmast though she stopped and peered. One of the steel shrouds had rusted, a yard up from the strainer. There were even some broken strands. The bottle-screw didn't look too good either. She prodded at it with her parasol. They ought to come and see Rand, and get that fixed. It was downright unsafe.

She half-pulled a belay pin from a rack, shoved it back. They sold things like that too; she was sure theirs would be better. There was good profit to be made here. She moved on. The deck was steel as well, with a sort of diamond pattern. It was so hot it was burning her feet. Crazy, for this time of the year.

The bows swept up, ended in bulwarks higher than her head. There was a massive winch, tall levers sticking up to one side. It was all gearwheels, their teeth covered with black grease. She thought it was the Kitewinch. It wasn't though, that was on top of the Tower. The Tower was braced to the deck by great tarred struts. She stared up at it. She didn't hate the Codys as much as she had. Not since a special String had been flown for her. They'd got this place in Southguard, afterwards; so she supposed sometimes they could do good as well.

Velvet edged round the winch. She thought how clever Mariner Ostman was, to understand things like that. She was sure she never could. She glanced back, over the high wheelhouse. There was a dusty look to the sky. Yellowish, almost; and dark clouds massing, low down in the west. She'd seen skies like that often enough before. The weather would break soon; there was going to be a gale. It was lucky *Kitestrength* wouldn't be sailing yet; after all she'd only come in at thirteen hundred.

There was a little hatch thing. She tugged at it. It opened. Below was a steep wooden ladder. She peered; then she took a firmer grip of her parasol. She adjusted her hat, swung herself over the coaming. She descended, placing her feet carefully.

His duffel bag was packed and waiting. He dumped it in the hall, walked through to the kitchen. Kari was washing up at the deep old sink; clattering dishes, slamming them one by one into the draining rack. She didn't look round.

He waited a moment. He said, 'Kari, I've got to go.'

She didn't answer.

He walked forward. He gripped her shoulders, turned her. He said, '*I've got to go …*'

She said, 'Then go.' She wouldn't look at him.

He took her chin, forced her head round and up. He said, 'It's just one trip.'

'I know,' she said. 'It's just this one. And then one more. And then another …'

He felt a gust of anger. He pointed at the windows. He said, 'The sea's been my life. And I'm giving it up. I'm giving it all up. For you. What more do you want? Tell me what else I could do …'

'You could put your kit back in the wardrobe,' she said. 'Right this minute. It's just as easy as that.'

He said, 'It's not as easy as that. You know it's not.'

She said, 'It's easy enough for me.'

He shook her. He said, 'Everything's easy to you. When you want it to be.'

She squalled at him. 'Easy?' she said. 'Easy? Running this place, and watching you go away, and wondering if you'll come back, and staying home in case you want a screw, and putting up with it if you don't. And washing your bloody shirts, and telling the neighbours no you're fine, and seeing bits of you cut off and wondering what'll be next. Yes, it's easy,' she said. 'It's easy, easy, easy …'

He slapped her. He saw her hair fly out. It brought him up standing too.

He'd never hit her before. He said, 'Oh, Kari, Kari … What's gone wrong?'

She clung to him. He let her cry it out. Then he steered her, very gently, into the lounge. He sat her down, and took her hands. 'Listen,' he said. 'I've been cleared for duty. And this is my last trip of the tour. After that, my contract's up. I can renew or not, exactly as I choose. But if I don't go, I'm Absent Without Leave. That means no pension, nothing. Everything I've done will be a waste. You know the Church, you know they don't give second chances. For God's sake, you were brought up a Var.'

She didn't answer; and he shook her wrists. 'We'll go to the Northguard,' he said. 'We'll go and see my folks. They'll find us something; or they'll know somebody who's selling. It won't be much at first; but it'll be a start. Afterwards … you can have your own family.' He pushed her hair back. 'Kari,' he said, 'have I ever let you down? Have I ever promised anything, and not kept my word?'

She looked up at him with reddened eyes. 'There's just one thing,' she said. 'You won't come back. Not this time.'

He brushed at her cheek. He said, 'Will you wait and see?' He swallowed. He said, 'I need you to, Kari. Just this once. Otherwise, I can't go on.'

She hugged him. Then she pushed away. 'Come on,' she said. 'You're going to be late.'

Walking down the High Street, he glowered at the sky. A storm was brewing; he'd known since zero eight hundred. Didn't even need to look up; he could smell it. Well, the sooner it came the better. Not even the Vars would order an offing then. If the voyage was aborted, he was through already. Nothing more to worry about.

He hefted the duffel. He thought about Addi, so many leagues away. Over the rim of the earth. What was she doing, now? Right this minute? What would have happened, if he'd gone with her? Would she have turned into a wife as well?

Kitestrength was in turmoil when he boarded. Cadets scurried about the deck, laying out cables and traces; others were atop the gantry in the bows. He saw a puff of vapour whirl above the winch. So they'd raised Kitesteam already.

He ran the First to earth in the wheelhouse. The Skipper was there, and the Mate. They were poring over a chart. The Chief Engineer gripped his hand. He said, 'Hello Nath, nice to see you back. How's the war wound?'

He said, 'Fine.' He flexed the finger. Some mobility had in fact returned. He nodded at the foredeck. He said, 'What in Hell goes on?'

The other put his hands on his hips. He said, 'Judge for yourself.'

He stared. A group of scarlet-robed men had appeared on the Kiteplatform. He could see the guns they carried from here. He said, 'Oh, no. That was all we needed.'

The Chiefie nodded. 'Yes,' he said. 'We drew a short course of Ultras.'

'When do we sail?'

The other looked grim. He said, 'Ten minutes ago. Better get below.'

The Skipper glanced at the sky. 'We can just about get on to moorings before that lot hits us,' he said. 'Given a bit of luck at least.' He turned back to the Mate. 'Double hawsers, Mister,' he said. 'We shall need 'em ...' The other said, 'Aye aye ...' He scurried off, bellowing orders.

Nath swung down the last of the ladders, to the gantry over the great gleaming engines. Like the deckplates, the walkway was floored with diamond-patterned steel. He glanced down. The oilers were at work already, each stripped to the waist, each with a greasy kerchief round his neck. They hurried from point to point with their red, long-spouted cans. He put his hands behind his back, checked the gauges quickly.

The Third was on duty; a slim, freckled youth. Came from the Easthold somewhere. He looked too young for the insignia on his jacket. But all Thirds were starting to look young these days. He said, 'We're not actually sailing?'

Nath said, 'Aye.' He whistled the boiler room. He said, 'Give us more steam.'

The Chief Stoker was gruff. He said, 'You're getting it.'

'OK, Rall,' he said. 'Thanks.'

'One day,' said the Third, 'this bloody Land's going to blow up. I've got my little hit list. Starting with the bloody Ultras ...'

Nath rounded on him. 'Run this ship, Mister,' he said. 'That's what you're here for.'

The wheelhouse speaking tube shrilled. He took the whistle from the mouthpiece. The Skipper said, 'What's our pressure?'

'Ten pounds under head, sir,' he said. 'Building well. Five minutes at the outside.'

'Can't wait,' said the other curtly. 'Quarter ahead.' The telegraph clanged at once; Nath swung the big brass handle to acknowledge, turned the first of the great valves. The engines woke up; the silver cranks rose, slow at first, sank into their pits. He checked the gauges again, looked over his shoulder. He said, 'Quarter ahead. *Mark* ...' The Third consulted his chronometer, made an entry in the engineroom log.

Velvet was appalled. She'd explored the first compartment, the vee-shaped space piled with big sausage-shapes of canvas. Spare sails, she presumed. A metal door opened on to a second, dimly lit by portholes to either side. There was a funny smell, like a garage. Steam pipes everywhere, shafts and wheels overhead. Flat leather belts led down to benches lined with machines. The drills she recognized; the others were strange to her. She shivered suddenly. She'd realized this was probably where the Mariner had hurt his hand.

She retreated. Better go back, before someone came and caught her. She gripped the ladder; and feet pounded overhead. She heard orders being called, then others.

Velvet clapped a hand to her mouth. This was what came of being nosey. Rand was always telling her, but she never listened. She wanted to go home now. Run to him and tell him what she'd done. He could spank her if he liked; he'd hold her then, and make a fuss of her. It was too late though, she was trapped.

She was seized by a wild hope. What was happening, what must be happening, was that they'd come aboard to make *Kitestrength* secure. They'd need to after all, with bad weather on the way. So she'd only have to wait a little while, then she could slip off. And never do a thing like this again.

There was a little alcove by the aft bulkhead. She huddled into it, gripped the parasol again. She looked up at the ports. It was getting dark already. She was sure even if someone did come down, they wouldn't see her.

She jumped. The deck beneath her was vibrating. There was a thumping noise too, deep and slow. It seemed to come from now-where at the back. She stared round wildly. For a moment she didn't understand. Then realization flooded. The engines had started.

More feet scurried overhead; and there was an order. '*Let go forrard …*' She heard it clearly, even in the little hold. They must be using one of those electric things to speak with. The engine beat increased; and the loudhailer sounded again. It said, '*Let go aft …*'

She curled into a ball, started to whimper. She was going to sea then; into the storm.

The Chief relieved him, which was sinister in itself. In times of peril, the First Engineer took the gantry; and a Second doesn't fill a Running Log. Nath made his way forrard, to his cabin. On the way, he glanced through a port. The sea was grey as slate, whitecaps beginning to break; and rain was lashing down already. He put a waterproof on, climbed to the wheelhouse. They'd already lit the lamps; they were swaying to the motion of the boat. He glanced astern, through the big square windows. The land was all but lost; a darker shadow, fading as he watched.

The Skipper looked at him keenly. He'd understood of course the significance of the relief; but he made no comment. He said, 'What's our offing, sir?'

The Master Heldon studied his wrist. 'We've not done badly,' he said. 'Should be picking up our marks in forty minutes.'

He glanced at the telegraph. Full speed ahead. Not that he'd needed the verification; the trembling of the hull told him the revolutions accurately enough. Nath almost smiled. On normal voyages, even of this short duration, they hoisted sail once clear of land; the wells round North Cape were drying one by one, fuel conservation was becoming a major factor. But this voyage wasn't normal. Even the Ultras, it seemed, had recognized that. At least the dispensation had saved him one unpleasant chore. The propeller was eight-bladed, ten feet or more across; raising it in its frame wasn't a job he relished, even on a calm, fine day. Lives had been lost at that, more than once; they probably would be again.

They contacted in less than forty minutes. *Spindrift*, the ship on Station, was firing rockets. He saw their answer arc into the gloom. The Skipper spun the helm. He'd pass her, turn against the tide, steam up to the buoys. A nasty operation; and with a crosswind too. Nath listened. He estimated half a gale already. He was glad, not for the first time, he wasn't Deck Crew.

One of the Ultras came in. He stood hands on hips and stared round. Nath left the wheelhouse, climbed carefully down the ladder. He couldn't stand their close proximity. Brave men's lives were being put at risk and for what? A whim, a fancy. There had to be a better way. He thought, not for the first time, 'It isn't the Realm that's mad. It's them.'

He took shelter in the lee of the bridge structure. *Spindrift* had slipped already; gratefully, he supposed. He knew he would be. A signal lamp winked from her stern. He translated the cyphers, automatically. '*You must be crazy …*'

There was an Ultra on the Kiteplatform. He raised a weapon. Shots crackled across the sea. The light went out abruptly; the signaller had prudently dropped flat. *Spindrift* turned contemptuously, trailing a faint wake of foam. She headed for the land.

The buoys were ahead. Nath heard the telegraph ring for Quarter Speed, then Engines Stop. He watched with something like awe. Thug and bully Yarman might be; but he was a good First Mate. As Heldon was a first rate Skipper. *Kitestrength* sidled in, the platform rolling against the almost-dark sky. The buoys were picked up, somehow or another; deckhands scurried, dragging the second hawsers forward. Astern, they'd be doing the same; but their task would be easier. Steam jetted from the foredeck winch as the cables were drawn in. The motion of the Kiteship altered at once. The rolling ceased; in its place was a shorter, sharper bucking. She plunged and yanked, snubbing at the cables. He heard the faint tinkle of the wheelhouse telegraph. He knew what the message would be. Finished with engines … He glanced up uneasily at the topload of rigging, canvas. They should have handed topmasts and to'gallants, steamed under bare poles; but there hadn't been time.

A loudhailer crackled from the foredeck. He couldn't believe his ears. It said, '*Stream …*'

Nobody but a madman or an Ultra would have thought of it. It was impossible of course; they'd even have grounded the Codys on the mainland. Nonetheless, they somehow managed to manhandle a Pilot on to the Tower. They coupled, paid out fifty yards; and the Kite collapsed with a crack. The cable snaked into the sea. They reeled it in; and the priest with the megaphone said, '*Stream* ...'

The second Pilot went the way of the first. A Cadet reeled to him, across the heaving deck. He said, 'My Lord, we cannot do it. It is impossible ...'

They'd rigged arc lamps from the wheelhouse front. So every detail showed clear. The Ultra took the pistol from his belt, barrel-whipped the boy across the face. Then again. The other crawled away. The priest said, '*Stream* ...'

Nath retreated to the engineroom. He was feeling sick.

Velvet wasn't too good either. An extra buffet came; the ship rolled and corkscrewed, and she finally threw up. Messily too, she was off balance at the time. She brushed at her front, and whimpered. 'Rand,' she said. 'Rand ...' She crawled back onto the canvas, lay staring into the dark. After a while she shut her eyes; but it didn't help, there were still little spots and flashes whirling about. She rolled on to her side. She didn't seem to be frightened any more, she'd just stopped caring. That was natural though. When you felt as bad as this, you didn't have time for anything else. The spasm came again. And again afterwards. The third was worst of all. Oddly enough though, she felt better for it. She wiped her chin and spat. She fell asleep.

The wind continued to increase.

He stared at the gauges. Still full head. He said, 'What about the Ultras?' and the Chief Engineer smiled grimly. 'They won't go near the boiler room,' he said. 'A fire slice is about the only thing they respect.' He glanced down at the slumbering machinery, shadowy in the swinging of the lamps. He said, 'Your engines, Third.' He jerked his head. He said, 'Time for a refresher.'

Nath followed, wondering. He'd never been in the Chief's cabin before. It was another of the unwritten rules. The other got a bottle and two glasses. The table was gimballed; the glasses still tended to slide about, one side of the fiddle to the other. He drank, and coughed. The Chief smiled. He said, 'Keep going. It's better when the teeth are numbed.'

He produced a box of the yellow, tobacco-filled tubes. Nath hesitated, and took one. Normally he didn't care for them; but tonight was different. In many respects. He lit up, and the Chief said, 'How's that lassie of yours?'

Nath frowned. He said, 'I don't know.' He sipped again, cautiously. He said, 'I'm going ashore after this trip. Did they tell you?'

The First looked at him. He said, 'We'll all be going ashore. Unless we look lively.' The wind roared; and he cocked his head. Tethered as she was, *Kitestrength* was helpless, exposed to the full fury of the sea. 'God,' he said. 'Listen to that ...' Through the crashing of the waves came the first dim growl of thunder.

Nath took another drag of the cigarette. He saw his hand was vibrating. He made himself be calm. He said, 'We're looking for a place up in the Northguard.' He grimaced. He said, 'Going back to the land.'

The other glanced at him. He said, 'If you're let to.'

He nodded. 'Yes, sir,' he said. 'I know what you mean.' He set his lips. The folk of the Realm were like folk down the ages. Wanting no truck with Gods, and less with Demons. Wanting to bake their bread, and till their fields, and raise their children in peace. He felt blind anger at the Ultras, at the Vars, at all who sought to impose their will on others. But maybe that anger was old as the hills as well. He said, 'Is there going to be trouble? Do you reckon?'

'There's trouble already,' said the Chief. 'You know that as well as I do. If it spreads, we're all for the chop. I used to think it wouldn't come in my time. But now I'm not so sure.' He drained the glass, poured himself another. He said. 'How's your little Island girl then?'

Nath was startled by the intensity of the vision that came to him. She waved and postured, held her arms out. She dropped to her knees. He knew there were tears in her eyes. He said, 'Chief ...'

The other waited.

He hesitated. Something he needed desperately to say. About Kari, and about Addi. But the words wouldn't form.

It seemed the First read his mind. He smiled again, briefly. He said, 'I sometimes think a woman's like a ship. She takes your breath away to start with. The lines of her, the glitter. Then they send you manholing. You see the worst she has to offer. You find out then, what you really think of the sea.'

He stared at his glass. He said, 'Why did you ask me in?'

The wind howled again. The Chief glanced at the bulkhead. Measured the angle as the Kiteship rolled. He said, 'It's never good to meet your Maker stone cold sober.'

There was a bang. It echoed through the ship. *Kitestrength* surged sideways, sickeningly. A crashing and grinding began at once. It sounded from the starboard bow.

The other flung the glass away. 'Bloody Hell,' he said. 'Come on, lad ...'

Before he reached the engineroom he'd realized what had happened. The port tackles had parted, she'd swung onto the other buoy. Only one hope. Release the starboard hawsers, winch astern. And hope the shortened moorings stood the strain. A few minutes of that pounding and she'd be holed.

The Chief glared at the gauges. 'Get on deck,' he said. 'They'll need all the help they can get. I'll take over here ...'

Nath said, 'Aye aye, sir.' He ran for the ladder.

The rain struck his face like slingshots. And *Kitestrength* was bucking and plunging, more wildly than before. Lightning blazed; he saw spray break over the fo'castle, a silver shower higher than the gantry. He began to work his way forward, hand over hand.

He clung to the wheelhouse ladder, peered aft. Lamps were rigged there too. Some sort of confused fight had broken out. He saw running figures, saw an Ultra felled. He heard, dimly, the clatter of the stern winch.

He climbed. Level with the windows, he pressed back. The Skipper was there, and the Mate. Both were backed against the bulkhead, their hands held high. The Ultra had an automatic levelled; they were expostulating fiercely, though he couldn't hear the words.

Nath glimpsed the big chronometer above their heads, and realization dawned. It was twenty-four hundred. This was the Holy Day, on which no work might be done. To save a woman in labour, to save a drowning man; or to save a ship from wreck. He should have expected no more.

He edged back down. He saw the stern party had backed away from the winch. The action spoke louder than words. He saw a hawser part; the severed end lashed viciously across the deck. That was the finish then. The others wouldn't last more than minutes now.

What happened was unexpected. He could tell by the instant alteration in her motion that *Kitestrength* was no longer tethered. Yet he'd heard no more shackles give. He realized what had happened. The endless fretting had finally taken effect; the buoy itself was adrift. He saw men hurry to the winch. They'd pay out cable, stream the thing as a drogue. It might be their last chance.

He edged his way round the lee of the wheelhouse. The Ultras had formed a cordon, forward of the winch. He saw the guns. The arcs were still burning; but they were scarcely necessary. The lightning was continuous; it lit the sea almost as bright as day. A loudhailer brayed through the thunder. '*Will of the Lord*,' it said. '*Will of the Lord …*'

He stared in disbelief. Passing to starboard was one of the Inner Markers. He wouldn't have believed their rate of drift. Even towing the buoy. But the tide was making, the gale itself had backed. It was blowing now almost straight onshore. He set his mouth. The Stanway wreckers would have good pickings, come the morning. They'd have no use for corpses though. They'd give them back to the sea.

He began to edge forward. Somebody must sacrifice themself, that was plain. If he could get near enough to their Bishop … He'd die of course; but it might distract the others. A few seconds was all it needed.

There was a cry. He stared again. Atop the launching platform capered a wild figure. A creature from hallucination surely, or a fevered dream.

Its hair, which was long and dark, flew wildly in the wind. It was bare to the waist; the water gleamed on its breasts. It raised an arm; instantly a vivid streak of lightning seemed to grow from the sea. The thunderclap was fearsome.

The apparition pointed, to the dark loom of the land. It crossed its arms above its head, a gesture of negation. It pointed at the ship, and the gesture came again. It struck a pose, one hip thrust out, waved an arm toward the open sea.

'*The Spirit of the Storm*,' boomed the loudhailer. '*On your knees, Brethren. On your knees before the Mother …*' The Ultras threw the guns down, cowered; and he wouldn't have believed the speed at which the deckhands moved. He saw a man's skull crushed; another writhed, a baling hook driven through his eye. Then mercifully the lights flicked off. The lightning blazed again; but the Kiteplatform was empty.

He swung back up to the wheelhouse. The Ultra lay groaning, blood plastering the side of his face. The Mate stood over him with a belay pin. The priest rolled over, tried to push himself to his knees. Yarman kicked him in the throat.

The Skipper was already blowing down the voicepipe. He said, 'Emergency revolutions, Chief.' A pause; and he shouted. 'To Hell with your bloody valves. *Emergency revolutions …*' A boiling began at once, under the Kiteship's stern. He grabbed a loudhailer. He said, '*Cut that bloody buoy loose …*' He swung forward, slammed one of the windows wide. '*Emergency*,' he said. '*Jettison Tower …*'

The charges had been well placed. Four thunderous reports; and the Tower sagged. It toppled, seemingly in slow motion. A mighty splash; and the Kiteship's bows rose high. Too high. The Skipper blew down the voicepipe again. He said, 'Ballast forward tanks.' He glanced over his shoulder. 'Stay here, Second,' he said. 'You might still be needed …'

For a long time, an eternity it seemed, it was touch and go. *Kitestrength* was throbbing from stem to stern, straining her every rivet; but she was already into the bight of Stanway Bay, the tide sweeping her to leeward. The Skipper had the wheel hard over. 'Come on, you bitch,' he said. 'Come on, you old sow. Come on …'

Slowly, agonizingly slowly at first, her head came round. The land, the dark loom of Mitre Head, was on her port quarter. Then it was abeam. She'd weathered the point. She wallowed in the cross sea; but the ballast tanks were filling, Nath felt a fresh stability. There was a sureness to her movement that hadn't been there before. She began to edge out from the land, to the safety of the open sea.

The Skipper heaved a long, slow sigh. He used the voicepipe again. 'Thank you, Number One,' he said. 'Standard revolutions.' He glanced down at the

Ultra. He said, 'My ship. My bloody ship …' He looked up at the Mate. 'Mister,' he said, 'she's still carrying too much deck cargo.'

The Mate grinned, and nodded. He bundled the Ultra to the door, dropped him down the ladder. The body hit the plates with a sickening thud. He swung down, started lugging it to the side. Others followed suit. There was a plashing of priests.

The Master Heldon looked across to Nath. His face was still set grimly. 'They all went over in the same big wave,' he said. 'One of the risks you take, going to sea.' He rubbed his face. Suddenly he looked unutterably weary. 'Thank you, Mr Ostman,' he said. 'Will you relieve the Chief? Ask him if he'd have the goodness to step up here for a momen'.'

Nath said, 'Aye aye, sir.' He saluted, and headed for the ladder.

The storm had blown itself out as quickly as it had risen. The only sign of its passing was the long, smooth swell. *Kitestrength* edged up to the quay. Hawsers were thrown, and secured; the throbbing of the engines stilled at last.

The morning light lay grey across the town. Nath swung down the forward hatch, clicked on a big handlamp. The forepeak was empty. As were the workshops beyond. He edged into the Kitehold. 'Velvet,' he called. 'Velvet …'

There was a flicker of movement. She tried to duck under his arm; but it was too late, he already held her scruff. She wriggled ineffectually, subsided. He looked at her. Her face was still pale; her hair was draggled, and she smelled of sick. 'Well, Mistress,' he said. 'And what have you to say for yourself?'

'I couldn't 'elp it,' she said. 'I was only lookin'.' She pouted. 'My skirt's all wet,' she said. 'You feel …'

He said, 'You're lucky it's not a good deal wetter.' He firmed his grip, began to march her toward the bow. He said, 'How did you know what to do? Who taught you a trick like that?'

She shrugged, as well as she was able. 'They were only Ultras,' she said. 'They're all a bit round the twist.' She looked up at him. 'Good act though, wadn't it?' she said. 'I quite enjoyed meself.'

'Yes,' he said. 'It looked as if you did.' He climbed the ladder first, waited for her to emerge. He resumed his grip.

Rand was waiting on the quay. His face looked haggard. 'My God,' he said. 'I guessed where she'd gone. If you knew what I've lived through …'

'I'd have traded,' said the Mariner dryly. He looked back at *Kitestrength*. Her soaring masts and yards. 'She saved the ship,' he said. 'And herself, and me. I suppose that makes her a heroine. But it doesn't mean you can trust her.'

'No,' said the other. 'I found that out already.' He dropped his hand on Velvet's other shoulder; they frogmarched her solemnly away along the quay.

8

Kitekillers

Velvet took her glasses off. They weren't her glasses actually; they weren't anybody's, she'd found them on a tip. They were very fine, with thin goldy-coloured frames. There was even a little chain, so she could hang them round her neck. She thought they made her look mature. There was only one problem; she couldn't see much through them. Everything looked all blurry.

They'd invested in one of these new fangled typewriters. It had seemed like just a toy at first; later though she'd realized how useful it could be. She twisted the big handle at the side, and the letter popped out of the top. She read it, carefully.

Dear Master Herringhold,
The bulbs what you ordered is ready.

She scowled. She'd known there was something wrong. She took another sheet of paper, retyped carefully.

Dear Master Herringhold,
The bulbs what you ordered are *ready.*

There, that was better. She signed it, '*PP Tremarest Holdings*'. She wasn't sure what the letters stood for; she sometimes suspected Rand didn't know either. But they were like the spectacles; they looked good. She addressed the envelope, stuck the flap with wax. She dobbed the big seal on to it, examined the results. That was the part of letter-writing she really liked best.

She put her hat on, headed through the shop. The air was full of cheeping; the little yellow birds they brought in from the Islands. Their cages lined the whole of one side wall. As she opened the door, a posh voice said, 'Good afternoon.'

She stopped. Then she scowled again. It was the big black bird they'd bought a few weeks back. That came from Tremarest as well. It was always catching her out. It seemed it could imitate anything; even the ringing of the door bell. She gripped her parasol. 'Naff orf,' she said.

The bird put its head on one side. It watched her stump off down the street. 'Naff orf, Miss Velvet,' it said.

She headed towards town centre. Not that Fronting had much of a centre really. Its name rather summed it up. One way, it fronted the Middle Lands; the other way it faced the Southguard. It belonged to neither. She'd been surprised when Rand had chosen it. Still, she'd been surprised at a lot of things. She'd been surprised when he'd given up the other shop. There'd been rows with Master Hoyland, certainly; they used to go at it hammer and tongs. Half the night, sometimes. It had still come as a shock though.

Very serious affair, it had been. There was even a solicitor, a Master Lanting. Tall and greyhaired, with a big shiny briefcase. She thought he'd given her some funny looks. She'd wriggled uncomfortably, wanting to get away; she'd never understood about things like this. It had been impossible though; there'd been papers to sign, all sorts of bits and pieces. She'd made her mark, frowning; a cross, like the Fishgard boatmen used to use. Later Rand had consulted her, very seriously, about what she wanted to do; but she'd merely shrugged. Her strongbox was nearly full; so it didn't matter. As long as she was with him.

The strongbox had been another slight cause of friction. Even with Rand. He kept his money in a bank; but she'd never fancied the idea. After all, if it wasn't there it wasn't really yours any more. You couldn't even count it. He'd asked her more than once, what would happen if the house burned down; but she merely shrugged. The bank might burn down as well. He'd said that didn't matter, it wouldn't make any difference; but she'd been unable to see that. The money would still go up in smoke.

The town was busy, for the time of the year. They held an Air Fair too; but that wasn't for weeks yet. She was beginning to see why Rand had wanted to come here. He'd been cleverer than she'd realized; with all the trouble in Middlemarch, and more starting in the Southguard, people had been moving out in a steady stream. There was a lot of money about. They hadn't had the shop long, but it had done really well.

She turned left, headed for the Var place. This posting of letters was a good idea. You paid so much a month, and they always seemed to arrive. They were faster than the carriers too; they had their own little vans, you often saw them about. They were painted maroon, same colour as the Launchers, with big insignia on the sides. She'd got to know their local man quite well.

She glanced up at the Codys flying from the Central Tower. She saw the wind had veered round to the south. Which meant good weather, for a day or two at least. Anyway that was what the Mariner always said. He reckoned on a good day you could smell the Island spice. Though she never had. She turned her nose up. He'd talked a lot about the Islands, particularly

Tremarest; but she hadn't been fooled. He'd got a bit of spare down there; you couldn't tell her much about seamen.

She handed the letter in, saw it stamped and signed for. She signed her own name on the sheet. VELVET, in big square lettering. That last was an accomplishment of which she was very proud. Learning to read had been a chore at first; learning to write had been even harder. The most difficult thing, she thought, that she'd ever tried to do. Rand had tried to show her, times enough; eventually he'd hired a tutor, Mistress Harken. She'd disliked her cordially; she had a feeling the sentiment had been mutual. She'd persevered though; she didn't like to be beaten at things. She'd chewed her quill tip, made inkblots by the score; but this was the result. She twirled her parasol. She was a real businesswoman now; she could even write her name.

Velvet headed back toward the town square. She hadn't been sure she'd like the shop at first, and living away from the sea. After all the sound of it had been in her ears all her life. It was all right though; in fact it had grown on her. And anyway her seafaring days were over. One experience had been enough. Also, she wasn't totally cut off. They handled mostly Island produce; even the seed corn and potatoes came from Tremarest. Rand had some good contacts; the Mariner had introduced him to most of them. There were other things as well of course; exciting things sometimes, apart from the birds. Great shells, all spikes and blotches, strange-smelling fibre mats; more of the funny floating stone, bolts of cloth with beautiful hand-printed patterns. She'd considered having some of it made up into a dress; but she'd decided against it finally. The great swirling flowers, in pink and violet and blue; somehow it wasn't really her. She had found a hat though, with funny little cork things hung all round the brim. She couldn't work out what they were for. They annoyed her eventually, bobbling about: so she cut them off. The hat was very nice though; it was made of a sort of grass.

The cloth had sold particularly well. With the proceeds they'd even bought a little van. It went out on delivery several times a week. There was a handcart too of course; Velvet used it herself sometimes, for small drops. Rand had scolded her once or twice, asked why she thought they employed a lad; but she'd merely shrugged again. She liked to get out and about, see what was going on; and anyway she was used to trucks. One way and another, her life had seemed to revolve round them.

In sight of the square she hesitated. A Hunter Waggon was parked by the town hall; scarlet and high-sided, with guns at front and rear. She could see the barrels from where she stood. There'd been quite a few of them about recently; they rumbled through the town all hours of the day and night. They worried Rand a lot, though she couldn't for the life of her see why. After all, they weren't doing any harm. They sold corn and seed potatoes, vegetables in season, Island fruits. They were just shopkeepers, the Vars wouldn't be interested in them. She gave the thing a wide berth nonetheless.

There was a closed carriage, drawn by a pair of handsome greys. She eyed it vaguely. She hadn't seen that one before; must be somebody else new in town. She made to pass it, and the window was rapped. She turned, curiously. The rapping came again.

She walked back; and the door was opened. Velvet gulped. She said, ''Ello, Mistress.'

'My little helpmate,' said the Lady Kerosina. 'I didn't know you were here. Get in'

She hesitated; and the other gestured. She obeyed, unwillingly. 'You livin' 'ere?' she said.

'We bought a little place a few weeks back,' said Kerosina. 'One needs the occasional breath of country air. I'll show it to you.' She rapped the roof, sharply; before Velvet could protest, they were jangling on their way.

Kerosina sat back and crossed her legs. She said, 'So what are you doing in Fronting?'

Velvet swallowed again. 'We got a shop,' she said. 'Leastways it's Rand's really. I got a sort of interest.' She gripped her parasol. 'Corn chandlers,' she said. 'We sells a lot of other stuff as well though.'

'Fascinating,' said the Lady Kerosina. 'Next time I run short of wheat, I'll come and see you.'

The carriage turned right, and left. The horses increased their pace. Velvet clung to a little plaited strap. 'I can't be long,' she said. 'Rand's expectin' me back. I only come out wi' the post.'

'You won't be long,' said Kerosina sharply. 'It isn't very far. It's only on the edge of town. If you can call this place a town. But at least it's quiet.' She eyed Velvet candidly. 'You've grown,' she said. 'You're looking well. So Rand's still looking after you.'

She nodded. She said, 'Yes, Mistress. 'E's ever so kind.' She looked down. 'Bit like 'avin a Dad, I suppose,' she said. 'Well, sort of,' she added.

The carriage turned again. She heard the crunch of gravel. The coachman reined; a brief wait, and the wheels clashed on to cobbles. Kerosina said, 'We're here.' She opened the door, climbed down. 'Don't stable, Jehan,' she said. 'The carriage will be going back to town.' The coachman said, 'Aye, Mistress.'

Velvet had followed. She stood and stared round. The house, as Kerosina had said, was not too large; but it was stone-fronted, with crenellations on the top and lines of big bay windows. A big Cody string flew from the eastern Tower. Velvet turned. Surrounding the entire place was a high stone wall, replete with more of the curious battlements. Men were patrolling it. They wore Kerosin livery, and each had a gun slung to his shoulder. It was more like a little fort than anything else.

The Lady Kerosina looked sardonic. 'One must take precautions,' she said. 'Even here. We're living in quite interesting times.' She opened a parasol. 'Walk with me, Velvet,' she said. 'It's been so long since I saw you.'

The grounds were really pretty; trees set all over, little twisty paths winding between. There were deep green pools, mossy head-high cliffs; in one place she saw a little waterfall. There were tall bushes, some of them in bloom already; between them she saw Island flowers. 'It's beautiful,' she said. She caught her breath. She said, 'What's that?'

They'd come upon the little house unexpectedly. It too was built of stone. There were tall crooked chimneys, windows with funny diamond-patterned panes; it even had its own Kitemast, from which streamed a tiny Cody.

'It used to be the Head Gardener's,' said Kerosina. 'But he moved out. Went with the other people.' She took a key from her handbag. 'It's empty at the moment,' she said. She glanced sidelong. She said, 'Waiting a tenant.'

The door had a rounded top. Like the door Velvet remembered in the arch. She stopped just inside. There were deep windowsills; just right for her driftwood creatures. She could twine flowers round them; there were enough in the garden already, but there'd be a lot more come summer. She hurried round opening doors. There was a big cupboard that would serve well as a wardrobe, a tiny sleeping cubicle. It was lit by more of the diamond-shaped panes; outside, a creeper tapped the glass. There was even a bathroom, with its own loo. In Fishgard, she'd always had to use the common.

There was a big metal box on the wall. She said, 'What's this, Mistress?' and Kerosina called back. 'A geyser,' she said. 'It makes the water hot.'

There was a brass wheel at the side. She turned it, and there was a *whoomph.* She jumped back, peered again curiously. Blue flames showed through a slot; and water had begun to pulse from a nozzle in the wall. She put her hand to it, snatched it away. It was almost scalding.

She turned the geyser off, went back. Kerosina sat on the settle, composedly. 'Well, Velvet,' she said, 'it's yours for the asking. Your own little house. Even when I'm not here. You knew that already though.' She smiled. She said, 'What do you think?'

Velvet swallowed. 'I'm with Rand,' she said. ''E needs me in the shop. 'E's bin ever so good to me,' she said. ''E taught me ter read an' write.'

The Lady Kerosina sighed. 'This is such a tedious little town,' she said. 'I'm bored with it already.' She leaned forward, whispered; and Velvet's eyes grew round with shock. 'I *couldn't,*' she said. 'I *couldn't.* I promised . . .'

The other looked at her. 'But you promised me as well,' she said. 'So you'll have to break your word to one of us.'

Velvet twined her fingers miserably. She wondered why life always had to be so complicated. It would go all right for a time; but something like this always happened. Kerosina had been good to her, she'd always been good to her; now she was offering her a real house, of her very own. But Rand had been good to her as well. She bit her lip. 'Look, Mistress,' she said, 'I do know somebody. It'll only be the once though. Then you'll'ave ter get someone else …' She twined her fingers again. 'I got the shop ter run,' she said.

The Lady Kerosina smiled. 'There's nobody as good as you,' she said. She sat back. 'Very well,' she said. 'Just the once.'

Letting herself back into the shop, the bird spoke to her again. Velvet glowered at it. 'I tol' yer already,' she said. 'Naff orf …'

It cocked its head, and made a noise like a bicycle bell.

It wasn't just the once of course. It was again and again. But she'd realized that as well. Once Kerosina had you in her grip, you didn't get away as easily as that. Sometimes it was boy children, sometimes girls; usually they'd scuttle away in shame and terror, but sometimes they'd creep back of their own accord. Then Kerosina would lock her doors, and laugh. It made it even worse.

Velvet raised the matter with her, several times; eventually the other's eyes flashed. 'I think I need some flowers for the patio,' she said. 'Perhaps tomorrow I'll call in on the Master Rand.'

She felt an instant surge of panic. 'No, Mistress,' she said. 'No, please …'

Kerosina stared at her. 'Velvet,' she said, 'you're an ungrateful little beast. Haven't you been paid good money?'

They were sitting in the main hall of the house. She looked at the carpet, traced one of the flowers with her parasol. 'I din' wan' it,' she whispered.

'But you took it,' said Her Ladyship. 'You took it, Mistress.' She sighed. 'What does it matter?' she said. 'What does any of it matter? We'll all be dead soon anyway. The wells are running dry; that will be the trigger.'

Velvet pouted. She didn't want to know. About wells, and triggers, things she couldn't understand. She wanted to feed the yellow birds, and arrange her shells in the windows, and just be left alone.

The closed coach trotted, forward and back from town.

The Minutemen were out; even here, in Fronting. Little contingents of them paraded the streets, muskets on their shoulders. Some claimed allegiance to the Vars, some to the Middle Doctrine. There was uneasiness when they met; but so far there had been no outright clashes. There'd be mutual glowering, as often as not a hurled exchange of insults; but one troop or another would invariably cross the road, out of the enemy's way. The Ultras were another factor altogether. They were more sinister; because nobody, not even the Vars themselves, knew the full extent of their authority. Their influence had been growing, that much was certain; there were rumours they'd even infiltrated the Middle Lands themselves. Rand heard the stories often enough; the taverns of the town buzzed with talk. As the taverns of any town buzzed with talk. The words of the Mariner Ostman came back to him once more. *We were saved. Just us, out of all the world. I sometimes wonder whether we were worth it . . .'*

There were other whispers. At first Rand turned a deaf ear. But finally they became too persistent to be ignored. He began taking note of Velvet's absences from the shop. She always took the mail down to the post, she had done since they'd opened. She'd leave about seventeen hundred, be back before they closed. It was a couple of hours now though, sometimes three. Once she wasn't back till nearly twenty-two hundred. She said there'd been a queue.

He turned on her, finally. 'Velvet,' he said, 'what's this I hear? About the Mistress Kerosina being in town?'

She wouldn't look at him. She stuck her lip out, stared down at the carpet.

'Velvet,' he said, 'what are you up to? Are you performing little services again?'

She pouted. She said indistinctly, 'I promised.'

'Yes,' said Rand, 'you promised.' A wait. He said, 'You're lying, child.' He paused again. He said, 'Look at me.'

She wouldn't.

He shook his head. 'All I tried to do,' he said. 'All the time I spent.' He swallowed. 'I'll tell you where I found you,' he said. 'In the gutter. You might not have realized it, but that was where you were. A thief, a procuress, a whoremonger, a liar. I made a home for you, I gave you a new start. The sort of chance you'd never had before. Not in your pathetic little life. For a time I thought it was working. I'd even begun to trust you. But you couldn't keep away, could you? You couldn't keep your fingers out of dirt.'

He'd never actually seen her lose her temper. He saw it now. 'What do you know?' she snarled. 'What do you fuckin' know? You an' yer Kites, an' keepin' yer nose in the air, an' lecturin' me an' tellin me 'ow ter go on. You ain't ever lived, not really. You don't know what it's all about, you don't know nothin'.' She jumped up, chest heaving. 'I'll tell you what it's about,' she yelled. 'I'll tell you what it's all about. It's about gettin' little kids, an' floggin' their snatches, an' gettin' some more an' some more after that because the first lot's wore out already. It's about nickin' things, an' tellin' lies, an' makin' it 'ow you can. Because that's what people are about . . .' She flung a vase across the room. It shattered. 'I ain't never made myself out posh,' she said. 'Only what I am. I tried ter play it straight though. I ain't never nicked from you. Not one bleedin' penny. You wouldn't believe that though, would yer? 'Cos I come out the gutter. An' you don't believe nobody out the gutter.'

She pointed through the window. 'Go up the church,' she said. 'Go an' light yer little lamps. Tell 'em yer 'oly. Make yer feel good, that will.' She panted. 'Made yer feel good what you done fer me, din' it?' she said. 'Go to 'Eaven fer sure, you will . . .'

If he hadn't seen her angry, she hadn't seen him. He was across the room in a flash. He slapped her, and again. She tried to bolt, but he took her by the scruff. He shook her, flung her down on the settle. 'All right,' he said. 'If you want it you can have it. You've been asking for it long enough.' He dragged at his belt. She writhed and yelled; later though she fell curiously quiet. He stood up finally. The rage was still burning. 'Get to bed,' he said. 'In the morning you can get out. The Mistress will find you a room. Useful to have you handy.' He blundered downstairs, slammed the outer door. He headed for the nearest boozer. His heels rang on the path; he heard the sound dimly, through the buzzing in his ears.

She didn't wait till morning. She began collecting her things at once. Clothes, the cashbox, a new pair of shoes. She filled the truck, hesitated. She dumped some of the little driftwood creatures on top. Just her favourites. She didn't see why she should leave them. After all they wouldn't answer back, or yell at her. She stumped off through the town. She wasn't crying; it was just that the tears would well and trickle. They dripped steadily from her chin. It wasn't the hiding. She'd had enough before, they never really hurt; the sting had gone off already. It was what he'd said. She'd had to go back and work for Kerosina, she'd been forced to; otherwise she'd have told on her, she didn't make threats like that lightly. He hadn't given her the chance to explain though, hadn't even asked. Just assumed the worst. She lifted her chin. If he didn't want her any more, she knew somebody who did. She'd get a house out of it as well. She'd be everything he'd called her; liar, procuress, thief. And never bother trying to be good again. There was more money in it anyway, than running a scruffy old shop.

At first light Rand walked down the Kiteport road. He found the handcart abandoned, by Kerosina's main gate. He pulled it from the ditch, stood looking at it. He stared up at the battlemented wall. Events had come full circle then, he'd known one day they must. 'It was bound to happen,' he said greyly. He trudged back into the town.

Summer was coming, but the days stayed overcast. He served in the shop, dealt with the occasional rep, worked on the accounts. After hours he loaded the van, went out on delivery. He saw no sign of Velvet. He was glad of that.

Now of course was the time for his Middler philosophy. Each act, dressing and shaving, eating, lying down, was an act performed; complete in itself, neither good nor bad. It led nowhere save to the next. The sum of awareness grew, the psyche altered; that in itself was of equal insignificance. It was useless though. The thought brought no comfort, didn't fill the nagging emptiness inside him.

Velvet's clothes, the ones she hadn't wanted, were still scattered about. She'd always been an untidy little wretch; it had been one of the maddening, endearing things about her. The woman who cleaned for him gathered them up. She turned to him finally, biting her lip. 'Where is she, sir?' she said. 'Where's your little girl?'

'She wasn't my little girl,' he said. 'She was never my little girl.'

She looked helpless. 'But what shall I do with these?'

The Middlers were always appealing for clothes for the paupers in their care. He supposed he ought to send them to the church. But he didn't have the heart. 'I don't know,' he said. 'Do what you like.'

The cleaning woman glanced at the bundle in her arms, and back to him. 'I'll put 'em in the spare room,' she said. She shook her head. She said, 'She had such pretty things.' He saw there were tears in her eyes. He wondered for a moment why.

It was true of course. She'd never been his, she'd been nothing to do with him. But nothing had ever been his. He'd loved his sister; and see what had happened there. He'd loved Janni, loved her with his heart and soul, loved her to distraction; and she'd been taken from him. Casually, by the crooking of a finger. He'd worked from month to month, from year to year; but for what? He'd ended as he'd begun, with nothing. The silence told him that, the silence of his rooms. The clock told him, with its ticking. He tried to remember happier times, set them against the gnawing loneliness; laughing with Janni, loving her, riding the horses. He failed again. Because those times had gone, ceased to exist. When the sun was shining, then it shone; when clouds eclipsed it, there was no sun.

He took to dropping into one or other of the local inns. Usually he'd make a night of it; though of course there always came a time when he had to leave. Let himself into the shop, and climb the stairs. So he started keeping a few bottles about the place. Wine and cider, even the Northland hooch. It did no long term good; but it dulled the pain a little. Like brandy on an aching tooth. He wondered what old Father Alkin would have thought. He'd probably have said it was a sensible idea.

News came from the north. There'd been riots in Streanling and Barida; Var Militia had taken over the coastal wells, oil production was now controlled by the Church. Middlemarch itself was a town under siege. Roadblocks had been set up on all approaches; strangers had been fired on indiscriminately. Shooting had been heard inside the town as well and many fires were burning, seemingly out of control. All the factions were armed; Vars and Ultras, the Middlemen, the Corps, Militia of various persuasions. But which of them actually controlled the battered city was unknown. 'It's the end of the world,' said a grimfaced Kiteman, shaking his head. 'It'll never be the same. Least, not in our lifetimes.'

Rand walked away. A part of him understood. The strange G8 affair had shown the way; pointed out the lack of overall control, the true weakness of the central authority. Since then the Kiteworld had been simmering, waiting for just such an explosion. Sometimes though he felt isolated, remote. It was as if the events weren't really happening, didn't in fact concern him. But of course his world had ended already. Not once, but many times.

He took the Falcon down to the Master Hummin, filled her to the brim. He piled jerrycans into the boot, added a gallon of oil. As he left the forecourt a Var patrol swung in. By morning the garage was sealed, the line of handpumps guarded by armed militia.

He dreamed of the flying of a great Cody rig. Its wings dwarfed anything he'd seen; even the wire of the Trace seemed thicker than his wrist. Lifter after Lifter sailed up, to clang against its cone. The wire thrummed; finally the basket climbed away. He saw Velvet was aboard. Tiny, and pathetic. She called to him, her voice thin as a gull's. She held her arms out. He called back, spread his arms in return; but it was too late. The winch was clattering, she was being drawn away. Higher and higher, into the drifting clouds. He shouted, despairingly; and the winchman turned. He saw it was Rone Dalgeth. 'I won again,' he said. 'I've taken her as well.' He swung a lever; the pawl cleared from the ratchet. Rand grappled, despairingly; then he was awake, and sweating. He staggered to the loo. He saw there was no rest, by night or day; now, she had invaded his sleep.

He frowned. The clattering came again, and faded. He knew the sound; steel halftracks on cobbles. Hunter Waggons from the Vars or Ultras; a whole convoy of them. It was like an army, grinding through the town. He frowned again. There was a rattling; distant, but unmistakable. Someone was using automatic weapons. He clicked the light off, pulled the curtains back. He saw the glow of flames, reflecting from the clouds.

The war came to Fronting with shocking suddenness. Next night Rand woke abruptly, wondered what had disturbed him. He wasn't left long in doubt. The sound came again. Gunfire. This time it was close though; it sounded to be in the street. He rose, dressed hastily. He snatched a glance at the clock. Zero three hundred. He hurried downstairs, turning on lights as he went; but before he reached the shop there was a massive crash. It came again, accompanied by the tinkling of glass. He was being broken into. He snatched up a crowbar that lay on one of the storeroom crates. It was a useless gesture though. He ran forward, saw what he was facing and dropped it. He raised his hands, slowly.

The intruders fanned out, guns levelled. Six hardfaced young men, their hair tumbling to their shoulders. A silence; then Brad Hoyland walked forward. Rand moistened his lips. 'Hello, Brad,' he said. 'Come for some seed corn then? I didn't know you'd gone back into farming.'

The Ultra stared back. The pale hair, so pale as to be almost white; the sharp-boned face, equally colourless eyes. The face of a fanatic. He'd been like it at College; all he'd needed was a Cause. He said, 'Where do you keep the Falcon?'

Rand gestured, briefly. He said, 'Round the back.'

'All right,' said the other. 'Open up. We're requisitioning.'

He moved ahead of them, prodded in the back by one of the guns. He unlocked the garage doors, ran the car into the yard. He'd have put his foot down, taken his chance; but it was useless, the gates were locked and chained. He slowed, set the handbrake; and one of the Ultras jerked his head. 'Right,' he said, 'out.' He heard the click as the other cocked his gun.

Hoyland spoke quickly. 'No,' he said. 'We can use a spare driver.' He ran round, climbed in. He pressed a pistol to Rand's ribs. He said, 'Do just what I say.' Rand nodded. He realized the other had saved his life.

The gate was swiftly dealt with. A hammering from one of the automatics; and the gunman put his heel to the splintered wood. It swung back; he eased the Falcon through, into a scene from Hell. Fronting was in uproar. A building was on fire; it lit the street as bright as day. There were running figures; and the air was full of din. Shots, and screams. He saw a man felled with a pickaxe handle. The assailant turned aside, fled into an alley. Rand realized things like that would be happening right across the Realm; old scores being settled, casual murder committed.

There was a big, squaresided vehicle. Four of the Ultras piled into it; the others dived into the Falcon. The van accelerated, moving fast. He followed.

More bodies lay about, in the path and roadway. He swerved round the first, couldn't miss the second. The nearside wheels passed over it, with a sickening double thud. Hoyland bared his teeth. 'That's it,' he said. 'You're getting the idea.'

The looters were active already. A shop window had been smashed, they were scrambling in and out. A gunman in the lead truck opened up. One fell; the others dropped their booty and ran. Rand said, 'What are you doing? What do you hope to gain?' and Hoyland said, 'Shut up.' The gun dug harder into his ribs.

The Middle Church was ablaze too; another big fire was burning behind the town hall. Hoyland said, 'Turn left.'

His throat dried. He'd realized where they were headed. 'No,' he whispered. 'No, Brad, you can't …' The Ultra laughed.

They pulled up short of the Kerosin Mansion, drew into the cover of some trees. The house was already under attack. Rand heard the clatter of automatic weapons, saw the answering flashes from the wall.

The van had pulled ahead. Two of the Ultras tumbled out, dragging what looked to be a heavy tube. They rammed the spiked tail into the ground, extended a pair of sturdy jointed legs. Hoyland prodded him with the gun. 'Out, fast,' he said. 'Leave the keys. Put your hands on top of the car.' He stepped back, barrelled Rand across the neck. He collapsed.

The first bomb was dropped into the mortar. A flash and roar. The missile fell short. The second though struck the big gates full on. Splinters flew, and one of the valves sagged inward. The gunner whooped, and elevated the barrel again. He began to bombard the grounds.

A man ran across, yelling. 'You fucking moron,' he said. 'We're already in.' He kicked the last bomb from the Ultra's hands. The other swore, rolled over sucking his fingers. Then he sat up. 'Kill the Pigs,' he said. He followed the rest, at the gallop. As he ran, he drew his pistol.

Rand hauled himself up slowly, leaned on the Falcon. One hand was to his head. He felt his neck, the warm stickiness there. He blinked giddily, stared round. At first things wouldn't focus; then awareness returned. He saw the shattered gates; beyond, the house was burning, shooting flames and sparks high into the sky. The flames caught the Cody rig, suddenly. Flashed from Lifter to Lifter. The String sagged, and began to fall.

The odd pistol shot still sounded; but in the main resistance seemed to have ceased. He staggered forward. One of the Ultras was curled under the gateway. The gun he had dropped lay an inch or two beyond his outstretched fingers. One of the new-style revolving arms as well. Rand checked it. One shot had been fired; the rest of the charges were intact.

He hurried through the grounds. There was a little house, set round with trees. He saw most of its side wall had gone.

He stepped through the opening. He had no torch; but the flamelight showed him as much as he needed to see. A body lay in the ruins. He recognized the dress. He'd bought it for her only a few weeks before. Other than that, identification was difficult. The corpse was headless.

Brad Hoyland was behind him. He licked his lips. He said. 'This shouldn't have happened.'

Rand straightened slowly, turned. 'No,' he said. 'It shouldn't.'

The other's eyes dilated. 'Rand,' he said. 'Now wait a minute, Rand. We didn't want to hurt her. But people do get hurt. It isn't our fault. It's the Pigs. They started it.'

He didn't answer, and the Ultra's face changed. 'All right,' he said. 'So we got the bourgeois bitch. Might as well get her tart.' He clawed at his waist, and Rand shot him through the heart.

They'd captured the Mistress Kerosina. They dragged her across the courtyard. One of the Ultras punched her in the face. She spat at him. They bound her to a kitchen chair, sat her where she could see her burning house.

They ripped her blouse away, and the Ultra giggled. He laid her shoulder open with a knife. Blood streamed instantly down her arm, began to dribble from her elbow. She looked at it incuriously. He cut her again. 'It's your tits next, Lady,' he said. 'Get ready …'

There was a little pressure on his back. 'Drop the knife,' said Rand gently. 'Step away. Slowly.'

The Ultra did as he was told. Finally he halted. He said, 'This far enough?'

'Yes,' said the other. 'I should think so.' He pulled the trigger. The Ultra shrieked, and tried to writhe away. He didn't get very far. You don't though, not with a shattered spine.

The rest had stood transfixed. He turned on them, and they bolted. He hurried to the Mistress Kerosina. He slashed the ropes, tore the ruined blouse into strips. He bound her arm as tightly as he could, took his jacket off and put it round her shoulders. She clutched it across her chest. 'I don't know why you bother,' she said dully. 'If you don't get me, the Vars will.'

'I'm sorry,' he said. 'It's all I can do.' She stared at him. Then she got up, walked off toward the flames. He ran back the way he had come.

A voice called, from the shadows by the gate. He hesitated; and she stepped forward. She said, 'Hello, Rand.' She swallowed. 'I knew they were coming for you,' she said. 'So I came too.'

He looked at her. Her hair was longer than he remembered it. She was wearing trews and a jerkin. A holster was strapped to her hip. So she was a gun girl too. 'Well,' he said, 'it seems to be my night.' He hit her. When she got up he knocked her down again. Janni crouched on hands and knees, hair hanging forward. He cocked the pistol.

Her voice was muffled. 'Yes,' she said, 'you'd better use it. Do it quickly though.' She shivered. 'You won't believe me of course,' she said. 'But I didn't have any choice. I had to go to him.'

He said, 'You had every choice.'

She shook her head. A drop of blood splashed on the cobbles. 'No,' she said. 'We'd have gone to Skyways. Both of us. And not come out again. He promised me.'

Rand set his mouth. 'Nice try,' he said. 'You could always spin a good tale though. He wouldn't have dared. Too much would have come out at the hearing.'

She shivered again. 'What hearing?' she said bitterly. 'He owned that place.' She touched her mouth. 'We were mad, doing what we were doing,' she said. 'It was obvious. It wouldn't have needed a hearing.'

He nodded. He said, 'I think I'm going to kill him.'

'You can't,' she said. 'He's already dead.'

'How do you know?'

She said, 'Because I shot him myself. Then we let them out of Skyways.'

He realized what he was holding. He flung it away, with loathing. He dropped to his knees, pressed with a kerchief and wiped. 'Janni,' he said. 'Janni, oh my God ...'

She stiffened. But he'd already heard it too. The shrill, rising and falling wail; the siren of a Battle Waggon, coming fast.

She scrambled to her feet. 'Quick,' she said. 'Quick, Rand ...' He ran with her, swung into the Falcon. He gunned the engine, moved off fast. Lights showed behind him, jizzing and bouncing. He hauled right, accelerated again. She said, 'Where are you going?'

'Kiteport,' he said. 'I've got contacts there.'

'It's useless,' she said. 'It's the same all over. Right through the Realm ...'

He swung the wheel. 'I'm not staying in the Realm,' he said. 'I'm going to the Islands. Tremarest. There's bound to be a ship ...'

She shook her head. She said, 'You won't make it, Rand.'

Everywhere, the night sky had blossomed fire. The flames were shocking, poppy-red. He detoured again and again, avoiding burning villages. The Falcon jarred and shook, wheels bouncing over potholes. Finally he found a better road. It ran south and slightly west. He said, 'This is for us.' He gripped her arm. 'We are going to make it, Jan,' he said. 'We've got to ...'

He stared. Ahead and to the right, a Cody string was rising. In place of the Observer's basket hung a great blazing symbol; the *ankh*, the looped cross of the Middle Doctrine. Beyond it was another and another. They stretched far into the west; the last bizarre signs of hope, in a crumbling world.

The night wore on. The road ahead became visible by degrees; grey cloud streaks grew overhead; between them was the lemon vividness of dawn.

She groaned. She said, 'Oh, no ...' She pointed. Lumbering toward them, jolting on the rough, was an Ultra Battle Waggon. It was moving fast, heading at an angle to cut them off.

He said, '*Get down ...*' He shoved her; and she ducked beneath the dash. He stared at the thing. The gap was closing fast. He changed gear, pushed his foot to the boards. The Falcon responded. He slammed back into top, held her as she bucked and leaped. He beat the big machine by fifty yards. As he passed, its forward armament set up a hammering.

Rand swerved, desperately. And again. Something spanged from metal. The windscreen starred, disintegrated. There was a rush of fresh, cold air. He swerved again; and a bend took the Ultras from sight. The firing ceased abruptly. They were clear; nor did he think the Cruiser would trouble to follow. They'd seen the Falcon's speed.

Janni uncoiled, slowly. He said, 'Are you all right?' and she nodded. She said, 'Yes, fine.' He gripped her hand. It was a miracle; the first of a very long night.

They rounded a further bend; and she pointed quietly. She said, 'Look. The sea.'

He glanced to the right. A pall of smoke was drifting from the west. His heart sank. That was Kiteport.

A mile on, the engine of the Falcon began to knock and miss. He coasted to a halt finally. The bonnet was instantly enveloped by a cloud of steam. He opened one of the long leaves and stared. The round that had passed between them had cracked the block.

Rand set his lips. He said, 'Come on.' He took her hand. He only looked back once. The Falcon was finished; but she'd served her turn. There was no emotion, no sense of loss. Strange, when he'd once felt such a pride in her. She was nothing to him now; she was a piece of worn-out steel.

The land was deceptive in its vastness. They walked an hour, but the sea seemed to be no closer. The sun broke through, for the first time in days. Long searchlight-beams sparkled from the water. It seemed ironic.

The road dipped, climbed again. Tackling the slope, Janni stumbled. He looked at her. The blood on her face had dried to long brown stripes; her skin looked chalk-pale by contrast. He dabbled the kerchief in a little wayside pool, wiped her neck and chin. Later he washed her hands. She clung to him. After a while he said, 'Come on. We can't stop now.'

They were on the high downs. The wind seethed in the short, cropped grass. Ahead, seeming still distant, the land edge was sharp-cut against the blue. He said, 'We're nearly there.' He pressed on; finally she shook her head. 'It's no good,' she said. 'I shall have to rest a minute.'

He sat with her. Wished he had a cigarette. He said, 'What happened to your folks?'

She looked at him expressionlessly. She said, 'They're dead.' Her eyes changed focus. 'Rand,' she said. 'Rand ...'

He stared back the way they had come. He saw it too. The red speck of a Battle Waggon. He grabbed her wrist, started to run. At an angle away from the road. It was useless, naturally. They'd already been seen; the thing altered course at once to intercept.

She collapsed finally. He dropped to his knees and held her. She whispered, 'I'm sorry.'

Rand kissed her. 'It's not your fault,' he said. 'At least I found you again. I'm sorry it didn't last longer.'

The great scarlet truck moved alongside smoothly. A little wait, and the engine cut. Silence fell; he could hear now, beyond the high plain of grass, the wash and crash of the sea.

She groped for the holster at her hip. He caught her wrist. 'No, Jan,' he said, 'it's useless. It only means you'd die that much quicker.'

A port opened in the Cruiser's side. Steps were lowered; and a tall man moved down them carefully. He wore the full robes of a Kitemaster. He was very old, his face lined and gaunt; but his eyes were brilliant, and he held himself erect. Two aides followed. They were also clad in scarlet; but they carried no guns. Instead, one held a great Staff of Power; slung on the other's shoulder was the sending apparatus of a wireless telegraph.

The priest walked forward. He stood awhile looking down, it seemed compassionately. Finally he spoke. 'Have no fear, my children,' he said. 'I am the Master Helman.' He smiled. He said, 'You gave us a long chase.'

Rand blinked, and swallowed. 'What's happening?' he said. 'What do you want with us?'

The other shook his head. 'What is happening,' he said, 'is that the Realm has become insane. But then, it always was a little mad. As to what I want with you . . .' He turned, and gestured.

Rand knew his jaw had sagged. A figure had appeared, in the sideport of the big machine. It was short, and inclined to dumpiness; it clutched a parasol, and wore a straw hat at a fetching angle. It said, ''Ello, Rand . . .'

He left Janni. He ran forward. 'Velvet,' he said. 'But . . . but . . .'

She clung to him. There were tears on her face. 'I wanted ter come back,' she said. 'I din' really want ter go. It was 'orrible. Bein' away from you. I daren't though. I din' think you'd want me.'

'You little fool,' he said. 'You silly little fool . . .' He shook his head. 'But how,' he said. 'The summerhouse . . .'

'Yeah,' she said. 'I know. Nasty, wadn' it? I seen it . . .'

He was conscious of not making sense. 'But who . . .' he said. 'It was your dress . . .'

Velvet looked a bit guilty. 'She liked ter do 'em up like that,' she said. 'Some o' the boys. Used ter turn 'er on.' She swallowed. 'I'd already scarpered,' she said. 'It was gettin' un'ealthy. Then the gentleman found me . . .'

He looked at the Master. 'But to do this,' he said. 'You're Vars . . .'

Helman smiled again. It seemed though there was infinite sadness in his eyes. 'The Vars, the Middlers,' he said. 'They're merely forms of speech. Folk see such things as the extremities of a ladder. But to me, philosophy is circular. Go far enough in either direction, and you meet your enemy.' He nodded to his aide. He said, 'Call them in.' The other inclined his head. He unslung the wireless apparatus.

Rand turned. Another figure had appeared in the doorway. She was tall and slender, with a mane of bronze-coloured hair. Her grave, lovely face was that of a child; but somehow he knew she was older. She hesitated at sight of the group, half-turned to the priest. She gave a little mewing cry. Helman moved forward. 'Her name is Tan,' he said. 'A *protégée* of mine for several years. She doesn't speak much; but she understands everything you say.' He took her hand. The girl stepped down. She moved a little awkwardly. Rand saw one leg was a mass of white scar tissue. The Kitemaster said, 'I want you to take her with you. A small boon.'

Rand shook his head. He said, 'Where to, Lord?'

The other said, 'You'll see.'

'Look,' said Velvet, awed. 'A Dragonfly …'

Rand stared. It was moving in purposefully, over the sea. He saw the silver glitter of it. The long, slim wings. Tan pointed, gave the little mewing cry again. Velvet took her hand. She said, 'She says it's pretty.'

The creature held course towards them. He began to realize the sheer size of it. It swept overhead, with a whirr and clatter; and he all but cringed. Helman laid a hand on his arm. 'Have no fear of it,' he said. 'It means you no ill.'

Velvet said, 'It's goin' ter *land* …'

It had banked, and turned. It was so graceful. It dropped down, low and lower; then it was bumping across the clifftop grass. He saw that what he had taken for eyes were the windows of a driving compartment; he could see the faces behind them now. On the thing's nose was a great spinning blade. Up close, the wings still glittered. He saw beneath its body were delicate spoked wheels. It moved toward the group, swung half away and stopped. A hatch opened in its side. Two figures climbed down; a man, and a woman. Both were fair; both wore tight fitting one-piece suits, as silver as the machine. 'They are from the World of Dragonflies,' said the priest. 'We've been in contact with them many years.' He smiled once more. 'You'll find it a very different place,' he said. 'You see they don't rob the earth, as we do. We began again, in the bad old way; and now we're paying for it. They take the Lord's true bounty; even their machines fly by the power of the sun. It will be strange, at first; but you'll walk free there, and live without fear.'

So there had been another people, all along. Rand said hesitantly, 'Will there be … others? Others like us?'

Helman nodded. 'We've been selecting carefully,' he said. 'For quite a long time now. Our world is dying; but many of its folk will be saved.' He nodded briefly to the west. 'A ship left yesterday,' he said, 'with some of your friends aboard. It was bound for Tremarest. It didn't sail under the Kites. They've served their purpose.'

The strangers approached. The taller spoke. 'I am Lanagro,' he said. 'This is Mada, my Lifepartner. Are these the folk you spoke of?' The Master said, 'They are.'

The woman made a little husky sound. She pointed. The stranger frowned. Then he hurried forward. He knelt at Tan's feet, looked into her face. He touched her ankle, placed his right hand gently on her knee. He moved the hand down, slowly; and she stared, amazed. Behind his fingers, the skin was no longer blemished.

One of the aides started back. He said huskily, 'A miracle.' But Lanagro smiled. 'No,' he said. 'A skill we have acquired. We have many others.'

Tan gave the little cry again. She pointed at the great machine. Velvet grinned. 'She says, can we get in?'

The Master nodded. He said, 'Take her, child.' He turned to the sky people. 'We send our best,' he said. 'We send Innocence, and Beauty. Cherish them.' Tan moved away a pace; then she ran back, impulsively. She dropped to her knees. She said, '*Thank … you … Lord …*' Helman touched her hair. He said, 'Go with God. Quickly, the machine is waiting.'

Rand said, 'Come with us, Master.' But the other shook his head.

'No,' he said. 'My place is here. In any case, I'm old. My life has run its course.'

He swallowed. He said, 'Try to save her, sir.'

'Save whom?'

Rand said, 'The Mistress Kerosina. She didn't ask to be the way she is. She didn't ask to be born.'

'I'll do what I can,' said Helman. He touched his shoulder. He said, 'Your feet are on the Way.'

Janni unslung the holster, laid it on the grass. 'Somehow,' she said, 'I don't think I'm going to need that any more.' She took Rand's hand.

The priest stood back and watched. The whirring of the Dragonfly's engine increased. It began to move, slowly at first. Its tail lifted; and it rose, lightly as thistledown. It banked once, swooped low overhead. He saw them wave, raised his Staff in salute. Then it was fading, across the sea. The last Helman saw was the silver flash of its wings.

He turned, nodded sombrely to his aides. They climbed aboard; and the big machine started up, rumbled away from the coast. It turned toward the smoke palls, hanging sullen on the horizon.

THE GRAIN KINGS

Weihnachtsabend	443
The White Boat	473
The Passing of the Dragons	491
The Trustie Tree	511
The Lake of Tuonela	522
The Grain Kings	541
I Lose Medea	588

For Anthony Whittome and Giles Gordon, who do the really hard part.

WEIHNACHTSABEND

1

The big car moved slowly, nosing its way along narrowing lanes. Here, beyond the little market town of Wilton, the snow lay thicker. Trees and bushes loomed in the headlights, coated with driven white. The tail of the Mercedes wagged slightly, steadied. Mainwaring heard the chauffeur swear under his breath. The link had been left live.

Dials let into the seatback recorded the vehicle's mechanical wellbeing: oil pressure, temperature, revs, k.p.h. Lights from the repeater glowed softly on his companion's face. She moved, restlessly; he saw the swing of yellow hair. He turned slightly. She was wearing a neat, brief kilt, heavy boots. Her legs were excellent.

He clicked the dial lights off. He said, 'Not much farther.'

He wondered if she was aware of the open link. He said, 'First time down?'

She nodded in the dark. She said, 'I was a bit overwhelmed.'

Wilton Great House sprawled across a hilltop five miles or more beyond the town. The car drove for some distance beside the wall that fringed the estate. The perimeter defences had been strengthened since Mainwaring's last visit. Watch-towers reared at intervals; the wall itself had been topped by multiple strands of wire.

The lodge gates were commanded by two new stone pillboxes. The Merc edged between them, stopped. On the road from London the snow had eased; now big flakes drifted again, lit by the headlights. Somewhere, orders were barked.

A man stepped forward, tapped at the window. Mainwaring buttoned it open. He saw a GFP armband, a hip holster with the flap tucked back. He said, 'Good evening, Captain.'

'*Guten Abend, mein Herr. Ihre Ausweiskarte?*'

Cold air gusted against Mainwaring's cheek. He passed across his identity card and security clearance, He said, '*Richard Mainwaring. Die rechte Hand des Gesandten. Fräulein Hunter, von meiner Abteilung.*'

A torch flashed over the papers, dazzled into his eyes, moved to examine the girl. She sat stiffly, staring ahead. Beyond the security officer Mainwaring made out two steel-helmeted troopers, automatics slung. In front of him the wipers clicked steadily.

The GFP man stepped back. He said, '*Ihre Ausweis wird in einer Woche ablaufen. Erneuen Sie Ihre Karte.*'

Mainwaring said, '*Vielen Dank, Herr Hauptmann. Frohe Weihnachten.*'

The man saluted stiffly, unclipped a walkie-talkie from his belt. A pause, and the gates swung back. The Merc creamed through. Mainwaring said, '*Bastard* ...'

She said, 'Is it always like this?'

He said, 'They're tightening up all round.'

She pulled her coat round her shoulders. She said, 'Frankly, I find it a bit scary.'

He said, 'Just the Minister taking care of his guests.'

Wilton stood in open downland set with great trees. Hans negotiated a bend, carefully, drove beneath half-seen branches. The wind moaned, zipping round a quarterlight. It was as if the car butted into a black tunnel, full of swirling pale flakes. He thought he saw her shiver. He said, 'Soon be there.'

The headlamps lit a rolling expanse of snow. Posts, buried nearly to their tops, marked the drive. Another bend, and the house showed ahead. The car lights swept across a façade of mullioned windows, crenellated towers. Hard for the uninitiated to guess, staring at the skilfully weathered stone, that the shell of the place was of reinforced concrete. The car swung right with a crunching of unseen gravel, and stopped. The ignition repeater glowed on the seatback.

Mainwaring said, 'Thank you, Hans. Nice drive.'

Hans said, 'My pleasure, sir.'

She flicked her hair free, picked up her handbag. He held the door for her. He said, 'OK, Diane?'

She shrugged. She said, 'Yes. I'm a bit silly sometimes.' She squeezed his hand, briefly. She said, 'I'm glad you'll be here. Somebody to rely on.'

Mainwaring lay back on the bed and stared at the ceiling. Inside as well as out, Wilton was a triumph of art over nature. Here, in the Tudor wing where most of the guests were housed, walls and ceilings were of wavy plaster framed by heavy oak beams. He turned his head. The room was dominated by a fireplace of yellow Ham stone; on the overmantel, carved in bold relief, the *Hakenkreuz* was flanked by the lion and eagle emblems of the Two Empires. A fire burned in the wrought-iron basket; the logs glowed cheerfully, casting wavering warm reflections across the ceiling. Beside the bed a bookshelf offered required reading: the Fuehrer's official biography, Shirer's *Rise of the Third Reich*, Cummings' monumental *Churchill: the Trial of Decadence*. There were a nicely bound set of Buchan novels, some Kiplings, a Shakespeare, a complete Wilde. A side table carried a stack of current magazines: *Connoisseur, The Field, Der Spiegel, Paris Match.* There was a washstand, its rail hung with dark blue towels; in the corner of the room were the doors to the bathroom and wardrobe, in which a servant had already neatly disposed his clothes.

He stubbed his cigarette, lit another. He swung his legs off the bed, poured himself a whisky. From the grounds, faintly, came voices, snatches of laughter. He heard the crash of a pistol, the rattle of an automatic. He walked to the window, pushed the curtain aside. Snow was still falling, drifting silently from the black sky; but the firing pits beside the big house were brightly lit. He watched the figures move and bunch for a while, let the curtain fall. He sat by the fire, shoulders hunched, staring into the flames. He was remembering the trip through London; the flags hanging limp over Whitehall, slow, jerking movement of traffic, the light tanks drawn up outside St James's. The Kensington road had been crowded, traffic edging and hooting; the vast frontage of Harrods looked grim and oriental against the louring sky. He frowned, remembering the call he had had before leaving the Ministry.

Kosowicz had been the name. From *Time International*; or so he had claimed. He'd refused twice to speak to him; but Kosowicz had been insistent. In the end, he'd asked his secretary to put him through.

Kosowicz had sounded very American. He said, 'Mr Mainwaring, I'd like to arrange a personal interview with your Minister.'

'I'm afraid that's out of the question. I must also point out that this communication is extremely irregular.'

Kosowicz said, 'What do I take that as, sir? A warning, or a threat?'

Mainwaring said carefully, 'It was neither. I merely observed that proper channels of approach do exist.'

Kosowicz said, 'Uh-huh. Mr Mainwaring, what's the truth behind this rumour that Action Groups are being moved into Moscow?'

Mainwaring said, 'Deputy Fuehrer Hess has already issued a statement on the situation. I can see that you're supplied with a copy.'

The phone said, 'I have it before me. Mr Mainwaring, what are you people trying to set up? Another Warsaw?'

Mainwaring said, 'I'm afraid I can't comment further, Mr Kosowicz. The Deputy Fuehrer deplored the necessity of force. The *Einsatzgruppen* have been alerted; at this time, that is all. They will be used if necessary to disperse militants. As of this moment, the need has not arisen.'

Kosowicz shifted his ground. 'You mentioned the Deputy Fuehrer, sir. I hear there was another bomb attempt two nights ago, can you comment on this?'

Mainwaring tightened his knuckles on the handset. He said, 'I'm afraid you've been misinformed. We know nothing of any such incident.'

The phone was silent for a moment. Then it said, 'Can I take your denial as official?'

Mainwaring said, 'This is not an official conversation. I'm not empowered to issue statements in any respect.'

The phone said, 'Yeah, channels do exist. Mr Mainwaring, thanks for your time.'

Mainwaring said, 'Goodbye.' He put the handset down, sat staring at it. After a while he lit a cigarette.

Outside the windows of the Ministry the snow still fell, a dark whirl and dance against the sky. His tea, when he came to drink it, was half cold.

The fire crackled and shifted. He poured himself another whisky, sat back. Before leaving for Wilton, he'd lunched with Winsby-Walker from Productivity. Winsby-Walker made it his business to know everything; but he had known nothing of a correspondent called Kosowicz. He thought, 'I should have checked with Security.' But then, Security would have checked with him.

He sat up, looked at his watch. The noise from the ranges had diminished. He turned his mind with a deliberate effort into another channel. The new thoughts brought no more comfort. Last Christmas he had spent with his mother; now, that couldn't happen again. He remembered other Christmases, back across the years. Once, to the child unknowing, they had been gay affairs of crackers and toys. He remembered the scent and texture of pine branches, closeness of candlelight; and books read by torchlight under the sheets, the hard angles of the filled pillowslip, heavy at the foot of the bed. Then, he had been complete; only later, slowly, had come the knowledge of failure. And with it, loneliness. He thought, 'She wanted to see me settled. It didn't seem much to ask.'

The Scotch was making him maudlin. He drained the glass, walked through to the bathroom. He stripped, and showered. Towelling himself, he thought, *Richard Mainwaring, Personal Assistant to the British Minister of Liaison*. Aloud he said, 'One must remember the compensations.'

He dressed, lathered his face and began to shave. He thought, *Thirty-five is the exact middle of one's life*. He was remembering another time with the girl Diane when just for a little while some magic had interposed. Now, the affair was never mentioned between them. Because of James. Always, of course, there is a James.

He towelled his face, applied aftershave. Despite himself, his mind had drifted back to the phone call. One fact was certain: there had been a major security spillage. Somebody somewhere had supplied Kosowicz with closely guarded information. That same someone, presumably, had supplied a list of ex-directory lines. He frowned, grappling with the problem. One country, and one only, opposed the Two Empires with gigantic, latent strength. To that country had shifted the focus of Semitic nationalism. And Kosowicz had been an American.

He thought, 'Freedom, schmeedom. Democracy is Jew-shaped.' He frowned again, fingering his face. It didn't alter the salient fact. The tip-off had come from the Freedom Front; and he had been contacted, however obliquely. Now, he had become an accessory; the thought had been nagging at the back of his brain all day.

He wondered what they could want of him. There was a rumour – a nasty rumour – that you never found out. Not till the end, till you'd done whatever was required from you. They were untiring, deadly and subtle. He hadn't run squalling to Security at the first hint of danger; but that would have been allowed for. Every turn and twist would have been allowed for.

Every squirm on the hook.

He grunted, angry with himself. Fear was half their strength. He buttoned his shirt, remembering the guards at the gates, the wire and pillboxes. Here, of all places, nothing could reach him. For a few days he could forget the whole affair. He said aloud, 'Anyway, I don't even matter. I'm not important.' The thought cheered him, nearly.

He clicked the light off, walked through to his room, closed the door behind him. He crossed to the bed and stood quite still, staring at the bookshelf. Between Shirer and the Churchill tome there rested a third slim volume. He reached to touch the spine, delicately; read the author's name, Geissler, and the title, *Toward Humanity*. Below the title, like a topless Cross of Lorraine, were the twin linked 'F's' of the Freedom Front.

Ten minutes ago the book hadn't been there.

He walked to the door. The corridor beyond was deserted. From somewhere in the house, faintly, came music: *Till Eulenspiegel*. There were no nearer sounds. He closed the door again, locked it. Turned back and saw the wardrobe stood slightly ajar.

His case still lay on the side table. He crossed to it, took out the Lüger. The feel of the heavy pistol was comforting. He pushed the clip home, thumbed the safety forward, chambered a round. The breech closed with a hard snap. He walked to the wardrobe, shoved the door wide with his foot.

Nothing there.

He let his held breath escape with a little hiss. He pressed the clip release, ejected the cartridge, laid the gun on the bed. He stood again looking at the shelf. He thought, *I must have been mistaken*.

He took the book down, carefully. Geissler had been banned since publication in every province of the Two Empires; Mainwaring himself had never even seen a copy. He squatted on the edge of the bed, opened it at random.

The doctrine of Aryan co-ancestry, seized on so eagerly by the English middle classes, had the superficial reasonableness of most theories ultimately traceable to Rosenberg. Churchill's answer, in one sense, had already been made; but Chamberlain, and the country, turned to Hess …

The Cologne settlement, though seeming to offer hope of security to Jews already domiciled in Britain, in fact paved the way for campaigns of intimidation and extortion similar to those already undertaken in history, notably by King John. The comparison is not unapt; for the English bourgeoisie, *anxious to construct a rationale, discovered many unassailable precedents. A true Sign of the Times, almost certainly, was the resurgence of interest in the novels of Sir Walter Scott. By 1942 the lesson had been learned on both sides; and the Star of David was a common sight on the streets of most British cities.*

The wind rose momentarily in a long wail, shaking the window casement. Mainwaring glanced up, turned his attention back to the book. He leafed through several pages.

In 1940, her Expeditionary Force shattered, her allies quiescent or defeated, the island truly stood alone. Her proletariat, bedevilled by bad leadership, weakened by a gigantic depression, was effectively without a voice. Her aristocracy, like their Junker *counterparts, embraced coldly what could no longer be ignored; while after the Whitehall* Putsch *the Cabinet was reduced to the status of an Executive Council …*

The knock at the door made him start, guiltily. He pushed the book away. He said, 'Who's that?'

She said, 'Me. Richard, aren't you ready?'

He said, 'Just a minute.' He stared at the book, then placed it back on the shelf. He thought, *That at least wouldn't be expected.* He slipped the Lüger into his case and closed it. Then he went to the door.

She was wearing a lacy black dress. Her shoulders were bare; her hair, worn loose, had been brushed till it gleamed. He stared at her a moment, stupidly. Then he said, 'Please come in.'

She said, 'I was starting to wonder … Are you all right?'

'Yes. Yes, of course.'

She said, 'You look as if you've seen a ghost.'

He smiled. He said, 'I expect I was taken aback. Those Aryan good looks.'

She grinned at him. She said, 'I'm half Irish, half English, half Scandinavian. If you have to know.'

'That doesn't add up.'

She said, 'Neither do I, most of the time.'

'Drink?'

'Just a little one. We shall be late.'

He said, 'It's not very formal tonight.' He turned away, fiddling with his tie.

She sipped her drink, pointed her foot, scuffed her toe on the carpet. She said, 'I expect you've been to a lot of house parties.'

He said, 'One or two.'

She said, 'Richard, are they ...?'

'Are they what?'

She said, 'I don't know. You can't help hearing things.'

He said, 'You'll be all right. One's very much like the next.'

She said, 'Are you honestly OK?'

'Sure.'

She said, 'You're all thumbs. Here, let me.' She reached up, knotted deftly. Her eyes searched his face for a moment, moving in little shifts and changes of direction. She said, 'There. I think you just need looking after.'

He said carefully, 'How's James?'

She stared a moment longer. She said, 'I don't know. He's in Nairobi. I haven't seen him for months.'

He said, 'I am a bit nervous, actually.'

'Why?'

He said, 'Escorting a rather lovely blonde.'

She tossed her head, and laughed. She said, 'You need a drink as well then.'

He poured whisky, said, 'Cheers.' The book, now, seemed to be burning into his shoulderblades.

She said, 'As a matter of fact, you're looking rather fetching yourself.'

He thought, 'This is the night when all things come together. There should be a word for it.' Then he remembered about *Till Eulenspiegel.*

She said, 'We'd honestly better go down.'

Lights gleamed in the Great Hall, reflecting from polished boards, dark linenfold panelling. At the nearer end of the chamber a huge fire burned. Beneath the minstrels' gallery long tables had been set. Informal or not, they shone with glass and silverware. Candles glowed amid wreaths of dark evergreen; beside each place was a rolled crimson napkin.

In the middle of the Hall, its tip brushing the coffered ceiling, stood a Christmas tree. Its branches were hung with apples, baskets of sweets, red paper roses; at its base were piled gifts in gay-striped wrappers. Round the tree folk stood in groups, chatting and laughing. Richard saw Müller, the Defence Minister, with a striking-looking blonde he took to be his wife; beside them was a tall, monocled man who was something or other in Security. There was a group of GSP officers in their dark, neat uniforms, beyond them half a dozen Liaison people. He saw Hans the chauffeur standing head bent, nodding intently, smiling at some remark; and thought as he had thought before, how he looked like a big, handsome ox.

Diane had paused in the doorway, and linked her arm through his. But the Minister had already seen them. He came weaving through the crowd, a glass in his hand. He was wearing tight black trews, a dark blue roll-neck shirt. He looked happy and relaxed. He said, 'Richard. And my dear Miss Hunter. We'd nearly given you up for lost. After all, Hans Trapp is about. Now, some drinks. And come, do come; please join my friends. Over here, where it is warm.'

She said, 'Who's Hans Trapp?'

Mainwaring said, 'You'll find out in a bit.'

A little later the Minister said, 'Ladies and gentlemen, I think we may be seated.'

The meal was superb, the wine abundant. By the time the brandy was served Richard found himself talking more easily, and the Geissler copy pushed nearly to the back of his mind. The traditional toasts – King and Fuehrer, the provinces, the Two Empires – were drunk; then the Minister clapped his hands for quiet. 'My friends,' he said, 'tonight, this special night when we can all mix so freely, is *Weihnachtsabend*. It means, I suppose, many things to the many of us here. But let us remember, first and foremost, that this is the night of the children. Your children, who have come with you to share part at least of this very special Christmas.'

He paused. 'Already,' he said, 'they have been called from their crèche; soon, they will be with us. Let me show them to you.' He nodded; at the gesture servants wheeled forward a heavy, ornate box. A drape was twitched aside, revealing the grey surface of a big TV screen. Simultaneously, the lamps that lit the Hall began to dim. Diane turned to Mainwaring, frowning; he touched her hand, gently, and shook his head.

Save for the firelight, the Hall was now nearly dark. The candles guttered in their wreaths, flames stirring in some draught; in the hush, the droning of the wind round the great façade of the place was once more audible. The lights would be out, now, all over the house.

'For some of you,' said the Minister, 'this is your first visit here. For you, I will explain.

'On *Weihnachtsabend* all ghosts and goblins walk. The demon Hans Trapp is abroad; his face is black and terrible, his clothing the skins of bears. Against him comes the Lightbringer, the Spirit of Christmas. Some call her Lucia Queen, some *Das Christkind*. See her now.'

The screen lit up.

She moved slowly, like a sleepwalker. She was slender, and robed in white. Her ashen hair tumbled round her shoulders; above her head glowed a diadem of burning tapers. Behind her trod the Star Boys with their wands and tinsel robes; behind again came a little group of children. They ranged in age from eight- and nine-year-olds to toddlers. They gripped each other's hands, apprehensively, setting feet in line like cats, darting terrified glances at the shadows to either side.

'They lie in darkness, waiting,' said the Minister softly. 'Their nurses have left them. If they cry out, there is none to hear. So they do not cry out. And one by one she has called them. They see her light pass beneath the door; and they must rise and follow. Here, where we sit, is warmth. Here is safety. Their gifts are waiting; to reach them they must run the gauntlet of the dark.'

The camera angle changed. Now they were watching the procession from above. The Lucia Queen stepped steadily; the shadows she cast leaped and flickered on panelled walls.

'They are in the Long Gallery now,' said the Minister, 'almost directly above us. They must not falter, they must not look back. Somewhere, Hans Trapp is hiding. From Hans, only *Das Christkind* can protect them. See how close they bunch behind her light!'

A howling began, like the crying of a wolf. In part it seemed to come from the screen, in part to echo through the Hall itself. The *Christkind* turned, raising her arms; the howling split into a many-voiced cadence, died to a mutter. In its place came a distant huge thudding, like the beating of a drum.

Diane said abruptly, 'I don't find this particularly funny.'

Mainwaring said, 'It isn't supposed to be. Shh.'

The Minister said evenly, 'The Aryan child must know, from earliest years, the darkness that surrounds him. He must learn to fear, and to overcome that fear. He must learn to be strong. The Two Empires were not built by weakness; weakness will not sustain them. There is no place for it. This in part your children already know. The house is big, and dark; but they will win through to the light. They fight as the Empires once fought. For their birthright.'

The shot changed again, showed a wide, sweeping staircase. The head of the little procession appeared, began to descend. 'Now, where is our friend Hans?' said the Minister. '*Ah* …'

Her grip tightened convulsively on Mainwaring's arm. A black-smeared face loomed at the screen. The bogey snarled, clawing at the camera; then turned, loped swiftly towards the staircase. The children shrieked, and bunched; instantly the air was wild with din. Grotesque figures capered and leaped; hands grabbed, clutching. The column was buffeted and swirled; Mainwaring saw a child bowled completely over. The screaming reached a high pitch of terror; and the *Christkind* turned, arms once more raised. The goblins and were-things backed away, growling, into shadow; the slow march was resumed.

The Minister said, 'They are nearly here. And they are good children, worthy of their race. Prepare the tree.'

Servants ran forward with tapers to light the many candles. The tree sprang from gloom, glinting, black-green; and Mainwaring thought for the first time what a dark thing it was, although it blazed with light.

The big doors at the end of the Hall were flung back; and the children came tumbling through. Tear-stained and sobbing they were, some bruised; but all, before they ran to the tree, stopped, made obeisance to the strange creature who had brought them through the dark. Then the crown was lifted, the tapers extinguished; and Lucia Queen became a child like the rest, a slim, barefooted girl in a gauzy white dress.

The Minister rose, laughing. 'Now,' he said, 'music, and some more wine. Hans Trapp is dead. My friends, one and all, and children; *frohe Weihnachten*!'

Diane said, 'Excuse me a moment.'

Mainwaring turned. He said, 'Are you all right?'

She said, 'I'm just going to get rid of a certain taste.'

He watched her go, concernedly; and the Minister had his arm, was talking. 'Excellent, Richard,' he said. 'It has gone excellently so far, don't you think?'

Richard said, 'Excellently, sir.'

'Good, good. Eh, Heidi, Erna . . . and Frederick, is it Frederick? What have you got there? Oh, very fine . . .' He steered Mainwaring away, still with his fingers tucked beneath his elbow. Squeals of joy sounded; somebody had discovered a sled, tucked away behind the tree. The Minister said, 'Look at them; how happy they are now. I would like children, Richard. Children of my own. Sometimes I think I have given too much . . . Still, the opportunity remains. I am younger than you, do you realize that? This is the Age of Youth.'

Mainwaring said, 'I wish the Minister every happiness.'

'Richard, Richard, you must learn not to be so very correct at all times. Unbend a little, you are too aware of dignity. You are my friend. I trust you; above all others, I trust you. Do you realize this?'

Richard said, 'Thank you, sir. I do.'

The Minister seemed bubbling over with some inner pleasure. He said, 'Richard, come with me. Just for a moment. I have prepared a special gift for you. I won't keep you from the party very long.'

Mainwaring followed, drawn as ever by the curious dynamism of the man. The Minister ducked through an arched doorway, turned right and left, descended a narrow flight of stairs. At the bottom the way was barred by a door of plain grey steel. The Minister pressed his palm flat to a sensor plate; a click, the whine of some mechanism, and the door swung inward.

Beyond was a further flight of concrete steps, lit by a single lamp in a heavy well-glass. Chilly air blew upward. Mainwaring realized, with something approaching a shock, that they had entered part of the bunker system that honeycombed the ground beneath Wilton.

The Minister hurried ahead of him, palmed a further door. He said, 'Toys, Richard. All toys. But they amuse me.' Then, catching sight of Mainwaring's face, 'Come, man, come! You are more nervous than the children, frightened of poor old Hans!'

The door gave on to a darkened space. There was a heavy, sweetish smell that Mainwaring, for a whirling moment, couldn't place. His companion propelled him forward, gently. He resisted, pressing back; and the Minister's arm shot by him. A click, and the place was flooded with light. He saw a wide, low area, also concrete-built. To one side, already polished and gleaming, stood the Mercedes, next to it the Minister's private Porsche. There were a couple of Volkswagens, a Ford Executive; and in the farthest corner a vision in glinting white. A Lamborghini. They had emerged in the garage underneath the house.

The Minister said, 'My private short cut.' He walked forward to the Lamborghini, stood running his fingers across the low, broad bonnet. He said, 'Look at her, Richard. Here, sit in. Isn't she a beauty? Isn't she fine?'

Mainwaring said, 'She certainly is.'

'You like her?'

Mainwaring smiled. He said, 'Very much, sir. Who wouldn't?'

The Minister said, 'Good, I'm so pleased. Richard, I'm upgrading you. She's yours. Enjoy her.'

Mainwaring stared.

The Minister said, 'Here, man. Don't look like that, like a fish. Here, see. Logbook, your keys. All entered up, finished.' He gripped Mainwaring's shoulders, swung him round laughing. He said, 'You've worked well for me. The Two Empires don't forget; their good friends, their servants.'

Mainwaring said, 'I'm deeply honoured, sir.'

'Don't be honoured. You're still being formal. Richard ...'

'Sir?'

The Minister said, 'Stay by me. Stay by me. Up there ... they don't understand. But we understand ... eh? These are difficult times. We must be together, always together. Kingdom and Reich. Apart ... we could be destroyed!' He turned away, placed clenched hands on the roof of the car. He said, 'Here, all this. Jewry, the Americans ... Capitalism. They must stay afraid. Nobody fears an Empire divided. It would fall!'

Mainwaring said, 'I'll do my best, sir. We all will.'

The Minister said, 'I know, I know. But, Richard, this afternoon. I was playing with swords. Silly little swords.'

Mainwaring thought, *I know how he keeps me. I can see the mechanism. But I mustn't imagine I know the entire truth.*

The Minister turned back, as if in pain. He said, 'Strength is Right. It has to be. But Hess ...'

Mainwaring said slowly, 'We've tried before, sir ...'

The Minister slammed his fist on to metal. He said, 'Richard, don't you see? It wasn't us. Not this time. It was his own people. Baumann, von Thaden ... I can't tell. He's an old man, he doesn't matter any more. It's an idea they want to kill, Hess is an idea. Do you understand? It's *Lebensraum*. Again ... Half the world isn't enough.'

He straightened. He said, 'The worm, in the apple. It gnaws, gnaws ... But we are Liaison. We matter, so much. Richard, be my eyes. Be my ears.'

Mainwaring stayed silent, thinking about the book in his room; and the Minister once more took his arm. He said, 'The shadows, Richard. They were never closer. Well might we teach our children to fear the dark. But ... not in our time. Eh? Not for us. There is life, and hope. So much we can do ...'

Mainwaring thought, 'Maybe it's the wine I drank. I'm being pressed too hard.' A dull, queer mood, almost of indifference, had fallen on him. He followed his Minister without complaint, back through the bunker complex, up to where the great fire and the tapers on the tree burned low. He heard the singing mixed with the wind-voice, watched the children rock heavy-eyed, carolling sleep. The house seemed winding down, to rest; and she had gone, of course. He sat in a corner and drank wine and brooded, watched the Minister move from group to group until he too was gone, the Hall nearly empty and the servants clearing away.

He found his own self, his inner self, dozing at last as it dozed at each day's end. Tiredness, as ever, had come like a benison. He rose carefully, walked to the door. He thought, 'I shan't be missed here.' Shutters closed, in his head.

He found his key, unlocked his room. He thought, 'Now, she will be waiting. Like all the letters that never came, the phones that never rang.' He opened the door.

She said, 'What kept you?'

He closed the door behind him, quietly. The fire crackled in the little room, the curtains were drawn against the night. She sat by the hearth, barefooted, still in her party dress. Beside her on the carpet were glasses, an ashtray with half-smoked stubs. One lamp was burning; in the warm light her eyes were huge and dark.

He looked across to the bookshelf. The Geissler stood where he had left it. He said, 'How did you get in?'

She chuckled. She said, 'There was a spare key on the back of the door. Didn't you see me steal it?'

He walked toward her, stood looking down. He thought, *Adding another fragment to the puzzle. Too much, too complicated.*

She said, 'Are you angry?'

He said, 'No.'

She patted the floor. She said gently, 'Please, Richard. Don't be cross.'

He sat, slowly, watching her.

She said, 'Drink?' He didn't answer. She poured one anyway. She said, 'What were you doing all this time? I thought you'd be up hours ago.'

He said, 'I was talking to the Minister.'

She traced a pattern on the rug with her forefinger. Her hair fell forward, golden and heavy, baring the nape of her neck. She said, 'I'm sorry about earlier on. I was stupid. I think I was a bit scared too.'

He drank, slowly. He felt like a run-down machine. Hell to have to start thinking again at this time of night. He said, 'What were you doing?'

She watched up at him. Her eyes were candid. She said, 'Sitting here. Listening to the wind.'

He said, 'That couldn't have been much fun.'

She shook her head, slowly, eyes fixed on his face. She said softly, 'You don't know me at all.'

He was quiet again. She said, 'You don't believe in me, do you?'

He thought, *You need understanding. You're different from the rest; and I'm selling myself short.* Aloud he said, 'No.'

She put the glass down, smiled, took his glass away. She hotched towards him across the rug, slid her arm round his neck. She said, 'I was thinking about you. Making my mind up.' She kissed him. He felt her tongue pushing, opened his lips. She said, '*Mmm* …' She sat back a little, smiling. She said, 'Do you mind?'

'No.'

She pressed a strand of hair across her mouth, parted her teeth, kissed again. He felt himself react, involuntarily; and felt her touch and squeeze.

She said, 'This is a silly dress. It gets in the way.' She reached behind her. The fabric parted; she pushed it down, to the waist. She said, 'Now it's like last time.'

He said slowly, 'Nothing's ever like last time.'

She rolled across his lap, lay looking up. She whispered, 'I've put the clock back.'

Later in the dream she said, 'I was so silly.'

'What do you mean?'

She said, 'I was shy. That was all. You weren't really supposed to go away.'

He said, 'What about James?'

'He's got somebody else. I didn't know what I was missing.'

He let his hand stray over her; and present and immediate past became confused so that as he held her he still saw her kneeling, firelight dancing on her body. He reached for her and she was ready again; she fought, chuckling, taking it bareback, staying all the way.

Much later he said, 'The Minister gave me a Lamborghini.'

She rolled on to her belly, lay chin in hands watching under a tangle of hair. She said, 'And now you've got yourself a blonde. What are you going to do with us?'

He said, 'None of it's real.'

She said, '*Oh* . . .' She punched him. She said, 'Richard, you make me cross. It's happened, you idiot. That's all. It happens to everybody.' She scratched again with a finger on the carpet. She said, 'I hope you've made me pregnant. Then you'd have to marry me.'

He narrowed his eyes; and the wine began again, singing in his head.

She nuzzled him. She said, 'You asked me once. Say it again.'

'I don't remember.'

She said, 'Richard, please . . .' So he said, 'Diane, will you marry me?' And she said, 'Yes, yes, yes,' then afterwards awareness came and though it wasn't possible he took her again and that time was finest of all, tight and sweet as honey. He'd fetched pillows from the bed and the counterpane, they curled close and he found himself talking, talking, how it wasn't the sex, it was shopping in Marlborough and having tea and seeing the sun set from White Horse Hill and being together, together; then she pressed fingers to his mouth and he fell with her in sleep past cold and loneliness and fear, past deserts and unlit places, down maybe to where spires reared gold and tree leaves moved and dazzled and white cars sang on roads and suns burned inwardly, lighting new worlds.

He woke, and the fire was low. He sat up, dazed. She was watching him. He stroked her hair a while, smiling; then she pushed away. She said, 'Richard, I have to go now.'

'Not yet.'

'It's the middle of the night'

He said, 'It doesn't matter.'

She said, 'It does. He mustn't know.'

'Who?'

She said, 'You know who. You know why I was asked here.'

He said, 'He's not like that. Honestly.'

She shivered. She said, 'Richard, please. Don't get me in trouble.' She smiled. She said, 'It's only till tomorrow. Only a little while.'

He stood, awkwardly, and held her, pressing her warmth close. Shoeless, she was tiny; her shoulder fitted beneath his armpit.

Halfway through dressing she stopped and laughed, leaned a hand against the wall. She said, 'I'm all woozy.'

Later he said, 'I'll see you to your room.'

She said, 'No, please. I'm all right.' She was holding her handbag, and her hair was combed. She looked, again, as if she had been to a party.

At the door she turned. She said, 'I love you, Richard. Truly.' She kissed again, quickly; and was gone.

He closed the door, dropped the latch. He stood a while looking round the room. In the fire a burned-through log broke with a snap, sending up a little whirl of sparks. He walked to the washstand, bathed his face and hands. He shook the counterpane out on the bed, rearranged the pillows. Her scent still clung to him; he remembered how she had felt, and what she had said.

He crossed to the window, pushed it ajar. Outside, the snow lay in deep swaths and drifts. Starlight gleamed from it, ghost-white; and the whole great house was mute. He stood feeling the chill move against his skin; and in all the silence a voice drifted far-off and clear. It came maybe from the guardhouses, full of distance and peace.

'Stille Nacht, heilige Nacht,
alles schläft, einsam wacht . . .'

He walked to the bed, pulled back the covers. The sheets were crisp and spotless, fresh-smelling. He smiled, and turned off the lamp.

'Nur das traute, hochheilige Paar.
Holder Knabe mit lochigem Haar . . .'

In the wall of the room, an inch behind the plasterwork, a complex little machine hummed. A spool of delicate golden wire shook slightly; but the creak of the opening window had been the last thing to interest the recorder, the singing alone couldn't activate its relays. A micro-switch tripped, inaudibly; valve filaments faded, and died. Mainwaring lay back in the last of the firelight, and closed his eyes.

'Schlaf' in himmlischer Ruh,
'Schlaf' in himmlischer Ruh . . .'

2

Beyond drawn curtains, brightness flicks on.

The sky is a hard, clear blue; icy, full of sunlight. The light dazzles back from the brilliant land. Far things – copses, hills, solitary trees – stand sharp-etched. Roofs and eaves carry hummocks of whiteness, twigs a three-inch crest. In the stillness, here and there, the snow cracks and falls, powdering.

The shadows of the riders jerk and undulate. The quiet is interrupted. Hooves ring on swept courtyards or stamp muffled, churning the snow. It seems the air itself has been rendered crystalline by cold; through it the voices break and shatter, brittle as glass.

'Guten Morgen, Hans . . .'

'Verflucht kalt!'

'Der Hundenmeister sagt, sehr gefahrlich!'

'Macht nichts! Wir erwischen es bevor dem Wald!'

A rider plunges beneath an arch. The horse snorts and curvets.

'Ich wette dir fünfzig amerikanische Dollar!'

'Einverstanden! Heute, habe ich Glück!'

The noise, the jangling and stamping, rings back on itself. Cheeks flush, perception is heightened; for more than one of the riders, the early courtyard reels. Beside the house door trestles have been set up. A great bowl is carried, steaming. The cups are raised, the toasts given; the responses ring again, crashing.

'The Two Empires . . .!'

'The Hunt . . .!'

Now, time is like a tight-wound spring. The dogs plunge forward, six to a handler, leashes straining, choke links creaking and snapping. Behind them jostle the riders. The bobbing scarlet coats splash across the snow. In the house drive an officer salutes; another strikes gloved palms together, nods. The gates whine open.

And across the country for miles around doors slam, bolts are shot, shutters closed, children scurried indoors. Village streets, muffled with snow, wait dumbly. Somewhere a dog barks, is silenced. The houses squat sullen, blind-eyed. The word has gone out, faster than horses could gallop. Today the Hunt will run; on snow.

The riders fan out, across a speckled waste of fields. A check, a questing; and the horns begin to yelp. Ahead the dogs bound and leap, black spots against whiteness. The horns cry again; but these hounds run mute. The riders sweep forward, on to the line.

Now, for the hunters, time and vision are fragmented. Twigs and snow merge in a racing blur; and tree-boles, ditches, gates. The tide reaches a crest of land, pours down the opposing slope. Hedges rear, mantled with white; and muffled thunder is interrupted by sailing silence, the smash and crackle of landing. The View sounds, harsh and high; and frenzy, and the racing blood, discharge intelligence. A horse goes down, in a gigantic flailing; another rolls, crushing its rider into the snow. A mount runs riderless. The Hunt, destroying, destroys itself unaware.

There are cottages, a paling fence. The fence goes over, unnoticed. A chicken house erupts in a cloud of flung crystals; birds run squawking, under the hooves. Caps are lost, flung away; hair flogs wild. Whips flail, spurs rake streaming flanks; and the woods are close. Twigs lash, and branches; snow falls, thudding. The crackling, now, is all around.

At the end, it is always the same. The handlers close in, yodelling, waist-high in trampled brush; the riders force close and closer, mounts sidling and shaking; and silence falls. Only the quarry, reddened, flops and twists; the thin high noise it makes is the noise of anything in pain.

Now, if he chooses, the *Jagdmeister* may end the suffering. The crash of the pistol rings hollow; and birds erupt, high from frozen twigs, wheel with the echoes and cry. The pistol fires again; and the quarry lies still. In time, the shaking stops; and a dog creeps forward, begins to lick.

Now a slow movement begins; a spreading-out, away from the place. There are mutterings, a laugh that chokes to silence. The fever passes. Somebody begins to shiver; and a girl, blood glittering on cheek and neck, puts a glove to her forehead and moans. The Need has come and gone; for a little while, the Two Empires have purged themselves.

The riders straggle back on tired mounts, shamble in through the gates. As the last enters, a closed black van starts up, drives away. In an hour, quietly, it returns; and the gates swing shut behind it.

Surfacing from deepest sleep was like rising, slowly, through a warm sea. For a time, as Mainwaring lay eyes closed, memory and awareness were confused so that she was with him and the room a recollected, childhood place. He rubbed his face, yawned, shook his head; and the knocking that had roused him came again. He said, 'Yes?'

The voice said, 'Last breakfast in fifteen minutes, sir.'

He called, 'Thank you,' heard the footsteps pad away.

He pushed himself up, groped on the side table for his watch, held it close to his eyes. It read ten-forty-five.

He swung the bedclothes back, felt air tingle on his skin. She had been with him, certainly, in the dawn; his body remembered the succubus, with nearly painful strength. He looked down smiling, walked to the bathroom. He showered, towelled himself, shaved and dressed. He closed his door and locked it, walked to the breakfast room. A few couples still sat over their coffee; he smiled a good morning, took a window seat. Beyond the double panes the snow piled thickly; its reflection lit the room with a white, inverted brilliance. He ate slowly, hearing distant shouts. On the long slope behind the house, groups of children pelted each other vigorously. Once a toboggan came into sight, vanished behind a rising swell of ground.

He had hoped he might see her, but she didn't come. He drank coffee, smoked a cigarette. He walked to the television lounge. The big colour screen showed a children's party taking place in a Berlin hospital. He watched for a while. The door behind him clicked a couple of times, but it wasn't Diane.

There was a second guests' lounge, not usually much frequented at this time of the year; and a reading room and library. He wandered through them, but there was no sign of her. It occurred to him she might not yet be up; at Wilton there were few hard-and-fast rules for Christmas Day. He thought, 'I should have checked her room number.' He wasn't even sure in which of the guest wings she had been placed.

The house was quiet; it seemed most of the visitors had taken to their rooms. He wondered if she could have ridden with the Hunt; he'd heard it vaguely, leaving and returning. He doubted if the affair would have held much appeal.

He strolled back to the TV lounge, watched for an hour or more. By lunchtime he was feeling vaguely piqued; and sensing too the rise of a curious unease. He went back to his room, wondering if by any chance she had gone there; but the miracle was not repeated. The room was empty.

The fire was burning, and the bed had been remade. He had forgotten the servants' pass keys. The Geissler copy still stood on the shelf. He took it down, stood weighing it in his hand and frowning. It was, in a sense, madness to leave it there.

He shrugged, put the thing back. He thought, *So who reads bookshelves anyway?* The plot, if plot there had been, seemed absurd now in the clearer light of day. He stepped into the corridor, closed the door and locked it behind him. He tried as far as possible to put the book from his mind. It represented a problem; and problems, as yet, he wasn't prepared to cope with. Too much else was going on in his brain.

He lunched alone, now with a very definite pang; the process was disquietingly like that of other years. Once he thought he caught sight of her in the corridor. His heart thumped; but it was the other blonde, Müller's wife. The gestures, the fall of the hair, were similar; but this woman was taller.

He let himself drift into a reverie. Images of her, it seemed, were engraved on his mind; each to be selected now, studied, placed lovingly aside. He saw the firelit texture of her hair and skin, her lashes brushing her cheek as she lay in his arms and slept. Other memories, sharper, more immediate still, throbbed like little shocks in the mind. She tossed her head, smiling; her hair swung, touched the point of a breast.

He pushed his cup away, rose. At fifteen hundred, patriotism required her presence in the TV lounge. As it required the presence of every other guest. Then, if not before, he would see her. He reflected, wryly, that he had waited half a lifetime for her; a little longer now would do no harm.

He took to prowling the house again; the Great Hall, the Long Gallery where the *Christkind* had walked. Below the windows that lined it was a snow-covered roof. The tart, reflected light struck upward, robbing the place of mystery. In the Great Hall they had already removed the tree. He watched household staff hanging draperies, carrying in stacks of gilded cane chairs. On the Minstrels' Gallery a pile of odd-shaped boxes proclaimed that the orchestra had arrived.

At fourteen hundred hours he walked back to the TV lounge. A quick glance assured him she wasn't there. The bar was open; Hans, looking as big and suave as ever, had been pressed into service to minister to the guests. He smiled at Mainwaring and said, 'Good afternoon, sir.' Mainwaring asked for a lager beer, took the glass to a corner seat. From here he could watch both the TV screen and the door.

The screen was showing the world-wide link-up that had become hallowed Christmas afternoon fare within the Two Empires. He saw, without particular interest, greetings flashed from the Leningrad and Moscow garrisons, a lightship, an Arctic weather station, a Mission in German East Africa. At fifteen hundred the Fuehrer was due to speak; this year, for the first time, Ziegler was preceding Edward VIII.

The room filled, slowly. She didn't come. Mainwaring finished the lager, walked to the bar, asked for another and a packet of cigarettes. The unease was sharpening now into something very like alarm. He thought for the first time that she might have been taken ill.

The time signal flashed, followed by the drumroll of the German anthem. He rose with the rest, stood stiffly till it had finished. The screen cleared, showed the familiar room in the Chancellery; the dark, high panels, the crimson drapes, the big *Hackenkreuz* emblem over the desk. The Fuehrer, as ever, spoke impeccably; but Mainwaring thought with a fragment of his mind how old he had begun to look.

The speech ended. He realized he hadn't heard a word that was said.

The drums crashed again. The King said, 'Once more, at Christmas, it is my … duty and pleasure … to speak to you.'

Something seemed to burst inside Mainwaring's head. He rose, walked quickly to the bar. He said, 'Hans, have you seen Miss Hunter?'

The other jerked round. He said, 'Sir, *shh* … please …'

'Have you seen her?'

Hans stared at the screen, and back to Mainwaring. The King was saying, 'There have been … troubles, and difficulties. More perhaps lie ahead. But with … God's help, they will be overcome.'

The chauffeur licked his mouth. He said, 'I'm sorry, sir. I don't know what you mean.'

'Which was her room?'

The big man looked like something trapped. He said, 'Please, Mr Mainwaring. You'll get me into trouble …'

'*Which was her room?*'

Somebody turned and hissed, angrily. Hans said, 'I don't understand.'

'For God's sake, man, you carried her things upstairs. I saw you!'

Hans said, 'No, sir ...'

Momentarily, the lounge seemed to spin.

There was a door behind the bar. The chauffeur stepped back. He said, 'Sir. Please ...'

The place was a storeroom. There were wine bottles racked, a shelf with jars of olives, walnuts, eggs. Mainwaring closed the door behind him, tried to control the shaking. Hans said, 'Sir, you must not ask me these things. I don't know a Miss Hunter. I don't know what you mean.'

Mainwaring said, 'Which was her room? I demand that you answer.'

'I can't!'

'You drove me from London yesterday. Do you deny that?'

'No, sir.'

'You drove me with Miss Hunter.'

'No, sir!'

'*Damn your eyes, where is she?*'

The chauffeur was sweating. A long wait; then he said, 'Mr Mainwaring, please. You must understand. I can't help you.' He swallowed, and drew himself up. He said, 'I drove you from London. I'm sorry. I drove you ... *on your own*.'

The lounge door swung shut behind Mainwaring. He half-walked, half-ran to his room. He slammed the door behind him, leaned against it panting. In time the giddiness passed. He opened his eyes, slowly. The fire glowed; the Geissler stood on the bookshelf. Nothing was changed.

He set to work, methodically. He shifted furniture, peered behind it. He rolled the carpet back, tapped every foot of floor. He fetched a flashlight from his case and examined, minutely, the interior of the wardrobe. He ran his fingers lightly across the walls, section by section, tapping again. Finally he got a chair, dismantled the ceiling lighting fitting.

Nothing.

He began again. Halfway through the second search he froze, staring at the floorboards. He walked to his case, took the screwdriver from the pistol holster. A moment's work with the blade and he sat back, staring into his palm. He rubbed his face, placed his find carefully on the side table. A tiny ear-ring, one of the pair she had worn. He sat a while breathing heavily, his head in his hands.

The brief daylight had faded as he worked. He lit the standard lamp, wrenched the shade free, stood the naked bulb in the middle of the room. He worked round the walls again, peering, tapping, pressing. By the fire-place, finally, a foot-square section of plaster rang hollow.

He held the bulb close, examined the hairline crack. He inserted the screwdriver blade delicately, twisted. Then again. A click; and the section hinged open.

He reached inside the little space, shaking, lifted out the recorder. He stood silent a time, holding it; then raised his arms, brought the machine smashing down on the hearth. He stamped and kicked, panting, till the thing was reduced to fragments.

The droning rose to a roar, swept low over the house. The helicopter settled slowly, belly lamps glaring, downdraught raising a storm of snow. He walked to the window, stood staring. The children embarked, clutching scarves and gloves, suitcases, boxes with new toys. The steps were withdrawn, the hatch dogged shut. Snow swirled again; the machine lifted heavily, swung away in the direction of Wilton.

The Party was about to start.

Lights blaze, through the length and breadth of the house. Orange-lit windows throw long bars of brightness across the snow. Everywhere is an anxious coming and going, the pattering of feet, clink of silver and glassware, hurried commands. Waiters scuttle between the kitchens and the Green Room where dinner is laid. Dish after dish is borne in, paraded. Peacocks, roasted and gilded, vaunt their plumes in shadow and candle-glow, spirit-soaked wicks blazing in their beaks. The Minister rises, laughing; toast after toast is drunk. To five thousand tanks, ten thousand fighting aeroplanes, a hundred thousand guns. The Two Empires feast their guests, royally.

The climax approaches. The boar's head, garnished and smoking, is borne shoulder-high. His tusks gleam; clamped in his jaws is the golden sun-symbol, the orange. After him march the waits and mummers, with their lanterns and begging-cups. The carol they chant is older by far than the Two Empires; older than the Reich, older than Great Britain.

'Alive he spoiled, where poor men toiled, which made kind Ceres sad …'

The din of voices rises. Coins are flung, glittering; wine is poured. And more wine, and more and more. Bowls of fruit are passed, and trays of sweets; spiced cakes, gingerbread, marzipans. Till at a signal the brandy is brought, and boxes of cigars.

The ladies rise to leave. They move flushed and chattering through the corridors of the house, uniformed link-boys grandly lighting their way. In the Great Hall their escorts are waiting. Each young man is tall, each blond, each impeccably uniformed. On the Minstrels' Gallery a baton is poised; across the lawns, distantly, floats the whirling excitement of a waltz.

In the Green Room, hazed now with smoke, the doors are once more flung wide. Servants scurry again, carrying in boxes, great gay-wrapped parcels topped with scarlet satin bows. The Minister rises, hammering on the table for quiet.

'My friends, good friends, friends of the Two Empires. For you, no expense is spared. For you, the choicest gifts. Tonight, nothing but the best is good enough; and nothing but the best is here. Friends, enjoy yourselves. Enjoy my house. *Frohe Weihnachten* ...!'

He walks quickly into shadow, and is gone. Behind him, silence falls. A waiting; and slowly, mysteriously, the great heap of gifts begins to stir. Paper splits, crackling. Here a hand emerges, here a foot. A breathless pause; and the first of the girls rises slowly, bare in flamelight, shakes her glinting hair.

The table roars again.

The sound reached Mainwaring dimly. He hesitated at the foot of the main staircase, moved on. He turned right and left, hurried down a flight of steps. He passed kitchens, and the servants' hall. From the hall came the blare of a record player. He walked to the end of the corridor, unlatched a door. Night air blew keen against his face.

He crossed the courtyard, opened a further door. The space beyond was bright-lit; there was the faint, musty stink of animals. He paused, wiped his face. He was shirt-sleeved; but despite the cold he was sweating.

He walked forward again, steadily. To either side of the corridor were the fronts of cages. The dogs hurled themselves at the bars, thunderously. He ignored them.

The corridor opened into a square concrete chamber. To one side of the place was a ramp. At its foot was parked a windowless black van.

In the far wall a door showed a crack of light. He rapped sharply, and again.

'*Hundenmeister* ...'

The door opened. The man who peered up at him was as wrinkled and pot-bellied as a Nast Santa Claus. At sight of his visitor's face he tried to duck back; but Mainwaring had him by the arm. He said, '*Herr Hundenmeister,* I must talk to you.'

'Who are you? I don't know you. What do you want ...?'

Mainwaring showed his teeth. He said, 'The van. You drove the van this morning. What was in it?'

'I don't know what you mean ...'

The heave sent him stumbling across the floor. He tried to bolt; but Mainwaring grabbed him again.

'What was in it ...?'

'I won't talk to you! Go away!'

The blow exploded across his cheek. Mainwaring hit him again, back-handed, slammed him against the van.

'Open it . . .!'

The voice rang sharply in the confined space.

'*Wer ist da? Was ist passiert?*'

The little man whimpered, rubbing at his mouth.

Mainwaring straightened, breathing heavily. The GFP captain walked forward, staring, thumbs hooked in his belt.

'*Wer sind Sie?*'

Mainwaring said, 'You know damn well. And speak English, you bastard. You're as English as I am.'

The other glared. He said, 'You have no right to be here. I should arrest you. You have no right to accost *Herr Hundenmeister*.'

'What is in that van?'

'Have you gone mad? The van is not your concern. Leave now. At once.'

'Open it!'

The other hesitated, and shrugged. He stepped back. He said, 'Show him, *mein Herr*.'

The *Hundenmeister* fumbled with a bunch of keys. The van doors grated. Mainwaring walked forward, slowly.

The vehicle was empty.

The captain said, 'You have seen what you wished to see. You are satisfied. Now go.'

Mainwaring stared round. There was a further door, recessed deeply into the wall. Beside it controls like the controls of a bank vault.

'What is in that room?'

The GFP man said, 'You have gone too far. I order you to leave.'

'You have no authority over me!'

'Return to your quarters!'

Mainwaring said, 'I refuse.'

The other slapped the holster at his hip. He gut-held the Walther, wrists locked, feet apart. He said, 'Then you will be shot.'

Mainwaring walked past him, contemptuously. The baying of the dogs faded as he slammed the outer door.

It was among the middle classes that the seeds had first been sown; and it was among the middle classes that they flourished. Britain had been called often enough a nation of shopkeepers; now for a little while the tills were closed, the blinds left drawn. Overnight it seemed, an effete symbol of social and national disunity became the Einsatzgruppenfuehrer; *and the wire for the first detention camps was strung . . .*

Mainwaring finished the page, tore it from the spine, crumpled it and dropped it on the fire. He went on reading. Beside him on the hearth stood a part-full bottle of whisky and a glass. He picked the glass up mechanically, drank. He lit a cigarette. A few minutes later a new page followed the last.

The clock ticked steadily. The burning paper made a little rustling. Reflections danced across the ceiling of the room. Once Mainwaring raised his head, listened; once put the ruined book down, rubbed his eyes. The room, and the corridor outside, stayed quiet.

Against immeasurable force, we must pit cunning; against immeasurable evil, faith and a high resolve. In the war we wage, the stakes are high; the dignity of man, the freedom of the spirit, the survival of humanity. Already in that war, many of us have died; many more, undoubtedly, will lay down their lives. But always, beyond them, there will be others; and still more. We shall go on, as we must go on, till this thing is wiped from the earth.

Meanwhile, we must take fresh heart. Every blow, now, is a blow for freedom. In France, Belgium, Finland, Poland, Russia, the forces of the Two Empires confront each other uneasily. Greed, jealousy, mutual distrust; these are the enemies, and they work from within. This, the Empires know full well. And, knowing, for the first time in their existence, fear …

The last page crumpled, fell to ash. Mainwaring sat back, staring at nothing. Finally he stirred, looked up. It was zero three hundred; and they hadn't come for him yet.

The bottle was finished. He set it to one side, opened another. He swilled the liquid in the glass, hearing the magnified ticking of the clock.

He crossed the room, took the Lüger from the case. He found a cleaning rod, patches and oil. He sat a while dully, looking at the pistol. Then he slipped the magazine free, pulled back on the breech toggle, thumbed the latch, slid the barrel from the guides.

His mind, wearied, had begun to play aggravating tricks. It ranged and wandered, remembering scenes, episodes, details sometimes from years back; trivial, unconnected. Through and between the wanderings, time after time, ran the ancient, lugubrious words of the carol. He tried to shut them out, but it was impossible.

'*Living he spoiled where poor men toiled, which made kind Ceres sad …*'

He pushed the link pin clear, withdrew the breech block, stripped the firing pin. He laid the parts out, washed them with oil and water, dried and re-oiled. He reassembled the pistol, working carefully; inverted the barrel, shook the link down in front of the hooks, closed the latch, checked the recoil spring engagement. He loaded a full clip, pushed it home, chambered a round, thumbed the safety to *Gesichert*. He released the clip, reloaded.

He fetched his briefcase, laid the pistol inside carefully, grip uppermost. He filled a spare clip, added the extension butt and a fifty box of Parabellum. He closed the flap and locked it, set the case beside the bed. After that there was nothing more to do. He sat back in the chair, refilled his glass.

'*Toiling he boiled, where poor men spoiled . . .*'

The firelight faded, finally.

He woke, and the room was dark. He got up, felt the floor sway a little. He understood that he had a hangover. He groped for the light switch. The clock hands stood at zero eight hundred.

He felt vaguely guilty at having slept so long.

He walked to the bathroom. He stripped and showered, running the water as hot as he could bear. The process brought him round a little. He dried himself, staring down. He thought for the first time what curious things these bodies were; some with their yellow cylinders, some their indentations.

He dressed and shaved. He had remembered what he was going to do; fastening his tie, he tried to remember why. He couldn't. His brain, it seemed, had gone dead.

There was an inch of whisky in the bottle. He poured it, grimaced and drank. Inside him was a fast, cold shaking. He thought, 'Like the first morning at a new school.'

He lit a cigarette. Instantly his throat filled. He walked to the bathroom and vomited. Then again. Finally there was nothing left to come.

His chest ached. He rinsed his mouth, washed his face again. He sat in the bedroom for a while, head back and eyes closed. In time the shaking went away. He lay unthinking, hearing the clock tick. Once his lips moved. He said, 'They're no better than us.'

At nine hundred hours he walked to the breakfast room. His stomach, he felt, would retain very little. He ate a slice of toast, carefully, drank some coffee. He asked for a pack of cigarettes, went back to his room. At ten hundred hours he was due to meet the Minister.

He checked the briefcase again. A thought made him add a pair of string-back motoring gloves. He sat again, stared at the ashes where he had burned the Geissler. A part of him was willing the clock hands not to move. At five to ten he picked the briefcase up, stepped into the corridor. He stood a moment staring round him. He thought, 'It hasn't happened yet. I'm still alive.' There was still the flat in Town to go back to, still his office; the tall windows, the telephones, the khaki utility desk.

He walked through sunlit corridors to the Minister's suite.

The room to which he was admitted was wide and long. A fire crackled in the hearth; beside it on a low table stood glasses and a decanter. Over the mantel, conventionally, hung the Fuehrer's portrait. Edward VIII faced him across the room. Tall windows framed a prospect of rolling parkland. In the distance, blue on the horizon, were the woods.

The Minister said, 'Good morning, Richard. Please sit down. I don't think I shall keep you long.'

He sat, placing the briefcase by his knee.

This morning everything seemed strange. He studied the Minister curiously, as if seeing him for the first time. He had that type of face once thought of as peculiarly English: short-nosed and slender, with high, finely shaped cheekbones. The hair, blond and cropped close to the scalp, made him look nearly boyish. The eyes were candid, flat, dark-fringed. He looked, Mainwaring decided, not so much Aryan as like some fierce nursery toy; a Feral Teddy Bear.

The Minister riffled papers. He said, 'Several things have cropped up; among them, I'm afraid, more trouble in Glasgow. The fifty-first Panzer division is standing by; as yet, the news hasn't been released.'

Mainwaring wished his head felt less hollow. It made his own voice boom so unnecessarily. He said, 'Where is Miss Hunter?'

The Minister paused. The pale eyes stared; then he went on speaking.

'I'm afraid I may have to ask you to cut short your stay here. I shall be flying back to London for a meeting; possibly tomorrow, possibly the day after. I shall want you with me, of course.'

'Where is Miss Hunter?'

The Minister placed his hands flat on the desktop, studied the nails. He said, 'Richard, there are aspects of Two Empires culture that are neither mentioned nor discussed. You of all people should know this. I'm being patient with you; but there are limits to what I can overlook.'

'*Seldom he toiled, while Ceres roiled, which made poor kind men glad* ...'

Mainwaring opened the flap of the case and stood up. He thumbed the safety forward and levelled the pistol.

There was silence for a time. The fire spat softly. Then the Minister smiled. He said, 'That's an interesting gun, Richard. Where did you get it?'

Mainwaring didn't answer.

The Minister moved his hands carefully to the arms of his chair, leaned back. He said, 'It's the Marine model, of course. It's also quite old. Does it by any chance carry the Erfurt stamp? Its value would be considerably increased.'

He smiled again. He said, 'If the barrel is good, I'll buy it. For my private collection.'

Mainwaring's arm began to shake. He steadied his wrist, gripping with his left hand.

The Minister sighed. He said, 'Richard, you can be so stubborn. It's a good quality; but you do carry it to excess.' He shook his head. He said, 'Did you imagine for one moment I didn't know you were coming here to kill me? My dear chap, you've been through a great deal. You're overwrought. Believe me, I know just how you feel.'

Mainwaring said, 'You murdered her.'

The Minister spread his hands. He said, 'What with? A gun? A knife? Do I honestly look such a shady character?'

The words made a cold pain, and a tightness in the chest. But they had to be said.

The Minister's brows rose. Then he started to laugh. Finally he said, 'At last I see. I understood, but I couldn't believe. So you bullied our poor little *Hundenmeister*, which wasn't very worthy; and seriously annoyed the *Herr Hauptmann*, which wasn't very wise. Because of this fantasy, stuck in your head. Do you really believe it, Richard? Perhaps you believe in *Struwwelpeter* too.' He sat forward. He said, 'The Hunt ran. And killed … a deer. She gave us an excellent chase. As for your little Huntress … Richard, she's gone. She never existed. She was a figment of your imagination. Best forgotten.'

Mainwaring said, 'We were in love.'

The Minister said, 'Richard, you really are becoming tiresome.' He shook his head again. He said, 'We're both adult. We both know what that word is worth. It's a straw, in the wind. A candle, on a night of gales. A phrase that is meaningless. *Lächerlich.*' He put his hands together, rubbed a palm. He said, 'When this is over, I want you to go away. For a month, six weeks maybe. With your new car. When you come back … well, we'll see. Buy yourself a girl friend, if you need a woman that much. *Einen Schatz.* I never dreamed; you're so remote, you should speak more of yourself. Richard, I understand; it isn't such a very terrible thing.'

Mainwaring stared.

The Minister said, 'We shall make an arrangement. You will have the use of an apartment, rather a nice apartment. So your lady will be close. When you tire of her … buy another. They're unsatisfactory for the most part, but reasonable. Now sit down like a good chap, and put your gun away. You look so silly, standing there scowling like that.'

It seemed he felt all life, all experience, as a grey weight pulling. He lowered the pistol, slowly. He thought, *At the end, they were wrong. They picked the wrong man.* He said, 'I suppose now I use it on myself.'

The Minister said, 'No, no, no. You still don't understand.' He linked his knuckles, grinning. He said, 'Richard, the *Herr Hauptmann* would have arrested you last night. I wouldn't let him. This is between ourselves. Nobody else. I give you my word.'

Mainwaring felt his shoulders sag. The strength seemed drained from him; the pistol, now, weighed too heavy for his arm.

The Minister said, 'Richard, why so glum? It's a great occasion, man. You've found your courage. I'm delighted.'

He lowered his voice. He said, 'Don't you want to know why I let you come here with your machine? Aren't you even interested?'

Mainwaring stayed silent.

The Minister said, 'Look around you, Richard. See the world. I want men near me, serving me. Now more than ever. Real men, not afraid to die. Give me a dozen … but you know the rest. I could rule the world. But first … I must rule them. My men. Do you see now? Do you understand?'

Mainwaring thought, 'He's in control again. But he was always in control. He owns me.'

The study spun a little.

The voice went on, smoothly. 'As for this amusing little plot by the so-called Freedom Front; again, you did well. It was difficult for you. I was watching; believe me, with much sympathy. Now, you've burned your book. Of your own free will. That delighted me.'

Mainwaring looked up, sharply.

The Minister shook his head. He said, 'The real recorder is rather better hidden, you were too easily satisfied there. There's also a TV monitor. I'm sorry about it all, I apologize. It was necessary.'

A singing started inside Mainwaring's head.

The Minister sighed again. He said, 'Still unconvinced, Richard? Then I have some things I think you ought to see. Am I permitted to open my desk drawer?'

Mainwaring didn't speak. The other slid the drawer back slowly, reached in. He laid a telegram flimsy on the desk top. He said, 'The addressee is Miss D. J. Hunter. The message consists of one word. "*Activate.*"'

The singing rose in pitch.

'This as well,' said the Minister. He held up a medallion on a thin gold chain. The little disc bore the linked motif of the Freedom Front. He said, 'Mere exhibitionism; or a deathwish. Either way, a most undesirable trait.'

He tossed the thing down. He said, 'She was here under surveillance of course, we'd known about her for years. To them, you were a sleeper. Do you see the absurdity? They really thought you would be jealous enough to assassinate your Minister. This they mean in their silly little book, when they talk of subtlety. Richard, I could have fifty blonde women if I chose. A hundred. Why should I want yours?' He shut the drawer with a click, and rose. He said, 'Give me the gun now. You don't need it any more.' He extended his arm; then he was flung heavily backward. Glasses smashed on the side table. The decanter split; its contents poured dark across the wood.

Over the desk hung a faint haze of blue. Mainwaring walked forward, stood looking down. There were blood-flecks, and a little flesh. The eyes of the Teddy Bear still showed glints of white. Hydraulic shock had shattered the chest; the breath drew ragged, three times, and stopped. He thought, *I didn't hear the report.*

The communicating door opened. Mainwaring turned. A secretary stared in, bolted at sight of him. The door slammed.

He pushed the briefcase under his arm, ran through the outer office. Feet clattered in the corridor. He opened the door, carefully. Shouts sounded, somewhere below in the house.

Across the corridor hung a loop of crimson cord. He stepped over it, hurried up a flight of stairs. Then another. Beyond the private apartments the way was closed by a heavy metal grille. He ran to it, rattled. A rumbling sounded from below. He glared round. Somebody had operated the emergency shutters; the house was sealed.

Beside the door an iron ladder was spiked to the wall. He climbed it, panting. The trap in the ceiling was padlocked. He clung one-handed, awkward with the briefcase, held the pistol above his head.

Daylight showed through splintered wood. He put his shoulder to the trap, heaved. It creaked back. He pushed head and shoulders through, scrambled. Wind stung at him, and flakes of snow.

His shirt was wet under the arms. He lay face down, shaking. He thought, *It wasn't an accident. None of it was an accident.* He had underrated them. They understood despair.

He pushed himself up, stared round. He was on the roof of Wilton. Beside him rose gigantic chimney stacks. There was a lattice radio mast. The wind hummed in its guy wires. To his right ran the balustrade that crowned the façade of the house. Behind it was a snow-choked gutter.

He wriggled across a sloping scree of roof, ran crouching. Shouts sounded from below. He dropped flat, rolled. An automatic clattered. He edged forward again, dragging the briefcase. Ahead, one of the corner towers rose dark against the sky. He crawled to it, crouched sheltered from the wind. He opened the case, pulled the gloves on. He clipped the stock to the pistol, laid the spare magazine beside him and the box of rounds.

The shouts came again. He peered forward, through the balustrade. Running figures scattered across the lawn. He sighted on the nearest, squeezed. Commotion below. The automatic zipped; stone chips flew, whining. A voice called, 'Don't expose yourselves unnecessarily.' Another answered.

'*Die konmen mit den Hubschrauber …*'

He stared round him, at the yellow-grey horizon. He had forgotten the helicopter.

A snow flurry drove against his face. He huddled, flinching. He thought he heard, carried on the wind, a faint droning.

From where he crouched he could see the nearer trees of the park, beyond them the wall and gatehouses. Beyond again, the land rose to the circling woods.

The droning was back, louder than before. He screwed his eyes, made out the dark spot skimming above the trees. He shook his head. He said, 'We made a mistake. We all made a mistake.'

He settled the stock of the Lüger to his shoulder, and waited.

THE WHITE BOAT

Becky had always lived in the cottage overlooking the bay.

The bay was black, because there a seam of rock that was nearly coal burst open to the water and the sea had nibbled in over the years, breaking up the fossil-ridden shale to a fine dark grit, spreading it over the beach and the humped, tilted headlands. The grass had taken the colour of it and the little houses that stood mean-shouldered glaring at the water; the boats and jetties had taken it, and the brambles and gorse; even the rabbits that thumped across the cliff paths on summer evenings seemed to have something of the same dusky hue. Here the paths tilted, tumbling over to steepen and plunge at the sea; the whole land seemed ready to slide and splash, grumble into the ocean.

It was a summer evening when Becky first saw the *White Boat*. She had been sent, in the little skiff that was all her father owned, to clear the day's crop from the lobster pots strung out along the shore. She worked methodically, sculling along the bobbing line of buoys; the baskets in the bottom of the boat were full and bustling, the great crustaceans black and slate-grey as the cliffs, snapping and wriggling, waving wobbling, angry claws. Becky regarded them thoughtfully. A good catch; the family would feed well in the week to come.

She pulled up the last pot, feeling the drag and surge of it against the slow-flowing tide. It was empty, save for the grey-white rags of bait. She dropped the tarred basket back over the side, leaned to see the ghost-shape of it vanish in the cloudy green beneath the keel. She sat feeling the little aches spread in shoulders and arms, narrowing her eyes against the evening haze of sunlight; and saw the Boat.

Only she didn't know then that *White Boat* was her name.

She was coming in fast and quiet, bow parting the sea, raising a bright ridge of foam. Mainsail down and furled, tall jib filling in the slight breeze. The calling of the crew came clear and faint across the water; and instinct made the girl scurry from her, pushing at the oars, scudding the little craft back to the shelter of the land. She grounded on the Ledges, the natural moles of stone that reached out into the sea, skipped ashore all torn frock and thin brown legs, wetted herself to the middle in her haste to drag the boat up and tie off.

Strange boats seldom came into the bay. Fishing boats were common enough, the stubby-bowed, round-bilged craft of the coast; this boat was different. Becky watched back at her cautiously, riding at anchor now in the ruffled pale shield of the sea. She was slim and long, flush-decked, a racer; her tall mast with the spreading outriggers rolled slowly, a pencil against the greying sky. As she watched, a dingy was launched; she saw a man climb down to rig the outboard. She scrambled farther up the cliff, crouched wild as a rabbit in a stand of gorse, staring down with huge brown eyes. She saw lights come on in the cabin of the yacht; they reflected in the water in wobbling yellow spears. The afterglow flared and faded as she lay.

This was a wild, mournful place. An eternal brooding seemed to hang over the bulging cliffs; a brooding, and worse. An enigma, a shadow of old sin. For here once a great mad priest had come, and called the waves and wind and water to witness his craziness. Becky had heard the tale often enough at her mother's knee; how he had taken a boat, and ridden out to his death; and how the village had hummed with soldiers and priests come to exorcize and complain and quiz the locals for their part in armed rebellion. They got little satisfaction; and the place had quietened by degrees, as the gales went and came, as the boats were hauled out and tarred and launched again. The waves were indifferent, and the wind; and the rocks neither knew nor cared who owned them, Christ's Vicar or an English king.

Becky was late home that evening; her father grumbled and swore, threatening her with beating, accusing her of outlandish crimes. She loved to sit out on the Ledges, none knew that better than he; sit and touch the fossils that showed like coiled springs in the rock, feel the breeze and watch the lap and splash of water and lose the sense of time. And that with babies to be fed and meals to stew and a house to clean, and him with an ailing, coughing wife. The girl was useless, idle to her bones. Giving herself airs and graces, lazing her time away; fine for the rich folk in Londinium maybe, but he had a living to earn.

Becky was not beaten. Neither did she speak of the Boat.

She lay awake that night, tired but unable to sleep, hearing her mother cough, watching between the drawn blinds the thin turquoise wedge of night sky; she saw it pale with the dawn, a single planet burn like a spark before being swallowed by the rising sun. From the house could be heard a faint susurration, soft nearly as the sound the blood makes in the ears. A slow, miles-long heave and roll, a breathing; the dim, immemorial noise of the sea.

If the Boat stayed in the bay, no sound came from her; and in the morning she was gone. Becky walked to the sea late in the day, trod barefoot among the tumbled blocks of stone that lined the foreshore; smelling the old harsh smell of salt, hearing the water slap and chuckle while from high above came the endless sinister trickling of the cliffs. Into her consciousness stole, maybe for the first time, the sense of loneliness; an oppression born of the gentle miles of summer water, the tall blackness of the headlands, the fingers of the stone ledges pushing out into the sea. She saw how the Ledges curved, in obedience it seemed to some cosmic plan, became ridges of stone that climbed the dark beach, curled away through the dipping strata of the cliffs. Full of the signs and ghosts of other life, the ammonites she collected as a child till Father Antony had scolded and warned, asked her once and for all time, if God created the rocks in seven days could He not have created those markings too? She was close to heresy, the things were best forgotten. She brooded, scrinching her toes in the water, feeling the sharp grit move and suck. She was fourteen, slight and dark, her breasts beginning to push at her dress.

It was months before she saw the Boat again. A winter had come and gone, noisy and grey; the wind plucked at the cliffs, yanking out the amber teeth of stone, sending them crashing and bumbling to the beach. Becky walked the bay in the short, glaring days, scrounging for driftwood, planks, broken pieces of boats, sea-coal to burn. Now and again she would watch the water, thin brown face and brilliant eyes staring, searching for something she couldn't understand out over the waste of sea. With the spring, *White Boat* returned.

It was an April evening, nearly May. Something made Becky linger over her work, hauling in the great black pots, scooping the clicking life into the baskets she kept prepared, while *White Boat* came sidling in from the dusk, driven by a puttering engine, growing from the vastness of the water.

'*Boat ahoy . . .*'

Becky stood in the coracle and stared. Behind her the headland cliffs, heaving slowly with the movement of the sea; in front of her the Boat, tall now and menacing with closeness, white prow cutting the water, raising a thin vee of foam that chuckled away to lose itself in the dark. She was aware, nearly painfully, of the boards beneath her feet, the flapping of the soiled dress round her knees. The Boat edged forward, ragged silhouette of a man in her bows clinging one-handed to the fore-stay while he waved and called.

'Boat ahoy . . .'

Becky saw the mainsail stowed and neat-wrapped on its boom, the complication of cabin coamings and hatches and rigging; up close she was nearly surprised to see the paint of *White Boat* could have weathered, the long jib-sheets frayed. As if the Boat had been nothing but a vision or a dream, lacking weight and substance.

The coracle ground, dipping, against the hull; Becky lurched, caught at the high deck. Hands gripped and steadied; the great mast rolled above her, daunting, as *White Boat* drifted slow, moved in by the tide.

'Easy there . . .' Then, 'What're ye selling, girl?'

From somewhere, a ripple of laughter. Becky swallowed, still staring up. Men crowded the rail, dark shapes against the evening light.

'Lobsters, sir. Fine lobsters …'

Her father would be pleased. What, sell fish afore landing 'em, and the price good too? No haggling with Master Smythe up in the village, no waiting for the hauliers to fetch the stuff away. They paid her well, dropping real gold coins into the boat, laughing as she dived and scrabbled for them; swung her clear, laughing again, called to her as she sculled back into the bay. She carried with her a memory of their voices, wild and rough and keen. Never it seemed had the land loomed so fast, the coracle been easier to beach. She scuttled for home, carrying what was left of her catch, money clutched hot in her hand; turned as *White Boat* turned below her in the dusk, heard the splash and rattle as her anchor dropped down to catch the bottom of the sea. There were lights aboard already, sharp pinpoints that gleamed like a cluster of eyes; above them the rigging of the Boat was dark, a filigree against the silver-grey crawling of the water.

Her father swore at her for selling the catch. She stared back wide-eyed.

'*The Bermudan* …' He spat, hulking across the kitchen to slam dirty plates down in the sink, crank at the handle of the tall old pump. 'You keep away from en …'

'But f—'

He turned back, dark-faced with rage. 'Keep *away* from en. Doan't want no more tellin' …'

Already her face had the ability to freeze, turn into the likeness of a dark, sculpted cat. She veiled her eyes, watching down at her plate. Above in the bedroom she heard her mother's racking cough. There would be spatters of pink on the sheets come morning, that she knew. She tucked one foot behind the other, stroking with her toes the contour of a grimy shin, and thought carefully of nothing at all.

The exchange, inconclusive as it was, served to rivet Becky's attention; over the weeks, the strange yacht began to obsess her. She saw *White Boat* in dreams; in her fantasies she seemed to fly, riffling through the wind like the great gulls that haunted the beach and headlands. In the mornings the cliffs resounded with their noise; in Becky's ears, still ringing with sleep, the bird-shouts echoed like the creaking of ropes, the ratchetclatter of sheet winches. Sometimes then the headlands would seem to sway gently and roll like the sea, dizzying. She would squat and rub her arms and shiver, wait for the spells to pass and worry about death; till queer rhythms and passions reached culmination, she stepped on a knife blade, upturned in the boat, and slicing shock and redness turned her instantly into a woman. She cleaned herself, whimpering. Nobody saw; the secret she hugged to herself, to her thin body, as she hugged all secrets; thoughts, and dreams.

There was a wedding once, in the little black village, in the little black church. At that time Becky became aware, obscurely, that the people too had taken the colour of the place; an airborne, invisible smut had changed them all. The fantasies took new and more sinister shapes; once she dreamed she saw the villagers, her parents, all the people she knew, melt chaotically into the landscape till the cliffs were bodies and bones and old beseeching hands, teeth and eyes and crumbling ancient foreheads. Sometimes now she was afraid of the bay; but always it drew her with its own magnetism. She could not be said to think, sitting there alone and brooding; she felt, vividly, things not readily understandable.

She cut her black hair, sitting puzzled in front of a cracked and spotted mirror, turning her head, snipping and shortening till she looked nearly like a boy, one of the wild fisherboys of the coast. She stroked and teased the result, while the liquid huge eyes watched back uncertainly from the glass. She seemed to sense round her a trap, its bars thick and black as the bars of the lobster pots she used. Her world was landlocked, encompassed by the headlands of the bay, by the voice of the priest and her father's tread. Only *White Boat* was free; and free she would come, gliding and shimmering in her head, unsettling. In the critical events of adolescence, after the fear her pride in the shedding of her blood, the Boat seemed to have taken a part. Almost as if from under the bright mysterious horizon she had seen, and could somehow understand.

Becky kept her tryst with the yacht, time and again, watching from the tangles of bramble above the bay.

The sea itself drew her now. Nights or early iron-grey mornings she would slide her frock over her head among the piled slabs of rock; ease into the burning ice of the water, lie and let the waves lift her and move and slap. At such times it seemed the bay came in on her with an agoraphobic crowding, the rolling heights of headlands grey under the vast spaces of air; it was as if her nakedness brought her somehow in power of the place, as if it could then tumble round her quickly, trap and enfold. She would scuttle from the water, thresh into her dress. The awkwardness of her damp body under the cloth was a huge comfort; the cliffs receded, gained their proper aloofness and perspective. Were once more safe.

As a by-product, she was learning to swim.

That in itself was a Mystery; she felt instinctively her father and the Church would not approve. She avoided Father Antony; but the eyes of icons and the great Christos over the altar would still single her out in services to watch and accuse. By swimming she gave her body, obscurely, to assault; entered into a mystic relationship with *White Boat*, who also swam. She needed fulfilment, the shadowy fulfilment of the sea. She experienced a curious confusion, a sense of sin too formless to be categorized and as such more terrifying and in its turn alluring. The Confessional was closed to her; she walked alone, carefully, in a world of shadows and brittle glass. She avoided now the touches, the pressures, the accidental gratifications of her body that came nearly naturally with walking and moving and working. She wished in an unformed way to proscribe at least a vague area of evil, reduce the menace she herself had sought and that now in its turn sought her.

The idea came it seemed of its own, unlooked for and unwanted. Slowly there grew in her, watching the yacht swing at her mooring out in the darkening mystery of the water, the knowledge that *White Boat* alone might save her from herself. Only the Boat could fly, out from the twin iron headlands to a broader world. Where did she come from? Why did she vanish so mysteriously, and why return?

The priest spoke words over her mother's grave, God looked down from the sky; but Becky knew the earth had taken her to squeeze and squeeze, make her into more black shale.

The Boat came back.

She was frightened now and unsure. Before, with the less cluttered faith of childhood, she had not questioned. The Boat had gone away, the Boat would return. Now she knew, that all things change, and change is for ever. One day, the Boat would not return.

She had passed from knowledge of evil to indifference; for that, she felt herself already damned.

The thing she had rehearsed and dreamed of blended so with reality that she lived another dream. She rose silently in the black house, hearing the squabbling cough of a child. Her hands shook as she dressed; in her body was a fast, violent quivering, as if some electric force had control of her and drove her without volition. The sensation, and the mad thumping of her heart, seemed partially to cut her off from earthly contact; shapes of familiar things, chairbacks, dressertop, doorlatch, seemed to her fingertips muffled and vague. She slid the catch back carefully, not breathing, listening and staring in the dark. It was as if she moved now from point to point with an even pace that could not falter or check. She knew she would go to the bay, watch the Boat up-anchor and drift away; her mind, complicated, reserved beneath the image others that would be presented in their turn, in sequence to an unimagined end.

The village was black, lightless and dead; the air moved raw on her face and arms, a drifting of wet vapour that was nearly rain. The sky above her seemed to press solidly, dark as pitch except where to the east one depthless iron-grey streak showed where in the upper air there was dawn. Against it the tower of the church stood tall and remote, held out stiffly its ragged gargoyle ears.

In the centre of the bay a shallow ravine conducted to the beach a rill dribbling from the far-off Luckford Ponds. A plank bridge with a single handrail spanned the brook; the steps that led down to it were slimy with the damp. Once Becky slipped on a rounded stone; once felt beneath her pad the quick recoil of a worm. She crossed the bridge, hearing the chuckle of water; a scramble over wet rock and the bay opened out ahead, barely visible, a dull-grey vastness. On it, floating in a half-seen mirror, the darker grey ghost of the Boat. She crossed the beach, toes sinking in grit, feeling with her feet among the planes of tumbled stone. The water rose to calves and knees, half-noticed; before her was a faint calling, the hard *tonk-tonk-tonk* of a winch.

Rain spattered on the dawn wind, wetting her hair. She moved on, still with the same mindless steadiness. The stone ledge, the mole, sloped slowly, water slapping and creaming where it nosed under the sea. She floundered beside it, waist deep, feet in furry tangles of weed. Soon she was swimming, into the broad cold madness of the water. As the land receded she fell into a rhythm of movement, half-hypnotic; it seemed she would follow *White Boat* tirelessly, to the far end of the world. The aches increasing in shoulders and arms were unnoticed, unimportant. Ahead, between the slapping dark troughs of waves, the shadow of the Boat had altered, foreshortening as she turned to face the sea; above the hull had grown a taller shade that was the raising of the gently flapping jib.

To Becky it seemed an accident that she was here, and that the sea was deep and the cliffs tall and the Boat too far off to reach. She nuzzled at the water, drowsily; but the first bayonet stab in her lungs startled something that was nearly an orgasm. She retched, and kicked; felt coldness close instantly over her head, screamed and fought for air.

And there were voices ahead, a confusion of sounds and orders; the shape of the Boat changing again as she turned back into the wind.

There were hands on her shoulders and arms; something grabbed in her dress, the fabric tore, she went under again gulping at the sea. She wallowed, centred in a confusion of grey and black, white of foam, glaring red. Was hauled out thrashing, landed on a sloping deck, lay feeling beneath her opened mouth the smoothness of wood. The voices surged round her, seeming like the lap and splash of the sea to retreat and advance.

'*That one ...*'

'Bloody fishergirl ...'

The words roared quite unnecessarily in her ear, receded in their turn. She stayed still, panting; water ran from her; she sensed, six feet beneath, the grey sliding of the sea. She lay numbly, knowing she had done a terrible thing.

They fetched her blankets, muffled her in them. She sat up and coughed more water, hearing ropes creak, the slide and slap of waves. Her mind seemed still dissociated from her body, a cool grey thing that had watched the other Becky spit and drown. She was aware vaguely of questions; she clutched the rough cloth across her throat and shook her head, angry now with herself and the people round her. The movement started a spinning sickness; she was aware of being lifted, caught a last glimpse of the black land-streak miles off as the boat heeled to the wind. One foot caught the side of the hatch as they lowered her; the pain jarred to her brain, ebbed. She was aware of a maze of images, disconnected; white planking above her head, hands working at the blankets and her dress. She frowned and mumbled, trying to collect her thoughts; but the impressions faded, one by one, into silence.

She lay quiet, cocooned in blankets, unwilling to open her eyes. Soon she would have to move, go down and rake the stove to life, set the pots of gruel simmering and bubbling for breakfast. The house rolled faintly and incongruously, shivering like a live thing; across beneath the eaves ran the chuckling slap of water. The dream-image persisted, stubbornly refusing to fade. She moved her head on the pillow, rubbing and grumbling, fought a hand free to touch hair still sticky with salt. The fingers moved back down, discovering nakedness. That in itself was a sin, to tumble into bed unclothed. She grunted and snuggled, defeating the dream with sleep.

The water made a thousand noises in the cabin. Rippling and laughing, strumming, smacking against the side of *White Boat*. Becky's eyes popped open again, in sudden alarm. With waking came remembrance, and a clawing panic. She shot upright; her head thumped against the decking two feet above. She rubbed dazedly, seeing the sun reflections play across the low roof, the bursts and tinkles and momentary skeins of light. The cabin was in subtle motion, leaning; she saw a bright yellow oilskin sway gently, at an angle from the upright on which it hung. Perspectives seemed wrong; she was pressed against a six-inch wooden board that served to stop her rolling from the bunk.

The boy was watching her, holding easily to a stanchion. The eyes above the tangle of beard were bright and keen, and he was laughing. 'Get your things on,' he said. 'Skipper wants to see you. Come up on deck. You all right now?'

She stared at him wild-eyed.

'You'll be all right,' he said. 'Just get dressed. It'll be all right.'

She knew then the dream or nightmare was true.

Tiny things confused her. The latches that held the bunk-board, she had to grope and push and still they wouldn't come undone. She swung her legs experimentally. Air rushed at her body: she scrabbled at the blankets, came out with a thump, took a fall, lost the blankets again. There were clothes left for her, jeans and an old sweater. She grabbed for them, panting. Her fingers refused to obey her, slipping and trembling; it seemed an age before she could force her legs into the trews.

The companionway twitched aside to land her among pots and pans. She clung to the steps, countering the great lean of the boat, pulled herself up to be dazed by sunlight.

And there was no land. Just a smudge, impossibly far off across the racing green of the sea. She winced, screwing her eyes; the boy who had spoken to her helped her again.

The skipper sat immobile, carved it seemed from buttercup-yellow oilskin, thin face and grey eyes watching past her along the deck of the Boat. Above him was the huge steady curving of the sails; behind the crew, clinging in the stern, watching her bold-eyed. She saw bearded mouths grinning and dropped her eyes, twisted her fingers in her lap.

Before these people she was nearly dumb. She sat still, watching her hands twine and move, conscious of the nearness of the water, the huge speed of the boat. The conversation was unsatisfactory, Skipper watching down at the compass, one arm curled easy along the tiller, listening it seemed with only the smallest part of his mind. The faces grinned, sea-lit and uncaring. She had jammed herself into their lives; they should have hated her for it but they were laughing. She wanted to be dead.

She was crying.

Somebody had an arm round her shoulders. She noticed she was shivering; they fetched her an oilskin, wrestled her into it. She felt the hard collar push her hair, scratch at her ears. She must go with them, they couldn't turn back; that much she understood. That was what she had wanted most, a lifetime ago. Now she wanted her father's kitchen, her own room again. Shipbound, caught in their tightly male and ordered world, she was useless. Their indifference stung; their kindness brought the welling, angry tears. She tried to help, in the little galley, but even the meals they made were strange; there were complications, nuances, relishes she had never seen. *White Boat* defeated her.

She crawled forward finally, away from the rest, clung to the root of the mast with one arm round the metal hearing the tall halliards slap and bang, seeing the bows fall and rise and punch at the sea. Diamond-hard spray flew back; her feet, bare on the deck, chilled almost at once. The cold reached through the oilskin; soon she was shivering as each cloud shadow eclipsed the boat, darkened the milk green of the sea. The dream was gone, blown away by the wind; *White Boat* was a hard thing, brutal and huge, smashing at the water. She could work her father's little cockleshell through the tides and currents of the coast; here she was awkward and in the way. A dozen times she moved desperately as the crew ran to handle the complication of ropes. The calls reached her dimly, '*Stand by to go about*', '*Let the sheets fly*'; then the thundering of the jib, scuffle of feet on planking as *White Boat* surged on to each new tack, changed the angle of her decking and the flying sun and cloud shadows, the stinging attack of the spray. The horizon became a new hill, slanting away and up; Becky looked into racing water where before she had seen the sky.

They sent her food but she refused it, setting her mouth. She was sulking; and worse, she felt ill. She needed cottage and bay now with a new urgency, an almost ecstatic longing for solidness, for things that didn't roll and move. But these things were lost for all time; there was only the hurtling green of the water, fading now to deeper and deeper grey as the clouds grew up across the sun; the endless slap and tinkle of ropes, the misery at the churning pit of her stomach.

They offered her the helm, in the late afternoon. She refused. *White Boat* had been a dream; reality was killing it.

There was a little sea toilet, in a place too low to stand. She closed the lid and pumped, saw the contents flash past through the curving glass tube. The sea opened her stomach, brought up first food, then chyme, then glistening transparent sticky stuff that bearded her chin. She wiped and spat and worked the pump and sicked over again till the sides of her chest were a dull pain and her head throbbed in time it seemed with the thumping of the waves. The voices through the bulkhead door she remembered later, in fragments, like the recalled pieces of a dream.

'Then we'll do that, Skipper. Hitch a few pounds of chain to her feet, and gently over the side …'

The voice she knew. That was the boy who had helped her. The angry rising inflection she didn't know; that was the voice of Wales.

Something unheard.

'How can she talk, man, what does she bloody know? Just a bloody dumb kid, see …'

'Make up the log,' said the skipper bitterly.

'Don't you see, man?'

'Make up the log …'

Becky leaned her head on her arms, and groaned.

She couldn't reach the bunk. She arced her body awkwardly, tried again. The blankets were delicious heaven. She huddled into them, too empty to worry about the after-scent of vomit on her clothes. She fell into a sleep shot through with vivid dreams; the face of the Christos, Father Antony like an old dried animal, mouth champing as he scolded and blessed; the church tower in the pre-dawn glow, the gargoyle ears. Then flowers dusty in a cottage garden, her mum bawling and grumbling before she died, icy feel of water round her groin, shape of *White Boat* fading into mist. All faint things and worries and griefs, scuttling lobsters, tar and pebbles, feel of the night sea wind, the Great Catechism torn and snatched. She moved finally into a deeper dream where it seemed the Boat herself talked to her. Her voice was rushing and immense yet chuckling and lisping and somehow coloured, blue and roaring green. She spoke about the little people on her back and her duties, her rushing and scurrying and fighting with the wind; she told great truths that were lost as soon as uttered, blown away and buried in the dark. Becky clenched her fists, writhing; woke to hear still the bang and slap of the sea, slept again.

She came round to someone gently shaking her shoulder. Again she was disoriented. The motion of the boat was stopped; lamps burned in the cabin; through the ports other lights gleamed, making rippling reflections that reached to within inches of the glass. From outside came a sound she knew; the fast rap and flutter of halliards against masts, night-noise of a harbour of boats. She swung her legs down blearily; rubbed her face, not knowing where she was. Not daring to ask.

A meal was laid in the cabin, great kedgerees of rice and shellfish pieces, mushrooms and eggs. Surprisingly, she was hungry; she sat shoulder to shoulder with the boy who had spoken for her, had, she realized, argued for her life in the bright afternoon. She ate mechanically and quickly, eyes not leaving her plate; round her the talk flowed unheeding. She crouched small, glad to be forgotten.

They took her with them when they went ashore. In the dinghy she felt more at ease. They sat in a waterfront bar, in France, drank bottle on bottle of wine till her head spun again and voices and noise seemed blended in a warm roaring. She snuggled, on the Welshman's knees, feeling safe again and wanted. She tried to talk then, about the fossils in the rocks and her father and the Church and swimming and nearly being drowned; they scuffed her hair, laughing, not understanding. The wine ran down her neck inside the sweater; she laughed back and watched the lamps spin, head drooping, lids half closed on dark-lashed hazel eyes.

'*Ahoy,* White Boat …'

She stood shivering, seeing the lamps drive spindled images into the water, hearing men reel along the quay, hearing the shouts, feeling still the tingling surprise of foreignness. While *White Boat* answered faint from the mass of vessels, the tender crept splashing out of the night.

She was still barefoot; she felt the water tart against her ankles as she scuttled down to catch the dinghy's bow.

'Here,' said David. 'Not puttin' you to bed twice in a bloody day …'

She felt her head hit the rolled blankets that served as a pillow; muttered and grinned, pushed blearily at the waistband of her jeans, gave up, collapsed in sleep.

The miles of water slid past, chuckling in a dream.

She woke quickly to darkness, knowing once more she had been fooled. They had slipped out of harbour, in the night; that heave and roll, chuckling and bowstring sense of tightness, was the feel of the open sea.

White Boat, and these people, never slept.

There were voices again. And lights gleaming, rattle of descending sails, scrape of something rolling against the hull. Scufflings then, and thuds. She lay curled in the bunk, face turned away from the cabin.

'No, she's asleep …'

'Easy with that now, man …'

She chuckled, silently. The clink of bottles, thump of secret bales, amused her. There was nothing more to fear; these people were smugglers.

She woke heavy and irritable. The source of irritation was for a time mysterious. She attempted, unwillingly, to analyse her feelings; for her, an unusual exercise. The wildest, most romantic notions of *White Boat* were true; yet she was cheated. This she knew instinctively. She saw the village street then, the little black clustering houses, the church. The priest mouthing silently, condemning; her father, black-faced, unfastening his broad, buckled belt. To this she would return, irrevocably; the dream was finished.

That was it; the point of pain, the taste and very essence of it. That she didn't belong, aboard *White Boat*. She never would. Abruptly she found herself hating the crew for the knowledge they had given so freely. They should have beaten her, loved her till she bled, tied her feet, slammed her into the deep green sea. They had done nothing, because to them she was worth nothing. Not even death.

She refused food, for the second time. She thought the skipper looked at her with worried eyes. She ignored him; she took up her old position, gripping the friendly thickness of the mast. The day was sunny and bright; the boat moved fast, under the great spread whiteness of a Genoa, dipping lee scuppers under, jouncing through the sea. Almost she wished for the sickness of the day before, the hour when she'd wanted so urgently to die. As *White Boat* raised, slowly, the coast of England.

Her mind seemed split now into halves, one part wanting the voyage indefinitely prolonged, the other needing to rush on disaster, have it over and done. The day faded slowly to dusk, dusk to deep night. In the dark she saw the cressets of a signal tower, flaring, moving pinpoints; and another answering it, and another far beyond. They would be signalling for her, without a doubt; calling across the moors, through all the long bays. She curled her lip. She had discovered cynicism.

The wind blew chill across the sea.

Forward of the mast, a hatch gave access to the sail locker. She lowered herself into it, curled atop the big sausage shapes of canvas. The bulkhead door, ajar and creaking, showed shifting gleams of yellow from the cabin lamps. Here the water noise was intensified; she listened sullenly to the chuckle and seethe, half-wanting in her bitterness the boat to strike some reef and drown. While the light moved, forward and back across the sloping painted walls. She began picking half-unconsciously at the paint, crumbling little brittle flakes in her palm.

The loose boards interested her.

By the lamplight she saw part of the wooden side move slightly, out of time with the upright that supported it. She edged across, pulled experimentally. There was a hatch, behind it a space into which she could reach her arm. She groped tentatively, drew out a slim oilcloth packet. Then another. There were many of them, crowded away in the double hull; little things, not much bigger than the boxes of lucifers she bought sometimes in the village shop.

On impulse she pushed one of them into the waistband of her trews. She scurried the rest out of sight again, closed the trap, sat frowning. She sat rubbing the little packet, feeling it warm slowly against her flesh, determined for the first time in her life to steal; wanting some part of *White Boat* maybe, something to hold at night and remember. Something precious.

Somebody had been very careless.

There was a voice above her, a moving of feet on the deck. She scrambled guiltily, climbed back through the hatch. But they weren't interested in her. Ahead the coastline showed solid, velvet-black. She saw the loom of twin headlands, faintest gleam of waves round long stone moles, and realized with a shock and thrill of coldness that she was home.

She saw other things too, heresies that stopped her breath. Machines, uncovered now, whirred and ticked in the cabin. Bands of light flickered pink, moved against a scale of figures; she heard the chanting as they edged into the bay, seven fathoms, five, four. As the devil-boat came in, with nobody at the lead …

The dinghy swung from its place atop the cabin, thumped into the sea. She scrambled down, clutching her parcelled dress. Another bundle was lowered, heavier, chinking musically. For her father, she was told; and to say, 'twas from the Boat. A bribe of silence that; or a double bluff, confession of a little crime to hide one monstrously worse. They called to her, low-voiced; she waved mechanically, seeing as she turned away the last descending flutter of the jib. The dinghy headed in slow, the Welsh boy at the tiller. She knelt upright on the bottom boards till the boat bumped the mole, grated and rolled. She was out then quickly, scuttling away. He called her as she reached the bottom of the path. She turned waiting, a frail shadow in the night.

He seemed unsure how to go on. 'You must understand, see,' he said unhappily. 'You must never do this again. Do you understand, Becky?'

'Yes,' she said. 'Goodbye.' She turned and ran again up the path to the stream, over the bridge to home.

There was a window they always left open, over the wash-house roof. She left the bundles in the outhouse; the door hinge creaked as she closed it but nothing stirred. She climbed cautiously, padded through the dark to her room. She lay on the bed, feeling the faint rocking that meant mystically she was still in communion with the great boat down there in the bay. A last conscious thought made her pull the package from her waist, tuck it beneath the layers of mattress.

Her father seemed in the dawn light a stranger. There was no explanation she cared to give, nothing to say. She was still drugged with sleep; she felt with indifference the unbuckling of her trews, heard him draw the belt slow through his hands. Dazed, she imagined the beating would have no power to hurt; she was wrong. The pain exploded forward and back through her body, stabbing in red flashes behind her eyes. She squeezed the bedrail, needing to die again, knowing disjointedly there was no help in words. Her body had sprung from rock and shale, the gloomy vastness of the fields; the strap fell not on her but on the headlands, the rocks, the sea. Exorcizing the loneliness of the place, the misery and hopelessness and pain. He finished finally, turned away groping to barge through the door. Downstairs in the little house a child wailed, sensing hatred and fear; she moved her head slightly on the pillow, hearing it seemed from far off the breathing wash of the sea.

Her fingers moved down to coil on the packet in the bed. Slowly, with indifference, she began picking at the fastenings. Scratching the knots, pulling and teasing till the wrapping came away. It was her pleasure to imagine herself blind, condemned to touch and feel. The fingers, oversensitive, strayed and tapped, turning the little thing, feeling variations of texture, shapes of warmth and coldness, exploring bleakly the tiny map of heresy. A tear, her first, rolled an inch from one eye, left a shining track against the brownness of the skin.

She had the heart of *White Boat*, gripped in her hand.

The priest came, tramping heavy on the stairs. Her father pushed ahead of him, covered her roughly. Her hand stayed by her side unseen as Father Antony talked. She lay quiet, face down, lashes brushing her cheek, knowing immobility and patience were her best defence. The light from the window faded as he sat; when he left, it was nearly night.

In the gloom she lifted the stolen thing, touched it to her face. The heretical smell of it, of wax and bakelite and brass, assaulted her mind faintly. She stroked it again, lovingly; while she held it gripped it seemed she could call *White Boat* to her bidding, bring her in from her wanderings time and again.

The sun stayed hidden in the days that followed, while she lay on the cliffs and saw the yacht flit in and go. A greater barrier separated her now than the sea she had learned to cross; a barrier built not by others but by her own stupidity.

She killed a great blue lobster, slowly and with pain, driving nails through the membraned cracks of its armour while it threshed and writhed. She cut it apart slowly, hating herself and all the world, dropped the pieces in the sea for a bitter, useless sacrifice. This and other things she did to ease the emptiness in her, fill the progression of iron-grey afternoons. There were vices to be learned, at night and out on the rocks, little gratifications of pleasure and pain. She indulged her body, contemptuously; because *White Boat* had come cajoling and free, thrown her back laughing, indifferent to hurt. Life stretched before her now like an endless cage: where, she asked herself, was the Change once promised, the great things the priest John had seen? The Golden Age that would bring other *White Boat*s, other days and hope; the wild waves of the very air made to talk and sing ...

She fondled the tiny heart of the Boat, in the black dark, felt the wires and coils, the little tubes of valves.

The church was still and cold, the priest's breathing faint behind the little carved screen. She waited while he talked and murmured, unhearing; while her hands closed and opened on the thing she carried, the sweat sprang out on the palms.

And it was done, hopelessly and sullen. She pushed the little machine at the grille, waited greyly for the intake of breath, the panic-scrabble of feet from the other side.

The face of Father Antony was beyond description.

The village stirred, whispering and grumbling, people scurrying forward and back between the houses gaping at the soldiers in the street, the shouting horsemen and officers. Sappers, working desperately, rigged sheerlegs along the line of cliffs, swung tackles from the heavy beams. Garrisons stood at alert right back to Durnovaria; this land had rebelled before, the commanders were taking no chances. Signallers, ironic-faced, worked and flapped the arms of half a hundred semaphores; despatch riders galloped, raking their mounts bloody as the questions and instructions flew. A curfew was clapped on the village, the people driven to their homes; but nothing could stop the rumours, the whisperings and unease. Heresy walked like a spectre, blew in on the sea wind; till a man saw the old monk himself, grim-faced and empty-eyed, stalking the clifftops in his tattered gown. Detachments of cavalry quartered the downs, but there was nothing to be found. Through the night, and into the darkest time before the dawn, the one street of the village echoed to the marching tramp of men. Then there was a silent time of waiting. The breeze soughed up from the bay, moving the tangles of gorse, crying across the huddled roofs; while Becky, lying quiet, listened for the first whisper, the shout that would send the soldiers to their posts, train the waiting guns.

She lay on her face, hair tangled on the pillow, hearing the night wind, clenching and slowly unclenching her hands. It seemed the shouting still echoed in her brain, the harangues, thumping of tables, red-faced noise of priests. She saw her father standing glowering and sullen while the cobalt-tuniced major questioned over and again, probing, insisting, till in misery questions became answers and answers made their own fresh confusion. The sea moved in her brain, dulling sense, while the cannon came trundling and peering behind the straining mules, crashing trails and limbers on the rough ground till the noise clapped forward and back between the houses and she put hands to ears and cried to stop, just to stop …

They wrung her dry, between them. She told things she had told to nobody, secrets of bay and beach and lapping waves, fears and dreams; everything they heard stony-faced while the clerks scribbled, the semaphores clacked on the hills. They left her finally, in her house, in her room, soldiers guarding the door and her father swearing and drunk downstairs and the neighbours pecking and fluttering over the children, making as they spoke of her and hers the sign of the Cross. She lay an age while understanding came and grew, while her nails marked her palms and the tears squeezed hot and slow. The wind droned, soughing under the eaves; blowing strong and cool and steady, bringing *White Boat* in to death.

Never before had her union with the Boat seemed stronger. She saw her with the clarity of nightmare, moon washing the tilted deck, sails gleaming darkly against the loom of land. She tried in desperation to force her mind out over the sea; she prayed to turn, go back, fly away. *White Boat* heard, but made no answer; she came on steadily, angry and inexorable.

Becky sat up quietly, padded to the window. She saw the bright night, the moonglow in the little cluttered yard. In the street footsteps clicked, faded to quiet. A bird called, hunting, while cloud wisps groped for and extinguished the moon.

She shivered, easing at the sash. Once before she had known an alien steadiness, a coldness that made her movements smooth and calm. She placed a foot carefully on the outhouse tiles, ducked through the window, thumped into the deeper shadow of the house wall. She waited, listening to silence.

They were not stupid, these soldiers of the Pope. She sensed rather than saw the sentry at the bottom of the garden, slipped like a wraith through darkness till she was near enough almost to touch his cloak. She waited patient, eyes watching white and blind while the moon eased clear, was obscured again. In front of her the boy yawned, leaned his musket against the wall. He called something sleepily, sauntered a dozen paces up the road.

She was over the wall instantly, feet scuffling. Her skirt snagged, pulled clear. She ran, padding on the road, waiting for the shout, the flash and bang of a gun. The dream was undisturbed.

The bay lay silver and broad. She moved cautiously, parting bracken, wriggling to the edge of the cliff. Beneath her, twenty yards away, men clustered smoking and talking. The pipes they lit carefully, backs to the sea and shielded by their cloaks, unwilling to expose the slightest gleam of light. The tide was making, washing in across the ramps and up among the rocks; the moon stood now above the far headland, showing it stark against a milky haze.

In front of her were the guns.

She watched down at them, eyes wide. Six heavy pieces, humped and sullen, staring out across the sea. She saw the cunning behind the placement; that shot, ball or canister, fired nearly level with the water, would hurtle on spreading and rebounding. The Boat would have no chance. She would come in, on to the guns; and they would fire. There would be no warning, no offers of quarter; just the sudden orange thunder from the land, the shot coming tearing and smashing …

She strained her eyes. Far out on the dim verge of sky and sea was a smudge that danced as she watched and returned, insistent, dark grey against the greyness of the void. The tallness of a sail, heading in toward the coast.

She ran again, scrambling and jumping; slid into the stream, followed it where its chuckling could mask sounds of movement, crouched glaring on the edge of the beach. The soldiers had seen too; there was a stirring, a rustling surge of dark figures away from the cliff. Men ran to point and stare, train night glasses at the sea. Their backs were to the guns.

There was no time to think; none to do more than swallow, try and quiet the thunder of her heart. Then she was running desperately, feet spurning the grit, stumbling on boulders and buried stones. Behind her a shout, the rolling crash of a musket, cursing of an officer. The ball glanced from rock, threw splinters at her back and calves. She leaped and swerved, landed on her knees. She saw men running, the bright flash of a sword. Another report, distant and unassociated. She panted, rolled on her back beside the first of the guns.

It was unimportant that her body burned with fire. Her fingers gripped the lanyard, curled lovingly and pulled.

A hugeness of flame, a roar; the flash lit the cliffs, sparkled out across the sea. The gun lurched back, angry and alive; while all down the line the pieces fired, random now and furious, the shot fizzing over the water. The cannonade echoed from the headlands, boomed across the village; woke a girl who mocked and squealed, in her bed, in her room, the noise vaunting up wild and high into the night.

While *White Boat*, turning, laughed at the guns.

And spurned the land.

THE PASSING OF THE DRAGONS

There's no real reason for an Epsilon Dragon to die. None the less, they do.

By 'real reasons' I don't, of course, include atmosphere, soil and plant pollution, direct and indirect blast effects and ultrasonic fracture of the inner ear. Most of the things that will do for a human being will do for a Dragon. They are, or were, more than humanly affected by high frequencies; the tympani were numerous and large, situated in a row down each side of the body an inch or so above the lateral line. Which you can see for yourself if you can get off your butt long enough to get down to the museum of the Institute of Alien Biology.

The other things that can kill a Dragon are more interesting, as I explained to Pilot (First Class) Scott-Braithwaite a few weeks after our arrival on (or coincidence with) Epsilon Cygnus VI. The specimen under consideration flowed and clattered into the clearing by the lab about thirteen hundred hours, Planetary Time. I was checking the daily meter readings, I didn't pay too much attention till I saw the three sets of whips a Dragon carries on its back flatten out and immobilize. It made the thing look like a little green and gold helicopter squatting there on the grass.

I picked up the stethoscope and the Röntgen viewer and walked outside. A Dragon has eight hearts, situated in two rows of four between the eighth and twelfth body segments. I attached the stethoscope sensors, studied the display. As I'd expected, the first cardiac pair had become inoperative. Pairs two and four seemed to be showing reduced activity; pair three, presumably, were sustaining residual body functions. Since breathing is by spiracles and tracheae, body function isn't all that easy to confirm. I used the viewer and stood up, leaned my hands on the knobbly back-armour. 'Well,' I said, 'our friend here is headed for the Happy Chewing Grounds. Or wherever they go.'

The Pilot (First Class) frowned. He said, 'How can you tell?'

I shrugged and walked round the Dragon. There was a slight injury, in the soft membrane between two body segments; a little fluid had wept across the armour, but it didn't seem critical. If Dragons were arthopods, as their appearance suggests, collapse from a minor abrasion would be understandable; but the body is no fluid sac, they have a blood-vascular system as well defined as that of a mammal. On the other hand the possibility of infection couldn't be ruled out. I fetched a hypodermic from the lab, drew off a fluid sample. Later I'd take tissue cuttings. They'd be clean, of course. They always are.

I'd brought the surgical kit out with me. I rigged a pair of pacemakers, set the collars on the probes to the standard twenty-five-centimetre penetration. I measured a handspan from the median lines, pushed the needles down through the joint membrane, used the stethoscope again. The trace bounced around a bit, and steadied.

He leaned over me. I suppose one might say, 'keen face intent'. He said, 'Working?'

I shrugged, I said, 'Any fool can make a heart pump. It isn't much of a trick.'

He said, 'Then it'll be OK.'

I shook my head. I said, 'It'll die.'

He said, 'When?'

I lifted one of the whips, let it droop back. I said, 'In thirty hours, twenty-eight minutes Terrestrial.'

He raised his eyebrows.

I said kindly, 'Planetary revolution.'

I walked back to the lab. I'd decided to run a cardiograph. Not that it would tell us any more than the thousand or two already on file at IAB. But it's one of the things one does. It's called Making an Effort. Or showing the Flag.

He was still standing where I'd left him. He said, 'I can't understand these damn things.'

Most of his conversation was like that. Incisive. Really kept you on your toes.

I started attaching the sensors of the cardiogram. You should listen to a Dragon's heart sometime. It's like the pulse of a star. Or maybe you're a fan of the Hottentots. They based their style on IAB recordings, so I'm told; so the Dragons, you see, have been of service to mankind.

He said, 'Why planetary revolution?'

I smiled at him. 'Do you know, Pilot, First Class,' I said, 'I have no idea.'

He frowned. He said, 'I thought you scientists had all the answers.'

His repartee certainly was a joy to the ear.

I said, 'I'm not a scientist. Just a Behaviourist.' I smiled again. 'Technician,' I said. 'Second class.'

He didn't answer that one. They don't encourage morbid self-analysis at Space School.

I walked back through the specimen lock. I'd had it rigged some time now. I'd been asked to take a living Dragon back to Earth. Not that it would survive phase-out. They never do. But that's what science is all about for most of us: a lot of little people doing what's been done before, and not succeeding either.

He followed me. He had that trick. He said, 'Can I help?'

I said, 'No, thanks.' I was thinking how difficult it must be for him, lumbered with a type like me. My teeth are less than pearly, my body is less than sylphlike; I don't play peloa, I drink my ale by the pint and what I say sometimes has some relation to what I think. It must have been hell.

He lit a cigarette. At least he had one insanitary habit. Maybe there were more. You can never tell, by appearances.

I switched the recorder on. The traces started zipping along the display. I turned the replay volume up. The sound thudded at us. He winced. He said, 'Do we have to have that?'

I said, 'It soothes me.' I gave the volume another notch. I said, 'You must have heard the Hottentots.'

He said, 'That's different.'

Man, was his conversation uptight. This was being a great tour.

I listened to the heartbeats. The rhythms phased in and out of each other like drums; or bells underground, ringing a change that was endless.

He said, 'And that thing's going to die?'

I didn't answer. I was thinking about the Dragon. Difficult to dissociate the notion of purpose from things that take exactly a day to die. Neither a second more nor less. But it's difficult to dissociate the notion of purpose from anything a Dragon does. Or did. For instance, they built cities. Or we thought they were cities. We were never too sure, one way or the other.

I ejected the sample into a centrifuge, locked the case and switched on. He watched me for a bit. Then he yawned. He said, 'I'm going to have a kip till contact time. Call me if you need me.'

I kept my back turned till the door had shut. With the din I'd set up he was going to be lucky. But some people can sleep through anything. Probably to do with leading a healthy life.

He started on the subject again at suppertime. He'd got a radio running; music was playing, from the room next door. The room we call Earth. My Dragon's jazz was still thumping in the lab. I changed channels, got the Hottentots. It made an interesting counterpoint. He changed back. He said, 'How many of those things do you reckon there are out there?'

'What things? Pop groups?'

He said, 'Dragons.'

I let a can of soup preheat, picked it up, burned my fingers and opened it. I said, 'A hundred, hundred and fifty. That was at the last count. Probably halved by now.'

He frowned. He said, 'What's killing them?'

I did rather take that as a silly question. Epsilon Cygnus VI just happens to have a mineral-rich crust containing about everything Homo Sapiens has ever found a use for, from gold to lithium. My species had blown in ten years back; now the rest of the planet was an automated slagtip.

I started ticking points on my fingers. I said, 'Ecological imbalance triggered by waterborne effluent. Toxic concentration of broad-spectrum herbicides—'

He waved a hand, irritably. He said, 'They've got a whole damn subcontinent to live in. There's no mining here.'

I said, 'So they die from minor abrasions. Maybe they're making a gesture.'

He looked at me narrowly. He said, 'You've got some damn queer ideas.'

I said, 'I'm an observer. I'm not paid to have ideas.'

'But you said—'

'I pointed out psychological factors may exist. Or there again, they may not. Either way, we shall never know. Hence my engrossment.'

He frowned again. He said, 'I don't follow you.'

'There's not much to follow. I'm fascinated by failure. It runs in the family.'

He shook his head. I think he was grappling with a concept. He said, 'You mean—'

'I didn't mean anything. I was just making light conversation. As per handbook.'

He flushed. He said, 'You don't have to be so bloody rude about it.'

I slung the can at the disposal unit. For once, I hit it. I said, 'I'm sorry, Space Pilot.' I smiled. I said, 'Us civvies, you know. Nerves wear a bit thin. Don't have your cast-iron constitutions.'

I don't have the stoicism of the upper bourgeoisie either. If I cut my finger, I usually whimper.

He flashed me a white grin. That's the most offensive sentence I can think of, so I'll leave it in. It describes what he did so well. He said, 'Forget it, Researcher. I'm a bit on edge myself.'

Oh, those lines! I was starting to wonder whether he had an inexhaustible stockpile of them. There must be an end somewhere, even to aphorisms.

I walked to the blinds, lifted the slats. Night on Epsilon VI is greenish, like the days. Like a thick pea soup, with turquoise overtones. The heartbeat thudded in the next room.

I picked up a handlamp. I said, 'I'm going out to check the patient.' The comic-opera habit was evidently catching.

He said, 'I'll come with you.'

I think his nerves were getting bad. He had an automatic strapped to his hip; on the way through the lab he collected a rocket pistol as well. There are no dangerous fauna on Epsilon VI; in fact at the time of writing I'm predisposed to believe there are no fauna at all. There used to be some pretty big lepidoptera, though. I said, 'You should have brought a scattergun. They're difficult to hit with ball.'

He said, 'What?'

I said, 'The moths.'

He didn't deign to answer.

The Dragon squatted where we had left it. I turned the lamp on. The halogen-quartz cut a white cone through the murk. Furry flying things blundered across the light. I swung the beam round. The jungle was empty.

He was standing with his hands on his hips, the holster flap tucked back. He said, 'What are you looking for?'

I said, 'The mourners should be arriving pretty soon.'

'The *what*?'

I said, 'Mourners. But again, I'm theorizing without data.'

'What do they do?'

I said, 'Nothing. Stand around. Generally they eat the corpse.'

He made a disgusted noise.

I said, '*Autre temps, autre mondes* ...' I switched the light off. I said, 'I like these field jobs, you know. They broaden one.'

He walked back ahead of me to the lab. I closed the door and bolted it, for his peace of mind.

I don't sleep too well these days. Like the poet says, old bones are hard to please. I lay and read a while. Afterwards I drank whisky. The site storeroom had a cellar like nobody's business. It should have had; IAB observer teams had been stocking it surreptitiously for a decade. I poured myself another good slug. No point leaving the stuff to rot; there wouldn't be any more folk coming this way. They'd cleaned up all the easy deposits on Epsilon VI; the archipelago on which we'd landed, a big curve of islands stretching into the southern ocean, was about the only land surface left unraped. It was also the last stronghold of the Dragons.

I put the glass down, sat staring at the dural wall. IAB had had assurance, of course, from Trade Control; but once assurances start arriving three times a year you know the end isn't far off. The principle of the thing's simple, as simple as all truly great ideas; while a single rumpled little Earthman with spiky yellow shoes can make a single rumpled little spiky yellow dollar, the killing goes on. Any killing. Next season they'd open-caste the islands; the Dragons had had their chance.

The Pilot (First Class) kept his light on well into the night. Maybe he was reading. I wondered vaguely whether he masturbated. I wasn't too concerned, one way or the other; but a Behaviourist gets into the way of collecting odd facts.

I'd turned the playback volume down but left it running. The Dragon's hearts thumped steadily through the thin metal wall. Toward the middle of the night the rhythm altered. I got up, pulled a jacket on and went outside.

There's no moon on Epsilon; but there is a massive aurora belt. The green sky flashed and flickered; it was like the brewing of a perpetual storm. The Dragon's whips vibrated faintly; the golden eye-clusters watched without interest. I used the stethoscope. The second and fourth heart pairs were dead. I applied a second and third set of pacemakers. Pair two picked up; pair four wouldn't kick over. I decided a stimulant couldn't do any harm. I went back to the lab, checked the chart, filled a syringe. I shot enough strychnine into the heart walls to kill a terrestrial horse. I saw the trace pick up and steady. Interesting. I thought vaguely I should have taken encephalographs as well.

The idea of stimulants was a good one. I went back, drank some more whisky. Then I dozed.

The mourners began to arrive at first light.

I heard the rustling and clattering and got up. I pulled on slacks and a shirt, stared through the lab port. The dawn was as green as the rest of the day; smoky emerald, fading to clear high lemon where Epsilon Cygnus struggled with the mist. A Dragon passed a yard or so away, jerking and lumbering like a thing at the bottom of an ocean. It was a big one, I judged a potential male. Dragons are parthenogenetic most of the time; over the years they sometimes develop sexual characteristics and mate conventionally. The analysis people had an idea it was to do with sunspot activity; but if there's a correlation we didn't give the computers enough hard facts to pinpoint it. The whole thing just made phylum classification a bit more entertaining.

The newcomer stopped a yard or more from the immobilized Dragon, and waved its whips. They were ten or twelve feet long, banded in green, orange and black. Ball and socket joints several inches across joined them to the body armour; round the base of each were tufts of stiff, iridescent hair.

The yellow eyes watched; the whips moved and stroked, touching the body of the dying creature from end to end. The head of the Dragon rotated, the jawparts clicked; then the thing reared its forepart into the air, lapsed into immobility. I'd seen the stance before. So had a lot of folk.

I opened the lab door, stepped outside. The morning air was cool and sweet. I walked up to the new arrival. The eye-clusters stared, like blank jewels. I wondered if it was seeing me.

I heard footsteps behind me. The Pilot (First Class) looked concerned. He said, 'Jupiter, is this the first?'

I nodded. I said, 'Good one, isn't he?'

He rubbed his face. He was wearing a white shirt, open to the waist. On his chest hung a heavy silver cross. Very fashionable.

There was a crackling in the jungle. Number two advanced slowly, through the moving coils of mist. It looked like a brilliant little armoured vehicle. The flowing of the clasper legs was invisible; you could have imagined readily enough that it was running on tracks.

It moved to the bunch of cables I'd stretched from the patient, and checked. The whips shook, stooped; rose again vertically above its back. It didn't seem to object to the cables overmuch; neither did it cross them. It turned, followed their line to the dying Dragon. The same ritual was observed. The whips rustled; then the creature arched itself, lapsed like its fellow into stillness.

The pilot (First Class) had his hand on the butt of the automatic. I shook my head. Dragons are harmless. Their mouthparts could take your arm off; but if you put your fingers between the mandibles they just stop working. I'd told him often enough, but it seemed he wasn't convinced.

He trailed after me back to the lab. He said, 'How many of these things do you expect to arrive?'

I said, 'Ten. Or a dozen.'

'What'll they do?'

I said, 'Like I told you. Stand around.'

He said, 'They're waiting for it to die.'

I set water on to boil. I said, 'Could be.'

He frowned. He said, 'They're obviously waiting.'

I laid out plates and cups. I said, 'It's by no means obvious. "Wait" as a concept depends on human-based time awareness. They may lack that awareness. In which case, they are not waiting.'

He said, 'It's a bit of a quibble though.'

I shook my head. 'Certainly not,' I said. 'Consider a proposition. "The rocks of the valley waited." That's more than a quibble. It's a howling pathetic fallacy.'

He glared at me. He said, 'If they're living, they have time awareness.'

I shrugged. I said, 'Try telling a tree.'

'I didn't mean that.'

'Then trees aren't living. Interesting.'

He said, 'You are the most argumentative bastard I ever met.'

I said, 'Hard words, Captain. In any case it's not true. For argumentative read definitive.'

He swallowed his temper, like a good skipper. My word, these boys have self-control. They're pretty fine male specimens, of course, all the way round.

By midmorning nine of the creatures had arrived. I set up the encephalogram, fixed the probes. A Dragon has a massive brain, situated behind and below the eyes. Capacity betters the human cranium by an average of twenty-five per cent. Nearly the same was once true of terrestrial dolphins. But they never learned to talk.

I watched the pens record. Something like an alpha rhythm was emerging.

By thirteen hundred Planetary Time the wave forms were altering, developing greater valleys and peaks. The crisis was approaching; but it was nothing new. I lit a pipe, walked outside. The heartbeats thundered from the open lab door. At thirteen-forty the first pair shut down. Then pairs two and three. I counted the beats on pair four. Then the glade was silent. I said, 'That's it, then.' I logged the time; Earth Standard and Planetary, hours and minutes from sun-up. I pulled the probes out, disconnected them, started coiling the cables.

He stood staring. He said, 'Aren't you going to do anything?'

I said, 'Like what?'

He said, 'Try it with a shot. Something like that.'

I said, 'You can if you like. Speaking from my human-based awareness, I'd say it was a waste of time.'

Dead, the thing looked just as it had when living; but the gold was fading slowly from the eyes.

He sat on the metal step of the lab, and lit a cigarette. He looked shaken up.

The jade-green ring of Dragons made no move. They stood poised through the afternoon, like so many cumbersome statues. Occasionally one or other of the pairs of whips would rise, tremble, sink again; but that was all. I cut tissue specimens for autopsy, stripped the pacemakers, autoclaved the probes. Then I scrubbed up and went through to the living quarters. He was sitting reading a glossy magazine somebody had left about. It had a full-frontal stereograph on the cover. She looked pretty good. I walked back to the lab, ran the tapes and started up. The heartbeat of the dead Dragon filled the air.

I heard him fling the book down. He stood in the doorway, staring. He said, 'Do we have to have that again?'

I said, 'We do. There might be a clue.'

'A what?'

I said, 'Think of it as a sort of Cosmic Code. It may help.'

We ate. The Dragons stayed in their circle. Afterwards he walked out. He didn't say where he was going, which is against the rules if you're going strictly by the book. There was a little vertol flier in one of the hangar sheds. I heard it start up, drone away towards the west.

I turned the replay volume up. The heartbeats thudded in the clearing. I got a heavy speaker housing from the lab, set it out on the grass, blasted the noise at the Dragons. It had been tried before, of course. They hadn't reacted then. They didn't react now. I dismantled the rig, put the gear away and shut down. The glade was very still, the veiled sun dropping towards the west.

I got my jacket, and a pair of prismatics. I walked due south, away from the lab. About a mile off, a rocky bluff thrust up through a mustard-green tide of trees. The front of the cliff, golden now in the slanting light, was riddled with holes. I used the glasses. A dozen were occupied; I could see the yellow masks staring down. The rest were empty and blank.

At the foot of the cliff was a roughly circular clearing. In it stood a dozen or more massive structures. The quartz chunks of which they were mainly composed flashed and glittered, throwing back the brilliant light. They formed columns, arcades, porticoes. At intervals openwork platforms pierced the towers; it made them look a little like gigantic rose trellises. Sprays of viridian creeper twined from level to level, enhancing the illusion. It was presumed the Dragons built them; though the proposition had never been proved. IAB had been interested in them for years, off and on. A docket went round whenever somebody had a bright idea. I'd seen nests, temples and freeform sculpture all put up as propositions. You paid your money, and you took your choice.

The city was the main reason for the siting of the lab. We'd put it a mile away initially in case the Dragons reacted to our presence. The hope had been wild and wilful; nobody had yet seen them react to anything.

I walked back to the lab. There was no sign of the Pilot (First Class). I set the coffee on again, picked up the girlie book, skimmed the pages. I was pleased to see they were letting a few white strippers back in on the act. Emancipation, like everything else, can go too far.

Towards nightfall I checked the port. The ring of Dragons had closed in; one of them was stretching its neck segments, nuzzling forward and back along the corpse like a cat skimming cream from a saucer. After a time the mouthparts settled to a steady motion. I logged the event.

The flier landed. A wait; and I heard the Pilot's footsteps in the clearing. He barged in through the lab door. He said, 'They're eating it. It's bloody horrible.'

I put the mag down. I said, 'The fact has been noted.'

He said, 'It's bloody horrible. And you reckoned those things were intelligent.'

'I can't remember reckoning anything. In any case it doesn't preclude the possibility.'

'You must be joking!'

I said, 'Perhaps it's a religious observance. Which would make it highly sophisticated.'

'A *what*?'

I remembered the cross round his neck. He was a neo-Catholic, of course. He had to be. I said, 'It has all the distinguishing characteristics.'

He sat down heavily, and lit a cigarette. He said, 'You're mad.'

'I wish I was. I'd get more fun out of life. Remember the Dream of the Rood?'

'No.'

I clucked at him. 'Dear me, And part of your course was the Humanities.'

He glowered. I smiled at him. I said, 'Teatime, Skipper. Your turn to undo the cans.'

He said, 'As a matter of fact, I'm not hungry.'

I said, 'Pity. I am. Force of habit, of course. But powerful. Rule One of the Behaviourist.' I got up, started banging pots and pans round in the galley. I said, 'Blood sacrifice. Eat, for this is my flesh. Also see Tennessee Williams. Mid-twentieth century. American.'

He stood. He said, 'I'm going to get cleaned up.'

I said, 'They probably have. It's a very old sofa.'

'*What?*'

'Nothing. Daddy has some timeslip trouble. Bear with an old man.'

He walked out. He'd started slamming doors.

I kicked the girlie stereo under the side table. Not so much from frustration as pique. One dislikes being constantly offered what isn't for sale.

He started singing in the shower. He always sang in the shower. His voice was very good. Light tenor. I expected he used a good aftershave too. I wondered just what the hell a Dragon would make of him anyway. Pink for skin, brown for hair, white for teeth. You could analyse the picture till it fragmented. Then you had a monster of your own.

The bath put him into a better humour. He emerged from his labours at seventeen hundred, Planetary. He was wearing a white uniform jacket, with the braids and brassard of his Order. He capered up to me, spun me round, slapped me on the back. Then he sat in a chair, legs asprawl, grinned and lit a cigarette. He said, 'Judy's coming through. On the Link.'

I said, 'I bet she's your fiancée.'

He looked hurt. He said, 'You know she is. You met her before lift-off. She's a model.'

I said, 'Ah, yes.' It was the Little Girl Look this year, Earthside. Which meant candid blue eyes, golden curls, tits like stoplights. I said, 'Thoughtless of me. I remember her well. A charming person, I thought.'

He looked at the chronometer on the lab bulkhead. He said, 'We're getting married. Straight after this tour.'

I said, 'I expect you are.'

He gave me a dirty look. He said, 'I suppose that fits a behaviour pattern too.'

I said, 'It very well might.'

He said viciously, 'Why don't you run a programme on it? You might come up with some new facts.'

I yawned. I said, 'Fortunately, I don't have to. I read tea leaves. Saves a lot of computer time.'

The buzzer sounded. He started the Richardsons. Earth Control exchanged the time of day; then Judy came on. She was as I remembered her. Love through the Loop; she had the sort of voice that can squeeze sex out of duralumin. He said, 'Hello, darling,' and she said, 'Hello, Drew.' Drew, yet ... I tried the full effect. Drew Scott-Braithwaite. I got up, went looking for the whisky. I needed something to take the taste away.

She said, 'How are you?'

He said, 'Fine, love, just fine.'

I poured three fingers.

She said, 'How's the project?'

He said, 'Fine.'

I walked out to the lab, started labelling and packing the heart tapes. She said, 'Who's that with you? I can't see, he's not in camera.'

He said, 'Researcher Fredericks. You met him at lift-off.'

She said, 'Are you looking after him?'

He said, 'He's fine.'

The speaker said, 'Give him my love.'

Drew said, 'She sends you her love.'

I said, 'That's fine.'

The Richardson operator said, 'Epsilon, you are in overtime.'

Judy said, 'Gosh, your poor bank balance. Darling, I must go. See you soon.'

He said, ''Bye, bunny. Take care now.' I heard the crackle as the link broke. The generators cut, whined down to silence.

He walked to the lab door. He said, 'That was bloody uncivil.'

'What was uncivil?'

He said, 'Walking out like that.'

I said, 'It was your call, not mine.'

'As if that mattered!'

'It mattered to me. Anyway, I had some work to do.'

His face darkened. He said, 'You might as well know, I don't like your attitude.'

I said, 'The fact is noted.'

He took a step into the lab. He said, 'I'm also very well aware you don't like me.'

I said, 'On the contrary. I don't give a damn. Now, if you please. You do your thing. I'll do mine. OK?' I pushed past him, got myself another drink.

He stood and stared for a bit, breathing down his nose. He said, 'What would you do if I belted you between the eyes?'

I said, 'Lose consciousness. Later, in all probability, sue you.' I turned with a whisky in my hand. I said, 'For Christ's sake have a drink, man. And let it go.'

He took the glass, shakily. His moods were starting to switch about a bit. Too much for my taste. Anyway, he cooled down in time. Sat and told me about the place they were buying in the Rockies, his old man having weighed in with a few thousand dollars to help the mortgage; and the Chrysler automat he'd picked up on his last Earth furlough, and all the rest. He didn't quite get round to how many kids they were planning for, but he sailed pretty close. He even gave me a standing invite to view the establishment after they got settled in; which would have been great if I could have afforded the fare. It was all great, life was great. I rejoiced for him. I couldn't help, though, having a momentary picture of the wedding night. You lie this way and I lie that, on sterilized polar sheets; while we devour, ritually, each other's bodies.

I walked out to the Dragons. Chitinous plates lay about; but the corpse had gone. The air was full of a sweet, heavy musk. One of the monsters was still in sight, moving away purposefully to the south.

Purposefully? I was getting as bad as Pilot (First Class) Scott-Braithwaite.

I walked the few yards to the landing vehicle. It stood canted on its fragile-looking legs, heat shields scorched by atmospheric entry. We still use conventional feeders, of course, even with the Richardson Loop; the Loop vehicle was parked somewhere out in orbit. We could probably slice it fine enough these days to make direct planetary landings; fact is, nobody's all that keen to be the guinea-pig. Get the Richardson axes a milli-degree or so out of true and your atoms could just get rammed cheek by jowl, so to speak, with the atoms of a mountain top. Nobody's quite too sure whether that would represent a paradox or not. The consensus of opinion is that it would, and there'd be a bloody great bang.

Travelling by Loop isn't too bad; no worse, I suppose, than allowing yourself to be wheeled in for a major operation. But somebody still has to make planetfall the other end, which is a process as primitive as firing a thirty-eight. That's why even middle-aged IAB researchers need pilots; though it's true to say we need them more than they need us. Still, it's nice to have some Clean-Limbed Young Men about the place. Restores your faith in the world.

I woke with a thick head in the morning. I lay in the bunk for a while wondering whether a touch of whisky would scorch the taste out of my throat. I heard the Pilot moving around outside. He called me a couple of times. I swore eventually and answered. I dressed, walked blearily to the lab door. He said, 'We've got a visitor.'

He was squatting on his haunches a yard or two away in the clearing. Beside him was a Dragon. It was one of the smallest I'd seen. The whips, longer in proportion than the whips of an adult, were folded across its back.

He was feeding it leaves off one of the palms; it was twisting its golden-eyed head and munching steadily. He looked up, grinning. He said, 'It's friendly.'

I said, 'It's eating.'

He frowned. He said, 'It's the same thing.'

I said, 'One statement is an observation. The other is a surmise.'

He said, 'Maybe it's thirsty. Does it want a drink?'

I said, 'They get all they need from vegetable fibres. You're wasting your time.'

He got a dish from the lab anyway, filled it with water and set it down under the thing's forelegs. He really thought he'd got some sort of green and gold, kingsize puppy dog there. The Dragon, of course, ignored it. He said, 'I've christened him. His name's Oscar. Do you know, I think he answers to it?' He crooned the name in a variety of voices, snapping his fingers and waving his arms. The Dragon twisted its head, keeping his hands in sight. He said, 'There, what about that?'

I said, 'Try throwing it a stick. Also, its ears aren't in its head. You'd be better off shouting at its arse.'

I put the coffee on to boil, and shaved. He played around with the thing half an hour or more longer. Finally he came inside. The Dragon stood where he had left it, motionless in the clearing. He watched it anxiously through the port while he was eating. He said, 'How old is he? I hope he stays around.'

I really think he was starting to get lonely.

We had a trip planned for the day. I strapped myself into the flier; he climbed in beside me, jetted up a couple of thousand feet and flew south. I sat with the instrument box on my knees and watched the treetops slide underneath. The sea became visible after a few minutes; a greenish shawl, fringed with an edging of paler lace. Farther out, a maroon stain spread across the horizon. A few biggish fish were floating belly-up. There were no other signs of life.

He turned west, following the coastline of the island. I waved to him to take the machine lower. Half a dozen clearings passed beneath, each with the curious towers of wood and stone. From above they looked vaguely oriental, like outlandish pagodas. Nowhere was there movement; the sites lay open, and deserted.

We crossed the sea again, flew over the northerly islands. Half an hour later I touched his arm. I'd seen a clearing bigger than the rest, glimpsed something bronze-green moving in the jungle. I said, 'Set down.'

He said, 'Here? You must be joking.' He took the machine in, all the same, skimmed to a perfect landing between two of the glittering towers. He killed the motors. I sat while the miniature duststorm we had created subsided, then opened the cab door.

The air struck warm. A Dragon surveyed me indifferently from the edge of the jungle. Another, the one I had seen, was lumbering a hundred yards or so away. I walked towards it. It turned, whips waving, headed back into the trees. I let it go.

Clustering on the edge of the clearing were a series of curious six-sided structures, like pale green organ pipes a few sizes too large. The Pilot stood beside them, dusting his immaculate slacks. He said, 'What are these?'

I said, 'Were.'

'Well. What were they?'

I said, 'Nests. Moonstone termites. They were rather a pretty species. But they produced a formic acid variant that upset the chronometers at Transhipment Base. Earth lost a couple of freighters; they're still out somewhere in the Loop. So we cooked up a little systemic. It was pretty good; did the job in a couple of years.'

He fingered one of the mortared columns, and frowned.

I said, 'Never mind, old son. Can't stand in the way of Progress.'

Beyond the clearing a low earth bank was covered by sprays of dense viridian creeper. Regularly spaced holes showed blackly. All but one were deserted; in the nearest showed a familiar green and gold mask.

He said, 'Are these places where they live?'

'What?'

'The Dragons.'

I said carefully, 'These are where they are usually to be found.'

He nodded up at one of the quartz structures. 'They build those?'

I said, 'It seems probable. Nobody's seen them at it yet.'

He said, 'What the hell are they? What are they for?'

I said, 'We have no idea.'

He said, 'There's got to be a reason.'

'That's a comforting philosophy.'

He glared at me. I was starting to get under his skin again. For a Pilot (First Class) he was pretty touchy. He said, 'Everything has a reason.'

I said mildly, 'Most things have explanations. But if we could explain why these things were built it might not strike us as a reason. Since we're hardly likely to explain them anyway, speculation is pointless.'

I walked forward. All the caves were tenanted; and all but a handful of the Dragons were dead. The bodies were flabby with decay, giving off the same sweet odour I'd smelled in the clearing. I counted forty-seven corpses. None of them showed any signs of damage. He frowned finally, pushed his cap back on his head. He said, 'Anyway, these weren't eaten.'

I said, 'Maybe there wasn't time. They all went together.'

'Do you think so?'

I said, 'It's possible.'

I sat on a rock and filled my pipe. He wandered off. A few minutes later I heard him call. I got up and walked in his direction.

There was a tower lower than the rest. On the timber staging were piled a dozen or more Dragons. I didn't care to approach too closely. The bodies were pretty far gone.

He said, 'That settles one thing anyway.'

'What?'

He gestured irritably. He said, 'They're burial platforms. It's obvious.'

I said, 'Or they climbed up there of their own accord. They were shuffling solemnly around, worshipping the sun, when they were struck with the same idea at precisely the same time.'

'What idea?'

I said, 'The idea our friend had in the clearing.'

'Which was?'

I said, 'You work it out.'

He said slowly, 'You think they're suiciding.'

I said, 'One possibility among many.'

He said angrily, 'It doesn't make sense.'

I said, 'Try not looking for the answers. You'll sleep easier.'

It was as if I'd challenged his Faith. He said, 'Everything makes sense.'

'Haciendas in the Rockies make sense. Laying women makes sense. Of a sort. Dragons don't.'

He shook his head. He said, 'I just don't understand you.'

'No,' I said. 'And we're the same species. Awe-inspiring, isn't it?'

He walked back to the flier. I followed him. We searched the rest of the islands, landed a couple of times. We found nothing living. It seemed our local group of Dragons now represented the universal population.

We were back at the laboratory by nightfall. The little Dragon still squatted where we had left it. He seemed overjoyed to see it; started scurrying about pulling down armfuls of leaves. He sat while I brewed coffee, prodding them patiently at its jaws. I thought he might sling a blanket roll beside it to make sure it didn't stray.

There wasn't much to do round camp. He fed Oscar and tried to teach him to sit up and beg; I logged the meter readings, processed fluid and tissue samples, collected droppings for analysis. The Dragons sat in their caves and watched us; we watched the Dragons. Each day at seventeen hundred hours Planetary we reported to Earth Control, and they reported to us. We listened to Earth news via the Loop; and twice more the Pilot's fiancée spoke to him. The second time they had a considerable heart-to-heart. I left them to it, risking his wrath; there were a lot of tears flying about Earthside, the thing seemed pretty private. I repeated the experiment with the heartbeat recordings, beaming a ring of loudspeakers on to Oscar. He didn't respond, which was hardly surprising, though the Pilot pronounced himself delighted with his progress. If you tickled his foreleg joints with a stick for long enough, he'd sometimes rear. It didn't strike me as exactly a critical development.

We took the flier across to Continent Three. It wasn't much of a trip. I remembered the place as vivid green, furred with trees. Now drifts of puce and ochre dust stretched to the horizon. Heavy automats were working. They looked like magnified versions of the Dragons. The wind was blowing strongly, racing across the ruined land; you could see the trails of dust smoking along the ground, dragging their long shadows over the dunes.

We didn't land.

He was moody at supper. It transpired he wanted to get back to Earth. Something had gone a bit wrong with his scene, he wasn't too specific about it. 'It's all right for you,' he said bitterly. 'Nobody gives a damn how long you sit staring at bloody great insects, you've got nothing to get back to. If it lay with me, I'd just report the damn things extinct and clear out. Nobody's going to know the difference anyway.'

I sucked at my pipe. It was pulling sour again. 'Can't be done, my son,' I said. 'Impatience of the young, and all that. Can't brush science aside, y'know.'

'Science,' he said. 'Two men stuck here on a bloody dustball, watching a handful of incomprehensible objects die off for no good reason. You might be devoted to research ...'

I chucked the pipe down, reached for the whisky. 'On the contrary,' I said, 'I couldn't care less.'

He stared at me. 'Then why're you here?'

'Because,' I said, 'I'm paid to be. Also, here's as good a place as the next.'

He shrugged. 'I'd say that was a pretty dismal outlook,' he said. 'It doesn't seem to me you've made much of your life. Anyway, that's your concern. I'm not going the same way, I can tell you.'

I said, 'Then you're a lucky man.' I filled a glass, shoved it across. He stared at me; then to my surprise picked it up and drained it at a gulp.

He called me next morning, early. I walked from the lab and stared. Oscar had immobilized; the whips thrust out at right angles from the body, producing that curious helicopter effect, and the eyes were lustreless. He was waggling greenstuff beneath the mandibles, but there was no response.

I set the meters up. It looked as if this might be one of the last chances we should get to gather data. The hearts failed, in their set pattern; I drove the probes, started the pacemakers, laid the syringes ready with the stimulants. The Pilot (First Class) took it hard. His pet was dying, certainly; there was no doubt of that. But the noise he made, you'd have thought he was losing a woman at the very least. He fumed and fretted, made trips out into the jungle to bring back this or that goody; he tried Oscar with tree leaves, bush branches, the pale green tubers that grew round the hangar sheds and landing pad. None of it, of course, made the slightest difference. The heart-pairs of the little Dragon faltered on through the night; the Planetary chronometers ran up their thirty hours; on cue, Oscar died.

The Pilot seemed broken up by the whole business. He vanished for a couple of hours or more; when I saw him again he was waving a whisky bottle. He took to his room, finally, in the afternoon. I presumed he was sleeping it off.

It was just as well. The funeral party arrived about fourteen hundred Planetary. They were commendably prompt. The ceremony didn't take long, the volume of the deceased being fairly small. They left the sherds of armour stacked neatly in the shadow of the lab; I heard the whips trail and rustle as they headed back south, toward the rock city and the quartzite towers. I labelled the new recordings, logged the time, took the routine call from Earth Control. I'd closed down the generators when I heard the lab door open and shut. I looked round, frowning. I'd no idea he'd managed to leave his room.

He didn't look too good. He had a bottle of rye in one hand and the rocket pistol in the other, which struck me as a bit unnecessary. Still, it was dramatic.

He flung the bottle down. It broke. He said, 'I was going to bury him. Those bloody murderers. With their bloody whips. Shaking their bloody whips …' He advanced, unsteadily. I suppose I should have told him to put that thing down before somebody got hurt. I didn't. It was the sort of line that would have come better from him.

He was fairly through his skull. I thought perhaps he didn't have too high a capacity; a lot of these clean-cut young men haven't. Also when they blow they really blow. He waved the pistol around a bit more and told me what was going to happen if I interfered within the next hour or so. I gathered a man had to do what a man had to do. Anyway when he finally staggered out I took him at his word. The girlie mag lay on the table; I got a bottle of whisky, poured myself a stiff one and started leafing through it. After all, there's nothing like curling up with a good book.

In time there was a hefty, rolling bang from the south, and another. Then some higher cracks that I took it were the automatic. I hoped he'd remembered to pack a few spare clips. After a bit the noise started up again, so it seemed he had.

I chucked the book down, lay back. I finished the bottle, sat watching the dawn brighten the green sky. It had been quiet a long time now; I wondered if he'd slipped on the bluff and broken his fool neck.

The lab door opened. He stood framed in the doorway, the gun still in his hand. His uniform was torn, his face haggard and dirty white. He said, 'I don't know what happened. I don't know what happened.'

I said, 'All?'

He said, 'It was their eyes. Staring. Their bloody eyes. They let me do it, they didn't move…' He rubbed a hand across his face. He said, 'If you waved at them, they didn't blink…'

I put the glass down, carefully. I said, 'One point, Space Pilot. Did you notice any signs of ritual behaviour among the survivors during the… er… event? If so, it should go on the report. You might have added to our store of Knowledge.'

He brought the gun round slowly. He said, '*You bastard. You bloody bastard…*'

I stayed where I was. I don't find life universally sweet, but that particular mode of exit has never appealed. I said as pleasantly as I could, 'I don't think that would be a good idea. I'm not worth it; you've still got Judy to think about.' The gun barrel wavered; and I smiled. 'If you've put all those rounds through that thing,' I said, 'it needs a clean. There's some water on next door; nip and sluice it through. I'll get some coffee going; you look as if you could use it.'

He stood a while longer, staring like a ghost; then it seemed it sank in. He turned silently, closed the door behind him.

'Next door' was my specimen lock. Amazing what autosuggestion can do. I clamped my foot on the floor switch, heard the bolts shoot home. He yelled something, started banging the wall; and I valved gas. A steady hissing, then a thump.

And blessed peace.

I bespoke Earth Control on the emergency frequency, explained the salient facts and got a clearance.

Lugging him to the shuttle wasn't the easiest part. I made it finally, strapped him in the couch, closed the hatches, ran through what countdown checks I could remember and gave myself back to Earth. Wire-flying through the Loop isn't a thing to be thought on too closely; but they made it. I transferred to the Richardson vehicle, tied myself down once more; and Earth pulled the tit, plastering our substance and the substance of the freighter thinly round the parameters of paradox.

When I regained coherence we were in stable Earth orbit, and the relief vessels were coming up to us. The Pilot (First Class) was awake, and saying quite a lot. He would probably have backed up speech with action in some unpleasant form or another, only I'd taken the precaution of tying him down again. I listened for a while; eventually I got tired. I switched his voice circuit direct to Earth Control, and he had enough sense left to button his lip. I spent the time till docking thinking how interesting we are as a species.

One and all, we build round ourselves little protective shells; but inside, when we're bottomed, we're really quite inhuman.

So IAB never got their Dragon. I was out of circulation for a time; when I got back I was told Trade Control had already issued authority for the automats to be programmed into the islands. Epsilon Development were losing money each day they didn't mine; they underwrote the cost of the station without too much complaint and endowed a research grant that will keep me in crusts for the next five years at least. I settled down to catalogue what had been learned of the humanoids on Proxima Centauri IX before Epsilon's power station ran supercritical; and the Dragons were forgotten.

Except that a few days later I had a visitor. I used the door sensors because only the week before there'd been a mugging a dozen floors below. But I hadn't got that sort of trouble this time. I opened the door and poured myself a whisky.

She was as pretty as her stereo. She'd been crying; and she was wearing the season's newest. I gave her a chair, but she wouldn't have a drink. She crossed her legs, tried them the other way. Didn't like that either. Finally she said, 'Remember me?'

I said, 'It's coming. Don't help me.'

She smiled. She said, 'I always expect Researchers to be much older men.'

I put the glass down gently, and sat at the desk.

She said, 'I've come from ... from Drew. I wondered if you could ... tell me a little more. He's so ... reticent. You know.'

I said, 'There's a report going in tomorrow. It's irregular; but I can arrange for you to see a copy. If you so desire.'

She swallowed. She said, 'I ... will have that drink, if you don't mind.'

I got it for her, sat down again.

She drank it, put the glass aside. She said, 'Researcher, the report ... You know why I'm here. Don't you?'

I said, 'I'm always willing to be surprised.'

She stood up, without fuss. She laid her gloves down, unbuttoned her blouse and pulled it open. Then she just stood there, looking at me.

I shook my head and opened the desk drawer. I thumbed through the report and started to read.

'Until day fifty-seven, the life forms designated Epsilon VI brackets three stroke two showed no awareness of the presence of the observing party, and no animosity. Their attack was both sudden and unexpected. My companion, Space Pilot First Class Andrew Scott-Braithwaite, behaved with conspicuous gallantry. To him, certainly, I owe my life; and my final employment of GS 93 was at his instigation, though he himself was imperilled by the release of the gas. Our subsequent return was logged by Earth Control ... etcetera.'

I tossed the papers over to her. I said, 'You read the rest. The style may be wanting here and there; but at least it's concise.'

She stared at the thing a moment, and burst into tears.

After she had gone Miss Braithwaite glided from the inner room. Miss Braithwaite is my secretary at IAB. She is also fat, fortyish and an optimist; but she cooks good suppers. Right now her eyes were misty with emotion; and she laid a hand shakily on my arm. 'Researcher,' she said, 'that's about the biggest thing I ever saw a person do.'

I patted her. 'That's all right,' I said. 'I'm like that.'

That's the sort of thing one has to live with.

They still have Pilot (First Class) Scott-Braithwaite down at the State Home for Bewildered Astronauts. But I did hear he's been seconded for another tour of duty. Apparently that boy was one of the worst cases of Loop nerves they'd ever seen. Had I not plastered the cracks, he would certainly have been an ex-spacer by now; and Judy would have had to cast those honest wide blue eyes around fairly rapidly. Because Drew's disability pension would hardly have maintained her in the Manner to Which. As things stand, I wonder which would have been the better turn to do him.

I wouldn't have thought he'd have blown like that; but you can never tell. After all, I once spent three years with a woman who closely approximated a Greek goddess. Appearances are deceptive; as a Behaviourist, it's the first thing you learn.

THE TRUSTIE TREE

His impressions on returning to awareness were two-fold: the play of light behind his closed lids, and the chuckle of water under the boat's forefoot. Though the orange flickering could be further analysed into a play of light and heat combined, while 'chuckle' seemed altogether too imprecise a metaphor. Rather the water sounds were like a series of little harps, struck continuously in some musical scheme that seemed always to be on the point of resolution. He toyed with the idea, and with another vaguely grasped; that of a relationship between the two effects. The pattering of heat against his face seemed contrapuntal to the altering, essentially liquid phrases of whatever melody the little bow-wave played. His mind annoyed itself with the unwanted pun, and he opened his eyes.

The trees here, lining the waterway, were of considerable height. To either side the slim trunks stretched away in aisles and arcades of golden-green; above, the small rounded leaves hung still like sprays of newly minted coins. He raised himself slightly, moving his elbows with care, and saw how ahead the canal stretched arrow-straight, infused with that same misty glow. The movement, though small, woke the pain once more. He rested a while, drifting his eyes closed. With concentration the stabbings could be made apparently to shift, from knee to ankle to thigh and groin. Though intellect understood, the animal brain could be confused. Logic suggested that by a similar exertion the agony might be reduced, perhaps to vanishing point; but the experiment, if possible, was beyond his powers.

To his left, slightly below the stretcher on which he lay, stood a cup and decanter of what appeared to be cut crystal. What it was the Kalti had given him he had no idea; but it was effective, though the swallowing of it turned lips and palate for an hour or more to purring velvet. He moved again, screwing his eyes; then stretching his left hand to the decanter base, reached with his right to withdraw the faceted stopper. He laid it down, transferred his grip to the cup, rested the neck of the decanter against its rim. Instinct bade him drink at once; but some perversity made him first reverse the process, replacing the stopper as carefully as it had been removed. Only then did he feel free to steady the cup to his lips. In his all but supine position, drinking posed an additional difficulty. He managed it by degrees, dribbling the precious liquid a spot a time into his throat. After the first sips it was easier; the action of the drug was immediate, and his hands were steadier. He set the cup down, rubbed his mouth and the unaccustomed fringe of beard. The stuff had a faint, antiseptic tang. He felt it must cling to him; and welcomed it. There were other scents, which he was pleased to mask; for he was a fastidious man.

He lay drowsily, feeling the trickling anaesthesia spread, watching the feathery gliding of the treetops. Between them the ribbon of sky was an intense, nearly metallic blue. From time to time birds, the little fishing birds of the swamps, flitted across his angle of vision, darting like sparks from bank to bank.

From where he lay, in the bows of the enormously long boat, the sound of her engine was all but inaudible, its pounding reduced to a murmur scarcely louder than the wash of ripples driven against the stone-lined banks. In places the stones had fallen in, releasing little slides of brownish-yellow mud. Between them, like moss-grown sockets, showed diminutive tunnel mouths. Birds scuttled beneath the trailing bushes; once a small furred animal plopped into the water, dived and was gone. He saw it surface some thirty metres ahead, a black dot trailing a smooth chevron of ripple. Later the canal narrowed between stands of tall orange-flowered bushes. The air was heavy with their musky scent. On Earth, no doubt, there would have been the steady drone of insects; but Xerxes, mercifully, owned almost no flying forms. He brushed his forehead, where a rivulet of sweat had started, turned his wrist to stare at the chronometer. The figures swam momentarily before his eyes; and he let his arm fall slack.

From the cabin at his back came the momentary rattle of some utensil; but none of the Kalti came near. Nor had they come near, since they lifted the brushwood stretcher into the bows; was it the morning before? They placed the decanter beside him and the cup, and said no word; these square, short, seamed-faced folk in black, with their broad-brimmed round-crowned hats and expressionless, slightly slanting eyes. They reminded him of old-fashioned nursery toys; or Chesterton's grim, simple little priest.

A breeze stirred momentarily, swaying the tops of the trees; and he wrinkled his nose. Twice now, of necessity, he had urinated through the stretcher; and there was the other stink, from the dressings on his leg. He wondered if in their way the Kalti were fastidious too.

He moved once more, settling his shoulders against the broad, sloping buttress of the cabin end; and was warned by the searing flash from his knee that the drink was a palliative only. He lay, breath held, while the pain throbbed through its many overtones, faded along the nerves. His leg twitched, and was still.

He returned to his contemplation of the gliding banks and trees; and a former notion, that of microcosm, came back to him, to some extent with greater force. The stately variation of perspectives, the sense of a progression both effortless and inevitable, gave the concept strength. *Like life*, he thought; but the idea was complex, defying further pursuit. To be expressed perhaps in the emblem-writing of the Kalti; but not in words. He thought idly then more intently of the pictograph blazoned on the name panels of the boat, the blue swirls fountaining above the white bar that is earth, security and God; and that can mean trust. Something growing was surely represented, a bush or tree. He turned the phrases round his tongue, lips moving; and a memory came, bringing with it first the tang of pain, later a pleasure curiously powerful and unalloyed. He spoke the new words aloud, tasting their flavour.

'I lean'd my back unto an aik,
'I thocht it was a trustie tree ...'

Then like a passage in the shadow-show his life had become, sense faded; and he slept.

When he woke the notion of the long hull beneath him, gliding so effortlessly night and day, was ready in his mind to comfort him. He welcomed it, as he welcomed the remembered words. A part of him, that in other times would have dominated, protested perhaps that never yet was boat called the *Trustie Tree*; but he was satisfied. He raised himself a little; and saw how beyond the upswept bow the woods drew back enclosing a broad pool, its surface still and milky green. At its far edge the canal plunged into a cutting of dark red rock; across the face of the little bluff, hung with creeper that trailed like Spanish Moss, hawked a solitary golden bird.

For two days, to his waking knowledge, they had met with no other boat; and the pool was likewise empty. None the less, he knew the marshlands to be full. He saw, vividly, the drifting of the endless black hulls, like particles drawn by a single current through the great vascular system of the Northern Continent's waterways. Midsummer was near, and the Kalti festivals at Bran Gildo and Hy Antiel. Somewhere beyond the cutting lay the low hill range that fringes the Salt Lagoon; and on the lagoon edge lay Bran Gildo itself and Earth Base, the trading complex and the Terran Hospital. He saw the city with equal brilliance, white walls clustered beneath green mops of palm, the watchtowers like squat terrestrial minarets; and wondered at the clearness of his mind.

As the long boat nosed into the cutting, the Kalti woman reappeared. She rigged a little canopy over him, of blue and yellow striped cloth, its edges frothed and scalloped with lace. He smiled at her as she worked and said, 'Bran Gildo.' She paused, crinkling her leathery face, and nodded; but made no other sign. After she had gone, and the diamond-lighted cabin doors were closed, he wondered why the protection had been necessary. Then as the sides of the cutting narrowed, shrubs and bushes arched dim overhead; and great spots of water began to fall, like an icy and persistent douche. He smiled again at that; for the Kalti were not unaware.

He fell to watching the strands of fern slide by to either side. Some, the longest, brushed the black-painted hull; others, disturbed by the faint air-mass the boat drove before it, swayed gently, discharging from their pointed tips their cargo of pellucid drops. The fronds were greyish, he saw; but the sides of the defile were by no means of uniform hue. Between the bastions of brick-red rock were lozenges of purple and maroon; through the strata ran veins of copper and dull gold. The updraught touched his face, dank-smelling and pleasantly cool. He closed his eyes, recalling just such another bluff, seeing, with the troubled yet very clear vision vouchsafed him, the flyer as it lay side-shattered, crumpled against the rock. De Valera's body, lying smashed amid a tangle of crimson-flowered cane; the burst and gutted first-aid chest; the saplings of the little clearing stripped of bark and foliage by the machine's descent. One spar of the flyer, driven javelin-fashion, had passed cleanly through the trunk of a tree; he remembered lying dazed, his back against a low earth bank, watching the trickling of dark sap or resin from the wound. In places the fluid, balked by a knot or stump, welled into tiny pools; in others it overflowed suddenly, streaking down glutinously a yard or more. Round him the air was motionless and warm; and somewhere a bird was singing. The image, arbitrarily recalled, filled him with a curious sense of desolation and loss; a sensation, he decided, that was primal as the pang of birth, the pain the thinking spirit must feel at the violence of the inanimate, the blindness of chance. He lay a day or more beneath the tree, while the impermeable dressing clamped to his leg turned first pink, then to poppy red. In the days that followed, the colour changed once more; and he covered the thing with bandages, roughly torn.

The violence of the descent, that disembowelled the flyer, had been indirectly his salvation. When the first shock and sickness passed, leaving only the pain, he commenced crawling laboriously between the twisted struts, finding here a treasure in the shape of a water flask or brandy bottle, there a morsel of food; an unsplit vacpak, a slab of emergency chocolate. He found a tube of white pills, that for an hour at a time partly relieved the pain; later he crawled to de Valera, fiddled with the wrist strap on the outflung arm. But the radio was dead as well. For all he knew, the flyer's main set might be unharmed; but it hung ten feet above his head, and was inaccessible. There were limits to what the white pills could achieve.

Later he wondered, as he wondered now, why he had not long since used the pistol at his belt, the standard nine shot semi-automatic space regs compelled him to carry. He could recall no driving will to live; yet the notion of violent self-destruction seemed none the less monstrous. He felt himself at one with the dead of all the ages; obscurely, it was as if his own extinction would make their ends the more complete. Later the thought was driven away by one still more irrational. He fumbled the gun from its holster, sat staring at it and trying to laugh. Held in his hand, the pistol still seemed a toy; that a bullet might be accelerated sufficiently to tear the flesh was a patent absurdity. How the conviction had come to him, he could not say. But come it had; and finally he put the rubber thing away, more useless than a catapult.

He rested in the shade, sipping from a water bottle, eating the little white tablets; and in time it seemed his strength grew rather than decreased. He wondered, disinterestedly, at the stubbornness with which the body clings to life. Finally, to occupy his mind and hands, he made shift to cut himself a pair of crutches from the tough stems of the bamboo. At first his mind, illogically obstinate, refused to admit that the things might have a purpose at all. Later, when their use was conceded, there was still no notion of actual employment. Their manufacture was an exercise, and nothing more; a gesture in the face of futility.

The knife he carried was barely adequate for the task; he discovered a machete in the remains of the Incidents Box that speeded the job a little. He made crosspieces for the tops of the poles, succeeded after several failures in lashing them more to less firmly to the shafts. Later he wrapped the makeshift joints with strip after strip of the flyer's silvery skin. The job finished, he set himself to fabricate slings. From them he suspended the last of the water bottles, and what ration containers remained; and finally he found himself, after a dozen false starts and as many pain-blenching falls, hobbling slowly and with infinite care away from the clearing, down the long slope into the forest.

*With the primarily agricultural economy of the Northern Continent must be considered the remarkable subculture of the Kalti, the Boatmen of Xerxes. The origins of this people are obscure. Reinhardt (*op. cit.*) argues a Southern derivation, detailing the many resemblances between the emblematic script of the Boatmen and the stelae of Barene and Defling in the subcontinent of New India. Agreement is by no means general however, and the field is a rich one for historian and ethnologist alike. The views of the Boatmen themselves add to rather than detract from the uncertainty. Some claim descent from a legendary ancestor, Bar-Zenno, sole survivor of a terrific and ubiquitous flood, while others assert that their forebears were once rulers of Antiel and Bran Gildo, till driven like the Tarquins to take refuge in the swamps with which the continent abounds. Their religious beliefs are likewise confusing to the outworlder, centred as they are on the notion of the Silent One, the Being who is at once Godhead, the epitome of the virtues and the tutelary spirit of the waterways, the canal complex on which from birth to death the Boatmen live, move and have* *their being. The symbol of his many manifestations is the* Bar-Ko, *the white or blue hyphen round which most Xerxian pictographs are built . . .*

He smiled and said to himself, 'The voice of the guidebook is heard in the land.'

The crutches served after a fashion; though after each few hours' travel he found he must sit and painfully re-tie the padded heads. Despite his efforts, the bamboo chafed him, so that the sides of his shirt beneath the arms became crusted with dried blood. He accepted the extra pain, unquestioning; for he had happened, dimly, on the first of several notions that were to sustain his journey, that of expiation.

The land at first trended steadily downward, aiding his progress. He knew approximately the direction in which he must travel; he made slow but steady time, guiding himself by the sun. Later, when he reached the lower ground, his difficulties multiplied. The soil here was spongy, clad with a carpet of vivid green moss; the tips of the crutches sank deeply, throwing his weight unexpectedly to either side. When this happened the tip of his maimed leg scraped the ground, and flashes like white fire woke inside his head. Once he fell, and lay for most of an afternoon before summoning the strength to continue. His water, now, was all but exhausted. More was to be had readily enough, by pressing his cupped hands into the moss; but it was tart and stinking, he didn't care to drink it. He contented himself with rubbing it on his lips, which still in time grew cracked and sore.

Also he found his mind was wandering. The simplest tasks he set himself, like the re-tying of the crutches, were hard to concentrate on and took far too long. Also it was becoming increasingly difficult to make his hands obey him; they wobbled and shook, possessed seemingly of a life of their own. These signs of impending collapse at first caused him acute distress. In time he came to view his state once more with something like dispassion. He was, he reminded himself, rather like the soldier in the poem, from whom successive pieces are carved and shot away until he is reduced to little more than a head. Later still, when the white pills were gone, he realized why the doggerel had at one time affected him with such horror. The soldier forgets to curse; even his God.

So he was reduced finally to crawling; in which condition earth banks assumed the proportions of low hills, bush clumps reared like the rain forests of an endless continent. Till on the fourth or fifth day his sense of the scale of things was once more altered; then it seemed, to his befuddled brain, that his body in its blunderings spanned light-years. He elbowed his way to Earth between the stars, thrusting aside whole galaxies. In this way he came to the water, on which the long boats passed like dreams.

He rested awhile at the crest of the final slope before scrambling and clawing the hundred metres or so to the bank. He sat the remainder of the day, nibbling his chocolate squares while his leg, resting in the cloudy water, was soothed to bearable numbness. The rushes whispered, rustling, and the black hulls puttered and thudded past, each like the next. First would come the rearing prow, with its knotwork and filigree; then the round portbrasses of the cabin, the endless cargo space tented with tarpaulin-like cloth; the engine house with its thin, vibrating chimney, so like the chimneys of the narrow boats that had once plied on Earth, and like them haloed by a haze of dieselblue. Finally the nameplates with their bursting hieroglyphs, the tiny stern grating, the steersman gripping his bright-banded oar. Through the day none of the Kalti so much as glanced at the bank; and he for his part waved and smiled, understanding with perfect amity. For the Silent One, who gave the *Bar-Ko* for his sign to men, sends pain and joy both in their season; all things are decreed to be.

Why they stopped their boat, the *Trustie Tree*, no one can say. Why they stilled their engine and drove their stakes, came thumping and squelching back along the overgrown bank, is a mystery as great as the Boatmen's origins. An hour or more they must have stared, the dumpy woman and the dumpy men, alike as pegtop toys in their suits of solemn black. No word passed between them, certainly; but at the end of that time they wove the stretcher, and raised him from the water with care. Once while lifting him aboard they jolted him. He – the central, thinking part – was indifferent; but the body screamed. They did speak at that; the clicks and guttural bangs that pass for syllables among their kind. They lashed the stretcher, and brought the drink; and then they let him be.

By early evening of the planet's short day the boat had cleared the cutting. The thudding of her engine, amplified by the close rock walls, faded once more; the ripples reasserted themselves. He saw he travelled now on a high embankment, twenty feet or more above the level of the surrounding land. To right and left, stretching to the horizon, ran a sea of sunbaked yellow grass, dotted with clumps of scrub and low, mounded bushes. Beside the embankment crouched thorny, bulbous-stemmed trees. From his vantage point he saw an animal break cover, trotting daintily; hornless, and something of the size and colouring of a terrestrial goat. He watched the grass heads wave, marking its passage. Some memory of Jefferies came to him then, and the sick magnificence of the Sun Life; uncomprehended before, realized now in a flash of insight. It seemed he too was one with what his senses recorded; the beast in the grass, the star hanging in the sky. The thought bred another, yet more fleeting and elusive. He understood, dimly, what world-union might mean to the Kalti and their flowing Tree, the boat that bore him; understood too his part in an ultimate scheme in which the very certainty of change, growth and death and birth, was an expression of the immutability of the Most High. The notion, as grandiose as it was vague, brought none the less a further upsurge of the pleasure that had buoyed him, a sensation almost of ebullience, a lightening of the spirit that seemed as carefree as a bird. He knew himself to be on the verge of greater revelations, and wished for pencil and paper with which to record his thoughts. There was nothing of the sort to be had; but no matter. In Bran Gildo, he would write of this. Later his leg set up a devil's hammering; and he drank some more of the anaesthetic wine.

When he opened his eyes again the Kalti woman had lit the great running lamps on either side of the cabin roof. To Planetary West a cauldron of dull light marked the setting of the sun. Ahead, breaking the dimness of the veld, low hills rose rounded against the sky.

The lamps were beyond his immediate range of vision. By twisting his head he caught glimpses of the filigree of brass, black against the brilliance of the coloured panes; red to the left, blue to the right. The glow reflected in moving ghostly patches to either side; beyond, a warmer diffusion more sensed than seen told him the cabin lamps were burning. The Kalti family, perhaps, was sitting to a meal; but day and night, the boat would never stop. He watched the hills grow slowly against the sky. Beyond lay the Salt Lagoon; beyond again, Bran Gildo. Rushingly, the *Trustie Tree* was swimming home.

For all but a fraction of the working year the Boatmen lead their solitary lives in the fastnesses of the canal country, transporting their cargoes of wood, coal and road stone across the swamps and plains of the Northern Continent. Only at the midsummer Feast of Bar-Ab does this most taciturn of races throw off its reserve. Then for a week or more the great fairs of Antiel and Bran Gildo glow with light. The streets fill; everywhere, on temple fronts, public buildings, inns, the flower-wreathed Bar-Ko *is seen. The festivities continue unabated from dusk to dawn; and here too the season's business is transacted. Marriages are arranged, contracts sealed, boats bought and sold. Though the Feast is evidently the successor of a much older solstice celebration, it seems fitting that it should be held now in honour of Bar-Ab, the vigorous and enlightened ruler of Bran Gildo who four Earth centuries ago first gave to Xerxes what has remained the planet's major transportation system …*

The canopy had been drawn back. He lay seeing the shapes of unfamiliar constellations. For some, he knew the Kalti names: the Anchor, the Fishing Net, Sista's Barge. The quadrilateral towards which the Barge for ever steered was the Great Pound; beyond were the Boatmen with his Oar, and the Hunter Bra'ad. As ever, the night sky of Xerxes held a faint greenish pallor; to the east, a broad silver streak heralded the rising of the planet's single moon. The hills loomed now to either side, black against the glow.

The sleep that claimed him was the deepest he had enjoyed. Round him, unheeded, were the night-sounds of the boat's passage; creak and thump of gates, rattle of paddle gear, roar of unseen sluices. The long hull ground and jolted, unheard; the shouts, rasp and scrape of footsteps, groan of ropes, seemed small as the flutterings of moths. The moon of Xerxes declined, sinking towards the west. Far below, the grass plain showed now pale as bone. The swamps, and the rising massif beyond, were a dark rim to the world; and still, by the hour, *Trustie Tree* climbed and climbed. As scores of her kind had climbed before her, and scores would climb after. Somewhere, far back in the hills, the mile-long reservoir that fed the summit was showing its reedy bed; in two weeks' time, when the last black hull had locked back to the east, it would be empty.

There seemed no sharp transition between the states of sleep and waking. He knew only that his eyes were open; and that he smiled at the boat, and the hills, and the sky. The sky was flushed now, chequered with pinkish light. At the zenith flickered the last star of the Pound; and a wind was on his face. A dawn wind, fresh and cold, overlaid with the great tang of the sea.

He sat up, nearly with a shout. Along the horizon, like a dimly shining sword, stretched the Salt Lagoon. Between hills and sea the land was dark, overlaid with the moving shimmer of mist; and from the dark, climbing towards him in a breathless sweep, rose the locks of the Bran Gildo flight. Beside each lock, the pale patch of its sidepond; above each the *Bar-Ko*, vaunting in its wrought-iron frame; and from pound after pound the gleaming stars, red and blue, red and blue, that were other boats, locking down to the city and the sea.

In the bows, poised impassively, stood the little Kalti boat-woman. He called to her, pointing and laughing; then it seemed the inside of his head took fire, catching brightness from the curious drink, so that he cried to her he was a sick Earthman coming home, and that the penance was done; that he was a Breton, and his forbears had been Bretons, and fishers of the sea. Some nonsense there was too of other boats, and the journeyings of the *Trustie Tree*; all of which she ignored, as was the way of her people. Though once she came to him, catching his chin in her pinching horny fingers, lifting his lids to stare into the pale-coloured eyes. She pulled at the stretcher, tugged the lashings that held it firm; rearranged the patterned quilting over him, turned back to the bow. Her presence warmed him; so he told her of Ben Cruachan, and the road that angles round the mountain's flanks, through the Pass of Brander to Dalmally and Glen Orchy and Rannoch Moor. He talked of finding Crearwy, and taking her there; and what it was like to love her, and how they went, and where they stayed. And the pink rocks of Iona and the Ross of Mull, the night boat raising a diadem of lights in Oban Bay. Many things, secret things, he remembered now; the wooden towns of

Wessex, the teashops and castles, fossils and chalk Gods; barrows crowning the grey ridge-sided downs, Portland tower bawling at the mist. He told her of the Star and the Mermaid and the Hare and Hounds; and renting the cottage for Crearwy who was Marie, the cottage with the yellow pine stairs and hearth of new Ham stone where they toasted legs and calves and laughed at the night-sound of the wind. And Kensington and Chelsea, Holland Park and Salisbury and the Great West Road. Once the Kalti nodded, over her shoulder, wielding the long-shafted hook; and once he thought she smiled.

So, encouraged, he told her the things for which he had never as yet found words; how it is when the Silent One has turned the wheel, when the laughter is dead and the loving and the wind blows empty on the downs, with nobody there to see. The warmth is gone, the stars remain; while over the years the object of love grows realler than when she lay all night at your side. Till you taste her lips, and smell her skin, and see her hair at every empty turn. And the whisky is there in the cupboard and the sandals she didn't want and her dress on the hanging rail. While *Trustie Tree* drove forward and down, forward and down, and the woman laughed and didn't understand. But how could they understand he asked himself, laughing in his turn; these folk who dressed in black, and used colours for their words?

Every year, they race the great Bran Gildo flight; a full day's work for a full-crewed boat, from Summit Pound to the Lagoon. From dusk to dawn the paddles crash, the sluices churn their streams of water and brown foam and stalks of weed. The blue haze rises, fed by the many exhausts; the shoremen curse, young and old alike, strain shoulders to the yard-thick beams, swing on the gates over the froth and boil. The cabin brasses dance, lamps sway and tick; feet are broken and hands, but the boats can't stop. Beyond lie the city and the sea, and a fever – the only fever ever to grip a Boatman – is in the blood.

The diesels bellow, the painted stern-oars dip; and through it all the boats sail out, at the end, between the reed clumps of the Salt Lagoon. The tide whispers and lops; the seabirds wheel; and Bran Gildo is half a night away.

In the noise and flurry, amid the roar of water, he at last understood that through suffering he was saved; so he sang, an old sea song – light on the engine room, no more – and laughed again because no hurt can last for ever, no time is too late, no clock runs that cannot be unwound. He knew the *Bar-Ko* and the Tree that sprang from it, the Tree that is life itself; he knew the words he would say, the healing, blinding words, sprung from wisdom that springs in turn from pain. They formed a pattern that glowed and flashed, Constantine's diadem of stars; a pattern that enclosed all things, Marie and the mountains, the *Bar-Ko*, Salisbury Spire, Earth Base, the Loop where they ravel the atoms of a man like coloured beads against a velvet sky. The tall reeds whispered to either side; the night birds called from the land;

and he was grateful, with all his heart, to the Kalti, and their Lord, and the great boats of the North.

'I lean'd my back unto an aik,
'I thocht it was a trustie tree ...'

The lamps, the engine-rooms, and Bar-Ab great prince, faded in his mind.

The early light lay grey and cold across the lagoon of Bran Gildo. A little swell was running, here so near the open sea; so the river boat, unused to open water, pitched and creaked, rolling to show her weed-stained sides. The light, brightening, gleamed on the complex knotwork at her bow, on her running lamps and burnished port rims. It gleamed on the stern oar, still held by the Kalti steersman; and on the painted name-boards, the *Bar-Ko* and the Tree. Beside the Kalti his woman stood head bent. The words she muttered were harsh and hurried as the gabbing of a bird; he frowned, inclining his own head in reply. She spoke again; then turned away, climbed to the catwalk above the cargo space. Along it she trudged, dumpy and foreshortened, secure as if she walked on land; while to either side the mist, thinning, disclosed the shapes of other boats, and others, and still more. On each prow, the headropes of the God; on each side, somewhere, the Sign; on each cabintop the fading gleam of lamps of beaten brass. At them the Kalti mother stared; then closed with her hard fingers the eyes of the man who lay in the brushwood stretcher, slipped the Ferryman's golden coin under the root of his tongue.

THE LAKE OF TUONELA

The dawn had been overcast, but by midmorning the weather had cleared. The small yellow sun of Xerxes burned in the planet's blue-green sky, waking shimmers and sparks from the little bow-wave the long boat drove ahead of it. The banks of the canal, lower here, were clothed with bushes and some stouter trees. Mathis, leaning his forearms on sun-warmed wood, felt their shadows stroke his cheek, touches of light and heat combined.

Here, in the bows of the vessel, the thud of her big single-cylinder engine was muted. He glanced back along the tented cargo space, turned once more to lean over the craft's side. The water was milky green; and some trick of light lent greater depth and perspective to the reflections than to the vegetation above. The tree leaves, small rounded sprays backlit to gold, passed smooth and silent fifty feet beneath the hull.

He studied the bow-wave, the fluctuating patterns within its stable form. The main crest curved from an inch or two before the vessel's blunt stem. Behind it the concave slope of water was glassy and clear. Some six inches ahead a smaller ripple began; the ends of this wavered, flicking forward and back in some pattern that seemed at the same time random and predetermined. Into it flowed the detailed images of branches; behind it the blue and gold melted into streaks that vanished in the deep green shadow of the hull.

He moved his shoulders, feeling the aches from the day before in back and arms. Thirty locks, in three flights of ten, had taxed his strength to the limit. The gates, unused for years, were grass-grown, nearly too stiff to move; also leaks had started, round the heel plates and worn paddle gear. Chamber after chamber refused to fill; it had taken the weight of the boat, butting at the timbers, to force the gates back. Locking down, the problem would be aggravated; but he had no intention of turning back.

He glanced at the chronometer strapped to his wrist, stared ahead again. For two days the canal had paralleled the course of GEM tracks, raw swaths of earth curving through the scrub and marshland that comprised much of Xerxes' Northern Continent; but the last of these had long since swung away. There were no signs of civilization, either Terrestrial or Kalti, and no sounds save the sporadic piping of birds. The boat moved through a silence that the thudding of the engine only seemed to make the more complete.

He wondered, with something approaching interest, whether his absence had yet been noticed. A week had passed since leaving the lagoon that fringed Bran Gildo on the seaward side, climbing the vast lock flight that leads inland from the city. Mathis shrugged. If an alarm had been raised, it mattered little enough. Hidden for most of the time beneath the lapping tangle of branches, the boat would be invisible from a flyer; while the canals of the Southern Complex forked and meandered endlessly, joined by watercourse after watercourse, some natural, others artificial. The hamlets they had served, the mills and tiny manufactories, lay deserted now, the scrub growing up to and lapping across their walls; once lost in that complex, a spotter craft might search for a week and be no wiser at the end.

The air was humid beneath the trees. He wiped at his face and arms. On Earth, flies and midges would have made life burdensome; but the few flying insects of Xerxes, jewel-like creatures resembling terrestrial dragonflies, had no interest in blood. He watched one now, darting and hovering beneath the miniature moss-grown cliff of the bank. The thing swooped, took something from the surface of the water, vanished with a bright blur of wings. The water, he noted, still flowed steadily. The current came via bypass sluices from the high Summit Level ahead. It was an encouraging sign.

In front of the boat a purple-flowered shrub hung low across the water. Her cabin passed beneath its branches with a scrape and rustle. A dozen times already she had been forced to a halt, while Mathis and his steersman used machetes to hack a way through the half-choked watercourse; but in the main the navigability of the canal after so many years' disuse was a monument to the half-legendary Bar-Ab and his engineers.

Four Earth centuries ago, so ran the stories, Bar-Ab had been Prince of Bran Gildo, the palm-fringed city by the Salt Lagoon. He it was who in war after war had swept away the barbarous tribes of the interior, driving their remnants into reserves or into the sea; he also who had given to Xerxes the vast network of canals that, till Terran Contact, had remained the planet's major transportation system. From his line the Kalti, the Boatmen of Xerxes, claimed descent, when they troubled to claim anything at all. From the first, Mathis had been intrigued by them; the little dumpy men and the little dumpy women with their wide-brimmed, round-crowned hats and suits of Sunday black. Though the Kalti were a fast-vanishing race themselves. In every direction, through the swamps, across the uplands with their mile on mile of spindly forest, ran the broad trackways of the Ground Effect Machines; their windy rushing was the night-sound of Xerxes now, replacing the churring of frogs and hunting birds.

Mathis shrugged, and lit a cigarette. From the hundred or so he had brought with him, he allowed himself just two a day. He smoked carefully and slowly, thinking back to his interview with Jefferson, the Bran Gildo Controller. Just ten days ago, now.

He'd pushed his request as far as a Behaviourist (Grade 2A) reasonably could; and been mildly surprised at the result. A small but important circus had assembled to consider the proposition; Ramsden, head of Biology; an Engineer/Controller from the survey section; and Figgins from Liaison, complete with Earth-style secretary. It had been Figgins who opened the attack; Figgins fat, and Figgins bearded.

'John, I feel I must make one point at the outset. This sort of thing is hardly your Department's concern.'

The Terran Complex, an air-conditioned cube of dural and glass, overlooked the brick-red ruins of the Old Palace; the place where Bar-Ab once sat, planning the network of waterways that would span a continent. A boat was passing, on the broad green moat that fronted the ruins, gliding above its mirror-image like a swan. A gay-striped awning covered it; on the foredeck lay a bare brown girl. Mathis shrugged. Difficult to keep his attention on the matter in hand. He said slowly, 'I never claimed my Department was involved. It's a personal project; and I've got a slab of leave come due.'

Figgins' secretary crossed her legs, looking bored. Ramsden, a neat, bald, compact man, ran his finger across an ornamental carafe – Kalti work – and frowned. The engineer doodled on a scratchpad. A little wait, while the Controller decided not to speak; and Figgins carried on.

'Speaking off the record,' he said, 'what would your object be in making a trip like this? What would you hope to prove?'

Mathis said, 'It's all in the report.'

Another wait. Nobody helped him.

The boat was nearly out of sight. He turned back from the window, unwillingly. The words sounded dry; meaningless with repetition. He said, 'We've been on Xerxes about one Earth generation. When we arrived we found a flourishing native culture. Backward on the sciences maybe but well up in the arts. We found a sub-culture, the Boatmen. They had a pictographic writing system like nothing we'd ever seen, and a religion we still haven't properly understood. One generation, and that culture is dying. I don't think we have that sort of privilege.'

Jefferson laid down the stylus he had been fingering. The click of metal on the rainbow-wood desk served to focus attention. Obscurely, Mathis wanted to smile.

The Controller said, 'I think we're rather wandering from the point. There are a lot of side effects to culture-shock that none of us much like. But they're inevitable given the situation in which we find ourselves.'

He glanced at Mathis, eyes bright blue beneath shaggy brows. It was a standard mannerism; a look calculated to convey old-world kindliness combined with shrewdness. 'We might not have learned as much as we ought from three hundred planets,' he said. 'But this much we do know. The day we made contact with Xerxes, existing social patterns were doomed. Mr

Mathis, you mentioned privilege just now. Let's all be logical.' He turned briefly to the big coloured map that covered most of one wall. 'The hinterland of the Northern Continent is largely swamp,' he said. 'In time, that swamp will be drained and reclaimed. Better standards of living are going to bring a higher birthrate, more mouths to feed. We shall need that land. As of this moment ... one Ground Effect Machine will traverse between Bran Gildo and Hy Antiel by any of half a dozen routes in a little under one day Planetary. It'll carry the payload of between five and six Kalti longboats, each of which would take a month on the trip. As I see it, our job isn't to resist a change that's already an accomplished fact. We're here to channel that change, help native cultures through a time of transition as smoothly and quickly as possible. In time, the Boatmen will learn new skills. Readapt. That's the way it has to be.'

Mathis said, 'In time, the Boatmen will cease to exist.'

The Controller nodded gravely. He said, 'That's also a possibility we must allow for.' He leafed through the docket on his desk. He said, 'You're asking for permission to take a Kalti boat through the Southern Complex by way of Hy Antiel Summit. And you still haven't answered Mr Figgins' question. What's your ultimate object?'

Mathis said, 'The word goes that that complex is no longer navigable. That isn't true; and I'm going to prove it. A tenth of what we spent last year on GEM terminals would restore it to full working use – and a hundredth of the labour. I want to see that happen; and I also want the matter of the Kalti culture raised at the next sitting of the Extraterrestrial Council. With your permission, I'm applying for a personal hearing. I want the Boatmen protected, and the entire Northern Continent declared a Planetary Reserve.'

The Controller raised his brows slightly. He said, 'Well, that's your privilege. Ramsden, what do you feel about all this?'

The biologist rubbed his chin. 'There's another factor, of course,' he said in his quiet, precise voice. 'Preservation equals stagnation; stagnation equals deterioration. This sort of thing has been tried enough before. In my experience, it's never worked.'

Figgins grunted. 'It seems to me,' he said, 'that you're starting from unsound premises anyway. These people, the Kalti, I haven't seen many of 'em clamouring for help. Could be they don't want the old way any more than we do. You preservationists are all alike, John. None of you can take the broad view.'

Mathis shook his head, still vaguely amused. How could he explain? If Figgins didn't understand, it was because he didn't want to. Study a Kalti pictograph, the swirls that were tenses, the shadings that were words, and the answer was plain enough. Through every design, like a great hyphen, slashed the *Bar-Ko*, the mark of the One who made water and earth, the green leaves and the sky. At the start of time, He decreed all things to be. If a man was to die, or a culture fail, then these facts were preordained; true a million years ago, and true for ever. This was all you needed; know it, and you knew the Boatmen.

But the Controller was speaking again. This time to the engineer.

'Mr Sito, do you have anything to add?'

Sito shrugged. 'I'd say the whole thing was a pipedream. That cut hasn't been used in thirty years; even the Boatmen don't seem to know much about it any more. I shouldn't think you'd get through to Summit Level; and if you did, do you know the length of that tunnel?'

Mathis said, 'Not precisely, no.'

The other made a face. 'That's my point. Those blighters dug like beavers. There's a tunnel up in the Northern Marshes, Kel Santo, that measures out at twenty kilometres. We've had to put scaffolding through nearly a kilometre to hold the roof; and Kel Santo's never been out of maintenance. Take a boat into Hy Antiel and jam, and you'd not walk back out. It isn't a chance I'd take.'

The Controller nodded. 'Yes, Mr Ramsden?'

The biologist said carefully, 'I have to point out it's not too healthy an area. Most of our cases of Xerxian fever have been brought in from the Antiel range. It's spread by a free-swimming amoeboid, gets into the smallest abrasion. Leave that untreated, and you're in trouble. I've seen some native cases; the medics call it the Shambles.'

The Controller said briskly, 'Right, I think that gives us all we need.' The stylus tapped the tabletop again, with finality. 'I'm not unsympathetic,' he said to Mathis. 'Far from it. As far as appeals go, I'll forward your case with pleasure; we all know every frontiersman has that right. But for the rest, I have to think, first and foremost, of the safety of Base personnel. Both your own and the party we'd have to send out if you went missing. So … request refused. I'm sorry.' He shuffled the papers together, handed them across the desk and rose.

Ramsden caught up with Mathis in the outer office. By mutual consent they took the elevator to the ground-floor bar. Earth interests on Xerxes were expanding steadily; they were brewing something on the planet now that tasted remarkably like whisky. The biologist called for doubles, drank, put the glass down and puffed a pipe alight. He said, 'Hm, sorry about that. Hardly expected anything else, though. Disappointed?'

Mathis smiled. He said slowly, 'Not particularly.'

The other glanced up sharply; and it occurred to Mathis that alone of the committee, Nathan Ramsden had understood his real purpose. Better, perhaps, than he understood it himself. He'd known the biologist a long time. Once, a thousand years back on another planet, he'd been in trouble. He rang Ramsden; and Ramsden had listened till the bursting words were done. Then he said quietly, 'I see. Now, what's the first thing I can do to help?'

The older man took another sip of the pseudo-Scotch. He said, 'As you know, it's not my custom to offer unwanted advice. But I'm offering some now. Go home.'

Mathis stayed silent. He was seeing the canals; the endless shadings of green and gold, puttering of the long black hulls, interlacing of leaf and branch shadows in the brown-green mirror of the water. By pictograph, an answer might be made. The white and blue swirls formed themselves unasked, inside his head.

Ramsden set the glass down. He said, 'This'll be my last tour anyway. I'm looking forward to putting my feet up on an Honorary Chair somewhere. You're still young, John; you've got a year or two left yet.'

Mathis said vaguely, 'I suppose we're as young as we feel.'

The biologist said, 'Hmm …' He waited a moment longer; then rose. He said, 'Drink up. I've got an hour before my duty tour; I've got someone I'd like you to meet.'

The steersman called behind him; a high, sharp sound, like a yap. The Kalti waved and grinned, pointing to the bank; and Mathis smiled, nodding in return. Ahead rose a line of hills, outliers of the Hy Antiel massif. An arm of forest swept down to the canal; it enclosed a grassy clearing, quiet and golden with sunlight. The Boatman swung the painted shaft of the stern oar, nosing the big craft in towards the bank.

In the Lagoon, close under the old white city walls, the long vessels lay tied each to each; the sun winked from brass-strapped chimneys and round portglasses, gleamed on the painted coamings of cabins. On each stempost, knotted rope-work was pipeclayed to whiteness; above each roof were the big running lamps with their filigree-work of brass; on each side, somewhere, was the mark of the God, the *Bar-Ko* with its sprays of leaves, gold and white and blue. Ramsden strolled beside the bright herd of boats, wiping his face and neck with a bandanna. He paused finally beside a craft tied up some distance from the rest, and called. 'Can't get my tongue round these Kalti names,' he said. 'I just call him Jack.'

The Boatman who bobbed from the diminutive bow cabin was slimmer than most of his people. His bland face with the dark, slightly tilted eyes looked very young; to Mathis, he seemed little more than a boy. He grinned, ducking his head, showing a half-moon of brilliant teeth. Ramsden said, '*Hoki*, Jack. *Hoki, a-aie?*' The Kalti grinned again and nodded, waving a slender hand. The biologist stepped across to the raised prow, dropped, grunting, to the foredeck. Mathis followed him.

Hoki, the coffee-like beverage brewed by the Boatmen, had not at first been to Mathis' taste; but he had grown accustomed to its sharp, slightly bitter flavour. He squatted in the cramped cabin, the thin-shelled, brightly painted cup in his fingers, waited while Ramsden mopped his face again. 'He speaks a bit of Terran,' he said. 'Not much, but I think you'll get by. His parents are dead. He's twenty-five; usually their marriage-contracts are settled before they're out of their teens but Jack's still working single-handed. Bit of an oddball, in many respects.'

The Boatman grinned again. He said, 'Too right,' in a clipped, slightly sing-song voice. He took Mathis' cup, poured more of the brownish fluid. The pot in which it was brewed, like all Kalti artifacts, was gaily decorated; the little discs of copper hanging round its circumference tinkled as he set it down.

Mathis looked round the cabin. It wasn't usual for Terrans to be invited aboard a Kalti boat. Nests of drawers and cupboards lined the walls. No inch of the tiny living space seemed wasted; there were earthenware bowls, copper measures and a dipper, a barrel for water storage, a minute stove. He wondered vaguely how Ramsden had come to know the Boatman. He seemed well enough at home.

The biologist lit his pipe again, staring through the open doors at the sparkling expanse of the lagoon. 'This man will take you to Hy Antiel,' he said. 'By the old route, through the Antiel Range. He's a bit of a patriot in his own way too, is young Jack.'

Mathis narrowed his eyes. He said, 'Why're you doing this, Nathan?'

The older man shrugged and raised his brows. 'Because,' he said, 'if you intend to go, and I feel you do, I'd rather you have a good man with you. That way you stand a chance of coming back.' He prodded at the pipe bowl with a spent match. 'Just one thing,' he said, 'if they drag you out by the back hair, as they probably will, I shan't know a thing about it. I've got troubles of my own already …'

He had one final memory: of sitting on the cabin roof of the great boat later that day, watching a vessel come in from Planetary West. Through the glasses she seemed to make no progression, hanging shadowlike against the glowing shield of water. The figures that crowded her rocked, as she rocked, slowly from side to side. From them drifted a thread of sound – a single note, harsh and unnatural, taken up and sustained by voice after voice.

Mathis touched the young Kalti on the shoulder, pointed. 'Jack,' he said, 'what's that?'

'*Kaput*,' said the Boatman unexpectedly, 'all finish.'

Mathis said musingly, 'All the decks were dense with stately forms …' He glanced down sharply. He said, 'You mean it's a funeral.'

'All finish,' said Jack. 'Yes. Bloody bad luck.'

The canal shallowed towards the edges, banked with fine silt. He heard the slither and bump as the flat-bottomed craft grounded, and shrugged. A few minutes' work with the poles would shift her, at first light. For safety's sake he still carried a line ashore. The ground, unexpectedly soft, wouldn't hold a mooring spike. He tethered the boat instead to a sapling at the water's edge. He sat a while watching the shadows lengthen, the gold fade from the little space of grass. From the cabin at his back came shufflings, once a tinkle as the Kalti worked, preparing the mess of beans on which the Boatmen habitually lived. With the dusk a little breeze rose, blowing from the hills, heavy with the scent of some night flower.

The Kalti bobbed from the cabin slide. 'All done,' he said. 'Too quick.'

Mathis turned, stared up at the high line of hills losing themselves in the night. 'Jack,' he said, 'are we going to make it?'

The Boatman nodded vigorously. 'One time,' he said. 'No sweat. Too bloody quick.'

He had conned De Witt at Base into knocking him up a generator and headlamp to supplement the lighting of the Kalti boat. It rested now on the forward cabintop, an untidy arrangement of batteries and wires. He ran a hand across the motor casing as he smoked his final cigarette. The canal was restless; cheepings sounded and close plops, once a heavier crashing of branches followed by the *swack-swack-swack* of a bird taking off from water. The banks, and the shaggy bushes lining them, were mounded velvet; between them the water gleamed, depthless and pale. It seemed the canal itself gave off a scent; chill, and pervasive. The moon of Xerxes was rising as he sought his sleeping bag.

The morning was difficult. The channel, much overgrown here, had silted badly; time and again the boat grounded, sliding to a halt. The pole tip sank in the softness, raising blackish swirls that stained the clear green. The Kalti, patient and expressionless, worked engine and steering oar, using the boat's power now to drive her forward, now to draw back from an impassable shoal. The sun woke shimmers from the thread of water remaining, while Mathis sweated and heaved. By midday, he guessed they had covered little more than a mile. They rested a while, drawn beneath a tangle of bushes; and he heard the echoing whistle of a flyer, somewhere to the north. He waited, frowning. For a time the machine seemed to circle, the sound of its motors eddying on the wind. Then the noise faded. It did not return.

By mid afternoon the condition of the waterway had improved. The boat resumed its steady pace, gliding still between high mounded bushes. Some of the branches bore viciously sharp thorns; Mathis, standing in the bow, swung a machete, lopping a path clear for the steersman. That night he was glad of his rest.

Next morning they reached the foot of a long lock flight that climbed steadily into the hills. The chambers were well spaced, the pounds between them a mile or more in length. Over each pair of gates the *Bar-Ko* rusted in its bright iron frame, a valediction from the long-dead Prince. Viridian creepers had wound themselves into and through the scrollwork of the supports; their long tendrils brushed Mathis' face as the boat glided beneath. On the following day they entered the first of the cuttings.

For some time the ground to either side had been trending steadily upward; now the canal sides, still heightening, closed together, becoming near-vertical cliffs of dark purple rock. The strata of which they were composed were seamed and cracked; between the layers massive trees somehow found lodgement. The root bosses, gnarled and lichened, glistened with water that oozed its way steadily through the stone. Above, the higher trunks were festooned with the brilliant creeper. Some inclined at precarious angles, meshing their branches with those of their fellows on the opposite bank. From them the tendrils swayed, dropping masses of foliage to the water fifty or sixty feet beneath. Later the cutting, still immensely deep, opened out; here lianas, as thick as or thicker than Mathis' arms, stretched pale and taut from the leaf canopy to the shelving rock. They did not, he saw, descend vertically but inclined on both sides at a slight angle to the water; so that driving between them was like passing through the forest-ribs of an enormous keel.

The cutting had one advantage; the height and density of the trees had thinned out secondary growth. The water still ran clear and green; the rock, though friable, seemed not to discolour it. Mathis sat in the damp warmth, hearing the magnified beat of the engine echo back from the high cliff to either side. In time he grew tired of staring up; then it seemed his sense of scale was altered. The bank beside which the boat slid, the foot or so of rock at the water's edge, became in itself a precipice, sheer and beetling. The sheets of lichen, the tiny mosslike plants clinging to the stone, were meadows and trees, above which the menacing shapes drifted like clouds. The tips of the great falls of creeper, touching the boat, discharged showers of drops that fell like storms of icy rain.

He thought vaguely of Ramsden, back at Base; the delight the biologist would take in the strange plant forms surrounding him. With the thought came another, less surely formed; a sense of loss, an aching regret at the necessity for actions. He knew himself better now; and understood more fully the nature of his journey. The notion, once admitted, remained with him, his mind returning to it with the insistence with which the tongue-tip probes the wound of an extraction. This seemed to be the truth; that because nothing, no homecoming, waited beyond the hill range he was drawn forward, because of desolation and emptiness he had to go on. The trees stretched their ranks over the edge of rock above him; beyond he knew lay others and still more, mile on endless mile of forest haunted by rodents and owls. There were empty hamlets, empty villages, empty towns maybe, lapped by the rising green, wetted by rains, warmed by summer suns. He experienced a curious desire, transient yet powerful, to know that land; but know it in detail, hollow by hollow, as he knew the lines of his palms. He wondered at the state of mind, not wholly new to him; and wondered too at a curious notion Ramsden had once expressed that the Loop, in scrambling a man, never reassembled the same being twice. The oddity was allied to another, better known; that over seven years or so the elements of the body, the pints of water and pennorths of salt, are wholly changed so that physically and intimately one becomes a different being. Yet the thinking part, whichever that might be, goes on for ever; hurting, and giving pain.

A mile into the cutting the engine stalled with a thud.

He was amused, momentarily, at the flash of panic aroused in him. The mind, it seems, insists on clinging to patterns once known; maybe to the point of death. The long hull was swinging and losing way, pushed by the faint current from ahead; he fended with the pole, felt the bottom bump gently against mud. He climbed to the catwalk above the cargo space, walked steadily astern.

Round the rear of the vessel, immediately above the propeller, ran a narrow ledge. The Kalti was squatting on it, gripping one-handed, groping with the other arm beneath the water. For the journey, he had affected Terran garb; a sleeveless woollen jerkin, printed with Fair Isle patterns and plentifully daubed with oil, and a pair of frayed and faded jeans. His harsh, longish hair hung forward; between jeans and pullover showed a half-moon of olive skin. He straightened when Mathis spoke, grinning his inevitable grin; Mathis wondered suddenly if it was no more than a reflex of the nerves. 'All stuck up,' he said. 'Jolly bad luck.'

Mathis climbed down beside him. The tip of a nobbled branch protruded from the water; below, its cloudy shape was visible for a foot or more before vanishing in the greenness. He tugged at it. It felt immovable. His reach was longer than the Kalti's; he felt carefully for the propeller boss, traced his finger back along the battered edge of the blade. The log was jammed firmly between propeller and hull.

The Kalti pulled the sweater over his head, balancing with care. He folded the garment neatly and slid into the water. Mathis followed, feeling the buoyant chill.

From this viewpoint, the black hull seemed immense. The mud of the canal bottom sucked at his feet; he grabbed for breath, ducked, surfaced again. He ran fingers across the curving, crusted planks, carefully, remembering Ramsden's injunction. The Kalti heaved at the branch. It moved anticlockwise an inch or so, jammed again. Half-rotten, the wood was difficult to grip. Mathis clung to the step, exploring again with his free hand. The edge of the big prop had bitten deeply into the waterlogged fibres. He shook his head, made washout motions with his palm above the water.

He paddled to where he could once more swing himself aboard. The ironwood grating at the stern lifted readily enough. Beneath it the shaft gleamed dully, secured to the primitive gearbox by a flexible jawed coupling. He fingered the heavy hand-forged bolts. The Kalti nodded, and grinned again.

De Witt had made up a toolkit for the boat. None of the set spanners fitted; he used an adjustable, working carefully so as not to burr the edges of the nuts. As he worked a light drizzle began, drifting in greyish veils from the heights above.

The nuts came clear, finally. He tapped the bolts back through the fibrous coupling plate, and gripped the shaft. It wouldn't budge.

He sorted the toolkit for the longest crowbar. A wooden wedge pressed against the gearbox end protected the coupling from damage. He leaned his weight carefully. The shaft stayed firm. He took a breath, jerked. The thing slid backward through the packing gland, with a faint creak. He reached behind him, pulled. The branch rolled clear and sank.

He eased the shaft forward, reconnected. He sat back, wiping his hands on a piece of fibrous husk. He said, 'Hoki, Jack?' The Kalti raised his thumbs. He said, 'Dear me, yes.' He scrambled forward, over the cargo space.

By mid-afternoon they were clear of the cutting. Beyond, the land fell away with startling speed to a steep and ragged valley. Across it strode an aqueduct, massive arches built of the same purplish rock. To one side, sluices discharged water from the canal lip with a sullen roar. The spray from the fall drifted back, obscuring the defile. Mathis, gripping the boat's rail, imagined the black hull, topped with the tilted brightwork of the cabins, sliding so high in the air. He saw the vessel from the viewpoint of an observer in the tangled valley bottom. Beyond the great structure the rock walls once more swooped together; and the Kalti moored for the night.

In the second cutting they were delayed again, this time by mud and weed. The weed, slimy strings of it twenty feet or more in length, wrapped itself persistently round the propeller, building a solid ball between blades and hull. As the obstructions formed the Boatman sliced them away patiently. Mathis poled dully, disinterested in time; later the machetes were once more brought into use. Finally the narrows were passed; the second cutting opened up ahead. The rock rose steeply, a hundred feet or more, clothed still for most of its height with living green. Through much of the day the far lip caught the sun; the feathery trees that lined it seemed to burn, haloed with pale gold. Later, clouds grew across the sky. The drizzle returned; and a thin mist, veiling the highest rock. In time the mist crept lower, rolling slowly, clinging in tongues to the water.

He was standing beside the steersman on the little stern grating. The Kalti grunted, pulling his lips back from his teeth. Mathis shook his head; and the Boatman waved an arm. '*Mutta-a*,' he said to the surrounding heights. '*Mutta-a. Kaput*.'

Mutta-a. Mutti, Maman ... The first sound any mammal's voice will make. Mathis said, 'You mean it's haunted.' Perhaps this was why the Kalti were disinclined to talk.

'*Mutta-a*,' said Jack, nodding vigorously. 'Rather silly.'

Mathis said, 'I can believe it.'

He walked forward. The mist, or cloud-base, had thickened again; the tree-limbs, some bleached, pushed through it, with curious effect. He was interested to find it was still possible to feel unease. He savoured the sensation with some care.

The huge walls angled to the left. The boat edged round the bend; and a black mouth showed ahead. The sloping hillside in which it was set climbed to unguessed height. Bushes clung to it; above were the trunks of the endless forest. The opening itself was horseshoe-shaped, its throat densely black. From fifty yards he smelled its breath, ancient, and chill. Mathis rubbed his face, then swung to the cabin top to start the generator.

This was the Tunnel of Hy Antiel.

He turned the handlamp. The ribbon of water ahead was tarry, non-reflecting. To either side the close brick walls were festooned with red and green slime; larger masses, leprous-white in the light, hung from the half-seen roof. As the boat brushed at them they broke with soft snaps. From the brickwork of the tunnel fell a steady chill rain.

He listened, turning his head. What he had not been prepared for was the din. The thudding of the boat's diesel echoed massively from the curved walls; but there were other sounds. A sighing rose to something like a roar, fled forward and back along the shaft. Maybe the boat had scraped the side, some sprag touched her hull; God only knew. The brick throat threw echoes back on themselves, lapping and distorting. At first the sounds had troubled him; but they had been travelling two hours or more, he had grown accustomed to the place.

He pitched the light farther ahead. For some time now a deeper roar had been growing in intensity. He saw its source finally; a curtain of clear water, sparkling as it fell from the roof. At its base the surface boiled and rippled, throwing up wavering banks of brownish foam.

This was the fourth airshaft he had seen. He ducked, tortoise-fashion, into the little bow castle, heard the cannonade pass down the long tarpaulins of the cargo space to the stern. The big boat rocked; the sighing came again, mixed with the fading roar.

Here, in the encroaching dark, the swimming sense of motion was intensified. A memory returned to him, odd and unconnected; and he nearly smiled. It was of a journey back from London to his home, when he was a tiny child. On the trip down the monorail whispered and clattered, flashing through tunnel after tunnel beneath the great complexes of buildings; but now the darkness pressed uniform and baffling against the rounded panes of the carriage. He had asked, finally, when this tunnel would end; and his father, momentarily surprised, had dropped a hand to his shoulder and laughed. 'It isn't a tunnel, John,' he said. 'It's the night ...'

He leaned back, head against the bulky survival pack. He felt tired and a little dizzy. Maybe it was the fumes that hung in the shaft. He lit his daily cigarette, and closed his eyes. He saw with remarkable clarity the white walls and green palm-clumps of Bran Gildo, the unused watchtowers pushing their dunce-cap roofs into the turquoise sky. It seemed he could smell the hot, spiced air, the fragrance of spike-leaved shrubs where the Terran girls walked with their pleated kilts and strapped native sandals and long bronzed limbs. From beyond the Palace walls came the sounds of the city's traffic, cartbells mixed with the whine of the electric buggies that were a gift from an ever-benevolent Earth. He opened his lids, seeing the slime-hung walls. The two images, so disparate, were yet interlinked; pieces of an equation that one day must be solved.

Later, he must have slept; certainly he dozed, for when his eyes once more opened the engine of the boat was quiet. The cabin lamps were lit; Jack banged and clattered at the little stove.

He rose, awkward in the confined space. For a moment he was disoriented; and the child's confusion returned so that it seemed the boat must have passed the tunnel. Then he saw how the lamplight glowed in fans across wet brickwork; the air he drew into his lungs was chill and stale. He turned to the Boatman; and the Kalti grinned. 'Too far,' he said. 'Not much good.'

They were moored to what seemed to be the remains of a little wharf. Lines of rusting iron rings were let into the brickwork. He swung to the cabintop, started the generator. The lampbeam showed the black, unrippling water stretching ahead. To the right, joining the main line at a sharp angle, was a second shaft. The stonework of the curving groin where tunnels met looked new and fresh. He pointed to the shaft; but the Kalti shrugged, making wash-out motions with his hands. He said again, 'Not much good.'

With the boat motionless, the silence of the tunnel was complete. He lay a long time hearing the quietness hiss in his ears. Finally, sleep came; and with it dreams. They were untenanted, yet precisely detailed. They concerned ancient buildings, places seen once on Earth. A gatehouse, lost in a wood of tall elms; a street of white-walled cottages; a flight of turf steps before a great stone Minster.

Finally it seemed he sat in an upper room of a very large house. The room, a study, looked out on wings of crumbling stone. Beyond were formal gardens, arbours framing leaden nymphs and gods. In the dream he knew with certainty that he would never leave the room, never rise from the chair; and that the light, the afternoon light, would never change.

The Kalti roused him. He was giddy and light-headed; and his eyes seemed gummy, as though he had not slept. He ate the bean stew the boy set before him with little interest. Afterwards he walked to where the jetty, if jetty it was, narrowed, the stone fairing into the smooth brick of the shaft. His purpose satisfied, he stepped back to untie the ropes from the heavy rings. The Kalti swung up the engine; he poled the bow from the wharf, and the journey was resumed.

Twice in the hours that followed echoing roars from ahead warned of fresh ventshafts. Each discharged its torrent of water into the canal; but staring up as the boat approached, Mathis could detect no gleam of outside light. One shaft seemed partially choked; fibrous roots hung twisting in the downpour, their tips pale and rotted. At eleven hundred the boat passed a line of low flood arches. Water from the canal lip poured beneath them in steady greenish sheets. Mathis turned the lamp. At first it seemed a black void opened beyond; but this was a trick of light. The rock, covered with some dark, non-reflectant growth, was very close.

The workings in the tunnel were complex, like none he had seen. He wondered at their age. He asked the Kalti, shouting above the engine; but the Boatmen shook his head. '*Mutta-a*,' he said. He spread his fingers, and again. Many generations.

The tunnel was very old.

To his other questions there was no reply. The tunnel was very long.

Later in the day the brickwork ended.

The effect was odd. Beyond the shaft sides, a jet half-circle seemed to form and widen. He watched the spreading band a moment, puzzled; then the tunnel was falling away behind. The engine noise, that for so long had pounded in his ears, faded as the stern of the boat drew clear.

He swung the big lamp left and right, discovering no sign of walls; the gloom ahead was likewise unrelieved. At last the abundance of summit water was explained; they had entered an underground lake, of unknown size. He wondered fleetingly if Bar-Ab and his engineers had known. Had they plotted the extent of the cavern, tunnelled to its brink; or had the miners burst into the void, startled and unsuspecting …

On impulse, he angled the light upward. Above, suspended it seemed from an infinite height, the *Bar-Ko*, dark red and dripping, marked the way. Beyond the great iron sign hung another; and another, dimly seen.

He nodded to himself. They had known.

The tunnel had been loud with noise. Running through the void, the opposite effect seemed to hold true. Silence, like the dark, pressed in on the boat; almost it seemed the cavern deadened sound, so that twice he scrambled to the cabin roof convinced the engine was no longer running. Each time he was reassured by the thumping ninety feet astern. Once he tried sounding, with the longest pole, but could touch no bottom. He turned his wrist in the beam of De Witt's spotlight, holding the chronometer close up to his face. He was surprised to see an hour had elapsed since quitting the shaft.

With time, the absence of sensation affected him strongly. The tunnel sounds returned, the whisperings and long sighs; but they were in his ears. Also it seemed that lights appeared, far across the water. It was as if a fairy army drove to meet him, yet for ever receded. He rubbed his face, knuckling at his eyes; and the lights were gone.

Finally a fresher breeze blew from ahead. Also he saw, above the endless line of markers, a fold of stone that was the dipping of the cavern roof. Ghostings of grey appeared to either side; then, suddenly, the cavern walls began to close back in. The slime-hung brickwork returned; and he stared behind him at the velvet dark. He said, 'The Lake of Tuonela.'

Tuonela, where dead spirits walk.

In the outer world the time was thirteen hundred. The abstraction counted for little here. He wound the chronometer, staring up while the bow of the vessel bumped gently at what looked at first sight to be the gate of a stop lock. The journey was ended.

The tilted beam of light rolled slowly, illuminating a slope of wet, smooth rock. At its summit, the side of the second great caisson showed its panels of rusting iron. More iron, columns and tie rods, rose into the dark. Beyond was an engine house. The round-topped windows stared like dim sockets; above them the buttressed column that was the chimney grew up into the stone, thrusting for the open air. Mathis grinned, showing his teeth. He said softly, 'The crazy bastards.'

He sat on the cabin roof and lit a cigarette. He felt closer to Bar-Ab and his men than he would have thought possible. He rubbed the beard-stubble on his chin and asked himself, how could they have done it? How could they carve through twenty miles of rock, with pickaxes and plumb bobs, and keep their line and level? Those engineers in kilts and plumes? Like the Incas, their priests used the Rope of Thorns. Like the Victorians, they knew black powder and the barrow run. Like both, they vanished. They left … this.

They built an Inclined Plane, inside a bloody hill.

A sound at his elbow made him turn. The Kalti's face was a pale mark in the gloom. He waved an arm at the monstrousness; the caissons, the engine house, the rails with their great red bogies. He said, 'Make go.'

Mathis threw the half-smoked butt into the water. Sito would have given his back teeth for this. 'Yes, Jack,' he said. 'We must make it go …'

There was coal; great bunkers of it, growing here and there a rich skin of mould. Coal, but no kindling. For that they stripped the powdering frames from windows, boards from the engine-house floor. Fuel oil from the boat's depleted tank would fire the furnace. The boiler they filled painfully, a bucket at a time. The top caisson already held water; the gate of the lower for a time refused to close. Mathis rigged a fourfold purchase from a mooring bollard, strained the thick iron partially shut; the boat herself, thundering in reverse, completed the job. Brown foam boiled; the big door closed, with protesting squeals. They lit the furnace then, sat an hour while pressure built to working head. Round the boiler were heavy riveted straps. In time the rivet heads began to sizzle and steam.

There was a bank of gauges, each set in a plate of foliated brass. The markings on the faces made no sense. It was guesswork, all the way.

Mathis edged the regulator forward. A rumbling; rust flew, in a thin rain. Below, the long chains stretched over the rock clanked to tautness. The boat slopped against the chamber side; the engine slowed as the ancient gearing felt the load. Steam roared from a union; and the boat was climbing, inching sideways up the Plane. The headlight, blazing, drew level with Mathis, began to pass. The Kalti heaved at the caisson side, adding his strength to the strength of the machine. He was happy. He had done what the strange Terri wanted; now others would come, with their engines that tore away rock and plucked down trees. And the long cuttings would once more fill. His head made pictures; he saw the blue and red stars that were the lamps of boats, sailing all night long from Bran Gildo to Hy Antiel.

A chain link parted, with a ringing crash. Mathis, sweating, wrenched at the emergency brake with blistered hands. The caisson, with its hundred-thousand-gallon load, lurched backward on the slope; and the Kalti's heels shot from under him.

'Oh dear,' said Jack. The bogies, gathering speed, severed his arm, ploughed crashing across his chest. The caisson took the water it had quitted with a thunderous splash. A tinkling; the headlight on the cabin roof swayed sideways and was extinguished.

*

The tunnel portal was set into a low, mounded hill. Beyond it the canal was fringed with low shrubs that blazed with smoky orange blossom. Above, saplings hung graceful and still, their sprays of rounded leaves catching the sunset light.

To an observer stationed at the tunnel mouth, the twin lamps of the Kalti vessel would have appeared at first like dim brown stars. For some time, such are the curious optics of tunnels, the stars would have appeared to grow no closer; then, suddenly it seemed, they swam forward. Between them the outlines of the boat became visible; the knotted headropes of the prow, the tilted cabin with its ornamented ports. Behind, sliding into the light, came the long tented cargo space; the engine-house, hazed with blue; the stern deck with its grating, the *Bar-Ko* vaunting white and gold on the rounded black sides. The steersman, in once-white slacks and shirt, leaned wearily on the painted shaft of the oar. His face was fringed with a stubble of beard; from time to time he glanced down, frowning, at a bundle near his feet. In places the canvas of which it was composed was soaked and dark; and a runnel of fluid had escaped, staining the boat's dull side.

To Mathis, the transition from darkness to the light seemed curiously unreal. He smelled the sweetness of the grass, heard the wind rustle in the tops of trees and frowned again, shaking his head as if to clear it. His brain recorded, but sluggishly. Ahead and to the left, twin hills marked the position of Hy Antiel. This was the Summit Pound; five miles ahead the lock flight began that led to the city, stepping in green steps down a green and grassy hill. He'd walked beside it often enough, it seemed in some other life.

He squinted up at the high dusting of gold. To the right showed the pilings of a mooring place. Little bushes surrounded it, throwing their branch-shadows across the water. He turned the oar, unused as yet to the boat's response, glided the long vessel to the bank.

He was uncertain of the forms to be employed. He chose a spot finally; a grassy knoll beneath the branches of a broad, spreading tree. He had brought a spade and mattock from the boat; he wiped his forehead, and began to dig. Later he drove a stake into the grass at the head of the fresh-turned mound. To it he lashed a crosspiece for the *Bar-Ko* sign; then there was nothing more to do.

He searched the Kalti's few possessions. He found a breech-cloth of silk, a scarf, a broad-brimmed, round-crowned hat; and a bolero crusted with pearly buttons, the sort of garment a Boatman would wear on a feast-day in Bran Gildo. In a bag closed by a drawstring were two brooches set with semi-precious stones, a nugget of what looked to be iron pyrites and a lock-key charm in gold. There were also a prayer-roll sealed with the *Bar-Ko* mark, and a much-thumbed packet of postcards showing bare-breasted Terran girls. These last he returned to the bag before tucking it carefully away.

He didn't wish to eat. Instead he brewed up the Kalti coffee, drinking several cups. Slightly alcoholic, the drink had a heady effect. He smoked a cigarette, saw to his mooring stakes and spread his sleeping-bag on the cabin roof. The spinning in his head was worse; he closed his eyes, and was quickly asleep.

He woke some time before the Xerxian dawn. To Planetary East, the first faint flush of green heralded the sun. The canal was a silver mirror, set between velvet trees; and Barbara watched him from the bank, her chin in her hand. The light gleamed palely from her hair.

He pushed himself up on one elbow, and smiled. 'Hello,' he said. 'Are you coming on board?'

She considered, smiling in her turn, before she slowly shook her head. 'No, thanks,' she said. 'I think once was enough. I don't think I could go through it all again.'

He said, 'I can't say I blame you. You're better off where you are.'

She chuckled. 'My word,' she said, 'you've certainly changed.'

He said, 'I suppose we all do.' He rubbed his face. 'I wasn't expecting you,' he said. 'Not here. I thought I'd travelled much too far away.'

'Oh,' she said, 'you know me, John. I'm the little crab who always hangs on. Remember?'

'Yes,' he said. 'I do.'

She was quiet a moment, watching along the canal. She said, 'This is a lovely place.'

'It needed you,' he said. 'It was rather pointless before.'

'Where were you going?'

He said, 'Hy Antiel.' He gestured at the bank. 'There were two of us. But …'

She said, 'I know.' She shook her head. She said, 'You haven't altered all that much, after all.'

'What do you mean?'

'Poor John,' she said. 'You never could understand, could you? About other people.'

He said, 'I didn't want it to happen. I didn't want him to be hurt.'

She said, 'You never wanted anybody to be hurt. But you always forgot.'

He said, 'I'm sorry.'

She said, 'I know. It doesn't matter.'

A little silence. Then he said, 'Please come aboard.'

She laughed. She said, 'No, not now. But I will stay with you.'

He said, 'Thank you.'

She said softly, 'It's more than you deserve.'

He said, 'You were always more than I deserved.'

He let himself sink back. Later she too dozed, her head resting on her arm. For that he couldn't blame her. It had been a long way, from Tuonela.

Sunlight lay in hazy patches on the water when he opened his eyes. He sat up slowly, pushing back the fabric of the bag, and saw how clever she had been. The light patch of her skirt was bright grass seen through a triangle of lapping boughs. The smooth rootstock of a shrub had made her ankle; and she had used a glistening branch for the sheen of hair. He moved, and she was gone. But there were many shadowed places on the canals, many quiet banks of grass; he found himself not without hope.

The shaking in his legs and arms was bad, but his head felt fractionally clearer. He started the engine, poled the boat from the bank. The canal was wider here and deep, curving gracefully beneath the overhanging bushes. The diesel chugged steadily; the wash ran slapping against earth banks studded with moss-grown holes. The *chikti* made them, the little burrowing mammals of the tropics.

Three miles before the flight a broad green arm of water opened to the left; the Coldstream branch, that once had served the villages to the south of Hy Antiel. He pushed the oar, leaning his weight steadily, watching as the bow began to swing. He had understood a final thing; that pain is life, and death is when the pain has gone away.

Ahead, the lapping of blue and gold repeated itself into distance. Beyond, dimly glimpsed, were the low hills of the watershed through which the canal, broadening and meandering, lost itself once more in the marshlands of the south.

THE GRAIN KINGS

1

The pamphlet was glossy and well thumbed. Harrison leafed the pages indifferently, glancing up from time to time at the bulkhead clock.

> *The principle of the combine harvester,* he read, *dates back to the early years of our century. The first machines were crude and small, and were usually controlled and operated by one man (see illustration opposite).*
>
> *A UN combine has been likened to a small township on caterpillar tracks. Aboard each great machine a crew of up to a hundred must eat, sleep and work for weeks at a time. The superstructure houses construction and repair shops, generator and boiler rooms, a sick bay, laboratories, a gallery; and for off-duty relaxation a restaurant, television lounge, bars and a cinema. A modern combine is big. It has to be; it has a big job to do. In Alaska alone, upward of a hundred thousand square miles of wheat must be harvested in not much more than a month. Wheat that is needed, desperately, to feed the teeming millions of our overcrowded planet.*

The wallclock pinged. Harrison yawned, tossed the booklet down and rose. A belted topcoat hung behind the door. He shrugged himself into it and left the cabin.

The corridor beyond, dim and quiet when he had come aboard, vibrated faintly. The lamps in their wellglasses glowed brightly; the combine had raised running voltage. He turned left and right, climbed a flight of spindly metal stairs. The companionway gave on to B deck and the observation lounge.

On deck he was assailed by an echoing clamour. He stood blinking vaguely, saw without surprise that the combine was in motion. Above and close, the big metal girders of the hangar bay slid past one behind the next; he stared up, seeing the yellow bowls of service lights glide by, watching the shifting, repeating perspectives. Ahead, the exit doors had already rumbled back. Daylight gleamed outside, faint as yet and grey. The opening looked like the slit of a pillbox. In a building so vast, perspectives tended to confuse the brain.

The tannoys in the roof were working again, gobbing out their words in big, bouncing chunks of sound. The lights gleamed on the combine's broad forward casings. On her stubby mast, red and turquoise identification lamps sequenced steadily, like the landing lights of an aircraft. Harrison found notebook and stilus, leaned against the deckrail. He wrote: *It doesn't fly, so it isn't a plane. It doesn't float, so it can't be a ship. It's something else, something different. Outside experience.* He sneered at the phrase, scored it through. Beneath it he scribbled; *Clearing hangar sheds, 07.30 hours. Loudspeakers working; difficult for the uninitiated to make out the words. They wouldn't mean much if they did. Big combining already has a language of its own.*

The observation deck was filling now. On the port wing O'Hara was angling his camera for a shot of the control-room windows. Alison Beckett had made her appearance, well muffled. Harrison flicked his fingers at her, walked over to the photographer. The combine was nearing the exit ramp. Red lamps sprang into brilliance round the edges of the great doors. He heard the main diesels catch and thunder. She'd been running on her auxiliaries then. The engine beats steadied to a pounding throb. He thought, 'We shall be living with that noise. For days.' He said to O'Hara, 'Don't forget the old man's hangar shots.'

O'Hara grinned. He said, 'The great sheds sink slowly in the west.'

Harrison said, 'You take the pictures. I'll write the copy.'

O'Hara rolled film, turned the Bronica, made an adjustment. He said, 'It's the pictures that matter, boyo.'

'Every one,' said Harrison, 'is worth a thousand words.' He turned away, hands dug into the pockets of his coat.

A combine is too big to be solid. Rather it humps its way across the land, like a jointed, gigantic steel carpet. Harrison watched the forward casings rise steadily, taking the slight slope of the exit ramp. As they nosed into daylight they changed colour from brown to orange-red. The pitch of the engines altered as the main bulk felt the incline.

Beside him stood a stubby, grey-haired man, an off-duty engineer. Harrison said, 'Why were the main diesels only started just now? I thought they'd need longer to warm up.'

The engineer glanced at him, took a pipe from his pocket, tamped the tobacco and struck a match. He seemed in no hurry to answer. Finally he said between his teeth, 'She doesn't run on her mains. They're running 'em up for start of cut. She goes anywhere on her crawlers.'

Harrison said, 'Thank you. I wasn't sure.'

The bulk of the machine was clear of the sheds now. The noise of the loudhailers faded abruptly. In the open air the thunder of the engines was less oppressive. Harrison stared round him. The sky was an indeterminate grey-blue. He saw, or thought he saw, the last spark of a star. The eastern horizon, flat, was slashed with searing yellow.

On the wing, O'Hara was lining up the hangar shots. He'd got Alison to pose against the rail. She was wearing a headscarf. One long strand of hair had come free, was moving in the wind. She put her glove up, tucked it aside. The bridge speakers clicked and said, 'Good morning.'

The voice said, 'I am Controller Cheskin. I welcome you on behalf of the United Nations Organization and the World Food Council. The machine on which you are travelling is an American-built Rolls-Toyota of the Dakota class. She develops a total horsepower of just over a hundred thousand, and harvests on a two-hundred-and-fifty-metre swath. Her codename to base is Combine Patsy. We are travelling east, fifteen degrees north at a speed of ten kilometres an hour. At zero nine hundred hours we shall be turning on to cut.'

The speakers crackled slightly. They said, 'Breakfast is now being served in the C deck restaurant. May I wish you all a pleasant and interesting trip. Thank you.'

Alison came over. She said, 'God, I'm frozen. Aren't you cold?'

Harrison said, 'Not too bad.'

'Coming to breakfast?'

He said, 'I've got some notes to get down. I'll take second tables.'

She said, 'You're too devoted.'

He said, 'I work better first thing.'

He walked back to his cabin, closed the door and hung the coat up. He lay on the bunk, hands clasped behind his head. Now, with the main engines running, the dural walls thrummed faintly. He closed his eyes, feeling the pulse of the combine. He remembered, arbitrarily, how someone once told him he made love to her at dawn, though the fleshly Harrison was two hundred miles away. He shrugged. The borderline between fantasy and fact is vivid and hard. Whoever holds it to be otherwise is either a liar or a fool. Probably the former. He lay now alone, a hardish pillow under his head. The counterpane was striped in sage green and orange, the cabin furnishings looked vaguely Swedish. The air conditioner whistled slightly, the clock hands stood at 08.05. Nothing and nobody would alter these facts.

He had a bottle of whisky in the bedside locker. He sat up, poured himself two fingers, grimaced and added the third. He thought, 'I should kick this early-morning drinking.' He drank, lit a cigarette, laid it in the tray. He was thinking about the flight up. He'd travelled, among others, in the company of a well-known divorcee. Her legs had been superb and she raised hell about the lunch. She left the plane at Kennedy. He thought, 'I should be over the other thing by now. Nine months is a good gestation.'

He opened his eyes again at ten hundred hours. The Scotch still stood on the locker; the cigarette had burned itself out half through. He thought, 'I missed start of cut.' But he could make that bit up. He reached for the notebook, considered for a time and wrote.

The main power system of a combine is diesel-electric. Motors situated above each set of cutter blades. Access from motor gallery forward; maintenance staff permanently on duty. He thought for a moment. Could they withdraw blade sets, service while in motion? He presumed so; still, it was a point worth checking.

The light through the cabin port was bright now. He buzzed the steward, asked for some coffee. While he was waiting he shaved. The coffee when it came was very good. He smoked a cigarette, stubbed it and walked back to the observation deck.

Climate control made these exercises possible. As he emerged into sunlight the combine was flowing past a radiator. The tower stood on tall black struts. Clamped to one of the stilt legs was a board with the legend *Danger. IOKV.* Below it was stencilled another warning: *Do not activate relays without blue and green authorities.* He wondered how service engineers reached isolated towers. Not by helicopter; the downdraught would flatten the wheat.

He stared above him. The sky had a hard, steely brilliance. The decks of the combine stretched out like a scarlet plain; ahead and to either side, the wheat was an immense level sea. He thought, 'Indian summer of technology,' and dismissed the phrase.

The radiator was well astern now. Ahead was a reef signal. The red disc bore a black triangle, point uppermost. He waited for the combine to change course. She didn't appear to; but the signal passed well to port. Beyond it, the smoothness of the grain was unmarred. He wrote: *Dural girders. Aluminium panels. Ground clearance zero. Patsy is a fragile giant.*

He thought, *Aren't we all?*

He watched the horizon, hazed with blue. Nothing to see; no way of marking progression. The combine was on cut; but from up here there was no way of telling. He listened, carefully. Maybe the engine rumble was a fraction deeper, there was a shade more vibration. The endless roaring he'd expected wasn't there. The machine moved majestically, a ship against a yellow ocean. He wondered again about the sea metaphor. As yet he had nothing on which to peg his story. No theme. He watched the cutter coamings a hundred yards away. They rose and fell steadily, rolling with the contours of the land. He imagined he could hear, above the diesels, the sibilance of the blades slicing wheat.

Two dolly-bird reporters came up from below. The taller looked Scandinavian. They glanced at him as they passed, leaned backs turned to him against the rail. They seemed to have a lot to chat about. He walked to the starboard wing, propped the notebook on his knee.

A combine works to a predetermined grid, he wrote. *Strictly, it's flying by wire. Control units, buried by the score, kick out a parcel of signal frequencies; underbelly sensors keep each machine on a true heading. Course and pattern of cut are predetermined at base; onboard computers see to the rest. The system's accurate; you can do a lot with a two hundred and fifty metre datum line.*

He touched the tip of the stylus to his teeth. He wrote: *Patsy's cutting on a two hundred kilometre grid. Two hundred up, two hundred down. When she gets back to start of cut she won't be running more than a yard from true.*

She could cut on a five hundred kilometer grid, or a thousand, or ten. Distance is no object; all we need is a big enough planet.

He thought, *I'm not getting anywhere.* He walked back down the companionway to C deck bar.

The room was wide and long, panelled in satin-finish dural. He'd read some of the Russian combines used mahogany and brass. Windows looked out through the underpinnings of B deck, across the main coamings to the wheat. There were chairs and tables set round, Audubon prints in thin black frames. A coffee machine sang and glugged on the countertop.

O'Hara was playing the Bandit. As Harrison walked in it paid fifty. O'Hara grinned a pale, square grin and said, 'What do I do with these?'

Swissy said, 'Use 'em for washers. Good for de car.'

Harrison said, 'Pint of beer. No, the English.'

Swissy said, 'D'American is very good.'

'I'll stick with this.'

Swissy rubbed his hands. He said, 'A dollar. T'ank you.' He pushed the glass across.

Harrison leaned on the bar and lit a cigarette. Swissy said, 'Where's de li'l girl?'

O'Hara turned back from the machine. He said, 'She's developing.' He winked at Harrison. He said, 'No point keeping these. The crafty bastard won't change 'em.'

Swissy said, 'Give you two dollar for 'em. Haven't counted.'

O'Hara said, 'I'd rather put them back.'

Swissy said, 'Anyway, she's tuned. Pay for t'ree dollar.'

Harrison said, 'You put more than that in it last night.'

Swissy smirked. 'Was wit' syndicate,' he explained. 'Get t'irty per cent anyway. Can't lose if I play wit' four.'

O'Hara said, 'He doesn't understand his systems any more than anybody else.'

Harrison drank beer. He said, 'Got your pictures for today then, Mike?'

O'Hara considered. He said, 'I didn't see you when we turned on to cut, boyo.'

'Quite so. How was it?'

O'Hara said, 'Spectacular.'

Harrison drank another pint, which tasted good. The missed-breakfast feeling was starting to leave him. By the third he was feeling nearly human, which wasn't in all respects a good idea. He walked to C deck restaurant, ate *entrecôte* steak with a scampi starter. You could say this for combiners' food – it was reliable. He signed the bill for the company and walked back to the bar. He had a tour fixed for the afternoon; he'd arranged to meet an engineer called Bertie Pritchard.

Bertie was short, boyish, greying and relatively tired. He looked like an ex-Navy man. He spoke with an explosive punctuation that could turn readily to a stammer. They propped the bar up till three. Swissy was back on duty. He was talking about the last execution in Berne. 'Dey climb up de trees,' he said. 'All de boys, you know? So dey see into de prison yard. Christ, an' down dey come den. Like de blowty apples.'

Somebody laughed.

Bertie said, 'You never *saw* a bloody *execution*.'

Swissy grinned. 'My fader tell me,' he said. 'You know, a man get his head cutted off, he don't stop wit' de blinking?' He mimed, rapidly. He did in fact succeed in looking like a severed corpse. 'Blinkin' de eyes,' he said. 'An' de mout' go, so; and out de trees dey come. Christ, like apples.'

Bertie said, 'Who are you *with*?'

'World Geographic.'

'Good outfit?'

Harrison said, 'Fair. Like the rest.'

Bertie said, 'Christ, listen to the basstard.'

Swissy was saying indignantly, 'Is true. In Zürich, used to know dis chap was apprentice to a butcher. Dey used to drink a lot of blood, when dey killing de calf. Dey go *ksss* on de li'l calf, an' catch an' drink in de glass. Do 'em good.'

Bertie said, 'You are a *repulsive* basstard.'

'No, is true,' said Swissy. 'Can't help what he tol' me, only tell de trut'. All de time.' He smirked. 'You listen, Bertie, you find out a lot. Tell you lot o' t'ings you never hear of.'

Bertie said, 'If you've finished, we'll get out of here.'

Swissy said, 'Chow, bot'. See you next time.'

In the corridor Bertie said, 'Where do you want to go first?'

Harrison said, 'It's your tour.'

They walked forrard. Over a bulkhead door was a stencilled sign, *Crew Members Only*. Bertie ducked through. He said, 'Mind your head.'

Down here, the quality of sound was changed. There was a heavy roaring; Harrison guessed they were close to the main diesels. Bertie turned right and right again. There was a short companionway. He took it at the trot. He said, 'Links. Don't get your *feet* tangled up.'

The corridor, articulated, flexed slightly, moving with the movements of the combine. From somewhere came a faint, persistent squealing. Already, Harrison felt lost. He said, 'How long does it take to find your way about?'

Bertie snorted. He said, 'They're crazy f-fucking objects. Pointless complexity. All the same.'

Harrison said, 'What do they cost?'

'Twenty million. *Give* or take. Everybody gets a nice slice of the pie. Watch your *feet*.'

There was a final hatchway. Harrison stepped through, and stared. They had emerged in the forward casings, directly above the cutter service gantry.

The noise hit him first. It seemed compounded of all frequencies; hum of motors, whirl and clank of chains, *whick-hiss, whick-hiss* of the blades, echoing rumble from the combine's tracks. To right and left, long glints of daylight reached under the coamings. The air was yellow, fog-thick; through it the cutters glittered dully, spinning silver drums. Beneath his feet flowed a jostling brown river; the conveyors, edging the grain tons a minute to the threshers in the great belly of the machine.

He watched the men on the gantry. They wore one-piece suits of something that looked like asbestos. Visors covered their faces; on his back, each carried a bulky pack. Tubes from the packs dived beneath the wearers' armpits. Harrison mouthed a question. Bertie shook his head. He said, 'Self-contained systems. Ocy-nitrogen. You can't filter that muck. It gets in everything.'

Harrison said, 'What do these boys earn?'

Bertie said, 'A hell of a lot.' He leaned back, hands in his trouser pockets. He said, 'It's all right while it lasts.'

Harrison said, 'Silicosis?'

'There's quicker than that. Heard of combiner's balls?'

Harrison said, 'No.'

Bertie said, 'It means you don't have any. No skin on the tops of the thighs. It gets up inside the suits. Can't bloody stop it.'

Harrison said, 'They're welcome.'

Bertie said, 'They're the toughest basstards in the world.'

Near at hand, a crew was swinging a blade unit down into operation. One man was beating at the motor housing with a gauntleted fist. Harrison saw him raise his arms, make wash-out motions. He stared down. The movement of the grain beneath his feet was giddying.

Bertie said, 'Seen enough? I can't stand this bloody stuff for long.'

Harrison nodded, stepped back through the hatch. The engineer dogged it shut. The noise diminished. Harrison said, 'Christ.'

Bertie clattered ahead of him, down a flight of steps. At their foot, the decking surged unexpectedly. Harrison grabbed for the rail. Bertie said, 'This is E deck catwalk. We're alongside the threshers. Nothing much to see. The process is totally *enclosed*.'

The catwalk was long, and dim. They glided, it seemed, at eye-level with the wheat. Down here you could really hear the whisper, the sibilance. Glass panels were rigged at head height along the gallery. Harrison leaned close, stared into the endless brown-grey aisles between the stalks. Bertie said, 'That's *virgin*, of course. Julie's coming up from the west. We're cutting east, towards the *Russkie* patch.'

Harrison said, 'It's a new viewpoint.'

Bertie banged the screen with his fist. He said, 'We had to fit these last trip. Had some stupid little *bitch* of a journalist. She put her hand out in it. Said it reminded her *of punting*.' He tittered, soundlessly. 'You should have seen it,' he said. 'A little *blood* goes a long way.'

Harrison turned away. He thought, 'It's graceful, and soft. Touch it, and it opens to the bone.'

Bertie walked ahead. He said, 'This *might* interest you.'

Harrison watched the complex assemblage of levers. The whole device seemed to stride. A rod was poised, plunged into a gap beside the main housings. A pause; and the forward travel of the combine brought the links upright. The rod lifted, gleaming; a dark earth sample was ejected, whirled away, before the corer dipped again. Harrison said, 'What's it taking?' He was still thinking about the wheat.

Bertie said, 'They're checking soil organisms. Bacteria count. It's called a Tom Thumb sampler.'

He opened a bulkhead door. Beyond, a link corridor led to a big darkened space. Heat gusted back, heavily. Harrison saw steel drums rotating behind protective panels of mesh. Lamps gleamed here and there, red-mauve. Bertie said, 'The intake is damped south of the conveyors. Here it's irradiated, and *dried*.' He gestured at the lamps. He said, 'Pig-rearing lights.'

They walked on. In the combine's belly, sound levels varied continually. Sometimes the clatter of an auxiliary room drowned speech, sometimes the roar of the tracks. They walked down a serviceway, its floor panels composed of thick steel mesh. There was a rich, earthy smell; inspection lamps showed stubble flowing a yard beneath. Bertie ducked through a hatch. He said, 'Main tracks.'

The combine jolted and heaved. He reached back, steadied Harrison's arm. He said, 'OK?'

Harrison said, 'Yes.'

Bertie said, 'Don't want to have to scrape you off a bloody *bobbin.* Not while I've signed for you.'

The tracks were also lit. Harrison watched the steel rollers on which they ran bounce and jump. The links, each plate the size of a dinner table, rose up smoothly, passed out of sight overhead. He said, 'How many tracks does she run on?' Bertie said, 'They're rigged on twenty-metre centres. You can do the *sum* yourself.'

In the main diesel room an engineer wearing padded earmuffs waved to Bertie from his gantry. Bertie waved back. Harrison looked at his watch. Already they'd been an hour on the trip. Bertie closed the door behind him. He said, 'We're now going *afft.* Crew's quarters on the left, and sick bay. Laboratories to the right. Can't go there; not my patch.'

There was a door marked *Latrine, male. Field use only.* A part of Harrison's mind recorded the words.

Bertie said, 'When are you seeing the old man?'

Harrison said, 'Tomorrow morning.'

Bertie said, 'He's a queer basstard. Why they let him get hold of this thing I shall never know.'

They passed another door. Bertie said, 'Galleys. Bakehouse.'

Harrison said, 'I shouldn't think there's any shortage of flour.'

Bertie said, 'Under UN regulations, we can't touch our output. They fly the f-flour up from base. Amazing, the workings of the Oriental *mind.*'

There was light ahead. Daylight. He pushed a door open. He said, 'The ass-*end* of the process.'

Harrison walked to the rail. They were on the stern of the combine. Behind and above, unfamiliar from this viewpoint, the control bridge jutted at the sky. Astern stretched the great swath of stubble; again like a wake he thought, the wake of some ponderous geometric ship. Below him, slipways disgorged the produce of the machine like vast parcelled eggs, each pallet the size of a truck. Flying cranes were busy in the middle distance, droning like headragonflies. He saw one settle its hooks into a bale, rise with it and lumber off to the south. The sun, already levelling, lit the great dust-cloud, turning the grains to gold. As they entered the brilliance, the service vehicles became shadows. It was blue, and red of coamings, and gold; everywhere, the blue and gold.

Bertie said, 'As far as I'm concerned, you've seen the lot. Anything you want to ask?'

Harrison said, 'Later on maybe. I'm still taking it in.'

Bertie looked at his wrist. He said, 'Can you find your own way back? Got to meet another party. We ran a bit late.'

Harrison said, 'Don't you have a duty watch?'

Bertie said, 'I'm just the bloody liaison man. Tell 'em why the *wheels* go round.'

Harrison said, 'Thanks for the trip. I shall be OK.'

Bertie said, 'See you in the Swiss *Embassy.*' He ducked through the doorway, and was gone.

There was a seat, to one side of the observation deck. Harrison slumped on it, pulled his notebook from his pocket, stared at it for a time and put it away. He closed his eyes; and for a moment he was on a ship. She had just this same easy motion; the thunder of her diesels was muted, as it was muted here; and she was coming into Oban, from Mull. The sea was millpond calm, big vees of ripples starting and starting and spreading for miles. He thought, *How often you hear that phrase, how seldom you see what it means.* He shut his eyes again. It had been bad all day. He thought, *We were going there together, only you couldn't quite make it. You weren't on that ship, you bitch, and you are not here.*

Aloud he said, 'That'll do you a lot of bloody good.'

He leaned back, lit a cigarette. He was remembering Cheltenham, and the caryatid figures in the Colonnade, and buying the big buckled lovely handbag for her and the flat she'd taken in the town. He inhaled, blew smoke. He remembered the first months after the break-up. Time had telescoped; he'd lost nearly a year of his life. He hadn't believed such a thing was possible. He thought about the place he'd found in London, and the absurdity of it all, the sheer absurdity. Once, years back, he'd had a really bad pain. He remembered laughing jerkily, in the middle of it; it seemed a ridiculous state of affairs that any one thing could hurt that much. He thought, *You sleep, not wanting to wake. But you wake. You get up, you get to the office, you trail back to your pad. You eat and speak and shave and wash and write words. Sometimes you can remember what you've done through the day. Sometimes you can't.* He remembered drinking sessions, sessions that started because the office had shut and just went on anyway; and empty Sundays and empty weekends and trailing out West for drag, the go-go dollies. He thought, *Is there anybody anywhere, for whom pleasure is real, existence meaningful? What happens, inside Bertie? Inside Swissy? Is it any different for them?*

He glanced at the last thing he'd written that morning. *Distance is no object,* he read. *All we need is a big enough planet.*

He thought, *I'm riding Combine Patsy. And Patsy is cutting a two-hundred-and-fifty-metre swath; and Patsy is a Wonder of the Age.*

Aloud he said, 'I couldn't bloody well care less.'

He looked at his watch. He'd caught himself wondering when the bars would open.

The sun was dropping toward the horizon. The air was keener now; astern, the dust-pall gleamed with a reddish light. He got up, walked back the way he had come. Finding his way through the combine's guts was a harder task then he'd realized. He passed along gantries he hadn't seen. Once he was challenged, made to show his press card. He got to his cabin finally. The thrumming of the walls felt familiar. He thought, 'Nearly like home.'

He took the Olivetti from its case, transcribed what notes he'd made. He added: *It's the dust you become aware of. It's in the air, a grittiness on the lips. It creaks underfoot as you walk. Nothing's really clean. Put a saucer down for an hour and lift it and you see the yellow bloom, the mark of where it lay. And this is only start of cut.*

He looked at his watch again. This past few months he'd got into the habit of marking the progression of hours and days. It was as if some bright point, some node of light and warmth, receded steadily; there was a compulsion to mark the regression. There were little anniversaries to be noted, transient things, affairs of hours, months. One day he supposed they would total years.

Loudspeakers were clattering somewhere in the combine. The sound reached him faintly, mixed with the humming of the cabin walls. He wrote: *In twenty minutes, if my mathematics serve me, we shall end our first pass.* He rose, took his coat down, put it on. He walked down the corridor, turned left and right, climbed the companionway to B deck.

The sun was low, the western hemisphere a bowl of dusty pink light. He thought, *Red sky at night, climatologist's delight.* The upper works and rigging of the combine were sharp-cut against the glow. Forward and below, the light seemed to permeate the coamings; the figures on the cutter housings were haloed with brilliance. The combine roared steadily, still forging to the north.

Alison was leaning on the rail. He joined her. She put her hair back, glanced up and half-smiled. She said, 'It's queer somehow. Oppressive.'

He said, 'Did you get your prints done?' She nodded, not answering. He leaned on the rail. He thought, *O'Hara gets an assistant. Maybe he needs one. I shouldn't take it out on her.*

The masthead lights began sequencing. He wondered vaguely why. The reflections hit her cheek and hair, scarlet, turquoise, scarlet, turquoise. He said, 'Was the stuff OK?'

She had a knack of not looking at him when she answered. She said, 'There's one advantage to big negs.'

'How do you mean?'

She said, 'You can always cut the middle out. It doesn't really matter where you point the camera.'

He thought, *Maybe she doesn't like O'Hara. But everybody likes O'Hara.*

The bridge speakers clicked and began to breathe. This time there was no formal announcement; it seemed they'd merely circuited on to Control. A voice said, 'Two minutes from end of cut.' He heard Cheskin acknowledge.

A helicopter moved up overhead. The downdraught battered from the metal deck. He thought, 'They have to fly grid patterns too. Always this business about flattening the crop.'

The speakers clicked again and roared. The chopper pilot was talking through a hamburger. He said, 'End of cut, Roger.' The machine surged back, fell away into the gloom astern. A klaxon began sounding somewhere. Alison said, 'All this fuss, just for turning round.'

Harrison said, 'It's a big machine.'

She said, 'They're just afraid they'll get on to somebody else's patch.'

Cheskin said, 'Time me, please.'

Another voice answered. It said, 'Forty five seconds, and counting.'

The klaxon cut out. Cheskin said, 'Stand by all stations. Ready on mains.'

The speakers said, 'Cut end . . .'

'Cease cut.'

The trembling of the deck eased. The speakers said, 'Half-speed on starboard auxiliaries. Phase differentials.'

Harrison heard the engine stations acknowledge. He turned away, becoming bored. Cheskin said, 'Reverse starboard auxiliaries. All ahead port.'

A couple of stars were visible. Harrison watched their sideways drift. The big cauldron to the west was moving too, swinging round behind the bridge. The combine was vibrating, straining. From below came a confused roar. The speakers said, 'Ninety degrees. One hundred degrees. One hundred ten.'

'Quarter speed on starboard auxiliaries.'

The sunset light was beginning to creep in from the right of the bridge. The combine nosed, questing.

The speakers said, 'I have forty degrees. I have thirty degrees. I have twenty degrees. Line-up good.'

Harrison said, 'Have dinner with me tonight.'

She looked up at him. She said after a pause, 'Yes. All right.'

Something bumped in his chest. He thought, *That's very odd.*

She said, 'Which restaurant?'

'C deck. They've got lobster thermidor. I don't know how old the lobsters are.'

She said, 'I'm a martyr to my stomach. I think I'm a compulsive eater.'

The speakers said, 'I have line-up.'

Cheskin said, 'All stations stand by. Confirm your line-up.'

The speakers said, 'Green board. I have line-up.'

Cheskin said, 'Outphase differentials. All ahead. Begin cut. Controller to log. Commenced second pass. I have eighteen, repeat eighteen, oh nine hours.'

She made a face. She said, 'Imagine that. Nine minutes late.'

O'Hara was weaving toward them across the observation deck. Harrison said, 'Where shall we meet?'

'Where do you want?'

He said, 'Swissy's bar. Twenty hundred.'

She said, 'You have a date.'

He went back to his cabin. He lay on the bunk and thought, *One in the eye for you, Michael.* He lit a cigarette, smoked for a while. Then he shook his head, sat up. He rang the steward for a sandwich, said, '*Gracias, Manuelo*' when it arrived and plugged in his shaver. He bathed and changed; by that time the wallclock read nineteen hundred hours. He picked up lighter and cigarettes, clicked the ceiling light off and walked round to Swissy's bar.

It was empty. Swissy was leaning on the counter reading a paper. He looked up and smirked. He said, ''Evening, Mr Harrison.'

Harrison said, 'Pint please, Swissy. English, not American.'

Swissy said, 'D'American is very good.' He drew the pint, set it on the bartop. He said, 'Looks good. Like in de picture house. Advertisement.'

Harrison lit a cigarette. Swissy said, 'Seen de paper?'

'What's new?'

Swissy said, 'Not'ing. Same blowty ol' t'ing. It don't go for my head.'

'What's that?'

Swissy said, 'Dey make big t'ing. Big fuss. 'Bout de combine. Dey say, Russia, America; blowty big row.'

'Where?'

Swissy showed him. The leader read:

Difficulties were prophesied today concerning the Russian-American grain link-up. Russia has lodged protests concerning what she describes as British-American infringements and infiltration. President Sukharevsky, in a strong note to the West, threatened Russian withdrawal from the World Food Council's biggest experiment to date, the Alaskan Grain Development Area. Harold Jenkinson, British Premier, expressed in the Commons his total disagreement with the Soviet attitude. 'The Alaskan Development,' he said, 'represents the biggest step so far in the cause of world unity and peace. The government of this country views these latest developments with disappointment, and grave concern.' Commentators feel the underlying cause of friction is the refusal of the United Nations select committee to accept Russia's demands for a controlling interest in the project.

Harrison put the paper down. He said, 'Like you said, Swissy. Nothing new.'

Swissy said, 'It be stupid. Blowty stupid.'

Harrison said, 'It doesn't go for my head.'

The dolly birds came in. They bought lager-and-lime and a Bloody Mary. Swissy said, 'I like to have dat one.'

'Which one? The blonde?'

Swissy snorted. He said, 'Ach, she be no good. Norwegian. Say, do dis, do dat … same like blowty German.'

Harrison said, 'Are you married, Swissy?'

Swissy shrugged. He said, 'Divowce. Only mistake I made.'

'How so?'

Swissy shook his head impatiently. 'She be no good,' he said. 'French …' He leaned on the bar and wagged a finger. 'I tell you dis,' he said. 'I never should have done it. Use to be on de boats. Go round de world, have a good time. Come back, to dis.'

Harrison said, 'Are you drinking?'

Swissy said, 'T'ank you. Have a half.'

Harrison paid. He said, 'Any children?'

'Ya, two,' said Swissy. 'Nice kids.' He produced a bulging, worn-looking wallet. He said, 'Nice kids, no?'

The pictures showed two rather chunky-looking little girls, the smaller gap-toothed. Both were dark. Harrison said, 'Why were you divorced?'

'Ach,' said Swissy, 'I don' know. Some t'ings go wrong, little t'ing, den get bigger all de time. Like I said, I never should leave de boat. Den she say, never should marry eider. I say bit late, bit blowty late for dat. Got de kids den, see? Working in hotel. Den a pub. Never was no good.'

Harrison said, 'Was this in France?'

'No, England. Cheltenham. You know it?'

Harrison said, 'I was there for a time.'

Swissy said, 'Have de children at school in England.' He waved his hand at the bar. He said, 'I do dis for dem. Make more money. Kids come first, all de time. Eh? Not so?'

Harrison said, 'I wouldn't know.'

Bertie came in. He said, 'Got it all written *down*?'

Harrison said, 'I'm working on it.'

Swissy said, 'Had a good day?'

Bertie said, 'Christ, no. Been trying to service an auxiliary since seventeen hundred. Wanted to pull it out of line, but that stupid basstard' – he gestured upstairs – 'won't have it. Says he's dropping behind schedule. As if it *mattered* …' He picked the paper up. He said, 'What's new?'

Harrison said, 'Why're you educating the children in England?'

Swissy said, 'Cause it's best. She start dat. De ex-wife. Maybe later I send 'em to Switzerland. I don't know.' He grinned. 'Christ,' he said. 'Have trouble wit' de family.'

'Why so?'

'Ach,' said Swissy, 'dey be pheasants. No, how you say dat?'

'Peasants.'

'Ah. Peasants. Be blowty peasants.'

'How do you mean?'

'Ah,' said Swissy, 'is difficult. Dey not understand. Dey t'ink I give de kids away.'

'You what?'

'Ah, well,' said Swissy. 'In my country, is no boarding school. State school only. All go dere, whatever parent. If you go odder school, eider parents dead, or prostitute … dat sort of t'ing,'

Harrison said, 'Can't you explain?'

Swissy said, 'My brodder understand. De rest … Christ, got two sister won't speak wit' me. I tell 'em, I no get de kids in de first place, den dere be trouble.'

'Because of being Catholic?'

Swissy brooded. 'Ach, yes, de Cat'olic,' he said. 'Be blowty rubbish.'

Harrison ordered another beer. He sat and wondered about his notes. The combine throbbed; but already it seemed he was accustomed to the noise. Only when he brought his mind back to it could he hear it. He thought, 'I should go on deck. Get the feel of the thing at night.' He remembered the reef markers. He'd been meaning to ask. He said, 'Bertie, those reef warnings. Are they necessary?'

Bertie looked at him blearily. He said, 'If you hit a b-bugger, you'd find out.'

'Can't the radar pick them up?'

Bertie said, 'Not under ten or twelve *feet.* These things only run a yard off the deck, and they're built of silver paper.'

'Couldn't they be levelled?'

Bertie said, 'If you'd tried picking all the rocks out of ten thousand fucking *miles*, you wouldn't ask.'

The Norwegian girl came to the bar with a glass. She said, 'Fill it, please.'

Swissy grinned. He said, 'For you, anyt'ing.'

Harrison drained his beer, lined up another. The bar was very quiet. The clock hands stood at 20.15. A couple of Americans drifted in. It seemed they knew Bertie. They sprawled across the bar, started an engineers' convention. He heard Bertie say, 'Well, what did you expect? The bloody *com* ring was shot.'

He wondered how long she'd be. He finished the beer, started on whisky. She walked in at 20.25.

She was wearing a little black dress. Her legs were delicious. Her hair gleamed; the bar lights made it look very blonde. Swissy grinned and said, 'Christ. Be all right wit' dat one.'

She said, 'I heard that, Swissy. 'Lo, John.'

He said, 'You're looking very nice, love.'

She said, 'I've got a great big ugly face. Compliments don't work.'

He asked her what she was drinking. She said, 'Scotch.'

He asked for a double. He said, 'How were the pictures?'

She perched on the bar stool. She said, 'I thought I wasn't going to make it. Big Brother wanted another batch put through.'

He laughed. He said, 'I thought you two got on.'

She said, 'He's the answer to the maiden's prayer. Didn't you hear?'

He stubbed his cigarette. She said, 'Have one of these.'

He lit up for her. He found himself starting to like her a little. He said, 'Where's the great man now?'

'Got a date. Or so he told me. I wished him luck.'

Harrison said, 'Swissy, do we have to book for the restaurant?'

Swissy said, 'Better, if you want table. No good eat at de bar. Not romantic.' He leered. He said, 'I fix it for you. Ten per cent.'

Harrison said, 'I'll buy your next beer.' It seemed a trite remark, and was. He thought, *Maybe I'm talking too much. Which is absurd. I'm dead; so I can't be nervous.*

Swissy used the phone. He said, 'Ya, two. Chow, Man'el.' He turned back. He said, 'Got you corner table. Gipsy orchestra.'

Harrison said, 'Have another drink.' While Swissy was pouring he said, 'I wish you'd accept compliments. It's very unnerving.'

She said, 'I'm funny. Somehow I can never believe in them.'

He said, 'You don't like yourself all that much.'

She said, 'Not much. Not often.'

The clock had moved round to twenty-one hundred. Harrison said, 'Let's go on.'

She stood up. She said, 'I'll see you round there.'

He said, faintly surprised, 'I'll wait.'

Bertie looked up and smirked.

Outside, Harrison said, 'That little man did nothing but stare at your legs.'

'Which little man?'

'Bertie. In the corner.'

She said vaguely, 'Oh, he's not too bad.'

Harrison said, 'It was a comment, not a condemnation.'

Walking beside her, he was conscious for the first time how tiny she was. It had never appealed to him before. He caught a waft of her scent. He thought, *It suits her.*

The restaurant wasn't too busy; half a dozen couples were eating, a few more sitting at the bar. The lighting was soft; they had no orchestra but piped music was playing. The tune was 'Blue Moon'. He wondered how old it was.

Manuelo showed them a corner table, held her chair. Harrison ordered Liebfraumilch. Manuelo offered him the glass. He sipped, knowing there would be nothing wrong. He said, 'OK, I'll pour.'

Manuelo said, 'Thank you,' and left them alone.

She said, 'Swissy said this means Maiden's Milk.'

Harrison said, 'I suppose it does.' He thought, *You're not like her. But you could be her. Face not your fortune, but the same big eyes.*

Over the main course she said, 'I'm glad you asked me out.'

Harrison said, 'You can't really be "out" in a combine harvester.'

She shook her head. She said, 'O'Hara can be a pig. I was getting really tired of him.'

He said, 'There's an easy answer.'

She said, 'It's not easy for me.'

He said, 'It will sort itself out. How's the lobster?'

'Mmm. John ...'

'What?'

She said, 'I am enjoying myself.'

He thought, *This is one of those Rare Moments.* Later he said, 'We could dance. Only there's no floor. Only I don't dance.'

She smiled, and opened her cigarettes. He lit up for her. She said, 'Was Swissy telling you about his family?'

'Yes.'

She said, 'He's divorced, isn't he?'

'I think so. *I* can't work it out. He's Catholic.'

She said, 'If he married outside the Church he'd have been lapsed anyway. Technically, he was living in sin.'

He said, 'You know a lot about it.'

She smiled, and pushed her hair back. She said, 'I'm a Catholic. Or was. I lapsed about a year ago.'

Harrison said, 'Why?'

She lifted her chin. She said finally, 'I don't know. I just couldn't see it any more. It's no good just doing it.'

He said, 'How did the family take it?'

'They're still trying to get me back. It's quite difficult.'

He said, 'How old are you, Alison?'

She looked at him. She said, 'Twenty-five.'

He said, 'I'm sorry. That was rather personal.'

She blew smoke. She said, 'I'm queer. I was always the rebel. My brother's much more conventional. He went into the family business. I moved out. Came up to Town.'

He examined his cigarette. He said, 'I was trying to work this afternoon. It wouldn't come. I think the photographic section's doing better.' He watched the fall of her hair and thought, *Get back behind me, you shadow, you bitch.*

She said, 'It'll come. I wish I could do that sort of thing.'

He offered the last of the Liebfraumilch. She shook her head. She said, 'Thanks. Reached my limit.'

He drank, slowly. In the restaurant the roar of the combine was very loud. Beside him, the long windows were blue with night. He said, 'Shall we have coffee in the cabin? The steward will send it up.'

She watched him a moment. She said, 'If you like. Yes, nice.'

He said, 'This place thrums too much. It gets into one's head.'

She said, 'It is noisy, isn't it? I suppose you get used to it.'

She walked ahead of him. They turned right, and right again. At the door he reached past her to click the light switch. She said, 'Oo, this is nice. Good heavens.'

'What?'

She said, 'What's this?'

He took it from her, carefully. He said, 'Rule one. Or so I'm told. Never wave a gun about till you know it's safe to.'

She said, 'Is it safe?'

He broke the cylinder. He said, 'It is now.'

She said, 'What is it?'

He said, 'Smith and Wesson. Point four five five.'

'It's a revolver.'

He said, 'Yes.'

She said, 'I've never handled a gun before. It's a beauty. Can I close it?'

He buttoned the intercom. He said, 'Just push it shut.'

The steward answered. Harrison said, 'Gaelic, Irish or plain?'

She said, 'Just plain.'

He walked to her. He said, 'Can I show you?' He broke the revolver again. He said, 'It's a very old one. It's what's called a fixed frame. With a hinged frame, the chambers open upwards.'

She said, 'It's not much fun waving an empty gun about.'

He opened the locker drawer. He said, 'Here.'

She said, 'Gosh. Can I do it?'

He thought, *I don't know quite what's happening.* He said, 'Go carefully, it's rather dangerous. Do it by numbers.'

She frowned, pushing the big cartridges home. Her hair fell forward, cascading. She shook it back. She said, 'Would it shoot now?'

He said, 'When it's cocked. So.'

She said, 'Oh, I see. The cylinder turns round.' She smiled. She said, 'I've found out about revolvers.'

He said, 'Hold it very carefully. Keep it pointing at the floor, else it's bad manners.'

She said, 'If I pulled the trigger now, it would go off.'

He said, 'Yes. But that wouldn't be a good idea so we'll … eject. So. Out come the cartridge cases.'

She said, 'I don't understand. Wouldn't they have been fired?'

He said, 'This part is the bullet. The shiny nose. This is the case. There's a cap at the bottom. When the pin hits it, it explodes.'

She collected the rounds carefully, gave them back. She said, 'It's safe now. Can I play with it?'

Harrison said, 'Most girls aren't interested in guns.'

She said, 'I'm not most girls.'

The steward buzzed with the coffee. She rolled back on the bed. She said, 'I'd like a gun. I'd like this one.'

'Whatever for?'

She said, 'To keep the ghosts away.'

He poured coffee. He thought, 'You are a funny little rat.'

She said, 'You know a lot about guns.'

'Not really. I think they're interesting.'

'Where did you get this one?'

He said, 'One of the German riggers at base. I think he was broke.'

She said, 'It would kill a person, wouldn't it?'

He said, 'I rather think it would kill anything.' He smiled. He said, 'Including ghosts.'

'Why did you buy it?'

He handed her the coffee. He said, 'It interested me.' He thought, *What was it Hans said? 'Your English law is stupid. Every man need a gun. For the one time.'* He said, 'For the one time …'

'What?'

He said, 'Nothing. Just a thought.'

She drew her knees up, sighted the revolver. He said, 'You look like Pussy Galore.'

She said, 'I feel like Pussy Galore.'

He thought, *And the dynamo's running, you little bitch. But that's not possible.*

She said, 'You like nice things, don't you?'

'How do you mean?'

She said, 'Like the gun.'

He thought, *This is out of the question, absurd.* He said, 'Alison, would you mind if I seduced you?'

She looked at him carefully. Then she put the Smith and Wesson down. She said, 'Not in the slightest.'

Harrison said, 'All right then. Better finish your coffee.'

She drank. He gave her a cigarette. They smoked for a while. Then he said, 'Were you serious?'

She said, 'Perfectly. Weren't you?'

He said, 'It was rather a silly question. I'm not sure how one goes about it.'

'Haven't you done it before?'

He said, 'I've been seduced. That's rather different.'

She put the cigarette down. She said, 'I don't want this.' She rose, walked over to him, sat on his knee. She said gently, This will do for a start.'

He lay back. She moved with him, softly. She was lithe, and light. She said, 'I'm sorry. I'm all hair.'

He said, 'Don't I know it.' He kissed her. She didn't mind his tongue. He found the cabin lights, dimmed to sleep level. In the half-dark, the thunder of the combine sounded louder.

She nestled, and kissed again. He found her dress clasp. She whispered 'No,' and didn't stop him.

The wine spun in his head. He said, 'Now I can say all the silly things. Like lovely, desirable, sweet. Nice little girl.'

She said, muffled, 'Nice big man …'

He stroked her, ran his fingers along her bra strap. He said, 'I'm not much good at this. Fumbly old job.'

The strap parted. She said, 'That wasn't bad for a novice.'

He worked her dress down, feeling satin skin. He thought, *I'm going to go crazy with this, because it's too good. These things don't happen.* Aloud he said, 'Move your arms.'

'Why?'

'They're in the way.'

She whispered, 'Please. No, please John …'

'What's the matter?'

She said, 'It's silly. I'm shy.'

He said, 'You can stop if you want. I don't want to spoil any friendships.'

She said, 'It won't. Honestly. This is nice. Please, John …'

She kissed him, wound her arms round his neck. He pulled at the dress, carefully. She sat up then, shivering. She said, 'Well, this is me. For what it's worth.' And he saw it was possible for a blush to spread, across the neck, down the shoulders and back.

He said, 'You're very lovely.' He bowed his head. She squeaked; and he knew he had to be gentle. Incredibly gentle. Her body was like a tight-strung wire; he could feel the responses start, little jumps deep inside her. She said, 'No, please. Not down there.'

He said, 'Yes …'

She caught his fingers. She said, 'I've got you now. You can't get away.'

He used a trick. She said, 'I shall fight you …'

He said, 'Alison, fight all night. That's what it's all about.'

He held her again, carefully. She lay back, head against the chair. She said, 'You are nice.'

He said, 'Alison, come to bed.'

'No!'

'I shall say please then.'

'John, *no*! It's no good, I just get stubborn. It's too early …'

'Then we'll go to bed later.'

She said, 'I'm not ready. Don't try to make me. I shan't do it.'

He said, 'Love, no one shall make you.' He stroked her back, gentling; and she relaxed again. He thought, *It could be her. She doesn't look like her, she doesn't act like her. But it could be her. I made it happen again.*

Her skirt had ridden up. She said, 'Don't look at me. I shall be decorous.'

He said, 'I'm enjoying you. Don't you like it?'

She said, 'No. Yes. I don't know …'

He said, 'What spectacular panties.'

She said, 'I'm a pantie fetishist. They always match my shoes. That's something you know about me now.'

He said, 'I shall blackmail you. Alison, come to bed.'

'*No!*'

'It's all right.'

She said, 'John, no. Don't do that.'

He said, 'You want it and you shall have it.'

'I don't. I don't.'

He said, 'Don't fib.' He thought, *Three years. She told me it had done me good. That's why I left her. But she was right. I know it now, I know how to make it good.*

She started to struggle. He said, 'Aren't I doing it right?'

She said, 'You're doing it too damned well … John, don't make me …'

He said, 'Girlie, you're made …' and she was moving against him, arcing her body. She pushed her head back, soundlessly; he thought, *Contact contact, flaring bloody contact …* And it was over; she relaxed against him with the longest, deepest sigh he had ever heard.

Later he said, 'Did I hurt you?'

She nuzzled and whispered, not opening her eyes. She said 'Only in the nicest possible way.'

He laughed, in the near-dark. He said, 'Your bottom's cold.'

She said, 'It's the only part of me that is.'

He watched the clock hands move, feeling her weight against him, hearing the great thunder of the combine. Once she stirred. She said, 'It's been a long time. I was only eighteen …' He stroked her till she was quiet. Much later, she pushed away. She said, 'I'm going to be a nuisance. I want to go back to my cabin now.'

He said, 'Stay in this one.'

'I can't.'

'You'll be all right.'

She said, 'You don't know O'Hara.'

'This isn't to do with O'Hara.'

She said, 'He keeps asking me, everybody asks me. The boss asked me. If he found out …'

Harrison said, 'Even O'Hara couldn't be that big a bastard.'

She said, 'Care to bet? Please, John …'

He said, 'Nobody shall make you do anything, lovie. You know that. Here …'

She sat upright, tousled. She said, 'I'm all undressed.'

He said, 'I like you that way.'

Her eyes looked huge. She said, 'I didn't know there were men like you.' She kissed him again.

Afterwards, he eased her to her feet. She tidied herself. He said, 'Lights on?'

She said, 'Yes. Trying to … find my comb.'

He swirled brightness back into the little cabin. The walls were the same, the bulkhead clock and the bunk; yet it was all different. Alive.

She stumbled, trying for her shoes. He caught her. He'd known she would be giddy. He thought, *I did it right. I did something right.* He said, 'You had a trip.'

Her eyes were very sleepy. She said, 'It was lovely. John, I must go.'

He walked her to her cabin. The corridor lights were dimming now, a part of Combine Patsy preparing for sleep. She opened her door, pulled him half inside, kissed him quickly with all her body. He said, 'My head will be rather full of you, of course. I shall want to see you. Is that proper?'

She smiled. She said, 'It's human. I never knew you were. Good night, John.'

He said, 'Good night.' He stayed till the door closed, softly; then he walked away.

In his cabin the bed was rumpled. He walked to the shower cubicle, rinsed his face and hands, lit a cigarette. He stood staring a while. The revolver lay where she had put it. He set it on the locker, twitched the covers straight.

Sleep was far from him. He walked back to C deck restaurant. The lights were out now, the place deserted. A bulb gleamed dully over the bar. Manuelo was drying a glass. He said, 'Coffee, Manuelo?'

The little man grinned and shook his head, jerked his thumb at the wallclock.

Harrison laid a dollar on the counter. He said, '*Por favor.*'

Manuelo grinned again, and walked to the dispenser.

He took the tall mug back to his room, sat and sipped. After a while he frowned, sniffed his sleeve. Her scent clung, faint and delightful. He thought, *I was trying to make her. To fill a hole in my life. But I didn't know what she was like. I didn't know what she was going to be like.*

He drank again. After a while he thought, *She trusted me. And she was shy.* The shyness had hooked him through the lip. He thought, *The other thing was never like that. It couldn't be.* A ghost had faded, seeming past return. He thought, *It was time. I went looking, and I made it happen again. A new thing.*

He finished the coffee, set the mug down, stood up. At the door he thought, *That wasn't her voice. Those weren't her eyes. It was all new. Like a flower, opening in the hand.* He wondered, *Are they all like that? When they're loved?*

He climbed to B deck. The air was rushing, intensely cold. Above, the bridge superstructure slid against an incrustation of stars. Darkness seemed to enhance the sense of speed. He saw the combine now as a great entity; he knew her blades spun and roared, her dynamoes hummed, her sensors probed with their electric fingers. He felt the exultation grow, and let it well. He thought, *I paid for tonight. It's mine.* He saw, with heightened vision, Combine Patsy and her sisters; Julie, Susannah, all the rest, strung like beads of light and warmth against the moving dark. He thought, *I'd forgotten. I'd sunk into the pit, and didn't know my need; and her hands raised me, unbeknown.* He thought, *It flies at sense and logic; it flies in the face of reason. But we love; and we rejoice, because it sets us apart from the beasts.*

In the east, already, a new dawn was making. The night air was reaching him; he stubbed his cigarette, and turned away. He thought, *We reap, and we thresh; grain for half the world. We are the Grain Kings, raised of old; and I a new God. A giant God, who was dead.*

2

He lay for a while in a floating half-awareness before opening his eyes. Sunlight slanted into the cabin from the one square port. The patch vibrated slightly, moving with the movements of the dural wall. He turned his head. The Olivetti stood on the side table; on the locker was the Smith and Wesson. These things pleased him. He studied them a while, unmoving. His awareness, his sense of colour and form, seemed unnaturally sharp.

The wallclock read 09.15. The intercom buzzed; he reached for the cord, lazily, thumbed the switch. The speaker said, 'Good morning, Mr. Harrison. Asked me to call you.'

He said, 'Joe. *Gracias.*'

He rose, padded to the shower cubicle. The stinging needlepoints enlivened him. In the cubicle the hum of the combine sounded loud. A can of shaving foam clattered softly against a glass shelf. He towelled, shaved, got out clean shirt and shorts, dressed. He found himself humming, vaguely, the theme from Thomas Tallis. He thought, *That's good music. English west country music.* He picked up his jacket, stooped to wriggle heels into shoes. He'd thought he would never go into the west again. Maybe now he would.

He let his thoughts drift round to her, by slow degrees. Before he'd kept her out of his head, deliciously. He looked round the cabin. He thought, *She was here, and she was naked. Funny little rat.*

He walked to C deck restaurant, ordered coffee, cereals and toast. He ate slowly, smoked a cigarette. At eleven hundred hours he was due to meet Controller Cheskin. He walked to the observation deck. The combine had turned once more on to a northern pass. He thought, Three since start of cut.' The sky was bright steely-blue, the red bridge coamings sharp-cut in sunlight. He watched rigging shadows move, thin dark stripes against scarlet paintwork. The wind buzzed faintly in the mast struts. The morning was very fair.

He thought, *Maybe she's sleeping it off.*

He walked back to C deck bar. The place smelled of polish and dust. Except for one of the American engineers, it was empty. Swissy grinned at him. He said, 'Here he come. De great lover.'

He was faintly startled. He said, 'What?'

Swissy said, 'How you get on wit' her? De li'l girl?'

Harrison said, 'We had a nice evening.' He settled himself on the bar stool. He said, 'Not beer, Swissy. Fruit juice.'

Swissy stopped, hand over the pump. He muttered, 'Got to keep up de strengt' …'

Harrison nodded vaguely. He was remembering the smoothness of her skin, dimly seen, the firm fullness under her scanties, later the bursting of soft dark down between her thighs. He thought, *These are my memories. It happened. Nobody can take them away.* He sipped orange juice. He thought, *I feel for her, rushingly. I didn't know how much I wanted her.* The images would revolve now quietly, hour on hour, till he saw her again; as she had lain quiet in his arms. He thought, *The smell of her was like a drawer of linen. Clean, lavender-fresh.*

Swissy said, 'Been up top?'

He said, 'It's a great morning.'

Swissy leaned on the bar. He said morosely, 'All right for some. I gotta work.'

Harrison said, 'I'm working all the time, Swissy.'

Swissy said, 'Yeah. T'ink about de li'l girl.'

Harrison said, 'You've got a one-track mind.'

The American glanced at his watch, nodded and strolled out. Swissy said, 'I t'ink after all I go back to de boats. Had good time den, real good time. Used to stop 'Frisco, Honolulu. Christ, was a place, dat. I t'ink I go Tasmania, or New Zealand. Lovely country.'

Harrison said, 'Why'd you leave home anyway, Swissy?'

Swissy said, 'Oh, some t'ings go wrong.'

'Family?'

'Ach, no. But some odder t'ing. Dey be pheasant anyway. I t'ink, fowk 'em. You know? See a bit of de world. Five years I was on de boats. Den I come ashore. After dat, go to England – Christ, was bad t'ing, dat.'

The wallclock pinged. Harrison said, 'Got to go. Seeing the old man. Keep my seat warm.'

Swissy said, 'Chow.'

At the bridge steps a guard with UN tabs on his shoulders scanned his press card. He said, 'Wait, please,' and walked away. Harrison stood idly, heard an intercom buzz. The guard came back. He said, 'Follow me, please.'

Here, higher in the combine, the endless sway and roll were more evident. Harrison glanced round him. Officers' country seemed no less spartan than the rest of the machine. He was high above the wheat; a port gave him a view of it, like a sparkling, brilliant-yellow plain.

The guard tapped a door, opened it. He said, 'Mr Harrison, sir.' Harrison stepped through.

The cabin was wide, and carpeted. To one side a wallfire glowed cheerfully; above it was an oil painting in a heavy, ornate frame. There were cupboards of china and glassware; shelves held a further display. Cheskin sat at a polished desk fronting the great range of windows. He rose as Harrison walked toward him, and held out his hand. He said, 'Mr Harrison, how pleasant. World Geographic, I believe.'

Harrison said, 'I' delighted to meet you, sir.' His mind was far away; down maybe with the racing, rolling wheat.

Cheskin said, 'Be seated, please. A drink?'

Harrison said, 'Thank you. Thanks very much.'

Cheskin said, 'Whisky perhaps.' He tinkled liquid from a decanter. He said, 'Your British whisky is the finest in the world.' He handed the glass. He said, 'Through peat, and over granite. I believe these are the requirements.'

Harrison smiled. He said, 'I've been told so, sir.'

Cheskin nodded briskly. He said, 'You will excuse me for not joining you. For me, it is a little early.' He pushed a box of cigarettes across the desk. He said, 'I have visited Scotland. A most lovely country. Sometime I hope to return, for the salmon fishing. Do you fish, Mr Harrison?'

Harrison said, 'Last time I tried, I managed a pike.'

Cheskin said, 'Ah. Yes.' He leaned back. He said, 'Have you been well looked after?'

Harrison said, 'Excellently. Mr Pritchard has been most helpful.'

Cheskin said, 'Good.' He steepled his fingers. He said, 'First, a few facts about myself. I am, as you undoubtedly know, Russian by birth. America has been for many years my country of adoption. I am a biologist and agriculturalist; during the Moscow crisis I served in the Russian army. My rank was colonel.' He smiled. He said, 'And you?'

Harrison said, 'Rather an ordinary sort of background, sir. Agricultural degree, then jobbing journalism here and there. I'm afraid I haven't led too adventurous a life.'

Cheskin said, 'I see. It is better that we know just a little of each other.'

Harrison's eyes had wandered. Cheskin caught the direction of his glance and turned. He said, 'Ah, the painting. Are you knowledgeable about paintings, Mr Harrison?'

Harrison said, 'Not really. But I think that's very unusual.' He was in a mood to be pleased by anything. He said, 'It's rather lovely.'

Cheskin smiled again. He said, 'It is not lovely. Rather, it is ugly. This is why I keep it.' He rose, walked to the picture. Its colours were sombre: flat reds, and browns. A table was set with a candlelit meal; a shirt-sleeved man sprawled across a bed, holding a stick over which a fluffy white poodle leaped. Cheskin said, 'It is, of course, a facsimile. The original was painted shortly before his death by a great Russian artist, Pavel Fedotov. You have perhaps heard of him?'

Harrison said, 'I'm afraid not.'

Cheskin said, 'He is not known much outside Russia.' He turned back to the canvas. He said, 'At twenty-five, Fedotov was a brilliant young officer of the Finlandsky Regiment of the Royal Guard. At thirty-seven he was dead, a pauper. This he produced in the last year of his life.'

He reached to touch the carved gilt frame. He said, 'The officer is drunk. The surroundings are squalid, suburban. As the dog jumps the stick, so his master is driven by boredom. By ennui. He too is a victim of his circumstances.'

Harrison said, 'I don't think I quite follow you, sir.'

Cheskin said, 'Though Fedotov was great, his life was wasted. The canvas serves to remind me of this. Effort misdirected is wasted. We must see clearly, rejecting dreams and the fantastic, holding at all times to the realities we perceive. We must not become such a man; jumping sticks, though we think we hold them for others.'

Harrison said, 'You seem very … aware of your homeland, sir. Have you never wished to return?'

On the desk was a silver-mounted photograph. It showed a blonde, plumpish woman with a dog. Cheskin frowned across at it. He said, 'While my wife lived, perhaps. Now it would be pointless.'

Harrison said, 'I'm sorry, sir. That was extremely personal.'

Cheskin shook his head. He said, 'This is a part of your profession.' He turned to the shelves. He said, 'Here is something that may interest you. It is very rare.'

Harrison rose, walked to him. The Controller lifted a glass drinking vessel, turned it in his thin ringers. He said, 'It is a joke, really, on the part of the glassblower. It was made sometime in the early eighteenth century. Above the goblet, you see, is a fabulous beast; you would call it a chimaera. To taste the wine, you must press your mouth to his. His body fills, as if with blood.'

Harrison took the piece, carefully.

Cheskin said, 'These are modern works, by Tatyana Navrina. The city in which she was born is now called Gorky. Its folkart is well known in Russia. Here you see a circular composition. Tatyana shows us the fox, the hare and the cockerel. Famous beasts in our folklore. They chase each other round and round, merrily. It is pointless and gay; yet also perhaps a little sad. Like a fairground entertainment.'

Harrison said, 'Do you have a large collection, sir?'

Cheskin said, 'I have a house in America. In New Jersey. Most of my pieces are there. These few, my favourites, travel with me.'

He walked back to the desk. He said, 'A little more whisky. Now, to your article. Have you collected all the information you will need?'

Harrison said slowly, 'I've collected a lot of information. I think the problem now is putting it together, making a shape. I was looking for something to peg the facts on, to get all this across. Maybe a theme.' He took the plunge, feeling good. He said, 'Yesterday I thought I'd got it.'

Cheskin said, 'Ah, this business of a theme. I find it most interesting. You had thought perhaps of a ship? Or an aeroplane?'

Harrison said, 'I suppose everybody does.'

'Yes,' said Cheskin. 'This is most important. Remember the painting. There are no themes; merely realities. This is a large combine harvester. With a model number, known characteristics. I can give you rates of cut and thresh, length of cut, passage time on cut, estimated return to Grid Base. Are these things not enough?'

Harrison said, 'I'm not sure.'

Cheskin said, 'You thought in higher terms? In terms of significance, of poetry?'

Harrison said, 'Don't you approve of poetry, sir?'

Cheskin smiled fleetingly, He said, 'There is perhaps a poetry. Unheard, unsung.' He brooded. He said, 'No. I have no objection to poetry. But it is necessary to apply the proper labels. We should know at all times with what we are dealing.'

Harrison said, 'I'm not quite with you, sir.'

Cheskin said, 'There is your English author, Kipling. You have surely studied his work. He might perhaps render such a theme. He understood much of machines.'

Harrison said, 'I'm afraid I'm no Kipling, sir.'

Cheskin said, 'Perhaps that is as well.' He turned the cigarette box thoughtfully in his fingers. He said, 'In Kipling's work the machines are made to speak. They cannot; but the poet is skilful, and so we believe. Soon too England speaks, as an old grey Mother. The sea speaks to the Danish women, declaring itself a rival for the affections of their men. The little banjo speaks; and what a harmless instrument! So the world, which is as it is, becomes re-peopled; with mirages, and Gods. Soon, for us, stones speak and trees; we feel the touch of phantom hands. Here is a paradox, Mr Harrison. We do not worship stones and trees; yet we listen to our poets.'

He rose, stood back turned, staring down across the miles on miles of wheat. A buzzer sounded on the bridge; Harrison heard the vague pealing of an intercom. Cheskin said, 'For me, the Grain Development Areas represent new hope. Here for the first time our many peoples work together, truly together, for the universal good. Here perhaps, if you search, you may find your poetry. This too is why none of us must be blinded. We must see, very clearly, what we do. We must see it as a good thing, perhaps a great one; but we must find no mystery. Moon and sun do not tug our brains, as they tugged the brains of earlier men. We reap, and we thresh. We are neither Gods nor ants. Our machines are our machines. As in this, so in our lives. Our hands work, our will directs the hands. The rest, our conceits, our grand words, are luxuries. We cannot permit ourselves such luxuries, Mr Harrison, if we are to survive. Dreaming, we are unaware; from unawareness spring grief, disaster, despair. For our own sakes, we must not dream.'

Harrison said slowly, 'I'm sorry if my ideas annoyed you, sir.'

Cheskin turned, and smiled. He said, 'I am not here to approve or disapprove of your ideas, Mr Harrison. I am not a censor. I merely warn.'

He walked back to the desk. He said, 'And now, if you have finished your drink, I will show you Control.'

At lunch, Harrison ran into O'Hara. He was sitting at a corner table in C restaurant, forging his way through a steak. He waved a fork, a chip impaled tastefully on the prongs. Harrison joined him, not particularly wanting to. He said, 'Hello, Mike. Where's Alison?'

O'Hara watched him palely. He said, 'I'm keeping her busy. It's good for her waistline.'

Harrison ordered Dover sole and a glass of wine. He steered the conversation on to safer grounds. There had been times when he'd felt a compulsion to belt O'Hara on the nose. Today, he might just do it.

He made his escape as soon as he decently could, walked round to C deck bar. Bertie was in evidence. He said, 'The *wanderer* returns. Have a beer.'

Swissy pulled a pint. He said, 'Is paid for.'

Bertie said, 'How'd you get on with the old man?'

Harrison said, 'This is good Russian beer. From the banks of our own Volga river.'

Bertie tittered. He said, 'I know the feeling.'

Harrison said thoughtfully, 'He's a strange bird though. I can't make out whether he loves Russia or hates it.'

Swissy said, 'All Russians funny bastard. Why he is hating it?'

Harrison said, 'I don't know. I had the feeling they maybe got rid of his wife.'

Swissy said promptly, 'Better off be single anyway. Dat way, get no trouble. Tell you sometimes, all de blowty trouble I have. Better off stay in Switzerland.'

Bertie said, 'If you will *do* these things …'

Harrison said, 'Are you married, Bertie?'

Bertie said, 'Yes, worse bloody luck.'

Swissy said, 'It don't stop him none.'

Bertie drank beer. He said, 'We've got a *treat* coming up this afternoon. We're meeting the Russians. Did he tell you?'

Harrison said, 'Yes. When will it be?'

Bertie said, 'Fifteen hundred hours. Or should be. We're getting near the end of the *patch.* We swing round north tomorrow. Start cut two.'

Harrison said, 'Are the Russian combines any different from ours?'

Bertie said, 'They cover the *ground* a bit quicker. Got a modified pickup system. They're bloody cagey about it too.' He drained his pint, and pushed it across for a refill. He said, 'You'll get a good enough view anyway. They should pass two swaths out.'

Swissy said, 'Funny bastard, dese Russian. Get on better wit' de German.'

Bertie said, 'You *are* a fucking German.'

Swissy said, 'I be Swiss German. You know dat.'

Bertie said, 'Oh Christ, don't *start.*'

Swissy said, 'I don't start not'ing. Is big difference. You go to Switzerland, you find out.'

Bertie said, 'You go to Switzerland. You're so bloody *fond* of it.'

Harrison looked at the clock. It read 14.30 hours. He wondered about Alison. He said, 'I'd better get on deck.'

Bertie said, 'That's what everybody will do. You'll get just as good a *view* from here.' He set his beer down, lit a cigarette. He said, 'What *did* the old man talk about?'

Harrison said, 'Mainly a painter called Fedotov.'

Bertie tittered again. He said, 'I expect you saw his glassware.'

'Yes,' said Harrison. 'I did.'

Folk began drifting into the bar in twos and threes. Harrison walked over to the windows. Bertie followed him. He said, 'Bring us a couple of beers, Swissy.'

Swissy said, 'You come fetch 'em. Odderwise, plenty more bars.'

Bertie said, 'Oh, do the *other* thing then,' and muttered something less detectable.

The wheat flowed past beyond the main coamings, silently. At 14.55 the intercom speakers crackled. They said briefly, 'Combine Valeri is in sight from Control, and will pass on schedule.'

Harrison wondered again about going up to B deck. He thought, 'Maybe she's there.' Then he remembered, if she was O'Hara would be with her. He decided to stay put.

Just before fifteen hundred somebody said, 'There she is.'

The combine was still well ahead, but coming up fast. Behind her, her dustcloud was a dark yellow funnel trailing on the land. She was big; God, she was big. She made Patsy, ungainly as she was, look elegant and low. On her side she wore the hammer and sickle of the Soviets, above it a big red star. The rest of her was grey; workmanlike, and blank.

Somebody said, 'Here comes bloody St Basil's.'

Bertie said, 'They were putting *onion* domes on 'em last year.'

Harrison said, 'Why did they stop?'

Bertie said, '*Track* weight became *excessive*.'

She passed abeam, trailing the long dustcloud. Somebody said, 'That's it then.' On Patsy's bridge a loudhailer was working faintly.

Bertie turned and shouldered his way out of the crowd. He said, 'That's damn funny.'

Harrison said, 'What's funny?'

Bertie said, 'She was cutting a swath too close.'

Swissy said, 'De blowty Russians never could steer. Not even de aeroplanes.'

Bertie said, 'I'm going to look *into* that. See you blighters later.'

Harrison walked to B deck, stood on the starboard wing. The combine had certainly passed a single cut away. He stared astern. The Russian was still visible, small with distance. The dustcloud smoked away across the stubble. Beyond, the land lay brown and bare to the horizon. He walked to the forward rail. The double swath remaining stretched like a golden road. Nothing to be seen; just the endless perspectives of the land, shimmering a little with heat haze. Patsy thundered steadily.

The bridge intercom had been left live. The speakers clicked and said, 'Mr Puustjärvi to Control, please. Mr Puustjärvi.'

He didn't feel like work. He walked down to D deck. They had a little gift shop there. It sold corn dollies, paperbacks, wooden Russian toys. He thought, 'Flowers were out, anyway. Right last time. Not this.'

A showcase held bracelets and some jewellery. He glanced across the display shelves and said, 'Good Lord.'

The stewardess smiled professionally. She said, 'Can I help you?'

He said, 'Does this shoot?'

She lifted the tiny revolver out. She said, 'They're bracelet charms. They fire blanks.'

He said, 'I shouldn't think they need a firearms certificate.'

She said, 'They didn't say anything when we bought them.'

He said, 'How much?'

'I think there's a ticket. Nine dollars fifty.'

He said, 'You've sold it.'

He walked back to his cabin, lay on the bunk, took the little pistol from its box. It had a hinge-frame action. He broke it and loaded carefully. The tiny thing made a very respectable crack. He thought, 'Good for the littlest ghosts anyway.'

He put the charm in the side locker, picked up his notebook. He made a rough draft of the conversation with Cheskin. At the end he wrote: *Strange to see the china cabinets. Impress of a personality that still isn't Western. After all these years.*

He pushed the papers aside, thought for a time. Then he reached for the intercom lead, pressed the button. He said, 'Joe, do something for me.'

'Certainly, sair.'

'Page E deck. Miss Alison Beckett.'

Joe said, 'It shall be done.'

The wallspeaker was covered by a plain grey grille. It clicked twice and buzzed. Then it said, 'Hello, John.' The voice had an unexpected huskiness.

He said, ''Lo, Alison. How's things?'

A pause. The speaker said, 'Fine.'

'Busy?'

She said, 'O'Hara took a lot of shots of the Russians. We're just starting on them.'

He said, 'Shall I see you this evening?'

'Mmm. Yes. Where?'

He said, 'Swissy's bar. About twenty hundred. We can go on a pub crawl.'

She said, 'Done. Sounds lovely. John, I have to go now.'

He said, ''Bye, Alison.'

The speaker said, 'See you later. 'Bye.' It clicked, and went dead.

He walked to C deck restaurant, ordered a coffee. He sat over it a while before going back. He spread the notes out, lit a cigarette and daydreamed. He wasn't seeing Cheskin's cabin. He thought, *The hell with it. It's there to be enjoyed. Like the aftertaste of brandy.* He thought, *I still can't believe it. But it happened.* Aloud he said, 'You never know what another person's like. Maybe a lot of chances get dropped that way.'

He started on a first draft of the article. It ran well. He read it back, made his corrections, started again. At eighteen hundred hours he bathed and shaved. He walked round to Swissy's bar. In the corridors, evening light lay flaring. Where sunlight hit the satin-finish panels they glowed with minute grains of gold. The noise of the combine was a steady muted rumble.

Bertie was there. He seemed a bit the worse for wear. Swissy had a copy of the *Swiss Observer.* He said, 'Dere. Tell you all about it dere.'

Bertie said, 'The one thing that's always struck me as *curious* is why nobody ever really understood the William Tell legend.'

Harrison said, 'What do you mean?'

'Well,' said Bertie, 'look at it this way. For the sake of a few bob a *week*, the basstard was prepared to risk nailing his son between the eyes with a bloody iron bolt. That's the Swiss for you. They haven't altered.'

Swissy said indignantly, 'He be blowty good bloke. I tell you.'

Bertie said, 'Why, you ass … oh, what's the use?' He drank his wine, grimaced, and pushed the glass across. He said, ''Nother glass of your exorbitant *plonk*. This time, try filling it.'

Swissy shook his head. He said, 'Drinking too much, Bertie. Too much not good for you.' He recorked the bottle, looking pained. He said, 'Anyway, what about ol' Winkelried?'

Harrison said, 'Never heard of him.'

'Ach,' said Swissy. 'All de schoolchildren, dey learned him. Was a battle sometimes, can't remember when. Against de Austrians. Austrians had de long spear, what you call it?'

Harrison said, 'Pikes.'

'Ach. Pikes. Anyway, was no good. Swiss only have de ball wit' spikes. So dey have to make a gap. An' Winkelried say, "Look after de wife an' kids." Den he take all de spear to himself, to de ehest. An' de odders run over him.'

Bertie said, 'I can see *you* doing that. Why don't you try?'

Swissy said, 'Christ, no. But was a good chap. He say just like dat, "Look after de wife an' kids …"'

Bertie said, 'You *told* it once.'

O'Hara walked in. He slapped Harrison on the shoulder. He said, 'Here's the man who chats up my assistants.'

Harrison thought, *One day I'll kill you and slice you, you bastard, and eat the strips. And I shall enjoy them.* He said, 'Have a beer, Mike.'

O'Hara sat and swung his legs. He was looking well manicured. The love life must be prospering. He said, 'You'll not get anywhere with her, boyo.'

Harrison said, 'Maybe I'm not trying to.'

O'Hara said casually, 'She's damn near married anyway. Reckon they'll get spliced next trip. Bloke out in Gloucestershire somewhere, breeds horses. Old man's got a packet. Didn't she tell you?'

Harrison looked at his shoes. He said, 'I don't really know much about her.'

A klaxon sounded overhead. Feet pattered on the decking. The bridge tannoys said, 'Duty officer to Control, please, Emergency stations.'

Bertie said, 'Christ.' He put his glass down and ran for the door.

Harrison swung off the stool. O'Hara got ahead of him. He turned right and left, following the Irishman. They collided on the companion steps. O'Hara said, 'No fucking camera.' He ran back the way he had come.

B deck was filling. Somebody pointed. They said, 'Right up. Up ahead.'

Bertie was back, with a pair of heavy prismatics. He trained them and swore. He said, 'The *basstards* shouldn't be there at all.' He handed the glasses across.

She was big, as big as the last. To Harrison she looked like a great lurching biscuit tin on tracks, grinding across the land. He lowered the glasses. She was easily visible now to the naked eye. He stared behind him, up at the bridge windows. There was a pale blur that could have been Cheskin's face. The light was fading fast, dying in long swaths and banners. The dustcloud ahead caught the last of the sunset, glowed orange against dull red. To right and left the stubble shone darkly, like a landscape seen on Mars.

The bridge klaxons blasted, driving sound at Harrison's shoulders and back. The intercom speakers said, 'All stations stand by. Maintain revolutions.'

The loudhailer seemed to solidify the air of B deck. The words rolled into distance, a barrage of thunder. Harrison said, 'What's he saying?'

Bertie tittered. He said, 'He's telling 'em to *f-fuck* off.'

Harrison said, 'She's on the next swath. She'll pass us.'

Bertie said, 'She's too close in. She's not even on the *grid*.'

The loudhailer bawled again, fell silent. The Russian machine was closing fast now. The light gleamed on her bridge wings and coamings. In the sudden quiet, the roar of her engines sounded clear.

Bertie turned, stared up at the bridge. He said, 'The crazy *basstard*.'

Harrison said, 'Why doesn't he swing?'

Bertie said, 'Because he can't, he's too bloody *late*.'

The Russian was nearly alongside. A final flurry from the loudhailer; and Cheskin spoke suddenly and urgently in English. He said, '*Emergency. Collision drill. Clear all starboard catwalks. Clear starboard casings. Hurry, hurry.*'

Harrison saw figures run crouching along the cutter housings. The grey superstructure reared beyond the bridge wing. Identification letters slid by; vast, curling, Cyrillic.

Patsy jarred, and shook. There was a report like a cannon shot, and another. The crowd on B deck surged back. Harrison saw steel handrail rise into the air, loop jerkily. The catwalk sheered, thunderously, back towards the stern. Something hit the deck wing. A glass screen starred and shattered.

Alison was there, holding his arm. He pulled her back instinctively, swung her away. Wire thrummed overhead. Bertie yelled, 'She's clear. She's clear ...' The superstructure was diminishing, sliding out of sight behind the bridge.

The deck wing was a mess of wire and glass insulators. Somebody said, 'We got her aerial array.' Bertie spoke feelingly, glaring up at the bridge. He said, 'I hope he broke *all* his fucking pots,'

The speakers said, 'Damage reports to Control, please. Reports to Control.'

A crewman was wrestling with the coils of thick wire. Another swore and turned, showed a wrist dribbling scarlet. Alison said, 'Oh, God ...'

Swissy was there in his white jacket, stogie clamped between his teeth. He said, 'Blowty Russians.' He turned to Harrison, grinning. He said, 'Like blowty Brand 'Atch ...'

The speakers said, 'Controller Cheskin. There is no major damage. There is no emergency. I repeat, there is no emergency. Please return to your quarters. We are continuing on cut.'

Bertie said, 'There'll be bloody *hell* to pay for this.'

Harrison swallowed. He said, 'Are you all right?'

She said, 'Yes. Yes, I'm OK.'

He said, 'Better come and have your drink. I think we need it.'

She shook her head, pushed her hair back. She said, 'In a minute. Got to go somewhere.'

He said, 'Are you sure you're all right?'

She said, 'Honestly. Go on down. I'll come.'

The bar was packed already. The American engineers were making most of the noise. A red-necked man with cropped hair was saying, 'Sons of bitches Russians.'

Swissy alone seemed unruffled. He was saying, 'Blowty Brand 'Atch' again. The phrase seemed to have taken his fancy.

Bertie was scribbling on the back of an envelope. His shoulders were shaking. Harrison jostled his way to the counter, called for a beer. He said, 'Why didn't he turn?'

Bertie said, 'Because he's bloody *mad*.'

Harrison said, 'What's so damn funny?'

Bertie seemed to be having difficulty controlling himself. He said, 'The Russians cut to a complicated *pattern*. Two ahead, close, and a follower. Always groups of three.'

'And?'

Bertie said, 'Well, we've encountered and *dealt* with two ...'

It dawned. Harrison said slowly, 'Then there's –'

Bertie nodded. He said, 'Another basstard somewhere dead *ahead*.'

Harrison said quietly, 'How long?'

Bertie said, 'You can't be sure, of course. O seven hundred tomorrow. Give or *take* ...'

Alison was back. She said, 'O'Hara's gone temporarily insane.'

'What for?'

'He wanted to wire his pictures out. There's a clampdown. Official news agencies only.'

Harrison said, 'We're not a news team anyway.'

She said, 'That's what I told him.'

He said, 'So the pictures ...'

She said firmly, 'Can wait till morning. I've had enough of friend O'Hara.'

Swissy leered at her. He said, 'Here dey are. De love bird.'

Harrison bought a whisky. He said, 'I tried to book a call to the old man. The booths were too crowded.'

She said, 'O'Hara did it for you. They'll page you when it comes.'

He said, 'That was extraordinarily good of him.'

The bar was getting fuller than ever. He was jostled, beer spilled on his sleeve. The red-necked man was saying, 'Shoot the bastards then. All the bastards.'

Somebody said, 'Anyway, why the hell'd they let Cheskin get Controller?'

The red-necked man said, 'Sucking the bastard British.'

Harrison said, 'Let's try D deck. We can still have our crawl.'

She said, 'It won't be much better.'

Harrison said, 'We can try. Chow, Swissy.'

Swissy said, 'Chow.'

D deck bar was quieter, to his surprise. She perched on a bar stool, looking fairly at home. He hadn't had a chance to see her properly before. She was wearing a fawn sweater, a tiny kilt with a big dress pin. She looked about eighteen. He watched how her hair moved against the woolly. The texture contrast pleased him. He said, 'You were terrific last night.'

She frowned. He said, 'Don't you want to talk about it?'

She said, 'It isn't that. You took me by surprise.'

He said, 'What?'

She turned her glass round on the counter. She said, 'I didn't know you thought of me like that. It never showed.'

'Like what?'

She said, 'Well, as a woman.'

He thought, *I can't have come back, after all these years, to this same arid place.* But his mind had spun already, added and made a total. He thought, *I can't believe. I won't believe. It's a joke that's gone bad, through too much laughing. Just a joke gone bad.*

He smiled and said the first thing that came to him.

'Manuelo wants to buy the gun.'

She grasped the subject-change eagerly. She said, 'It fascinated me. I've never handled one before. I'd love to fire it, just once.'

He said, 'You were very good with it. But I don't think you'd like it when it went off.'

She said, 'I wouldn't mind. Not if I was ready.'

'You'd flinch anyway.'

She said, 'Is that wrong?'

Harrison said, 'It makes you miss the target.'

He opened his cigarettes. She said, 'No. Have one of these.'

He lit up for her. She blew smoke. She said, 'We could have done it just now, if we'd known the collision was coming. Nobody would have heard.'

He thought, *Stop being desperate; for your sake, if not for mine.* He said, 'It's already an international incident. It would really have loused things up if the Russkies found a forty-five slug stuck in the works.'

The intercom speaker said, 'Mr John Harrison, World Geographic. International call.'

He said, 'Excuse me.' There were booths outside in the corridor. He walked to the nearest, closed the door. They took a time establishing the connection. Finally London came through. He listened and said 'Yes' several times. Then he put the handset down, stood staring at it. He thought, *The mouth moves, and the facial muscles. The words form, while the odds increase to the power of n. Then you walk away. They call it maturity.*

He went back to the lounge. He said, 'That's about it then.'

She said, 'What's happened?'

He said, 'I'm being recalled. They're sending a bigger gun.'

'Who?'

He said, 'Bill Goldie.'

She made a face. She said, 'When do you have to leave?'

He said, 'Day after tomorrow. They're flying him from Tokyo. I take the helicopter back.'

She said, 'I think we're stopping on.'

He said, 'I think so. From what they said.'

She looked at him blandly. She said, 'You're not getting all up tight about it, are you?'

He stared back. He thought, *Just twenty-four hours, and I've learned you all over again. My ducky little ball of solid brass.* He said, 'No, I'm not getting all up tight.'

She said, 'I'm sorry about on deck. I was scared.'

He said, 'You had every right to be.'

'I didn't think Swissy would ever stop laughing.'

Harrison stubbed his cigarette. He said, 'Would you like to eat?'

She said, 'Not tonight, honestly. I couldn't.'

His skull felt blocked; too much personal stuff going through. He remembered Bertie and his envelope. He wondered if he should tell her. He said, 'What do you want to do?'

'I don't know. I don't mind, really.'

'Shall we go back to Swissy's?'

She brightened. She said, 'I like him. Yes, all right.'

Outside he said, 'I'm afraid it wasn't much of a crawl.'

She said, 'I'm enjoying myself. I just don't show things much.'

The Americans had gone. Bertie still sat at the bar. He looked in a bad way; his eyes were starting to run. Swissy said, 'Ah, here she come. De untouchable one.'

Alison said, 'Supposition, Swissy. Mere supposition.'

Bertie brightened momentarily, and greyed back over.

Swissy said, 'I was just telling Bertie here, 'bout dis duel. Last duel dey ever have, in Switzerland.'

Bertie said cloudily, 'Another of his horrible *bloody* stories.'

'No, is true,' said Swissy. 'Interestin'.' He turned back to Harrison. 'Dey have de doctor dere,' he said, 'an' one man, he get de end of his nose cutted off.' He started to giggle. 'An' before dey can sticked it back on,' he said, 'is eaten by de Alsatian dog.'

Alison said, 'I still don't understand about bullets. About part stopping in the gun.'

Harrison started drawing on a beermat.

Later she said, 'I know the lot. Matchlock, wheellock, flintlock, percussion cap. Then bullets. The percussion cap's still a bit dodgy.'

Harrison said, 'They only get more complicated. Just remember all guns are really clockwork.'

She said, 'I like finding out about totally new things.'

Swissy said, ''Bout time you give me de bar back.'

The time had passed, as any time passes. Harrison stood up. He said, 'G'night, Swissy. Bertie.'

Swissy said, 'Chow.' Bertie hiccupped faintly.

Outside she said, 'Bertie always looks so unhappy. Like a singularly mournful puppy.'

Harrison said, 'Maybe he is unhappy.'

They'd reached his cabin without the question being raised. Which he supposed was another hurdle crossed. He thought, *I'm not going to leap on you now every time I get the chance. But you're not to know that, of course.* He opened the door, thumbed the lights to full. He said, 'Coffee?'

She sat on the bed. She said, 'Please. I mustn't be long, though. I feel whacked.'

He murmured something like, 'I wouldn't wonder.' It didn't much matter what he said; he'd lost interest in the words.

She drank her coffee, when it came. Afterwards he held his hand out. She looked uncertain. He said, 'Nobody shall take your clothes off. I won't let them.'

She walked to him, sat across his knees, relaxed. The pressure was back, and the warmth. She looped her arms round his neck and said, ''Lo.'

He kissed her. Her mouth was very soft. He thought, *Here we are again then.* He said, 'Were you very mad?'

She said, 'I'm never mad. I just don't react when I should. I think there must be something wrong with me.'

He thought, 'If I stayed surprised for two hours and twenty minutes, I should see a doctor.' He touched her knee.

She said, 'No, John, please. Not tonight.'

He said, 'Very decorous.'

She said, 'I just wanted body contact. It's comforting.'

They lay silent. He watched the wallclock and rubbed her behind. Finally she stirred. She said, 'I was so worried.'

'What about?'

'You. And us. Being friends.'

He said, 'As far as I know, nothing's altered that.'

She said, 'I just don't know about … being lovers. I've had so many.'

He said, 'Lovers?'

'No, boys. Well, men. I didn't want you hurt.'

He thought, *You lying, two-timing bitch and mother of bitches to be, that is the bloody last straw.* Aloud he said, 'I wouldn't worry too much about me.'

She pushed against his shoulder. She said, 'I'm better at … well, talking. I'm a great free thinker. That's why it wouldn't be fair.'

'What wouldn't be fair?'

She frowned. She said, 'The physical attraction thing. It always goes. It's only once. Then …'

He said, 'It must be very frustrating for you.'

She said, 'I've lost a lot of friends that way.'

He thought, *How much do you want? Just how much?*

She drew her finger across his lips. Then she put her mouth up. He evaded her. She punched his chest, chuckling. She said, 'Oh, you … man …'

The wallclock pinged. He thought she'd move but she didn't. After a while she said, 'I don't think I shall ever marry. I don't know. I'm too independent or something. It just isn't me.'

He said very gently, 'My dear, all I have done so far is remove your knickers. There are rather a lot of steps between that and publishing the banns.'

She stiffened, and relaxed. He thought, *You put your hand out to the flower; because it's perfumed, and lovely, and you're human. And you feel the cold, bristling worm. At last, I know the Enemy.* He felt tireder than he had thought possible; he wanted her weight, that was just a weight, shucked off.

He massaged, gently, the firm swelling of her woolly. She half put his hand away. She said, 'Don't, please.'

He said, 'This isn't sex. This is friends.'

She said, 'It's in between.'

He thought, *And you're starting to tighten behind the nipple.* He said, 'Come on. I'm taking you home.'

She sat up carefully, smoothed her skirt. She said, 'I shall have to find my comb.'

They walked up to B deck. The diesels roared, in the night. Overside, lamps were slung. Riggers were working, swinging in belts over the moving stubble. Most of the rubbish had been stripped clear. The combine's side gaped for thirty yards or more, iron brackets showing like bones.

The sky was crusted with stars. Not the same stars. She looked up. She said, 'What a lovely night.'

He walked her to her cabin. She stepped forward, kissed him quickly. She said, 'Good night. And thank you.'

He thought, *And that, God preserve us, was the Regretful Parting Peck.*

He said, 'Good night.'

He walked back to his pad, sat on the edge of the bunk. Then it hit him. He thought, *Last fling of lonely middle aged man.* He picked the revolver up, broke the cylinder, loaded five. He closed the piece and cocked, hearing the creak of oiled steel. He laid the gun to his face, felt coldness touch temple and cheek. He thought, *I should have barrelled her across the ear and got stuck in while she was giddy. It would have come to the same thing.* He broke the gun, worked the ejector. The cartridges fell to the bedcover, lay fatly shining. He got up, opened the locker door. The whisky was two-thirds gone. He slid the big gun into his pocket, walked to C deck restaurant. Manuelo was closing up. He said, 'Manuelo. Bottle of whisky. On my bill.'

Manuelo grinned, made a note on a pad. Harrison took the bottle. He said, '*Gracias.* And Manuelo ...'

'Mr Harrison?'

He held the revolver out, butt foremost. He said, 'Here.'

The little man's face lit up. He said, 'Mr Harrison. *Gracias, gracias.*'

Harrison said, 'Good night, Manuelo.'

He walked back. On the way he thought, *To her, it's dirty. She couldn't step right out. They never do.* He opened his cabin door, sat on the bunk. He raised the bottle, squinted through it at the ceiling light. He thought, *When she hooks her Mister Right, it'll still be dirty. Only there'll be children, for excuses.*

He finished the whisky, cracked the new bottle. He thought, *There's two cold spaces now. Hers, and the gun's. Odd to become attached to a material object. Any object.*

The wallspeaker clicked, hummed a moment and faded. He thought, *Odd, too, what a jump that should give the heart.* Later he decided he had imagined the sound. He thought, *We could have worked. For a little while. Now all the rest comes back. Like rubble, cascading in the mind.* He said aloud, 'I wonder if he did break his bloody pots?' He remembered the Fedotov painting. He'd thought he'd been doing the taking. But he'd been giving again. So much more than he could afford. He said, 'Now, I jump the stick. It isn't even original.'

His lids felt warm and heavy. He lay on the bunk knowing he wouldn't sleep. The combine was a monstrous weight, useless tracks grinding, useless blades spinning, useless bolts and nuts and chains and levers and wheels. He thought, *Cheskin knows. As well as I.*

He palmed the ceiling light to dim. He didn't want any more whisky; and he wasn't drunk. He lit a cigarette. The first drag brought phlegm up into his throat. He finished the thing anyway, lay back. The cabin walls trembled and thrummed. He closed his eyes and remembered how her bare hip felt under her skirt. He said, 'Get out, please God. Get out, get out, get out of my skull.'

He fell asleep.

The cabin was grey, when he opened his eyes. He felt chilled to the bone. Maybe the air conditioning had failed. He swayed upright, glared at the clock. He thought, *Another day, another dollar.*

The hands stood at 06.35. He said, 'In time for the show.' He walked to the shower cubicle. He looked as rough as he felt. He shaved, washed his face, changed his shirt. He thought, *Last night little Alison bestrode the grain, and was a Queen. Her eyes were stars, her flesh the good brown earth, her hair the golden crop.* He slapped his pockets, located matches and cigarettes. He thought, *I saw a goddess, from old time. She enjoyed the touch-up.*

The corridor vibrated faintly. He closed the cabin door, turned left and right. He thought, *One thing, only, is dirty. And that she didn't do. She'll give herself clean, the bells will ring her clean. They call it morality.*

He said, 'And I let her get away with it.'

B deck was crowded. The figures stood muffled, not speaking, watching to the north. The light was growing, across the waste of stubble. He thought, *Bertie wasn't the only one with an envelope and pencil.*

He stared ahead. There was nothing. The dawn-streaks in the sky were high, clear green. He thought, *Maybe she isn't on track. Big anticlimax kick.*

Beside him stood the grizzled engineer he'd spoken to on the first day. He said, 'There's nothing there then.'

The man sucked his empty pipe. He turned, looking faintly surprised. He said, 'They've had radar contact for half an hour. She's there. Reciprocal course.'

High in the combine's rigging a red light started to blink. It lit the backs of the people on the deck. The engine beats stayed steady. He wondered about Alison. He thought, *If she needs a pair of comforting arms, there's always O'Hara.*

The wind stung his eyes. He rubbed, peering. There was something, after all. A smudge, on the wide, smudged horizon. On Patsy's mast, the identification lights started to sequence. The smudge made no response.

He could see her clearer now. High and square, like her sisters. Bone-pale. Somebody said in a conversational voice, 'Vostok class. Combine Ilya.'

Harrison looked back at the bridge windows. There were faces, staring ahead. He heard the loudhailer circuit start to breathe. The engineer said, 'We're privileged. We're seeing the start of World War Three.'

The path, the swath of uncut wheat, stretched ahead. The gap was closing now with increasing speed. Harrison clenched his fingers on the deck rail. He thought, *He understands; and I know him. They took his wife, they took his birthright. Now they take his grain.*

He could make out the long rectangles of the bridge windows. Below, the Russian's forward coamings looked higher than the deck on which he stood. He thought, *Combine Ilya.* The words made no particular sense.

The bridge speakers said, 'Eight hundred metres, sir. Closing speed constant.'

The loudhailers rumbled briefly, and were quiet. The engineer said wonderingly, 'Right on our bloody track.'

The combine was towering now against the horizon. Seen head-on, her silhouette was oddly complex. The speakers said, 'Five hundred metres, sir. Closing speed constant.' The voice was starting to edge up in pitch.

Cheskin said, 'Main beams, please.'

Brilliance burst, above Patsy's cutter coamings. The Russian's bridge windows reflected back a dazzled glare. The speakers said, 'Three hundred metres, sir ...'

Abruptly, the combine bucked. A rumbling; then a tearing, crashing shock. The deck rail hit Harrison in the chest. He clung, stupidly. Somebody yelled, '*Reef*...' Round him people were tumbling stiffly, legs and arms thrust out. He saw the forward casings fly apart, plates hang in the air like petals of a red steel flower. Something black came ploughing and shrieking. The air was full of din. On C deck promenade the windows bowed and banged.

He saw the body fly out below him, plunge to the main coamings. It seemed they opened to receive it, snapped like a mouth. The victim poised a moment, impossibly. The eyes blinked rapidly; it was as if Swissy once more gave his impersonation of a severed head. Then he was gone, into the tracks.

The emergency beacons were glaring, orange-pink bowls of fire. The klaxon sounded, huge and harsh. The Russian was slowing, slowing. Her prow reared over the coamings like a grey-white cliff. Then she was halted; and the noise of her many motors was a roaring, confused and dim.

The bridge speakers said, 'Emergency procedure, all departments. Give me full dampdown, please.'

There was a deepening whine as Patsy's diesels died.

Harrison laid the suitcase on the bed. He sorted used shirts, shorts and socks, slipped them into a polythene wrapper. He folded handkerchiefs and ties, packed a box of quarto and half a dozen books. He closed the case, slid it to one side. He sat at the table, sorted the transcript sheets into order and pinned their corners with a staple. Somebody tapped the door. He said, 'Come in.'

It was Bertie. He sat on the bunk for a time and puffed. He said, 'Christ almighty, what a bloody day.'

Harrison said, 'There's some whisky in the locker.'

Bertie poured two fingers. He said, 'I don't know where the other *glasses* are, you'll have to get your own.'

Harrison helped himself. He said, 'Cigarette?'

Bertie said, 'Not at the m-minute.' He drank Scotch, grimaced. He said, 'D-did you see old Swissy take a dive?'

Harrison said, 'Yes.' He looked at the papers, frowned and laid them aside. He said, 'Were there many other casualties?'

Bertie said, 'Six in the cutter casings. They're still picking the *bits* out.' He stared at the Scotch. He said, 'Christ, I needed that.'

Harrison thought, 'I wish there was something I could think of to say. But it doesn't get to me. Any of it.'

Bertie said, 'Swissy's a lucky basstard.'

Harrison turned. He said, 'That's one way to look at it.'

Bertie said, 'Quite seriously. The basstard got away with it. They got him out. I think he lost a foot.'

Harrison said, 'Good God.'

Bertie finished the whisky at a gulp and stood up. He said, 'I've got to get on. Just thought you'd like the news.'

Harrison said, 'How badly are we damaged?'

Bertie said, 'It just about took her *guts* out. H-hell to pay.' He shook his head, clucked sorrowfully and closed the door.

Harrison called sick bay. The speaker said impersonally, 'The patient is sleeping. His condition is satisfactory.'

Harrison said, 'Thank you,' and broke the link.

The wallclock pinged. He frowned at it. In thirty minutes Cheskin was due to make a statement. He wondered if there was anywhere he could get a beer.

C deck was a shambles of girders and wire. To his surprise, the bar door was ajar. Manuelo was behind the counter, shovelling glass into a bucket. He said forlornly, 'Not much on, Mr. Harrison. All bottles go smash.'

Harrison said, 'Christ, what a mess. Any beer?'

Manuelo said, 'American.'

Harrison said, 'That's fine.'

He walked to the windows. The glass had gone. Below, they had a heavy tackle rigged. Crewmen were lifting aside a buckled hatch cover. Ahead, the forward coamings were split as clean as by an axe-cut.

He finished the beer, got another. A tired-looking party of men came in. They were blackened with oil, one had an arm bandaged. Manuelo said, 'Sorry, sirs. American beer only.'

Harrison lit a cigarette. Sun patterns were moving on the dural walls; the polished panels glistened. He took the glass back to the counter, walked up to the bridge.

A flying crane was hovering alongside the combine. The downdraught beat at his clothes. He showed his pass to the security man, stepped into the cabin. The crane moved away.

The place was hazed with cigarette smoke. He found a seat. The dolly birds were there; one flashed him a frozen sort of smile.

Cheskin was sitting behind the desk. He said, 'Mr Harrison. Now, I think we are all here.' He looked at a paper. He said, 'At o seven fourteen hours this morning, the combine ran afoul of a hitherto-unmarked reef. We have sustained heavy damage to engines and plant, and can no longer function as a field unit. I regret to inform you that nine lives were lost. Under the circumstances, other injuries were remarkably slight.'

Somebody said, 'Have the Russ – the Russians been helpful, sir?'

Cheskin said, 'A medical team from Combine Ilya is at present working with our own sickbay staff. The seriously injured are being flown to base hospital. We are in contact with combines Maya and Valeri. Both have offered assistance, which is not at present required.'

An American said, 'Can you define our present position more closely, sir?'

Cheskin said, 'Certainly. We are proceeding to base under our own auxiliary power. Tankers are withdrawing reserves of diesel fuel, which may not be jettisoned in this area. Civilian personnel will not be evacuated; there is no danger, and the situation is under control.'

Somebody said, 'Can you tell us anything as yet about the Russian encroachment?'

Cheskin turned. He said, 'It is by no means certain an encroachment has taken place. It is possible a computer error was responsible. At the moment this is my personal opinion, and is not for publication. A full-scale investigation will, of course, be held.'

The American came back to the attack. He said, 'This reef, sir. Was it not detectable by radar?'

Cheskin said, 'Under the circumstances, no. It was masked by the bulk of the approaching vehicle. Yes?'

The question was barbed. 'Under the circumstances, I'd say this machine was a write-off. Where do you put the blame?'

Cheskin glanced up tiredly. He said, 'An investigation will be held. Until its findings are known, I cannot answer you.' He paused. He said, 'I am Combine Controller. I will naturally assume such responsibility as may be necessary.'

There were other questions. They tended to pass Harrison by. Finally Cheskin looked at his watch. He said, 'I have to inform you full communications have been restored. You may cable your stories if you wish. Thank you, gentlemen. And ladies.'

There was a rush for the door. Harrison let himself be left behind. At the door he turned. He said, 'Controller.'

'Mr Harrison?'

Harrison said, 'Had the reef not intervened, would you have closed down?'

Cheskin rose, stood hands clasped behind him. He stared down for a time at the ruined deck. Finally he turned. He said, 'I find your question difficult to understand. There would, of course, have been no other choice.'

Harrison said, 'Thank you, sir.'

Cheskin nodded. He said, 'Goodbye, Mr Harrison.'

Harrison walked back to his cabin, stood staring. But the packing was finished. He thought, *Once more, I'm killing time. It does seem a waste.* He got the Olivetti out, started reworking his notes. He thought, *While I'm doing this, the thing's still alive.* Finally, he got himself a meal. He had to wait a goodish while; C deck restaurant was still suffering malfunction. Afterwards there was some whisky to finish. He sat and swilled the glass round and thought, *So life goes on. Habit is a wonderful thing.*

The intercom buzzed. He thumbed the control, said, 'Harrison.'

The speaker said, 'Mr Harrison, this is Sick Bay. We have a Mr Hauser asking for you; are you available?'

He thought, 'I don't know a Mr Hauser.' Then he remembered. He said, 'I'll come at once.'

C deck looked tidier now, but D level was still a shambles. Repair crews were working with cutters; he stepped over a mess of cables, ducked through a bulkhead door.

He nearly ran into her. She said, 'Oh … hello, John.'

He smiled. He said, 'All right?'

She said, 'Just about. I got knocked down. I'm bruised all over.'

'How's O'Hara?'

She said, 'Developing. The scoop of the year.'

He said, 'I'm going to see Swissy.'

Her eyes widened. She said, 'I saw it. It was horrible. You mean he's not …?'

He said, 'Apparently, he's still kicking. With one foot.'

She said, 'I'll come too.'

Harrison said, 'I don't suppose they'll mind.'

Emergency beds had been set up in the corridors. There was a clanging and clattering of trolleys A nurse met them; a striking girl, dark-haired and high-cheekboned. On her shoulder tabs were neat red stars.

Harrison said, 'A patient was asking for me. Mr Hauser.'

She said, 'Yes.' She smiled. She said, 'I'm sorry. Small English. With me, please.'

She walked ahead, opened a door. She said, 'Doctor say – very short.'

Harrison said, 'Thank you.'

The room was tiny, not much more than a cubicle. Swissy looked very sick. A cage had been rigged over his legs; beside the bed a blood drip was set up.

He said feebly, 'Ah. De love bird.'

Harrison said, 'How are you, Swissy?'

He said, 'Had a foot gone. Christ, when I go t'rough dat t'ing, I t'ink dat's it. No more take de piss out of Bertie.'

Alison said, 'I'm … terribly sorry, Swissy.'

He waved a hand. He, said, 'I get over it. Same like everyt'ing else.' He closed his eyes, wearily. He said, 'Always a way. Eh? Not so?'

Harrison said, 'Is there anything we can do?'

Swissy said, 'Ya.' He fumbled beside the bed, held out an envelope. He said, 'Little t'ing. You don't mind?'

Harrison said, 'I don't mind.'

Swissy said, 'Dey fly me out tomorrow. Don' want de kids to know. Tell 'em myself, in a bit. But dey need money.'

Harrison said, 'I'll go and see them.'

Swissy said, 'No, don't matter to see 'em. But send it on. Is in dollar. OK?'

Harrison said, 'OK.'

Swissy said, 'Christ, dat li'l one … only twelve, but she know how to spend. Know what she want already.'

Harrison said, 'It'll be done. Get some rest, Swissy.'

Swissy said, 'Ain't got much blowty choice …' Bye, Al'son. Don't do not'ing I wouldn't.'

She said, 'Chow, Swissy.' She walked through the door. Harrison closed it after her.

She leaned on the wall and rubbed her face. He said, 'Are you all right?'

She nodded. She said, 'I just don't like hospitals.'

They walked back the way they had come. He said, 'I'm flying out tomorrow.'

She said, 'Yes. I know.'

He said, 'Meet me for a drink tonight? End-of-term party.'

She said, 'I suppose so … Haven't you got a lot to do?'

'It's done. Goldie takes over, anyway.'

She said, 'Swissy's bar, if it's open. About twenty hundred.'

Harrison said, 'OK.'

She said thoughtfully, 'It won't seem the same.'

He said, 'No. It won't.'

He walked back up to B deck. He was surprised, vaguely, to see it was evening already. The combine was heading nearly due west across the miles of stubble. He turned away from the pouring redness. A hundred yards off, a massive recovery tractor paced the crippled machine. A helicopter swooped low, belly lamps winking. He leaned on the rail, watched the slow flowing of the ground. He missed, now, the thunder of the mains; Patsy seemed somehow less than half alive, a crawling red shadow in the dusk.

A tanker moved away, left behind a rich gust of fumes. As the light faded, the torches working on the ruined forward housings sprang into prominence. He watched the white glare shift and flicker, the sparks fall like hot coals. He stayed still a long time, smoking, till the land was wholly dark.

The wind was rising, keening in the rigging. He pushed his jacket sleeve back, looked at his watch. He walked to his cabin, used the dry shaver and washed. He went to the locker, slipped the little charm into his pocket. He thought, *We must be ships, passing in the night; but elegantly, so elegantly. Nobody gets hurt.*

Halfway to C deck he thought, 'I hope she's stood me up. It's about time.' But he pushed the door open knowing she would be there.

She wasn't *that* kind of girl.

I LOSE MEDEA

The first trouble was the ghosts. You wouldn't think a field of cloth of gold would get itself all that haunted but there they were all right, whole formations of them drifting round like smoke puffs and congregating above the hedgerows. I drove from the gate bumpety-bump, clank, bump, up across the swell of land to where you could see the barrows in the distance and the big stone circles crowning the downs, and the glower low down on the horizon that meant just there was the sea. Then Medea said, 'Stop, this is fine.' I don't know how she could always tell the exact place she wanted to be. I stopped the car and put the engine off and sat a minute thinking, *We're here. We got here at last.*

But the light looked as if it was nearly ready to fade so I didn't fancy sitting around too long. I got out and unlocked the boot and pulled the lid up and Medea started throwing canvas out on the grass in rolls like big grey sausages. Then there was the holdall with the mallet and the spare hanks of nylon line and all the framing and stuff. Some of the framing was round and some was square, I could never remember at the start just how it all went except there were two big wishbone-shaped pieces that made the tent gables. I found the bits for them and fitted them together and laid them out alongside the rest.

Medea was looking good, she was wearing white stretch pants and a dark blue top and had a kerchief bound through her hair. When she squatted and started pulling the canvas into shape you could see a big half-moon of brown back. She got the tent laid out OK, then she changed her mind and said we were pitching wrong way on the slope or something and started in again turning it all round. This was the thing about Medea, she never had much of a sense of time.

The ground sloped down towards the back of the field and there was a high tousled hedge with a gap in it and a stile, and a couple of trash bins stuck at angles in the grass. I looked across and started feeling a bit annoyed because the smoke puffs were separating above the hedge and quite a few starting to drift our way. Medea got the tent lined up and crawled inside with the ridge-pole and one of the uprights, you could see the canvas writhing round like a sack with a good-looking ferret in it. I'd have nipped in after her but I was getting worried about the ghosts, one or two of them were looking nasty. There was one big grey chap with horns, I could see from his expression he was just looking forward to coming over our way and dropping a hundredweight of fog on top of us, which was all we needed. I called to Medea to hurry up a bit and she said something muffled inside the canvas, something about having got the wrong pole. I couldn't see how that could be because she'd got all the sections marked with bits of surgical tape with numbers on them, and tied in bundles with lengths of the nylon cord.

The big chap was certainly extremely nasty but fortunately for us he was none too well organized. He'd got himself caught up on the briars and stuff in the hedge, he'd get one part free then something else would catch and he'd roll over snapping and writhing like a horizontal column of bonfire smoke. But I could see he was making it by degrees and I was getting really mad with that slow old Medea. Thing is, your own Field Spirits take over as soon as you've got something up that looks vaguely like a roof and then you're OK, but till then they're just plain disinterested. You can be anybody's meat, whether you're on their patch or not.

Some of the nasties were fairly close. I broke up a couple of little ones with one of the awning stays and swirled them round a bit on the grass but there were some bigger jobs I didn't fancy tackling on my own. I turned the car round to point at the hedge and put the headlights on to main beam. The big chap flattened and streamed down the other side out of sight, but I knew that wouldn't last for long. I called to Medea to come out. I said, 'I'll get the thing up, you do the other stuff. We're getting surrounded here.'

She crawled out with her jumper pulled half up her back and her hair all tousled. She had a whole bundle of bits in the car, crucifixes, lightning conductors, old cavalry sabres, that sort of thing. She started walking round sticking them in the grass and muttering. She set up an interesting crossfire of emanations, but I couldn't see the effect lasting much longer than the headlights so I humped into the tent and started straightening things out. The tent was one of those with a built in groundsheet which are fine when they're up but can be a nuisance if you don't know for sure what you're doing. I got the upright located and stood up and slipped the ridge pole on top and called to Meclea to put the end guy on and a couple of side lines, and after that it wasn't so hectic. With the second upright in place the tent ridge filled out nicely and the Field Spirits there were a pair of them, husky-looking blighters as far as you could see went thundering down past us cracking whips and such and the locals just shredded up and blew. The big chap went really amorphous, the last I saw of him he was streaming off into the valley like a snake of thick white mist. He was mad too, he kept looking back at us with his yellow eyes. Somebody was in for a bad night, but as it wasn't us I didn't worry too much.

I'd got pretty hot and sticky, pitching camp is not a thing I go for though it's usually worth the effort afterwards. Also cloth of gold is great stuff but hell to get pegs into. I bent three all up and had to knock 'em straight again with the mallet, but eventually things got more organized. Medea had unloaded the rest of the stuff from the car, the twin-ring burner and the lamp and the big gas bottle and hanging larder and all that. I'd got the second ridge-pole up and guyed and the tent inner pegged down tight, all we had to do was rig the fly and the bell end and we were there. I lit a cigarette and sat back for a bit to cool off. There was a strip of light now along the top of the downs; the grass shone gold, nearly technicolored. There were a lot of people up there, you could see the priests in their white robes, very distant and sharp and clear. The stones looked good, the lintels dark against the glow, and the incense smoke threading straight up in the still air. Our field was very peaceful now with the ghosts gone, there was a smell of dog roses and hay.

We got started again and rigged the rest of the canvas and I went round and shifted a couple of pegs Medea had put in wrong. Then we got the stuff inside and lit the lamp and it all started looking more like home, beetles and moths blundering in knocking their fool heads against the light. I said, 'I'll get some water,' and Medea said, 'I'll come with you,' so we walked diagonally across the field to where there was a tap on a standpipe and an old enamel bath. There was a notice scrawled on a board saying not to empty detergents into the bath, I suppose because the cattle sometimes used it. The 'S' on the notice was printed the wrong way round, I'd never actually seen that done before. Medea had taken her shoes off, as she walked she kicked up little flurries of embers and dark sparks like jewels. Round the bath the ground was all muddy and churned up and she sloshed through that as well, mud never seemed to stick to her. Not for long, anyway.

While we were filling the water carriers I said, 'We shall have the place to ourselves,' which was a classic case of speaking too soon because a Land Rover came down the farm track nearly at once, towing a great long trailer. The car was full of young Danes, leastways I think they were Danes, they nearly all had fair hair. They all piled out laughing when they saw us and called to help unhitch the trailer because it was too long to swing in through the gate. But I wasn't having any of that. I said to Medea, 'Maybe if they can't get in they'll go off someplace else.' They had a maypole on the trailer, so it looked as if they wanted to be hectic. What with the war starting any minute it didn't seem there was going to be much rest and quiet.

The girls all had hip-length pants and little blouse tops in white and turquoise blue. They got the trailer unhooked and started shoving it about trying to angle it to get it through the gateway. It was a big trailer too, one of those lattice-sided things they used to call a Queen Mary. I took the water carriers from Medea and we walked back to the tent. She said she wanted to get the bed straight and hang our stuff up and get supper on, all of which things she was better at doing by herself. I walked over to see how the Danes were getting on. They were in the far corner of the field by the copse. They'd got the trailer in position and the maypole cleared for lifting. Up close you could see what sort of thing it was, I mean what it was all about. It was garlanded with flowers and green boughs and the tip all painted shiny ochre, lying there against the cloth of gold. They had some transistors stood about, one on the cab roof of the Land Rover, but fortunately the sound wasn't travelling very far.

I said we'd had some trouble with ghosts but they got shooed off and we didn't think they'd be back. They gave me some beer, they had cans and cans of it all strewn about. After I'd drunk it I decided I'd walk on up to the main road and see how the war was getting on.

The light was changing all the time now, which pleased me. The sky had turned a sort of pinky bronze, the sort of colour you get if you hold a candy wrapper up close to your eyes. There was a farmhouse on top of the hill, all little and twisted and built of stone like something in *Snow White.* It had very tall ornate chimney stacks, where the light caught them they burned orange like flames. Somebody had hooked a wire across the farm-track. It had a spring one end to keep it tight and a piece of white rag hung in the middle so you could see it was there. I hoped this meant no other people would come in because I had a proprietary feeling about that field of cloth of gold, having been there several times before. I stepped over the wire and walked on up the track. There was an old outhouse I hadn't really noticed before, it had a vintage Morris motor-car in it which pleased me a lot because I like old machinery. It was a pretty sad-looking Morris though, somebody had dumped a stack of old sacks on the roof and one tyre was flat. I wrote my name and Medea's name in the dust on the bonnet before moving on.

What made the campsite so secluded was the copse on the landward side, beech saplings I think they were. They weren't all that tall, but the lie of the land made it impossible to see much beyond. Once I got to the lane though the first of the castles came rearing back into sight, it wasn't really so far off. It was pretty huge; it always surprised you how big it was, it didn't matter how many times you saw it. There was a slip of moon behind it in the sky, in that light the stone didn't look any more substantial. The whole building looked sort of translucent, as if the light was really pouring through. Some of the windows flamed and reflected like diamonds, others were dark.

There were seven castles really, Stretching away in a big curve into the distance, though only the first four were visible; the others were lost in the haze, or occulted one behind the next. The nearest, the big one, was silent though the next in line was working very hard. They had cranes rigged on the battlements and you could see loads of stuff going up and the empty slings swinging back down. That castle was really busy. I think it was prepared for trouble, which it was certainly going to get.

I couldn't see any guns from where I stood so I walked on up to the main road. There was a little wooden structure on the verge like a shop counter standing all on its own where you could buy jam and marmalade sometimes, and pots of cottagemade lemon curd. It was all sold out when I got there though, except for a bunch of flowers which looked pretty sad, and anyway I didn't want them. There was a blue Sellotape tin with some sixpences and florins and ten-shilling pieces in it, so it looked as if they'd had a busy day. I lit a cigarette and wondered where the batteries were, but after a while I saw them down below the road some couple of hundred yards away. There was a gate and nobody seemed to be worrying too much, so I opened it and walked on down. There were a lot of vehicles parked, and a steam traction engine with half-tracks. The guns were big things with angular shields in front of the breeches, I think they were eighteen-pounders. The crews all wore shabby peaked caps and khaki uniforms and queer-looking tightly strapped puttees. They had an officer with them, a captain. He looked harassed and red-faced and kept making notes on a clip board. There was a lot of running about and shouting; a fatigue party was filling sandbags from a big pile of sand dumped to one side of the emplacement, others were farther on down the valley hammering stakes into the ground and stringing coils of barbed wire between. It seemed too there was some trouble with the field telephone; a man with headphones on was cranking a handle and saying, 'Hello, HQ,' but nothing was coming through.

I watched them getting the guns lined up for a time. There were shells stacked about on the grass, big ones with shiny yellow cases. I wanted to see the crews open fire but they didn't seem anywhere near ready so I walked on to the next emplacement, which one of the gunners had said was called the Tudor Lines.

Of the two groups the Tudors seemed the better organized. One party was unloading tall wickerwork cylinders from a cart; another was arranging them as a breastwork in front of the guns, and filling them with earth. The guns were enormous things with ornate brass barrels, all rings and straps and curlicues. The gunners wore dusty brown leather costumes and shoes with big buckles and queer flat shiny leather caps. Behind the emplacement two men were mixing powder in a tub. They were using wooden spades so there wouldn't be a spark, but the whole operation still looked risky to me.

I'd expected some really heavy pieces to be brought to bear and so wasn't too surprised when I saw Mons Meg. A little farther on though they had the Dardanelles Gun, which struck me as a bit unnecessary. They had the breech and barrel shored up on stacks of timber and were trying to align them preparatory to screwing them home. They weren't having too much success, which considering the size of the piece wasn't surprising. The gun captain was standing up on top of the barrel trying to jiggle it into line by stamping on it. I called up to him that what he needed was a jack but he was too busy to listen, so I walked back to the eighteen-pounder lines to see if I could borrow one. They didn't seem altogether keen. I got one eventually from one of the supply trucks, though I didn't really see why I should bother since it was my rest that was going to be disturbed. Anyway I lugged it back across the grass and the Tudors were extremely pleased once they got the hang of it. They lifted the muzzle of the gun into line and a dozen started in with crowbars, ramming them into the sockets on the breech and twisting to get the thread started. But that didn't work too well either, as the thread was corroded through being left out in the weather so many years. I left them chipping away at the screw with cold chisels, and greasing it with butter and lard.

The RA captain was studying the nearest enemy position through a little pair of field glasses. He had longish fair hair that had strayed down outside his cap, and he was looking extremely annoyed. I said, 'What you need are some tanks,' but he just looked blank. Then I had another idea and said, 'I mean Land Ships,' but that didn't please him any better. He jumped down from where he was standing and started waving a revolver and shouting something about breaches of security. The revolver was a nasty-looking Webley .38, so I walked over to the nearest of the gun crews in case he started pointing it at me.

It seemed they'd got the land line working because shortly afterwards the order came through to fire. The first gun went off with a big crash and lurched back some distance from the breastwork of sandbags. One of the crew knocked the breech open; out came the shell case sizzling, in went another shell. This time I stood well back behind the line of flight. I found I could watch the shell in the air quite easily; for some reason it seemed to be making a lot of smoke. It was very accurately aimed; I thought it was going to hit the target dead centre, but at the last instant it veered like a side-winder missile and swerved behind the keep. I was expecting a fairly healthy bang over there, but instead the thing fizzled out nearly with a plop in midair. Or rather it didn't exactly fizzle out; it sort of dwindled to a dot and vanished, and the sky shut behind it. Wherever it had gone, it was obviously not going to do much good. I said to one of the gunners, 'At this rate you'll be here all week.' but he seemed very optimistic, he told me they just hadn't found the range. They set to at once loading the gun again and I walked back the way I had come as nothing else seemed likely to happen.

The Danes had got the maypole set up; they'd built a bonfire, which was against camp rules, and were making a lot of noise. Dusk was settling, but the flames lit their corner of the field cheerfully. On the crest of the downs the stones stood sharp and ragged like teeth, but nobody was moving up there, it all looked very grey and cold and far away.

Medea had cooked a paella, one of those dried, packeted things. She said, 'About time too,' when I stepped into the tent, and started ladling the saffron-coloured rice on to a plate. She was wearing a big chunky sweater now, I thought how good she looked. I'd have shut the tent flap because it all looked bleak and miserable out there and it was worrying me, but I knew she'd want to see out so I let it be.

We'd got a bottle of wine, a Beaujolais; she'd put it by the cooker to warm and forgotten it, and it had really got hot. If you've ever tried drinking hot Beaujolais, it burns your throat right through. Also all we'd got was plastic cups, which didn't help the taste, and what with that and the barrage banging away over the wood I started getting annoyed again, though I'd nearly got over the business with the ghosts. I said, 'It's wrong to drink this with paella anyway, you should have got some white,' and she said if I didn't like it I didn't have to drink it, then she had a big snuffly thing and I had to go over and comfort her though I didn't feel very much like it. However I really enjoyed stroking her, she was really very nice, and afterwards she finished her paella and we had a cigarette and laughed about the Beaujolais being so hot. She sat a while with her head on my shoulder and watched the last of the light drain away over the downs, then she said, 'I want to go to bed, you shut the tent flap.'

I took the awning stays down and brought them inside and started lacing the canvas shut. She looked good getting undressed, with the greenish-yellow light from the lamp making big shadows on the canvas walls and the moths and bugs all zooming about. The barrage was still going on, I'd nearly got used to it; but just as I was putting the light out there was a big rolling crash louder than the rest, then another, then one you felt through the ground that made that old field of cloth of gold really shake and ripple. She said, 'What's that?' and I said, 'The Dardanelles Gun, they must have got it screwed together.' It didn't look as if we were in for a very peaceful night.

Anyway the noise died down after a time and you could hear birds hunting and the crickets in the grass. I liked it lying there with her in the sleeping bag, feeling how smooth and firm her hips were. We made love several times, she was good to love, she was cool and she didn't get smelly and all that. Finally I got tired, so I rolled over on my side and went to sleep and she tucked in back of me with her arms round me, very comforting.

It didn't last all that long though, because the next thing I remember was her stepping on my ankle which woke me up very sharply. There was a lot of din going on that I couldn't at first place. I sat up and saw she'd lit the lamp and was trying to deal with all these cats, and boy there were some cats. We had cats like Bishop Hatto had rats. They were everywhere, six or eight were jumping up trying to claw the larder down, others were cleaning the bits off the plates we'd forgotten to wash, they were up to all sorts. It was raining too, the drops pattering and slashing on the canvas and the bell end of the tent leaking all over, I suppose where Medea had touched it while she was trying to deal with the cats. I started yelling, 'Get rid of these cats, get rid of these damn cats.' I grabbed for a few myself but it was no good, they just smoked off through your fingers worse than those old ghosts. Then I saw there were some three or four starting to drag the garbage bag out under the tent flap so I shied something at them that turned out to be her handbag, bits and pieces flew all over. Then we really had a row. She had her arms full of cats but you could see she wasn't really trying to push them out, not all that hard. I said, 'They are your damn cats and you could get rid of them if you wanted.' Anyway she started in crying again, really crying; then she started pulling the tent flap undone, she said she'd sleep in the car or outside someplace because I didn't want her either. Then the field guns let fly again over the hill and it was hell in there, I tell you. So I let her go which was a pity, she was only wearing a sweater and nothing below the waist and she looked really nice. I lay back and tried to get some rest in between the ground shaking. I remember thinking, 'She's got to be taught a lesson, she brought those damn cats on purpose.' I was still plenty mad.

I think I dozed for a time; anyway, when I sat up the lamp was still burning, hanging where she'd left it, and the rain was thudding down and the tent was empty. I felt really bad about her, I mean having sent her out in the rain and all. I got up and put some things on and started calling her, but there was no answer. Then I remembered she'd said she would go to the car. I ran out to fetch her but she wasn't there.

I really got upset then. I was mad with myself for going to sleep, it seemed most heartless under the circumstances. I ran down to the stile where the ghosts had been and called again but there was nothing, only the wind. There were some big trees in the next field, really big, you could hear the wind boom in the branches. The flashes from the field guns kept lighting the sky, but they weren't bright enough to see by. Rain was trickling down my back and I was getting soaked. I looked back up the field and you could see the lamp on and the light glowing through the canvas, it all looked homely and warm, it was terrible she wasn't there.

I went back and put a blanket round my shoulders and sat shivering, listening to the rain. I must have got really confused then because I remember thinking I'd sent my cat out in the dark and it wasn't her fault at all, just me and my bit of bad temper. But there was nothing to be done, once a cat's gone it's gone in a big way, as I expect most of you know. I lay on my side after a bit. I kept thinking, 'Come back, Medea, it's all right,' and trying to set up a sort of mental beacon for her to home on if she couldn't see the light. I didn't think I'd sleep, but eventually I dozed off again.

I was warmer when I opened my eyes. I lay there for a bit feeling good, thinking about the breakfast we were going to have; cereals and marmalade and toast, and oatcakes and Scottish cheese. Then I remembered and sat up feeling terrible. I went out to the car but there was no sign of Medea, the whole field was still and empty and the dew all grey on the grass and rough.

I put the kettle on and made some coffee but I didn't want it, with her things all scattered about like that it just wasn't the same. I thought I'd better take the car and go and look for her, though really I had no idea where to start. I got in anyway and started the engine and I was just turning round when one of the Danish boys came over shouting and waving his arms. He said a girl had cut her throat in the night and would I come and see. I asked was it Medea, that was how bad I was feeling. He said no it wasn't, but I still had to see.

I looked across to the corner of the field. It was still shadowy there, the ground being low and beneath the spinney. The little tent in which it had happened, being soaking wet, had taken up some rather nasty colour from the groundsheet, which colour was staining upward in fans across the canvas. They had lit lamps inside which made the whole effect somewhat worse, they should have known better. I said, 'I don't want to see a thing like that,' and drove away.

I'd forgotten the wire across the track till I drove into it, giving the car a scrape across the paintwork. Anyway I didn't stop, I was too concerned about Medea. There was no sign of her in the lane, so I drove up to the main road. It was broad and white and empty. There was a Shell filling station to one side, but it was shut. I drove the car to the batteries, turned into the gateway and got out. I stood looking over the gate. They'd had more success than I had expected. The nearest castle was a ruin, great shells of wall pierced and fretted with windows and high doorways, all still and vague in the early light. The other castles were still fighting; I saw some nasty-looking stuff drift over, like soft, dark flak.

The eighteen-pounder emplacement was a mess. The grass had been churned into mud and the guns were filthy, all streaked with black and big chunks of mud sticking to the wheels. There were shell cases scattered everywhere and the crews were sitting about in greatcoats looking huddled and miserable. A man with a bandage round his head was cooking sausages over a stick fire, but they none of them looked as if they wanted to eat.

The captain had got his Blighty one sometime during the night; they had him on a stretcher, tucked round with bright red blankets, and there were a couple of nurses. He was propped up with a greatcoat for a pillow, he had a cigarette in his hand and was shouting something about getting more sandbags, but I didn't like his colour. His cap was off; I saw his hair was grey rather than yellow. I asked him if he'd seen Medea and he said no, nobody had come that way.

I went on to the Tudor Lines but nothing was moving there at all. The fires were out, and the big cannon strewed anyways across the hill. One was cocked up on its carriage pointing at the sky, and the muzzle and barrel all smashed. Round it the grass was black and trampled and there was a smell of burned powder, like fireworks.

They had some little gay-striped tents, each one topped with a pennant, but I didn't feel much like looking inside. I walked back the way I had come. As I passed the captain, he pushed himself up on one elbow. He shouted, 'They were going to send us naval support. They promised us naval support.' Then he started to cry, big tears rolling down his face. I felt very sorry for him, but there was nothing I could do.

I got back into the car and drove off. I thought, I don't know why, that she'd probably gone down to the coast, to one of the bays. Trouble was there were several bays, I had to look into them all. I drove to four but they were all the same, there were stands of gorse and bracken, drystone walls, little farmhouses and barns with tractors parked outside. The sea was pale silver, very cold-looking, and it was still only halfway light.

The fifth bay was big, with cliffs of crumbling grey clay. I drove the car as near the edge as I dared, got out and looked over. I saw her at once, lying down there tiny as a moth. Beyond her the beach was a wide half-moon stretching to the sea. The sea was still, nearly unrippling. There were big mirror-streaks of swell moving in, lazy and calm; and out in the bay a ship of the line was practising at the greatguns. The broadsides rolled out fleecy clouds of smoke; the noise of the barrage came in dim across the water, like thunder a long way off.

I started climbing down the cliff. There were gullies, crisscrossing, and the paths were very slippy. I reached the beach near where a little stream ran out under a plank bridge, soaked itself away across the pebbles. Beside the bridge was an old concrete pillbox. The beach was littered, there were sprags of wire, bits of old dried seaweed and half-bricks and broken bottles and big boulders that had tumbled down out of the cliffs. Nearer the water the sand was smoother, firm and grey. I kept wondering what Medea was doing there anyway because it was none too warm and she was wearing this little white cotton bikini, very small. I called her but she didn't answer.

I reached her, squatted down. She was lying on her side, back turned to the sea and her head on her arm. I touched her ankle. She was very light, I think she must have been hollow. When I touched her her whole figure moved, sand and bits of dark grey shale started trickling into the depression where her hip had been. I remembered the whole thing then, about snipping her out of a calendar page and pasting her down so carefully. I was really upset because it was all my fault, I'd just stopped thinking of her in the round and that had been enough. Though what with the war and all I suppose it was understandable.

Anyway she was still three-dimensional, which was something. I started moving round her in a rather ungentlemanly way, being curious to see what she looked like from behind. Which was my second big mistake because I took my mind off her again just for a second and it gave her a chance to flatten right out. She was supported at the back by a framework of scantling, very neatly made. The wood was new, pinkish yellow, and two struts were pushed down into the sand to keep her firm. I started getting really depressed then because Medea hadn't been the sort of exercise you can do all that often; I mean, these days even good calendar pages aren't all that easy to come by.

The frigate seemed to be drifting in closer to the cliffs, I looked up and she was getting really vast. She was turning too, showing the black and amber stripes along her side and her row of gunports. It wasn't a good place to stop but I was still worried about Medea. I thought for a bit but I couldn't see how I was going to take her with me, she was too big to go in the car even with the hood down and naturally being a soft-top there was no roof-rack. It seemed I was just going to have to leave her there, which was a great pity on top of all that had happened. It was raining again, a thin, misty drizzle, I could see her buckling pretty soon and getting spoiled.

In the end I turned her round so at least she was facing the sea, and propped her with a couple of stones. I ran back the way I had come. As I got to the top of the path there was a boom and the whole cliff shook. I looked back and saw shingle and bits of rock fly up in the air. I was really sorry then, I felt I should have tried to take her with me instead of leaving her to get blown apart. I should have guessed they'd use her as a mark.

I sat in the car for a bit and thought things through. The first problem was the tent, which had of course been hers. Also there were her things, her clothes and all the rest. It seemed probable the whole lot would have vanished, leaving my gear just strewn about on the grass. I sincerely hoped so, as I wasn't relishing the prospect of burning the camp. Killing a pretty woman now and then is all very well but getting rid of her possessions afterwards is quite another thing. However there was plainly only one answer, I had to go and find out. The drizzle had misted the windscreen so that I couldn't see, I started the wipers and drove that damn old car away up the hill.

If you've enjoyed these books and would like to read more, you'll find literally thousands of classic Science Fiction & Fantasy titles through the **SF Gateway**

✶

For the new home of Science Fiction & Fantasy . . .

✶

For the most comprehensive collection of classic SF on the internet . . .

✶

Visit the SF Gateway

www.sfgateway.com

Keith Roberts (1935–2000)

Keith Roberts was an English author and illustrator, who did more than most to define the look of UK science fiction magazines in the sixties. He won four BFSA awards for his writing and his art, and edited the magazine *Science Fantasy* (later *Impulse*) for a time. He was also nominated for Hugo, Nebula (twice) and Arthur C. Clarke awards. He is perhaps best known for his seminal alternative history novel, *Pavane*, praised by George R. R. Martin: 'No alternate history novel of the past thirty years comes close to equalling *Pavane*.'